The Mule
on the Minaret

Alec Waugh has written more than forty books.
The list of them includes

FICTION

The Loom of Youth (1917)
Kept (1925)
The Balliols (1934)
No Truce with Time (1941)
Guy Renton (1952)
Island in the Sun (1956)
Fuel for the Flame (1960)
My Place in the Bazaar (1961)

GENERAL

Hot Countries (1930)
Love and the Caribbean (1959)
In Praise of Wine (1959)
The Early Years of Alec Waugh (1963)
A Family of Islands (1964)

THE
MULE
ON THE
MINARET

A Novel About the Middle East

BY

ALEC WAUGH

FARRAR, STRAUS AND GIROUX † NEW YORK

CONTENTS

PART I

The Land
of Milk and Honey

In the bazaars of Damascus and Baghdad, they tell this among many other stories about the legendary Hoja Nassiral-Dia. It happened on a certain day, that Hoja, traveling from Homs to Hama, reached shortly before noon, an unfamiliar village. In the market place was a vociferous, gesticulating concourse. He was warmly welcomed. "Stranger," they said, "we are in trouble. The Muezzin is sick and we have no one to summon us to prayer. We are a small village; we have known one another all our lives and we know that not one of us is worthy to ascend the minaret. But against you, a stranger, we know nothing. It would be proper for you to do so."

"But I have my mule with me," protested Hoja. "If I leave him at the foot of the tower he will be stolen."

"Then you must take him up with you," the villagers insisted.

So Hoja did as they requested. He climbed with his mule to the top of the tower and from its balcony summoned them to prayer. There was peace in the noisy market place.

But when he would continue his journey, he discovered that it is one thing to lead a mule to the top of a minaret, but quite another to lead him down. So he called on the villagers to help him. They shook their heads. Hoja was indignant. "But you told me to take the mule up with me." They laughed. "The man," they said, "who takes his mule to the top of a minaret, must bring it down himself."

1

ON AN EVENING IN LATE NOVEMBER, in the year 1962, the voice of
the announcer boomed across the airport waiting room at New
York's Idlewild.

"Pan American announce the departure of their flight number 2
for Frankfurt, Beirut, New Delhi, Bangkok and Tokyo. Will
passengers please proceed to their aircraft by Gateway Number 7."

Among the eighty or so men and women who obeyed the summons was an Englishman in the middle sixties, of rather more
than medium height; sparse, with thick white hair, clean shaven,
long nosed; caricaturists often presented him as a bird. He had an
authoritative manner. As he walked down the corridor, a couple
of newspapermen hurried forward.

"Professor Reid?"

"That's right."

"May we take your picture, please?"

"Of course."

As the photographer arranged his camera, the other began the
standard questionnaire.

"You are going to Baghdad for the Al Kindi celebrations?"

"That's right."

"As England's first historian-philosopher?"

The Professor smiled. "As the only one available." A scholar of
New College, Oxford, he had taught for nearly forty years now in
a red brick university, Winchborough in Sussex. He was currently
completing a two years' exchange professorship at Columbia. A
disciple of Arnold Toynbee, he had, under the signature N. E.
Reid, published a number of substantial volumes that had earned
him the respect of his colleagues but no great measure of popular
recognition. The moment called, he felt, for a display of modesty.
"They would have preferred an Oxford or a Cambridge don," he

3

said. "But no one cared to go; though I don't think it would be tactful to print that."

"Why didn't anyone else want to go? This is off the record."

"Baghdad isn't particularly comfortable. Most of our Orientalists had links with the old regime. It's only four years since the King was murdered."

"Then why do you want to go? That question needn't be off the record, surely."

"I was there for three years in the second war. I'm curious to see in what ways it's changed."

"You must have several friends there."

"I had, but I don't know what's become of those that are still alive and aren't in exile."

"Will you try to get in touch with them?"

"I'll leave the first move to them. It might not be convenient for them to know an Englishman; but that again is off the record."

"You are breaking your journey at Beirut. Were you in Lebanon as well, during the war?"

"For seven months."

"You won't have any difficulty in meeting your old friends there."

"I'm trusting not."

"Fine, thank you very much, Professor; I'm most grateful. Is there anything you'd like to add?"

"I don't think so. Thank you."

"Bon voyage."

The camera clicked again, and the Professor walked towards the gangway.

He smiled as he fastened his seat belt, and settled luxuriantly into the deep wide seat which the generosity of the Iraqi Government had accorded him. He stretched out his legs towards the footrest. It was the first time that he had travelled otherwise than tourist. It was ironically appropriate that he would be returning in such resplendent style to a country where he had served so austerely as a soldier, to read the final chapter of a story that, for him, had started twenty-one years earlier in Beirut.

†

Twenty-one years ago, November 1941, in the early afternoon, and he was standing in the hallway of a block of flats that had been requisitioned by the military. He was one of a dozen officers

4

who had been, two months earlier, hurried out from London to the Middle East as a matter of the utmost urgency to staff the newly formed Spears Mission. After a seven weeks' journey, in convoy around the Cape, they had at last, on a day of wind and rain, arrived. An orderly was reporting their appearance.

From above them on the uncarpeted staircase came the clatter of high heels; a clatter that ceased suddenly. Reid raised his head. On the first floor landing a tall, dark-haired young woman wearing a short sheepskin coat, had checked at the sight of the cluster of officers below her.

"Who on earth are you?" she asked. She had a rich contralto voice.

Reid was then a captain and there were a couple of majors in the group, but he had become their spokesman during the voyage out.

"We're the new members of the Mission," he informed her.

"You are; you really are, at last."

She sat down on the top stair and stared at them; then burst out laughing. She had a full, gay laugh which made him realize that though she was not pretty she was attractive. He noticed that her eyes were blue.

"Did any of you," she asked, "read a last-war book by Ian Hay called 'The First Hundred Thousand'?"

"I did."

"Do you remember a chapter about the practical joke department in the War Office?"

"Of course."

"The department is still functioning. In August, after the collapse of the Vichy forces, we needed a dozen officers for our Mission. It never occurred to London that Cairo had a pool of highly competent officers, invalided from the desert. Within five days we'd filled our vacancies. In the meantime London was busy ransacking every Corps Headquarters for extra bodies. Before we realised what they were doing, you had sailed. It's been the autumn's biggest laugh."

The autumn's biggest laugh! It might have been that for the Middle East, but for Professor N. E. Reid it was the biggest blow delivered him since the war began. Two months back, when he had received his posting orders, he had felt that every personal problem in his life had been if not solved at least shelved for the duration. Now once again the gate swung open.

The tall girl stood up. "Is anybody looking after you?"

"An orderly is doing something."

"That probably means Colonel Weston. You're in good hands. I'll be seeing you all later. Good luck."

She came down the stairs with something that though not a stride was definitely more than a walk. Reid pictured her on skis. Every head turned as she went by. A subaltern at Reid's side drew a long slow breath. "If that's a fair sample of Beirut, we're not on a bad wicket."

Simultaneously, there appeared at the head of the stairs a slim, short, very dapper man, adorned upon his shoulders by a crown and star; above his left hand breast pocket was an array of ribbons. He appeared to be in the early fifties. He paused, as the young woman had, looking down on the miscellaneous collection of military personnel that the practical joke department of the War Office had landed on his doorstep. Then he smiled; there was a twinkle in his eye.

"Welcome, gentlemen; though I'm afraid that you'll hardly regard as welcome the news I have for you. If you'll follow me into my office, I'll try to put you in the picture."

He led them into a room with a view over the harbour. Three years ago the flat, of which this was the main sitting room, had no doubt commanded a high rent. It looked very bleak now, with its uncarpeted floor, its windows uncurtained but with black-out blinds, its bare furniture, and walls decorated with security posters against careless talk. An oil stove was smoking in the fireplace; over the fireplace hung a framed admonition: "Think, plan and act in terms of March 1942."

The Colonel seated himself on his desk. He had a breezy manner.

"Now, tell me: how much do you know about all this?"

Once again Reid was the spokesman. "Only what we were told five minutes ago by that charming young lady on the stairs."

"And that's about all there is to know. It's what we used to call, when I was a subaltern, a G.M.F.U. grand military fuck-up. Not the first and not the last. We must make the best of it, and that should not be hard. Don't feel that you are not wanted here: you are. You are all of you handpicked. Middle East is, at the present moment, the most important area in the war. It is the one place where we are hitting back at our enemies and, what is more, hitting back effectively. It may be several years before we can

6

open a second front in Europe; but on this front we shall be fighting continuously until the whole sector has been cleared. No one can tell how the situation will develop. One thing is certain, it will develop; that means opportunities for you all. It is a question of waiting, patiently; it won't be for long; and during that period of waiting you can be very sure that we shall find means of keeping you occupied and useful."

He smiled, and the group smiled with him, but Reid's smile was wry. He had heard this kind of speech before; many times before, during the last twenty-seven months.

In 1916, as a schoolboy of eighteen, he had gone to Sandhurst. He had no intention of making the army his profession. But taking a short wartime view, it had seemed the simplest and most effective way of getting a commission. He had been gazetted as a regular army subaltern. As a result, in 1919, in order to take up at Oxford the scholarship that he had won before he joined the army, he had transferred to the regular reserve—the R.A.R.O. Every subsequent first of January he had duly and dutifully reported in writing to the War Office and in September 1939 he had been recalled, as a Lieutenant, to his regiment, along with a dozen other forty-year-old reservists, to the concerned embarrassment of the Colonel, whose speech of welcome at the depot had been very like the one that he was receiving now from Colonel Weston.

"I am delighted to have you here," he had said. "I am sure that in a very little while we shall find the particular way in which to make the best use of you. You are none of you young enough for a Lieutenant's job. It's a question of athletics. You can't play rugby football after thirty. At the same time you haven't enough military knowledge for the job to which your age entitles you, a half colonel or at least a major. But it's only a question of time. I'm sure of that."

A little later, he had called Reid aside for a private interview. "I recognise, of course," he had said, "that you are in a very different position from these others here. You are someone in your own rights and very much so. You are a person of achievement and distinction. We don't want to waste you as a garrison adjutant in a remote back area. There must be exactly the right place for you somewhere, but it takes a little time to find it. You are, perhaps, a rather hard man to place."

A hard man to place. How often had not that been said to him during the last two years; at the end of each of the various courses

7

—at Matlock, Swanage, Hendon—to which he had been sent by colonels despairingly confident that there must be the right niche for him somewhere.

A hard man to place. Who could recognise it better than himself? And hadn't he, each time he had been forced to take stock of himself, been exposed to the same sense of guilt, the inner voice that whispered, "You've no right to be here. You're doing no good. The army hasn't any use for you. You are an encumbrance. You ought to be in Winchborough, teaching."

How eagerly after a year as staff-captain in the military section of the Ministry of Mines, to which he had been posted as the result of a chance meeting at a cricket match, an appointment for which by taste and training, he could scarcely have been more unfitted where he had fulfilled subordinate clerical duties for which in peacetime an untrained eighteen-year-old girl would have been hired at fifty shillings a week, how eagerly he had welcomed this appointment to the Spears' Mission for which he had been selected on the grounds of his French and his historical familiarity with the area. At last, at last; here was work which would justify his remaining in the army. He could shelve his problems for a little longer. He had sailed with a clear conscience and a high heart; now once again he was back where he had started.

"Don't feel despondent," Colonel Weston was concluding. "It's now just after three, and the Chargé d'Affaires wants to see you at five o'clock. The General, by the way, has gone back to London. There are two things that I must explain: firstly this is a Legation; that is to say though you were soldiers under military discipline we are under civilian control. General Spears is now a Minister and except on special occasions, will wear civilian clothes. Secondly, because this is a Legation and also because we are here mainly for liaison purposes, we do not live in messes but in hotels and flats. We find it easier to meet the Lebanese that way and it's easier with the French. Their *popote* is very different from our mess. They prefer their club, where they can entertain women. You, of course, are all honorary members of it, so I've arranged for you to stay in hotels and pensions for the first few days. That won't be inexpensive and in a week or so when you've found your feet you'll be able to make more suitable arrangements for yourselves. I've put the elder ones into the St. Georges, the younger ones into a convenient pension."

He picked up a list from his desk and read out his dispositions.

8

"I suggest, therefore, that you go to your billets and get settled in. Back here, don't forget, by five o'clock. The Chargé d'Affaires is Cartwright, Frank Cartwright, seconded from the Sudan Service. Oh, yes, I forgot. There's some mail for some of you; it came by air and beat you to it."

The letters were spread out on a table. One of the envelopes was addressed to Reid, in a familiar back-sloping script. At the sight of it, he half-closed his eyes. Rachel. It had all begun again, the resumption of a domestic problem across two thousand miles.

†

The St. Georges was on the waterfront, modern, five-tiered, set like a citadel, each bastion turned to catch the sun. The rain had ceased, but the sky was overcast and the sea beat choppily against the shingle.

Johnson, a Sandhurst contemporary of Reid's, though they had been in different companies, fell into step beside him.

"Bad show," he said.

Johnson was large, corpulent, balding, red-faced, with heavy features. He and Reid had spent a good deal of time together on the ship. He was the kind of Englishman who will maintain a strict barrier of reserve for days, and then suddenly late at night, after a fifth whisky, tell you the whole story of his life. Reid could guess at what was passing in his mind.

Johnson, like himself, had set high store by this appointment, though for different reasons. Johnson had had a difficult time during the 1930s. He had transferred to the Reserve in 1931 because he had seen no future in the army. Promotion was slow, pacifism was in the ascendant. Men who had commanded brigades during the war were still commanding companies. But 1931 had not offered favourable auguries to a man of thirty-four with no civilian experience. The motor firm in which he had invested half his retirement gratuity went into liquidation. His second venture in real estate, undertaken during the boom in luxury flats, fared better, but the boom did not last. Too many blocks of flats were built. Johnson had welcomed his recall to khaki.

But the last two years had been no more satisfactory than the preceding eight. He was out of touch with the training and tactics of the modern mechanised army. He was not sent to join his regiment in France. He was found, instead, a number of administrative posts. But he had never been to the staff college; he was unfamiliar with staff duties. Younger men slid ahead of him. He had begun to anticipate a dreary, routine war that would leave him at its close several years older, less receptive, less elastic, with no compensating record of achievement. He had seen his transfer to the Middle East as the door of opportunity.

"Anything may happen there," he had said to Reid in one of his hours of expansion. "Britain is going to consolidate the Middle East. The French have had their day. The Arabs will turn to us. Through the Mission we shall meet important people; that's how you get on, through meeting the right people."

He was in a roseate mood, halfway through his fourth whisky. Fantastic dreams out of the Arabian Nights circled in his imagination. "Anything might happen, anything." And now the cloud-based castle had dissolved.

They walked down the hill in silence. As they turned into the carriage drive Johnson sighed. "There are times when I envy the man who has a safe job waiting him after the war."

†

Frank Cartwright was on the brink of fifty. He was of medium height, thin, grey-haired, clean shaven. He had the drawn look of a dedicated man. He received the new arrivals in a room that was no larger than Colonel Weston's, but that looked larger because it was furnished in the style appropriate to the reception of local dignitaries. There was a carpet on the floor; there were comfortable arm chairs; there was a long settee. The posters of the King and Churchill had been framed. Cartwright was neatly but unobtrusively dressed in a dark grey suit.

"I welcome you on behalf of General Spears," he said. "He wanted me to assure you how happy he is that you are here. He is very sorry not to be able to welcome you in person; he has a great deal to settle up in London; he does not expect to be back till February. He is confident that when he does, he will find each and every one of you happily and usefully employed. The Middle East is an expanding area."

For a couple of minutes Cartwright enlarged on what Colonel Weston had already said. His manner was friendly, but diplomatically remote. Reid sensed in him the man who had had, all his life, to weigh his words; to strike a balance between what he himself believed, what his hearer wanted to hear, and what authority in the background required of him, so that he could best persuade his hearer, who often was an adversary, that the interests of that hearer and of the authority in the background were in the last analysis identical. Walking a tight rope, he had remained an honest man.

He echoed and amplified Colonel Weston, then he changed his appeal. "I imagine," he said, "that you are all familiar with the general background, with the T. E. Lawrence legend. In the first war the Arabs were roused against the Turks; they were promised their independence, but at the Peace Conference the Arab World was divided up into spheres of interest; France getting one chunk, Britain getting another; while a national home for the Jews was set up in Palestine. There are very many mixed opinions on the wisdom of those treaties. You'll form your own opinions. Nearly everyone who comes out here becomes a violent partisan on one side or another. That doesn't concern us at the moment. We can't go back to first causes. We have to consider the present situation in terms of wartime needs."

He explained the genesis of those needs. Britain had promised independence to the countries over which she had been given a protectorate, and she had kept her promises. Iraq was independent by 1931, though it had remained a sphere of influence with British technical advisers in the ministries and with Britain retaining naval, military and air force bases. France on the other hand though it had granted independence to the Lebanon, had not implemented its guarantee. That had been the position in September 1939, with the French maintaining a large body of troops in the Levant, just as the British were in Egypt.

"The eastern flank of the Mediterranean was," Cartwright explained, "well protected, of course, but the situation changed completely in June 1940 after the Armistice, with Syria and the Lebanon under the control of the Vichy Government. Our lines to India were threatened; so was our conduct of the whole war in the Western Desert. The Germans had designs upon Iraq. There is a very strong pro-German element in Iraq, just as there was an anti-British element in Beirut. We had to move first, and fast. I think history will show that we forced the war in Iraq, before the pro-Germans and anti-royalists in Baghdad were ready, while here in a joint action with the Free French we attacked the Vichy Levant.

"We won the campaign, but we put ourselves in a very awkward situation diplomatically. In the first place the French have always been touchy about our position in the Middle East. They consider that they were here first. Perhaps they were. You remember their song, 'Partant pour la Syrie.' The French are resentful because the entire campaign in the first war in Mesopotamia was organised and fought by us. They've put up a statue to themselves along the waterfront, but they did in fact very little fighting. They've always believed that we had designs on Lebanon, and on Damascus. Read a novel like Pierre Benoit's *Chatelaine du Liban*; and they have this argument in their favour. Feisal, who was our protégé, laid claim to Damascus. Anyway they are convinced that now we're here, we're going to stay here. We have to convince them that that is not our game at all. And it isn't, I'm convinced on that point. Sometimes in the diplomatic world one has to give answers that aren't wholly true. This isn't one of them. But the French distrust us. You've got to remember that."

He paused; he looked round him with an easy smile. He had delivered a lecture but it had not sounded like a lecture. "And now," he said, "I'm going to add something that you are at liberty to ignore. It's my particular hobby-horse. But you must remember that I have been living in this area all my adult life. I came here in Allenby's army in 1917. My roots are here. I tend to see issues through Arab eyes. I want you to remember this. We are in Arab territory, not our own. The Arabs are for the most part our friends, though they have deep reason to distrust us. They are very different from us; in culture, in religion. Many of them think of us as infidels. Our war is not their war. We, as English, have only one concern, to defeat the Axis powers. But for the Arabs, the defeat of the Axis is incidental. It is a part of their long history. In 1914 they had no concern with European politics. We, because we were at war with Turkey, fomented and aided the simmering Arab revolt against the Turks; we made the Arabs certain promises which we did not keep. They feel, many of them, that they were tricked. This time they are on their guard. They do not care whether European democracy survives, apart from its effect upon the Arab world. One of our first duties is to persuade them that an allied victory is to their advantage; but there is a further, in my opinion, very important point. The problem of Anglo-Arab, perhaps I should say Arab-European relations, will not end with the defeat of Hitler. You see that notice over the mantelpiece, 'Think, plan, act in terms of March 1942.' That is very sound advice. Take a short view in wartime. But remember that in terms of Anglo-Arab relations what we are doing today will have its repercussions in 1965. Take a long view there.

"That's all I have to say," he finished. "I expect you'd like to have a look round the place. I'm handing you over for the evening to one of our officers in the economic section. He'll show you the ropes. Tomorrow's free, of course. If you'll come round on Monday around ten, we'll see what news we have for you. Reid, if you'd stay behind a minute. . . ."

The moment the room was empty he drew up a chair beside his desk. "Now this is a pleasure," he began. "I've always hoped that we should meet one day. I was delighted when I heard that you were coming out, but tell me, when they posted you out here from London, did you know what exactly you were posted to? I mean, what did they think that you were coming here to do?"

"They talked about the publicity and propaganda section. They thought that as a historian-philosopher I'd be able to understand the Arab point of view."

"That certainly makes sense, but in point of fact we don't have a propaganda section; we have on paper, as part of the establishment, but that section is mainly occupied with making digests out of local papers and B.B.C. reports and looking after the security of the building. We aren't issuing any propaganda, at the moment, though that may come later. I don't think that that section is at all your tea. We've got to find exactly the right thing for you. After all, you're in a different category from these other chaps."

Reid's heart sank. Here it was again: the same old story. A special person for a special job: with a special job that nobody could find.

"I've arranged," the Chargé d'Affaires went on, "that for the first few weeks you should work in the political section, which is my special pigeon. One of our chief jobs is to prepare a bi-weekly summary of political events, which is sent out on a limited, high level distribution list. This summary is a digest of the reports that are sent in by our political officers all round the country. It is a job that needs doing carefully. It isn't a dog's body's job, far from it; at the same time it isn't a whole time job. It'll give you plenty of spare time and I'd suggest that you read up some of our back files and also one or two of the specialised histories that may have missed your notice. In that way you could put in a couple of months, very profitably, until the General returns. He's bound to have a number of new ideas. Till then we're in the position of a caretaker administration. We can't undertake anything drastic or decisive. I know he'll be very pleased to find you here: as I am; and one day next week I'd like you to come up to dinner at my house. We might fix the day now. Let's make it Wednesday. In the meantime there's a chap here who wants to meet you. Nigel Farrar. He knows friends of yours. I'll take you to his office."

He got up from his desk, walked towards the door: then checked.

"I'd better ring him first. He may have someone with him." He called the number. "Is that you? Cartwright here. I've got Reid with me. Is it all right for me to bring him round? Fine. Right away."

On the door of Farrar's office was a notice: "Economic section." Farrar was a captain, tall, dark, clean-shaven; with his hair worn short. He had bright eyes, and the air of an alert rodent. His uniform was new, neat and well-cut, yet he did not have a military look. He appeared to be in the early thirties. He welcomed Reid briskly.

"It's fine you're here. I've been looking forward to this ever since I heard you were on the way. Thank you very much, sir."

"Then I'll leave you to gossip over mutual friends."

"Thank you, sir. Thank you very much."

Farrar had a quick but easy way of talking. He gave the impression of being in a hurry, but also of being on his way to something he expected to enjoy. Reid felt that he would like him.

"Who are the friends we have in common?" he enquired.

"As far as I know, we haven't any. Though we must have mutual acquaintances. Everybody knows everyone in England."

"But you told Cartwright you knew friends of mine."

"I know: it's my security training. I never tell the truth when a lie will do as well."

"Doesn't that get you into muddles?"

"Less and less often; and it's very good for one's memory. Keeps one's mind alert: I know a lot about you. I thought it would be fun to know you. But I didn't want to put it to the boss like that. I'm sure that by the time the evening's over we'll have established contacts. We might have dinner together if that's agreeable. In the meantime let's go up to my flat and have a drink. I hate talking in offices."

The flat was a five minutes' taxi-drive away, up hill. Reid looked from one side to the other. It was a curving road with tramlines running down its centre. On one side it sloped steeply to the sea; the other side was flanked with modern buildings.

"You don't seem to bother about the blackout here," Reid said.

"How could we, in an Arab city? If the streets weren't lit they'd be unsafe to walk in: robbery with violence along every block. They do issue instructions about not having naked lights facing the sea, but no one bothers much, even though there are submarines."

Farrar's flat was on the second floor of a walk-up block of flats. There was no hallway and no porter. It had two entrances: "Very convenient," Farrar said.

It was a four-roomed flat: it was sparsely furnished. There were no pictures. There was an immense desk, and a steel filing cabinet. But there was only one small wardrobe: and the second bedroom contained nothing but a military camp-bed.

"I've only just moved in," said Farrar. "I'm not settled yet, as you observe."

Reid looked round him, puzzled. He had heard that some of the Mission officers lived in flats; but he had presumed that they either shared them—what was the word they used in the Far East, "Chummeries"—or else lived in a pension. The rent and furnishing of a flat of this size must be considerable.

"Do many of you have flats of this size?" he enquired.

"Not very many."

"I suppose I shouldn't ask you questions, or perhaps I shouldn't ask you questions at all, because you'll give me devious answers."

Farrar laughed. "I'm going to like you. I'll make you a promise. I won't tell you a lie unless it's absolutely necessary. That reverses my usual practice of never telling the truth when a lie will do just as well."

"That's very civil of you."

"Not at all. The Austin Reed service: excuse the pun. Now, what'll you drink? I've almost everything. Have you tried Arak yet? It'll save you a lot of money if you can learn to like it. It's rather like Pernod, white and it clouds when you pour water on it. A taste of aniseed. They serve side dishes with it, *messé*. It's something you sip, not quaff, and you have to keep nibbling when you're sipping or you'll find the room spinning round you; but a couple of mouthfuls will put you straight. It's very strong. The troops aren't allowed it. The Arabs sell what they call spiked oranges into which Arak has been injected. Arak leaves a lining to your stomach and if you've drunk a lot at night and start the day with a glass of water, the water will mix with that lining and be the equivalent of raw spirits on an empty stomach. One glass before a meal is fine; try it, I've got some cheese here."

He raised his glass. "Here's to your first drink in Beirut. Now about myself. I'll put my cards on the table, in terms of our gentleman's agreement. That notice on the door you may have noticed, 'Economic section,' doesn't mean a thing. I'm not in the Mission. The Mission is my cover and I don't think I'll be allowed to keep it for much longer. The Mission will be a Legation soon, and 'the cloak and dagger boys'—that's what I am—will have to find other roosts.

"This is the way it came about. I'm in oil: or was until a year ago. I was at Stowe and New College; so you see how I know who you are. I got a second in mods. and a third in greats. That wasn't enough for the Home Civil. But oil was prepared to find a place for someone with an honours degree, who could bowl 'Chinamen'; I was a 'Tic' and can sport a Vincent's tie. . . . Anyhow, I came out here; with the I.P.C. in 1934. Men in oil are, as you know, a reserved occupation. When the war started I was told it was my duty to stay put. That seemed fine to me, when nothing was happening anywhere. It didn't seem so fine in the summer of 1940 when the whole fabric slipped. I'm not a death or glory boy, but I like to be a part of what is happening. I nosed around, I felt I'd like to be in khaki, and just when I was thinking that, a fellow turned up here who could do just that for me. 'You won't get the V.C.,' he said. 'You won't charge a redoubt at Omdurman, but the right man in the right place is worth a division in the wrong.' Have you heard of an organisation based on Pelham Street? You haven't. I'm delighted. That means that our security is good. I won't say what we do. Perhaps we're not a quarter as important as we think we are. But if we're a tenth as important as we think we are, there's no need to worry about dodging your share of the war effort. If you think I've a chip on my shoulder or a sense of guilt because better and older men than I, are shivering in foxholes, it's the 'don't give it another thought' department. In every deal someone has to pick up the good hand and I'm the lucky guy this time. Probably in 1955 the boot will be on the other foot. The wretch of today will be happy tomorrow! For the moment all's fine with Ferdinand, and listen now, this is where you come in."

He stopped. He looked thoughtfully at Reid.

"I hadn't meant to bring this up right away. But why waste time? You're O.K. I can see that. The point is this. How would you like to share this flat with me? It won't cost you much. Not nearly as much as the St. Georges. It has to cost you something because of Whitehall redtape book-keeping. I've an accountant here: he'll work out a round sum: including a certain amount of food and a reasonable amount to drink. You'd be on your own. There's that 'entrée independent.' You can bring your friends here. It would be much more comfortable than an hotel."

"Of course it would. It's very generous of you. But why are you asking me? Why not someone in your own outfit?"

"That's the precise point. I don't want to be associated publicly with my outfit. They won't let me stay much longer with the Mission but it was very useful for me to have had this link with it, and if you came to stay here—you, a professor in civilian life and a member of the Mission—it would continue in the public eye my association with the Mission. The kind of cover that I need. The moment I heard you were coming, I thought: 'My man.' "

"I don't suppose that there'd be any point in my asking you for what kinds of activity you need a cover?"

"Scarcely, and the less you know the better. My organisation has a dozen different names. If ever you see anything called 'I.S.' for Inter Services something or other, you can be pretty sure that it's some 'cloak and dagger' racket. Half the time I don't know what I'm doing myself. By that I mean I don't know whether the boys up top are giving me the right reasons for what I'm doing. In this game one is only told as much as is necessary to do one's job. I take things as they come. It's a cosy job, in a place like this, or shall I say as long as Beirut stays a place like this. Did you see that notice on the Mission walls: 'Think, act and plan in terms of March 1942'? You read that, I guess, as an admonition against being idle in the winter months. I read it another way. 'Nigel,' I said to myself. 'In a few months' time the whole of this seaboard may blow up, with Germans pouring in from every side. Make the most of the good times while they're around. 'The long night cometh, starless, void of sun.' I think you'll like it in this flat, and you'll meet a number of agreeable people. But don't decide right away. Case the joint for a day or two. Now let's go and see the town. It isn't raining so let's walk."

The sky was clear now, and a waxing moon glistened and glittered on the water. It was strange once again to be looking down on the Mediterranean: so much was familiar, so much was new.

At the foot of the road ran a street, lined on one side by shops and restaurants.

"This is the student quarter," Farrar said. "That's the American University—the A.U.B.—across the way. I use its library quite a lot; and I sit around in the student cafés. Most of them are jabbering in Arabic. My Arabic is shaky; I don't get half of what they are saying, but I learn something just by looking at them. Often when I'm reading secret reports the characters in my file become puppets in a game; they cease to be real people. Looking at them across a café, seeing how they move their hands when they talk, makes them real again."

The road turned to the right as they descended. Most of the houses were modern; solid cement structures; but now and again there was a house built on the Turkish pattern, in dark yellowish brick, with high arched windows; some of them with coloured glass.

"They're delightful inside," Farrar said. "A large central hall, usually with a fountain playing: low divans round the walls, piles of rugs and carpets, small rooms opening off. Typifies a whole way of life. That's a fine example."

He pointed to a house that stood at the head of the road which housed the Mission building. It had an exotic, ecclesiastical flavour. "A big shot in local politics lives there. I can't remember his name. Names are a great problem. They aren't pronounced the way they are spelt, or rather the Arabs have a different alphabet. One doesn't always know which is the important name, so that in an office they get filed incorrectly. That's why bad boys slip through our hands so often. We won't go past the Mission. I'll take you down a back street. Careful how you tread."

It was a needed warning. There were deep gutters beside the sidewalk: the paving stones were often broken. The streets were dimly lighted. There were few pedestrians: "Everyone's in the night club quarter," Farrar said.

The night club quarter, or at least the European section of the night club quarter, ran along the waterfront: it was barely two hundred yards long. Restaurants, hotels, shops, bars, dance clubs jostled close against each other. Then the street became a promenade along the water, with larger hotels and shops facing it.

"This is typical of Lebanon," said Farrar, "—of the mixture that is Lebanon. There's the Kit Cat which is an international hot spot with a floor show and reasonable food. Next to it is an open Arab kitchen where you can get meat off a skewer; or rissoles containing heaven knows what and all kinds of sour vegetables. Then across the way there's a café without a license where you get those sweet cakes that look so indigestible and aren't; and note the different kinds of clothing: the Moslems with their baggy trousers and red tarbooshes. Look at the Lebanese girls with their black hair loose upon their shoulders; they may be just as good Moslems as those veiled shuffling figures."

He paused on the pavement opposite the Kit Cat Club. A quartet of Australian soldiers with big-brimmed hats were looking at the advertisements of the floor show: a group of little boys were clustered round them, holding out their hands with cries of, "Hullo, George, give five piastre." There were flower stalls; and an air of bustle.

"Beirut's enjoying a boom," said Farrar. "Eight months ago it was dead. The French were in mourning, after their defeat. There was a Pétainist killjoy atmosphere. *Famille, travail, patrie* . . . no goods, no tourists, empty shop-windows, nothing. Now it's all changed. British and Australian troops on leave with their pockets full; goods coming in from Egypt and from India. Offices opening up. Employment at the Docks; a railroad being built, a need for all kinds of services, and the prices haven't gone up yet, still based on the Vichy franc. It won't last long. Let's make the most of it. Think, act and plan in terms of March 1942. There are still good Bordeaux wines at the French Officers' Club. That's where I'd suggest we go."

The French Officers' Club was along the waterfront, half way between the night club section and the St. Georges. It was a large barrack type building, with, on the first floor, a library and sitting rooms that were, so Farrar informed Reid, rarely used. "Heaven knows what happens on the top floors," he said. "I've never had the good luck to find out."

The dining-room was large and high; over half of the tables were occupied. There were more British uniforms than French.

"And the dinner's on me," said Farrar. "I can charge you up once against the firm. After that it's Dutch. When did you drink

19

champagne last? Not since you left England? Good, there's still some left. This place is run by the man who owns the Lucullus Restaurant, which is about the tops; he knows what's what. And I'll tell you another place here where you can get good wine; the Egyptian wagonlit. They've a stock and they're not hoarding it, they're working through it at a reasonable profit. There'll never be another Krug '28. Let's have a fling with it. And really it's about time you said something now. I've talked my head off."

Reid smiled. It was his role in life, after all, to listen while his juniors talked. He would lecture for an hour without interruption. Then there would be the tutorial, when he tried to be a receptive stimulant to young men and women, uncertain of themselves in one way, desperately self-assertive in another, desperately self-conscious, testing themselves against his response; he had to make it easy for them, yet he had to be critical. He had to be a kind of *sage-femme*, bringing their ideas to birth. In conversation he did not attempt to force his ideas on other people. He wanted to know what they thought. He preferred to hear Farrar talk. Besides he could learn far more from Farrar than Farrar could from him.

"Let's start with oysters," Farrar said. For seven weeks Reid had eaten three meals a day in the Belgian ship s.s. *Leopoldville*; for the first three days he had been enchanted by her Continental cuisine, but by the end of the first week he had come to find the same range of meals monotonous. In Cairo he had been restricted in his choice of restaurants by the limited means at his disposal. This was the first real dinner that he had eaten since he left England.

He concentrated upon its excellence—so exclusively that he had little time to look round the room. It was not till the end of the meal that he noticed three tables away the tall blue-eyed young woman who had welcomed the missionaries on their arrival. She was with a group, of which she was the only one not in uniform. One of the women was a nursing sister, with grey skirt and blouse, red collar and wide white cap; the other wore the grey-blue of the Motor Transport Corps. The three men were Army officers. She herself in a burgundy red dress had an exotic air in the varied conformity of her group. Reid called Farrar's attention to her.

"Who's that? The one in red?"

"Diana Benson."

"What does she do in the Mission?"

"The same as I do."

"Cloak and dagger?"

"More or less."

"She looks rather striking."

"She is striking. Her father's a retired general: East Kent, very county. She's a rebel: drove an ambulance in Spain during the Civil War."

"For the loyalists, I suppose."

"No, that's the funny thing; for Franco."

"She's a Catholic then."

"No, she did it to be different. She's got a minority complex. All her friends were for the left, so she went with the right. I don't suppose she cared much either way, but she wanted to be where things were happening."

"There's no ring on her left hand."

"There are a lot of men here who'd be delighted to put one there; she's popular with chaps."

"Is she wild?"

"I wouldn't say so, but she's twenty-five. Something must have happened. You might find her interesting. I'll see what they're doing afterwards."

Farrar walked over to their table; as he leant over it he saw Diana Benson raise her head and look in his own direction. Her face lit up. He saw her nod her head.

"That's O.K.," said Farrar on his return. "The nursing sister has to be back early and the other girl is tired, but Diana'll bring two of the men to the 'Chat Rouge' afterwards."

The Chat Rouge was a small underground *boîte* opposite the St. Georges, run by a Russian refugee, who strummed mournful songs on a guitar. It was ill lit, heavy with smoke, with low divans round the walls. It was reminiscent of Paris in the '20s.

"Ten minutes of this and I'll fall asleep," said Reid.

But within five minutes Diana Benson had arrived. Seeing her on the stairs he had realised that she was tall but he had not realised how tall she was till she came into the small low room. She had to bend to get through the doorway; she was taller than both her escorts, and they were not short. Yet she did not seem large or cumbersome when she was curled up beside him among the cushions.

"You won't believe it, but I've been looking forward to this for seven years," she said.

"Looking forward to what?"

"To meeting you."

"How did you ever come to hear of me?"

"Does the name Margaret Spencer convey anything?"

"Margaret Spencer?"

"One of your pupils."

"Margaret Spencer." Yes, the name returned; and vaguely the face and the appearance that went with it. But she was one of many, very many. She had not been remarkable in looks or in achievement. He could not even place her year. He had not thought of her once since she went down. "Was she a friend of yours?" he asked.

"A kind of friend. We came from the same part of Kent; she used to rave about your lectures, the way you humanised history and philosophy, so that they weren't cold and abstract, so that they were alive, a part of living. Then your tutorials: she said it was wonderful reading out her essays to you. The way you would listen and nod, and then ask one or two questions: somehow those questions managed to be personal. 'There I was supposed to be talking about Kant,' she'd say, 'and I *was* talking about Kant, yet at the same time I was talking about myself, about my own problems. It's wonderful to have someone to whom you can really talk about yourself.' That's what struck me so. To have someone to whom you could really talk; not to a contemporary. That isn't the same thing: someone older, wiser, who can explain one to oneself. 'If only I had someone like that in my life,' I used to think. I was so excited when I heard you were coming here. It's too late now, of course. You're a soldier, not a professor, and. . . ." She paused, breathless. Her eyes were shining and there was a glow in her contralto voice.

He looked at her through the dusk. She was not actually pretty, but in flashes she had beauty; she had it now, in the aftermath of her eager outpouring.

"Didn't you go to a University?" he asked.

She shook her head.

"Why not?"

"My father was too anxious that I should."

"Did you make it a rule always to do the opposite of what your father wanted?"

"There have to be exceptions to every rule."

"And that's why you drove an ambulance for Franco?"

"Oh no, that was part of the same project. My father would

have so enjoyed being able to say in the Rag: 'There's my daughter now, joined up with the Spanish Bolshies, got guts, of course. I'll give her that; but to think of my daughter among all that rif-raf.' I robbed him of a grievance. That's a hard thing to forgive. But how did you know I'd driven an ambulance for Franco?"

"Farrar told me."

"He did. And what else did he tell you about me?"

"That your father was a general; that you came from East Kent. Huntin', shootin', fishin'. That you were a rebel."

"That's true enough."

"What were you rebelling against?"

"Everything. The general complacence. Do you know East Kent?"

"Scarcely."

"It's lovely country. I'll give it that. The Oast Houses and the hop gardens. The Garden of England; and Canterbury itself—with all that English history: but don't they know it, these Men of Kent, so self-assured, so circumscribed. Unless you were born in Kent you don't exist. The Band of Brothers; that's typical of Kent. In any other cricket-playing county it would be Gentlemen of Kent and any resident could join; but not in Kent, you have to have been born there to belong: either a Kentish man or a man of Kent. It's fine, all that tradition, but it's stifling."

Once again her rich voice glowed; this time with anger. She was like a panther.

"I don't suppose that you're the only child," he said.

"Oh no, there are five of us. I came fourth."

"They're not like you?"

"Only my youngest brother. At least he could have been. There was one side of him that would like to have worn long hair and corduroys and listened to jazz music, but he let the other side have its way. He went into the Navy though: not the Army; the Navy's freer."

"Your other brothers are in the Army?"

"I'll say they are; both of them with red flannel on their tunics and my sister's married to a captain in the Blues. I'm the one apostate. Oh, listen to that thing he's playing. Austria in February '39. That's what it takes me back to. Kitzbuhl and the skiing. That's another thing that drove my father mad. My being friends with Austrians. 'We'll be at war with them within a year,' he'd say. 'All the more reason to be friends with them now,' I'd answer.

To think that it was only thirty-three months ago. It seems another century . . . oh well. . . .

"Yes?" She looked up quickly. One of her escorts was asking her to dance. "Yes? Oh, well, yes, thank you."

She slid on to her feet. He watched her as she danced. She managed her great height gracefully. It was awkward, always, for a man to dance with a woman taller than himself. But Diana had evolved her own technique. She danced at a right angle to him, his right hand against her right waist, her left hand on his shoulder, her right arm hanging free. They looked very natural, and at ease on that minute floor. Reid wondered whether they meant anything to one another. On the man's face was a yearning look. But she seemed simply to be someone who liked dancing. He sat back among the cushions. One of the escorts was on his other side, turning away from him, gossiping with Farrar; he started to listen and then ceased to listen; the music thudded softly and he felt drowsy. He looked at his watch. Ten to twelve. And he had woken that morning at six o'clock in Haifa. Eighteen hours and he was tired. He leant across to Farrar. "I'm through. I'm packing up. Thank you for a wonderful evening, and I'll let you know very soon about that offer. I'm pretty certain it will be 'yes.' "

"I hope it will be. I'll be on the St. Georges terrace tomorrow before lunch. Let's meet there for a drink."

"Fine, I'll be there."

Diana was still on the floor. He waved his hand to her. There was a bright, welcoming expression in her eyes.

Outside the air was cool and clean; the moon had set but the sky was starlit. The snow on the mountains glistened. The main rooms of the St. Georges were empty. His bed had been turned down. The fact that a nightmaid had been in his room emphasised the unreality of his presence in wartime in this luxury hotel. Quarter of a century ago, a subaltern in the line, he had read Siegfried Sassom's "Base Details":

> "When I am old and bald and short of breath
> I'll live with scarlet majors at the base . . .
> Guzzling and gorging in the best hotel."

He shrugged. Time's revenges.

On his dressing table was the envelope that had been awaiting him at the Mission. He had not opened it during the ninety minutes when he had been getting himself settled into his new quarters. It wouldn't be the kind of letter to be read in a hurry, he had told himself. He would read it in solitude, at the end of the day, "when he had tidied all things for the night." He picked up the envelope; he turned it over; he hesitated. Once again he thought, "Not now. Later when I'm ready for it; in the morning, when I'm fresh." He put down the envelope. He undressed slowly, savouring the peace of this luxurious bedroom after the confined conditions of a cabin shared with three other men. He opened the window. It was a relief to be able to open a window after seven hermetically sealed weeks of blackout restrictions. He turned off the main centre light, got into bed, opened the Oxford Book of English Verse, turned to Tennyson's *Lotus Eaters*, but he had not read seven lines before the print began to blur. He switched off his bedside light. "Than tired eyelids upon tired eyes," he thought, and was asleep.

2

REID SLEPT LATE, waking to a room bright with sunlight. The air was cool and fresh. He rose and closed the window. He drew back the curtains. The Mediterranean was unruffled now. Craning his neck, he could see the long curve of the water-front, the line of the low roofs, the cypresses by the cemetery, the snow-capped mountains at the back. He might have been in Nice. 'I'll have my breakfast brought up here,' he thought.

He turned to pick up the telephone, but he saw the unopened envelope propped against the mirror. "No," he thought, "I must read this first."

As he slit the flap of the envelope he felt his nerves contract. The familiar handwriting, the familiar writing paper; elegant, from Smythson, browny grey, with the address, "Hirst Farm, South-wick," in red, and in the left hand corner a drawing of a miniature telephone before the number, and a railway train beside the name "Hassocks S.R.R." Then the date: Monday, 8th September; only three days after their last night in London.

"Darling," it began. "I've just got back here and I can't believe it. The house is so full of you. It doesn't seem credible that you won't be coming down here next weekend. How long is it going to be? How can it not last several years? We shan't stop until we've won; and we haven't begun yet to start winning it. James will be at Fernhurst then, and Mark, too, probably. . . . They'll be strangers to you; and we, how shall *we* seem to one another? We'll look the same, won't we, unless you get very fat. I can't imagine myself getting fat, with these grim rations here. Will we have changed underneath? You'll be leading such a different life, and I'll be leading so very much the same life . . . in the same house, with the same neighbours, going to the same shops, making an occasional trip to London, with the children's height-marks on the door going up each holidays. The same life except that you won't be here—and of course that is an immense 'except'; while you'll be doing so much, seeing so many new places, meeting so many new people. When you come back you'll have so much to talk about that in a way there'll be no point in your talking because I shan't understand about them. I, who'll have the same silly gossip about the rector, and Mrs. Hawes, and Simon Long. . . .

"And then there's all this security, so you can't tell me where you are or what you're doing. I shan't be able to picture you; . . . only two days ago . . . and already I don't know where you are . . . and I'm afraid that long, long journey is going to be very grim and dreary for you; being away from all your friends and interests. I do think it unfair that twice in a lifetime you should have had this happen to you.

"But you do realise, don't you, darling, how proud I am of you? It's wonderful that they should think you important enough to be sent all that way upon that Mission. It's different from a whole regiment being sent. This is so very special, going all by yourself. Dear one, please never forget how proud I am of you, or how proud the boys are. It means more to them than either of us can guess, to be able to say at school, 'My father's in the army; he's in the Middle East.' "

Reid let the letter fall forward on his knees, overwhelmed with a sense of guilt. There was, after all, no need for him to be here. He could easily have applied for an exemption. He would have, had his home life been happier.

On the surface it had been a successful marriage. Rachel was seven years younger than himself. They had been married eleven years when the war broke out. They had two boys, born in their first thirty months of marriage. Rachel was small and dark. Her mother, who had been Jewish, had died in the 'flu epidemic of 1918. Her father, a successful London architect, had remarried, and by his second marriage had three children. But through her mother Rachel had received a share of a trust fund that brought her in an annual income of twenty-five hundred pounds. Their marriage, that was to say, was materially well established since Reid was able to supplement his University fees with editorial work. In his agreeable eighteenth century house in Southwick he was in a position to indulge his taste for entertaining. Rachel was an excellent hostess.

No marriage could have been more suitable. Each was eminently eligible. Each was at the marrying age, he thirty, and she twenty-three. Each was a flint waiting for the tinder. Yet it had been, for both of them, a romantic courtship; he had spoken of it as the "coup de foudre."

"We both knew right away. It all happened in the thirty seconds that it takes to walk from a head-waiter's desk to a table in the window."

And what had happened to it? Their honeymoon and the picnic time that they had in their new home afterwards had been a rich enchantment. Within five months she had told him she was pregnant. For him, as for her, it had been welcome news. There had been a dream quality about those months with Rachel changing inperceptibly, becoming another person, no longer a playmate to make love with but a precious invalid to be adored and cherished. During the last weeks an ethereal beauty had transfigured her. He had not thought it possible for him to love anyone so much . . . and yet . . . and yet. . . . How was it that after his son had been weaned he had never been able to get back to the gay atmosphere of courtship? He had watched her change from a playmate into an invalid: he had adjusted himself to that change, but he was not able to readjust himself to this second change, from invalid to playmate. He could not get back to his old feelings for her.

Why, why, why? She had not lost her figure or her looks. She was as active on the tennis courts. In herself she had not changed. She had not become overwhelmingly maternal. She did not, as young mothers often did, neglect him for the child. The difference was not in her, it was in him. He no longer wanted to make love to her; it was an inconceivable situation but there it was. He had continued, naturally, to make love to her. But the spontaneity, the zest had gone.

On the surface they were a happy couple. They never quarrelled; they had similar tastes. They liked doing the same things, they liked the same people. She enjoyed, when he came back at the end of the day, sitting with him over a martini and exchanging the gossip of the day. She shared a half bottle of wine with him at dinner. She was interested in his career. She seemed contented. She was gay and cheerful. She never sulked. When he compared his marriage with other people's, there seemed to be nearly everything right with it. All except this one thing. Making love was a delight no longer; it had become a duty.

He had sometimes wondered whether a psychiatrist might not be able to help him. But he distrusted psychiatrists. The whole of his childhood and youth would be explored. And at the end of it all he would be informed that he had a fixation about his mother; that once Rachel had become a mother the idea of making love to her partook of incest; and because as a child he had suppressed his desire to make love to his mother, there was now a repugnance in the idea of approaching Rachel. And perhaps that might be the explanation; but what good would it do him if it were? Was it so important to know the cause of one's problem? Wasn't it better to recognise what the problems were and learn to live with them—in the same way that driving an old car there was no need to know how, when and where the gears, the brakes and the clutch had been strained and damaged? The point was to learn how to handle a car that possessed those disabilities; so he had let it stand. And always at the back of everything there had been this drain upon his energies, this strain upon his nerves, this recurrent, incessant burden; a subtle persistent poison. So that his first reaction on that September morning, when he opened a War Office letter and read the calling up notice, had been one of an unqualified relief. No sense of regret, of loss at the abandonment of his career, of separation from his home; only the thought: "At last, at last." War had produced the solution to a problem to which there had seemed no solution.

He picked up the letter again. He re-read the sentence. "How proud the children are. It means more to them than either of us guess for them to be able to say at school, 'My father's in the army. He's in the Middle East.'" Once again guilt overcame him. What right had he had to leave them at a time so crucial for them, for

28

a personal whim, because he hadn't learnt to live with his own problem?

"I keep thinking about that last night," the letter ended. "I couldn't believe it was the last night. It seemed so like every other night. I couldn't believe that in twenty-four hours' time I should be back here, having seen you off at Euston and that you'd be on your way north in a train to Glasgow, bound all those miles away. Perhaps it's best, isn't it, that it should have been like that; that it should have seemed an ordinary evening, not an occasion, something to be taken as part of the routine of marriage."

Was that really what she thought, or was it an alibi, a cover, an attempt on her part to make him feel that everything had been as it should have been on that last evening? Did he ever know really what she was thinking? That was one of the strange things about marriage. In a way you knew somebody so well; you knew what would amuse them, and what annoy them. You learnt what to avoid, and what to do. You talked in a kind of shorthand. But did you know what went on underneath? Did you ever talk openly with one another? In every marriage there were scenes; you were anxious to avoid their repetition, unless yours was one of those marriages that are fed on scenes, that are kept electric and alive by scenes, a kind of self-tortured torturing. You recognised the danger signals of a scene; you saw it on the horizon. You learnt how to avoid it. And that was what you called in marriage, "getting to know each other"; but in fact it was not that at all. It was a learning how to elude each other. You never put your cards upon the table. Because you had scenes no longer, you boasted that you had no secrets from each other; and then suddenly a chance remark would draw aside the curtain and you would realise that you had no idea what the other person had been feeling.

How did he know what Rachel had been feeling through that long, last day? They spent it in London, coming up from Sussex in the morning. They had booked a room at her club, the International Sportsmen's, to which during war-time, members were allowed to take their husbands and to which she had often come up during his year at the Ministry of Mines. They had seats for "Blithe Spirit"; the curtain went up at 7. They had a sandwich first, arranging because of the difficulty of getting taxis, to dine afterwards at Grosvenor House. It was a usual routine for them. There was no point in departing from it. Yet all through the day he had been thinking, "This is an occasion. This must be an occasion. This is our last night. We shan't be seeing each other again for four, five years; we shall look back to this night so often, reliving it, remembering it. It must be made special for her. The right kind of last night will be her assurance that we'll re-start life happily when the war is over." Balzac in his physiology of marriage had said that everything depended on the first night. Didn't everything in a wartime separation depend on the last night? It must be right for her.

He glanced at her more than once during the play. She was laughing with every appearance of lightheartedness at this lighthearted comedy. She appeared not to have a worry in the world. It might be any evening. He had noted it with irritation. How could he make it an occasion if she was not in the mood for an occasion?

That was what he had thought then in London, but here, ten weeks later in Beirut, her letter in his hand, he wondered. He must have seemed as unconcerned to her as she had to him. Beneath the calm surface, she may have been torturing herself with doubts, saying to herself, "I must make this night memorable for him, so that he'll think of me the way I want him to, during this long separation. But how can I, on my own, after thirteen years of marriage, if he treats it like any other night?" She might well have been thinking that, in the same mood of despair, under the same pressure, hopelessly trying to break out of the inexorable pattern that marriage had established.

By the time they were back at Grosvenor House his nerves were taut.

"I think we should have champagne," he said. "Heaven knows when I shall have another chance of drinking it."

He cursed himself the moment he had said it. Why had he put it that way? Why couldn't he have made it personal; have said, "Let's wish ourselves luck with Bollinger."

"What would you like with it?" he asked. "Oysters?"

She shook her head. "You won't get any game on a troop ship. Let's split a grouse."

"Hot grouse, or cold?"

"I'd prefer it cold."

"So'd I."

The amber wine sparkled. He raised his glass. "Good luck to us," he said. The wine was light and gay. It sent a reassuring glow along his veins. "It's going to be all right," he thought, adding as a corollary, "It's got to be all right."

But later as he lay in bed watching her at her dressing table, he was conscious only of exhaustion. There had been so many little chores during the last few days, the inoculations, the tropical kit, the issuing of a passport, the packing, the deciding what to take and what to leave. He was like a runner at the end of a long race.

She brushed her hair slowly in long sweeps. He always enjoyed watching her brush her hair. It was like watching an artist before an easel, the slow creation of a thing of beauty. It tranquillised his nerves. By long habit drowsiness came over him. She stood up. She was wearing a transparent nightgown: with the light behind her he could see in silhouette her soft curved outline. In just that way in their first year of marriage he had seen her in silhouette against a lamp. She was ten weeks pregnant, but her figure had not begun to change. Her breasts had lifted the bodice of the nightgown so that it hung away from her body, veiling but not hiding it. He had seen nothing lovelier. At the same time he had thought, "I'm seeing it for the last few times and this one glimpse of it is a chance effect of lighting and of grouping. It may not come again; and in a few more days that line will have been distended. It will never return wholly, the perfection of the breasts will vanish, gone for ever." The sense of imminent loss had struck him. "Look thy last on all things lovely," and he had opened his arms, hungrily.

The memory of that moment returned poignantly, as she lifted her hand to switch off the light. She pulled back the curtain, and a shaft of moonlight lit the room. She turned towards him. The club room had twin beds; at Hirst Farm they shared a bed, though he had a dressing room. She hesitated: he flung back the sheets; she slid in beside him. She nestled herself against him and his arms went round her. His heart was heavy. The words that he wanted to say deserted him. Gently, very gently, he stroked her shoulder. "Darling," he murmured, "darling." His fingers ran the length of her arm in a slow caress. So often in the past he had soothed her this way, wooing her to sleep. On her, too, the compulsion of habit began to work. Her breathing became regular and gentle. She mustn't go to sleep, he thought, not tonight. She mustn't, mustn't; but his fingers could not stop their slow caress. Her breathing became steady. She's asleep, he thought, asleep. He

31

slid his arm slowly from beneath her shoulders. She did not stir. He edged away from her. He had a sense half of relief, half of despair; weariness returned. He closed his eyes. In a few minutes he was asleep himself.

He was roused, he did not know how much later, but the room was dark, by a slight movement at his side. She was trying to slip out of bed.

"I'm sorry," she said. "I didn't mean to wake you. I thought you'd sleep better by yourself."

He did not answer. He drew her back beside him. Once again she nestled up to him. Once again he began to stroke her shoulder, but this time it was different, and they made love gently, tenderly. Within a very few minutes, still in each other's arms, they were asleep.

Thirty hours later Rachel, back in Southwick, was writing the letter that he held in his hand; and that last night was the pledge that they had made each other, the amulet that would have to protect them against loss of faith during this long separation. He shrugged. What was there that he could do about it now?

†

He was finishing his breakfast when the telephone bell rang.

"Is that you, Prof? This is Gustave. Sorry to bother you so early, but I wanted to catch you before you left. Could you spare me a minute?"

Gustave was the subaltern—one of those billeted in a pension —whose eyes had followed Diana down the stairs.

"Where are you speaking from?" Reid asked.

"The lobby."

"Then come right up."

If he were in a dressing gown he would have an easier excuse for getting rid of Gustave. Gustave tended to be garrulous. The fact that he had acquired the nickname Gustave was indicative of his personality. He was short, wiry, athletic; he looked to be in the early thirties, but was actually only twenty-four. He had dark, curly hair; his cheeks were pale. He had a foreign look. His father was an Englishman who had entered the cotton business in Alexandria before the first world war. His father was dead. His mother might be anyone. It was an Alexandrian marriage. Who

32

could assess an Alexandrian background? Greek, Armenian, Jewish, what you will. Gustave had been to an English school, to Stowe, but his guardian had chosen Grenoble for his university. Gustave had been in France when the war broke out; he had hurried back to England. Commissioned quickly, he had asked for a posting to the Field Security Personnel, had commanded a section in the north of England, and then. . . .

Like most of those posted to the Mission he had been the victim of mischance. He had been on a parachute course, broken a bone in his ankle and been in hospital six weeks. When he returned to duty his section was in another's hands. He had awaited a fresh posting; none had come. When Spears' Mission had applied for volunteers, the adjutant had said, "Might not this be the thing for you, Gustave; Middle East, Egypt? Don't you speak Arabic? Shall I put in your name?"

Reid, from his experience of two wars, knew well how this kind of thing came to happen. Colonels did not recommend "duds" when applications for special appointments reached them, but they put barriers round the men they really needed. Gustave's colonel probably had nothing specific against Gustave. His foreign background?—Yes, perhaps, in part. Alexandria? Who was his mother, after all? And why Grenoble? Why not an English red brick university? A certain foreignness, some basic difference? A sense that he was not quite one of them? If he had not had that accident no one would have considered having him supplanted. But since he had had that accident, what a lucky chance. For five weeks Gustave had been at a loose end. He had felt humiliated. Like all the other missionaries he had been proud and excited, restored in his own self-esteem, by his new appointment. Now he was back where he had started, like the rest of them.

"I'm sorry to bother you with this," he said. "It's outrageous of me. It's quite unimportant in the long run, but at the moment . . . I did think it would save time. I've always thought of you as the senior of our group. Not in rank, of course, but what does rank matter? You've got a name. People know who you are. In ten years' time these majors and colonels will be again the nobodies they were three years ago; I shouldn't say that, of course, but there it is."

"Gustave, let's get to the point."

"I know, exactly, Prof, but I had to lead up to this. You were very decent to us younger fellows on the boat; you never gave yourselves any airs though you had a perfect right to."

"Please, Gustave, please."

"I know; I'm sorry. I *will* come to the point. You stayed behind afterwards with the boss. You were the one he picked. He recognized you as our spokesman. What did he say was going to happen to us?"

"He didn't discuss the matter."

"Then why did he ask you to stay behind?"

"He had some things to say to me, personally."

"Oh," Gustave stared, abashed, speechless; his eloquence punctured. Reid smiled. He quite liked Gustave.

"You've something on your mind. Let's have it. If I can help, I promise you I will."

"Thanks awfully, Prof . . . you . . . well. . . ." he hesitated. Then in a rush it all poured out "I'm in a rather different position from these others: through being half Egyptian. I've all these relatives in Alexandria and there are some in Cairo. One wants to cut a dash before one's family. I've an idea that they don't set much store by me. My mother was a cut above the old man, at least in their eyes; most of them are anti-British, too. You know how it used to be, when my father came out: Kipling and the white man's burden. Kick the brown johnny off the pavement. That's all over now. Jack's as good as his master. They'd like to look down on me if they could, and I don't want them to. Thing is, you see, it's all my fault, but when I learnt I was coming out I overplayed my hand. I told them that I was going to be a big shot with Spears. For the first time in my life they were impressed. They respect force, and that's what the Mission stands for, in their eyes. I boasted, yes, let's face it, boasted. That puts me in one hell of a position now."

"What can I do to help?"

"Now, that's exactly what I was wondering myself. But there's one thing I don't want; to be sent to the intelligence pool in Cairo, as a lieutenant. I'd told them, you see, I'd be made a Captain. It seemed a reasonable bet. I assumed that by the time any of them saw me I would be one. But if I get sent down to Cairo next week, it is just more than my vanity could stand. I'd rather go to Damascus as a corporal than to Cairo as a subaltern."

He spoke lightly, jocularly, with gestures; he employed a jargon that he fancied was fashionable, but that jarred on Reid's perceptions. He seemed to have cast himself as a P. G. Wodehouse character, and was getting the idiom wrong. He exaggerated his predicament. But it was a predicament none the less. Reid recognised that. He had let Gustave talk a lot; it was up to him now to help him out.

"I see your point," he said. "But I don't see at the moment what I can do. We're all in the same boat. Cartwright told me that I was a hard man to place, because I was too senior in civil life for certain posts and lacked the military training that would fit me for a job on my own level. It'll be much easier for them to place you than to place me. You are young, athletic, active. On a long term basis, you haven't any need to worry; but I do see your point about not going back to Cairo now—and as a subaltern. I'm dining with Cartwright on Wednesday. I'll make a point of saying something; I'll put it tactfully."

"Prof, you're wizard. Bless you."

"Don't bank on anything."

"I won't."

As the door closed behind Gustave, a thought crossed Reid's mind. Farrar: they'd both been at Stowe. The bond of the old school tie. Gustave might be the right man for cloak and dagger.

†

It was half past ten before Reid left his room. Johnson was in the lounge, with a paper in his hands, but he did not appear to be reading it. His eyes looked like slits. Reid presumed that he had made a heavy night of it.

"How did you make out?" he asked.

Johnson shook his head. "As you might expect. They took me to the Australian Club. It was the first time I'd had whisky at a reasonable price for weeks. I exceeded. It was good whisky, though. I'll be all right by lunch. What's more important, how did you make out?"

"Why more important?"

"Because you saw Cartwright. What had he to say?"

Here it goes again, thought Reid.

"Nothing in particular, just casual gossip. Then he introduced me to a man in the economic section who knows friends of mine. He took me to the French Club."

35

"I see. So you learnt nothing about what's cooking for the rest of us?"

"Nothing. But I can't believe there's any cause to worry. He's probably got something suitable worked out. He looks that kind of man."

"I see. . . . Well . . . what about a stroll? I could do with some fresh air."

They strolled along the waterfront. Yesterday in the rain and dark Reid had had no chance of making an assessment of the town. He found it now a cheerfully haphazard conglomeration of architectural styles. There were examples in the French idiom of the worst uses to which the 1920s had put concrete in terms of hard, rectangular lines; most of such buildings, originally ochre-tinted, had been discoloured by rain and sun. There were the bazaars, tranquil, cool and arched; the spires of Christian churches mingled with the domes and minarets of Moslem mosques. Here and there the broken stonework of a Roman column testified to a legendary past. A mingling of races and of cultures, and each race, each culture, had contributed its patina to contemporary Beirut.

It was a bright, warm day. They walked slowly, but Johnson was breathing heavily. He soon returned to the problem of his employment. "I'm in an awkward spot," he said. "I've been a major for two years; but only a temporary, not a war substantive one. If I don't get on somebody's establishment soon, I'll revert to my real rank as captain. That means a big drop in pay and in allowances. I've got a wife, and I don't have a firm making good the difference between my salary and pay. Unless I'm found a job within a fortnight I'll be 'waiting to be posted'; back to captaincy; and they may antedate it to the day of sailing. That's why I'd be so very grateful to you if you could let me know how the wind's blowing. You're in a different position. In peacetime you and Cartwright move in the same world, on the same level. He'd tell you things he'd not tell me. I'm out of my depth here. One battalion of my regiment is in India, the other is back in England. I've got no influence. I've no strings to pull; at least, I don't think I have. That's why I'd be so grateful if you'd sound out Cartwright. You'll see more of him than I shall, and, what's more important, on a different basis."

"I'll do my best."

To himself Reid smiled. None of them imagined that he himself had any problems. In their eyes he was an established person, with a job waiting him in England. They pictured him as someone who could accept with equanimity a wartime inconvenience. Well, let them go on doing so, and in point of fact, Gustave's and Johnson's problems were more serious than his own. This was Johnson's last chance of self re-establishment. His own problem was not material. It was personal.

†

Farrar kept his noontime appointment with Reid punctually. The terrace of the St. Georges faced the waterfront. On Sunday morning it was the town's fashionable rendezvous, with tables set out under striped umbrellas, and smart French officers, many of them with the blue kepis of the cavalry, clinking their heels and bowing from the waist to smartly-dressed women, Lebanese and European. It was impossible to believe that a few hundred miles away in the Western desert troops were lying out in foxholes.

Farrar stood on the steps of the terrace, looking round him. He pointed out to Reid a group of three, a middle-aged couple and a young man.

"I'm going to introduce you to them. She's of Turkish origin, married to a Lebanese. Her sister is in Istanbul. That's her nephew, Aziz. He's come down to study in the A.U.B. He's not doing very well. He's an idle gentleman, and I suspect that he's taking advantage of being away from parental scrutiny to enjoy the flesh-pots. His parents are Moslems, but his aunt's husband isn't. Let's go over. Amin Marun's the name."

The aunt was plump, pale skinned, with large dark eyes. She must have been extremely pretty as a girl. The uncle was big shouldered, fat, with flabby cheeks; his dark hair was beginning to turn white about the ears. The boy was tall and gangly, with spots on his chin. He had a long, hooked nose. He might become handsome at the age of thirty.

"I want to introduce Captain Reid," said Farrar. "He arrived yesterday to join the Mission. He's an English professor. He should be able to advise Aziz about his studies. I'm wondering whether Aziz might not do better in an English university, in Alexandria, say."

"What is he studying?" Reid asked.

"History."

"There might be better historians in Alexandria."

"That's what I was suggesting."

"But we want Aziz here with us," the uncle said.

"Perhaps he would work better if he was on his own."

Amin Marun shook his head. "That's the English theory, send boys to boarding schools. We don't agree with that. We believe in maintaining the atmosphere and influence of the home."

"But if Aziz fails in his exams again at Christmas—"

"He's not going to fail."

"I hope he isn't. But if he does I should consider Alexandria. That's why I brought Captain Reid across. He is a man of influence in scholastic circles. He might be of assistance. His brother was out here in the first war; fought in the Mesopotamian campaign. He's beginning to wonder now whether it wasn't a waste of time."

"How do you mean, a waste of time?"

"He thinks it would have been better if that part of the war had been avoided. We ought to have stayed friends with Turkey and maintained the Ottoman Empire."

"Did I say that?" said Reid.

"You inferred it and I'm sure that Madame Amin would agree with me that basically the Arabs were better off under the Ottoman Empire?"

She shook her head, as her husband answered for her, "The Turks aren't Arabs."

"They are Moslems."

"That isn't enough. Italy hasn't the right to rule France because both are Christians."

"But under the Ottoman Empire the Arabs were one people."

"One subject people."

Farrar shook his head. He turned to Reid with a laugh. "I can never get Amin Marun to agree with me. The idea of Arab independence started in Beirut. His father was one of the founders of the movement. But revolutions aren't necessarily justified because they succeed. I'm sure that Madame Amin would agree with me on that point. She was brought up in Turkey. The Turks would never have divided the Arab world into separate spheres of influence as we Europeans have. The Sykes-Picot agreement was about the most discreditable diplomatic performance of the war. And think how much worse it might have been. Suppose Russia had had her share, as she was intended to, with the Arab world divided up, not between two countries but between three. And I can tell you this. We haven't finished with Sykes-Picot yet. Not by a long chalk, now that the Russians are in the war again. Stalin is as much an imperialist as any Czar. There are just as many private treaties in this war as in the last. I know this for a fact. There's going to be at least one new Republic in the U.S.S.R. when the war is over and that's Kurdistan. The Kurds are crazy for it. They're sick of being divided up between Syria, Turkey, Persia and Iraq."

He enlarged his thesis: "To keep Russia in the war we have to promise her what she wants; the Kurds are the cream in her coffee."

Reid let him talk, but afterwards at lunch in the Cercle he remonstrated. "I never said that the Arabs were better off under the Turks. I don't believe it for a moment."

"I'm sure you don't. I was using you as a decoy. I wanted to lead up to that corollary about the Kurds."

"Yes, and what about that now? Is it true?"

"Of course it isn't."

"Then why on earth?"

"The oldest trick in counterespionage. Didn't they tell you about it during that course at Matlock? If you want to find out if someone is indiscreet you tell him under a vow of secrecy something that isn't true. If you then hear the story from another source you know that that person broke his vow of secrecy. My Kurdish nonsense is a variation on that gimmick. If that story crops up in the Turkish press or in any of the confidential summaries from Istanbul—we're on very good terms with one section of their foreign Ministry—I shall know what Madame Amin is about."

"Do you know that she is in contact with someone there?"

"I suspect she is. We're censoring her correspondence but we've found nothing yet. She probably sends her messages, if she sends them, through someone here."

"What'll you do if you find that she is sending messages?"

"Nothing, for the moment. I'll have to decide—or rather other people will have to decide for me—what is the best use for her. When a policeman is chasing a murderer, the moment he has his man, he claps the handcuffs on. It's different in our game. We could use Madame Amin as a broadcasting station. We could send up to Turkey—and Turkey is neutral, don't forget—the kind of information that we want the Germans to have, true, half true, altogether false. If we were to find some excuse for arresting Madame Amin, we might frighten and send underground a number of people whom we want to watch. We rarely arrest small fry. They are more useful at liberty. They may lead us to something; and, of course, as I said, I've no idea whether she is passing on information; or, if she is, whether she is passing it on innocently. She can be useful that way too. She's a push-over from our point of view. Born in Turkey, married to a Lebanese, all her family in Turkey—somebody must be using her. I want to know where and how. . . . What did you make of the boy, by the way?"

"I hadn't any chance of making anything. He didn't say a word."

"Is he queer?"

"How on earth should I know?"

"Schoolmasters have a nose for that kind of thing."

"I'm not a schoolmaster."

"I know you aren't, but you know that world. What would your guess be?"

"I'd say 'no.' "

"You would. I was afraid you would."

"Afraid?"

"Forget it. If he had been, it would have been more simple. But in this world things don't always work out simply. And when they do, there's usually a snag. One waits and bides one's time. I've all the time there is. Now about this afternoon. This is your range-taking day. What about the racecourse?"

There was racing every Sunday. If it had been difficult that morning on the terrace of the St. Georges to believe that a war was being fought, a few hundred miles away, it was even harder that afternoon when the same elegant creatures whom he had seen that morning at the St. Georges were sauntering now in different frocks under the fir-trees, past the paddock. At the far end of the racecourse was the low yellow *Residence* where General Catroux lived, with its Circassian guard in comic opera uniform at the gateway. It was like a film-set. And after the races there was a *thé dansant* at the St. Georges, with the same smart officers, the same smart women, again in different dresses.

"This is their big day of the week and this is how they spend it," Farrar said. "And this is our one free day a week and this is how we spend it. There's really no alternative, with petrol scarce. There's a nine hole golf course but one loses balls so fast that one can't afford to play often enough to strike any kind of form. But it's a good life even so. Now, what about that flat of mine?"

"I'd like to move in very much."

"Fine. Give me a couple of days, to get in some more furniture, and we are fixed."

To be living in a semi-luxury flat in this frivolous little beach resort was certainly an odd footnote to last year's *"drôle de guerre."*

†

Reid moved in on the Wednesday. There was now in the spare room, a double bed, a wardrobe and a desk; there were a couple of rugs on the floor.

"We'll get some pictures soon; but that's a start. You've your own entrance to the bathroom, which has two doors so that you can lock me out, and you've got a private key to the flat, so that you've all the privacy you could need if you want to entertain a floosy."

"I don't fancy that I'm likely to."

"You never know; and remember this: shortage of females is the central problem of the Middle East. But it isn't here. Make the most of Beirut while you can. You might be posted to Baghdad one day."

That night Reid dined with Cartwright. Cartwright had a bungalow five minutes' drive from the Legation, which before the war had been owned by an Englishman in the I.P.C. It was furnished in the English style: with heavy club armchairs, photographs of school groups, and an oar over the mantelpiece.

"This should make you homesick for college life," said Cartwright.

There was no other guest. "I thought it would be more pleasant just to ourselves," he said. "I have to do so much official entertaining and being entertained; it becomes an effort, always trying to find what interests the others so that I can keep the conversation moving. Always the search for a common multiple; usually it's a very low one. I'm sure we'll find that we have a good deal in common."

Cartwright was three years older, but they were contemporaries in this, that they had had no adult life before August 1914. Cartwright was to have gone up to Oxford that October. They had grown up quickly in wartime, and over half of their contemporaries were dead.

"I was looking at the old Fernhurst register the other day," said Reid. "Of the forty-four boys who went to school with me in September 1911 only nineteen are alive, and I suppose in your case there'd be even fewer: your generation was in France in time for the Somme; mine didn't get there till Passchendaele. The survivors of the Somme came back for a second dose of medicine. For the most part, the survivors of Passchendaele hadn't recovered in time for the victory campaign."

"The lost generation, in fact."

"Weren't there a number of lost generations, each different in a very definite way?"

"I guess there were, but I'll tell you this. I believe that those of us who did survive are younger now than our immediate successors. We had no youth, no carefree period. But in recompense we got a delayed adolescence. Some of those bright young people are beginning to look middle-aged."

They compared notes; they had many friends in common, although their lives had followed such separate streams.

"I hear that you are going to live with Farrar," Cartwright said. "I'm surprised at that."

"He's a lively fellow."

"He's that all right. I don't know what he's doing half the time, and I don't want to know. But he won't be able to go on doing it much longer in the Mission building."

"He's aware of that."

"I'm glad he is; he certainly keeps queer company. But you'll live well with him. And I don't suppose you'll be staying here very long."

At that point Reid recalled his promises to his fellow missionaries. "Do you think it's going to be difficult to place us all?" he asked.

Cartwright shrugged. "I can't imagine that it will. This is a developing area. One has to have reserves in case of an emergency. You remember yourself in the last war when you were at the front how much of the time you spent doing absolutely nothing. It was part of an officer's job to see that his men did not get bored. It is not so very different with staff work. Someone like myself is working harder at this moment than he ever has done in his life, so are a large number of officers at M.E.F. in Cairo.

Yet I know perfectly well that in the Mission building half of the officers, who have to spend eight hours a day beside a telephone because someone responsible has to be there to answer it, don't do six hours' real work a week. It is precisely the same in Cairo. There's waste and idleness in wartime. It can't be otherwise. Someone worked out once how many men were needed in back-areas to keep one man in the firing line, and how many bullets were fired for every casualty."

"So you don't think the fellows need to worry?"

"Of course they don't. Something'll turn up. Every establishment is trying to enlarge itself so that the ones at the top can go up a rank; you can't have a major-general without twenty-eight lieutenants in the basement. You could work out a multiplication table: twenty-eight lieutenants rate fourteen captains, fourteen captains rate seven majors, seven majors rate four colonels, four colonels rate two brigadiers, two brigadiers rate one major-general."

"Some of these surplus missionaries are rather worried at the moment. They think that no one's worrying about them."

"They are dead right there: nobody is."

That answer did startle Reid. He was not used to hearing men in authority answer so unreservedly. Cartwright was lolling back in his chair, his feet raised upon an Arab cushion. He was wearing the pointed local slipper with the heel turned in. He had a cigar between his fingers. He was utterly relaxed. "Why should any of us be worrying about them?" he said. "We are extremely busy people. We've no spare time; as things are at the moment they can't help us; our work is distributed among the staff we need. If we try to make work for them we clog up our own machinery. We do our best to welcome them; we give them an office they can sit in. We report their presence here to the appropriate authorities. If we hear of anything that would be likely to suit them we'll, of course, put them on it. In the meantime they can look around on their own behalf. They are almost certain to find something soon."

"You don't feel any responsibility for them?"

"Why should I? We're not an employment agency. It's not our fault they're here. It's London's."

"Isn't it rather bad luck on them?"

Cartwright shrugged. "Is it? I don't know. There are casualties of all kinds in wartime. These are not very serious casualties. At the most it only involves them in the loss of temporary rank for a few weeks. They'll soon recover that crown or extra star; they're not unemployed in the sense that a civilian is when a firm cuts down its staff. They are drawing their pay; they have their allowances. They are better off here than they'd be in England. It's not as though they were professional soldiers with careers at stake. A temporary soldier's war record does not count for much three years after the war's over, unless he's put up a terrific black or won the V.C. No one knows who was the subaltern and who the colonel in the long run. It doesn't really matter what happens to them, here. And from the short point of view they'll all of them be all right in six months' time."

Had Cartwright's little speech been transcribed by a shorthand-typist it might have seemed arrogant and insensitive; but it did not sound that way, spoken in a quiet, sympathetic voice, accompanied by a smile.

"This isn't quite the impression that you gave them in that welcoming address of yours; when you told them they were all hand-picked men."

Cartwright laughed. "One has to cheer people up. By raising their morale, by telling them they're wanted here, they're much more likely to find themselves a job than if they went around with a hangdog look thinking no one wants them. Hand-picked? Yes, I know, but in what cattle pen? Be honest now: was there in that whole consignment a single outstanding person, except yourself, of course; they are all of them sound, responsible, efficient—if they hadn't been, they wouldn't have been sent out here—but if they really had been outstanding they wouldn't have been sent: their colonels would have seen to that. Except, as I said, yourself. And you've special talents for which the service ought to be able to find some use. They didn't apparently find the right use in England. We must try to do better here. But, as I said, you're a hard man to place."

Reid smiled ruefully. "You're not the first person who's said that."

"I guess that's true; let's hope that I'm the last. But even if I'm not . . . well, does it matter much? When it's all over, you'll go back to your old life, refreshed. It may be that you'll think in retrospect that this whole episode was a lucky break, a half-time breather; and you're bound to be enlarged by this, by becoming a part of the Moslem world. It may add a dimension to you. I'm not worrying about your enforced idleness on your own account;

I'm simply feeling that from the service point of view, in terms of the war effort, it's a waste."

Reid returned to his flat to see a line of light under the door of Farrar's sitting room. It had been agreed that when Farrar did not want to be disturbed he would lock the door; and that Reid should retire quietly or remain in his own room till Farrar's visitor had left. Reid turned the handle, pressed and the door opened.

Farrar was seated at his desk, with an array of stamps spread out.

"I did not know you were a philatelist."

"I'm not, and what a word to use. I'm an investor; a contrabandist; these are my blue chips. I don't trust currency. But stamps are like diamonds: they're easy to smuggle across frontiers. I'm laying in provisions for my old age. How was it? Did he do you well?"

"Extremely."

"What gossip did you pick up? Anything I can turn to my nefarious purposes?"

Reid shook his head. "We were two venerable quadragenarians comparing notes about the first war and our youth; but there is a young fellow in the Mission building whom you might use. He was at Stowe; born in Alexandria; twenty-four years old."

"A Stoic. Ah, let's look him up. What is his name?"

"Sargent. S-A-R-G-E-N-T, initials A.Q."

Farrar had the old Stoics address book on his shelf. "Twenty-four, you say; then he must have gone there in '30 or '31. Just after I'd left, but he must have known quite a number of men that I knew. Sargent, A.Q. That's it; September '31. Not the same house as I. Left 1936. So he had five years there. Doesn't look as though he'd been expelled, stayed out his full time. Address c/o Barclay's Bank, Paris. That's plain enough. Tells us damn all. Now tell me what you know about him."

Reid told all he knew. "There's something endearing about him; something feminine. Perhaps it comes from his mother. He was nicknamed Gustave."

"That might add up to something in the long run. Nicknames often do: they are usually appropriate. Names often aren't."

"It doesn't always follow. I was nicknamed Moke at school. Would you call that appropriate?"

"I'd say I wouldn't. Moke? How did that come about?"

"Ned. Donkey. Moke."

"I get it. Prep school, I suppose."

"Yes."

"Of course. That wouldn't mean a thing. At Fernhurst, did you have a nickname there?"

"I've never had another nickname."

"You haven't? No, I guess you wouldn't. You're not a nickname person, somehow. Prof. That's another matter. It seems right here. The disparity of age and your distinction. But Gustave now; he's touched you somehow, made you feel protective. Do you know why?"

"He's weak and vain. He was anxious to cut a dash before his relatives in Alexandria. He's only a lieutenant, but he told them he was coming out here as a captain, as a diplomat. He daren't tell them that he's a subaltern in the intelligence pool in Cairo."

"Ah, now you're talking."

Farrar stood up. His eyes brightened. He began to stride up and down the room.

"We're on to something there. A man's Achilles' heel. A man's point of vanity. If once we find out what he needs from us, we've got some chance of getting what we want from him. If only more people would realise that simple truth, but they never do. The average person makes an acquaintance. His first thought is, 'What can this man do for me; what can I get out of him?' He'd be so much wiser if he'd think, 'Is there anything I can do for this man that no one else can?' If he finds that out, and does it, then he can start asking himself what he is going to get in return. It's a very true fact that there isn't anyone so important that you can't do something for him that no one else can. It may be something very simple. Like meeting a professional actor, or being taken into the pavilion at the Oval. Something that you and I take for granted. Now we know where we are with Gustave. He wants to cut a dash in Alexandria. If we see that he does, and then later threaten to spoil his performance for him . . . Anyhow, we'd better have a look at him; ask him up for a drink. Don't tell him we've anything in mind. I'll have to have him checked in London. He's probably all right on security grounds; M.I.5 must have checked on him before he was passed for F.S.P. Cairo can check on his Egyptian contacts. Cairo can authorise me, if it wants, to take him on. But we must see him first. Try and get him for Friday night. I'll ask along a girl or two; I'll get a line on him from them."

"Diana Benson, I suppose."

He shook his head. "It's best for her not to come up here."

"Why not? Everyone knows that she's your secretary."

"There's no need for them to know that she's my friend."

"You went over and spoke to her in the Cercle in front of everyone."

"That's different. The Cercle's a public place. This flat's a private place; it's probably watched. I have to be careful of who comes here and how often."

Reid was conscious both of irritation and disappointment. The whole thing seemed so silly. "But doesn't my being here make a difference? I'll have friends of my own, won't I? Couldn't she be one of them?"

Farrar grinned. "My dear fellow, but of course she could. And if you and she arrive together and by your *éntree independent*, no one will be happier than I. Fine for you both. But I don't want her here as a party guest. You may think I overdo security, but it's as well to be on the safe side. I'll bring along some lively girls, I promise you. I'll ask them for six-thirty. Warn Gustave to be here at six; that'll give me a half-hour's innings with him."

†

Gustave arrived promptly and there ensued between him and Farrar a conventional Old Boy's meeting.

"I was delighted to hear there was another Stoic here," said Farrar. "There must be quite a few, but I haven't found them yet and, of course, as the school only opened in the 'twenties we haven't got any high-ups. That's a bit of a nuisance. I'd like to feel there were a few major-generals and Air-vice marshalls I could play Old School Ties with. That's where Etonians have such a pull. There's always an Old Etonian on the top of every woodpile. At the bottom too, for that matter. Maybe, though, the fact that we are so few is a special bond. That's one of the reasons why my father sent me there. It's more exciting to build up a tradition than to carry one on. And with a headmaster like Roxburgh it couldn't not succeed. What a man he was. Did he ever surprise you by wishing you 'happy returns' on your birthday?"

"As a matter of fact, he did; in my first term, too. I've never been more touched by anything. I ceased to feel I was an outsider."

"That was one of J.F.'s special lines. I asked him when I came back as an Old Boy how he managed it. He explained. He had a big desk diary. He had every boy's birthday entered there. Each morning he'd consult it. Evans-Pritchard and Morton minor, he would say. Then if, in the course of the day, he ran across them, he'd wish them 'happy returns.' He didn't go out of his way to find them, but as often as not he did. Wonderful public relations, as you say. It made a kid feel differently about the place. You're, of course, quite a lot younger than I am. I looked you up. I'd left two years before you arrived, but a good many must have over-lapped. 'Laddie' Lucas, for instance, must have been the big blood your first term."

Reid as he listened savoured the dramatic irony of the situation. Gustave had no idea that he was being interviewed.

The door bell rang. The door opened upon two young women and a youngish man. The girls certainly fulfilled Farrar's promise. Their prettiness was typically Lebanese; they were of medium height, slightly plump, pale skinned, with dark luminous eyes and black hair, shining and worn loose upon their shoulders. There was a marked family resemblance.

"These," said Farrar, "are the Miss Koumayans. They are not sisters, they are first cousins; but they are more inseparable than sisters. The elder, the one on the right, is Annabelle, the younger Veronique. They are a self-protective unit. They chaperone each other and their defense is completed by Annabelle's brother, François. You may not know this, Prof, you are new to the Middle East, but Sargent with his Alexandrian background will be very familiar with it. The Lebanese young lady of good family is more strictly guarded than the most prim Victorian damsel. They roll those lustrous eyes, they indulge in verbal audacities. But it is impossible to be alone with them. It puzzles the Englishman a lot at first. He thinks he's got a date. He hands his girl into a taxi; he follows, glowing with expectation. Then, wham, from the other side, there's a cousin or brother, slipping in to perch on the seat facing him. Is not that true, Annabelle?"

"Of course, and why not? Why should one of us want to be alone with you?"

"There are certain things that cannot be said in public."

"That is where you are so wrong, my naughty captain. There is nothing that cannot be said in public, if you are sufficiently adroit, and veil your meaning cleverly."

48

"But some of us are not that adroit."

"You do not then deserve the attention of a subtle woman."

She spoke in a light flirtatious manner. Reid was reminded of Edith Evans in the rôle of Millamant. It was clear that she and Farrar knew and understood each other very well.

"You make things very difficult for the simple British officer."

"But I do not want to be bothered with a simple officer. They are so tediously the same. They say, 'I want to be alone with you so that we can really talk.' But it is not in order to talk that they want to be alone."

"There, Prof, didn't I tell you? Verbal audacities, but nothing else."

"Ah, my incorrigible captain; always hankering for that forbidden garden. Think how it might disappoint you. Think how happy we are with this innocent badinage and its *sous-entendus*."

Her voice had retained its tone of raillery, but her eyes were gentle. They like each other quite a lot, Reid thought. But already Farrar had changed the subject.

"I've had an idea that the Lebanese speak a highly corrupt Arabic. Now here's the test. Lieutenant Sargent was brought up in Alexandria. He speaks Egyptian Arabic, which as everyone knows is the purest Arabic. He'll tell me if I'm right or not. Now come along, Gustave, put them through their paces."

There was a lot of laughter; the sally was a useful ice-breaker. Gustave's Arabic was clearly very fluent. It was, Reid presumed, Farrar's method of putting Gustave to a language test. The Koumayans would report later on his accent and on how grammatically he spoke.

They were still speaking in Arabic when the last guest arrived —an English girl, Jane Lester, a driver with the Hadfield-Spears ambulance. She was in her very early twenties. Her husband had been taken prisoner at Dunkirk. They had been two months married.

She was in uniform. She was little and lithe and blonde. She looked very tired. She was, Reid suspected, one of those girls who lose their looks when they are tired.

"I've been on the road seven hours, Damascus and back; I'll have a whisky, Nigel, and a strong one."

She took two fast gulps at it; and it was as though a hand had smoothed out the drawn lines round her mouth and eyes. Reid changed his seat so that he could be next to her.

49

"Your husband is a prisoner of war, they tell me. I was one in the first war."

"Where?"

"In Germany, in Mainz."

"For long?"

"Eight months. I was taken in the big retreat."

"That wasn't long."

"I know. I was very lucky. But I didn't know I was going to be so lucky. At first I thought I might be there for years. I probably felt very much as your husband felt during the first four months."

"And how did you feel?"

"Shame at first, humiliation. Doubt as to whether I should be there at all. I was taken in a group. Our whole company was surrounded. I wasn't in command, but I wondered if we oughtn't to have fought to the last man; as the Germans did in their pill boxes at Ypres. At the same time I had a feeling of relief that it was all over; my life had been spared; I could do the things I'd dreamed of doing; I could go up to Oxford. And that was the feeling that persisted; it lasted during the weeks it took me to get settled into my permanent prison camp. Then suddenly I thought: 'I'm here for the duration. That may be for two years, three years, four years; the best years of my life behind barbed wire.' But that was in the summer of 1918; within a very few weeks, I knew that the war would be over soon. Your husband hasn't that consolation."

"Indeed he hasn't."

"Nor have you?"

She looked up quickly. There was a look of gratitude in her eyes, as one might have for a doctor who had made a quick diagnosis.

It must after all have been the same for her: the anxiety when her husband was posted missing, the weeks of waiting; then the relief of learning he was a prisoner; safe, safe, safe; one day he would come back to her. There had been that month or so of exaltation, then gradually the recognition of the chancery in which she found herself; the war might last for four, five years, and for all that period she would be neither wife, nor widow; in cold storage, she who was little older than a debutante.

"Did you ever make your bob?" he asked.

"I was going to in 1940; if there had been no war."

Neither realised for the moment how quickly they had made

their conversational transition. They had been following their own thoughts, reaching the same point without the need of words. There was now animation in her face. Youth had returned to it. She had nearly finished her whisky. She must have been desperately tired when she came in.

"Let me freshen that drink," he said. He had a feeling she would be grateful if he did the talking for a little, so that she could relax. "What's your husband's profession?" he enquired.

"A regular soldier. That's bad luck, isn't it? He'll miss promotion. He'll be out of date when it's all over."

Reid thought of all those regular officers who had been captured on the retreat from Mons. They had never made up the ground that they had lost; particularly the elder ones. But perhaps that was partially their own fault.

"At a first glance it looks like that," he said. "But there's another angle; Louis Napoleon spent three years in prison; do you know what he said about them?"

"What did he say?"

"That he had been educated in the University of Ham. He read there the books that otherwise he'd never have had the time for. That happened to me at Mainz. It was a prelude to Oxford. I met there for the first time first class minds on equal terms. Gerard Hopkins was there; so was Hugh Kingsmill. I had eight months of solid reading. I read all the major Russian novelists, except Tolstoy. I read Flaubert and Balzac. I was introduced to Walter Pater. I heard good talk four hours of the day. If I hadn't done that reading then, I don't know when I would have; Hopkins and Kingsmill were my university. I went up to Oxford with a flying start. Not only that: I made up my mind about myself. I knew what I wanted to do: to learn enough to be able to interpret History and Philosophy in terms of one another. It's not the same for your husband, as a regular army officer. But there's a great deal of solid reading he might do, military history and strategy that the average subaltern never finds the time for. Can he read German?"

"Yes."

"Then he can read Clausewitz and Schlieffer. When his time comes for the Staff College he may look on this period as a blessing in disguise."

"Let's hope so. But it's hard to take a long view in wartime."

He knew what she meant. She was inhabiting a vacuum. He

looked across at Farrar. A good deal of laughter was coming from his group. Gustave was doing most of the talking. He was recounting an incident that had taken place when he was on a training exercise in England, and making high fun at the expense of his major whom he described as "the old Perisher."

"There was I in that sunken road. It was raining; my men were soaked and as near mutinous as makes no difference. I'd no idea where we were; lost my bearings, couldn't find my position on the map. And then, at just that moment, who should show up but the old Perisher himself. He looks me over and he looks my men over and he doesn't say a word. Petrified, was I petrified. Believe *me*—" He pronounced "me" as though it were a French word. Reid found it hard not to wince. It was a piece of music-hall slang that was seventeen years out of date. "And then what do you think he says, that old Perisher of mine? 'Now what would you do if an enemy platoon appeared over that ridge?' What would I do? Had I a clue? The old cerebellum wouldn't work. I squeezed the lemon and not a drop came out."

He told the story with gusto and animation. The girls listened with amused expressions. Farrar was smiling. Gustave might be the right character for the curious harlequinade he was conducting. Reid turned back to Jane. "Do you have anything to do with the Mission?"

"Only in as far as May Spears is the general's wife. We're completely independent."

"Do you know Diana Benson?"

"We share a flat."

"Then you know her very well."

"Does anyone know her very well?"

The evening wore on. Seven-thirty became eight-thirty. The two girls stood up. "Time for us to go," said Annabelle. "Why don't we take Lieutenant Sargent with us, so that he can compare a Lebanese home with an Egyptian?"

At least he's made a good impression there, thought Reid.

"Now we can relax," said Farrar as he closed the door behind them. "Jane, stay for supper?"

She shook her head. "I'm all in. I want to pack up, have a bath, get into pyjamas, read my mail and darn my stockings. But I'd like one more drink before I go."

It was her fifth. She was a different person now. "What a day," she said. "Seven hours on the road. It's exactly what I was looking for when I joined the outfit. I wanted to be so exhausted at the end of every day that I'd fall flat upon a mattress and stay there till reveille. But this is becoming more than I had bargained for. If May wasn't such a darling I'd throw in my hand; but she is a darling. We all love her; and the thing's worth doing, which so few things are."

She finished her whisky in one long swallow, then stood up.

"I'll drive you home," said Farrar.

"I've my car."

"Exactly. I will drive it."

"How will you get back?"

"I'll take a taxi. Charge it to the firm. Off we go. I'll be back in twenty minutes, Prof. Then we'll eat right away."

He was back within fifteen. "That girl wasn't fit to drive," he said. "She's drinking much too much."

"She's got a good deal on her mind, I suppose."

"Not only on her mind, poor thing. Still, there it is. I'm hungry; where's that soup?"

The cook was a Lebanese, short, dusky and half Turkish. He was a good cook and his discretion had been guaranteed. "I wouldn't be in his shoes if he tried to double-cross us," Farrar said. "Cloak and dagger means cloak and dagger."

"And how did Gustave strike you?"

"He'll do; other things being equal."

"How about his Wodehousian slang?"

"All right out here. The epitome of gilded youth, the Bright Young Person as the Egyptian sees him. His Arabic was fluent; and those girls liked him. He's likeable all right. I wonder if he gave you the full reason for not wanting to go back to Egypt?"

"It sounded a sound reason."

"I daresay; but there's often a truth behind the truth. I'd like to know if there is, in this case. It would double his value to us, if there is."

"Don't you believe anything that anybody tells you?"

"Not till I've checked on it."

"You certainly lead a complicated life."

"This is a complicated war and I'm in a complicated branch of it."

"I wonder how you keep track of what you're doing?"

"I don't. It's guess work; or at least it's preparation. Do you play chess?"

"Not very seriously."

"But you know how you develop your pieces, aiming at the centre of the board; with your knights out and your bishops cleared, so that you are covering the maximum of squares. You don't know how the game will develop because you don't know what your adversary is planning; but you are as ready as you can hope to be at that stage of the game before a piece has been taken. Your enemy may give you an opening to attack, or he may blunder into your defences. But you've done all you can by covering the greatest possible number of squares. That's not an exact parallel. But it'll do. I'm making all the preparations that I can; and you've got to remember this, that I haven't been here very long, less than half a year; there was no real organisation here till the Vichy French had gone. France was always suspicious of us; unnecessarily suspicious, as the French tend to be. I won't have my system working for at least a year and just when I've got it working the way I want, they'll probably transfer me to Teheran or Haifa. What did you think of the Koumayans?"

"I didn't have much chance of thinking anything."

"I know. Gustave was talking all the time."

"Tell me about them."

"There isn't much to tell. They're of Armenian origin. That's obvious from the name. Their fathers are local notables with a number of irons in a great many fires, in the way of Lebanese economy, which has its ramifications in every country, in most cities. There's a big colony in Brazil, there's a big colony in Brooklyn. A shipload of wool is bought in Sydney; it's shipped for Singapore; halfway to Java it has been resold and is scheduled for Ceylon. But it never gets to Ceylon. It is re-bought in mid-ocean and headed for Aden. It may eventually turn up in Capetown; and somewhere at the back of each transaction there's a Lebanese drawing his minute commission. That's how Lebanon survives, on that endless flow of commissions from all round the world. No one knows how rich any Beiruti is, or rather how rich he would be if he didn't gamble; but I'd say that either of those girls would be a very advantageous proposition for any young British officer looking for a *dot*."

"Are they Christians?"

"Greek Orthodox. So there's no complication there. Which did you think the prettier?"

"I don't know that I really thought about it; there didn't seem much to choose."

Farrar laughed. "There are times when I envy you, Professor. You are so invulnerable, so immune. You meet two very pretty girls and don't bother to ask yourself which you'd prefer if you had the choice. It's your being married, I suppose; you're fixed, you're settled. There's nothing to be done about you. The score's added up. Have you ever thought how it is for me?"

"How what is for you?"

"This whole woman problem in the Middle East."

"You tell me how it is for you."

"In the first place Beirut is an exception. The Lebanon has Christians, Maronites, Greek Orthodox. Women don't live behind veils in purdah as they do in Syria, in Iraq and in most of Egypt. But even here there is a great dearth of women. Beirut is French so it has houses of call like the Mimosa; but they are dreary, and what's the alternative? There are some light-hearted ladies bent on a good time; not worrying about tomorrow; wives with husbands somewhere; an occasional nursing sister, a girl in an embassy or in a show like ours. But those are the exceptions; most of the young women have marriage very definitely in mind. That's for the younger ones. There are also quite a number of older ones in the middle thirties who are desperately anxious to be married; it's their last chance. There weren't nearly enough men to go round when they came out. The men they should have married had been killed in the war; it was the period of the bright young people when a large number of the bright young men were queer; it was the period of Freudian psychology when young things talked about releasing their inhibitions: they released them right enough. Half of them got involved with married men who left them on the shelf. London, before the war, was simply stocked with disappointed unmarried women in the early thirties. A number of them are out here now; to every woman there are twenty men, most of them from the desert who haven't seen a woman for six months. This is their chance.

"All of which adds up to a very pretty problem for poor Nigelo. After all, he's not getting any younger. He's over thirty, and that's the age when one should be getting married. I run the danger of being a quadragenarian by the time the war is over—when will it be over? And if you were me, would you see much to be said for marrying one of those young women in the services: two weeks' honeymoon and then you go your separate ways; what an opportunity for her to play wild and loose, with a temptation at every turn. A girl like Annabelle Koumayan presents a very definite temptation to somebody like me. She's young, she's unspoiled, she's as near to being rich as makes no difference. And I can tell you this, for her a British officer has the charm of novelty. She hasn't seen so very many of us yet. I've quite a number of things upon my mind in addition to chasing subversive elements. That's why I say you're lucky, Prof; you can take this war in your stride."

3

ON THE FOLLOWING SUNDAY, Reid was duty officer. It was in the main a sinecure. It involved sitting by day and sleeping by night beside a telephone, but the duty officer's sleep was rarely interrupted. The bed in the telephone room was comfortable, and Reid watched his fellow missionaries depart at eight o'clock without regret. He was prepared to enjoy a quiet evening by himself. He had brought a packet of sandwiches and a half bottle of local wine. It was the first meal that he had had by himself since he had left England. It was also his first opportunity for quite a while for a period of uninterrupted reading. He was not only surprised, therefore, but resentful when the telephone bell rang shortly before ten.

"Spears Mission. Duty officer," he said.

There was a laugh from the other end. "How very official you do sound." It was a female voice, a deep, contralto voice.

"Who's that?" he asked.

"Diana."

"Diana who?"

"Benson. Don't you remember?"

"Of course. I hadn't expected you to call."

"And you've never heard my voice on a telephone before. Nigel told me that you were duty officer. I thought that you might be lonely. I also wondered if you'd heard the news?"

"What news?"

"About America being in the war."

"With whom?"

"Japan. The Japs have bombed Pearl Harbor."

"Where's that?"

"Somewhere in Hawaii. Half their fleet's gone down."

"And are we in this too?"

"I gather so. Anyway there's that Berlin-Rome-Tokyo axis. Everyone will be in it in three days; at least that's what the boys in my group are saying."

"It's the biggest news in the world's history."

"That's what I knew you'd feel. That's why I wanted you to know. I asked where you were tonight and Nigel told me that you were duty officer. I couldn't bear to think of you all by yourself, not knowing. I had to ring you up."

"I'm touched."

"I think you should be. Do you know what I thought? If I call him now he will remember me all his life, because he'll never forget today. It's the day that's changed the world. All through our lifetimes people are going to talk about this day, and when people are exchanging war memories, when they ask, 'When did *you* hear, how and where?', you'll say, 'There I was, a Spears Mission duty officer in Beirut, cut off from everyone and everything, and a young woman took pity on me.' You'll forget a great many things, but you'll remember that."

Yes, he'd remember that, and indeed the news was so startling, so unexpected, that he wanted to be alone to absorb it, to think about it by himself. At the same time he did not want to disconnect the line; to lose that rich, full voice.

"I ought to ring off and let you get back to your party. But I'm selfish. I want to go talking on," he said. "It's tantalising, hearing you but not seeing you; yet at the same time you seem closer on the telephone."

She laughed. "I've had that said to me before. I wonder if my voice is wrong for my appearance."

"That's not the impression it gave me. Next time we meet. . . ."

He checked. ". . . Why don't we have lunch one day?"

"That would be nice."

"Or dinner?"

"Dinner would be nicer."

"What about Tuesday?"

"Tuesday would be fine."

"Shall we meet at the St. Georges at half past eight?"

"The St. Georges at half past eight."

"We might try the Lucullus."

"We might indeed."

There was a pause. "I've got to be firm with myself," he said. "I mustn't keep you from your party."

"Thank you—and in forty-eight hours' time. . . ."

"In forty-six and a half. Good night."

There was a click from the other end. He stared at the receiver. Three seconds ago it had contained that golden voice; now it was a metal instrument. He put it back. The day that changed the world. Indeed, that was what it was: the world had become a different place; America and Japan were in the war, and all over the world at this moment people were thinking in consternation, "How will this affect me?"

To the millions of Americans and Japanese who would be involved, whose lives would be uprooted, the tens of thousands who would lose their lives, this was a night of black calamity; and how else but with heavy hearts could the Germans and Italians learn of the acquisition of that ally and this foe? For them the end of the war was immeasurably further off; but for the beleaguered British, standing alone, apart from their unlikely and uncertain alliance with the Russians, how could they not welcome today's news gleefully? The war had become infinitely complicated. Territories that had thought of themselves as safe, were now in peril. Australia and Malaya were in the front line. The war's worst fighting lay ahead, but who could doubt for a second the ultimate outcome of the fighting now that America was in it, and on our side?

There had been many times during the autumn of 1940 and the spring of 1941 when, in terms of mathematics, it had seemed inconceivable that England could win the war. The most that could be hoped for was a stalemate. Defeatism was not admitted. Officious persons would report to the police those who spread apathy and despair. His colonel in the Ministry of Mines was careful to say, not "when the war is over" but "when we have won the war." At the intelligence course at Matlock when they had been working out exercises in their halls of study, the problem would be set with the exordium: "It is the year 1942. We have invaded the Continent." He would think to himself: "What with?"

How should a Briton feel tonight in view of the immense dis-

aster that had befallen civilisation and the incalculable consequences of that disaster? How was the world's greatest Englishman,
who was himself half American, feeling at this moment? Was
there any doubt that, it must be dinnertime in London—he was
raising a glass in a spirit of thankfulness to heaven? It was a new
war now, even in this little *oubliette*, where the war had loitered
for a while and to which war might return if the Germans struck
southwards in the spring.

†

Diana Benson was already in the lounge of the St. Georges when
Reid arrived. She was at a desk, writing a letter. "I won't be four
minutes," she said. "I hate writing letters in offices when I'm likely
to be interrupted." He watched her as she wrote, bent low over the
paper, intense on concentrating. To whom was she writing? What
was her life, in that way? As Farrar had said, a girl such as she
didn't reach the age of twenty-five without having had something
happen. When he had made that remark on the telephone about
her voice, she had said, "I've had that said to me before." The in-
flection in her voice told him that it was a man who had said that.
What kind of man, he wondered? To what kind of man did she,
a rebel, turn?

She rose from her table and came over.

"Shall we have a drink here first?" he said.

She shook her head. "There's bound to be someone in the bar
we know who'll insist on standing us a round. We'll never get
away. That's the worst of this town, everyone knows everyone."

Outside the hotel a trio of little boys came forward with a shout
of "Taxi?" She shook her head. "Let's walk. I can do with exercise:
that's another of the troubles of this place, you don't get nearly
enough of it in the winter. There's swimming in the summer. But
it's a problem now."

"What do you do for exercise in England?"

"Sailing, riding, skiing."

"You can get skiing here, can't you, at the Cedars?"

"It's difficult to arrange and it is tantalising too: only for a few
hours and every other week. It reminds me of things I can't do
any longer. I suppose it'll all come back. I wonder."

The Lucullus was along the waterfront, past the night club section. You reached it by a flight of stairs. It was simply furnished,

59

with straight-backed chairs and rectangular wooden tables. It had a broad window facing on the sea, the kind of place of which you would say in France, "It must be either very bad, or very good, since it can afford to be so unpretentious." The room was half-full, mainly with civilians. Diana looked round her, then sighed with relief.

"No one that I know here; or at least no one that I know well enough to have him come across for coffee. That's another of the troubles of this place: there're not enough women to go round, not enough that speak English anyhow; and every officer thinks he has the right to attach himself to a table at which there's a female whom he knows: 'the freemasonry of wartime living' is their name for it. No respect for privacy. It's terrible where there's dancing. You go out with someone presumably because you want to be with him, and man after man comes up and asks you if you'll dance. One doesn't want to be rude, one's sorry for him. He's an exile; and any moment, if he's young, he may be posted to the Western Desert. But it is a bore, a crashing, crashing bore. It's so exhausting, too, dancing every dance. I'm glad you picked on the Lucullus."

There was an undertone of irritation in her voice. Yet at the same time she was smiling. She had a sense of humour. She could laugh at herself. She could be a formidable person, he suspected, when the indignation deepened and there was no corrective smile to balance that fierce undertone.

He handed her the menu. "Have you any views about the kind of meal you'd like?" he asked.

"Something as the main dish that I could drink red wine with."

Leaning across the table on her elbows she held her glass between both hands and raised it to her lips as though she were a priestess officiating at a pagan altar.

"You told me a little about your father; you didn't tell me anything about your mother," he was saying.

She shrugged. "She's the kind of woman that men like my father marry. It worked out very well."

"What am I to take that to mean?"

"They can speak in shorthand to each other. They don't need to explain themselves. They were brought up in the same world. They think the same things important. They have the same loyalties, the same dislikes. When my father sees someone whom he wants to see again, he knows instinctively whether it's the kind of man he can have down for the weekend or whether he should take him to his club. He never asks himself whether or not my mother'd like him. He knows at once. It's very restful, and on the whole it makes for a much fuller life than you'd expect. They both like quite a lot of people, and worth-while people too, which doesn't always happen in a marriage. Husbands and wives are so afraid of bringing to the house someone of whom the other will disapprove that they play for safety, they ask guests of whom no one could disapprove and the people of whom you can say that are negative; the life of the house is reduced to a lowest common multiple excluding all that was most alive and individual in both wife and husband. Each leads a narrower instead of a fuller life after marriage. That didn't happen with my parents. For them life didn't contract with marriage; it got a longer radius because there were two, working on the same plan together."

"It was a happy household?"

"I'd say so, yes. There was a constant going and coming. I make fun of huntin', shootin', fishin'; but a lot of fun goes with them: the parties, the dressing up, and hunting itself is a fine outdoor business. There's a thrill to it; you feel so well afterwards."

"Yet it's exactly against that kind of thing that you rebelled."

"I rebelled against the worship of it. Why on earth should they think they are the salt of the earth because they like fox hunting; why should blood sports be sacrosanct? It's fun; gorgeous fun. Why can't they accept it as fun, without making a religion of it?"

"Because of that puritan streak that prevents the English from enjoying anything for its own sake. There must be some justification: it's good for one's health; it helps to build an Empire; Waterloo and the playing fields of Eton."

"Perhaps you're right. But it made me mad. It was all so complacent."

"Did you have rows with your parents?"

"Arguments, rather than rows, I'd say."

"With your mother or your father, or with both?"

"With my father mainly. I enjoyed arguing with him; with my mother I felt there wasn't any point. She didn't talk my language. I puzzled and depressed her. She gave me up as a bad job. She couldn't understand how she had produced me. But with my father it was different. I was a challenge to him. And he enjoyed a challenge. He was a fighter. He wanted a foe he could respect.

'Honour as you strike him down,' and I've an idea I represented that side of him that never had been released. I was the equivalent of the man that he took to dinner at the Rag instead of having down to Hatch for the weekend, and maybe he preferred the man he didn't ask down to Hatch. Then, again, in terms of marriage, he wouldn't have wanted to marry anyone except my mother, but there was one side of his nature that was precluded by that marriage; only a part of himself was in it—the major part I'll admit—and I fancy that I was the expression of that part of him that was left out. How do I know what his life has been? There must have been someone in his life. I've always wondered who she was. An Anglo-Indian perhaps, someone impossible, someone opposed to all he stood for. But he'd always remember her. He'd ask himself what would have happened had he married her? He'd have prejudiced his future, his career. In those days you had to marry wisely. He had no doubt that he had chosen wisely. But he must have asked himself: 'Suppose I had?' Something in him died, but yet it hadn't really died. It was reborn in me. So he had to fight me to prove to himself that he had been right in stamping down that side of himself. . . ." She checked. Again her eyes were bright. But this time behind her warmth there was no undertone of indignation; there was a welcoming receptiveness. Just as earlier he had thought how formidable she would be without that balancing sense of humour, now he thought how devastating a man would find it if this wealth, this depth of feeling, was turned on him, in love. Who could resist her? Who would want to resist her?

She sighed. "It's just the way Margaret said."

"Margaret?"

"Margaret Spencer. That pupil of yours. You've forgotten her; but you meant so much to her. And it's just the way she said. How you made it easy for her to talk about herself; she hadn't realised before the kind of person that she was. It was the same with me just now. I hadn't realised until this very moment that what my father loved in me was that side of himself he'd never dared become. . . . Why haven't I seen that before? . . . Why have I seen it now? It's the way Margaret said."

She checked again; her eyes were glowing. "I don't believe I've ever envied anyone as much as I envy Margaret this minute. Even though she never had the chance of meeting you the way I am, she heard you lecture. I've missed that. I've only seen one side of you. I haven't had, probably never will, the chance of comparing

62

the two 'yous': the one that stands upon a platform, that expounds, explains, with everyone seated round you, with you their master and you leading them. Then two days later in a tutorial the rôles are changed: it's the pupils who are expounding to you; yet they couldn't expound unless they had heard you lecture first. This life out here must be very strange to you after all those years as a professor."

"I find it very strange."

"And the work so very different. Does it interest you at all?"

He hesitated. Interesting? It had the attraction of novelty. As he studied the Mission files he had had the fascination of being taken behind the scenes, but it was a quarter time employment.

"Don't you sometimes feel that you are wasted there?" she said. "Isn't there something more useful you could do?"

"For the last twenty months I've felt that I wasn't doing anything that couldn't have been done just as well by a fifteen year old schoolgirl."

"You'd be glad to change then, if you were offered genuine whole time work."

"Of course I would."

"That's what I thought. I've an idea. . . . No, I won't tell you what it is. Don't count chickens before they're hatched. But if it does work, it would be fun for all of us."

They made an early evening of it. He was back at the flat before half past ten. He let himself in by the independent entrance. A light shone under the door leading into the flat. He could overhear voices. He turned the handle of the sitting room door gently, pressed and there was no resistance.

There were two guests: a plump, greasy-looking Levantine, and the young student whom he had met two Sundays ago at the St. Georges terrace. Farrar welcomed him warmly.

"I was hoping that you would be back before we broke the evening up. Of course, you remember Aziz, and this is Abdul Hamid Aral. I don't quite know how I should explain Abdul Hamid. How should I explain you, my good friend?"

The Levantine chuckled. He rubbed his hands together. They were podgy hands, with long pointed polished nails. He wore a ruby ring on the little finger of his left hand, and a sapphire on the fourth finger of his right. "I have many irons in many fires.

My ruby is ignorant of my sapphire. There is an Arab proverb: 'The man is wise whose acquaintances are numerous but whose friends are few.' "

"I hope that I am one of your friends, Abdul Hamid."

"There is another Arab proverb: 'The friendship is strong that has not been tested.' "

Reid laughed. "The Arabs have another saying: 'There are only seven plots in the world. And every story that has ever been told is a variation upon one of those seven plots.' "

"That doesn't sound very pertinent," said Farrar.

The Lebanese chuckled. "All truths are pertinent. All truths are reflections of Allah's wisdom."

He looked roguishly at Reid. There was a conspiratorial gleam in his eye that Reid did not particularly fancy. Reid turned to Aziz. "How are the studies going?"

Aziz flushed. "How can I tell? I do my best."

"What does the tutor say?"

"He's preparing a thesis. He's only interested in himself."

"That's why I said he should try Alexandria," said Farrar.

"Why did you come to Beirut in the first place?" Reid asked.

"It was an excuse to travel. I felt shut in in Turkey. When my father was young, Turkey was so large; Turkey is so little now."

He seemed resentful. There was an aggressive tone to his voice. Yet there was no suggestion of a whine in it. He was a type with which Reid was familiar. Was there all that difference between a Turk and an Englishman? One assumed that there was because of the difference in religion. But possibly many Turks accepted the teachings of Mohammed as casually as many Englishmen accepted the implications of the catechism they had learnt at school.

"Is this your first visit to the Lebanon?" he asked.

The young man nodded.

"You might have chosen a better time. It can't be at its best in wartime."

"No country is at its best in wartime. In Turkey too there are restrictions. We cannot tell how long we shall be at peace."

"What do you plan to do when the war is over?"

Aziz shrugged. "I do not look ahead so far. I cannot guess what kind of a place the world will have become."

"But you know that whatever kind of place it does become it will be useful to have a good degree."

"That is what my instructors tell me."

64

"And that," Farrar interrupted, "is why I suggest Alexandria. You'd find more stimulus."

Later, after Aziz and the Lebanese had left, Reid asked Farrar why he was so insistent about the young man's going to Alexandria. "There really isn't anything to choose between the two universities."

"I daresay not, but it might be useful to have him under our supervision for a little. Eventually he'll go back to Turkey. We need Turks who'll be helpful to us. He's the kind of chap who is likely to get into mischief. He might be lured into the kind of mischief that might put him into our power."

"You certainly have a lot of irons in the fire."

"Only a very few of them are hot, as yet."

"What about Abdul Hamid?"

"My contact with my cut-out."

"What's a cut-out?"

"What did they teach you in that course at Matlock?"

"Nothing that has any bearing on what you seem to be about. What is a cut-out?"

"The point in intelligence beyond which you don't know the sources of your information. Abdul Hamid brings me information. I accept most of it as accurate. He gets that information from a man whose name I know, but whom I've never met. That man is the cut-out. What happens after him I've no idea. If there's anything shady to be done, he fixes it. I rely on Abdul Hamid to choose me a reliable cut-out."

"What an extraordinary amount of things go on beneath this roof, of which I've no idea."

"That's why you're so useful to me, old boy; you're so transparently honest that nobody can believe that I'm not, too. How did Abdul Hamid strike you?"

"He seemed intelligent."

"He's that all right. Did he strike you as being devious?"

"A number of Lebanese strike me as being devious. He didn't seem any more devious than the rest. But I did think him sinister."

"Sinister? Yes, perhaps that's the word, 'sinister,' and that's what he should be in this racket."

THREE WEEKS LATER Reid was again duty officer. He woke with a feeling of anticipation. He looked forward to an evening by himself. He also looked forward to the possibility of Diana telephoning. A week earlier he had volunteered to take Johnson's place, Johnson having an opportunity to meet a Sandhurst contemporary who might prove useful, and once again shortly before ten the telephone had gone. "I've just finished such a good dinner," she had said. "I felt so sorry for you all alone in that bleak room. I didn't want you to feel abandoned."

There had been warmth and gaiety in her voice. It had filled the room with colour.

"By the way," she had said, "I don't know your Christian name."

"Noel. But I don't use it."

"Why not?"

"It doesn't seem quite like me."

"Doesn't it? It does to me. You sign your books with your initials."

"Don't you think that's the right signature for the kind of book I write? Noel is too flowery."

"What does your wife call you?"

"She doesn't call me anything."

"Just 'darling'?"

"Yes, just 'darling.' "

It was the first time that he had spoken of his wife to her. It was the first reference that either of them had made to the fact that he was married.

"So no one's ever called you Noel. That's what I'll call you, then," she said.

They had gossiped for ten minutes, then she had rung off. "I can't occupy that line any longer. Suppose General De Gaulle rang up from Cairo." The room which had seemed so private and cosy fifteen seconds earlier now seemed bare and cavernous. "I wonder how she knew I was 'orderly dog,' " he thought. He had not been on the duty roster.

It was a bright clear day, after a week of rain. Spring was still six weeks distant, yet it was difficult to believe that the short Lebanese winter was not already over. The breeze had a scent of flowers. In the Rue Jeanne D'Arc there was a new animation about the workmen repairing a building partially ruined in an air raid; about the women in large straw hats propelling mules laden with provisions; handcarts were pushed beside the pavements; long, shining cars were honking irritably; a clothes shop selling the remnants of its smart Paris stock stood next to an open kitchen where savourous stews were simmering and bubbling in low wide saucepans. Shabbiness and elegance walked side by side. There were Moslems with baggy trousers and red tarbooshes; there were young women with their black, greased hair swinging low upon their shoulders; there were veiled shuffling women with black skirts sweeping the ground; there were beggars with misshapen limbs squatted against the walls; there were men in tattered clothes, thin, grey-skinned, who might have belonged to any race; there were Arabs in long robes with their head-dress held by a golden fillet, carrying in their right hands a string of yellow beads; there were men, tall and portly, sleek and prosperous, in well-cut European suits. The whole scene was rejuvenated by the sunlight and the air of spring.

He turned right at the end of the street. Usually he caught a 'bus here, but he had left the flat early. He had time to walk. He slackened his pace as he went by the University. It had the typical look of an American college; red brick, spacious, square-towered with sloping grounds. The morning classes were about to start, and the street was crowded with young men and women hurrying with their satchels and their piles of books, laughing, chattering.

He paused at the main entrance, watching them. There were Turks, Indians, Syrians, Egyptians, French. There were a few, but only a very few, with the very black skin and large pouting mouths of Central Africa. The large majority had grey, slightly darkened skins with delicate features; often with their cheeks disfigured by the scars of the big boils that were endemic to the Middle East and India. They were an attractive comely lot. They were pursuing their education just as their predecessors had done four years ago, planning their futures and careers; just as his former students were at Winchborough—except with this one difference, this basic difference: English students stood on the brink of war. These did not; this war was only theirs incidentally.

He had been here six weeks now, and had already begun to feel himself a part of this vast world, new to him, of the Middle East. And he was beginning to see it in terms of itself: a world of its own; alien, if at times friendly, to the West.

His in-tray was filled with papers. He might well have given the impression of being a busy person. Cartwright had told him that he would be mainly occupied with the composition of the weekly summaries, which would be a half-time job, and that the rest of his time could be devoted to the study of back files; but in point of fact a good deal of work had devolved on him, simply because he had an office and a desk.

He had for instance the men's mail to censor. In the first war he had looked forward to the censoring of mail, before he was commissioned, because he had thought that it would give him an insight into his men's minds, and that his knowledge of human nature would be enlarged. He had been disappointed and surprised by the dullness and lifelessness of the letters. They had been bare bulletins of facts, presented without personality. He had wondered whether in this second war a higher standard of education and a keener sense of independence among the new recruits would produce livelier letters. He was soon to find that it was not so. The letters that lay on his desk every morning were little different from those which he had read in 1917. Everything really personal went into the green envelopes that were censored not regimentally but at the base; the letters that came to him were in the main replies to letters that had been received from home ("Well, darling, I bet you enjoyed yourself that day Bert took you to the picnic"); health reports ("I seem to have got over my attack of 'gippie tummy'"); comments on the war news ("Well, mum, I don't think it'll be long now. We'll soon be giving Gerry a taste of his own medicine. Six months I give it"). There was a Lance Corporal who had been out fifteen months who numbered his letters to his wife, she numbering hers to him, whose letters consisted entirely of acknowledgments. "Darling, I have wonderful news. I have received your numbers, 35, 36, 37, 39, 40; I wonder what happened to your number 38. I hope not enemy action. I am so relieved that you have got my 51, 52, 53, 54, 55. How well the mail is working nowadays." He wrote in a large spidery hand, and the provision of that amount of information practically filled the airgraph so that he was forced to wind up with his invariable, "Well, darling, I must now close. Keep your chin up. Won't be long now." Reid wondered what the wife's letters were like. Did

68

she too merely repeat a list of numbers, or did she contribute news and comments?

He had also to deal with the various suppliants who presented themselves to the Mission offices. Everyone who had a grievance felt that here was the right audience for it, and every service branch in Beirut when faced with a conundrum said, "Oh, try Spears Mission." There were consequently innumerable Lebanese complaints about houses that had been bombed or looted in the campaign, about lorries that had been requisitioned and abandoned. Photographers applied for permission to develop snapshots for the troops. Officials claimed that their loss of office under the Vichy regime was due to their pro-British sentiments. One of these claims he had copied out and filed among his records:

"I know Your Excellency that it is the Syrian authority to which I should apply for my return to work. But what can I do if the said authority is unwilling to consider my grievance, and does Your Excellency's conscience consent and get restful while there is a person complaining of deprival and injustice in a country over which the British banner waves?

"I belong to a family occupying the first place in the Moslem and Arab worlds and the history certifies that; which thing prevents me from doing low work not corresponding with my social position.

"I do swear by the life of his Majesty the King and Emperor, and by the glory of that most noble British nation whose civilisation has been spread all over the world, and whose noble instruction has been distributed among mankind, that I should return with the British flag waving to the function of a district officer in compensation for the prejudice and injustice which I have undergone.

"I do come before Your Excellency, just as an Arabian comes before a mighty Emir and I should find in you refuge and support, and if the field of functions will not accept me there is no doubt that the British generosity would welcome me, closing my letter by saying with all my heart, long live Britain, defender of oppressed men, and long live the Allies and God save the King."

There were also a number of chores which normally would have been disposed of by an A.D.C. There were the sudden visits of important personages for whom air passages had to be booked, cars ordered and trains met. There would be diplomats in transit with a retinue of prams and nurses. He was, that is to say, occupied, and he was not bored. Yet he knew that his work could have been carried out just as effectively by a junior freshman. I've no real right to be here, he thought.

Pleasantly, placidly, the morning passed. Shortly before eleven there was a tap upon his door. Gustave responded to his "Come in." Gustave's eyes were bright and his cheeks were flushed.

"That chap you share a flat with, Farrar; is he bogus?"

"What do you mean by that?"

"Well, you should know. Mutual friends and all that, isn't it?"

"We have friends in common."

"So I deduced. You know my methods, Watson, but what's his racket?"

"I didn't know he had one."

"Ah, come now, listen. How could anyone without a racket be living in the style he does on a captain's pay?"

"Some people have private means; he was out here before the war, with I.P.C. He hasn't told me anything, but I daresay they make up the difference between his pre-war salary and his army pay."

"I see." Gustave hesitated.

"Why do you ask?"

"I want to know what's cooking."

"What's cooking where?"

"Oh, come now, you know that."

"I've not the least idea what you are talking about."

"You haven't, honest?"

"I assure you, honest."

"Oh." His face clouded. "I thought it was something you'd fixed up between you."

"I'm still in the dark."

"If you are then, Prof, there's no more to be said. I came to thank you. If it hadn't been for you, asking me up to have that drink, I wouldn't have met Farrar and this wouldn't have happened."

"What's happened?"

"My going to Cairo for an interview; if things work out, and Farrar says they should, I'll be working in his outfit there, and as a captain."

"Which is exactly what you wanted, isn't it?"

"I'll say it is."

"Congratulations, then. Good luck."

"Thanks; and it really is all due to you. Even if you didn't wangle it. You're a good guy, Prof."

So that was another of the missionaries settled. By now they had most of them found employment, as Cartwright had prophesied, all except Johnson and himself: the two first-war veterans.

There was a tap upon the door. A corporal with the mail. "Three for you, sir."

They were all on the new airgraphs by which a large sheet of paper was reduced by photography to the size of a small postcard. They were the first of these that he had received. One was from Rachel, one from his father, the third, in larged printed capitals, was from his younger son. He opened his son's first:

"Dear Daddy, Happy Christmas. I am excited. What will Santa bring. No prize for me this term. Much love, Mark."

He opened his father's next. His father, a widower and treasury official, had retired a few years before the outbreak of war. He lived in Hampstead and had been given half-time employment as a censor. He left his home every morning at half-past-nine, lunched at the Athenaeum, and was home by half-past-four. He missed the discomfort of crowded tubes and buses and did not have to travel in the black-out. He wrote on a cheerful note:

"It seems rather shocking for me to admit it, but I am actually having a more entertaining existence than I had three years ago. The hours are not long. The work makes no great demands on me; it is routine work, but it is not uninteresting. I am in the Italian section, and there is something a little special about everyone who is writing or being written to in Italian. I feel I am in the swim, and when I lunch at the Athenaeum, I have something to contribute to the conversation—without, I hasten to assure you, indulging in careless talk; moreover I don't have to hurry over my lunch, as the important figures in Whitehall have to. In fact the war came at a lucky time for me. If it had come eight years ago, when I was head of my section, I should have been putting in a nine to ten hours day, six days of the week. I might have finished up with a Knighthood, but I don't fancy that I should have lived to enjoy it very long."

Timing, his son thought, everything was timing, and it probably was true that his father, at the age of seventy-two, was leading, because of the war, a more satisfactory life than he could have anticipated for himself when he was fifty. He made a point of writing cheerfully, but in actual fact he was relatively cheerful. He had a sunny nature, and he had good health.

"I had a telephone talk with Rachel the other day," his letter ended. "She is having, I suspect, a rather dreary time, poor dear, but she is being very brave about it. I am hoping that after Christmas she will bring the boys up to London for a day and that I shall have a chance of seeing them. Children forget so quickly. I want them to have a real memory of their old Poppa."

A rather dreary time; poor Rachel. And it was his fault that she was having it.

The telephone rang beside him. A female voice was at the other end. "Is that Captain Reid? Will you please hold on a second for Mr. Cartwright?"

Reid's spirits lifted. Was this the call that he expected daily? The news that an appointment had been found for him? "Is that you, Reid? Cartwright here. It's very short notice, but I wondered if you were free for lunch today?"

"I'm afraid I'm duty officer."

"Too bad. I have a friend from London. I think you'd have interested one another. Well, it can't be helped. Another time. He's going to be here two weeks. There should be another chance; when I know his plans I'll let you know."

There was a tap on the door. It was Johnson, his eyes narrowed and his cheeks flushed.

"Busy?" Johnson asked.

"Not particularly."

"Mind if I sit down?"

"Of course not."

Johnson took out a cigarette and lit it. He drew the smoke deep into his lungs, breathing it slowly out. "Nothing came out of that fellow in Ninth Army," he said at length.

"I'm sorry to hear that."

"So am I. I was banking on it; thought I had the thing sewn up. They said I wasn't young enough. That means that I'm not fit enough; out of training; well, so I am. I don't know what's going to happen to me."

He checked. Reid said nothing. What was there he could say?

"The British Council are looking for men," said Johnson. "One or two of our group have got in on that. But then they're scholars. The British Council wants men who can teach something. What could I teach? All I can do is look after troops; and I'm too old for that. I've led the wrong kind of life for office work. You, of course. . . ." He paused; he looked at the heap of files in Reid's in-tray. "You're trained for this kind of work; I'm not. It's a continuation of your peacetime life. But me. . . ."

Reid made no reply. They all say the same thing, he thought, that it's different for me. They all imagine I've no problems because I've an established position in peacetime England, because I've a job waiting for me. Well, let them go on thinking it. It was hard to enter imaginatively into lives alien to one's own. That was one of the historian's functions, to explain to the public why men and women of whom their taste, training, instincts disapproved, acted in the way they did.

He waited. Johnson stubbed out his cigarette, stood up, moved towards the door, hesitated. "I suppose you haven't any whisky, have you?"

"As a matter of fact, I have."

It was the custom for Mission officers, during the last half-hour of the day, to take a drink in their offices before going out to dinner, but it was the first time that a morning drink had been suggested. He took a bottle of whisky from his deep bottom drawer.

"You don't mind, do you, if I don't join you?"

"Not in the least, not in the very least."

Reid handed him the bottle and a tumbler. "Help yourself."

The tumbler was squat, wide and solid. Johnson poured himself out a half-inch shot, checked, then poured another quarter-inch. He sat down again. "You're sure you're not in any hurry?"

"Dead sure. This is only half-time employment."

"But you're on the establishment."

"Yes."

"That's all that matters. As long as a man's on the establishment and doesn't put up a black, and you're not the kind of man man who does put up a black, there's nothing to worry over. Half-time employment; think how fresh you'll feel when you get back to your university."

Johnson did not mix any water with his whisky. He lifted his glass and took a quick, deep gulp. He blinked and shook his head.

"I needed that. One good thing about being out here is getting whisky at a reasonable rate. It's in very short supply in London."

Four more gulps and the glass was empty. "Thanks, I'm better now. I fell among friends last night." He rose; walked briskly to the door. He certainly did look better.

Reid picked up the last letter. Rachel's; it was strange to see her handwriting reduced to such minute proportions.

"Darling," the letter read. "They tell me that this kind of letter will get to you more quickly than an ordinary airmail letter, because it can be flown out to you direct, whereas an airmail letter goes part of the way by sea. Do tell me if that is so. Your airgraph reached me in ten days but I haven't had a real letter yet. I'm longing to hear what you are doing, if you are allowed to tell me, that's to say. It's wonderful for you to be out there and have a real use found for you at last. I know how exasperated you got at that Ministry of Mines, putting letters into envelopes. It was painful to watch you sometimes, you looked so frustrated. I'm sure that one gets more tired by things that bore one. I'm so glad for your sake that you are where you are. But it is dreary here without you. Those weekends made such a difference, and then there were your telephone calls; even when you were in London you seemed very close. I didn't realise how much those calls meant until now, when I haven't got them. But I mustn't grumble. You're not to worry about me. I'm all right. I'll get used to it, but it is a change for me. We've been so very much together. It isn't as though you were one of those husbands whose work took him away from home. How quickly I've got to the end of the sheet. Have I written so small that it won't be clear? Do let me know, or better still send me back this airgraph so that I can see what it looks like. All my love, my darling."

He stared at the small cramped script. Johnson and Gustave envied him his immunity. They thought he had no problems. Never in forty-three years of living had he felt less certain of himself.

As duty officer he was allowed to absent himself from the office between twelve and one. He strolled down the hill to the St. Georges. It was warm enough to sit out on the terrace; he allowed himself the indulgence of a bottle of canned American beer that in New York would have cost ten cents but here cost two Syrian pounds. With the official rate at nine to the British pound, he could not afford one very often. What a cool, clean bite it had, and how good it was sitting out here by himself, without the usual throng of men in uniform. On the beach below a group of children, taking advantage of the unseasonable sunlight, were playing in the sand under the watchful guardianship of their nurses. A few tables away three Lebanese men in Western suits were talking slowly, seriously, over small cups of coffee. They would remain there over those same cups for an hour, talking in the same deliberate unhurried manner, settling, most likely, a deal in which very large sums of money were at stake. For two thousand years similar men had sat, under the shadow of Mount Hebron, weighing the ultimate value to themselves of the fratricidal strife of Greeks and Romans, Phoenicians and Carthaginians. The triremes passed and the percentage of profit stayed, and his heart warmed towards this astute fickle, frivolous and charming people that had been true to itself, at the expense of interlopers. He could understand why so many Englishmen had been attracted to the Middle East.

Back in his office, in the silent deserted building, he busied himself with the reading of the Mission files. There was so much here for him to learn. It would be easy for him with his sense of history and of philosophy to yield to the fascination of this new world. He could justify himself in staying on. The Government had sent him here. He was the Government's responsibility. If the Government could not find adequate work for him, that was the Government's fault, not his. He could revivify, rejuvenate, recreate himself. He could enlarge himself. He would have more to give the world when the war was over. And in point of fact he soon would be able to find enough work to keep his days occupied. Already the half-time occupation that Cartwright had offered him had become three-quarter time. In another month it would have become full time. Give a conscientious man a desk and a telephone and he would soon find himself employment. That was the whole theory of increased establishments. A staff of five could easily cope with all the work required. Double the staff and within a month each member would somehow or other, by duplicating duties, have managed to be busy. That was bureaucracy. Taking in each other's washing. It might be one way to solve the white collar class unemployment programme. But it wasn't good enough for him, in wartime. He could not postpone the issue any longer.

That evening as soon as the office closed and he had moved in to the duty officer's room, he spread out a sheet of writing paper. He addressed it to the Dean of Winchborough University.

"Dear Gerald," he wrote. "Thirty months ago when I told you that as a Reserve officer I was likely to be called up shortly, you strongly advised me to apply for a postponement. The University,

75

you said, would support my application. Education was a first necessity and the authorities were not going to repeat the mistakes of 1914 and let all the young schoolmasters go to the front and leave education in the hands of the elderly and unfit. I argued in reply that if I had felt like that I should have resigned from the R.A.R.O. several years ago, that I had undertaken an obligation to be on call if I was required. Later, when my calling up papers came, you said, 'Don't forget, if you ever feel that you would be of greater service here than in the army, you've only got to let me know and I'll start wheels moving.' Well, I think the time has come. Since May 1940, I haven't, except when I was on courses, done a single full day's work."

He enumerated the various posts that he had filled.

"Here," he continued, "it is the same thing over again. I am doing work that any fifth form boy could do a great deal better. So, I take you at your word. Will you get the University to apply for me? I fancy that that is the correct method of procedure. It will be very good to be back again among you all. I hope that I shan't find myself too rusty."

He read it over; then put it in the envelope. He did not seal it down. He would ask Cartwright if it could be sent back to England in the diplomatic bag. It might need censoring. He didn't think it would, but it was more tactful to leave it open. And now for supper.

He had brought a packet of sandwiches from the flat and a half bottle of Lebanese red wine. He enjoyed this kind of picnic. He sipped the wine slowly, savouring its flavour. It was more than adequate. The French were responsible for this. The Lebanese had cause to be grateful to the French. He made his meal last over half an hour. Back in the chill of England oppressed by the blackout, by rationing and restrictions, he would often feel nostalgic for the Levant. He'd miss these duty hour periods. But if he did not send this letter now he would despise himself.

It was close on nine; he tidied up his desk. Evenings such as this provided him with a good opportunity for letter writing. It was a week since he had written to Rachel. Should he tell her about his application? Better not. Wait till the news came through officially. She would fret at the long delay. Better keep it a surprise.

"Darling," his letter started. "Here's another week gone, with nothing of much interest happening. You don't know the people that I'm meeting. Gossip about strangers can be very dull and anything that is of genuine interest would be cut out by the censor, so you see. . . ."

The telephone beside him rang. Diana, he wondered? And his heart contracted. That was another thing that he would miss, and miss a lot.

It *was* Diana. But her voice was abrupt and businesslike.

"Are you free for lunch tomorrow? You are? That's fine. You said, didn't you, that you'd like to leave the Mission if you got an opening somewhere else. The man who runs our show is up here now. We call him 'the Controller'; Gavin Stallard. Have you heard of him? No, well, I don't see why you should; you move in different worlds. I've mentioned you to him. He wants to meet you. Don't say anything about it yourself, wait for him to bring it up. It's very possible he won't. Not at the time, or maybe not at all if he thinks 'better not'; but it should work out, I think you'll like each other. Tomorrow at Ajalami's, one-fifteen."

She rang off quickly. She had not called up to gossip but to give a message. He looked at the envelope on his desk. Maybe he would not need to post it, after all.

Ajalami's was on the edge of the old town. The kitchen was in the open, at the end of a souk, with tables set out under the protection of a high curved roof. Slices of meat were roasted on skewers over a charcoal fire. There were cauldrons of rice and steaming vats of stew. The cook scooped the rice up in a bowl so that when inverted on a plate it was a rounded hillock over which the stew could be poured or slices of meat and fish arranged. It was unpretentious, excellent and expensive.

"I hope you don't mind my bringing you to a place like this," said Stallard, "but I'm only here for three days and I don't want to eat at the St. Georges the same kind of meal that I can eat at Claridge's."

Stallard was tall, broad-shouldered, with a heavy jowl. He was clean shaven but his chin was already darkening. He looked about fifty. He was the kind of man whom in London you would expect to see wearing a black pin-stripe suit, a stiff white collar, with a bowler hat and a rolled umbrella over his arm. He was now wearing a light check suit that had faded, but sat well upon his shoulders. He had on a striped shirt and a Brigade tie. His manner was genial and outgoing. His nose was lined with red veins. You had the impression that all his life he had eaten and drunk rather more than he should, but had kept his weight down by violent exercise. Reid's first thought was: "Possibly a *faux bon homme.*"

Stallard ordered himself an Arak. "You needn't have one if you don't want. Whisky's much better for you, but in England I'm one of the lucky few who can get it still. I've got a number of wine merchants. How that pays off! Each gives me a couple of bottles a month. Do you remember what Dr. Johnson said about debts: 'concentrate them; have two or three major ones, not a lot of little ones. You can dodge the cannon balls, you can see them coming, but the bullets will get you down.' That may be good advice in peacetime, but it's not in wartime, at any rate where spirits are concerned. Think of all those poor wretches who used to buy their gin and whisky from the local grocer. They are stranded now. What'll you have, Diane? Arak, like me, or something different? Gin and Italian, fine. How much longer shall we be able to get Italian? And what for you, Reid? The same? Fine. It'll take me a little time to finish my Arak so we'll make them doubles. Ah, but it's something to be back here for a little. I shall go back to England with such gusto after two weeks of this. It'll stop me creeping up the wall. When this war began I made up my mind on one point: to keep on the move. No sitting in a Whitehall office for fifty weeks a year. Half my friends are round the bend already. Sitting on that narrow island, with the blackout, the bombing, and the restrictions: a new restriction of some kind every month. Heaven knows what state they'll be in by the time the war is over; an advanced state of claustrophobia."

He sipped his Arak, with slow appreciation. "What'll we eat?" he said. "I'd suggest that we each order something different, treat the whole mélange as *hors d'oeuvres,* put it in the centre of the table and have picks at it: after all, that's what the Arabs would do, only I'm not suggesting that we should eat it with our fingers. Will you let me order?"

Reid wondered what exactly Stallard had done before the war; who he was and what his background was. The Brigade tie came from the first war; he had had a pre-first war life. He belonged to the generation of Raymond Asquith that had acquired a mystical significance to his own, which had not seen active service until 1917 by which time the fine flower of that earlier world had been mown down at Loos and on the Somme. Stallard had found himself presumably in 1919 at the age of twenty-seven with scarcely a contemporary. He had shrugged and done his best to do a deal with the mammon of unrighteousness. Who was to blame him on that account? What had he done between the wars? Endless committees, endless boardrooms, first in a junior then in a leading capacity; the man who always knew the right moment at which to intervene; when the others had talked themselves to a standstill he would interject his "Now, I've been thinking this: surely between our various divergent views we have one shared objective, out of which perhaps we could decide on a temporary probationary policy. . . ." He was the catalyst, and such as he rode the storm.

"Timing's everything," he said. "For me the war came at exactly the right time. I wasn't a regular officer in the first war so there was no R.A.R.O. nonsense in my case. I was forty-seven, there was no question of my being put in charge of a platoon, but you were in a different position, so you were automatically called up in that first September. How did it all turn out? How did it happen that you find yourself here, twenty-nine months later?"

Reid proceeded to explain. Stallard was a good listener. He had no doubt interviewed many hundreds of applicants for jobs. He knew how to show interest and at the right moment ask the question that would make it easy for the applicant to talk.

"I see," he said finally. "Yes, I see. It's a typical War Office miscalculation. From your point of view it was rather a pity that you were in the R.A.R.O. If you hadn't been. . . ." He paused. "Take my case as an example. I'm in business, a company director, a lot of irons in a lot of fires. I hadn't much doubt after Munich that we'd be in a war in eighteen months, so I went round to White's and asked a few of my contemporaries what they were going to do about it. I soon found out that the War Office was running an intelligence course in the evenings for men of a certain age with a certain experience of the world who spoke one or two foreign languages. That means I got in on the ground floor and I was in touch with the men who were running my present racket. So that when the balloon went up, they said, 'You'd better come in with us,' and as the army, or rather as the services, expanded, I found I was in a lift that was going up. Now you, on the other hand, because you were in the R.A.R.O., didn't make any effort after Munich. You said to yourself, 'The army knows where I am; if it needs me, it'll send for me.' If you hadn't been in the R.A.R.O. you'd have probably done in the Athenaeum what I did in White's. You'd have started asking questions. I don't know much about the Athenaeum, but it is, I take it, very full of high level civil servants, permanent officials, the men who run Ministries. They would have put you into touch with the right people. The Ministry of Information had its staff ready to take over the day war broke out. Then there was the Ministry of Economic Warfare; the British Council was enlarging too. The important thing would have been that men like that wouldn't have offered you a job unless it bore some relation to your capabilities and status. You would have moved along on your own level. As it was, you reverted to the position that you had held twenty years before, without being as well equipped to fill it as you were then. Have I diagnosed the case correctly?"

"I guess so. I'd never thought of it that way before. I've accepted myself as someone whom it was hard to place."

"Which is just what you were, but only because you were trying to find yourself a niche below your level; though actually you weren't trying to place yourself at all. You were waiting to be placed. First war psychology that: you offer your services to your country unreservedly and your country decides how it can make the best use of you. And for a fighting man that's the pattern still; but we're not fighting men, you and I, and careers in wartime are run in just the same way as they are in peacetime. You have to manoeuvre yourself, pull strings. You wouldn't have got where you have in your own field if you hadn't known how to plot a graph. But that's in the past, we can't alter that. The thing is to see what we can do about the present. Now Diana tells me that you are not very happy in the Mission."

"I'm happy enough. But I don't feel I've anything to do there. I'm marking time till they find the right niche. I've been there five weeks. Nothing seems to be happening."

"That's what I'd heard. I was wondering whether you'd like to come in with us. We're expanding here. We've got a new establishment. There's a vacancy that you can fill. Do you know anything of the kind of thing we do?"

"Very little. Farrar's most discreet."

"That means that you are taking a jump in the dark. But . . . well, I'll take a parallel. Are you a Mason?"

"No."

"I am, and if you asked me why I became one I'd find it difficult to give a convincing answer. You are not supposed to join because of any advantages that it might bring you; there are advantages, of course, but no good Mason would consider that. I felt it must be a good thing because of the kinds of men who were Masons. That's how it is with us. You know Nigel and Diana, and you've met me. That's a reasonable cross section. A secretary, a section chief and the controller."

"Should I be working under Farrar?"

"You'd be working parallel, under instructions from Cairo."

"Would I be still in uniform?"

"For the time being. And you'll still rank as a captain. Sometimes we give local rank if you have to meet 'high-ups' on level terms, but here you'd be more useful if you went about as someone not particularly important. But in terms of pay, now, that's another thing. You are expected to entertain, you have to travel; that comes out of service funds and there are no questions asked. It's a cosy enough game. The Mission won't mind letting you go, I suppose?"

"They'll be relieved."

"Then we'd better break the good news to Nigel."

"Nigel's not going to regard it as good news," Diana said.

That surprised Reid. "I thought we were getting on rather well together."

"Precisely. You were getting on far too well. You were his cover. He took you everywhere and no one questioned him because they knew who you were. He didn't mind having to leave the Mission building as long as you stayed on. But now you'll have to leave; and that isn't all; you'll have to leave the flat as well. He'll not want to appear in public with you, and he'll set about finding someone else from the Mission to share his flat."

"Is that really necessary?" Stallard asked.

"Nigel thinks it is. He's the most security-minded man I've ever struck, even in our racket."

"It's a fault on the right side."

Later that day the controller explained to Reid in broad outline the scope and purpose of the work he would be undertaking.

"There are two main branches of intelligence: M.I.6, that acquires information about enemy plans and movement, that operates in enemy territory; and M.I.5, which is us, that keeps information about our troops from getting to the enemy. Now, in our high echelon there's a lot more to it than sticking up posters about careless talk. That's the dreary obvious side of security. It's necessary, very necessary, but it's a bore. The exciting side is ours, finding out what the German-Italian equivalent for M.I.6 is doing, stopping them, outwitting them and, when the occasion comes, sending back false information that will mislead them. It's fascinating work. Think what it means if you can fool the Germans into keeping, in Thrace, a couple of Divisions that are desperately needed in Sicily. I think you'll have fun with us, and what's far more important, as far as you are concerned, you'll be in the war as a belligerent at last."

"Shall I ask Cartwright about this?"

"If you like. Perhaps you'd better. No, on second thoughts it had better come from me. I'm applying for you, after all."

†

That evening Cartwright rang down to Reid. "Can you spare me a couple of minutes?"

Cartwright was smiling genially. "You work even quicker than I do," he said. "Stallard was the man I wanted you to meet. I thought he might have something for you. I'm delighted that he has. I don't know the one half of what his outfit does, but they *are* handpicked. It'll take a week or so before your posting is through. But there isn't any need for you to wait for that. The sooner you move across to them the better."

Two days later there was another letter from Rachel, this time sent by air mail, acknowledging the first letter he had written from the Lebanon. It was dated December 28:

"Dearest, It was a great relief to get your letter, to know that you had arrived safely, and to be able to picture your new life. How far away it all does seem. I've thought of you so much these last few days. It's the first Christmas that we haven't been together, and on the surface it all looks so much the same: the kids coming back for the holidays, the Christmas tree in the drawing room, and the staff coming in at five o'clock for their presents and Christmas cake and port; there were the same candles and decorations on the tree; and I went to the midnight service and tried to work out what time it was with you. It's so silly but I always forget whether the clock goes back or forwards; the kids seemed to be having as much fun as ever; there was a rich array of presents. They miss you. But children take such a short-termed view of things; they only see the next thing on the list. Did you know that the Montereys were getting a divorce? I talked to Dorothy about it the other day. She told me that she had spent twenty minutes explaining to the children what it was all about. They listened quietly; when she had finished there was a pause. The children ruminated. Then the elder boy said, 'Does that mean we shan't go to St. Ives this summer?', St. Ives being his family home. Is that pertinent? Perhaps it isn't. But I thought it interesting. That's the way children are; a short, short view; and, of course, when you come back they'll pick up the threads as though there hadn't been an interval. And perhaps that's the way it should be. But it depresses me in a way. It makes everything seem so temporary and short-lived. But really there isn't anything to worry over. They both had good reports. I'll forward them by sea mail. They are happy and well; they are having a good holiday; there are parties and Christmas trees. Parents can't be bothered to do anything for themselves these days, but they see to it that the children don't feel too great a difference. I'm glad now that I didn't take them to Canada after the fall of France. I was very tempted, as you know, with talk of invasion. I was so afraid that they might be starved. You were uncertain yourself, weren't you? You couldn't tell what was going to happen to yourself, you might have been posted anywhere, but nobody thinks now that there's any real likelihood of invasion and with America in the war we shan't starve. If we'd gone to Canada they might have found it very difficult to settle back into English life. They'd have absorbed a different way of living; there might, too, be a certain amount of resentment towards them on the part of those that stayed here. Who can tell? And after all we had that year together. It was a happy time, wasn't it? One of our really happiest, I thought. We seemed so close to one another; perhaps the idea of danger helped. I so looked forward to those weekends. Peace-time weekends were always fun, but it was different when it meant your actually coming home instead of just not going into Winchborough; and I used to look forward all the week to those Fridays when I came up to London. Oh, I'm very glad we had that year."

He shrugged as he put the letter down. His face wore a wry expression. Was she writing as she really felt, or as she thought she ought to feel; or was she simply forgetting what she did not want to remember? They had been happy times, admittedly. He had looked forward to those Fridays, and Southwick was much more enjoyable when he wasn't there all the time. Yet even so he had never known any real peace of mind once the danger of invasion had passed, when bombing had become intermittent and he had recognised that he could not stay permanently in the Ministry of Mines; that he had outlived his use there; and that he might have to apply to be returned to his professorship. Well, that was behind him now. He was in the war at last, if what Stallard had said was true.

5

REID HAD READ RACHEL'S LETTER in a fourth floor office in a building that from a side street running parallel to the waterfront looked on to the St. Georges, on the one side, and the playing field of a girls' school on the other. The three lower floors were occupied by the M.E.S.C. (Middle East Supply Centre).

"It's as good a cover as you could have," Stallard had explained. "Lebanese of all denominations are going there every hour of the day. It won't excite any curiosity if one of our secret boys is seen going through the door. It's much safer than the Mission."

Reid also moved from the flat above the University to a room in the old town. Abdul Hamid found it for him. It was part of a large family flat owned by a Lebanese professor at the University who had two small children; the cost of living was rising and his salary was stationary; he was glad of the extra money. "He also hopes that you will buy material for him from the Officers' Shop and groceries from the N.A.A.F.I. That is strictly against army regulations, but the law does not apply to you in your present position."

Reid's lodging consisted of one large room with direct access to the bathroom; it also had an independent entrance, "very convenient," Abdul Hamid explained with a leer. "No one will feel embarrassed about visiting you."

It was a congenial place. Through one window as he lay in bed he could see the high minaret of a mosque; through the other at the end of a long vista of houses he could see the sea. Every morning while it was still dark he would be woken by the voice of a *muezzin*. Always an early riser he would make no attempt to get back to sleep. He would lie among his pillows brooding while the quick dawn broke. On the balcony of the house across the street two girls in long, white dressing gowns, with their black hair flung loose over their shoulders, would hang their mattresses over the

84

side of the balcony and beat their carpets. By six, tramcars would be running in the streets. By seven, the honking of car horns had begun. Breakfast was served to him in his room. When he left the flat at eight, the shops were open and the streets were crowded with veiled Moslem women; with Lebanese girls, their black Bryl-creamed hair worn long upon their shoulders; with Arabs walking two and two, in fezzes, swinging their beads, sometimes their little fingers intertwined. Along the sidewalks would be vendors of hollow bread, shaped in crescents, and shoe blacks with their little brass-bound caskets. His twenty minutes' walk took him up the noisy main street, down which the trolleys ran. At the pivotal traffic point where a policeman stood under an umbrella, he took the road that ran south to the sea. It was Beirut's Piccadilly. At its head was Tanios, a kind of Fortnum and Mason where Duty Officers would procure picnic sandwiches. There were bookshops there and libraries. Kassab's—the Liberty's of Beirut—several Indian silk-shops, and Terses where you brought brocades.

At the foot of the street he turned left along the waterfront. He had spent a good deal of his time on the French Riviera. It was oddly familiar to be taking morning after morning just this walk. The luxury hotels reminded him of the Croisette; the small sailors' cafés of Antibes; the night-club section past the Normandie had an air of Juan les Pins. Two hundred yards beyond the fashionable *plage* of the St. Georges was another beach highly unfashionable, like the stretch of shingle under the railway between Villefranche and Cap Ferrat. There was a cemetery like Mougins' with tall cypresses. Bougainvillea trailed over high garden walls, the sky was blue and at the back of it all a perpetual backcloth, like the Esterelles, were the high snow-capped mountains of the Lebanon. It was as though the whole run of the coast between Cannes and Monte Carlo had been telescoped in essence into the limits of this few minutes' stroll.

The office staff consisted of one other officer, a lieutenant called Finchley, the son of an English business man, and an Egyptian recruited in Cairo who acted as accountant and administrator with no share in the intelligence side of the office's work. Diana handled the personal correspondence. There was a corporal in charge of the files, two typists and a batman chauffeur. Reid had a room to himself, while Diana shared a room with Finchley who said that the sound of typing did not disturb him.

"It's nice that I'll be seeing you every day," he said to her.

"That's what I've been thinking."

"But I was beginning to enjoy my evenings as Duty Officer."

"Only beginning? I'd liked them from the start."

†

On his last morning in Beirut Stallard laid out his plan of campaign to Reid and Farrar.

"You are as much on the same level as a G.2. (ops.) and a G.2. (1); and it seems a little invidious to leave Nigel in charge of that flat and all the greater amenities involved by it, but as I see it a flat will be of much greater use to you, Nigel, than it would be to the Professor. Nigel, you're an extrovert: you talk a lot; not too much, not at all too much. It's gay, I like it. You're different, though, Professor: your forte—Diana put me on it and I noticed it myself—is your capacity to make people talk; you draw them out. You're at your best in tête-à-têtes, or as a chairman for a group of three or four; the result of the tutorial system. I'd say that quiet lunches and dinners rather than cocktail parties were your line.

"Then again, Nigel speaks reasonable Arabic and he knows this parish. My idea is that he should find the people who can be useful to us and then hand them over to you; I picture Nigel as a public relations man, seeing groups of people, picking the two or three who might be suborned, intimidated, generally recruited, then saying to you, 'Prof, try your luck with him.' It's wise not to have the two of you living in the same flat, and there's no need to let the world know that you are working in the same outfit. But there's no need for you not to go about as friends. Some people carry security to an extreme. They are so anxious to deny information to the enemy, that they wouldn't allow an attack in the Western Desert for fear that the Germans would discover what kinds of tank we have. If you were to stop going around together, people would imagine that you had quarrelled. There's no point in that; besides, when they realised that you were working under the same roof they would be suspicious. No, none of that. It's all very simple. Explain that the Professor is forty-three years old, that he's used to a quiet life, that he needs evenings by himself and that you're too social for him. And I'd say by and large that was pretty true. That's the general strategy, it's up to you to work out the tactics. Good luck to you both, and remember this is an important area. It looks a pretty playground at the moment; it won't be so pretty if Rommel breaks through to the canal and the Turks decide to join the Axis. On your toes, in fact."

No, thought Reid, he isn't a *faux bon homme.*

On his first morning in the M.E.S.C. building, Farrar handed Reid a file marked "Amin Marun."

"Before I came up here they kept me for a month in Cairo with their files. You've met Amin Marun; if you read their file you'll have a good idea of the way we work. There are a few things to remember first. If a report is marked 'A+' it means it comes direct from Abdul Hamid. If it's marked 'A' it means it is a good report. Anything marked 'B' is something to be taken with a caution. 'C' is no more than a rumour. But if there are a lot of 'C's, it is worth investigating."

"Do all reports come through Abdul Hamid?"

"Not all of them, not by any means. We have a number of representatives scattered through the country. We also correspond with our branch in Istanbul. They have a link with the Turkish War Office whom we call 'Aunt Mildred.' She is very useful to us. There are code names that you'll find the clue to in another file. Ask Diana about that. I'd read it all through first, as though it were a novel; then take it slowly a second time, make notes and after that ask questions. By the way, T.B. is me."

"Why?"

"Short for Toby Belch."

It was a bulky file but after half an hour's study of it, Reid was reaching the conclusion that it contained very little solid information. There was an opening entry stating how Farrar had met the Amin Maruns at a party given by a Lebanese merchant who possessed a consignment of dates in Basra that he wanted to transport to Syria. There was an account of the Amin Marun background, which he already knew. There was a description of Aziz.

A copy of the Office's weekly summary was sent to I.S.L.O. M.E.F. with a limited distribution list. "It is believed," Reid read in it, "that there are possibilities in a young Turk who is staying with his aunt, the wife of a Lebanese merchant. He is a problem child and if we could find some way of exerting pressure on him he might serve as a channel for false information to Turkey. On the other hand, by judicious blackmail, we might force him to give us valuable information on his return to Turkey. A lot depends on whether he passes his next exams. If he fails I shall suggest that he goes to Alexandria. He might accept the suggestion out of a reluctance to return to Turkey. I think he has no sympathy for his father. In Alexandria, without the security offered him by his aunt, it would be easier to detect what his special weakness is. When we have detected that, it will be easy to decide what is our most fruitful method of approach."

A report marked 'A' from his English teacher at the A.U.B. stated: "A low potential: no feeling for the language: no wish to acquire it. Well behaved in form." A 'B' report from a fellow student ran: "Speaks fluent French but does not write it grammatically: does not interest himself in community activities: not popular, not unpopular, a cypher." Another 'B' report indicated that he kept late hours, that he often looked tired at morning classes.

Interspersed with these reports about Aziz were entries about the aunt and uncle. Censorship had been put on all mail entering the Amin Marun household and addressed to Aziz at the University. Madame Amin's correspondence had been submitted to a V.I. lamp but there were no indications of secret writing.

It all, in Reid's opinion, amounted to very little. His interest began to wane. Then suddenly his attention was startled by an 'A+' report.

"I had been asked," it said, "to make any discovery I could about Aziz's love life. I called at the company's flat after dinner; we drank several whiskies; the atmosphere was cordial. The professor joined us later; we talked for a little, then I offered to see Aziz home. 'It's early,' I said, when we were in the car. 'Why not go somewhere for a drink.' He shook his head. 'I've had enough to drink.' 'I know a place where we can find nice girls.' 'No, thanks.' We drove towards his home. I did not hurry. I put my hand on his knee. He made no response. I moved my hand higher. Still no response. I paused, waited. He shifted. He crossed his legs. It was not that he repulsed me; I do not believe he was aware that an advance had been made towards him. He is a very curious young man."

Reid stopped, astounded. He re-read the report. It could only mean one thing.

He crossed the passage to Farrar's room.

"This file," he said. "Is this the truth?"

"The truth, the whole truth, and nothing but the truth."

"This report of Abdul Hamid and Aziz, in the car?"

"Sinister was the word you used."

"But we're encouraging this, abetting a crime."

"Steady, now, steady; we're abetting nothing, and it's not a crime here, remember. The places where it's a crime are very few. No one worries about it in a Moslem world. It's the women they worry about, not the men. It's difficult for a young Moslem to find a girl friend. He has no alternative."

"Then if that's the case, why seduce him, if it gives you no blackmail hold as it would in England?"

"Seduce is a big word. A young man like Aziz knows his own mind. He's one thing or another or perhaps both things. We want to find out the kind of young man he is. Then we know what use to make of him."

"I see."

"You'll find more sinister things than that in our files before you're through."

"I'll be on my guard." He turned back towards the passage; as he did, the door of the next office opened and Finchley walked out through it. Diana was alone. He went straight in.

"Are you doing anything for lunch?" he asked.

"I'm not, no."

"Then would you have lunch with me? It's short notice; but this file has been a shock to me."

"Which file is that?"

He handed it across. She glanced at it. "Oh, yes, I know. I can understand, one has to get used to that kind of thing in this game."

"So Nigel warned me. Shall I pick you up at one?"

He returned to his study of the file. There was a report from Aunt Mildred on Aziz's father. "He appears to be a conventional, efficient, but not very brilliant army officer. He is employed in Q. He lives quietly, rarely entertains; is unpolitical; he plays bridge in the army officers' club, but he does not gamble. He appears to have no mistress, is not believed to be homosexual. The only suspicious thing about him is that his life is so obviously respectable. In a detective story the last man you would suspect is invariably the murderer. Nothing is known about his wife. She follows the routine of a strict Moslem. She is never seen in a public place alone; she appears to be absorbed by her family."

There were translations of the letters that had passed between

89

her and her sister, and between Aziz and his mother. Aziz wrote to his mother every Friday and to his father on the last day of every month. The letters were without any interest. There were accounts of Farrar's various meetings with the Amin Maruns, including the one at the St. Georges when he had explained that Kurdistan was to become a Russian sphere of influence. "If any echoes of this report reach us from Turkey we can be sure that it is due to her." There followed a note that made Reid smile. "I believe the Prof. will be very useful as a piece of ground bait. He will be unsuspected because he is himself unsuspecting. He also appears to have a knack for making people talk about themselves. He may be able to break down Aziz's reserve."

†

They lunched in Sa'ad's. It was a grey, cloudy day in tune with the long, dark, narrow room with its balcony in which no one ever seemed to sit. There was no one there in uniform and the restaurant was quarter full. Reid sat with his back to the light. Diana was wearing her dark office clothes with a white shirt-waist fastened at the throat by a gold brooch, set with an oval reddish stone. She had a tired preoccupied expression, as though she had something on her mind.

"I wonder if they've any Bols gin," she said. "It's the kind of thing they might."

They had.

"I had it on a Dutch ship once. I liked the look of the bottle, then I started liking it for itself."

"Where was the Dutch boat running?"

"Tangier to London."

"What were you doing in Tangier?"

"The kind of thing one goes to Tangier to do."

They laughed together. It was nice to be able to talk in shorthand in this way. Once again he found himself wondering what kinds of love affairs she had had; had they been many, had they gone deep, had they left scars?

"I'm missing those duty-officers-talks even more than I had expected to," he said. "I felt so close. Do you yourself feel that you're more yourself when you're on the telephone?"

She smiled. "I feel very natural on the telephone. Something went wrong with my spine when I was ten. I couldn't walk. I had to be taken out in a wheel chair; I had to do special exercises. It's all right now, but for two years I was cut off from all the games and sports that I should have been enjoying at that age. But it didn't cut me off from my friends. I'm gregarious; they enjoyed bringing me their stories, they'd embroider them, of course. They'd make themselves more heroic and dramatic; half of the fun of their adventures was the coming round to tell me about them afterwards. I couldn't visit them, of course. But I could call them up. I spent hours talking on the telephone. Those were my happiest times. The moment the house was empty, I'd start calling up all my friends. I loved the telephone. It saved me in those days. I love it still. I sometimes think, even now, that I'd rather talk to people on the telephone than go and see them. I feel closer to them that way."

"I feel very close to you now."

"You do? I'm glad you do. I feel close to you: in the way I always dreamed I'd be. It's funny, isn't it, that I'd made this dream picture of you through hearing Margaret talk about you."

"I must re-meet this Margaret some day."

"I shouldn't. There'd be no response. She's settled down, marriage, children. You were a stepping stone for her, a sounding board. And, oh, how I wanted just that for myself."

"You didn't find it?"

"No, I didn't find it. I was looking for someone, for something, I didn't know what. I'm not sure if I expected to find it, but the looking for it was the thing that counted. 'The quest,' I'd call it, and I needed so much someone to whom I could talk about the quest. It's wonderful to have found you here; and wonderful that you'll be here for a long time, that there's no need to hurry anything, that we're living in a small self-contained world where we get asked to the same parties, where meetings aren't planned. That's one of the things that maddened me in England, or at least my part of England. Everything was so cut and dried; these people to meet these people, and not those people; everything on time, everything to schedule; on the day a son's born, put him down for Eton and the M.C.C."

She checked. She laughed. "There I go again. That old hobby-horse of mine. And you encourage me. You shouldn't. I'll begin to bore you."

"You could never do that." But he changed the subject.

"Were you in this game before the war?"

"On the brink of it. I knew that war would come. I wanted to be in it, but I didn't want to be in uniform. I knew that my father would want me in the A.T.S. He'd have got me a commission easily: I was on my guard; and exactly what I had expected to happen, happened. On that first Sunday in September, after we had listened to Chamberlain's broadcast, my father got up from his chair, walked over to the fireplace, stood with his back to it, his hands in his pocket. 'That's that,' he said. 'Now we've got to decide what each of us has to do. What are your plans, Diana? To drive an ambulance again?' 'Not this time. I report for duty tomorrow as a civilian at the Foreign Office.'

"You should have seen his face. It was one of the best moments of my life. He was so certain that at last he'd be in the strong position, that I'd have to come to him: with the game played on his home ground. But I managed to work this out for myself."

Reid laughed. "This is one of the most extraordinary love-hate relationships I've ever heard of."

"There's not much hate about it. It's mostly love. We get a huge kick out of one another. He couldn't do without me."

"Does he know what your Foreign Office work consists of?"

"He's a pretty good idea. His friends at 'the Rag' could tell him."

"Wasn't it a shock to you to discover the kind of work it was?"

"I guessed at it."

"But things like that file today."

"You can't make an omelette without breaking eggs."

"But to try to corrupt a young man."

"That's the schoolmaster in you talking. Is it worse to teach a young man bad habits which he'll outgrow if he hasn't got a special bent that way, than send a platoon of infantry on a forlorn attack, as a diversion, to mislead our enemy? Both involve sacrifice; both are necessary."

"One seems a cleaner way of fighting."

"Cleaner? Is there such a thing as a clean fight, in modern warfare? With gas and flamethrowers and bombs. It's not like Agincourt and Crécy; when a battle was a series of private duels, begun and ended in a day." She spoke scornfully, angrily. Her eyes were flashing. She was genuinely roused. He had never seen her in quite the mood before. She checked and flushed. "I'm sorry. I sometimes get worked up. I don't know why it is. Let's change the subject. Have you heard any news about the General coming back?"

Had she, he wondered, lost a lover in the war? Was that why she was so intense? Later he returned obliquely to the subject.

"Has anyone you cared for a good deal been killed in the war?" he asked.

"Killed as far as I'm concerned. He was on the other side."

"A German or an Austrian?"

"A German."

"What happened to him?"

"I don't know. I don't want to know. He wrote to me once through a friend in Switzerland. I didn't answer."

"Too risky?"

"No, it wasn't that, it was just that it was over. Things could never be the same again. Best cut it out. Some of the girls I knew went on writing to their German friends. During that phoney war period they'd talk of how it would be all over within a year. 'Christmas 1940 we'll be packing our skis again.' I knew better."

"Was that how you met him, skiing?"

"At Kitzbuhl."

"I've never skiied. I've always wished I had."

"There's nothing like it. It's so beautiful, and you feel so well; and everyone looks so handsome. He was tall and blonde, the Nordic type. He took his skiing so seriously. That was one of the loveable things about him, because he wasn't very good; but he'd try so hard; his forehead would wrinkle. It made him such a little boy, his being so serious about it; but then in the evenings with his accordion, when he sang, he was so different then, so in his element. The way he rocked to the music; that's how I felt he ought to be, that's how I felt Germans ought to be, young and gay in the things they have a knack for, not being serious and solemn about things that they're no good at. The Germans are no good in the long run in the things that they take seriously; they'll lose this war in the end; they're bound to with America against them, and then in twenty years they'll start taking themselves seriously again and once again they'll make idiots of themselves with furrowed foreheads. Why can't they stay Bohemians? But he was wonderful after those hours in the snow; he seemed like a legendary god; his blue eyes were so blue and he looked—I can't say that he looked incandescent—but that's really what I do mean: he looked as though something had been lit up inside him."

"You may meet him again, you know."

"I may; but I hope not. It wouldn't be the same thing. Keep things in their setting."

"You sound very ruthless when you talk like that."

"Ruthless? Do I? I've had that said to me before; perhaps it's true. But I'm someone who knows what she doesn't want, even if I don't know what I do want. Perhaps that makes me unfair to men, to some men. I've tried to figure it out. I know I'm mean, but I can't keep being mean. I've an unsolved question on my hands. I meet a man. I think he has the answer. I throw myself into something; then I come up for breath and find I haven't found the answer; and I'm resentful. Which is unfair of me. I asked more of him than he had to give, and I try and console myself by saying that for a few days or weeks I gave him more than he deserved to get. But he's not grateful, damn it. He thinks I'm mean. Oh, I don't know, I reckon that I don't fit in, but I think the balance is equated. I hurt myself more than I hurt anybody else. But . . . oh, well . . . ruthless: that's the word they use." She checked. She leant across the table. She put her hand over his. She pressed it. "Let's hope you never have to use that word to me."

That evening Reid went round to the Amin Maruns. He had an open invitation to look in whenever he liked. In London it would never have occurred to him to call on an acquaintance without telephoning first, but he suspected that Madame Amin led a limited social life and welcomed visits. There was no reply when he rang the bell; but there was a light beneath the door, and he could hear the sound of music. He waited for a minute or so, then rang again. This time more lengthily. There was a pause; then he heard the sound of feet, a latch clicked. Aziz was in the doorway. His face was flushed; he looked awkward, embarrassed and resentful. "I'm sorry to keep you waiting," he said. "I very much wanted to hear a record through. It was only a matter of half a minute, to the end of the first side."

"I'm sorry to have disturbed you. May I sit quietly and hear the other side?"

He watched Aziz as he listened. To himself music had little specific meaning. He enjoyed it as an agreeable background to his thoughts, but he could see that to the younger man it was something altogether different. There was a taut expression on his face.

94

He was leaning forward; his lips were moving, his eyes alight. He seemed entranced. This was the real boy, he thought.

Reid waited till the record had run down. He allowed a minute to pass before he spoke.

"That certainly was something," he said at length. Aziz made no reply; he was seated on the floor, on a cushion, his heels tucked under him. He shook himself as though he were emerging from a trance.

"Yes, that certainly was something."

Again there was a pause.

"Not to appreciate music is to lack a sense," said Reid. "I've no idea what I lose through not understanding it."

Aziz looked round, staring blankly, uncomprehendingly. "It's my whole life," he said. "I can't imagine life without it. I wouldn't want to live without it."

Reid had found in his tutorials that when a young person had begun to talk it was best not to interrupt him with questions, not to attempt to draw him out. If a pupil felt the atmosphere congenial he would talk, on his own account. There was a pause of a full minute. Then Aziz started.

"Music is the one thing I can be sure of in this uncertain world. It is indefinite. It does not try to explain anything, yet it resolves everything. All these people, in all these countries, are trying to lay down formulae. Who is not with us is against us. You must be a Nazi or a Communist or a Catholic. There is only one God, Allah. Everyone who does not believe in Allah is an infidel. So many voices, so many words in search of a definition. Music has no concern with that. All these separate chords and notes and dissonances are woven together, to achieve a pattern, and a harmony. There *is* a meaning; but it is not a meaning that can be expressed in words; for everyone it has a different meaning; yet everyone is held by the same arrangement of notes and chords, is led through those discords to a final climax. An audience becomes one person. Sometimes I feel the whole world is mad, that there is no point in anything. I wonder why I should compete in this insane rat race. Then I come back here, I put on a record; I listen and gradually I forget my troubles, peace descends and I have a feeling that everything that is incongruous, antipathetic, antagonistic in our modern living is resolved; *sub specie aeternitatis,* under the lens of eternity. If you get far enough away from quarrels and disputes you can see that they are trivial. When I was a boy I couldn't understand how the earth could be round when there were so many mountains, until a master took a football and rubbed a very little mud on it—said, 'That football is the world, the Himalayas on the earth's surface in relation to the earth are a tenth the size of that film of mud. If you were a big enough giant to catch the world as a goal keeper catches a football you would feel, in spite of the Himalayas, that it was smooth and polished. If you were far enough away from the world to look at it through a telescope it would seem as perfect a sphere as the moon seems to us.' I have always remembered that. Music takes us so far away that troubles as vast as the Himalayas barely seem a roughness on a surface; when that record was running a German, an Italian, a Jap, an American, a Briton, if they had been sitting beside me listening would have felt at one with another. Music makes me believe that there is a meaning in the universe. Nothing else does."

"One day love may."

"Will it? I've been told it does. But I've thought that was one of those magazine fiction panaceas. Marry, settle down, have a family, be a good citizen; what that really means is 'dull your mind with domesticities and duties.' Love is the opium of the thinking classes."

Reid shook his head. "It can be; but it needn't be. It can do what music does. It can put you in tune with the long rhythm of life itself, of birth and death and rebirth; the whole cycle of creation. When you are in tune with that, everything else falls into place."

"Have you found that yourself?"

Reid hesitated. Had he, he wondered; not he suspected in the fullest sense. Intimations of immortality; but not more than that. He replied evasively. "One does not need to experience something to know its truth. You can be vouchsafed a glimpse. I am convinced that there are several doors to that detached peace you were talking of, when you are far enough away from the human race to feel yourself a part of it; religion gives it to you. Priests and nuns know it, and all dedicated people know it. Though I've not known that kind of peace myself, I know that it exists, just as I know that it can be reached through love."

"I see. Dedicated people. Do you think Hitler had it?"

"In early days, maybe."

"When did he lose it?"

"Perhaps there is such a thing as evil. Perhaps the powers of darkness do exist."

There was another pause. There was a ruminating expression on Aziz's face. Reid waited, certain that Aziz had more to say. He had.

"I have not yet fallen in love," he said. "I wonder when I shall. How long shall I have to wait?"

There was an eagerness in his voice that carried Reid back to the autumn of 1913 when as a schoolboy he had read the first volume of "Sinister Street" and his heart had warmed to the description of Michael Fane's love affair with Lily, when they had walked in Kensington Gardens on a misty evening and Michael had slipped his hand inside Lily's muff. He had wondered how long he would have to wait before a similar experience came to him. Here, twenty-eight years later, a young Turkish student was asking him the self-same question. Was there all this difference between one people and another, between one generation and another?

†

That evening, Reid dined at home alone with Farrar.

"I can tell you what makes Aziz tick," he said to Farrar. "It isn't anything to do with sex or drugs. It's music."

He recounted their conversation earlier. Nigel listened with absorbed attention.

"Now we know where we are," he said. "Now we've got something we can work on. I knew that you'd be the man to help me out. You can make people talk."

"I don't see how it's going to help you."

"Don't you? I do. Every man has his Achilles' Heel. I don't mean a weak spot; but a vulnerable side. Indulge his hobby and you've got him. We always think of sex and drink and drugs as the way to get a man into our power; but there are other things. Snobbery, for instance. Most people think snobbery means wanting to meet peers, but there are a lot of people who don't care for titles but will go miles to meet a film-star or a footballer. Find out what a man wants, show him that you can give it to him and then exert the pressure. Music—now, let me think.

"Has he any musical ambitions? Are there records that he can't get in wartime or that he can't afford; is there some special record player? We must find out what he needs. Then we can give it to him and then we've got him. Now, next time that you see Aziz, what you've got to do is this."

He stood up. He began to stride backwards and forwards, up and down the room. He had a lean, lithe stride like a caged animal's.

†

A week later Reid again called on the Amin Maruns. This time Aziz was out; only the aunt was there, which was as he had hoped. He had timed his call so that her husband should be absent. Over the inevitable coffee he told her how much he had enjoyed his talk the other evening with her nephew. "He is a very stimulating young man," he said.

"I am glad you find him so. To us he is a problem."

"But aren't all intelligent young men precisely that? You know what Maeterlinck said, 'If a man is not a socialist at twenty he has no heart; if he is a socialist at forty he has no brains.' "

"My nephew is not a socialist."

"I didn't say he was. I used the phrase loosely. I meant that every young man is against the existing order; he is in revolt against what his elders stand for. You'll remember, I'm sure, what Byron said: 'I have simplified my politics into a detestation of all existing governments.' "

"Byron's own end was most unfortunate."

"To the Greeks he is a hero."

"He is not to the Turks."

Reid sidetracked that.

"As a professor," he said, "I am in constant touch with the young, and since I am no longer young I'm able to take a long view. I can see how this student and the other has turned out. I have not found that on the whole the exemplary student has turned out best."

"That is little consolation to the parents or relatives of students who are not exemplary, at the time when they are proving headstrong."

"I would not have described Aziz as headstrong."

"Nor would I. He would be easier if he were."

"Is he thinking of making music a career?"

"How could he? What kind of an income could he earn through music?"

"Has his family no money?"

"A little; enough, if he were prepared to accept the kind of position to which he is by birth entitled; if he were to become a soldier or, as we would all prefer, a civil servant, he would be able to obtain a bride who would bring to the marriage a dowry that would ensure their comfort. But music is another matter. What parents would wish to see their daughter married to a musician?"

"Does he play the piano or the violin?"

"He plays the piano, but only as several hundred others play it; and even if he played it well, really well, how could my sister tolerate her son as a pianist, a public performer in a restaurant or café? Oh no, no, no. In Europe it may be different. A pianist may have a social status, but not here in Turkey, in the Levant."

"Has he any ambitions as a composer?"

"I don't think he has. He has no ambitions whatever as far as we can see. That is what worries my sister and myself. He has this passion for music. He wants to spend all his spare time listening to it; and he wants to spend all his spare time with young people who share this passion. Do you know what time he gets back at night? One, two, three in the morning. How can he expect to come fresh to his studies six hours later?"

So that was how he spent his nights. How far wide of the mark they had been in picturing him drinking, wenching or taking hashish.

"I hope you don't think I'm being impertinent," Reid said. "I've no right to be asking you all these personal questions, but I was very struck with your nephew. I'm used, you see, to dealing with young men. I know their complexes: how self-conscious they are, how reserved, how on the defensive; yet suddenly so expansive. They so want to give, to pour out everything; yet they are afraid of being laughed at. They won't expose themselves to ridicule. Yet they are hungry for friendship and affection. The first time I met Aziz he didn t say a word, but the other evening when I found him alone, when we were listening to music, he was so warm, so outgoing. He has such an attractive smile."

"Ah, but he has, hasn't he?" Madame Amin's own face brightened suddenly, lit by a smile reminiscent of her nephew. It took fifteen years off her. He could picture her fascination as a young girl, before indolence, boredom, middle-age and over-eating had coarsened her. He thought of Thomas Hardy's poem, "Wives in the Sere." A half minute, and the smile, the look of youthfulness, had vanished. She was once more an ageing, discontented woman. "I wish he would meet some nice young woman who would make him see some sense," she said.

Reid smiled. There it went again, that invincible belief of the middle-aged that youth should be put in chains, harnessed to conformity, the wide wings clipped. English rebels used to complain that the Public School system stifled individuality, turning out everyone according to a pattern, that of the Embryo Empire builder. But wasn't it the female of the species who demanded uniformity, turning men into husbands and providers? And they were right nine times in ten; that was what most men needed—to be like other men. There were some men, however, who were born to break the pattern. Perhaps Aziz was one of them.

Farrar was delighted with Reid's report. He paced backwards and forwards in the room of the flat in the Rue Jeanne D'Arc. "I get it. I think I get it. The boy makes sense. He knows his aunt is right. He can't make a living out of music. He probably doesn't want to. He doesn't want to professionalise his hobby. But music is the one thing he cares for. Without music his life would not be worth living. That's what he said. Now, Prof, it's up to you. You must find the angle from which we can attack. Find out what he needs. There must be something we can give him that no one else can. We've got to find what it is. There must be something."

A few days later Reid received an invitation from Amin Marun to a Tabooli party. He was delighted at the prospect. "Unless you have had Tabooli in a Beiruti house, you cannot understand the Lebanon," he had been told.

Tabooli was more than a Lebanese speciality; it was a Lebanese ritual. It was served at a quarter to six with arak. A large dish contained what looked like a mixed green salad. It was composed of wheat, pounded up with vegetables, it was eaten with the fingers, scooped up with lettuce leaves. It had a fresh cool taste, with an after flavour of onions. With it were served balls of kibbé —a minced meat mixed with corn. The meal was taken slowly, one sip of arak to one mouthful of Tabooli. A glass of arak was expected to last half an hour. Eventually the Tabooli and the arak were cleared away and tea was served with biscuits and very sweet sticky cakes that had an almond flavour. Later on, Cherry

Heering was offered. The party was scheduled to break up at nine o'clock, so that the guests could dine or not dine afterwards as they chose.

Amin Marun had invited a dozen guests. At the start Aziz contributed nothing to the conversation. He sat silent, sulky, inattentive, exactly as he had at that first meeting. Reid waited till the room filled up and he had an opportunity to change his chair and sit by Aziz on a sofa.

"Do you find more opportunities here for hearing music than you had in Turkey?" he enquired.

"Many more. That's what makes it so exasperating."

"Makes what exasperating?"

"The fact that I can't get my hands on all there is."

"I don't follow that."

"In Turkey we are cut off from Europe. There are currency difficulties. We cannot buy all we want from Germany and communication with England is very difficult. I had to make the best of what there was. But here I should not be cut off from England, and the best records are being made in England now. But I cannot bring Turkish currency across the frontier, and my aunt does not realise how much they matter to me. I did not worry in Turkey because they were out of reach. But here they should not be. They are available to others. I sometimes feel I shall go mad, because I can not hear the music that I need. You cannot memorise music, as you can a poem. You have to go on hearing it."

His face was white, his eyes were blazing.

"He talked," Reid was to tell Farrar later, "like a drug addict deprived of his drug."

Farrar exulted. "Now we've got him where we want him. Listen. This is how we'll play it. Not through Abdul Hamid. Aziz has met him and distrusts him; or he should. At any rate, they can't be friends. We'll use a friend of his, Fadhil, whom you haven't met. The Koumayans entertain a lot. They know Aziz. They can invite him to a party; then, on the day that he's coming I'll arrange to have Fadhil asked."

"The Koumayans aren't in our show, are they?"

"Of course they aren't. They'd be horrified if they knew what I was about. I've told them I'm in propaganda; and of course, in a way, I am. My having been at the Mission was a help in that regard. They are very pro-ally. I can ask them to meet people here of whom they wouldn't have acknowledged the existence three years ago. On occasions I can persuade them to invite a friend of mine."

"Do they get anything out of this?"

"Nothing on the surface, except the self-satisfaction of making a contribution to the cause. We all like to think we're doing something of use in wartime. Though of course there are little things that I can do for them: permits, for instance; and there are some articles that are in very short supply here. When I go into Cairo I don't return empty handed. And finally, my dear Prof, incredible though it may seem to you, Annabelle Koumayan thinks this decadent piece of masculinity a dish."

Next morning Reid paid a visit to the Mission. He liked to maintain his connection with it. He also had an opportunity of reading English newspapers, seeing the latest news reports and reading the daily bulletin that was issued by the Mission's Propaganda Section. The news could not be worse. Japanese forces were seeping south. Singapore had fallen. Java was next upon the list. In the Western Desert Rommel was again in the ascendant, and on the Eastern Front the Russians were in retreat. Reid had not now the slightest doubt of the eventual outcome of the war. With the United States in the field the Axis could not win. But how long would it last? Every battle, every defeat seemed to add another year to its duration: the enemy had to be forced back over so vast a territory.

On his return he paused in Diana's office. "A message for you from the boss," she said. "That party at the Koumayans' has been fixed for Tuesday. Six o'clock; and all the interested characters will be there."

"Doesn't it seem very trivial that we should be arranging a party for interested characters when the whole of our Eastern Empire is threatened?"

She smiled. "Five years ago, did the fact that there were two million unemployed barely subsisting under the means test, prevent your enjoyment of a chateau-bottled claret?"

It was the first time that Reid had been to the Koumayan house. It lay on the high main road that led to the Place des Martyres. It was constructed of ochre brick; a high wall shut it round; a high ironwork gate opened on to an ornamental garden. The house was arranged in the old Turkish manner; a large central hall with small rooms opening off it. The walls of the main hall were hung with carpets and gilt-framed portraits.

When Reid arrived there were some thirty other guests. He recognised very few of them. There were only one or two British officers; those were captains. Farrar was on his guard against having rank pulled on him. There were, however, three French colonels. The remainder were French civilians or Lebanese. Tea and cakes and sandwiches were being served at a large ornately silvered table. A small corner table provided ice, soda and scotch whisky. The attendance round this table was continuous. Reid supposed that Farrar was responsible for its steady sustenance. Little Scotch could have been available since the fall of France.

He looked for the Amin Maruns. Aziz was standing in a corner. His aunt and uncle were seated together on a sofa. They were not talking to each other. Marriage was curious that way, he thought. Husbands and wives went out to parties, felt they must protect each other; sat together; consumed nourishment, then went home and discussed a party they had not in fact attended. They might just as well go out to a café and watch the world drift past. They would see more variety that way.

Nigel was ubiquitous; gracious, dominant, peripatetic, acting as a host, though he was not a host, effecting introductions, moving from one group to another; he certainly looked as though he were a public relations officer.

To his surprise Reid noticed Diana across the room. He moved across to her. "So you are allowed to this kind of party," he remarked.

"It wouldn't do, would it, for me to avoid all his parties. People would start asking questions. We have to appear in public sometimes as business acquaintances."

"I suppose that I shall one day see the point of these elaborate precautions."

"Don't try. Use your common sense. It's refreshing to have one man in the office who relies on that."

"It's a relief that security doesn't limit *us* to a business acquaintanceship."

"That was my one fear when I fixed your coming to us. It was in fact my one condition. I said to the controller, 'The Prof. may have to leave his flat, but he's not going to stop seeing me.'"

"You actually said that?"

"Of course I did." Her look was frank. There was a twinkle in her eyes. He had the sensation of something underneath his heart going round and over. He turned away. He looked across the room, searching again for Aziz. He found him, at length, seated, talking to a youngish man who was wearing European clothes. He might have been a Frenchman by his appearance. He wondered if that was Fadhil. Diana had followed his glance. "It seems to be going all right," she said.

He noticed at the end of the evening that the Amin Maruns left alone. He took another look for Aziz, but did not see him. He looked in vain, also, for the young Frenchman. He presumed that they had slipped away together. I'd give a lot to be invisible, he thought.

Next day he asked Farrar about Fadhil. "He looks as though he might be a Frenchman. Is he?"

"I fancy he is, but he won't admit it. If he did they'd conscript him for the army."

"What does he say he is?"

"Egyptian; that could be anything. I don't know too much about him. In point of fact I don't want to know too much. Abdul Hamid swears he can be trusted. That's enough for me. He has been here several years. Since the beginning of the war he has had a teaching job at the University; a wartime job because they are short of staff. He has no real qualifications, but it isn't difficult to teach elementary English."

"Is he married?"

"I don't think so; not so as you'd notice it, as they used to say."

"What about his parents?"

"All his relatives are in Egypt."

"For a man as security-minded as you, you take a great deal on trust as far as this gentleman is concerned."

"I trust Abdul Hamid. That is sufficient. He has a hold on Fadhil. Fadhil wouldn't dare doublecross him. Abdul Hamid is a very tough operator."

"I wish I knew what had happened between those two."

"We'll know soon enough."

†

They learnt five days later. Aziz and Fadhil had made friends quickly. In fact, they had recognised each other, through their association at the University, though they had never met.

"I've noticed you," Fadhil had said.

"I'm surprised at that. There are so many students."

"Perhaps, but there was something different about you. You looked as though you didn't quite belong there."

"Is that unusual at the A.U.B.? We're a very miscellaneous collection; a dozen different nationalities."

"Yes, but there's a common multiple. They are all desperately anxious to graduate with honours. You do not seem very anxious."

"Is that a recommendation?"

"Normally it wouldn't be; but you didn't look an idle person. I felt that you had other interests. I wondered what they were. What are you studying?"

Aziz told him; for a minute or two they exchanged notes on the professors who took his classes; then the talk became personal. Very soon Fadhil edged the conversation so that it was Aziz himself who brought up the question of music.

"I have some new records in my flat," said Fadhil. "I wonder if you'd like to come back and hear them?"

Fadhil had a small two-room apartment near the University. It was in a recently built house. It was on the fourth floor. It was barely furnished, with a settee and two armchairs, but the shelves were filled with books, and though the floor was covered with cheap threadbare matting, a good carpet was hung over the settee. The room was heated by an open charcoal brazier. It was chilly. "We'd better keep our coats on," Fadhil said. On the table there was a high pile of records.

"I wonder if you've heard this. I got it at Christmas. When I was in Cairo." He had brought back six new records. He played them over. There was an entranced expression upon Aziz's face.

"If only I could get records like that," he said.

"You can, if I can."

"I never go to Cairo."

"I do. I can get them for you."

"I couldn't afford them. It is a question of currency. My parents can't send money out of Turkey. They don't even pay my expenses with my aunt. My aunt has no money except what my uncle gives her. I'm dependent on him. He only gives me a bare minimum."

"Then why not earn some money?"

"How could I?"

"There are ways; there are always ways; most of us have sidelines that are more profitable than our apparent jobs. Do you think I could afford trips to Cairo, a record player like this and all those records on my salary at the A.U.B.? Of course I couldn't. My sideline is an import-export agency, mainly with Turkey. It is very possible that you could help me there. I'll think it out. There may be ways in which we could serve each other's purposes. I don't like to think of you being deprived of music. I'll see what I can do."

Reid read the report in Farrar's office.

"So you see," said Farrar, "what did I tell you?"

Three days later Fadhil produced his offer.

"As I told you," he said to Aziz, "I'm carrying on trade with Turkey. It's legitimate business; you needn't worry about that. But there is a good deal of information that I need about conditions in Turkey that I find it hard to get. Censorship is strict, security regulations are strict. Turkey does not want the whole world to know the secrets of its economy. Germany is doing a considerable trade with Turkey. I am in competition with the Germans. I need to know what goods are being imported from Germany and at what price. I also want to know what Turkey is selling to Germany. I'm wondering if you couldn't help me with just that information?"

"How would I set about it?"

"Have you any friend in a government department, in the Board of Trade say, who would have access to that kind of information?"

Aziz thought. He had very few friends of his own age, and friends of his own age would not have been of much help in a position like this; they would not occupy posts of sufficient prominence. But through a music club he had met a number of older men, some of whom were employed in government service. One of these was in the Istanbul branch of the Ministry of Commerce.

"In a junior position, though," he explained to Fadhil.

"That wouldn't matter. It is the most elementary information that we require. We are not asking him to divulge state secrets. It is simply routine information, only it is difficult for me to get it. A newspaper man could find out easily. Do you know any journalists?"

"I'm afraid I don't."

"In that case we had better make use of your friend in the Ministry of Commerce. He should be able to help us. But there is one complication. We have the problem of the censor. It would not do to have you making such enquiries in a letter that might be opened by the censor. We want to avoid that kind of complication. It will save a great deal of trouble if the messages are sent up in secret ink."

Fadhil explained how this could be done. Letters were written with a pen that looked like a safety match. The head of the match was covered with a chemical substance. A pen of this kind could be carried in the slot inside a soft collar which normally held a bone stiffener. The acid that developed this writing could be poured inside a bottle of after-shave lotion.

"A friend of mine," said Fadhil, "is shortly going up to Istanbul. He will carry the materials; and he will give them to your friend and explain to him how to use them. Your friend will then write to thank you for the presents you have sent him. That is your signal to open operations, and you can begin writing letters that contain questions written in secret ink which your friend will answer. The correspondence can then proceed smoothly. Is that perfectly clear?"

A perplexed look crossed Aziz's face. "You are sure that this isn't a black market deal?"

"It isn't a deal at all, as yet. It's certainly not black market."

"Then why should there be the need for this deception?"

"Because it's wartime. If it weren't wartime, you'd be able to move your money where you chose. It's your own money, isn't it? It's not the government's. They make these restrictions in wartime to protect the many; but those restrictions press upon the individual. The individual has to protect himself. You want those records, don't you? There is no reason why you shouldn't have them. This is the easiest way to get them."

There was a silence.

"Could this possibly get my friend into trouble?" Aziz asked.

"How could it? The secret ink matches and the secret acid will not be detected at the frontier. How could they be? Nor will your correspondence be detected, provided the letters are such as two friends could be expected to exchange."

"Isn't that against the law?"

Fadhil shrugged. "In wartime everything is against the law. A number of stodgy people get themselves good jobs drawing up these regulations: sensible men elude them. Do you think that I, a professor at a University, would lend myself to something that was underhand, that I would imperil the safety and future of a student? I see your point, of course, I see your point and I respect it. If you don't want to help me in this way I shall understand, perfectly; but I do believe that we could help each other. Think it over. Let me know in two days' time."

Farrar chuckled when the report of this meeting reached him. "We've got him. I bet you a hundred to one we've got him. You look distressed, Professor. Yes, I understand, this fellow appeals to you, as one of your own students did. You've been a guest at his aunt's house. The obligations that a guest incurs, I know, I know. But this is wartime."

"And who is this reputed friend of Fadhil's who is acting as a go-between?"

"One of the Pullman porters on the Taurus. We call him Chessman. Most of them are working for one side or another; some of them are working for both; but we trust Chessman."

"What happens to the package when it gets to Istanbul?"

"That's up to our boys in Istanbul. Our job's done when we hand over the package to the Pullman porter. They'll tell us how the case proceeds."

Half a week later Abdul Hamid reported that Aziz had accepted Fadhil's proposition. He had resisted a little longer on the grounds that his friend would be reluctant to send the information in such a subterranean manner. "He will be suspicious. He will not like using this secret ink."

Fadhil swept away his objections. "My friend is very persuasive. Let us leave it to him. In the meantime you must write a letter to your friend, explaining that this friend of yours is shortly visiting Istanbul, asking him to give him any assistance that he may require; a straight-forward letter that will not disturb the censor. This kind of thing—"

The letter that Fadhil dictated was intercepted by the censor, photographed, sent on its way and entered in the Aziz file.

The letter ran:

"Dear Ahmed, I am working very hard and the date of my examination is very close. I have so much to say that I have very little to say; nothing that can be said in a few words. But I have found a way of giving you my news. A friend of mine is shortly visiting Istanbul. His name is Ismail Hilli. He has few friends in Turkey and he would be very grateful for any help that you can give him. He is in the export-import business. He has my complete confidence. Your affectionate friend, Aziz."

Another document had preceded it in the file. Fadhil had said to Aziz, "That is fine; now we are started. In a few weeks we shall be embarked on a correspondence which will prove useful to all of us. I want to prove to you that I can be trusted. Take any two records out of this pile. You can then make a list of the records that you most want. When I go to Cairo I will get them for you. There's one extra point, however. I'll need a receipt for the records that I give you, for income tax purposes. I can then explain to the inspector that you do secretarial work for me. It is more satisfactory if the receipt is made out in money. We avoid complications that way."

The document that was entered in the file read:

"Received from Fadhil, 20 Syrian pounds in return for services in connection with trade with Turkey."

It was dated and it was signed "Aziz."

6

THE LETTER ANNOUNCING this operation was opened in the Instanbul office of the I.S.L.O. by an English girl in her early twenties called Eve Parish. She was the youngest daughter of a minor Treasury official. She was small, trim figured, with pale cheeks, brown hair, and hazel-coloured eyes. She was short-sighted and wore large horn-rimmed spectacles. She was not a girl whom men stared at in the streets, but at cocktail parties one man at least would ask to be introduced to her. She had been in Instanbul for a year and was the liaison link between her branch and the British Embassy. She recognized at once that this operation which appeared to have been undertaken very light-heartedly in Beirut had a number of Turkish complications which the Lebanon and Cairo offices had not foreseen. She opened a main file for the operation; she already had files open for the Amin Maruns; and for Fadhil. She cross-checked the references to the main file, then took the collection to her office chief.

Her chief was a man of forty, tall, thin. with receding brown hair that had grown grey beside the ears. He had a long thin nose and a tight mouth; he had an air of distinction, but he suggested bloodlessness. His hands were long, with thin pointed fingers and carefully tended nails. It might be assumed that he was proud of his hands since he displayed them prominently. He did not exactly fidget, but he was invariably playing with some object on his desk, a pen or a paperweight. This playing did not fuss his interlocutors; on the contrary, it put them at their ease. It had a mesmeric property.

He had had no military training. He was a Wykehamist, a scholar of New College, Seconded from the Treasury to the Ministry of Economic Warfare, in which capacity he had been posted to Istanbul. He spoke in a slow precise well-modulated voice. He was neither liked nor disliked. It was recognized that he was extremely competent. He was appreciative of work well done. He might have been expected to be sarcastic but he never was. Eve would have felt more at her ease addressing him as "Sir", but he insisted on being called by his Christian name, Francis, his full name being Francis Mariott Sedgwick. He was not the head of the section, the head was in Ankara, but he was the most important member of it. In the last Honours List he had received a C.B.E. He was married, and on his desk was a framed photograph of a formidably handsome young woman wearing the feathers of a Court presentation. Eve could not imagine such a formal couple indulging in connubial practices, but the marriage had produced two sons.

Outside his door he had a light that flashed red when he was busy, green when he was free. The light was green. Eve handed him the files. "These are marked urgent," she said, "I think they are important." He nodded. "Good." He looked at his in-tray, and at the engagement calendar on his desk. "I have not much on this morning. Come back in half an hour." He pressed the red light button as she left the room.

On her return he pointed to a chair. "Take the weight off your feet," he said.

He never liked to have anybody standing beside his desk. That was one of the things she liked about him. "Well, what do you make of this?" he asked. And that was another of the things she liked about him. He gave his subordinates a feeling of responsibility. They were not cyphers. She had expected to be asked that question, and she had her answer ready. "Won't the Turks be annoyed if they find that we, on our own, are making use of one of their employees?"

"Precisely: they would not like it at all. Any more than we would like it if Turkish Intelligence were to seduce one of our people in Baghdad. It is most important that we should stay on good terms with the Turks. Aunt Mildred is a valued friend. They should have realised that in Beirut. Have you any suggestions?"

"Only to refuse; to say that the operation is too dangerous."

He shook his head. "This plan has Cairo's backing. We have to take their orders. We want to keep on good terms with Beirut. Farrar's a clever fellow. The controller thinks a lot of him; besides, there are possibilities in this. We may be able to use this young Turk ourselves. The story's only starting. No, we must retain Aziz without involving the Turkish civil servant. What's his name? Ahmed Bahjat. He must never know anything about it. I haven't worked out the details yet. But my general idea is this: to keep these secret inks here, and send round a message to Ahmed, saying that Aziz's friend has arrived and has brought a present. One of our boys will take round that present. Ahmed will thank him for it. That will be the signal for Aziz to send him letters. We shall know from Beirut what the questions are. Ahmed will get these letters, but he won't know there's any message there in secret ink; he will regard it as a piece of routine correspondence. Fadhil will see to it however that it is a letter that requires an answer. That answer will be intercepted by the Lebanese censor, and one of Farrar's boys will write in secret ink the answers to the questions that Aziz sent up. Aziz will develop the letter and hand over the information to Fadhil. In return he will receive a supply of records. Everyone will be happy. Do you see any objections to it?"

She thought. There was only one objection to it that she could see and that was so obvious that it must have occurred to Francis. "When Aziz comes back to Turkey, and meets Ahmed, he'll learn that Ahmed knows nothing of this deal in secret messages."

"I've thought of that. We shall have to be on our guard. We'll have to intercept Aziz and tell him what has happened. By that time he should be in our power. We can't tell yet how this case will develop. It might be something big. We are not in any hurry."

"Are you going to explain all this to Beirut?"

"Not for the moment. We'll wait till we've delivered a present to Ahmed and he has sent off his thank-you letter to Aziz. When is Chessman due here next?"

"On Monday."

"Good. When he comes we can decide what to do. I shouldn't be surprised if Master Aziz did not provide us with some lively entertainment."

On Monday Chessman arrived with the secret ink matches and the bottle of acid for developing the secret messages. On the train, in his brown uniform, his braid, his gilt and his peaked cap, he was an impressive personality. But off parade, in a drab suit, with a soiled shirt and a frayed tie, he looked a depressed number of the white collar class. He was middle-aged, with a scraggy moustache. He was the kind of man whom you would never notice in a crowd; which was precisely the effect he endeavoured to produce in public. At home he wore a brocaded smoking jacket, a tarboosh, and gilded slippers, as he puffed ruminatively at a large water pipe, in the intervals of sipping at a sweet, very strong coffee.

On his arrival at the I.S.L.O. building he was shown at once into Eve's office. He placed the packet on the table. "You know about this?" he asked.

She nodded. "Is there anything more you need?" he asked.

"No, that is all and as always we are very grateful."

"In Beirut, they suggested that there might be a special errand in connection with this errand."

"We have made different arrangements here."

"Very good." He stood up, hesitated.

She said, "I will give you a receipt for Suki."

Suki was the secretary adjutant of the department. Eve scribbled on a sheet of paper, "Chessman's mission completed," and initialled it. She handed it to Chessman with a smile. In return for that chit, Chessman would receive a sum of money, then Suki would burn the chit. Eve presumed that some tally was kept of these transactions. The office was allowed so much a year out of secret funds, and Whitehall presumed that it was spend advantageously; but if for security reasons, every chit had to be destroyed the moment the purchase had been made, what was there to prevent Suki from entering in her ledger a larger sum than she had actually paid to Chessman, and herself pocketing the difference, since the entries in the ledger were in code and the ledgers were destroyed each month, only the total being carried forward? Eve wondered, then she smiled, picturing Suki, a prim, angular spinster, who had worked in Turkey before the war on behalf of the R.S.P.C.A. Who could imagine her embezzling public funds, even for the benefit of homeless cats?

Eve walked down the corridor, carrying the package. The light over Sedgwick's door was green. It always astonished her that it should be so often green. Did he take work home at night? He was nearly always accessible. He greeted her with a smile.

"Well?"

"Chessman's package."

"Good. It may come in handy one day. Sit down, please. Now what do you think I've been thinking about all this—" He paused. He looked at her with a teasing smile.

"How can I tell what you've been thinking?"

"Indeed, how can you? I've a brand new idea. I have acquired a very pleasant toilet set—Yardley's Lavender—exactly the article to appeal to a young Turk. We'll send this round by hand to Master Ahmed, explaining that his friend's friend had to cut his visit short. He'll be delighted with the gift and is sure to thank Aziz for it. And shall I tell you by whom we'll send it round? By you. It is so unexpected and so unusual that the authorities will assume that there is nothing fishy about your visit. Do you remember Poe's story, 'The Purloined Letter'? A room was shortly to be ransacked by the police, so the owner put the letter that they were looking for in a torn and dirty envelope and stuck it in a pipe rack. So here's the package, off you go. You'll have no difficulty with your passport in getting into the Ministry of Commerce. On the way back you might look in at the Embassy and collect any mail there may be for us. You don't mind running errands, do you?"

"I enjoy a change of atmosphere."

"I thought you would; and it's really much more secure to have correspondence carried by you. A dispatch rider on a motor bicycle is always likely to be poleaxed by a German."

It was a chill bleak day, but the grey drab city was never without its charm for her. She loved its precipitous cobbled streets, its huddled houses with their narrow balconies, its sudden vistaed glimpses of the Bosphorous; the sense of its many fortunes. Whenever possible, she went on foot about her errands.

As Sedgwick had predicted, she experienced no difficulty in getting into the Ministry of Commerce. She filled in two forms and was then conducted by a uniformed attendant into a long bare room, in which a number of youngish men were seated at high desks, writing.

"Which is Ahmed Bahjat?" she asked the guide.

He pointed to a small, youthful man with a puckish look. He did not seem as surprised as she had expected him to be at her arrival. "Do you speak English?" she enquired.

"Of course."

She explained her purpose. "I come from the friend of Aziz, Ismail Hilli, who was going to have brought you messages from Aziz. Unfortunately he could not stay in Istanbul as long as he had hoped. But he wanted you to know that Aziz is happy and in good health. Aziz has also sent you a present. He thinks that you will like it. It is something that you would not be able to get easily in Istanbul. Ismail Hilli was most anxious that you should send Aziz a note to tell him that you had received his present, but he did not want you to mention in your letter what the present was. He got it, you see, through a friend from the officers' shop in Beirut. Civilians are not supposed to be able to make purchases in the officers' shop. If the Lebanese censor were to read the letter it might get Aziz's friend into trouble. So will you be careful to say no more than present?"

"I will be very careful to say no more than present." He spoke with a correct accent. This, she supposed, was one of the results of the Attaturk régime. Thirty years ago a young civil servant would not have spoken English.

Ahmed showed no curiosity as to how the package had been delivered to her. Francis had been right. If you were brazen enough suspicion was not roused. And, after all, was there anything so very remarkable in an English girl employed in a government organization delivering by hand a package acquired across a frontier in a British shop to a member of a neutral and friendly power? Ahmed had not even asked her name.

The British Embassy was five minutes away. The Ambassador had transferred the chancery to Ankara, but a section of his staff still functioned in what was now officially the consulate general. Eve always enjoyed her visits to the ample dignified building with its yellow ochre entrance and its V.R. above the gateway, with its spacious garden, its high ceilings, its marble staircase, its glassed-in courtyard. It had a perdurable quality. She always made her visits last as long as possible.

As she was walking down the corridor, her errand finished, a voice called after her. "Hullo there, Eve; I heard you were in the building. I thought you were on your way to me. It looks as though you weren't."

It was a light-toned, half mocking voice. Its possessor was a tall slim young man, wearing a well-worn but well-cut dark blue pin-stripe suit and an old Etonian tie. His name was Martin Ransom; he was a career diplomat and a second secretary at the Embassy. He looked down with a friendly smile. "Turkey suits you. You look prettier every time I see you."

"Perhaps that's because you don't see very many other European women."

"That may be so, and do you know what is the most maddening thing about it all? Nine times out of ten when I do see an attractive woman she's an Austrian, a German, or an Italian, which means that I mayn't speak to her. Every new country that joins the Axis cuts down my acquaintance automatically."

"The war won't last forever."

"That's what I tell myself. But in the meantime it's highly inconvenient. Why do we meet so seldom?"

"We move in different worlds."

"That's my complaint. Why do we? It must be at least a month since we've met."

"It's two weeks."

"It seems a month. It's too long, anyhow. Let's dine tonight."

"I'm sorry, no, I can't."

"Why not?"

"Because. . . ." She hesitated. She had not an excuse ready. She could not say "another party". He would ask what party, and there wasn't one. In a small world like theirs everyone knew what everyone was doing.

"You are not doing anything, now are you?" he insisted.

"Well, no."

"But you'd planned a quiet evening for yourself. You were going to wash stockings, answer letters, cut out a pattern, iron a dress and be asleep by ten. Can't you do all that as easily tomorrow?"

There was in his voice a note of mocking tenderness. He likes me, she thought, he really wants me to go out with him. I do attract him. And, after all, why shouldn't I? I can cut out that pattern another day. It isn't as though I go out so often. This isn't London. And it was a relief to find an attractive man who was neither married nor a pansy. It was only that. . . . It was only what? That she didn't like to be asked out on the spur of the moment? Ten minutes ago she was the last person on his mind. If he wanted to see her why couldn't he call her up, ask her to fix a night, as other men did? But then he wasn't like other men in that way. He planned ahead, his pocket diary was necessarily black with entries, yet he always had spare time. He had his answer ready. "Three quarters of my social life is concerned with duty. The quarter that is free I keep unmortgaged." And that was logical.

"No," he was saying, "there's no good reason why you shouldn't dine with me. I'll call for you at eight o'clock."

There was a sudden masterfulness in his voice that contrasted with its casual elegance and which she rather liked. He was a man all right.

Eve shared a flat with an English girl Kitty Lang who worked for the British Council. Kitty was twenty-two years old. She was large and plump and bouncy. She had auburn hair and was always laughing, at nothing in particular, out of sheer exuberance. Every-one liked her, she liked everyone. "I'm having the time of my life," she always said.

The British Council had been showing a film of historic beauty spots that afternoon and Kitty did not return to the flat till Eve had finished changing. She raised her eyebrows at the sight of Eve's grey green marocain. She knew her friend's wardrobe well. This was for special dates. "For whom this glory?" she enquired.

"Martin Ransom."

"Then I'd say not wasted. He'll appreciate it. I'll envy you as I sit here with my knitting."

"I wish I could envy myself."

"Why can't you? He's fun. He'll do you well."

"I know; but it always ends in the same argument."

"Why not let him win the argument for once?"

"Oh, you know me."

"If I were in your shoes there wouldn't be much argument." Kitty made no bones about her conduct. "The war came at just the right time for me," she would say. "I'm going to settle down one day; be a fine wife and mother; the crown, the altar, and the hearth. But I mean to have a good time first. And that might not have been too easy for me in peacetime. One gets talked about. One disqualifies oneself for what one really wants. One has to be discreet. Nobody cares a damn what you do in wartime. When it's all over you can wipe the slate clean and start afresh. Besides, in wartime, no one looks ahead. You're here today and gone tomorrow." There was a quizzical but at the same time affectionate expression on her face.

"Do you know how I feel towards you sometimes? Maternal. Isn't that odd for me? Ah, the bell: your beau. Good hunting."

Martin had changed and shaved. He exuded an atmosphere of lavender water and clean linen; and he had exchanged his pin-stripe suit for grey flannel trousers and a cashmere sports coat, he was no longer wearing an Old Etonian tie. He had shed his uniform, in fact.

"You look so elegant, and I so casual. But I spend so much time on parade. It's a relief to me to be myself."

But was this really himself, she asked herself? Wasn't the real self the pin-stripe suit and the black tie with the thin blue stripe, the young man of good family, with a career, who at the right time would marry the girl who would be appropriate to that family and that career? And why in heaven's name should he be any different? He was not trying to fool anyone. Take me on my terms, or do without me. Well, and why shouldn't he say that? All the same, it was pleasant to see him in that soft warm coat that one would like to snuggle up against and that foreign jig-jag tie, the kind of tie of which a woman would think, "Dare I buy him that?" I'll buy him a tie like that next Christmas, she decided.

"I thought we'd dine at Abdullah's," he was saying.

Abdullah's was the smartest winter restaurant in Istanbul. It was quiet, and good, and exceedingly expensive, there was no music and no dancing. It was patronised by rich Turkish merchants and members of the diplomatic corps with substantial private incomes. Germans went there, but very few Italians.

"Let's do ourselves well. Let's do ourselves very well," he said, "and instead of cocktails let's start off with a half bottle of Turkish white wine. It isn't bad and I like its name: 'Aphrodite'."

†

"I've a feeling," he was saying two hours later, "that the waiters are getting restive." He scrutinised the bill that lay beside him. "It's supposed to be bad manners to think about money when you're with a woman," he had said to her. "Waiters bank on that.

117

They slip in little extras." And indeed every three or four times he found something wrong. This was one of them. He beckoned the waiter over.

"My guest had only one glass of brandy."

"I apologise, Mr. Ransom."

"That's quite all right."

He never got cross on such occasions. He was too delighted at having his point proved. Yes, he had everything worked out, she thought. She was impressed, yet at the same time nettled, by his assurance. It contained a challenge.

"Well, are we on our way?" he said.

As they sauntered down the crowded street he slid his hand under her arm, pressing it against his side. "I always have a good time with you," he said. He lowered his voice half-a-tone, as he always did when he had something personal to say. It was one of his greatest attractions for her.

His car was a two-seater, low and red. She settled herself luxuriantly into the bucket seat. It would be very pleasant to go for a long drive into the country in this smooth, swift car. It was something they had not done. They had first met in November. Perhaps in June. . . . But would he be still dating her in June?

His flat was a little way out and to the north; but he turned his car to the right not to the left. So that's that, she thought. She had started the evening resolved not to go back to his flat. She did not want a repetition of that last time. But she had expected to be asked. She was piqued that she had not been asked; and a little saddened, too. Had he given her up as a bad job? Was tonight's dinner the start of the slow tapering off? By the time June came, there might not be a question of picnics in the country.

He did not talk; she was grateful to him for that. She did not want to make casual conversation. But when he drew up outside her flat he did not jump out to open the door. He leant forward across the wheel, both elbows on it, his hands falling loose on the far side. He turned his head towards her.

"There are times in life when one feels one's living in a vacuum," he said. "An old self's dead, a new self hasn't come to life, or rather hasn't started to emerge. One has to wait until it does; then you can find out what that new self is, what that new self wants; but till it does you can't get on with that new life." He paused. He was speaking very slowly and his voice had again dropped half a tone. "I was in that position myself two years ago. It's a curious time; you feel that nothing really matters; there are so many months to be lived through: that and no more than that. I'm wondering whether that isn't the position that you're in now."

She turned to look at him. His expression in the half-light was fond, was almost brotherly. What can he know about me, she thought; but even as she thought it, she recognised that it was a silly thing to think. Of course, he'd have made enquiries about her. He was that kind of man. He didn't take things on chance. He'd want to know what he was taking on. And she supposed that more people than she guessed, knew about Raymond.

"It's a curious time," he was continuing, "but it can be quite amusing in its special way. There's an interval to be filled in; there's no reason why one shouldn't decorate that interval." He paused again. "If I'm right in what I guess, I could help you to decorate yours, quite amusingly."

There was a twinkle in his eye. The brotherly look had gone, but the fondness stayed.

He looked at her steadily for a moment, then turned away; opened the door, swung his legs into the roadway, handed her out on to the pavement. He walked beside her to the entrance of her block.

"You're very sweet, and very dear," he said.

Kitty was still up when Eve returned. She raised her eyebrows. "So I gather he lost the argument?"

"There wasn't an argument."

"That's dangerous; you must be on your guard."

"I know, I know."

She slumped back in an armchair, letting her arms fall limply over the sides. "I sometimes wish I weren't myself," she said.

"Don't all of us?"

"I doubt if you do."

"Perhaps not too often."

"When did you start this game?"

"Eighteen."

"Was it with somebody important?"

"Not particularly."

"Not a *grande passion*?"

"Heavens, no. A kind of date."

"You weren't in love with him?"

"I liked him well enough. It was a hurdle I had to carry. It seemed as good a time as any."

"How long did it last?"

"How long did what last?"

"The affair."

"It wasn't an affair. I saw him once or twice, but it was rather awkward. He lived a long way out, and with his parents. It became more trouble than it was worth. Besides, there was someone else."

"How soon was it before you really fell in love?"

"I never have."

"Oh, come now, surely—"

"No, honest, no. It's been exciting, romantic, sometimes there's been a risk. But that feeling you read about in books—that I haven't known."

Eve sighed. "If I could have started off your way I'd find life a great deal easier than I do right now."

Kitty laughed. "There have to be some recompenses for my kind of life."

"I wish there were more for mine."

"There are times when I envy you."

"I doubt if I do myself . . . but, all the same, since that's the way it is. . . ."

Since that was the way it was, she had to make the best of it. There hadn't been for her, as there had been for Kitty, a first and easy hurdle.

Across two winters she recalled another February evening, a night of fog in London during the phoney war. They had dined, she and Raymond, at the Café Royal, in the Grill Room, with its panelled mirrors that had reflected Wilde and Whistler. It was a Saturday. The room had been half full. They had lingered over their coffee. They had planned to go to a French film at the Curzon, but when they came out into the street they found that the fog had thickened. The chances of getting a cab were slight. "Let's go back and play records," he suggested.

He had chambers in Albany. He had a key to the door on Vigo Street. He lived on the second floor. His rooms were warm. There was no central heating but he had left on the electric heaters. She appreciated his extravagance. She liked him for having thought: "We might come back; I couldn't bring her into a cold room."

The fireplace was high piled with logs and coal. He lit the papers under it and the flames leapt high. He turned down the high centre light and switched on two small lamps. Their soft light mingling with the firelight, glowed in the glass of a tall Queen Anne bookcase and glinted on the silver thread of the blue damask curtains that screened the high broad window. He put on a stack of records; he turned the volume down. She made a pile of cushions on the floor, and leant her head against the sofa. He poured her a liqueur and sat behind her, his hand on her shoulder, stroking sometimes her arm, sometimes her cheek, sometimes her hair. It was a peace, a happiness deeper and wider than anything that she had known: outside, the fog, the blackout, the chill, the slimy pavements, the shouts of "Taxi", the ill-tempered, ill-mannered homegoers stumbling against each other; and here this calm, this beauty, this soothing of every nerve.

"Darling," she said, "when we are married it'll be in London, won't it?"

"I suppose so, yes."

"Then let's come back here afterwards. Let's honeymoon here."

"Why not?" She sighed. May. What a long time to wait, until his divorce came through. If only this were May, with this their wedding night. Could they ever be closer than they were this minute, until they were really one. His fingers were stroking her cheek, gently, tenderly, but with a vibrant pressure; the music ebbed and swelled, plangent, evocative through the warm firelit dusk. Why wait?

"Darling. Do you know what I wish?" she said. "That this were the start of our honeymoon, that we'd been married this morning in that grim little unromantic room. Darling, do you know what I'd like?"

She paused. The suggestion would have to come from her; his sense of chivalry, based on his greater age, would hold him back.

"I'd like us to pretend we had," she said. "I'd like us to start our marriage now."

His fingers on her cheek deepened their pressures. He drew a long, slow breath, and then stood up.

"I want to read you a poem," he said, "by a Victorian, who wrote one good poem and nothing else."

He crossed to the high bookcase and took out the Oxford Book of Victorian Verse.

> "Come, let us make love deathless, thou and I,
>   Seeing that our footing on the earth is brief,"

he read in a full cadenced voice. He had not turned down the phonograph. Its rich tones were a harmonious background to the poetry.

> "Seeing that her multitudes sweep out to die
>   Mocking at all that passes their belief.
> For standard of our love not theirs we take.
>   If we go hence today
> Fill the high rich cup that is so soon to break
>   With richer wine than they!"

He finished the poem and then came back to her. Once again his arm was about her shoulder.

"If this was seventy years ago," he said, "when that poem was written, when England was starchy, stuffy, stodgy, I'd be the first to throw my challenge to decorum, to say, 'We're different. We make our own rules; we live our own lives, in our way.' But the world is a different place today. Everyone is so casual; they say those things don't matter; but they do. I don't want us to be like everybody else: I want us to make our gesture; to prove that we are different; to wait till we can say to the world: 'In the eyes of the world, we belong to one another.' That's what one has to mean today by 'richer wine'."

She had felt so proud, so confident. She and he were different; they were proving it; and then only ten days later, he had slipped on a curbstone in the blackout.

"With richer wine" . . . "to decorate an interval". She contrasted the alternatives. Raymond had set the highest store by the very thing that Martin was disparaging, but only because he set high store by her; he would have been no doubt ready enough to decorate an interval with others by whom he had set as little store as Martin did by her. Yet what Martin was offering would constitute a certain happiness, a certain kind of happiness. It was something that sooner or later she would have to come to; a virgin at twenty-three. She knew all the arguments against her status. And yet, and yet . . . Raymond had put her on a pedestal. She did not want to come down from it too casually.

7

A WEEK LATER the censorship in Beirut intercepted a letter from Ahmed Bahjat to Aziz.

"Dear Friend, I thank you for your kind present which I appreciate greatly. I await eagerly the day when once again we can listen to Bach and Beethoven."

The letter was photographed and filed. Three days later, the reply to Ahmed was intercepted.

"Dear Friend," "The day of my examination approaches. I await it anxiously. I greatly fear that I shall not pass. This is my last chance. I do not know what will happen to me if I fail. Some English friends have suggested that I should go to the University in Alexandria. They assure me that the English professors there are excellent. But I feel that I had better return home. The difficulty is that I have no ambition. I cannot persuade myself that a University degree is all important. I do not want to be a bureaucrat."

The letter was put under a V. I. lamp and revealed the following sentence:

"State chief exports Germany to Turkey Quantity and price."

Farrar rubbed his hands.

"And that," he said, "ties our little deal up very prettily. We have now the proved admission that Aziz, a Turkish citizen, has been handing over to a belligerent, information that in the event of war might prove useful to the enemy."

"And what use are you going to make of this admission?"

"I don't know yet. It depends a little on Aunt Mildred. While Aziz is here he is not of very much value to us. He can't tell us anything we need to know, and he can't spread false information to the Germans."

"Do you still want him to go to Alexandria?"

"Not now that we've got him in our power; the sooner he goes back to Turkey the better. Once he's there we can decide what to do with him."

"What are the possibilities?"

"Your guess is as good as mine. I'd like to make a double agent of him.

"When he crosses the frontier we could have one of our agents pick him up, tell him he's on the carpet, that he, a Turk, has been selling information to the Lebanese. If the Turks find out, it'll be a long prison sentence, if not death. He'll have to play our game. We've got photostats of his letters and we've got his receipts. The great thing is to get him across the frontier. Next time you are with Madame Amin find out what chance there is of his going up to Istanbul for a holiday. It wouldn't be a bad idea for you to give her the idea: put it into her head. It's curious how often people have to have ideas given them; something in the sub-conscious needs bringing to the surface."

"Galsworthy had never thought of being a writer, so he said, until a woman suggested it. 'Why don't you write?' she said. 'You're just the person.' You'd have thought a born storyteller like Galsworthy would have known it from the start."

"Exactly. And it may very likely not have occurred to Madame Amin that it might do Aziz a lot of good to see his parents."

"What do you propose to do about his friend, Ahmed?"

"Keep an eye on him. He might be of some use to Aunt Mildred. He's in Turkey and we can put the pressure on him. But that might be risky at the moment. We don't want to start too many hares. Keep him on ice a little. And one thing, Aziz must never suspect that we know anything about this business. He can still go on sending routine information to Ahmed. When Aziz returns he'll be contacted by quite a different person, someone whom you and I don't know. There's going to be a whole lot of amusement out of this operation. Believe you me."

That afternoon there was a letter from Rachel:

"Last week," (she wrote) "I went up to London, for the first time this year. There isn't much reason now that you aren't there. How gay those Fridays were; and London itself was more gay then. There was a feeling of challenge in the air. We were in the front line ourselves; the bombing gave an edge to everything. But now the war has gone in other directions and we're left high and dry; there's a certain listlessness about it and now that the bombing is over people are coming back to their London flats and houses. That means that everything is crowded. There are all these foreigners here, too; you see far more foreign than British uniforms in the streets. It is hard to get a table in a restaurant and when you do, you get dreary food and very little of it. Taxis are scarce; it isn't really much fun going out.

On Saturday, I am going down to see the boys. They seem to happy enough and doing well, but it is not easy to tell from their letters. They simply say, 'Thank you for your letter. I had a letter from Daddy. He says he likes Middle East. It has rained a lot. The ground is too wet for football so we go for runs. I do not like runs. Gainsford's father has given him a new model aeroplane. No more news. Love.'

But it isn't as satisfactory going down to see them by myself. I'm with both of them all the time and if one of them has something special to say to me he's afraid of saying it before the other. When you are with me, each gets a chance of being alone with each of us. This is one of the many little ways in which I'm missing you. And it's so hard to foresee any ending to it at all. Unless it's we and not Hitler who have the secret weapon.

One result of that trip to London by the way is that your father suggested I should take on a job in the Ministry of Information. I believe he's right. Then I could let the farm. What do you feel? I believe the boys would get more out of their holidays in London; and there's no danger of bombing any longer, and I hate doing nothing for the war."

That evening he went to the Amin Maruns in the early evening; one of the pleasantest features of his work with Intelligence was that he did not have to keep office hours. His duty allowed him visits to prospective clients.

Aziz was in a surly mood. One of the spots on his chin was bleeding and he kept dabbing it with his handkerchief. Reid asked when his exams began.

"On Monday week."

"They last about a week, I suppose."

"Yes."

"And how long will it be before you hear the result?"

"Three weeks."

"You'll take a holiday, I suppose? Will you go back to Turkey and see your family?"

"I hadn't thought of it."

His aunt looked up quickly at the suggestion. "It might be a good idea, you know." She turned towards her husband. "What do you think?"

"An excellent idea." He said it forcefully. He appeared to welcome the idea. Perhaps he would be glad to have his own house to himself again.

Reid turned to Aziz. "Are you going to the concert at the A.U.B. tomorrow?"

Aziz shrugged. "They aren't playing anything that I care to hear." He had retreated behind his habitual indifference. It was hard to believe that he had been so outspoken on the evening when they had talked of music. But then he had been alone. Reid remembered Rachel's complaint that the two boys could not talk when they were together; the one inhibited the other. Aziz would not talk in the presence of his aunt and uncle.

†

A copy of Aziz's letter to his friend reached the Istanbul office three days later; three days before it could be expected to reach Ahmed since it would be delayed inevitably by the Turkish censors. Eve entered it in the file and took it down the passage. Sedgwick read it thoughtfully. "We've got to take Beirut into our confidence," he said.

Eve nodded.

"Is there anything that strikes you immediately about this?" he asked.

"That Ahmed may not answer it?"

"Precisely. Would you yourself if you got a letter like this from a casual friend?"

"It does not call for an immediate answer."

"Precisely. You would put it away for a week, two weeks, till you had some news to send. You might even not answer at all."

"That's so."

"Aziz can't expect an answer for a few days; Ahmed has to find the answers to these questions. We have two weeks before we need start worrying; then he'll probably write again. But we must let Beirut know. And there's another point: Aziz may come up here. If he does, we must ensure that he doesn't go to Ahmed until we have warned him. We've got to find the best way of warning him, and what do you think is, in my opinion, the best way of warning him."

He paused. She was sufficiently familiar with his methods to recognise this question as rhetorical. He did not expect an answer

to it. "We'll continue," he said, "with our technique of the purloined letter. You are the one to warn him."

She opened her eyes wide. "Surely that's risky?"

He shook his head. "It's far too obvious to be risky; and it has
this advantage: if Aziz ever does compare notes with Ahmed he'll
find that there has been the same intermediary each time. I don't
suppose that he will compare notes, but if he does this will give
him confidence. You have to remember that he had no idea who
brought up that present. He was simply told that it was a friend
travelling by the Taurus. You will give him a changed version of
that story. You will say that this man Ismail Hilli changed his
mind at the last moment. He had a qualm of conscience, and of
fear; it wasn't fair to Ahmed. It might get him into trouble with
the Turks so he substituted a genuine present for those secret inks,
and flung the original package through the window. He did not
want to be connected with the transaction so he asked you to
deliver it. Now I know all this sounds highly involved, and if you
had a skilful barrister putting you under cross-examination the
whole transaction would be torn to shreds in a few minutes. But
this young man isn't a skilful barrister. He is by all accounts more
than a little dumb. He'll believe what you tell him. He has no
training in counter-espionage. He'll swallow it."

"And how am I to meet him?"

"Beirut through Fadhil, must explain that there has been a
muddle and that before he sees Ahmed he must contact you."

"But where does he contact me?"

"The obvious place: your flat."

"But, surely. . . ."

He interrupted her. "There couldn't be a safer place. I had the
possibility of this in mind when I suggested that you should share
a flat with that girl from the British Council. A number of Turks
visit that flat, presumably."

"They certainly do."

"It is reputed that she is a free-hearted young person with a
number of beaux. One more or less would not excite curiosity.
We will give him the telephone number of the Perapalas Otel.
He will let you know when he arrives. You then make your own
appointment."

"I see."

"Do you foresee any complications?"

"Not in the way you put it."

"Let's hope there'll be none. And of course there may not be any immediate need of this. It may be a long time before the young man comes up here. Our job is to be ready for him when he does. I'll draft out a letter to the Beirutis."

"I still don't see what is the real purpose of this exercise."

Sedgwick shrugged. "It's early days to tell. Let's call it ground bait. We've got this young man in a position where he has to do what we want. We can put the pressure on at any time. It may never come to anything. In the meantime we can keep him upon ice."

†

Diana whistled when she registered the letter. She took the file into Reid. "Here's a headache for you," she announced.

He read it, then took it down to Farrar. "I'll leave this with you," he said. "Let's have a gossip when you've digested it."

Farrar was back in his office within ten minutes. "Sometimes one can be too clever at this game."

"Who's being too clever, we or they?"

"By 'they' do you mean our boys in Istanbul?"

"Of course."

"I'd say it was fifty-fifty. We probably ran a risk in the first place. Whatever we do, we mustn't upset the Turks. And again we worked too fast, suggesting that Aziz should go up to Istanbul after his exams. I'd have liked to have got back a letter from Ahmed first, even though it means writing in our message in secret ink ourselves. As it is, this whole operation with Fadhil has to be closed down."

"Does it matter?"

"Not very much. Fadhil has to be told. He had better start grumbling about the delay, but he might give Aziz a few more records. I rather like the chap and there's a good deal of trouble on its way to him. Oh, well, it'll be summer soon."

Spring comes suddenly to the Lebanon. In December when heavy waves had dashed upon the waterfront and in January when winds had swept down from the mountains, when draughts had whistled under ill-fitting doors, when bare floors and staircases had been cold under the feet and the Arabs wrapped tight in their djellabahs had huddled over charcoal braziers, Reid had wondered

128

whether winter was not preferable in England where houses were constructed in view of the cold with sandbags to keep out the draughts, with heavy curtains, radiators, open fireplaces. He had never felt so cold, so uncomfortable in England; but Farrar had smiled knowingly. "Don't worry, spring will come on the fifteenth of March."

"How can you say that? Seasons vary. This may be a bad winter."

"It is already. But ask any Arab. He'll tell you the same thing. Spring comes on the fifteenth of March."

And sure enough, within a week, it happened; one day it was wet and cold, with the skies grey, and with sudden gusts of wind scattering papers across desks, and then, sixty hours later, the sky was blue and the sun was shining, the gardens were bright with flowers and larks were singing; the air was soft and scented. Was not this the promised land of the Old Testament that flowed with milk and honey?

"Think, plan, act in terms of March 1942," said Farrar. "Well, here we are."

In the last week in March there was to be a security congress in Damascus, a high level gathering from Palestine, Egypt, Transjordan and Iraq.

"Let's go up a couple of days before," said Farrar. "There are people we ought to see. We can do with a holiday, and let's take Diana. She needs one, too."

Damascus, if you went to it straight, was a three and a half hours' drive across the mountains, but in three and a half months Reid had not been outside Beirut.

"We'll make a scenic tour of this, we'll take in Baalbec," Farrar said.

Baalbec was deserted; there were no tourists, no guides, no charges for admission. They wandered among the empty terraces and temples and stared with appropriate awe at the seven majestic pillars that stood against the sky; that perhaps were more impressive now in their lonely abandoned grandeur than they had been when they were part of a complete building; their size was more apparent. They dwarfed the surrounding ruins, as they could never have done in the days when they were part of a symmetrical, harmonious design.

They lunched in Zahlé, at an open-air café beside a river that ran noisily through a tree shaded valley underneath the mountain.

The sun fell in dappled colouring across their table. Diana was dressed as though she were on a hitchhike, in dark green velveteen corduroy slacks and a short primrose jacket. She had knotted a pink silk handkerchief in her hair. "I'll promise to dress respectably in Damascus," she assured them.

It was the first time he had seen her so relaxed. "I wish I could have seen you in your skiing days," he said.

"I looked much like this."

"That's what I was thinking."

They smiled at one another across the table. Farrar noted the smile; for a moment he ruminated, then he reassumed his casual, careless manner.

"Let's do ourselves very well," he said. "This is all in the course of duty. It is on the house."

But actually they lunched very modestly. Some of the best Arak comes from Zahlé, and they had an Arak lunch, with mezze and river trout, with little squares of Kibbé and thick black coffee at the end. "We'll make up for it tonight," said Farrar.

They drove in the mid-afternoon across the Bekaa valley.

"This is where the opium comes from," Farrar said.

They saw little along the road; occasional military transport, and in the plains a hooded Arab driving a herd of goats. They came into Damascus late in the afternoon; a green oasis in the desert, it had, in spite of the mountains backing it, an air of Oxford with its mosques and minarets and gardens.

"Shall we see Abana and Pharfa?" asked Reid.

"You'll see Abana; a trivial stream."

They were staying at the Omayyed, a hotel built by the French in modern Oriental style. It had wide lounges and deep armchairs and carpets. In its hall there was a vast mural of Syria, showing in relief its links of air and rail and car with Europe. There were advertisements of flights from Amsterdam. "That's ironic now," said Reid.

"This is even more ironic," Farrar said. He pointed to the writing desk on which were set out the 1939 instructions as to the dates on which you could post airmail letters to Saigon.

They dined that evening in the French Officers' Club. "They still may have some French wine left," said Farrar.

The Damascus cercle was very quiet after the Beirut cercle. There were not many British officers in Damascus and only a small French garrison. The diningroom was high and dimly lighted but it had an air of France. It was a quiet, cosy dinner. At the end of it Farrar said: "Listen now. I hope you two won't mind, but I've a number of old friends here whom I'd like to see. Could you look after yourselves tomorrow, go sight-seeing or whatever you like, and then we'll start in fresh on Thursday after breakfast? O.K. Fine."

A long, long day with nothing to do but loiter. It was the first such day that Reid had had for longer than he could remember. Had he indeed had one since the war?

"You've been here before, haven't you?" he asked Diana.

"Only once for half a day."

"That's enough to let you act as guide."

It was a warm, clear day and the sun brought a glint of gold into the high ochre brown mountains that screened the city from the northern winds. They went to the Souks first. "They are arranged in sections, according to the trade," she told him. "This, by the way, is the street that was called straight."

There was a steady roll of noise, the rattle of harness, the tinkle of camel bells, the honking of horns, the raising of impatient voices, the murmur of gossip. Cabs and carts and camels jostled pedestrians into the gutter. But the salesmen in the small theatres of their shops contributed little to the general din. They sat impassive among their goods, cloth or corn or leather; spices or silks or carpets; they were wrapped in heavy, coarse brown cloaks, usually with the peaked headdress lowered over the shoulder, the head protected by a tightly fitting skullcap. They did not solicit custom, though they bargained endlessly; that was their game and they enjoyed it. But their pride would not allow them to invite refusal. If you were interested in their goods they would display them for as long as you chose to look, in a spirit of Arab hospitality. Their time is yours, you are their guests. They do not press you to buy. Sometimes they will offer you a cup of coffee, but the offer of it entailed no obligation. Salesmanship was dignified in the Souks.

"We're coming to the goldsmiths' section," Diana said. A succession of gnome-like figures were beating the yellow metal into brooches and bangles that were sold by weight. The yellow under the electric light was so vivid that it seemed unreal. The designs of the articles were so commonplace and tasteless that you felt you were being offered brasswork in a county fair.

"This is the street where they sell high quality goods," she told him. This is their Rue de la Paix."

They went into a large silk shop. "I must get something here," he said. The owner spread out a succession of exquisite brocades. Reid took out his wallet. "I wish I'd brought more money."

"Don't worry about that," the salesman said. "I will always cash a cheque on a British bank."

"Even in wartime?"

"Especially in wartime."

He hesitated between a red and a pale blue material.

"Is it for your wife?" Diana asked. He nodded.

"Is she fair or dark?"

"She's dark."

"Then I should take the red."

Often in a gap in the Souks would be a doorway, studded with brass.

"That's probably the home of a rich Damascus merchant; many of them live here in the Souks." One such house, the Azid Palace, was on show to tourists. It was a large, low building, or rather it was a succession of low buildings with courtyards and fountains playing; off it opened rooms with painted ceilings and rich harmonising colours. There was a spacious air of leisure and deliberation. It was hard to realise that the din and traffic of the Souks were only a few yards distant.

"The Arabs know how to live," he said.

"We'll go to the citadel afterwards," she said. "Then you'll see how much space there is between the actual framework of the Souks. It's rather like looking down on England from an aeroplane. You see how much land lies between the ribbon developments of all those roads that radiate from London."

Now and again they would catch in the Souks glimpses of the old wall itself, with ironwork let into the great stone gates. At the entrance to the Souks was a single Roman column. Paul of Tarsus may have rested his hand against it. There was a money-changer on whose table a shabby-looking Arab produced from the folds of his djellabah a bag containing sovereigns. "So that's where our gold's got to," said Reid. They climbed up the citadel. He could see the pattern of the bazaars from the arched domes of the corrugated iron that protected them. He could discern the outline of the old city from the arrangement of the mosques. "I'm glad you've seen Damascus the first time with me," she said.

They took an arak at a sidewalk café. A vendor of soft drinks went by, his goat-skin bright with brass.

They lunched at an open air French restaurant.

"I wonder what kind of a meal they get now in the South of France in a restaurant like this," he said. He put his parcel of brocade on the empty chair.

"She'll like that," she said.

"I hope so."

"Do you know, that's the first time you've ever mentioned her?"

"Is it? I suppose it is."

"It's funny. I've told you so much about myself. I know so little about you."

"There isn't very much to know. It's a very humdrum kind of life."

"I can't even picture it."

"That's only because you didn't go to a University. It's lecturing and tutorials, a certain amount of routine research."

"But your home life; what's your house like?"

"Eighteenth century, rectangular and convenient."

She looked at him thoughtfully, with the half-flicker of a smile, a fond, protective smile. "You aren't going to tell me anything, I know. I rather like it that way: for you to be somebody I think and guess about and make pictures of."

"Make pictures of me?"

"But of course I do." Her eyes were steadily on his; there was a look in them that he had not seen in her eyes before. It made him feel nervous and excited as he had done in the days when he played cricket as he waited with his pads on in the pavilion.

"I'd like to see a film this afternoon," she said.

Hedy Lamarr and James Stewart were showing in "Come Live with Me."

"Have you ever seen that?" he asked.

"No."

"I have, but I could see it several times. The way she says, 'Perhaps your orchids help.' "

"Don't spoil it for me."

They had had an Arak before lunch at a sidewalk café and they had drunk a bottle of red wine with their meal. Drowsiness stole over him. He fought against it; he wanted to hear her say, "Perhaps your orchids help," but the bright light of the screen held him in a hypnotic spell; his attention faded; every nerve cell was at rest, he did not feel he had a trouble in the world. He was conscious of her scent, heavy, fleeting, evocative; a wave of Jasmin, it increased his drowsiness; his eyelids closed.

He woke, when the lights went on, with a start. "I hope I didn't snore," he said.

"I'd have woken you if you had."

The sun was low in the sky when they came out into the street.

"It's my turn for a rest," she said. "Let's meet in the bar at seven."

He left her in the door of the Omayyed and strolled through the new part of the city. Peace of a quality that was new tranquillised his every nerve cell. He made no attempt to analyse it. He was content to wrap its mantle round him.

They dined in the hotel. The large ornate room was practically empty. They took a table in the corner.

"I feel as though there were no one in the whole world except ourselves." he said.

"Haven't you ever had that feeling even when you were in a crowded room?"

"Have I? I suppose I have. I wonder."

"If you haven't, you've been unlucky."

"I've been so lucky in some things, that perhaps I have had to be unlucky in others."

"Have you, though, really? Have you been unlucky . . . in that, I mean?"

He did not answer for a moment. He did not know how to answer. Had he been unlucky? It was a question that he had never asked himself. He had been worried about his marriage but most men he imagined, worried about their marriages. He answered her obliquely: "I don't think I'd want to be anybody else. I don't wish that I had someone else's life. If I can say that, I can say I've been lucky, can't I?"

"That doesn't mean that you don't feel that there are some things you've missed."

"Is there anyone in the world who doesn't feel that he's missed something. Don't you yourself?"

"Yes, but I'm still hoping that I'll get it. You're talking as though you never would get it."

The waiter was at their side with a wine list.

"They've still got some French wines on their list," he said. "What is your favourite wine?"

"Red Burgundy."

"Mine, too. They've got a Richebourg '34."

It was a rich, full wine; velvet-smooth, with a lingering flavour on the palate.

"I wonder what's happening there now," he said. "Have you heard the story of the French colonel who ordered his men on their way to battle to present arms to the Clos de Vougeot? 'Mes enfants, it is to preserve such beauties that you are about to fight.' Think of it now. The slopes of gold, with Germans there."

They were eating a roast chicken, that did not interfere with the wine's flavour. He felt once again a sense of being in tune with the entire universe. As always when she drank, she held the glass between her hands, raising it reverently to her lips. He returned to the earlier subject of their talk.

"They used to complain about Victorian novels that end with marriage bells; marriage wasn't an end, the critics said, but a beginning. Yet really it is an end, a man with a career, after a certain point, sees the way clear ahead; only a certain number of things can happen to him unless there's a calamity of some kind, in most careers, at least. No one could have foreseen that Churchill would have had this fantastic St. Martin's summer; but he's the exception. That's why the early chapters of an autobiography are more interesting than the later ones. A young man of promise might become any one of a dozen things. He might be a lawyer, a politician, an administrator, and it's usually chance that decides what he will become. He is leaving his flat in a hurry; the telephone bell rings. Shall he answer it? He almost doesn't. It is an invitation to a party, where he meets the person who will reorientate his entire life for him. If he hadn't answered that telephone he would never have met that person, his life would have been completely different. That's what one asks of an autobiography, to be told how a man got set originally on the road he's followed. One sees him as he is today, in the round, one wants to know how he became the person that he is."

He enlarged the subject, embroidered on it, drawing illustrations from the past and from contemporary events. She listened, her eyes wide: her lips slightly parted as though she were breathing in a rich, keen air. When he paused, she sighed.

"This is what I've always wanted; to hear you talk as your pupils hear you. That's what I've been missing all this time. Now I see what Margaret meant." Her eyes were shining, her face gave a curious illusion of transparence as though there were a lamp inside it. "Go on," she said. "Don't stop."

The chicken was followed by a cheese ramekin that enhanced the flavour of the Burgundy. He had left a little wine in the bottle. He poured it into his own emptied glass. There was no sediment. "That's luck," he said. He poured half of the wine into her glass. He raised his glass, touching hers with it. "I shall remember today as long as I remember anything," he said.

"It's been a dream day." The contralto in her voice struck a deeper tone, a tone he had never heard before. His whole being was flooded with an emotion he could not control. He had no power over his voice.

"Another such day," he said, "and I'd be in love with you."

She sighed; a long, slow sigh that seemed to rise from a deep well of happiness.

"How I've been waiting for you to say just that. How I've despaired of your ever saying it."

He stared, astounded. "But I had no idea. . . ."

"Darling, I know; it's that that makes you irresistible." She checked; she leant forward across the table, resting her elbows on it, cupping her face between her hands. "I knew from the very start," she said. "That first evening in the night club. This is my fate, I thought. You were saying how everything turns on chance; a telephone that rings at the last moment; taking a bus rather than a taxi; now there's that muddle in your posting. We'd never have met but for it. No, please don't say anything. Accept it; there's nothing to be done. It's wartime; we're lucky, very lucky, not to have to make plans, not to have to discuss a situation. We're lucky, darling. Oh, so very lucky."

He stood outside her room. Her height made him feel awkward. He took her hand, lifted it, turned the palm over, held it against his mouth. It was soft and scented. She allowed it to rest there for a moment; then she turned towards the door. She paused on the threshold, smiled, raised her hand to her lips. Good night."

He had a glimpse of her room, with the moonlight shining on to her mosquito net. Then the door shut it out.

He leant on the window sill of his own room. The light from hers fell in a long oblong on the courtyard. His heart was thudding. He picked up the receiver of his telephone. "Room number 26."

There was a chuckle from the other end. "If you hadn't called within three minutes I was going to jump right out into that courtyard."

"Can I look in and tuck you up?"

"Of course."

She had flung back the mosquito net. The room was filled with moonlight. She was sitting up among the pillows. She opened her arms to him.

8

REID RETURNED TO A MESSAGE from Amin Marun: Aziz was going to Istanbul for a holiday, would he come round to say "au revoir." He showed the message to Diana. "It seems strange coming back from that to this," he said.

"Perhaps it's as well there should be contrasts."

"This is the kind of thing that makes me hate myself."

"We all have to hate ourselves at times."

"At those times it's a great relief to me to have you down the passage."

"It's a relief to me."

"I say to myself pretty often, 'I couldn't stand this place if it weren't for Diana.' "

"Please go on saying that."

There was a warm look in her eyes. His whole being was flooded with peace and beauty.

"Are you lunching anywhere?" he asked.

"I'd planned to boil an egg at home."

"Why not a steak at Sa'ad's instead?"

"That sounds a very nice idea."

After lunch he said, "You've never seen my flat. Don't you think it's time you did."

"I do, most certainly."

"We've two hours before our office opens."

"We have."

"Is there any reason why we shouldn't go round there now?"

"I can't think of one."

†

Reid found Madame Amin in the liveliest good humour.

"This is your doing," she said. "It seems silly but till you asked me if he was going back to Turkey, it hadn't occurred to us to let him go. It's because of your English system of the boarding school. We think in terms of day schools. But you're right; it is a good idea to send them home between their courses."

Reid, as he looked at Aziz, had a sense of Aeschylan tragedy. Could you find a more poignant example of dramatic irony? Aziz was excited, happy; feeling himself important as one always does on the verge of taking off. All these people one tells oneself will be here tomorrow, doing the same things, meeting the same people, but I shall be in another universe. If one felt that in peace-time, how much more did one in wartime when so few were allowed to travel independently.

Reid moved across to him. "It's strange to be a neutral in this war; hardly anyone in this room could make your journey without elaborate visas; without having immense influence; belligerents on both sides exist behind iron curtains. I don't suppose that there's one person in this room who could if he wanted continue his journey in that train through the occupied countries into Germany. Do you remember the Kaiser and the Berlin-Baghdad railway? It's ironic, isn't it, the way it has come out? It's a strange war. It was very different in Napoleon's day. Think of Byron going on his Grand Tour right through the war."

Aziz made no reply, but his eyes were shining.

"If you fail," Reid went on, "do give Alexandria a second thought."

"I will."

"I guess at the moment you're so relieved at the thought that your exam is behind you that for better or for worse there's nothing you can do about it, that you're so excited at the thought of going on a journey that you don't much care what'll be happening in three weeks."

"That's about it." He grinned and there was a friendly openness about the grin that confirmed Reid in his sense of guilt. This boy had confided in him in a way that he had not with his family and friends; this openness was to be rewarded with betrayal.

"When will you be back?"

"If I've passed, I shall be back in the following week."

"Then I hope we'll see you the first week in April."

"Let's hope so."

†

The Istanbul office was warned by a coded signal that Aziz was on his way. Eve called at the Perapalas Otel daily for his message. At last it reached her. She made a date with Aziz for the following evening at five o'clock.

"What should I serve him at that hour?" she asked Sedgwick.

"Coffee is never wrong, but whisky is more effective." He paused. His eyes twinkled. "He's a Turk, remember. Make sure that Kitty arrives at six."

At a quarter to five Eve was taut with expectation. This was her first essay at genuine secret service work. Up to now she had done all her work on paper. She had formed her own impression of the characters whose activities she catalogued. Now she was to see a dubious performer off his guard. She only regretted that from every account he must be rather dingy.

Because she had counted on his being dingy, she was pleasantly surprised. He was taller than she had expected. He was neatly dressed; his linen was clean; he had a tie that was obviously expensive; his shoes were freshly polished. But what struck her most was his air of personal distinction. He seemed somebody.

He looked round him curiously. It was very possibly the first time that in Turkey he had been alone in a drawing room with a young woman who was "convenable". He noticed the coffee tray and cakes. He also noticed the decanter and glasses on the sideboard.

"Would you prefer whisky to coffee?" she enquired.

He hesitated. She suspected that he would have preferred whisky but that decorum counselled the choice of coffee.

"Perhaps whisky later, then," she said. He sat on a low cushion stool, his feet drawn under him; his elbows rested on his knees, the coffee cup held between his hands. He looked up at her, his eyes bright, his head slightly cocked.

"I expect you are very puzzled about all this," she said.

He inclined his head.

"You have never met this man, Ismail Hilli, who was supposed to deliver a package to your friend Ahmed?"

139

"No, I have not met him."

"Do you know what was in the package that he was supposed to deliver to your friend?"

Aziz hesitated. She put him at his ease. "You can be outspoken with me," she said. "I know what was in it. I am employed here by the British Council. You know, of course, what that is."

"I know."

"I can understand why you should feel puzzled that you had to adopt such a secret method to obtain this information for your friend . . . what is his name? Fadhil, isn't it? The censorship is tiresome these days. They make the conduct of business difficult and there are risks attached. What would a Turkish censor say if he detected secret ink upon a letter? The betting is a thousand to one against. But there is that one chance, as Ismail realised. After all, Ahmed is in the government's employ. It would ruin his career. So this is what Ismail decided. He knew that you wanted messages and a present given to Ahmed; so he exchanged the package. He kept the handkerchief you had sent to Ahmed, but he flung away the inks. He sent a box of real toilet water instead; and then at the last moment he felt nervous again. Ismail is a good friend of mine but I have to confess that he is very timid. Scarcely a man at all. He felt that he did not want to be mixed up in this business in any way. So he asked me to deliver the package."

"Which package?"

"The one with the real toilet water."

"Then Ahmed knows nothing about the scheme at all."

"Exactly."

"But I wrote to him only a week ago, asking for information about German exports."

"The questions were in secret ink, of course."

"Naturally."

"Then that's all right. Ahmed will never know it. He will think it an ordinary letter, and throw it in the waste paper basket."

"I see."

There was a puzzled expression on his face. She watched him closely, anxiously. Was this story of hers carrying weight? It had seemed flimsy enough when Sedgwick had set it out for her in the office. It seemed much more flimsy when she was recounting it herself. Why should Ismail have bothered to substitute another package? He could easily have brought round the handkerchief alone. A sudden idea struck her.

"He substituted the package because he thought it should be a more substantial present, since he wasn't delivering it himself. Would it have been worth my while to run that errand simply for a handkerchief? I think that was rather nice of him, don't you?" she finished lamely. Was that a sufficient explanation? Was it convincing? Perhaps she would have done better not to attempt an elaboration. The parable of the purloined letter. Present the whole issue in the most straightforward way. Wasn't that one of the first tenets in intelligence. Don't make your alibis too watertight? They had made that mistake with an agent whom they had sent into Bulgaria with so many cards and permits, each one genuine, that the Gestapo had been suspicious. How could any one man have acquired so many cards? It had settled that agent's score.

She waited for Aziz to speak. He was still looking puzzled. There was something very touching and youthful about his expression. He was really very handsome. She felt protective, and possessive. In a sense he was her victim. He was hers. "I've led him into this," she thought.

"So that's how it is, you see," and her voice softened.

He nodded. "Yes, I see." His puzzled expression changed to one of thoughtfulness. "This means I can't give Fadhil the information he needs."

"I'm afraid it does, unless. . . ." She stopped. She was going beyond her commission.

"Unless what?" he asked.

She had been going to suggest that she might correspond with him; but what was the point in that, and very likely his letters were exposed to the Turkish censorship.

"Unless," she said, "you were to ask me what you need to know. I'm in the British Council. I very likely could find out. If we did it by conversation, that's to say, not through the mail: the mail's too risky. What did you ask for in that letter that you sent to Ahmed?"

"What Turkey was importing from Germany."

"I daresay I could find out that for you. How long will you be up here?"

"Two and a half weeks."

"Then why don't you come and see me before you leave?"

He nodded pensively. He's believing this, she thought. It seems incredible, but he really is. Sedgwick was right. The more obvious the better.

"What about that whisky now?" she said.

"I would like that, please."

She put the ice in first so that he could not tell how heavy a shot of whisky she put on to it.

"There," she said. "And now what about a little music? Would you like to see my records?"

She had a high pile on the lowest bookshelf. He ransacked them eagerly. "Could we have this?" he said. She watched him closely as he listened. He was utterly absorbed; his expression changed; it seemed as though his whole face had been smoothed over. She had never seen a corpse, but she had read that a few hours after death the face assumed an ethereal beauty with the lines and strains of life removed: a recovery of lost innocence, a discovery of peace. Music had the same effect on Aziz. He was almost beautiful. He had a rarified spiritual look. Once again she had that protective feeling towards him, mingled now with a sense of guilt and of forboding. He was in a trap and did not know it, a trap that she had baited. How long would he be able to retain the utter peace of spirit that now enveloped him? "I must try to make amends," she thought.

They were still playing records when a key clicked in the lock.

Kitty's return dispelled the mood. So soon, Eve thought. The record was nearly finished. Eve did not put on another one. Kitty only enjoyed dance tunes and songs from musicals. Kitty fixed herself a drink and embarked on a narration of the day's events. Her conversation was directed exclusively at Aziz. She was a different person when there was a man in the room. Aziz listened with an air of interest, but he too had become a different person. That rapt poetic absorption had disappeared, and he soon rose to take his leave.

"You'll come again, won't you, before you leave?" Eve said.

"You can be sure of that."

Kitty looked at her enquiringly as the door closed.

"No case of repelling boarders this afternoon, I gather."

"Clearly not."

"Anyhow, he does not look the type."

"You didn't think he was attractive?"

Kitty shrugged. "Gaunt, morose, self-centred. Maybe all right in the middle thirties, but he's got a long way to travel."

Eve was relieved that Kitty had not been impressed by Aziz. It proved to her that Aziz was someone special.

Early next morning Eve was summoned into Sedgwick's office. "How did it go?"

She told him.

"And you really believe that he accepted your explanation?"

"He seemed to."

"Time for the next move."

"What is the next move?"

"To put Chessman on to him. We have to work fast. Only two and a half weeks to play with."

Two mornings later, Aziz was called to the telephone soon after his father had left for his office and while his mother was still in bed. A quiet masculine voice came over the line. "You do not know who I am. But I shall be sitting at a corner table of the Café Brazil this afternoon at twenty minutes to four. I shall be wearing a dark overcoat, and a grey felt hat. I am a man in his middle forties. I have a small dark moustache. I shall be alone. I shall be reading a German paper. Do not recognise me. Sit in another part of the café. Keep an eye on my table. After seven minutes I shall get up and leave. Stay at your table for another six minutes, then leave the café. A grey four-seater Chevrolet will be drawn against the kerb. Get into it. I strongly advise you to do this. If you do not, the results for you will be unfortunate. We are in a position to make things most unpleasant. I use the name Ahmed. That is all the explanation I need give." The voice was quiet, almost gentle, but it was very firm.

It was a dark day. It was raining. The blinds of the Chevrolet were drawn. The car kept turning. Aziz had no idea where he was being taken. The drive lasted about twenty minutes. Suddenly, the car stopped. "You can get out here," said the man beside him.

Aziz stepped out into a long ill-lighted street lined by apartment buildings; the homes of artisans and minor office workers. The hallway was bare. There was no porter. There was no lift. "On the second floor," he was told. "Number 17." It was a small, rectangular flat. Two rooms, a kitchenette, a bathroom. It was warm and comfortably furnished. There was a low table set with a coffee pot and coffee cups.

"You can take off your coat," said the man. "You will be here a little time. I hope that it will prove a cordial meeting. We will start with a cup of coffee."

Aziz sat on the low settee. He had not spoken a word since he had stepped into the car. It was strong, very sweet, thick coffee. "Now," said the man. From his pocket he took two sheets of paper. He handed them to Aziz. "You will recognise these." One was a photostat of the second letter that Aziz had written to Ahmed. The second was a photostat of the same letter under a V.I. lamp showing the writing in secret ink. "I will not tell you my name. There is no need for you to know. I am a member of the police force though I have another job. I have a friend in the censor's office. He brought me this letter unofficially. No public report has been made yet of this letter. I want to ask you a number of questions before deciding what to do with it. Now I presume that Ahmed has the necessary acid to develop this secret writing?"

Aziz shook his head. He explained what had transpired. "I see," said Chessman. "Then Ahmed has no knowledge of this operation?"

"None."

"All he knows is that he received an unexpected present from you?"

"That is so."

"Now this man Fadhil from Beirut: what do you know about him?"

Aziz explained how he had come to meet him.

"The Koumayans? Who are they?"

Aziz explained that they were an Armenian family whom his parents knew. "They have no contact with this case."

"It is simply, then, an issue between you and Fadhil. Ahmed does not enter. This man Ismail Hilli, now: what about him?"

"I have never met him."

"You know nothing about him?"

"Nothing."

"There may, of course, be no such person. This English girl, now, who told you what had happened: Eve. What was her surname? Parish, yes, Parish. What about her?"

"She is in the British Council. She shares a flat with another girl, Kitty something or other."

"If you go there again—and I think you should go there again—you should find out what this Kitty's name is and all you can about her. Now then, I think we have the position clear. Let us review it. . . ."

He paused. He looked at Aziz quizically. He raised his left eyebrow. There was friendliness in his smile. "Don't be frightened," he said. "I do not want to bully you. But I do want you to realise that you have put yourself in a very difficult position. You are a Turkish citizen, studying in the Lebanon, which was once a part of Turkey. You have tried to evade censorship regulations in order to provide a Lebanese subject with commercial information that he could not obtain through ordinary channels. That is a serious offence. You have also attempted to persuade a Turkish citizen, who is a loyal servant of the state, to provide you with this information. For him this would be a very serious offence. For you it is no less serious, to attempt to seduce a servant of the government. In wartime it might even be a capital offence. I do not want to threaten you, but I do want you to realise that I can do you a very great deal of harm." He paused. His look was still quizzical, but friendly. "Luckily for you," he said, "you are in a position to be of use to me, so that there is no need for us to reach extremes." He paused again. "I told you that I had another job. I have two other jobs. The one about which everybody knows; the third about which very few know. I provide the German Embassy with various types of information. In the last war, as you know, we were the allies of Germany. My family and I have still the warmest feelings for the German people and their ideals. It was a great misfortune to us and to the whole world that through American intervention, Germany lost the war. This time Germany has Japan on her side, so she cannot lose it. This time, luckily for us, in Turkey, we are now neutrals; but we need not neglect our former friends. I presume that you have no particularly friendly feeling for the British or the French?"

"Why should I have?"

"Indeed, why should you have? Your father fought the British in the first war. Your uncle was killed by them. They dismembered the Ottoman Empire. But for them you would be the heir to a rich estate. The sooner they lose this war, and they will lose it, the better for us all. You would welcome, wouldn't you, an opportunity to help hasten the ending of the war?"

"I would welcome it."

"It is a relief to have you say that. Then I do not have to threaten you. And I could threaten you. You realise that, don't you? If I were to hand over this letter to the police you would be arrested within an hour. And who would believe your story about a member of the secret police who is working for the Germans? You do not know my name. You do not know my address. You do not know my occupation. They would laugh at you. Even if they half believed your story, how could they do anything to me? How could they find me? I am invulnerable. But luckily I do not have to threaten you. You are happy to collaborate; and it will prove profitable for you. The Germans are rich and generous. Did this tradesman pay you any money?"

"He gave me some gramophone records."

"The Germans can do better than that. They will give you money with which to buy gramophone records. How many records did this man Fadhil give you?"

"He has given me four so far."

"We can do better than that. But the Germans pay by results. You must remember that. Money will arrive when you deliver your first instalment; and with that money will be this photostat. Is that quite clear?"

"It is clear."

"You are prepared to meet my friend at the German Embassy?"

"I am prepared."

"Then we will meet three days from now. At the same time, but at the Café Florian."

Next morning Eve took down in shorthand Chessman's account of the interview. As she transcribed the notes she experienced the same mounting excitement that she had earlier at her flat: an excitement compounded of the same conflicting ingredients; the basic espionage drama of the operation, the sense of protective pity, a curious possessive thrill, the thought, 'this is my victim'. She could picture Aziz sitting there while Chessman wound his ropes slowly round him; her finger held the knot while he brought the ends together; yet mingled with a gloating that was near to cruelty was the consoling tenderness, the knowledge that she could make amends assuaging the wounds she had inflicted. And in three days' time she would be taking down Chessman's account of the interview with the German. What a tightening of knots!

The meeting took place with the same smoothness. Again there was only one man, the same man in the Chevrolet. "Our friend is meeting us at my apartment," he explained. "He will be wearing civilian clothes, but he is a soldier. Address him as Herr Capitaine."

The Captain was tall and spare, clean shaven, with light coloured hair that he wore long. He did not look particularly German. He did not look particularly anything. He leapt to his feet as Aziz and Chessman entered, clicked his heels, stretched out his right arm and barked, "Heil Hitler." Aziz and Chessman followed suit.

"Do you speak German?" the Captain asked. Aziz nodded. "Good, then we will speak German. It is said that many Turks speak French now instead of German, as they did thirty years ago. That will be altered when our victorious armies have established the Pan-German peace. I am glad to see, young man, that you cherish the ideals and traditions of your ancestors. I have brought with me a bottle of schnapps. Let us have three small glasses and let us toast the glories of the Third Reich and its friendship with our good friends in Turkey."

The spirit was poured; glasses were clicked; "Heil Hitler", and then drained.

"Let us now sit," said the Captain. "Our friend here, whom I call Heinrich though it is not his name, tells me that you are ready to help our noble cause by supplying information from the Lebanese; let us consider what information you can give us. Your aunt is a rich woman. Does she entertain?"

"Yes, she entertains."

"Whom does she entertain?"

Aziz described the social milieu in which his aunt and uncle moved. The German nodded. "That could be very useful. We want to know how the Lebanese feel towards the French. They, of course, are anxious to be rid of them. They are technically independent, but the French are in control everywhere. They own all the public services. They control the banking. The Lebanese are astute. They will try to get the British on their side; they will foment ill feeling between the French and British. That should not be difficult. The French have an hereditary distrust of the British. They have always believed that the British want to take over Syria and Lebanon from them, so that the sphere of British influence can run straight from Cairo to Aleppo. They believe, and very likely they are correct in thinking so, that the British are welcoming this opportunity to enlarge their raj. It is very important that we should know what the Lebanese are planning; or rather what they are concocting. Trouble in the Levant would be of the greatest assistance to our forces in the Western Desert. We want to exacerbate those differences of opinion. It will be useful for us to learn how we can do that most effectively. We can do it with propaganda. We can also send funds to subversive elements. Information from you may be extremely useful. Do you know anybody in Spears Mission?"

Aziz nodded. "There are two officers I know very well. One of them was a history and philosophy Professor at an English University. He is often a guest at my aunt's house. He has been sympathetic and kind to me."

"And the other?"

"A younger man. He worked for an oil company before the war."

"Do you know what their duties are in the Mission?"

"Propaganda. Public relations."

"Excellent, excellent. See as much of them as you can. Anything they may have to tell you is of interest. General Spears is an important figure. He has Winston Churchill's confidence. His point of view is accepted in London. It was he who established de Gaulle as the leader of the Free French movement. But we believe that he and de Gaulle are no longer the best of friends. Keep close to those two officers; you may learn a lot from them. There are other points, of which you might not recognise the importance, but of which we should; for instance the kinds of troops you see in the streets. If there are Indians try to find out from what part of India they come. If you see more or fewer Australian hats, let us know that. Unusual movement of military transport; shipping; the arrival of any large liner. Nothing is too trivial to tell us.

"Then there is another thing: keep on the look-out for any young Lebanese who are coming up to Turkey and might be of assistance, who would do for us what you are doing. If anyone expresses, I won't say pro-German sentiments, but anti-French, anti-British sentiments, let us know about them. If they come up here, we'll contact them.

"Now, our method of communication. Correspondence through the post is dangerous, even with secret ink, even if the secret writing is done very well. These censors have a trained sense. Something in the letter may strike them as peculiar. There seems no purpose in it. They keep a watch on the man who wrote it. If another of his letters looks unnatural, they test it for secret ink. We cannot risk that. You saw what happened to your letter to Ahmed. We must suppose that the first letter had wakened the censor's suspicions. He tested the second letter. We must be on our guard. We will follow another method. You know the Turkish café in Babedris. Go there every Monday evening at 6.15. Take with you a copy of the *Palestine Post*. Go to a table in the centre of the room; order a coffee, put your paper down beside you. Make your coffee last half an hour. It may be that a man with the *Palestine Post* will sit beside you. After a little while he, too, will put down his paper, wait a few minutes, then prepare to leave. You pick up his paper instead of yours. You will take the paper back to your home. On the inside page where there is blank paper you will find some questions in secret ink. You will also find instructions as to where you are to deliver a copy of the *Palestine Post* with your reply to the questions. The same method of the exchange of papers will be followed. But you cannot be certain that every Monday somebody will arrive at your table reading the *Palestine Post*. If no one arrives you must go away after half an hour. But no matter what happens you must go there every Monday, and always there must be some message in secret writing on your paper.

"It may be that strangers will sit at your table. If that happens there is no remedy. You must sit at the table just the same. The staff of the café must become accustomed to your attendance. I would advise you to go on other days of the week; to become a client, in fact. But always, whatever happens, you must be there every Monday at 6.15. Is Monday at 6.15 a convenient time for you?"

"I will ensure that it is."

"Excellent. Then that is all." He rose to his feet, clicked his heels, extended his right arm, barked "Heil Hitler."

"We then took our leave," Chessman concluded.

When Chessman had gone, Eve stayed behind. "There's one thing more. It's a confession really. I'm afraid I went beyond my instructions, but when Aziz was looking despondent about not being able to take back information to Fadhil, I suggested that I might be able to get those facts for him and that he could take them back by hand. I suppose I shouldn't have said that?"

"I suppose you shouldn't, technically, but one has to trust one's instinct sometimes; instinct is more often right than wrong, far more often, nine times in ten I'd say. This was before he'd met Chessman, I assume."

"Yes."

"And of course he was worried about those records. The situation is different now; but all the same it might be as well for him to continue his transaction with Fadhil. It will keep the two operations separate in his mind. And it is important that he shouldn't confuse the information that he is getting for Beirut from Turkey with what he is getting for Turkey from Beirut. This may help him to keep them separate. The poor fellow probably does not know which way to turn at this actual moment. But . . . how did you leave it at the end?"

"He was going to call me before he left."

"Did you feel that he would?"

"I have some records that he wants to hear."

"In that case, maybe he will come. Well, let's see. If he does come it can't do any harm. It may do good."

"There's no reason why he shouldn't see me, is there?"

"None at all. He's seeing our boys in Beirut. He thinks that they are in public relations. You're in the same position that they are. The more tags we have on him the better."

"In that case then. . . ." She hesitated. "Do you think the operation is important?"

He shrugged. "We can't tell yet. It's another iron in the fire, we contact the Germans through him. Our boys in Beirut will photostat those copies of the *Palestine Post* before they reach Aziz. We shall learn from them what the Germans want to know."

"But we can't send up the answers we want them to have."

"I know we can't."

"Mayn't he send up some information that we would rather they didn't have?"

Sedgwick shook his head. "Nine times in ten it does not matter what they know as long as we know they know it. If Aziz did tumble on to something genuinely secret—he is very unlikely to, but he might—then we would have to burn the newspaper. The man who collects the paper in the café is going to take it to Farrar before he takes it to the Germans. It will be interesting to know what Aziz finds out. We must not forget that he is a genuine spy. He'll be doing his best to make discoveries. We are well up on the deal. We shall be learning what the Germans don't know and what they want to know. They're working in the dark, we're working in the light. What did Aziz want for Fadhil?"

"A routine question about German imports. The quantity and price."

"I can find that out easily. I'll give it to you tomorrow."

†

In Beirut the reports were received with mixed feelings on the third floor of the M.E.S.C. building. The situation was not developing as Farrar had intended, though it was possible that it could be developed in that direction later.

"We want to send up to the Germans the kind of information that we want them to have. I hoped that we should be able to do that through Aziz; now we can't. We shall have to find another agent for that purpose. That should not be impossible. The Germans want Aziz to give them names of men going up to Istanbul who would be likely to work for them. We must see that Aziz meets such a man. It is up to Abdul Hamid to find him for us. It may take a little time, but there's no hurry."

He paused. That morning the wireless news had reported that Burma had been overrun. "It's strange, isn't it, that I should be saying there's no hurry, when in one area every second counts. Twelve months ago everything was touch and go here in the Middle East, particularly in Iraq. Baghdad had been evacuated; the women and children were in an R.A.F. cantonment at Habbanya; prominent civilians were in a state of siege in the British Embassy; German aircraft were at Mosul. German staff officers were in Baghdad itself; the former German consul was back to organise the take-over. It was a question of days, one might say of hours, whether the British relief forces got there before the Germans. But we did get there and the revolution collapsed. The same thing happened here in Lebanon, a few weeks later, when we attacked the Vichy French. Everything turned on a few hours; while in Malaya the rubber planters were coming down to Penang and Singapore for wild weekends; they weren't bothering about us. To-day the situation is reversed. Everything is tranquil here. Everything is tranquil in Iraq. As long as Rommel is held in the Western Desert, we can afford to say, 'There isn't any hurry,' "

He shrugged. "In Paris they talked about the 'drôle de guerre'. We've got one here all right."

On the following morning the examination results were out. Aziz had passed. The news reached the office through Abdul Hamid. Reid promptly rang up Madame Amin.

"I suppose you have heard the news."

"Indeed I have."

"Congratulations."

"We are so happy and so proud."

"Do you know how soon Aziz will be back?"

"The new term starts in ten days' time."

"It must be wonderful for you to know that you'll have him back."

"Wonderful. Wonderful. He'll be so happy, too. We are going to have a welcome home party for him. We are getting out the invitations now. Of course, there'll be one for you, and Captain Farrar. I'm so grateful to you for the sympathy and kindness that you've shown him. I attribute his success to you, in part. You gave him confidence. You restored his faith in himself. He always speaks most highly of you."

Reid was glad that she could not see his expression at that moment. "I suppose," he thought, "I'll learn to play my role: to smile, and smile and be a villain."

A week later, in the early afternoon, Eve waited impatiently for Aziz. He was catching the train that evening. On the morning before she had picked up a message at the Perapalas. Would she telephone him at his home that afternoon? She found herself trembling when she heard his voice. Its foreign accent was more marked over the wire. It had a rhythm, a lilt she had forgotten, or had not been conscious of when he had been here in person, when she had been more aware of his looks, his manners.

"I've found that kind of cigarette that you were looking for," she told him.

"What cigarettes?" He sounded puzzled.

She chuckled. He was not used to the security trick of calling everything by a different name.

"You remember; you must. You can't get them in the Lebanon. A special German make."

"Of course, of course," and his voice lightened eagerly. "I'll call for them tomorrow."

"Come early, so that we can have some music."

The following morning she returned from her office with a large bunch of roses. As the flat was centrally heated they rarely used the fireplace, but today she laid a fire; she tidied the writing desk and bookshelves. She arranged low round cushions by the settee. Though twilight had not yet fallen she drew the curtains and switched on the two small reading lamps. It looked very cosy. "I'll light the fire at three. I'll have a record playing." She had no idea what would happen this afternoon. But she felt something would, something decisive. Anyhow, the stage must be set as though it would.

In the hall there was a bare hard light. He started when he came out of the hall into the softly-lit warm room, with the firelight flickering on the ceiling, on the roses and on the polished woodwork of the bookcase. He checked, looking round him. "It all looks different today," he said.

She smiled. "It's the same flat. But perhaps it seems different to you because it isn't strange to you any more; you feel at home here. Let me take your coat." She took it into her bedroom. He followed her.

"Is this where you sleep?"

She nodded. It was a bed-sitting room rather than a bedroom, with a divan pushed into the corner. There was a writing desk and two easy chairs. On the walls were reproductions of English painters: A Constable, a Moreland and a Turner. There was no washbasin. It looked like a schoolgirl's room. On the desk there was a picture of a man in uniform. He went across and looked at it.

"My father in the first war," she said. "He was wounded at Dardanelles."

"My uncle was killed at the Dardanelles, and my father fought there."

They looked at one another thoughtfully, then smiled. It seemed a bond rather than a cause for enmity. The music was swelling to its climax. "Do you know this?" she asked.

He shook his head. She told him what it was.

"I wish you could have heard it from the start," she said. "Another time. Look, before I forget. Here's this list for you."

His eyes widened. It was a long list. He read it slowly. "This is more than I could have got from Ahmed. Are you sure that this is accurate?"

"Quite sure. I got it from the consulate."

"But isn't it classified material?"

She shook her head. "It's a publicity handout. Our office was trying to prove to the Turks that we were more important to them than the Germans by showing how much more was imported from Britain than from Germany."

He read it to the end, then grinned. "They'll be very pleased with this when I get back to Beirut."

"Ismail losing his nerve was really a piece of luck for you."

"A great piece of luck for me."

This was, indeed, she thought, a fantastic double-take in dramatic irony. He believed that she had no idea that his second letter to Ahmed had been intercepted in censorship and that through that interception he had become a German spy. He was reminding himself that he must be desperately careful not to reveal his true position, that he must play the role of the Lebanese student finding commercial information for a friend. He had no idea that she knew exactly what he was thinking; she knew all that he knew and a great deal more, because she knew that he was now a pawn not in the German machine but in the British. It was more than a double-take, it was a treble-take. And again there came over her that sense of pity and protective tenderness. He had no knowledge of his plight. Two weeks ago he had been relatively innocent. He had been trying to evade censorship, but now he was acting for a power that might one day find itself at war with his own countrymen. Aiding an enemy in time of war: the Turkish authorities would have short shift with that. And I'm responsible.

But it won't happen, she reassured herself. I shall protect him. I'll be in the background, watching, if danger threatens; I'll see he's warned. They shan't throw him to the wolves. Sedgwick might be ruthless. But she was there. If he only guessed how dependent he was on her.

Her smile grew fond. "I've prepared an English tea for you this afternoon. You've probably never had one. Sit down. The kettle will be on the boil almost at once."

She explained to him the ritual of English tea; how you first warm the teapot and the teacups with hot water; how the water must be brought to the boil only just before you make the tea otherwise you boiled all the good out of the water. How you put into the pot one teaspoonful of tea for each guest and then one extra one for the pot; how you let the tea draw for five minutes before you poured. "A great deal depends upon the water," she explained. "There are special blends of tea for places with special water. Thomas Lipton once brought back a barrel of water from Hamburg to find the right blend for it. The Customs officials would not believe that the barrel contained only water. I don't suppose this tea was blended specially for Turkish water. Tea never tastes as well out of England."

But it did taste very well, and she had prepared Marmite sandwiches and produced a plum and sultana cake as a contrast to the over-sweet, sticky almond and sugar cakes of the Levant. And the logs glowed in the grate and music played softly from the gramophone; their talk ceased; not for many months had she felt so at one with anyone. She shook herself. She stood up. "I'll clear this away. No, don't you bother. I won't wash up. Choose some records while I tidy up. We'll have a little music, then a whisky. You aren't in any hurry, are you?"

"I'm not in any hurry."

Nor was she. She had asked Kitty not to return too early. She leant against the settee, her back propped with cushions. She watched the expression of his face change as the music ebbed and flowed. Once again under the impact of the music, a spiritual expression came into his face. He was not handsome, but he was beautiful at such a moment. It was just as it had been at the earlier meeting, except that the moment's magic was intensified by the change in his position. She had thought of him as her victim then; he was now her prisoner though he did not know it. That indeed was a large part of his fascination for her. He did not know what cords she had fastened round him, cords that would tighten in his absence. There was no escape for him, no escape from her.

The record finished. "I'll get your whisky now," she said. On her return from the kitchen she sat beside him.

"Are you excited about going back to Beirut?" she asked.

"Not very."

"You'll be glad to see your girl friend, won't you?"

"I haven't a girl friend."

"What, a young man like you? And I'm told that the girls in Beirut are very pretty. They are very pretty, aren't they?"

"They are all right."

"No girl friend, though?"

"No girl friend."

"Because you are faithful to your girl friend here."

"I have no girl friend here."

"Then where is your girl friend?"

"I have no girl friend anywhere."

She raised her eyebrows in mock astonishment. She was enjoying this teasing of him in the same way, so she suspected, that an experienced man would enjoy teasing an inexperienced girl. He's actually blushing, she thought. Yes, he is.

"Haven't you ever been in love?" she asked.

He shook his head.

"But you find girls attractive?"

"Oh, yes."

"What kinds of girls do you find attractive? Dark, fair, thin, plump?"

He laughed, a little nervously. "I have not thought about it."

"Are you sure you haven't?"

Again he laughed, that same nervous laugh.

"If you haven't, they have," she said.

"They? Who do you mean?"

"The girls."

"What girls?"

"That's what I'm wondering. Which girls you attract. It's a curious thing, so I've been told, that very often very young girls don't like young men. They prefer older men, men of experience who can put them at their ease. It's vice versa, so they say; young men prefer women with experience. Is that true in your case? Do you like married women?"

Again he shook his head. He looked awkward, yet at the same time he seemed to be enjoying it as though he were being tickled.

"I think I can guess the kind of girl you'd like, who'd be right for you; a girl about five years older who's had some experience. That's what you need. Shall I tell you what I'm going to do, when you come back. . . . You are coming back, aren't you?"

"Yes, I'm coming back."

"I can be much more help to you than Ahmed could have ever been. But that's not the only reason, is it, that you'll be coming back?"

"That's not the only reason."

"I wouldn't be at all happy if it were; I'd be very hurt. But you will come back. I know you will, and when you do I'll have a party and ask two or three of the kinds of girl I think you'd like, about twenty-three to twenty-six, who've been about. There are quite a number of them in the various Ministries; and then you can see which you'd prefer. The only trouble is," she paused and her eyes were twinkling, "the trouble is that I might get jealous. I've a suspicion I could use you for myself."

She saw, at that moment, a look in his eyes that was partly anticipation, partly fear: the kind of expression that a mature man might see in a young girl's eyes when he first approaches her; a girl who is terrified of what may transpire, but who will never forgive him now if he draws back.

"Yes," she repeated. "I'm very sure I should be jealous." She swung round off the low round cushion and knelt on it. She was higher than he was now, and she looked down on him. It gave her a heady sense of power. His eyes were shining. She lowered her face slowly over his, let her mouth rest on his; gently at first, then with a strengthening, deepening pressure. She let her lips open slightly, let the tip of her tongue slide between them. She lingered, then drew back her head. "He'll never forget this," she told herself. "Never, never, never."

†

The party to welcome Aziz's return was fixed for seven o'clock. It would go on till ten to accommodate those who worked late in offices. Reid and Farrar agreed to go there early. Reid had a dinner date afterwards with Diana.

"I'll be able to give you a first hand report," he told her.

"Do that," she said.

Reid was curious to see whether he would be able to detect any difference in Aziz. Surely there would be some signs of change. But to his surprise on the surface Aziz was unaltered. He was as silent and detached as ever. He made no effort to do more than acknowledge congratulations. The only obvious change in him was superficial; he had exchanged his usual heavy black winter suit for a light grey summer one. It did not suit him. Black went better with his mournful countenance. Reid waited till the press of guests had thinned.

"Congratulations. It must be a relief," he said.

"It is."

"Are you glad to be back?"

"In most ways, yes."

"Did it seem strange being in a country that was not at war?"

"There's not all that difference. Istanbul is full of uniforms."

"But isn't there a different tension in the air? The men here who are in uniform may be in action any day."

"There's the same tension when you've a military dictator, and Turkey may be in the war at any moment."

"How do your friends there think the war is going?"

"It will be a long war they say."

"But they have no doubt as to the result, I hope?"

Aziz shrugged. "They are not sure. They guessed wrong in the first war. Some of them think that Japan and America cancel each other out, that Russia might make a separate peace, which would leave Germany in control of Europe."

"Do many Turks think that?"

"Several do."

"You don't yourself, I hope?"

"I am not qualified to judge."

Reid hesitated. It would be interesting in the light of that admission to read the reports that he sent up on the blank spaces of the *Palestine Post*. He looked at Aziz more closely; perhaps there was a change in him after all, though not the kind of change he had expected. There was a kind of glow about him. I wonder, he thought, I wonder.

"Is your heart still moving on an even keel?" he asked.

For a moment Aziz looked puzzled, then remembering their last talk, blushed. Reid laughed. "I don't believe it is. You remember the prophecy I made?"

Aziz's blush deepened. "Your prophecy has not been fulfilled."

"But is it unfulfilled?"

Aziz smiled, but did not answer, and at that moment Madame Amin bustled up. "Aziz, dear, the Commandant has just arrived. You remember who he is, don't you?"

Reid moved away. "I've no doubt," he said to Diana afterwards, "that he is at least half in love."

They were dining in Sa'ad's. It was their favourite restaurant. They liked its privacy; they liked its food; they liked the fact that it was more patronised by Lebanese than French and British. "It's curious, isn't it, that we should be so excited about what he has been doing in connection with our operation, but that to himself this operation may be far less important than this girl, whoever she may be. You would expect a young man who has been exposed to such a shock to have a look of strain or guilt. Instead of that there's an inner glow about him, because he's met a pretty girl."

She laughed. "Perhaps the shock wasn't so serious to him after all; perhaps he is rather glad to be working for the Germans. Perhaps he considers he has had a lucky break; he's being paid to do something that he's always wanted to. Have you thought of that?"

"Frankly, I hadn't."

"There are so many different slants on every situation."

"There are times when none of it seems real to me."

"Perhaps none of it is."

"The only thing that does seem real is you sitting across this table from me, holding your glass between your hands. And yet if I had been told thirty months ago that I should be here in the Middle East, working in the Secret Service, decoding cyphers, recruiting spies, sending messages in secret ink, all that which now seems so unreal would have seemed quite probable. Yet the one thing that is real, you sitting here, is the one thing I could not have imagined happening. It is so foreign from everything that I had pictured for myself."

She did not speak. She lifted the glass to her lips and sipped it slowly. Her eyes softened. Her silence was supremely eloquent. She evoked poetry in him. As he spoke, as his sentences took shape he had the sensation of swinging incense before a shrine. She seemed to be saying, "Yes, go on. Go on. Now is your chance of saying it. I am receptive, responsive, waiting to be wooed with words. The chance may not come again; I may not be in this mood again, with you."

He swung the censor higher.

"I could not have believed that anyone like you existed: you with your deep rich voice; you who are so tall but do not look tall, of whom I cannot think in terms of height, only in terms of beauty, of grace; the way you walk; the tones that come into your voice; the viols in your voice. You are like no one I have known; that I should meet you at all, that is a miracle, but that miracle of miracles you should be dining with me, and alone. I had no conception that. . . ." He checked. She had half closed her eyes. She lowered her glass and her lips parted, as though she were drinking in his words.

"All my life," he went on, "I've been giving lectures. Sentences build themselves for me as I'm talking, but I never believed that I could talk like this, that I could have this sense of being lost but found, of being drowned but salvaged; of losing all identity but at the same time being myself, completely, for the first time in my life. Every time I see you I feel I am seeing you for the first time; there is that same shock along my nerves and senses that I knew when I saw you standing at the head of the Mission stairs; everything is for the first time always; a new adventure, a new landscape, the opening of a porthole on a long dreamed island." He stopped and smiled. "Do you know that we've barely finished our soup; that this is our first glass of wine; that no man makes speeches till he has reached the coffee and liqueur?"

"That's what I've been told."

"I've broken all the rules, in fact."

"That's what you've done."

"You make one break rules, you know."

"That's what I've been told."

"You don't mind my breaking rules?"

"I'd have been furious with you if you hadn't."

He stopped again. Her eyes were dilated and very tender. "You are coming back with me, aren't you, afterwards?"

"That's why I've come here, isn't it?"

9

SPRING COMES SWIFTLY but gently to the Lebanon. Then suddenly the heat of summer falls: the hot, dry wind, the *Hamseen*, from the desert is followed by a clinging humid heat and the rich Beirutis hasten into the cool of the hills, into Aley and Brumana. On a May morning, with the fan whirring in the office, Reid studied the Amin Marun file. It had received a number of entries in recent weeks. The first folio contained an account of the first Monday in Tanio's café. Chessman had brought down a marked copy of the *Palestine Post*. The paper was brought to the Beirut office. It contained a special enquiry about Australians. Had any of them been observed recently? The paper was delivered by a friend of Abdul Hamid. It was intended that the paper should be brought on each occasion by a different bearer. Aziz was instructed to deliver his reply in the Bassoul Café on the following Thursday. He reported that he had seen a number of men in uniform wearing Australian hats, but that he did not think they were fighting troops. He thought they were working on the railway that was being constructed from the Turkish frontier to Cairo. He considered that the Lebanese did not consider the British armies in the Western Desert were strong enough to resist Rommel. They were wondering what their own position would be if the canal were to be captured. They believed that the British and French would evacuate the seaboard and set up a defence line on the Tigris, maintaining contact through Basra with Persia and the Russian front. Farrar had pencilled on the folio, "I wish the Germans would ask him for the sources of his information. I wonder if he made this up."

The next folio was a report from Fadhil. "Aziz brought me the following list of exports to Germany from Turkey. I have compared the list with the one supplied by Istanbul. The two lists are identical. Aziz is reliable to the extent that he does not tamper with material. He might have held back some of the information that he was given so that he could use it on a subsequent occasion. His account of his experiences with Aunt Mildred tallied with the account that we had already received. He assumed that I knew of Ismail's sudden attack of panic, but not that there had been an exchange of packets and that Ahmed had received a box of toilet water by hand of Eve Parish, nor that I knew that Eve had promised to supply him with information. He told me about this and suggested that he should supply me with information through Eve. I asked him how he was going to collect this information. He told me that he would take my enquiries by hand on his next visit. I asked him when that would be. As soon as he could manage it, he said. I objected that that might be several weeks, since he could not go up to Istanbul till the end of the next term at the A.U.B. He knew that, he said, but it would be worth my while to wait because the information that he got from this British source would be much superior to anything that he could get from any of his own friends. I asked him why he did not correspond in secret ink. He told me that it was too risky. I pooh-poohed this nervousness. He was being more nervous than the wretched Ismail. What danger could there be? I was aware that he had every reason to be nervous of the Turkish Censorship, since it had, so he believed, detected his correspondence with Ahmed. But he did not know that I knew this. I pressed the point. I was very anxious to see whether he would betray his real cause for being cautious about the censorship. I mocked him, I told him he was a coward. I hoped to irritate him into explaining his reasons in self defence. He did not, however. He remained surly and impassive. Yes, he agreed, he probably was a coward. He could not help it, that was the way he was. He adopted a take it or leave it attitude. I recognized that I was much less important to him now that he was in the pay of the Germans. I tried to catch him out on this point, to force him into an admission that he did not care whether he worked for me or not.

'Listen,' I said. 'These gramophone records are important to you.' He said that of course they were. 'Well, don't you realise that I can't continue to supply you with them unless you are giving me in return the information I require? It is a matter of exchange.' He realised that, he said. 'Don't you realise,' I went on, 'that in business you have to have your facts on the hour? Situations are fluid. The market changes from one day to the next. If there are going to be these gaps I shall be in the dark. This list is very valuable. I do not question that, but it may be out of date within a month. Come now, won't you think it over? When you go up in August, won't you take up those writing inks and arrange a regular system of communication in the way that we had planned with Ahmed?'

"But I could not draw him. He said that he was sorry, that this was the best that he could do. The risk was too great. He insisted that the information he was getting from this new source was so authentic that it was well worth my while to wait for it. It would have been impossible for me to suspect from his manner that anything unexpected had happened to him in Istanbul. He appeared to have changed his mind in view of Ismail's sudden panic and the advice he had received from Eve. My conclusion is that he is a pretty cool operator."

The next folio was a report by Farrar:

"I have decided to keep a close watch on Aziz. He has an invitation to drop in to the flat whenever he likes, which is convenient for him, as the University is close. He often has an hour to spare and does not want to go back home. He is very fond of the Prof. and we have a number of good records. He has come to think of us as a second home. I have been experimenting as to his quickness to pick up significance of gossip. The other day, for example, I said to the Prof. that we should invite Major Strudwick to dinner in a day or two. Strudwick is a G.2 in the 7th Australian Division. He was bound to be moving soon, I said; they wouldn't keep such fine fighting troops on garrison duty when there was need of them in the Western Desert. I did not stress the point at all, but Aziz caught on to it. In the next *Palestine Post* instalment he reported a rumour that the Australian Division was to be shortly sent to the Western Desert. As far as I know no such rumour is current in Beirut. It is possible that Aziz might be useful in a deception scheme. But one cannot be certain that he will get the nuance of our conversation; moreover, we have to be on our guard against careless talk.

"I am in search of a direct double agent whom Aziz can introduce to the Germans. It is not easy to find one; we cannot approach a Frenchman; that would cause difficulties with our French colleagues. Moreover, we could not trust a Frenchman. He would almost certainly be acting for some group of Frenchmen. A Lebanese is the obvious choice, but not through Aziz's mediation. They would be awkward with each other. My inclination is an Armenian. Aziz would not think of him as a compatriot. Armenians are children of no-man's land. Their hand is with everyone's and against everyone's. They are mercenary; they have to be. They live by their wits. I have my eye on a cousin of Annabelle K's—Alexis Belorian. He is twenty-three years old. He has just graduated from the A.U.B. He is studying law. His parents are rich. I am asking Abdul Hamid to furnish a report on him. He is handsome, dark, dapper, very much a ladies' man, a *coureur des jupes*. Might be just the man for us."

Folio 15 was a report by Abdul Hamid:

"Alexis is popular; generous, a spendthrift. He is having a romance with the thirty-four year old wife of an elderly merchant, I will call her Freida, who contributes to his support. He is also involved with a dancer at the Kit-Kat, who must be exceedingly expensive. Freida knows about the dancer and is intensely jealous. Alexis has persuaded her that it is to her advantage that he should have this public liaison. It disarms suspicion. Her husband's jealousy can thus be kept asleep. Alexis is clever; he got a good degree at the A.U.B. He is ambitious and he is industrious, but he is burning the candle at both ends. He is reputed to be unscrupulous, but not blatantly dishonest. He has no political affiliations but he has probably an hereditary hatred of the Turks. He has no respect for the law, but he would do almost anything for money."

Folio 16. A report from Farrar:

"I have asked Annabelle about Alexis. He has for her the attrac-

163

tion of the bad sheep of the family. She is glad that she is not too closely related to him, but is rather proud that he is a relative. He is often discussed by people who do not know that there is a relationship. He is always discussed with raised eyebrows. Annabelle encourages them to say the worst they know; then when they have been thoroughly disapproving she will say: 'I can't deny the half of what you say, but there is another side to him. I see the other side because he is a rather distant cousin. There's a great deal that's very sound about him. One day he'll marry a nice girl and settle down.' "

In the margin Farrar had pencilled: "Is it not extraordinary how women continue to believe that a man has only to marry to reform? They fall in love with a man because he's different, then they try to make him like everybody else. They then grumble either because he stays himself or because he is no longer the man they fell in love with."

Folio 17 was also a report from Farrar:

"I suggested to Annabelle that she should bring round Alexis as a chaperone instead of Jacques. She twinkled. 'I will bring Alexis as well as Jacques, but do you think Alexis could be trusted to stay with me if he saw a pretty girl across the room?'

" 'Could we not run that risk?'

" 'Now, Nigel, you are no better than Alexis.'

"She brought Alexis round. It was not the first time that I had met him, by any means, but it was the first time I had had an opportunity of a real talk with him. He is certainly an amusing creature, with a cosmopolitan attitude, although he has not travelled much. He is noticeably but not ostentatiously well dressed. He is slight, slim, moustached, with a pale complexion. His hair is thick and has a wave in it. He gesticulates as he talks. He has a highly masculine manner. He talks a lot but is prepared to listen. I asked him about the Dashnaks, a secret society organised to establish an Armenian state. I told him that I had read a reference to it in one of Michael Arlen's stories and also in one of William Saroyan's. I supposed that he must have met a certain number of them. He laughed. 'I used to hear them talking together when I was a boy. They split into two groups, you know, in the way that the Russian emigrés did. They had Bolsheviks and Mensheviks. We had Dashnaks and Henshaks.' I asked if they really amounted to anything. He shrugged. 'I suppose they had a chance after the Russian revolution, but even if they had set up on their own they'd have been absorbed in one of the Soviet republics. They wouldn't have been any better off.'

" 'What was their programme, then?' I asked.

" 'They had an idea that the White Russians would drive out the Bolsheviks. What a hope.'

" 'Do you know what's happened to them now?' I asked.

" 'I've no idea.'

"I let the matter drop. I knew that the Dashnaks had had their headquarters in Paris and that when the Germans had occupied Paris their files and records had been taken over. I decided to bring this point up later when, if ever, we discussed solid business. I instructed Abdul Hamid to approach Alexis on our behalf. He was to be asked, I explained, whether he would be prepared to assist the Allies in the propaganda field; it would be secret work, but it would not be dangerous. It would involve trips to Istanbul, which we would finance. He would receive reasonable recompense for his co-operation."

Folio 18 was from Abdul Hamid:

"I interviewed Alexis. He is the adventurous type of playboy. He is ready to engage in anything lively and lucrative that is not criminal. He has no political affiliations. He is the buccaneer type." In the margin Farrar had pencilled, "And that is the boy for cloak and dagger."

Folio 19 recorded that a meeting had been arranged in the apartment in Rue Jeanne D'Arc for the 12th April.

Reid closed the file and carried it down the passage to Diana. He found her reading a February copy of *The Times*.

"Do you remember," she said, "that story of Maugham's about the man in the jungle who insisted on having a fresh copy of *The Times* by his breakfast table every morning? They arrived in a batch, numbered, once a month, and he rationed himself to one a day. Ordinarily he did not mind a paper being three weeks old because he did not know what had been happening in the meantime. But he found it very tantalising during the war; he would read about the beginning of a battle, and there under that pile, would be the paper that could have told him how it had turned out. He had the strength of character to control his impatience. We're in a different position. We get *The Times* five weeks late, but we know what has happened. I'm reading a leader about the impregnability of Rangoon."

She was alone; he sat on her desk swinging his leg over its side.

"Do you think," he said, "that in six weeks' time we shall be evacuees in Malta, reading a bland editorial about the loyal Arab states?"

"It gives a zest to the good times we're having now."

"I don't need any added zest."

†

The meeting with Alexis took place in Reid's flat, instead of in the Rue Jeanne D'Arc.

"We'll centre this operation here," said Farrar. "The more centres that we have the better. Scatter ourselves, that's the programme, and we don't want Alexis to associate us with the M.E.S.C. Not yet, anyhow."

The meeting was fixed for six o'clock. Alexis was to be brought by Abdul Hamid. Farrar and Reid were to arrive there earlier and independently.

"We don't want to be seen together in this part of town," said Farrar. It was the first time that Farrar had been inside Reid's flat. He looked round him approvingly.

"You've made yourself comfortable in here," he said. He noted the rugs, the pictures and the screen that Reid had hired.

"It doesn't look like a bedroom. Yet it looks as though the stage has been set for an assignation. Prof, I've an idea that you're one of those still waters that run deep."

He winked. Reid wondered if Farrar had any idea how much he and Diana were seeing of each other. Farrar had made no reference to it, but then he was not the kind of man who would.

The doorbell rang. "Now let's see if he starts," said Farrar. "It'll be a test of his self control."

Reid opened the door. The stairway was dark, and Alexis blinked as he came into the lighted room. Then he raised his eyebrows. "This is certainly a pleasure that I did not expect."

"I'm glad it is a pleasure," Farrar said.

"It is not only a pleasure, it is a relief. I prefer to do business with those whom I can trust."

He was completely calm. He did not wait to be offered a seat; nor did he take the nearest one. He looked round, decided which would be the most comfortable and brought it forward. Abdul Hamid looked enquiringly at Farrar. Farrar nodded. "That'll be

166

all, thank you." As the door closed, Alexis looked round him brightly.

"Now, what is all this about?" he said.

Farrar smiled. "You had no idea that you would be meeting the Professor and myself?"

"How could I have?"

"You did not know we worked in the same office?"

"I only knew that you were friends."

"What did you think we did?"

"I hadn't thought about it."

"Surely your cousin Annabelle must have told you something?"

"I did not ask her; was there any reason why I should?"

"There was no reason, you are very right. I only asked you because I was curious to know how much is known about us. I told your cousin that I was engaged in propaganda. I am. We both are. But propaganda has many angles. Some of it is public. Some of it is obscure. The most effective propaganda is that which is not presented as propaganda. You know, for instance, that a full page advertisement of a new brand of soap is less important than a paragraph in the news section of a paper stating that a well-known personality uses it. Again, there are certain angles of propaganda that are so discreet that it becomes a branch of the secret service. Part of my work, of our work, I should say, consists in spreading rumours. It is in that connection that we want your assistance. You told Abdul Hamid that you would be prepared to help us."

"Under certain conditions."

"Exactly; and very sensible conditions. It must not be criminal, it must be lively and it must be lucrative. We can certainly meet those conditions; and there is another thing, too, which I can promise; it will not be dangerous. We want you to present yourself to the Germans in Istanbul as a man who wants Germany to win the war and is anxious to help them by sending information about movements of troops, and about political and social trends. Some of the information that you will send up will be accurate; a part of it will be only fairly accurate. We have to give them a certain amount of correct information so that they will believe the inaccurate information, that we shall give them from time to time. As you know, we shall be soon opening a second front; we do not know where, we do not know when. It is very important that we should mislead the Germans as to our intentions. If they do not know where the blow or blows will fall, they will have to guard every vulnerable point. If they think we have more forces here than we actually have they will anticipate an attack across the Turkish frontier or through the Balkans and will have to maintain a large body of troops in this theatre. In consequence the places where the attack will fall will be thinly held. On the other hand, if we do decide to attack through Turkey, it is important that the Germans should not know that we are massing a large body of troops; they must not suspect that attack; we want the Turkish frontier to be thinly held. The Germans must be misled. We are hoping that you will help us to mislead them."

"But how shall I contact the Germans?"

"Leave that to us. We will lead the Germans to believe that you are a man who would be ready to help them. They will contact you when you are in Istanbul, and arrange for you to send them answers to the questions that they send you; they will also give you instructions as to the kind of information they require. We will give you the reports that we want sent up there."

"But how are you going to lead the Germans to expect that of me?"

"That is what I am going to explain. The Germans have their agents in Beirut who are looking for anti-British Lebanese. We know who some of them are. It is not necessary for you to know who they are; in fact it will be much better for you not to know. But we are going to arrange for you to meet some of them. We will warn you of the occasions when they will be present. I shall then want you to pose as being anti-British. There is every reason for an Armenian to be anti-British. The British did not intervene during the Armenian massacres at the end of the nineteenth century. Britain has always been pro-Turkish. The Turks consider that they made a great mistake in fighting on the German side in the last war. It cost them their empire. As an Armenian you could easily feel that you are likely to profit by a German victory, particularly as this involves a defeat of the Russians. I gather you did not know this, but the Germans have decided to sponsor the Dashnaks. They took over all the Dashnak records when they captured Paris. They had approached the leaders of the movement. They have promised them that after the war they will establish an independent Armenian state, at the expense of Russia. No such promise could be made by Britain. She is Russia's ally. An Armenian has every reason to be pro-German. Have any of your family been Dashnaks?"

"Some of them must have been."

"Then find out which of them have. Find out any details that you can. Concentrate on the Dashnaks; they are your reason for being pro-German. It is our belief that if you indulge during the next few weeks in a certain amount of anti-British talk you will find yourself approached by a German agent, either here or on your next visit to Istanbul."

"But you can't expect me suddenly to become violently political when all my life I have been saying that politics were for the professional politician."

"You have not got to be violent. You have only to indulge in this kind of talk on special occasions. We will tell you when."

"It all seems improbable to me."

"So does everything else in this kind of work. We are all of us working in the dark, but sometimes we get glimpses of the light."

"But mightn't I get into trouble with the authorities here if they found I was working for the Germans? I've always read that the spy is always disowned by his own people if he gets into trouble."

"I have thought of that. I will give you a document, stating that you are doing secret work for the British Government. Keep that document in a strong box and you will be safe."

"That sounds fair enough. And what about my salary?"

Farrar smiled. "To some extent payment is by results. You will have to trust us. But I am ready to make you an advance of one thousand Syrian pounds. I do not think that you will find we are ungenerous. I have the money ready for you in notes, and here is a receipt, a matter of book-keeping. And don't, by the way, attempt to correspond with us. We will find ways of reaching you. I know we can rely on your discretion. It is very much in your own interests after all."

When he had left Reid looked enquiringly at Farrar. "I know that I'm only a new boy in this game, but it seems to me that we've told our new friend too much."

"How could he do us damage?"

"He could doublecross us with the Germans."

"What good would that do him? He is in this for money. He wouldn't get any more money that way. If he were a stout patriot that would be another matter. He might change his allegiance.

But he is a child of no-man's land. And that receipt gives us a whip hold over him. He is not breaking any laws, but he would be a watched man in the Lebanon if the police ever learnt that he had been employed by us. We're batting on a pretty wicket."

"The plot thickens," was Eve's comment when the report of this meeting reached her. It excited her, but at the same time it raised qualms. Aziz was getting in very deep. She felt again imperiously the need to cherish him, to make amends. The new term ended in early June, but he might not come back here right away. Istanbul was intolerably hot in the summer. He might prefer to stay on in the Lebanon, going back into the cool of the hills, to Aley or Brumana. The next term did not start until October. He might wait until September. It was a long time to wait.

The green light was showing over Sedgwick's door. She handed him the file. "From Beirut," she said. He nodded, pointed to the in-tray.

"I'll take that when I've an hour clear," he said. "It'll need thinking over." She hesitated. He raised his eyebrows interrogatively. "Yes?" he said.

"I was wondering. Perhaps this isn't the right way to bring it up, but I've been abroad solidly for two years now."

"Oh, yes, well, so you have . . . I suppose," he deliberated. "I should hate to lose you. You're the most valuable member of the staff, to me at least. And you know what is going on; it takes three months to train a secretary. But you are entitled to repatriation. . . ."

"Oh, no, I don't mean that. I like it here."

"In that case. . . ." He paused, that familiar look of interrogation in his eyebrows.

"I like it here," she said. "The last thing I want is to leave this office, but I was wondering . . . you see, I haven't had a holiday in all this time. If I could have a little local leave. . . ."

The look of relief on Sedgwick's face was highly flattering to her vanity.

"But of course, of course, I should have thought of it before. Careless of me. I get so wrapped up in our work here that I forget that my staff have personal problems. Where would you like to go: Ismir, Bursa?"

"I thought Beirut."

"Why not? It's very pleasant at this time of year. The real heat

170

comes later. We can call it a liaison visit, so that you won't have to pay your fare; and the office there can find you accommodation. You could actually turn the trip to very good account. It's always easier to do business with somebody one knows. When you get their letters, you can read between the lines. And you can see that Turk of yours at the same time."

Was there a twinkle in Sedgwick's eyes when he said that? If there was it was a fleeting one. He looked a stuffed shirt, but he had a sense of humour.

When the news reached Beirut, Farrar said to Reid, "Prof, this is a good chance for you to take a breather. Why don't you and Diana drive up to Aleppo and meet her?"

There was no flicker of a smile when he said that. He might be a fine poker player, the Professor thought. He must know. Yet there's never any suggestion in his manner.

†

Eve's heart was beating fast as Diana drove over the beach road, south of Tripoli. In two hours she would be in Beirut. It would be four o'clock; she would ring Aziz up at five. In three hours she would hear his voice. She had not warned him that she was coming. She wanted to take him off his guard, to hear the tone of his voice when he heard hers. There had been no correspondence. They had both kept to their promise. How much had he been thinking about her? Had he been thinking about her at all? Had she exaggerated the importance of the episode? Had it meant anything to him at all? Had it only meant so much to her because of this long restraint, because of the barriers that she had built round herself? For the very reason that she was not like Kitty, she might be seeing the whole episode out of all proportion.

So she argued with herself, preparing herself for disappointment, but she could not believe that for him she had been just an episode. She kept looking at her wristwatch. In one hundred and fifty minutes I shall know; in a hundred and thirty minutes; in ninety-seven minutes. But don't fool yourself, she said. In ninety minutes this girlish dream of yours will have exploded. You'll be back where you started; an inexperienced girl who holds men off because she's been cherishing a girl's dream of the ideal; a girl who's going to shrivel into an old maid if she isn't careful. So she communed to herself as the car swung down the winding road and she made conversation with Diana and the Prof.

In seventy minutes you'll know; in sixty-three minutes you'll know. But she could not still the beating of her heart. She could not believe that she was not on the brink of the most decisive hours of her life. A sense of acute premonition struck her.

Diana unlocked the door of her flat; Eve looked about her. It had a large central room on the Turkish style, with rooms opening off it. It was conventionally furnished with rugs, and a drawing room suite; on the walls were posters supplied by the British Council. There was nothing personal about it. Eve drew a long, slow breath into her lungs. "My dreams are going to live in this room for a long time," she thought.

"I share this room with a girl who works with the Spears Ambulance Unit," Diana was saying. "She keeps odd hours. I never know when to expect her. But she'll be away for the next three days; that I do know."

Eve's room was even more impersonal than the flat itself. It was a room in which a succession of visitors had stayed for a night, two nights, for a week. They had left nothing behind them except a scrubbed and polished air, as though each young woman had been resolved to leave it a little more tidy than she had found it. Eve was glad that she had brought some photographs and one or two knick-knacks: a small ivory elephant, two silver Hindu gods, a Dresden shepherdess. She would soon feel at home here.

"I expect that you'll be glad of an opportunity to unpack and bathe and rest," Diana was saying. "I have to go to my office, but I'll be back at eight. The Prof. is taking us out to dinner at the French Officers' Club. You'll see the world and his wife there."

Eve drew into her lungs, a long, slow breath of relief, as Diana closed the door. At last, at last. There was the telephone. In seven minutes now.

She was resolved not to call him up till five. That was the time she had decided during the long drive south. Five o'clock, she had told herself. She made a rendezvous with destiny at five o'clock. She must keep her pact. She looked up the Amin Marun number. She pencilled it on the pad. She sat beside the telephone, her eyes upon her wristwatch; first on the minute hand, then on the second hand. Who could have thought a minute could take so long;

thirty, forty, fifty, fifty-five, at last, the sixty. She lifted the receiver, dialed.

There was hardly a second's interval between the evenly-spaced buzzing, the click of a raised receiver and a voice answering in French. The answer came so quickly that she was not ready with her reply. Often though she had rehearsed the tone in which she would say in English, "Good afternoon, Aziz, guess who this is," the words stuck in her throat. Once again the voice came in French. "I am listening. Who speaks?" She opened her mouth. But she could not fill the role, casual, light-hearted, detached, affectionate, for which she had cast herself.

"Aziz," she cried. "It's Eve," with her voice risen sharply.

"Eve." His voice had dropped, and there was warmth in it, an excited warmth she had not heard before. "Where are you calling from?"

"Here, Beirut."

"Where in Beirut?"

She gave him the address. "When did you arrive?"

"Twenty-five minutes ago."

"Oh, Eve, Eve."

He stopped; there was a silence that was over-charged with happiness. Then they both started, simultaneously; and both stopped simultaneously. There was another pause.

"You first," she said.

"But I can't think what to say."

"I'll wait till you make up your mind," and she was laughing now.

"What are you doing here?" he asked.

"I've come on leave."

"For how long?"

"Two weeks."

"Are you going to be very busy?"

"That depends on you."

Once again she was in the saddle, controlled, teasing him, sure of herself. "I want to see Beirut," she said, "and I don't want to be shown it by my compatriots. I want to go to the amusing little places, where the English are shy of going and eat the kind of food that they distrust. And I want to swim, and I want to go to Balbaak; and I want to hear your new records. So I'll be very busy if you've got time to spare for me. Are you working very hard?"

"Not very hard."

"Shouldn't you be?"

"I'll work after you go back."

"But haven't you got to go to lectures?"

"It isn't necessary."

"Then we'll be able to bathe tomorrow?"

"Of course."

"And lunch after we've bathed?"

"Of course."

"And then come back here and listen to some music?"

"Where's here?"

"A flat that I've been lent; with two other English girls who work here. They're out all day. They won't be in our way. Will you call for me here, tomorrow?"

And that was that, she thought. She had a sense of complete relief. The trouble that had fretted her for so long was now resolved. How right she had been to wait. "And fill the cup that is so soon to break with richer wine than they."

Eve had asked Diana where to swim. "Is your beau rich?" Diana asked.

"I wouldn't think so."

"Then I'd go to the Bain Militaire."

"Can my Turkish friend go there?"

"You can as a British official. Take him as your guest."

The Bain Militaire lay two-thirds of a mile along the coast in a small bay that had been appropriated by the military. Two long arms of rock contained a narrow stretch of waveless water that washed languidly against a stretch of sand. There were bathing cabins and beach umbrellas and a floating raft, and just before the bay opened into the sea there were steps fixed into the rocks and a high diving board. Halfway up the cliff there was an open air restaurant where they served omelettes and *filet mignon*. On the crest of the cliff there was a succession of small fish restaurants. There was a bar by the bathing strip and many of the officers brought sandwiches. On the rise of the hill behind, there was an old-world lighthouse painted blue and white, which had long since ceased to serve a useful purpose, though the red light flickered still. It seemed a piece of decoration like the barrage balloon that floated above the port.

Eve and Aziz swam out to the rocks where the bay ended. He was a stronger swimmer than she had expected; nor was he as thin as she had expected, he was lean and wiry. There was a medicine ball on the beach; she watched Aziz and a young Lebanese throw it back and forth. She noted how the muscles of his stomach tightened. They lay side by side together in the sand, feeling the sun beat against their shoulders. They did not talk together a great deal. There was no need. They were sure of one another. They were treading a one-way street.

She foresaw precisely what would happen. They would lunch later in the café restaurant on the cliffs; not a heavy lunch, a *filet mignon*, a salad and some cheese. They would divide a bottle of red wine. They would exchange casual gossip. They would feel drowsy. They would go back to the beach, stretch themselves and doze in the shade of an umbrella for half an hour, the sun would lower over the sea; a breeze would waken them. By the time they got back to the flat Diana would have left for her office. For three hours they would be alone. She would put a record on the gramophone. They would sit on the floor on cushions in the manner of the Orient; the music would weave its spell about them; they would turn to one another.

It would be the first time for both of them. She ought to be feeling frightened. But she wasn't, because he was so young. If it had been an Englishman of her own age she would have been, yes; on both sides there would have been awkwardness because each would have been worried by, would have brooded over, the fact of their inexperience. She had read so often, heard so often, that a young girl should be initiated by a mature experienced man: that was what she had pictured for herself, that would have been her destiny had there been no blackout; but there had been and that was that, and because she had been foiled then, because she had learnt during those following months to set a store by what Victorians had called "the giving of herself," she had been unable to accept the casual suggestions of the average predatory male. She had also a feeling, not exactly of shame but of embarrassment at the incredulous, almost contemptuous, tone that would have come into a man's voice, his "What, don't tell me you're a virgin; you, at twenty-three." Her vanity had shied at that. "I'll wait," she had thought, "till the right thing comes."

She had often laughed at herself, often had her moments of self doubt; particularly since she had shared a flat with Kitty. She had seen herself shrivelled, with those awkward movements of old maids who had allowed their body's suppleness to stiffen. But it had been worth it. She knew that now.

Aziz was lying on the sand, his face turned away from her. What a clean, smooth line that was, running broad from his shoulders, slimming to the waist, curving out over his hips, stretching out into the long, thin legs. She wanted to pass her hand slowly over it. "I will," she thought. "I will."

Yesterday as the car had bumped over the uneven mountain road, she had thought, "In ninety minutes' time . . . in seventy-three . . . in sixty." Now in a different context she repeated, "In an hour and a quarter's time, in three-quarters, in half an hour." She was going into this with her eyes open. She had no illusions about the nature of the experience that awaited her. She had received confidences, she had read those little books. She would get no pleasure from it; at least to start with. On the contrary she would be hurt, perhaps a lot. That did not matter. That was something to be borne. She would not wince. She would not make it difficult for him; her pain would be a cause of pride. It would give her a sense of power. He was younger than she was. He was feeling timid, but she was not. She was the initiator. She shook his shoulder. "Time we were going back," she said.

His long, shuddering gasps relaxed into a deep and steady breathing, but his heart was still thudding over hers. His head was buried in her shoulder. She opened her eyes. She loosened her hold about his neck. On his shoulder was a fleck of blood where her nails had cut him. She smiled. That had been as the supreme pain tore her. She had exulted then, matching his pain with hers. "You too," she had thought. "You too."

She had felt no pleasure, but an intense pride had engulfed her. This was what she had waited for. She was relieved of an intolerable burden; and his excitement, his cries, his broken sobs, the bounding and plunging of his body were the reward for those months of waiting. He would never forget this hour, ever. She intensified its delight for him; responsive to him, with her hands moving on his shoulders, her movements in tune with his, her voice breaking into sighs. It was worth the waiting; abundantly worth the waiting. How different it would have been if she had let some casual philanderer take her in his stride, to be remembered afterwards, if at all, as one more scalp upon a bedroom wall.

Slowly, exquisitely slowly, the moments of relaxation came. He turned over on his side, his head laid back among the cushions, his hands crossed behind his head. His face wore a transfigured look. That was her doing. She had revealed him to himself. He was in a trance. And he does not yet know the half of it, she thought. It will get better, it will go on getting better. I shall see to that. He was hers; hers to transform, hers to exalt.

But for that missed footstep in the blackout, it would have been Raymond's privilege to initiate her into the ritual of love; she would have responded to his technique. She would have been the violin on which he played the melody. She would have taken the impress of his tastes; that would have been her pride and happiness. At the same time those tastes in him, those predilections, would have been implanted there by her predecessors. She would have inherited their personalities. This was very different. Aziz would take her imprint, and because of her complete inexperience, no limit would be set upon the range of her adventurous curiosity. He was in her power, not she in his; it was heady knowledge.

She slid off the couch. "Don't move," she said. She put another record on the gramophone. She was thirsty. On the sideboard was a bottle of red wine that Diana had opened the night before. She filled a glass and took a long, slow sip. It warmed her blood. "You thirsty too?" she asked. He nodded. She filled the glass. Looking down at him, she had an inspiration. She took a long, deep sip and held the wine in her mouth. She knelt beside the couch, put down the glass, bent over him. As she lowered her head, he guessed her meaning, opening his lips as her mouth met them. Slowly she let the wine glide over his tongue and palate.

It was a halcyon time. The sun shone out of a pale blue sky; breezes blew from the north; the *Hamseen* was stagnant in the desert. They saw each other nearly all the time. They went on picnics. He borrowed a car and they drove out to the Cedars. It seemed unbelievable that there should be snow there still; that they should be skiing in mid-June; within half an hour of the tepid Mediterranean. But then so much seemed unbelievable in the Lebanon, "the land of milk and honey" that had beckoned the prisoners out of Egypt.

Most evenings they would take coffee or an aperitif on the terrace of the St. Georges. It was hard to believe that such a cosmopolitan playground could be flourishing in wartime. In one way the war seemed further off here than it had in Turkey. Yet the Lebanon was actually the back area of a battle zone. The Legation was heavily guarded with barbed wire against an enemy commando raid. You could hear the boom of guns in the Mediterranean. The streets were filled with men in uniform.

There were other reminders of war. One morning Aziz said, "I've got another list of questions that I'd be grateful if you'd answer for me."

"You'll have to come up to Istanbul to get the answers."

"I know."

"How soon will you come?"

"My term ends in June."

"It is very hot in Istanbul in July."

"I know that well."

"But you won't wait till the cool weather comes?"

"I shall not wait."

She asked him to introduce to her some of his Lebanese friends.

"I have some good friends who are Armenians. I will take you there."

It was to a tea party that he took her. Almost all the guests were in civilian clothes. Eve did not recognise any of them. A young, very self-confident man made a dead set at her. He was the kind of man she almost disliked. He was good looking, urbane, witty. But she resented the air of complacence that he exuded. He had no doubts about himself, he assumed that any woman would be flattered by his attention.

"I haven't seen you in Beirut before," he said.

"It is the first time that I have been here."

"Where do you come from?"

"England."

"I know that. You could cut your accent with a knife. What are you doing in the Middle East?"

"I'm in Istanbul, attached to the British Council."

"Then how do you come to be here?"

"Aziz brought me here."

"Aziz? And who might he be?"

"That young man, a Turk, talking to our hostess."

"Our hostess happens to be my cousin. Aziz, yet, I do know him now I come to think of it. Madame Amin's nephew. How long are you staying here?"

"Another ten days."

"Too little, and I suppose you are very busy here. Belle of the ball, no less. But I'll be coming up to Istanbul quite soon. I'll call you at the Council. You probably won't be so busy there. I didn't catch your name."

"Eve Parish."

"Miss or Mrs?"

"Miss."

"Fine. That's encouraging. Mine is Alexis Belorian. I'm not married either. You'll be hearing from me."

Having made his point, he moved away. Alexis Belorian, so that was who he was.

A little later in the afternoon she saw him talking to Aziz. Their talk appeared to be animated. She moved across to them. Alexis was talking with an arrogance which was almost insultingly detached. "I see your point; you are a Turk. You belong to a real race, as I do. But you have a country of your own, a diminished country, but still a country. I, on the other hand, have not. That is the difference between us. I am a child of no-man's land. I don't care who wins the war or loses it as long as it doesn't involve another Armenian massacre. And I would say, by and large, that I would sooner the Germans won; they're too busy massacring the Jews to bother about us. The English basically have always been on the Turkish side. The last war was a mistake, as far as both of them were concerned. The Turks and the English understand each other."

Aziz flushed angrily. "You have no right to say a thing like that, here in the Lebanon."

"And where have I a better right? What is the Lebanon's story but the record of one invasion after another? Everybody's overrun it; everybody always will overrun it. It has no defence. We shrug our shoulders and charge our conquerors one per cent. As an Armenian, I'm more Lebanese than the Lebanese. I don't really care who wins the war, but by and large I would as soon the Germans did, and I guess forty per cent of you in Turkey feel the same."

"How do you know what we in Turkey feel?"

"I often go there. As a matter of fact, I'll be going there in a month or so. I need to keep my eyes and my ears open." He moved away.

"I wonder who that was," Aziz said.

"I can tell you that: Alexis Belorian. He's a cousin of our hostess."

"Really, so that's who he is."

His eyes flashed. She knew what he was thinking. She was thrilled and tremulous. Yet at the same time she felt qualms, on his account. He was getting in very deep.

Once she visited the office in the M.E.S.C. building. It was curious to meet in the flesh men whom she knew so well on paper, particularly the Professor; Aziz had spoken of him so much. He was the one person for whom Aziz had seemed to have a genuine attachment. She felt a kinship with the Professor because he was the only one in the office who had understood and appreciated Aziz. He had found the clue to him. The love of music. It was ironic that that understanding, that appreciation, had been Aziz's undoing.

She wished that she could talk to the Professor about Aziz. She wondered whether he was inquisitive about her relationship with Aziz. Diana suspected something, she was very sure. Had Diana said anything in the office? Presumably she had; or at least she must have to the Professor. But even of that she could not be sure. Diana had great reserves. She was not a gossip. It might well be that she maintained her office standards of security in her private life; if, in their kind of racket, you could be said to have a private life.

On her official visit to the office she did not discuss Aziz or either of the operations in which he was involved. Her interview was personal and social. Farrar asked her about the clubs in Istanbul, about the cafés, how much night-life there was. Was it difficult to get certain foods? What about beer? He had had some Turkish beer in Iraq. It had cost five shillings a bottle and had tasted of straw. Did they ever meet the Germans? How did the Germans seem? Arrogant and boastful, he supposed. What about the Americans? Did she see anything of them? At the end of his questionnaire, Farrar said, "From what you tell me, I shall do my best to avoid being posted there. I fancy Ferdinand would wilt. Not enough of the fleshpots for his 'little heart of clay'."

She had no idea whether Aziz was apprehensive about his equivocal position. She never saw moody expressions on his face. He seemed tranquil, self-composed. She rarely discussed the war with him; they did not discuss anything very much. They listened to music; they swam, they picnicked, they motored into the country. They made love; but they did not talk about making love.

"Once," he said, "I told Professor Reid that music gave me a peace of mind that nothing else did because it was not precise; not to be explained in words; it brought you into harmony with the whole universe, but did not lay down rules about the universe. It took you to the core of understanding. You understood the mystery of existence. When I told him that, he said, 'There are those who say that that same paradise can be reached through love.'" He paused. "I think the Professor was right," he added.

They made love with an assiduous frenzy; she threw herself into love-making with an unslaked zest. She still had not experienced that acute, devastating ecstasy, that death in life, that utter apotheosis of every nerve cell of which she had read in books. But the very fact that she had not, quickened her absorption in this new pastime. She concentrated upon his response, not her own, devising new ways to heighten and prolong his pleasure. Though she was inexperienced in the practice of love, she was not ignorant of its theory. She had read and lingered over a number of the semimedical books that had appeared in the late 'thirties. Her ignorance had increased her interest in them. She had brooded salaciously over the delights she had denied herself. She had sometimes looked at girls like Kitty and had thought, "Has she done that; has she tried this?"

She recalled those moments. Now that she was freed from the stable, she would gallop with a loose rein over open country. She would admit no bridle. No device would be too bizarre. She rolled certain French words on her tongue as a wine taster rolls the wine round his mouth: *Outré* and *dévergondée*. They were self-expressive. Sometimes she felt that she was being ridden like a steed over open country; at others that she was herself in the saddle driving her mount towards the winning post. Had she been with a compatriot, or a man older than herself, an inherited modesty would have placed its check on her; but with this foreigner, this inexperienced foreigner, who was three years younger than herself, she could abandon herself to an utter shamelessness. The word "shame" did not exist for her. She studied his responses, learning what he liked most, what most excited him. Had she been concerned with her own pleasure she could not have been so solicitous of his. No other woman would be able to boast that she had taught him anything.

The knowledge that this thing between them could have no future gave it a special favour. They were divided by age, race, religion; sooner or later they would go their separate ways. She felt no jealousy on that account. On the contrary, she relished the prospect of his dissatisfaction with her successors. They would seem tepid after her. She wished that he could have an affair with Kitty, she could imagine Kitty's astonishment when Aziz said, "Ah, that little Eve, she was unique."

He did not use the big words of love; he could not express himself with ease. But she had little doubt of the hold that she had placed on him. There was no sense of tragedy about their parting. They were sure of one another. She joked over his promise to come up in August. "If you want any new records, you'll have to come up, won't you, to get the answers to those questions."

It had been arranged that Eve should be driven to catch the Taurus at Aleppo by the girl in the Spears unit who shared Diana's flat. Diana, at the last minute, decided to come too.

Jane was late. "I'm sorry," she said. "I made a night of it. What a relief not to be driving on real duty. Where duty is concerned, I'm the punctual soldier. But a routine drive like this." Her voice was a little blurred. There were lines under her eyes. As soon as they were on the main northern route to Tripoli, Diana offered to take over.

"That's very civil of you," Jane said. In ten minutes she was asleep.

High on a distant hill, they saw the Crak des Chevaliers, a forlorn relic of the Crusades.

"Do you want to make a detour?" Diana asked.

"Why bother?"

Diana laughed. "Yet think of all the tourists who in peace-time spend vast sums of money to visit the Levant, and include that castle as a 'must'. Can you picture us in ten years confessing why we've never seen Petra or Isfahan or the arch at Tesiphon. Simply because it is so easy, we don't bother."

They paused at Homs where the great water wheel turned slowly with its cranking chains. They had come south by this same road two weeks earlier, but then Eve had been too excited to notice what she was seeing. So much had happened to her during these two weeks; she was a different person because of what had happened to her in Beirut. Yet for Diana they had been two weeks like any other. Wasn't there a poem of Hardy's on those lines: "For them it had been an ordinary day"? Yet how could she tell if it had been an ordinary fortnight for Diana? Did she herself look any different? When she was back in Istanbul, would Kitty stop in her tracks? "Good heavens, kid!"

They reached Aleppo in the early evening. The train left next morning. They had booked in a Y.W.C.A. hostel.

"I'm packing in," said Jane. "I don't often get a chance of an early night like this."

"We, on the other hand, are going to do ourselves extremely well. This dinner's on the house," Diana said.

The hotel where they dined had been the headquarters of the Turkish General Staff during the first war. It had a stolid sober air. "And I suppose," Diana said, "that there are still officers on the German roster who dined here then; one or two of them a year ago, when the Free French campaign hung in the balance, must have thought, 'Maybe we'll be dining in there again next month.' Perhaps some of them actually did come back here with the Axis Armistice Commission."

The dining room was very empty. Aleppo was now a railhead, little more; a junction for the Taurus. Eve felt a little awkward sitting alone with Diana. It was the first time that they had been more than casually together. "There should be some real wine here," Diana said. There was: a Burgundy that was full and warm, like its own rich colour. Diana lifted her glass between her hands, breathing in its bouquet reverentially.

"Jane's missing something," Eve said.

Diana shrugged. "Poor Jane. Every time she has an evening free, she gets the way she was last night. She's resolved to stay out of mischief while her husband is behind barbed wire; she wants to be able to say to him at the end of the war, 'Darling, nothing happened, nothing.' But he's almost certainly resigned himself to something happening. He has already rehearsed his little speech, his 'Darling, let's forget everything that's happened in the last six years and start again where we left off.' Hundreds of husbands all over Europe are preparing to say just that. Jane's an ass not to accept the general pattern."

They continued to discuss Jane as the level of the wine sank below the label.

"It's difficult for her," Diana said. "She was crazy about her husband. They'd had a two weeks' honeymoon, and that was that. A perfect honeymoon. And when you get down to brass tacks, that means she liked love-making; suddenly to be deprived of it, just

183

when you'd started to enjoy it, and not to know when you'd have a chance of it again. . . . It's easier for a widow. She must be heart-broken, but she can say to herself, 'One day I'll get over this.' There's an interval and life begins again. She can look at a calen-dar and think, '1942. I should be a new self by then.' Jane can't do that. She's in a vacuum. She does not know when the war will end. It might last ten years. Think of those French officers in Napoleon's time."

Diana did most of the talking, and Eve, as she listened, won-dered as so many men had done, what Diana's own life was. She was so assured, so composed. She had no inhibitions, yet she never talked about herself. You felt that she had come to terms with the problems her life had brought her, her background, her height, her conflict with conformity.

"And Jane's a man's piece," she was continuing. "She attracts men and they attract her. She likes dancing. She's not a prude. She's only twenty-four. She's tempted, just as we all are, and there's the heat; and the men outnumbering the women twenty-five to one. Healthy, good-looking men who scarcely ever see a woman; ravenous young men. Think of the strain on her. No wonder she drinks like that."

"Is that why she drinks so much?"

"I've presumed it is: to damp down the fire. It's also a form of self-defence. She encourages the men to drink. When they want to leave a restaurant she'll say, 'Oh, no, let's stay a little longer. I'd like to see that cabaret again.' That means another brandy; then another; both get a little high. Then she can pull an act, become sentimental and self-pitying: maybe it's not an act. She is self-pitying and sentimental at that point of the evening. A man feels sorry for her and chivalrous; and won't take advantage of the wife of a brother officer who's behind barbed wire. It's all very noble and self-sacrificial, but it's also very silly and self-de-structive. She's ruining her health. Soon she'll be ruining her looks. That husband of hers won't be all that grateful when he's met by a plump, bloated spouse; even if she is virtuous. He'd prefer, after five celibate years, to be welcomed by a lively wanton."

"How often is she like the way she was last night?"

"Too often for it to be comfortable. She's careful on the nights before she's taking out an ambulance. But one day she'll get an unexpected summons. That's the danger. Her reactions may not be fast enough. She's all right at the moment, but she's on a slippery slope. I wish to heaven she'd fall in love with someone."

It was said in the most detached way possible, yet it was said with warmth. There was no note of the cold analyst. Once again Eve found herself wondering about Diana's own life.

"Does the Prof. know Jane well?"

"Fairly well. Why?"

"Mightn't he do for Jane? He's a married man. With someone to forget. They're in the same boat, in their separate ways."

Diana smiled. "Somehow I can't see the Prof. and Jane in that galley."

Their glasses were nearly empty. It was getting late. "Do you worry much about the future?" Eve asked.

"It doesn't do much good worrying, does it?"

"Doesn't it? I find I have to, or rather I can't help it. Before the war one could make decisions for one's self. Now decisions are made for one. One lives from day to day. One can't make any long term plans. At school I was told that I must discover what I wanted out of life and then try and see if I couldn't get it. One can't do that any longer, can one?"

Once again Diana laughed, a rich ironic laugh. "I never could," she said. "I've never known what I wanted out of life. I've only known what I didn't want, and I knew that from the start."

10

A FEW DAYS LATER Diana received a report from the official analyst. It contained the photostat of a message sent up to Istanbul by Aziz. "Strongly pro-German anti-British Armenian called Alexis Belorian visiting Istanbul shortly. Will try inform you E.T.A. Young man, expensive tastes, good family, believe easily bribed." She shrugged. She filed it, entered the cross reference in the other appropriate files, then brought it to Reid's office. "This is what you were hoping for."

He read it carefully, then whistled.

"The captain does hit the nail on the head. He'll be dancing round the office when he sees this."

"Is he alone now?" she asked.

"Yes."

"Let's break the good news to him together."

Rarely had Reid seen a man more overjoyed. Farrar jumped to his feet, and began to stride backwards and forwards like a panther.

"Wonderful. Wonderful. Better than I dared hope for, and so soon. I felt that we couldn't fail. Yet I couldn't trust myself to hope. We've made it. You know the Arab proverb. 'If the camel has got nose under the flap of the tent, the body will soon follow.' We can't miss. Alexis is the tops . . . all that Cole Porter stuff; the Coolidge dollar, Whistler's Mama. Poor Aziz. He'll get no reward for this. Let's mention him in our wills. Let's have him endowed. Let's open a Trust Fund in Geneva. We're sitting pretty. Man, are we sitting pretty. We'll have Alexis in Istanbul within a month. Not sooner. Give the Germans time to bait the trap. They are so slow and thorough. They'll have to make enquiries about Alexis. We must see that when he is there he'll be visiting people whom they can trust. We must give him a sound cover story, so that he'll have a water-tight alibi for going up there, and one that will give him an excuse for going up again. It won't be difficult. We must have a steady talk with Alexis. Then he must convince the Germans that he has sound sources of information. We must build him up a team of notional characters."

"What are notional characters?"

Farrar stared, pretending to be dumbfounded.

"You don't know what a notional character is?"

"How should I?"

"What did they teach you in Matlock? A notional character is . . . well, let me explain. This should have been lecture No. 5 in counterespionage. When you have a double agent who is working under your control, he has to have sources for his information. And he has to be able to convince his employers of the validity of those sources. For instance, he might say, 'I know an Irishman whose father was murdered by the Black and Tans. He hates the British. He drinks heavily. In his cups he is boastful, arrogant and anti-British. In his resentment against the British, he is often indiscreet. He is inclined to say things like, 'Would you believe what these miserable creatures are doing now,' and out comes a piece of secret information. Now that Irishman doesn't exist. He's a notional character. But he has to exist for the Germans; he has to be a real and convincing character. That is what we have to do for Alexis, build up a cast of notional characters so that he has as many sources of information as possible. He should be able to give naval, military and air force information. He should also be able to give some clues to diplomatic situations. He ought to have a pipeline on to the Spears Mission.

"What we have to do—and I'd say that this is the kind of thing you'd do far better than I—is to imagine the kind of person that a chap like Alexis would know. He's only twenty-three. We mustn't have him moving in too exalted circles. The thing has to be convincing; and his cast can grow. He must be devious. He must try to find the kind of person who can help him. It won't be too easy for us to create that cast, but let's remember this: the men who are going to read these messages are completely in the dark. Any news is welcome. I'll work on a character or two. You do the same. Then we'll compare notes and make a composite picture out of the two. There's no desperate hurry. He can't be expected to send back messages right away. He hasn't got his team lined up yet. Besides, he doesn't know yet what they want to know; or rather we don't know yet what they want to know from him.

"Do you remember that golfing cartoon of Reynolds', of the man in plus-fours sitting in his study, and his wife admonishing their children, 'Sh, darlings, don't go in there. Daddy's gone round in par and he wants to think about it.' That's how I feel; I want to sit and brood. The heavens are opening and I see new worlds. No one can tell where this day's work will end."

A soft reminiscent smile came into Eve's eyes as she opened the envelope that brought Beirut's report on the Armenian operation. It transported her to that halcyon fortnight. There had been times since her return when she had wondered if it had ever happened. Istanbul looked the same, her office looked the same, her flat looked the same. So did Kitty. So did Sedgwick, so did everyone in the office. The talk was just the same. And she supposed that to all of them she must have seemed the same. Sedgwick had invited her to his flat for an evening drink. "Now tell me everything about it," he said. "Who is doing what, and when, with whom and how?"

He had asked her about Farrar, about the Prof. Had she seen General Spears? How were relations between Spears and Catroux.

She answered as best she could, but she fancied he would have learnt more from a monthly intelligence summary. It was surprising how little she had to tell him. In Beirut, as in Istanbul, they were all leading their day-to-day life, caught up with their day-to-day problems that in two years would have been shelved or solved, and all of it was superficial because none of it had any root in the real life of the men and women who were conducting it. Their real lives were in England, waiting to be resumed when the war was over. She had nothing to tell him about the real life of the Lebanon. She could only talk about its restaurants and night clubs, the skiing at the Cedars, the bathing at the Bain Militaire and the cost of whisky, just as she had talked to Nigel Farrar about the hot spots of Istanbul; and whereas Farrar had said, "Pray God I'm never posted there," Sedgwick had said, "Clearly that's the place to go for leave."

Everything was the same and nobody noticed any difference in her. Kitty had been in a dither because two beaux had planned to arrive simultaneously for a leave; she did not want to lose either but neither was more than what she called a "passade"; "all right for when one's in the mood for them, but not worth having a nerve storm over." Kitty had been so full of her own problem that she had scarcely bothered to ask Eve about her leave. Had any of it really happened?

And then here was this report to remind her that it had. There was the report of Aziz's meeting with Alexis at the Koumayan tea party, presumably the Prof's, since she had been interviewed by the Prof. on the following day. She could hear her own words coming back to her, she could hear that bumptious young Armenian exerting his obvious charm, and she remembered the way Aziz's eyes had flashed. He had resented the Armenian's arrogance, his sexual confidence. It was a male's instinctive hostility towards a rival. She had relished that. And now the two rivals were locked together on paper, in a file.

The telephone rang. She gave it the official answer: "Interservices Liaison Office."

There was a laugh at the other end. "How very formal that does sound."

For a moment she was puzzled. Then she recognised the voice. "Martin, what a surprise."

"Ah, surely not. I want to hear all about your leave. When can I hear it?"

His voice had its habitual tone; his perpetual façade of courtship. Usually it managed to annoy her. It was so very much a manner; the diplomat in an hour of relaxation. But this time it rather pleased her.

"I'd love to, any time," she answered. "I'm not very busy."

"What about Tuesday then, next week?"

Tuesday was five days off. This was unlike him. Normally he would ask her out for that same evening, or at the most the following day because of some change of plans. To be asked five days ahead was a genuine date.

"Tuesday would be fine," she said.

"Then I'll call for you at half past eight. No special clothes; a quiet evening."

It was a warm, clear evening. The heavy summer heat had not descended yet. He had the hood of his car down. "Let's drive along the Bosphorus," he said. He chose a restaurant on the water, a few miles beyond Terapia. The terrace was sheltered and Eve took off her coat. He raised his eyebrows. "That certainly is something."

She had bought in Beirut a length of blue brocade, adorned with cedars, out of which she had made a jacket.

"It's the first time I've worn it. I thought you were the right man for it." She would not have said that a month ago. He might have thought it "forward". But the remark slipped out naturally. He laughed. "That's a most flattering tribute." He seemed genuinely pleased. "The food here won't amount to much after what you've been enjoying in the Lebanon, but it's a pleasant place."

The waiter handed her a menu; but he did not give her time to study it.

"Why don't we have simple Turkish things? That's what they do best. Imam Baialadi—the Imam swoons and Doner kebab. Plus one of their honey-rich desserts. How's that?"

She nodded. She was grateful to him for making up her mind for her.

"And now for the wine," he said. He studied the list with a student's care. "When I was here the other day they told me that they were expecting some new German wines. Yes, a Moselle, 1939. That's something you couldn't get in the Lebanon. Isn't it strange to think that they were gathering these grapes in the same week that their aeroplanes were bombing Warsaw? The two sides of Germany."

It was a clean, fresh wine, with a faintly sweet aftertaste. "No," he said. "I question if you got anything as good as this in Lebanon. I've heard a lot about their red wines. How were they?"

He asked her about the restaurants and the cabarets in the same way that Sedgwick had; but her answers seemed much livelier than they had in the I.S.L.O. offices. He was animated and interested. He made amusing comments; his wit evoked wit in her. He laughed outright several times. She had never thought of herself as being particularly funny; but she did feel that she was being funny now. She had felt that she was boring Sedgwick, she knew that she was entertaining Martin.

As her office's contact with the British Embassy, she had no secrets from him, though he had, inevitably, quite a few from her. In consequence, she was able to be open with him in a way that she could not be with her other friends. She could never remember offhand the sources of the information that she possessed; whether she had read it in a newspaper, heard it on the German radio, or acquired it from an intercepted message in a code that had been broken. She was forced therefore to confine herself to gossip on trivial subjects. It made her self-conscious sometimes. She must seem so terribly trivial and limited; with Martin she could give herself free rein.

He asked her about the Beirut office. "How are Farrar and the Professor getting on? They seem a curiously assorted pair."

"I'd say they dovetailed very well. The one completes the other."

"Their summaries are certainly well written now. How's Farrar's love life?"

She laughed. "I'd say a little confused. There's a young Armenian that keeps him guessing. He never can get alone with her. She's chaperoned by her brother."

"Isn't that rather a strain on him?"

She pouted. "I don't think he's too disturbed. Lebanon's French, remember. There are accommodations handy."

And that was again something that she would have hesitated to say a month ago. She had avoided references to sex. She was afraid of their being given a personal twist. Her inexperience had put her at a disadvantage. She had felt that he might laugh at her. She was on her guard. But now she felt no embarrassment.

"So on the whole, Beirut is not a man's paradise after all," he said.

"The competition is very keen."

"That's disappointing. I'm going there on leave next month."

So that, she thought, is why he asked me out to dinner. A month ago her pride would have been hurt. She had been fooled, fancying herself invited for the sake of her own company, without any ulterior motive. But now she was amused. How true to type he ran. Her answer came back pat: "I don't think you'll need to worry."

"That's another very flattering tribute."

"Oh, come now. Don't be modest. You know your value well enough. You're quite a dish."

He looked at her quickly, searchingly. It was the kind of remark that, put in a letter, might have been interpreted in a hostile manner. But her voice held no catty undertone. It was frank and friendly; almost affectionate. She might have been teasing him, as a sister would.

"It's a question of meeting the right people and I've got just the person for you." She launched on a description of Jane Lester. "She's pretty and she's perplexed. She needs someone who'll be firm with her, who'll stand no nonsense. You'd be performing an act of charity, and from your point of view there's one supreme advantage. She's married to a prisoner-of-war. There's no possibility of your finding yourself involved."

Once again he looked at her quickly, searchingly. Once again she had used words that might, in a letter, have been misread. But, again, there was no snide undertone. She met his look with an open smile. She had a surprising feeling of self-confidence, of being in the stronger position. She leant back in her chair. "I'd very much like to read a novel of which you were the hero."

That did surprise him. He could not think of an appropriate answer. "That's one of the strangest things that I've had said to me," was, at length, the best that he could manage. "Why do you say that?"

"Because I'm inquisitive. I can see you, as you are to-day, thirty and a second secretary. You've been to the right school and the right college. You got the right degree; you have the right connections. The road stretches straight ahead. Nothing can stop your being an ambassador. You won't make any mistakes. In four or five years' time you'll marry exactly the right girl: she'll embellish your career and help you with it. She'll probably have a certain amount of money; that kind of girl always does. And you'll really be in love with her. You won't propose to her because she's the right kind of girl. It will be a romance, for both of you. At the point when you're beginning to feel the need of a wife, the right kind of woman will appear. It'll be most romantic and unplanned. Because that's the kind of thing that happens to your kind of man. You have a sense of self-direction; it councils you, warns you. It's the daemon, the inner voice that guided Socrates. I see you now, a complete, polished product." She paused. She was slightly dazed by her own garrulity. But she was enjoying herself, as she never had before with him. He was staring at her, astounded. She revelled in it. He smiled. It was a respectful smile.

"All this is very flattering," he said, "and I am not contradicting you. I am not denying your estimate, but if that is what I am, and I suspect it is; and if you have so clear a picture of me, I am wondering why you should be inquisitive about me, why should you want to read a novel about me: since you already know how the story ended."

"Ah, but that's just the point. I want to know how it began. You know those novels that start with a picture of a man in old age or middle life and then suddenly switch back, to explain how he reached that point? I know what you are, and what you are going to become, and I can see you as a little boy of nine going off to his preparatory school in your grey flannel shorts and blazer; and I can see you at Eton in your ridiculous tail coat, and high hat and stiff white collar. That's all clear, the alpha and the omega. But there must have been a crisis along the way. There must have been a watershed, when you asked yourself whether this was what you really wanted, whether there weren't other things in life? What happened then? Was there some girl who was quite impossible in terms of the life that had been planned for you, but who offered you another kind of life that might have been more worth while; or it may not have been a girl, it may have been a don at Oxford who opened up to you—what's the cliché?—other vistas— a life of scholarship and research. You, with your great talents, might have had a quite different career, that might actually have been more in keeping with your real self."

She paused again. At the start, she had leant back in her chair; she had been nonchalant and casual. But now she leant forward across the table, her elbows rested on it, her face cradled between her hands. The tone of her voice, too, had changed. It had deepened. It had grown warmer; it had softened; it had lost its irony.

"Something must have happened," she went on. "There must have been some crisis. That's what I'm curious to know: what was it? What made you what you are?"

She was exalted in a way that she had never been with him before. Up till now she had been his junior, his inferior, a little secretary, with whom he'd have liked to go to bed but didn't much mind whether he did or didn't. There were many others. He had set the pace. And she had been on her guard. But now she was setting the pace; and it was heady knowledge; she had become aware of herself, conscious of her powers, fulfilled, knowing what she amounted to. And that mocking look had left his face. There was surprise, but there was admiration; a feeling that he, too, in his turn was conscious of her powers, recognising her for what she was; no longer seeing her as the potential plaything of an idle hour but a separate and distinct human being. Their eyes met and held each other's. A month ago he would have found some ready light-hearted reply that would have changed the tempo of their talk. He did not now.

"Something's happened to you," he said. "You're a different person. I'd like to read the story of your last three weeks."

And that, too, was heady knowledge; that he, of all people, he who had been so casual, should recognise the change in her. Nobody else had seen it; but he had. "Maybe I'll tell you, some day," she said. And then they changed the subject and again their talk was casual.

They made it an early evening. As she stood up by the table, she remembered how often the last twenty minutes of an evening had marred the three preceding hours; either he would try to persuade her to come back to his apartment "for a night-cap"; or he would want to drive out along the Golden Horn and see the moonlight with all that that involved; or else he would be sarcastic and contemptuous. She had found herself dreading the last twenty minutes as she sipped her coffee. She had often declined to join him in a liqueur because she had been afraid that it would deaden her reactions, making her say something she would regret. But this time she accepted a cognac and sipped it slowly, appreciatively, feeling the fire along her veins. Nothing could spoil tonight.

He held the door of the car open for her, then, walking round in front, sat down beside her. He said nothing as he put the car into gear. He did not ask where she wanted to be driven. He drove towards her flat. He did not speak during the drive. But, outside the building, he leant forward across the wheel, as he had after their last dinner. Then he turned towards her, raised his hand under her chin, lifted her face to his and kissed her very gently on the lips.

Her sleep was cradled by fond dreams.

11

IN BEIRUT, Reid was at work on the creation of his first notional character.

"Lucille Moumahnan," he wrote, "is a Lebanese girl, twenty years old. She is employed as a nurse in the military hospital. Many of her patients are men in the armed forces, French and British, who were wounded in the June campaign. They are often visited by their comrades in arms. She has many opportunities of over-hearing gossip. Alexis has known her slightly for a little time. He is going to develop this acquaintanceship. She is pretty. He enjoys her company, and he would not be averse to an entanglement. She can inform him as to which units are still in the area."

Reid re-read what he had written; it seemed satisfactory. He stated on his second notional character. "The father of one of Alexis' ex-fellow students, an Armenian, has been recruited locally as a typist in the Spears Mission. He has been put into uniform. He was carefully vetted before he was enrolled. He is thoroughly pro-British, and anti-Turkish. He is anti-German because the Germans were the Turks' allies in the last war. His son shares his views. The father believes that the only chance of a united Armenia lies through the British. The father does not have access to secret documents; he is employed on routine typing; but he has opportunities of overhearing gossip. He talks about the office when he gets home. He knows nothing really very secret, but he knows a little. Alexis has found that by posing as being anti-British he can goad the son, André, into pro-British tirades. He will say, for instance, 'The British are doing nothing in this war. They held back their air force in the Battle of France. They are letting the Russians do all the fighting now; and in a year's time they'll be making way for the Americans.' When Alexis says that, André's eyes blaze; he starts enumerating all that Britain has done and is doing with her fleet, her air force, in her factories; he draws on the information that his father has given him. Every now and then he will back up his argument with an incident that has not been reported in the press. Alexis is not going to become a friend of André's. He gets more out of him as an adversary."

He re-read what he had written, then went down the passage to Farrar's office. "Here's my attempt. Can I see yours?"

"Certainly. You won't find them very scholarly. Don't put me on the carpet for their English."

"Alexis' mother," so the first page started, "entertains French and English officers. One of these, a Frenchman called Dupré, is a major in the Commissariat. He is a man of forty. He is married. He has two young children. He is a career officer. He would have preferred to stay with his regiment, but he was not popular with his brother officers. He was not *sportif*. He was not fun on parties. When an application list for transfers to the service side of the army came in, his colonel suggested that he should apply for a transfer. He was posted to the Lebanon in 1938. When the 1941 campaign was over, and he was offered the choice between returning to France or becoming a *rallié* under de Gaulle he was in a quandary. He had no sympathy for de Gaulle or for the British. Yet he was afraid if he went back to France he would be relegated to the reserve, on the same principle that his colonel had suggested his transfer to the Q branch. He has two young children. He had their interests to consider. Also his wife's, to whom he is devoted. Finally he became a *rallié*. Now he regrets his choice: he resents the de Gaullists who are getting the best appointments; he speaks little English and dislikes the British for having disturbed a comfortable way of life. Why could not they have been practical like the French and accepted the fact of their defeat, and waited for time to adjust the balance? He is at outs with everyone. He feels at ease in Alexis' family because they are Armenians. It is the one house in Beirut where he can be outspoken. He is often indiscreet. Alexis feels that if he listens carefully, he will learn something of interest to his friends across the frontier."

Farrar's other notional character was very different. "A young

Alsatian lieutenant, who had been in England in hospital when the Vichy Government had signed the armistice. He had been acting as a liaison officer with Gort's staff at Arras, had been wounded in the first bombardment on the night of May 10th, had been sent to the base at Boulogne and had been evacuated with the early sections of G.H.Q. He was still in hospital when he had been offered the opportunity of returning to France on his recovery. Like Dupré, he had been in a quandry, though of a very different kind. He thought of himself as an Alsatian first. He wanted to be a part of whichever country owned Alsace-Lorraine. His great-grandfather had been a Frenchman. His grandfather had started as a Frenchman, then been forced to change his nationality and become a German. His father had been brought up as a German and had fought in the German army against the French; then in 1919 he had been informed that he was now a Frenchman. He had shrugged. He had said to his son, then aged eight, 'My dear son, we have been born into a difficult age. Remember that you are Alsatian first, and French or German second.'

He had never forgotten that. Because Alsace was French he had tried to be a loyal Frenchman, and had fought under the tricolour. But when, as he lay in hospital, he learnt that France had lost the war and that Alsace had been returned to Germany, his loyalty to France ebbed. He had no wish to return to a France that did not own Alsace. In Metropolitan France he would no longer feel himself a part of her; on the other hand, if he rallied to de Gaulle though he would be fighting against Alsatians, he would be joined to a party that was resolved to restore Alsace to France. He finally decided that since he was wounded and in hospital, it would be simplest to stay where he was.

But his heart was not in his new assignment; 'a plague on both your parties'; he wanted the war to stop; he did not particularly care who won, he wanted the French and Germans to cease their century-long squabble and let him, an Alsatian, live peacefully in the valleys of his fathers. He was a discontented man; he had done his best to be a good soldier in the Free French Forces. He had fought gallantly against the Vichy Forces. But when the campaign was over, and the attempt was made to recruit members of the Vichy Forces to de Gaulle, he had felt envious of those Frenchmen who had the opportunity of returning to Metropolitan France. How would he choose now if he had the opportunity of going back? He did not know. It was a pointless question for him to ask himself, because he no longer had the choice. But when the ship drew outwards with the band playing on the quay he was not at all sure that he did not envy those on board. He did not know how the war would end; if it ended in a stalemate, as well it might, with Alsace left in German hands—after all, Germany had as much right to it as France in terms of history—might he not be better off as a Vichy Frenchman than as a de Gaulle rebel? The Germans would have friendly feelings for the Vichy soldiers who had honoured the armistice; he would find it easy to cross a frontier and become an Alsatian again. When he had made that snap decision in a London hospital he had not had the time to weigh all the alternatives; he was weak and in pain and wanted to be left alone. He wished he could have that choice again; but he hadn't and that was all there was to it. He was disgruntled, apathetic. He was not in a mood to place a check upon his tongue. He would talk against the allies, in the privacy of a neutral home; he might easily let slip a secret.

Reid took the material back to Farrar. "You've gone into much greater length than I have," he said.

"I know, and your characters are easier material than mine; yours can be sent up to Turkey almost as they stand. I'll have to make a precis out of mine. But I find that I only make these nominal characters real to myself by writing about them at length; it's surprising how real nominal characters can become, sometimes you can't believe that they don't actually exist. They're more real to you than the people you're seeing every day. In a month or two I'll be wanting to take that wretched Alsatian down to the St. Georges bar, give him a lagoon-sized Martini and tell him to cheer up."

"That's rather the way a novelist feels about his characters."

"You'd know more about that than I would; but this I know: if these notional characters aren't real to me they won't be to the Germans. We're going to have fun with this, and it's a relief to feel that what's real fun for us is helping do the Germans down."

†

A fortnight later, Farrar paused at the end of a long conference. "Prof. I'm wondering if you don't need a holiday."

"Do you think so? Have I been missing points?"

"Lord, no, but if I were you, I could do with a change of air;

you are much more tied to the office than I am. I'm always getting away for a night or two, and much of my work is outside this office. There's another point, too. I've seen a great deal more of the country than you have. Before the war I covered the whole of Lebanon and a lot of Syria. It's useful in our job to have seen the country. It's hard to tell what difference it makes, but these characters that we are dealing with cease to be real, or never become real if we only see them as folios on a file."

"How are you suggesting I should set about it?"

"That's what I'm coming to. You know about this wheat scheme Spears is running."

"Roughly."

"That's about all you need to know. They're short of officers to run it and they're borrowing, on a short lease, from neighbouring units. It won't be more than three weeks to a month. How does that strike you? It won't be hard work. It amounts to a leave."

"It sounds fine, but I don't know anything about wheat."

To Reid that seemed a highly pertinent objection. In 1918 thousands had died in the Lebanon of starvation, in the streets and hedges. Vast fortunes were made by the Damascus merchants who hoarded the wheat and forced the prices up. Now in 1942 the people were terrified lest the horrors of the last war should be repeated. The merchants were hoping to repeat their "coup". In the previous winter, the situation had been saved by the importation of Australian wheat. But the present situation in the Far East had made impossible the resumption of this remedy. The Spears Mission had therefore devised, initiated and sponsored a scheme by which all the wheat and barley in the country was to be bought by a central office—the O.C.P. (Office des Céréales Panifiables)—and distributed at a fixed price to the public; the produce of the entire country, being registered, village by village, by a series of wheat commissioners. Reid felt that such work lay outside his province. But Farrar shook his head.

"You're the regular army officer, not me, but I sometimes believe that I'm much more familiar with the way the military machine works. Staff officers are always being posted to administrative branches of which they have no previous experience. A major, who has taken a six months' duty leave to learn Malay and study the terrain north of Singapore, is summoned back to the War Office. He believes he is going to be a G.2 in the Far East section. Not at all; he is in the department that deals with income tax. It is the army's way of keeping juniors in their place, showing them how little they know, and how much there is for them to know. By the time the major is an expert on income tax, he is posted back to active service as a D.A.Q.M.C. You'll do fine as a wheat commissioner; all they need is someone to show the flag. I frankly envy you."

"Where do I go?"

"You are based on Damascus. You're actually in Deraa: that's where T. E. Lawrence pulled off many of his shows, blowing up the railway."

"When do I start?"

"As soon as you can. Tomorrow if you like?"

"You seem to have got it cut and dried."

"It's an emergency. If there was a famine here now it would be fine for Hitler."

"All right, tomorrow then."

"By the time you come back those notional characters should have come to life."

Reid went down the corridor to Diana's room. "Could you break any date you may have for tonight, and dine with me?"

"I have no date, but if I had one I'd have broken it. What are we to celebrate?"

"Nothing, except that I'm going to be away for a month."

"Ah, so that O.C.P. deal has come through."

"You knew about it?"

"Nigel discussed it with me. He thought you needed a rest."

"Do I look washed out?"

"No, but you're over-conscientious. You feel that you must justify being in a warm climate, with plenty to eat, and no air raid danger. Just in the way that civilians in the first war worked themselves to death in offices because they weren't in the trenches. You work much harder than you need. So Nigel cooked up this plot. You'll have an interesting time; you won't be over-worked. What's more, it will be important work. You'll come back with so much energy that we shan't know how to rein you in. Certainly there's something to celebrate tonight."

For once they did not dine at Sa'ad's. Instead they went to the Lucullus, where they had had their first meal together. "That's only six months ago. What a lot's happened since then," he said. "And do you realise that for the last four months we've seen each other every single day except for that one trip to Aleppo. We've seen more of one another than most married couples do in their first five years of marriage."

"I know we have."

"In a way, I'm rather happy about this separation."

"You are?"

"It'll give me a chance to think about you."

"What am I to take that to mean?"

"It's surely very simple. I've had no quiet time to sit and brood, recreating times together, remembering things you've said, and clothes you've worn; living it all over, day by day, and night by night, savouring the whole magic of it, the whole magic of you. You can see that, surely?"

"Yes, I can see that."

"And there's another thing. I can write you letters. Do you know that I've never written you a letter? I've never needed to."

"You've written me some very charming notes."

"That isn't the same thing."

"Notes can be very dear."

"But a letter, with a whole hour before me, with nothing to interrupt me, to be able to tell you all I feel about you."

"Never seek to tell thy love, Love that never told can be."

"Aren't letters different?"

"Are they? I wouldn't know. I never write them."

"But you'll write to me when I'm in Deraa?"

"Will I? I wonder."

"At least a note."

She was smiling; never had he felt so understood before; understood so that there was no need for explanation, yet at the same time an overwhelming necessity to explain.

"If I hadn't met you, my life would have been half lived," he said.

"Think that. Go on thinking that."

They lingered late over the table. Only one couple remained, when they left the restaurant. It was hot, but a breeze was blowing off the sea.

"I'd like to walk back," she said. "Oh, but no, there's an arabana." It was a very ramshackle barouche. It rocked and jolted over the uneven roads, swinging them against each other. They were holding hands. She paused on the pavement outside his building. A waxing moon was sinking over the rooftops.

"I'd like to stay the whole night," she said.

He woke earlier than she, woken by the voice of the Muezzin. It was not yet dawn. He could barely distinguish her features in the dusk. She was turned towards him, breathing gently, her hair ruffled on her forehead. He did not move, fearful of disturbing her. He wanted to wait, watching her features grow distinct minute by minute as the room lightened. What was that poem of Ezra Pound's about life having nothing more exquisite to offer than the joy of waking together? Soon there would be the rattle of tramcars; and the two girls on the roof across the street in their long white dressing gowns would hang their mattresses over the balcony and beat their carpets; and Diana would stir and stretch out and raise her arms above her head, and blink, and then smile and, turning, open her arms. Could life hold for him any lovelier moment?

12

DERAA, WHITHER REID HAD BEEN CONSIGNED, was the Hauran's head-quarters of the O.C.P. The Hauran was a long, broad undulating plain, sheltered by the mountains of the north that rose every so often into a protuberance on which a village stood. One of the chief granaries of the Roman Empire, the villages had been built on and over and out of the ruins of Roman houses. Everywhere there were signs of Rome; stones with Roman inscriptions supported the flimsy fabric of a mud-built cottage. Columns rose unexpectedly out of a dingy side street. Sometimes the head of a column showing a few feet above the ground would demonstrate to what extent succeeding generations had superimposed layer after layer of mud and rubble on the original Roman site.

There were five other depots to which the villagers could bring their wheat. It was the duty of a wheat commissioner to supervise at these depots the weighing and guarding of the wheat and barley, and to ensure that the villagers were paid their due, and that the wheat they brought was clean. It was also his task to publicise the scheme, to visit the various villages, interview the local head-men—the *moukhtars*—explain the scheme to them, convince them they were being squarely treated, show by his presence that the British were behind the scheme. He also had to move in close liaison and co-operation with the French *services speciaux* officer for the district.

Reid's main assignment, however, was to see that an agreement was reached between the chief notables, the *mohaffez* of the district, the French S.S. officer and himself, as to the amount of wheat and barley that the region was able to produce. The figure was intended as a minimum. No cereals could be sold except through the O.C.P. But the Damascus merchants were anxious to lay up large stocks as capital; the villagers were anxious to stock their cellars. The scene was set, therefore, for a black market. It was in the immediate personal interest, both of villagers and merchants, to fix the figure as low as possible. As long as their cellars were stocked they did not mind if the inhabitants of Damascus starved.

Before Reid had been in the area three days he realised that it was impossible for one new to the country to form any idea in the course of a few weeks as to the productive capacity of the region. Grounds were measured and assessed by a complicated system which was different in every village. The nomenclature was a mixture of Arabic, French and Turkish. It was impossible to tell on which system—old Turkish, older Arabic or modern French— the assessment was being made. The O.C.P. had given what it considered a fair estimate of the potentialities of the neighbourhood and the notables had given their bid which was less than half that figure. It was going to be, he recognised, a question of bargaining. The eternal bargaining of the Orient.

Reid had a car and an interpreter at his disposal. He drove round the area supervising the weighing and the payment, re-checking the wheat for impurities by taking a large handful between his hands, tossing it over and seeing how much sand lay between his palms. He knew that there was cheating and that the black market was being fed. Every day stories would be brought to him of someone having boasted in the coffee shops of the fortunes that he was making at the scales. He knew that there was no way of checking on these stories. Diana had told him that he was over conscientious; perhaps he was, but he had a sound store of common sense. He knew that he would go off his head if he made himself a rigid enforcer of the law. The most that he could hope was that by looking important, by making an occasional "scene", the prestige of his uniform would deter a few of these malpractitioners. He would stand looking grim, then suddenly pounce and interrogate someone whose face he did not like and hope that he was performing a useful service.

He let himself relax, accepting his assignment in the spirit that Farrar had offered it. He was a privileged tourist, enabled to see the countryside and meet its inhabitants in a way that no tourist could ever hope to do. He enjoyed the long drives into the country, over the flat boulder-strewn plain of the Hauran. For miles it would be the same, field after field of growing wheat and maize, the earth showing red between the stubble where the crops had been cut or the ground left fallow. There was the animated noise of harvest. Where the ground was barren, a group of Bedouins would sit idle, under and about their long, low tents. There were no treees, no gardens, nothing green. Along the road were stone shelters like sentry boxes to protect in winter the guardians of the fields. Camel trains laden with wheat, led by small boys on ponies, went by with a jingling of bells. There would be four to five camels in each train; their long necks seemed to move in and out of their loads. The villages were low, grey-black, one-storied build-ings of mud and boulders, peaked by the spire of a minaret, sur-rounded hedgewise by a succession of low walls, some mud, some of brick. Inside these walls the wheat was being threshed. A pony or a mule was driven round in circles, drawing a broad, flat board on which stood the driver—a child or an old man. A fine yellow dust rose as the wheat was tossed into the air. Mile after mile, village after village, it was the same.

The villages were farmyards, little else. There was no sanitation as Western civilisation understood the word. There was a large central pond, usually of Roman origin, where clothes were washed and cattle drank. The houses were gaps in a mud wall. There would be a pen or two for the hens and cattle. There would be a roofed-in pen or two for the family. The village women did not wear veils. They were shapeless bundles of old clothes, with blue tattooing on their chins and lower lips. The children rolled hap-pily in the dust.

Yet in the house of the headman, the *moukhtar*, in even the smallest village, there was a sense of leisure, of graciousness, of culture, of inherited immemorial manners. His reception room, though it was only a roofed-over cattle-pen, would be high and cool. There would be carpets on the floor and stools and cushions arranged against the wall. In the centre would be the ashes of a fire where coffee had been made and where the coffee pots still remained. Old men would be puffing at *narghiles*, very old men who sat there day after day, doing nothing, rarely speaking, but whose age entitled them to be present when the *moukhtar* received his guests. There was a constant drifting in and out and much shaking of hands. Children would sit in the doorway and stare inquisitively but without offence at their strange visitant.

Reid came during these trips to appreciate Arab dignity. When an English tourist returned from the Levant or from North Africa with a *burnous* which he employed as a dressing gown, the result was usually unfortunate. The square cut collar made the neck seem too long and the short sleeves gave an appearance of discomfort as though the gown would slip off at any moment. But worn with a white veil and head rope as the Arabs wore it, the brown *burnous* with its gold threadwork at the neck was comfortable and appropriate. The long flowing dress with high-collared silk shirt and embroidered bodice gave the whole costume a surprisingly masculine effect.

Though he could speak no Arabic, Reid learnt to appreciate Arab oratory. The first piece of advice he had been given when he began lecturing had been, "Get a table in front of you. Have something to hold on to, so that you won't distract your audience with awkward gesturings with your hands." He had often heard the old school of actor complain that the modern actor could not use his hands; all he could do was tap a cigarette against a case and light it. The Arabs, in contrast, had mastered the management of their hands. When an Arab was listening, his hands would be busy with his beads. He would draw back the beads in twos with his left thumb, then push them forward with his right. But when he spoke, he would amplify his meanings with a series of effective, eloquent, often unexpected gestures. When he was enumerating a succession of points, he would hold out his hand, the back facing the audience, and draw his fingers one by one into his palm. When he wished to beckon anyone towards him, he would stretch out his arm, his fingers pressed, then draw back his elbow as though he were drawing that person to himself.

He learnt during those weeks to appreciate the ritual of Arab hospitalities. One is always offered something, coffee or curdled milk. The coffee was bitter but surprisingly refreshing. You only took a sip of it. The cup was replenished until, by a turning of it between your hands, you indicated that you had had enough. Though the Moslems did not take alcohol, they usually kept a bottle for their guests. Reid soon learned to decline the offer of it. What might be proffered as a sweet local wine might turn out to be a tumblerful of neat Damascus brandy, and it would be bad manners not to finish what you had accepted.

No matter at what hour he would arrive, he would be offered food. If he had nothing else to do, but only if he had nothing else to do that day, he would accept. The preliminaries were endless. "We will go into the fields," the notables would say. "We will measure off so many square metres of ground. We will pluck the corn, thresh it, weigh it, then you will realise that this land only produces five mouds to each moud sown, and that if we agree to yield you twenty-five thousand tons, we shall run the risk of finding ourselves without any reserve for a bad winter. We will make our examination; then we will return here and you will find lunch ready."

But lunch would not be ready. The Arabs did not divide time into separate divisions like hours and parts of an hour. Besides, it was bad manners to be in a hurry. For an hour, for two hours, for three hours maybe, he would wait. He would pay elaborate compliments; he would acknowledge and reply to elaborate compliments. On the manner in which he accepted and made these speeches would depend, he was well aware, that particular village's reaction and response to a scheme on which the welfare and security of a whole countryside depended. The scheme would be judged by his behavior. It was supremely important that he should make the required effort. But his ears were strained listening for the approach of food. At last was brought the water in which his hosts could perform the ablutions that would precede their prayers. Then the meal could be set out on the floor.

Arabs sit upon their heels, and it is bad manners—it is more than bad manners, it is an insult—to point the soles of your feet at anyone. It is not easy for a European to sit upon his heels. Reid was not particularly supple. He curled himself up as best he could. Fortunately the meal did not last long, though there was a great deal to eat. The moment that food arrived all conversation ceased. Reid soon became accustomed to this kind of banquet. You help yourself, he learnt, with your right hand to what is set before you. There would be two kinds of rice and curdled milk and several sauces. There would be a salad or two soaked in vinegar, with cucumbers stuffed with rice; there would be chicken and possibly a whole roast sheep stuffed with roasted nuts and rice. There would be flat, grey-brown bread with which to scoop up the sauces. The host will help you to the choicest morsels. The eye of the sheep is a great delicacy. As a tribute to your importance, he will extract it for you and pop it into your mouth with his own fingers. It looked repulsive, but it was, Reid found, mercifully tasteless. After the meal a servant brought a bowl of water and soap with which to wash his hands. In the richer villages he was also offered scent for his hands and forehead.

So it went on, day after day. The sun beat down out of a cloudless sky. The hard glare of the parched earth dazzled him. But in the evening, shortly before sunset, a breeze would blow from the still snow-capped Hebron. Reid would close his eyes, wearied by diplomacy, savouring the calm of this last hour when the outline of the hills would be subdued, merging into a succession of level layers of rich, soft colours, dominated by a purplish brown; the camel trains would move in slow silhouette against the sunset and the dust of the chaff about the villages was flacked with orange.

Reid was housed in the town major's office. There was no furniture in the room he shared with the local transport officer, except a table. He had his camp bed and a camp chair. He was living very much as he had done a quarter of a century back in Harrowby Camp, Grantham, as a machine gunner. There were rarely more than five others in the mess. The food was dreary; the town major sharing the British view that local foods and vegetables were messy and unhealthy and likely to upset one's digestion. He preferred to open a tin and spread tomato ketchup on its contents. He had access to a cache of whisky and usually arrived at the table with a glazed expression. The conversation was as dreary as the fare; the day's wireless report, news from England, gossip about local personalities, reminiscences of England. Yet for Reid the final two hours of the day were a reward and recompense for the strains that the long day had imposed. At last he was by himself.

The house had been built before the first war, and on a Turkish pattern; two stories, with all its rooms facing on a square of grass out of which a date palm grew. After dinner, he would sit on the stone pathway under the gallery outside his room, with the Oxford Book of English Verse. At night he slept under a mosquito net, but there were not enough mosquitoes to be troublesome; the bare electric bulb in his room gave him enough light to see the page. He would read a poem or two, or a section of a familiar poem, then he would let the book fall forward on his knees, his mind abroad, thinking over the letter that he would write before he went to bed. He would write for forty, sixty, ninety minutes— a serial letter that he would mail every third day or so.

He had never written in this tone before, with such an exuberant flow of words, such a wide vocabulary. As a historian he was well aware of the deficiencies of his writing, the lack of flexibility, the absence of warmth, the limited vocabulary. He knew that he could never hope for the large sales that certain popular historians achieved. He did not resent it. He was not that kind of writer, because he was not that kind of man. Writing was not his métier. He was a teacher, not a writer. His special merit lay in the lecture room and in his tutorials; and in the way he contrived that the one should amplify and round off the other. He had no illusions about himself. But just as he had become a new self during his picnics, his dinners, his twilight hours with Diana, so now he became a different writer seated here at this desk, letting pour forth, night after night, this torrent of adoration. He described his day to day events, the places he had seen, the conversations, the bargainings; right through the day he had kept thinking, "I'll tell Diana that tonight." When anything amusing happened he had thought, "That'll make Diana smile." When anything had occurred pertinent to British or French relations with the Arabs, he had thought, "That will interest Diana."

His whole day was interpreted in terms of his love for her. She was beside him all the time. She was never absent from his thoughts. When she reads these letters, he thought, she'll understand, she'll appreciate what she means to me. These letters could only have been written by a man to whom she was the earth and stars and the revolving heavens. During the months when they had been seeing each other all the time, the "big words" had rarely managed to get said. They had not even had an opportunity of talking on the telephone as they had when he was Duty Officer at the Mission. She might very well have thought that for him the whole episode was just a "war-time affair". She would know better now. The best of their romance lay in the future. He was impatient to return. Yet at the same time he savoured the delay. Every week, every day apart would heighten the thrill of their reunion. He did not, therefore, pester Farrar with enquiries about his return. All in good time, he thought, all in good time.

During the third week of his absence he returned to Deraa to find a message asking him to telephone the Director-General in Damascus. The line was faulty and it was a garbled message that he received. Apparently there was a tense situation in one of the depots, where the British officer in charge was quarrelling with the French *Services Spéciaux*. Neither spoke the other's language fluently; the Briton was a major while the Frenchman was a captain. The major was trying to pull rank. This was particularly unfortunate because promotions were not so rapid in the French army as they were in the British, and the status of a French captain could be higher than that of a British major. The Director-General was not quite clear himself as to the cause of the dispute. It was something to do with the Quaimaquam. The Frenchman appeared to be siding with the Syrian. At any rate, what was needed was a bilingual catalyst to smooth out the situation. Would Reid drive over there first thing next morning?

He set off without enthusiasm. Though he was drawing the pay and allowances of a major, he still had three pips upon his shoulder and he suspected that this major would try to pull rank on him. His second war service experience had warned him that majors in back-areas tended to be touchy. They were often reservists who had found themselves out of date when they were recalled to the colours, or they were men with long service who had been promoted when Hore Belisha had introduced his army reforms in 1938, who had grown indolent during the long years when the army had been neglected, had been unable to meet the sudden pressure placed on them in the campaign that had preceded the evacuation from Dunkirk and had been by-passed when the army was reformed in England. There were also quite a few younger officers who had been on active service with their regiments when war had broken out, had been wounded in the Western Desert, were not fit to rejoin their units and had failed to play their cards cleverly in the Cairo rat race; there were also a number of elderly warrant officers who had recently been commissioned, had a sense of social inferiority and were on the look-out for affronts. Altogether majors in back-areas after three years of war tended to present a tricky problem.

It was a considerable relief therefore to Reid to find that the major in question was his old fellow missionary, Johnson. Johnson seemed as relieved that the visiting catalyst should be an old companion. Figuratively, he fell upon Reid's neck.

"My oath, this is a relief. I was expecting one of those bright young know-all from Whitehall who've never been on a parade ground. Have you seen the objects that they've been putting into uniform? Consuls with red flannel, vice-consuls with crowns; makes an old soldier like myself want to vomit; I guess it does you, too. Thank God, you're Sandhurst; you'll understand this muddle."

"What is the muddle?"

Johnson's account of it was far from explicit but Reid could read between the lines. Johnson had been in too much of a hurry. He had wanted quick decisions and that was not the way in which a Quaimaquam was used to doing business. He had bridled, had made difficulties, had imposed delays. Johnson had got angry, a fatal thing to do with an Arab. With a Frenchman it might work, on the right occasion. If an Englishman threw his hat on the floor and stamped on it, a Frenchman might be delighted because it was so un-English. But with the French officer he had been studiedly polite, addressing him as "Mon capitaine" and thereby possibly stressing the difference of rank. He had assumed that the Frenchman would take his side, but to his indignation the Frenchman had appeared to be siding with the Syrian.

At that point Reid interrupted. "He's worked in this area for eight years. He knows how to treat these people."

"That's just the trouble. He knows how to humour them in peacetime, how to jolly them along. But this is wartime; we need that wheat in a hurry."

"It's wartime to us; it isn't to the Arabs. Their wheat's their capital. They'd be just as happy selling it to the Germans as they would to us."

"But we can't afford to humour them at a time like this."

"We've got to if we want their wheat. Do you mind if I hunt up that Frenchman?"

"Naturally not. Oil on troubled waters, that's what you're here for."

The Frenchman was petulantly indignant. "I have been living and working with these people for seven years. I have learnt to love and trust them; as they have, I hope, learnt to love and trust me in return. They are proud and sensitive, like their own Arab steeds. They can be managed but they cannot be coerced. A pressure of the knee, a touch upon the bit and they respond; but tug at the mouth, stab at their flanks with spurs—ah, fatal, fatal. Such delicacy is needed, such address. We have made our mistakes here.

We are not perfect. It has been a hard task that we have set ourselves, we Frenchmen. The Druses for instance: how to reconcile their traditions with the Arabs'; ah, what patience, what finesse; but gradually, slowly, listening, counselling, I have managed to adjust all their differences so that the country can know prosperity and peace. Divide and rule: that is maxim. Keep the separate tribes separate from each other, sometimes stressing their differences so that they will come to feel that they can only preserve their own identity, their own traditions through our overall authority. 'As long as France is here,' I say to them, 'you are safe. We will preserve your rights. But if we were to leave. . . . Ah, this disastrous tide of Arab nationalism. It will destroy your way of living, it will not tolerate your independence.' That is what I tell the Druses; and they believe me. They know that I am right. But the Sheikhs have to trust me too, and the Bedouins. I tell them that we have our eyes upon the Druses, that France will not tolerate aggression; that we will protect their flocks and grazing grounds. We play one against the other, and it is in their interests that we we should; as long as we are here they will know peace.

"But it is a very delicate mechanism; very, very delicate. It has to be watched and oiled and tended. Can you not understand my indignation when your compatriot, who knows nothing of this country or these peoples, tries to force his English ideas on us? My machine is geared to a certain pace; it cannot be forced. In two weeks he can ruin the work of seven years."

Reid let him talk on, till the first flood of invective was spent; then, as with Johnson, he interrupted. Had his colleague—he was sure the captain would not object to the use of the word colleague since they were working to a common goal—had his colleague, he wondered, seen any service in the Far East? No, he had not. Perhaps if he had he would be a little more sympathetic to the British major's tactlessness—if tactlessness was the right word; obtuseness perhaps was better; or should we make a combination —obtuse tactlessness. Much of the major's service had taken place in India; he had had to deal with a country that contained a servile class, a coolie class; they even used the word "untouchable". The British major was accustomed to shouting at coolies. He did not appreciate the difference between Arabs and Indian coolies. He was an elderly man, he was set in his ways. In addition, not only was he rather deaf but his French was not nearly as good as his colleague's English; yet his pride insisted on his speaking

French. He did not catch the exact nuance of the discussion, and he himself often used the wrong words. It was altogether a most delicate situation.

"But I am sure, my dear colleague, that if we could spend a half hour with the major before our conference with the Quaimaquam we shall be able to smooth out all our difficulties. The major understands that the conduct, the strategy, the tactics of the negotiation must lie with you, in view both of your long experience here and of France's privileged position in this country. The major has not, alas, had what I regard as one of the supreme good fortunes of my life: the opportunity to mix on equal terms with my opposite numbers in your country. As a University professor, I recognise, I proudly acknowledge how much my life has been enlarged and enriched by my association with the culture and traditions of your country."

Did I lay it on too thick, Reid wondered. His experiences during the last nine months, particularly during these last three weeks with their endless oratorical exaggerations, had accustomed him to the fanciest flights of hyperbole. He looked cautiously at the French captain. A smile that was like a purr hovered on his lips. Perhaps one could never lay it on too thick. Perhaps that was the mistake the English made abroad, and with foreigners. They laid it on too thin.

At any rate there was a definite atmosphere of cordiality when the conference began. Reid opened it. He addressed the Quaimaquam. He spoke in French. Technically, his French was slip-shod. His use of the subjunctive was mercurial and he imposed arbitrary arrangements on his syntax, but he was extremely fluent, his vocabulary was extensive and he could understand quickly-spoken French. He had an idea that the French liked his kind of language from a foreigner, and he suspected that General Spears would have been more popular with the French had he not spoken their language a great deal more correctly and a great deal more idiomatically than they did themselves. Reid spoke now with great rapidity. He explained to the Quaimaquam that Major Johnson, a most distinguished British officer, had spent the greater part of his service in India, on the north-west frontier, that he had not been long enough in the Middle East to appreciate how different were the conditions here, in the centre of an older and deeper culture, to which the mingling of the minarets of Islam and the arches of ancient Rome proudly testified. He had not realised this at first; it is not easy to overcome a lifetime's training; but the days that he had spent here, in this ancient city, in the company of the Quaimaquam and of our so talented French colleague, had now convinced him of the necessity of a very different approach.

Reid turned to Johnson. "You will endorse that, I am very sure." Reid knew very well that Johnson had not been able to follow a third of what he had been saying, but from the way in which he pitched his voice, from the smile with which he spoke, Johnson had no alternative to agreeing. With the same technique on the few occasions when he did speak to Johnson in English, he was voluble, with an eating of his words, and with the use of obscure colloquialisms that made him completely incomprehensible to the French. "Don't worry," he told Johnson. "We've got them on a sticky wicket; the ball is turning. It'll be lifting in half an hour when the top has caked. If we keep the runs down for that half hour we'll have them where we want them. Play it slow."

Both Johnson and the Frenchman thought that they had made their point, and in a sense the Frenchman had, because when the eventual conference began it was played within the immemorial traditions of the Orient. Nothing was decided, everything was postponed. Yet an atmosphere of cordiality had been created. Eventually there would be a satisfactory conclusion.

It was four o'clock before the meeting was dissolved. They had had nothing to eat, although cups of coffee had been proffered frequently.

"And now," said the Quaimaquam, "it will be my privilege and honour to invite you to join me in my humble meal."

The meal, Reid knew well, would be anything but humble. He also knew that no preparations for it had been set in motion. He looked interrogatively at Johnson. Johnson shook his head. "Let's get out of this, old boy. If I don't get a strong whisky soon I'll be round the bend."

At considerable length Reid explained the predicament in which he and his compatriot found themselves. Major Johnson occupied a very confidential position in the O.C.P. He was, in fact, General Spears' special representative. General Spears was insistent that he should receive from Major Johnson tonight a report on this day's conference. General Spears recognised the importance of this meeting. He insisted that the report should be made to him on a direct confidential line; the nearest such line was in Damascus. The legation office closed at eight o'clock. Major Johnson must, therefore, return to Damascus right away. "And I myself, alas, have to accompany him, because the Director-General wishes us to discuss with him the outcome of this conference. He will be delighted to learn how harmoniously our deliberations have proceeded. I hope, however, that His Excellency will at a later date offer me an opportunity of accepting the hospitality of his house."

He stressed the need for hurry. Yet it was a full half-hour before the car door was closed. "Did I hear you saying that you had to come back to Damascus? Wasn't that your alibi? Well, why don't you? And let's give ourselves a decent dinner. It's a long time since I've had a chance to reminisce."

†

The dining-room of the Omayyed was almost empty. It was late, but here there was no problem about early closing hours. "Let's go into the bar," said Johnson.

He looked tired, and drained, and old. Reid found it difficult to remember that they were contemporaries. He had finished his first whisky, while Reid's glass was three-quarters full.

"Don't wait for me," he said. "I'll catch up with you on the wine."

"Wine. That's something I've never understood. Too much time east of Suez. Stengahs and Gin Pahits. Ah, those long evenings before dinner; with the fans whirring, and the shouts of 'Boy!' That was the life." By the time he had finished his second whisky, Reid's glass was still not empty. Johnson looked younger now, refreshed, and his voice had assumed a mock self-pitying tone, as though he were laughing at himself. "You know, old boy, I didn't understand a great deal of what was going on today."

"I didn't think you did."

"Did it matter?"

"Not in the least. They're in the right humour now. You'll get your wheat all right."

"Why couldn't I have understood that, at the start?"

"Why should you have? It's not the kind of thing you were trained for."

"I feel awfully out of my depth at times."

"Don't we all."

"You don't seem to."

"That's all you know."

213

"Ah, but it is different for you, Prof. You are used to listening to people. I'm not. I give orders or am given them. Half the time I don't know what I'm doing or why I'm here. The O.C.P. Office des Céréales Panifiables, indeed; if they were told that in 'the Rag' how they would laugh. Oh, well, I'll have one more whisky. You can take nearly all the wine."

The dining-room was completely empty, by the time they reached it. There was a long five-course dinner; Johnson wrinkled his nose. "Now that I've got to the point, I'm not really hungry. A steak'll do for me. What about you, Prof?"

"A steak'll be fine for me."

"And about that wine. You get yourself half a bottle. I'll stick to whisky. Grain and grape. Choose a decent wine. This is on me. You got me out of a scrape today."

He returned to the incident before the meal was over. "I suppose I made an ass of myself," he said, "but damn it all, those Froggies get my goat. We're fighting this war for their sake as much as for our own. But I wonder half the time how much they're really in it. That Frenchman this morning doesn't care half as much about beating the Germans as about keeping on the right side of these Syrians so that this area can remain a French sphere of influence when the war is over."

"Can you blame him? He's given seven years to getting to know these people, and how to handle them, in France's interest."

"But Syria is now an Independent Republic."

"Nominally, on paper, but don't you remember that first war phrase about 'a scrap of paper'? Nobody knows what the post war world's going to be like. That Frenchman's trying to carry on the traditions that he's been raised in."

"He ought to have one idea in his head: the quickest way to beat the Huns."

"Try to look at it from his point of view. Suppose . . ." Reid paused, searching for a parallel situation. "This isn't an exact parallel but it'll do," he said. "Suppose the position was reversed; suppose England had been invaded first, and overrun, with France still in the war; suppose the Germans had established a puppet government in London, with Moseley as Prime Minister; suppose the King had felt it his duty to his people to stay in England as a constitutional monarch. He might have thought that; but suppose Winston had gone to Ottawa and announced that Britain would go on fighting, with her allies, her Dominions, and her colonies. He would announce that the King was a prisoner and it was the duty of a loyal subject to see that he was freed. It isn't a fair parallel, but let it pass. Now suppose that some colonies join the Free British movement and some don't. Some colonies think that their first duty is to the constitution. After all, the Vichy government is a legal one. Now suppose that you are a district officer in Malaya, and that Malaya has not rallied to the Free British movement. You take your orders from Whitehall and you continue to administer your district in terms of Malaya's welfare and Britain's interests. Your life in 1941 wouldn't be very different from what it had been in 1938, like that French officer's today.

"Then one bright morning Winston's Free Britons and the French decide that they cannot afford to have Malaya providing all this rubber for Whitehall, half of which goes to Germany. So they decide to liberate Malaya; and a group of Free Britons from Australia with a much larger French Force from Indo-China launch a campaign to win it, take over the country and establish an allied condominiun in Singapore. You find yourself in exactly the same place, doing the same work, only your orders are coming from a source that is partially French. You wonder whether it is entirely French, since France is supplying the Free British movement with funds and weapons. Don't you think you would be suspicious of the French at times, asking yourself whether the French, at the back of their minds, might not be toying with the idea of taking over Malaya and, in the Peace Treaty, incorporating it with their Far Eastern Empire, Cambodia and Indo-China? Don't you think you might feel it was your duty to resist French influence, to remind the Sultan of how much he owed to Britain? I think you would, you know, or at least I think you might. We aren't fair to the Vichy French. They feel that their duty is to Metropolitan France, to the people they grew up among. I'm very glad that I wasn't a Frenchman of forty-two in the summer of 1940. I don't know what I would have done. There's another thing, too; now that we've got Russia and America on our side we know that we can't lose. Two years ago could you really visualise the conditions under which we could win?"

"I never thought about it. I simply thought: here we are and here we stand."

"But then we're not logical and the French are."

"Prof, you're a damned good professor."

They moved into the main coffee lounge. Only four tables were occupied, one of them by a group of Arabs who sat over their cups of coffee, pulling at their beads, talking, talking, talking. "I'm going to have a whisky," Johnson said. "What about you?" Reid shook his head. "I don't often drink after dinner. I've done very well."

Reid had lost count of Johnson's whiskies. They were very small, and Johnson was completely sober. At the same time, whiskies were expensive in hotels. Usually officers only drank it in clubs, or out of the ration allowances that they drew from N.A.A.F.I. He was surprised at Johnson's extravagance. This was an occasion, he supposed, but even so—

A boy was walking from the reception desk intoning a name. "That sounds like you," Reid said.

Johnson started forward. "Yes. Who—what was that?"

"Major Joneswan. Major Joneswan."

"That must be."

Reid stretched back in his chair, his mind abroad. It was the first time that he had been here since that visit with Diana all these weeks ago. He had lived in the memory of this hotel so often. It looked exactly as it had on that first afternoon. I shall remember this room as long as I live, he thought.

Johnson returned with a worried look upon his face. "The Spears Mission duty officer," he said. "They want me in there tomorrow, by six o'clock. I wonder why. I hope to God I haven't put up a black. Six o'clock is an inconvenient time. I shall have to stay the night. Leave here after lunch; that means missing my siesta. I'm no real good if I've missed that; and I may need to be good."

"Why don't you go in the morning?"

"I could, of course; but no, that really would be awkward. There are things I have to do here first. Besides, they want some papers in Beirut that'll need sorting out. It must be after lunch, but. . . ." He paused, frowning, then suddenly his face brightened. "Look, I've an idea. Why don't you come in with me? You could take the wheel while I have a kip and vice versa. What's wrong with that?"

What indeed was wrong with that? A night in Beirut, then come back next morning; either with Johnson or with public transport. He'd only miss one whole day. There were things that he could find to do tomorrow. And he needed to keep in touch with the office. He needed to know how all those irons were heating in those fires. And, anyhow, what was one day off duty? He was too conscientious. Hadn't Diana told him that? He wouldn't be missed here for a day. A night in Beirut. He saw himself walking into the office at six o'clock, saw the look of delighted surprise on Diana's face; hear her exclaim, "Why, Noel," saw himself perched on the edge of her desk, his leg swinging free, laughing down at her. "I couldn't stay away too long. I was getting impatient. You know how it is when you're reading a daily serial and miss two instalments."

"But have you left that wheat job?"

"Heavens, no. I'm only down here for the day."

"For the day?"

"Till tomorrow morning, that's to say."

"Oh, till tomorrow morning."

"Just time to catch up on the files."

"I see, to catch up on the files."

"Those two instalments."

"Exactly, those two instalments."

Her eyes would be twinkling. He knew her so well that he could foretell almost to a sentence, almost to an intonation of the voice, how the talk would go. Yet somewhere there would be a difference; a subtle undertone. She had read his letters. They were moving on a different level. But when he would ask her casually, "I suppose you're not by any lucky chance free tonight?" she would answer, just as casually, "I can make myself."

"At Sa'ad's then, at half past eight."

"At Sa'ad's."

And he would swing himself off the desk, and wave his hand and as he walked down the passage to Farrar's room his heart would be thudding fiercely. Soon, very soon, he would be thinking. . . .

"I'd be enormously grateful if you could," Johnson was continuing. "It seems silly of me; but I am a little anxious about the whole concern. I do need that little spot of shuteye. If you'd like me to ask the D.G.—"

"Don't worry. I can make it."

Next morning the heat was tempered by a breeze blowing off the hills. Reid sauntered through the souks looking for a piece of brocade, remembering how he and Diana had walked here on that fateful day.

They left shortly after lunch. The long valley of the Bekaa

dazzled him; he had forgotten that such a colour as green existed. Soon, very soon, he thought. He had not rung the office to warn them that he was on his way. He wanted the surprise to be complete. He would have no difficulty in getting a room at the St. Georges at this time of year. Perhaps Jane would be away. But anyhow, there were no problems there, not in Beirut, in wartime. Johnson drove for a quarter of an hour; then handed over the wheel. "Just forty winks," he said. He was asleep within two minutes. A minute later he was snoring. He looked old and helpless. He ought to have been holding some staff sinecure in a garrison town. A camp commandant perhaps; somewhere along the line, he had missed his chance and now it was too late.

Johnson had said, "Forty winks," but it was more likely to be a ninety minutes stupor from which he would wake querulous and heavy-lidded. Reid did not disturb him. He was happy with his own thoughts. Soon, very soon. The sun lowered in the sky. Five o'clock. He pictured Diana arriving at her desk, unlocking her cabinets, setting her desk in order. It was for her a routine afternoon like any other. How little she knew. There was a mist over the sea. Cyprus was invisible. He had been told that Flecker's reference to the "hidden sun that rings black Cyprus with a lake of fire" was a factual description, that the long spur of land north of Famagusta was ringed by fire at sunset. He had never seen it. He would not tonight.

Beirut was only a mile or two away. The roofs and towers of the city stretched below him. By an optical illusion the long promontory of sand beyond gave the impression of an incline rising to a peak. It was time to wake up Johnson. He nudged him. "It won't be long now," he said. Soon, very soon, he thought.

He left his bag with the hall porter at the St. Georges. "I'll let you know in the next hour if I'll need a room," he said. He walked slowly up the short hill leading to the Rue Georges Picot. Outside the Mission building was the usual bustle of cars, military and civilian. Poor Johnson, he thought. "Good luck," he said.

Never had his own mind been more at peace. At that moment, he knew well, Rommel's forces were streaming across the desert towards Alexandria. It was for Britain one of the darkest weeks since the fall of France. Yet his heart was headily exultant. Life was offering him its richest wine. At Damascus five months ago he had stumbled upon a mystery. Now he was approaching it with open eyes, knowing what lay ahead. "I shall remember this moment all my life," he thought.

Diana was on the telephone when he came into her room. She was listening; she raised her head at the sight of him; a look of blank astonishment came into her face. She stared, frowned, looked down at the file in front of her, then began to talk. It was a routine matter concerning the arrival of a French admiral from Alexandria. She seemed to know well and be on good terms with the man at the other end. She was laughing and there was the familiar richness in her contralto voice. Her telephone technique was in full deployment. A piece of business that she handled on the telephone always went more smoothly than one carried out by correspondence. "Good," she was saying. "Good. We'll do that. You can rely on us. We'll do our share if you do yours. Yes, I wish you were here to discuss it. But it's nice to have heard your voice. Good luck."

She was laughing as she replaced the receiver, but the frown returned as she raised her head. "What on earth are you doing here?" she asked, the warmth had gone out of her voice. It might have been a different person speaking. "You weren't expected for two weeks."

"I know. I've come in for the day."

"Why?"

"To see how everything was getting along."

"There wasn't any need. Everything's under control."

"I know, but . . . a friend was motoring in for the day, so I thought I'd take the opportunity."

"I see. There's nothing wrong, is there?"

"No, there's nothing wrong."

They looked at one another. Her face wore an expression that he could not fathom. It was resentful, but it was more than that. It was inimical.

"Are you doing anything tonight?" he asked.

"Nothing in particular."

"Could you dine with me?"

"I suppose so, yes."

"Sa'ad's then, at half past eight?"

"All right."

They were still looking at each other. There seemed no more to be said. He turned away; then checked. "By the way, is Jane here?" he asked.

"I don't know. I suppose so. Why?"

"Oh, nothing, nothing."

Farrar was equally surprised to see him. "I thought I heard your voice. Why on earth are you here?" It was said in astonishment, but also, Reid suspected, on a note of irritation.

He explained. "It seemed too good a chance to miss."

"If you like motoring, I suppose so. I was just about to write to you, as a matter of fact. I've warned the Mission that we'd have to have you back within a fortnight. They're insisting on their pound of flesh. August 15th. Everything is all right there, isn't it?"

It was practically the same conversation that he had had with Diana, except that Farrar was his usual cheerful self.

"How's everything?" Reid asked.

"Everything's fine."

"Any development in any of our projects?"

"Nothing very dramatic yet. Except that Alexis is leaving for Istanbul next week."

"That should be important."

"I think we'll have plenty to keep you busy with when you get back. By the way, are you doing anything tonight?"

"Dining with Diana."

"Of course, yes, well—"

There seemed no more to say. He had meant to ask to read the files, but he felt, suddenly, that he wanted to get out of the office altogether; to sit on the terrace of the St. Georges for this last, loveliest hour, and drink a cool glass of imported beer.

Diana called out as he walked down the passage, "Could we make it five past instead of half past eight?"

That means, he thought, that she's not going back to her flat first.

She arrived punctually; in the same clothes that she had been wearing at the office. She was, as always, neat and tidy; but she was very definitely not dressed for a date.

"What would you like?" he asked.

"A double pink gin."

His spirits sank. He knew what that meant. "I'm going to have beer," he said. "That sounds stupid, but beer is something you can't get in Deraa."

"How is it in Deraa?" It was said in the same tone of voice

with which Royalty, going round a military hospital, will ask, "And where were you wounded, my poor man?"

Reid felt his irritation rise. Two could play at that game. "It has its points. I've come to realise why nearly all Englishmen who come to the Middle East feel a warm kinship for the Arabs."

"And why is that?"

"Their manners in the first place. Their recognition of the bonds of guest and host." He enlarged upon the subject. He recounted his experiences. He might have been lecturing to a group of pupils.

She listened attentively. "How interesting. I always thought the English felt a kinship with the Arabs because they loved horses and were homosexual."

The waiter laid a menu on the table. "The food in my Mess is drearily British and I'm tired of Arab food. I'm going to have something French," said Reid.

"Then why did you come here? You should have chosen the Lucullus."

She ordered curdled milk, to be followed by minced lamb mixed with chopped onion and parsley and broiled on a skewer over charcoal. He ordered a fish soup, a vol-au-vent and a bottle of Lebanese red wine. "You'll have to drink most of that yourself," she said. "I don't feel like wine tonight."

"Would you like a pink gin instead?"

"As a matter of fact, I would."

His temper was mounting fast, but he was resolved not to show it. If he had to make conversation, it was something he was well qualified to do.

"There's always," he said, "a snag to every scheme no matter how carefully it's been worked out. Have you heard what the snag was in the wheat scheme?"

"No, I have not."

"A most unlikely one. A shortage of cash; no, not currency, but of paper money. No notes have been printed since the war began. They were flimsy notes and they have started to disintegrate; since the British occupation the amount of money in circulation has been quadrupled. We had plenty of gold in the banks, but when we had to pay out every week several thousands of Syrian pounds in small denominations there simply weren't enough notes available. We've cabled England for some more; but that takes time. One of my chief jobs every morning is the provision of enough notes to meet the demands of all the depots. That's funny, isn't it?"

"Hilarious."

He could have smacked her across the face. But he maintained the same brisk tone of party conversation.

"There's a lot of money in the Hauran now. When a Haurani is in the black, he does one of three things. Can you guess what they are?"

"You tell me."

"He kills an enemy, marries a maiden or runs off with a friend's wife. In each case the recompense to the family is about the same."

"I think that's cute."

"I thought you would."

It went on like that. He had never seen her in this mood before. He was so angry that he did not ask himself why she was in this mood. She had drunk her second gin quickly. He did not offer her a third. He poured her out a glass of wine. She barely sipped it. The waiter presented the sizzling skewer. Its aroma was rich and pungent. The pastry of his vol-au-vent was starchy.

"Have you heard any good Arab proverbs recently?" he asked.

"Have you?"

"I like this one:

'My enemies have done me much good:
May Allah keep for me mine enemies.
They found out my faults. I avoided them.
They competed with me. I reached higher places.' "

"That's excellent. I must remember that."

He gulped at rather than sipped his wine. It had a pleasant flavour, but he might have been drinking Coca-Cola for all the effect it had on him. She said, "The Duke of Gloucester was here last week. The Mission gave a tea party for him. The women were very perturbed as to whether to wear gloves or not."

"What did you do?"

"I hadn't any gloves."

She isn't the same person, he told himself. Her voice had a different tone. Her eyes were bright and cold. An alien spirit had taken possession of her form and features.

"What would you like as a dessert?" he asked.

"Just coffee."

"I'll have some cheese to finish off my wine with."

"Do that."

"You haven't finished your first glass of wine yet."

"I warned you, didn't I?"

"I'm not complaining."

The waiter brought an imported American cheese.

"Black market, from the American PX?" said Reid.

"That's what I'd suppose."

It was a Cheddar with a clear, sharp tang. But he did not linger over his wine. He signalled to the waiter. "My bill, please."

He had drunk five-sixths of the bottle, yet he was completely sober. He looked at his watch. Usually when he dined with Diana the time passed so quickly that they would be astonished at the lateness of the hour. "It can't be; twenty past eleven!" But it was now barely quarter past nine.

"I've had a long day," he said. "I'll be turning in."

"Me, too."

They drove back to her flat in silence, sitting in opposite corners of the Arabana. "Don't go away," he told the driver. They stood on the pavement, facing one another. In the dusk of the partial blackout, with her eyes veiled and her features shadowed, she became for an instant the Diana he had known. His anger fell away and a thudding surging wave of love came back. She held out her hand, as she would have to an acquaintance. "Thank you for my good dinner," she said.

"Thank *you*. See you in two weeks."

"Yes, see you in two weeks."

He watched her turn her key. She waved from the doorway. The door closed behind her. "No, I'll walk," he told the driver. It was a warm, still night. The sound of dance music jangled from the night club quarter. It was very early for Beirut. He was very far from drowsy. He wished he were in London now, with all the alternatives that London offered. He had recently been elected to a supper club off St. James's that was housed in what had been the kitchen quarters of a small Mayfair house. Its membership contained a number of young politicians, mainly Conservative; there would be officers from the Brigade, and White's. The long table in the dining-room had room for only a dozen diners. But there would be a group of members gossiping over their port or preprandial sherry, clustered in the warmth of the large kitchen fireplace. He would be certain to hear some interesting "behind the scenes" talk there; or he could look in at the Athenaeum, planning to sit in the long drawing room, turning over magazines; but almost certainly he would meet there unexpectedly someone he had not seen for half a dozen years. In London, there was no such thing as an empty evening: but here there were only night clubs and bars and the empty lounges of hotels. The St. Georges was probably the least unsatisfactory.

As he came through the main doorway a figure in uniform at the far end of the lounge left his chair and came across. Johnson. "Ah, there you are," he said. "I was thinking that you'd be looking in here before long."

Reid was glad to see him. Johnson would take his mind off his own problems. He still felt dazed. He did not yet realise what had happened and he did not want to know.

"How did it go?" he asked.

"Not too well. At least, I don't think it went too well. You can't tell with these Legation people. They are so smooth. When I was a subaltern and my captain had me on that mat, I knew exactly where I was. He tore me off a strip, and then it was all over. On parade, on parade, off parade, off parade. No bad feelings afterwards. But these damned fellows are so polite. They tell you to take a chair, they offer you a cigarette; they ask you about old so-and-so, and then about some Frenchman in the Jebel Druse and before you know where you are you're being cross-examined. I'm tired, let's have a night-cap in the bar."

Again Reid ordered himself a beer. "What did they want to see you for?" he asked.

"That's what I'd like to know: to get themselves in the picture was what they said; to learn who was who, and what was what. But I think they wanted to have another look at me, to size me up. I'd put up a black, and they wanted to know if I was the kind of chap who'd put up another one. That's how it seemed to me."

"Who was there?"

"A chap on the economic side, a half-colonel; a civilian in uniform, you know the type. The chargé d'affaires looked in for half a minute, only time to say 'Hullo'. I don't think that he was in on it. Then there was the vice consul from Damascus. Another civilian in uniform. He said that he happened to be in Beirut this week. I don't believe that for a moment. I bet he came down specially to report on me."

How self-important some fellows are, Reid thought, imagining that busy people have nothing else to do but worry about their concerns.

"Was there anyone else there? Reid asked.

"One of the secretaries, I didn't catch his name. They were all so damned polite, asking me question after question; questions that seemed all right at the time, but didn't seem so good when I thought about them afterwards."

"What kinds of question?"

"About the French and about France. Which parts of France I knew the best. Had I any personal friends in the wine country. If I found the Frenchmen I had met in France very different from the type of Frenchman I was meeting now in the Hauran. It couldn't have been more affable, but when I thought it over afterwards I realised that they had been finding out that I knew practically nothing about France and the French beyond what I picked up in the first war in the trenches. Shall I tell you what they're saying now, right this very minute? 'We've got to find a replacement for that man Johnson.'"

And maybe he's right, thought Reid. Maybe that's exactly what they were saying, right this minute. "How did you get the job in the first place?" he asked.

"Influence, pulling strings. There was a chap in the M.S. office that I knew. They needed officers in a hurry. And I had the right qualifications, the right school, Sandhurst, India, 'the Rag'. That's the trouble about me: on paper I look the kind of man they want; then they find out I'm not. Something breaks down somewhere. I can get jobs but I can't keep them. This isn't the army as I knew it. Regimental soldiering. That's the stuff I know: handling men, how to mix well in a Mess, sense of discipline, always properly turned out, respect for the King's uniform. This staff racket's not my game. This talk of a job: soldiers don't have jobs, they are posted to duty. They go where they are sent. Theirs not to reason why. . . . I'm all at sea, old boy."

He paused. He had looked old that afternoon, as he had slumped, snoring, in the corner of the car; he looked older now, leaning forward across the bar. He had reached the end of his tether, his short tether.

"It's different for you," he said. "You're used to files and reports and monthly summaries. You know what they're talking about. I don't. You can read between the lines. I can't."

That's what they all say, Reid thought. That it's different for me because I've led an academic life; because I'm used to paper work. Actually that very fact makes it the more difficult. They feel that there must be the right job for me somewhere, so they don't give me the job that is about half right, and that I could perform reasonably well. Men hard to place. I'm every bit as hard to place as Johnson. I'm lucky to be where I am.

Johnson had not stopped talking. "Have you heard that there's a new general order coming out, by which officirs of 45 who aren't needed, can go back to civilian life? I'll be forty-five next year. Do I want to go back to civilian life? Damn it, I don't know. Bowler-hatted. I don't care for that, going back to England in wartime, with nothing to do; joining the Home Guard, doing fire-watching. I don't fancy that. I must be on the look-out for something else. I see that. Is there any opening in your racket, on the administrative side?"

"Not here in Beirut. Perhaps in Cairo."

"What about Baghdad?"

"There might be, I don't know."

"Well, keep your eyes skinned; and I'll keep in touch. An adjutancy; someone who knows about allowances. Who can find his way through general orders. You'll think about it, old boy, won't you?"

"I'll think about it."

"That's good of you. God, it's a relief to deal with someone who speaks the same basic language. What time do we start tomorrow?"

"As early as you say."

"Directly after breakfast, then?"

"Directly after breakfast."

By nine o'clock they were on the road. The Bekaa valley looked as green and cool as it had the day before; and once again Damascus with its towers and minarets had a look of Oxford. Reid was still in a daze. He could not believe that that dinner had ever happened, that he had sat opposite Diana making conversation; that his blood had seethed with irritation, that he had wanted nothing more than to raise his hand and strike her across the face; when only four hours earlier his heart had been singing with exultation, when he had seen himself on the brink of the richest ten hours of his life.

What had happened. It had been a nightmare. Had it been his

fault? Perhaps it had. He should have warned her. It had been one of her bad days. Those two pink gins. He had taken her off her guard. He should not have allowed his disappointment to make him irritable. He should have been exceptionally considerate. He should have wooed, cajoled her into a cosy mood, when they could have talked with a freedom, an intimacy, that was not possible when they were "on a date"; a different kind of freedom, a rare, a special freedom. He remembered a time two months ago when she had said ruefully as they started out, "I'm afraid I shan't be any use to you tonight." He had said, "Then let's make it an occasion for an especially good dinner." It had become one of their most memorable evenings, when he had felt himself a disembodied spirit, moving in a clear limpid air, in an ethereal universe. Never had they been so close, in spirit. It was his own fault, surely, that they had not recaptured the same peace last night. She had been edgy and he had missed her mood. He had lost his temper. He had set out deliberately to rile her. Their dinner had been a battlefield. He had given as good as he had taken. It was his fault.

So he argued with himself as he drove through the bright green valley of the Bekaa. It was his fault. It was all his fault. When he got back to Deraa he would write her a long letter, not of apology, but of explanation; of implied explanation. She would read between the lines and understand, and in two weeks' time he would be in Beirut with a long tranquil late summer to be enjoyed. The world was rocking with premonitions of disaster. But they, for all they would care, might have been stranded on a Pacific atoll.

They reached Damascus shortly before one.

"What would you like to do?" asked Johnson. "Lunch at the Cercle, then a siesta in my office?"

Reid shook his head. "I don't want to be back too late; I'll miss lunch, an Arak in a café will be enough for me."

He went to the same café where he had sat on that first morning with Diana. A shoeblack importuned him and he was too lazy to resist. He sipped the cool clouded liquid and nibbled at his mezze. A vendor of lemonade went by; under his left arm was the large bronze jug from whose mouth projected a block of ice, pink-tinged across its base; under his right arm was the brass bound tray of glasses. Over his shoulder was slung the jug of water from which he could wash his glasses. He clattered two cups together as he walked. Every time he made a sale, he sang. It was the same man probably. Nothing was changed. Of course nothing was changed. In two weeks' time he would be in Beirut, seeing her every day, seeing her every hour of every day. They would laugh together over their ridiculous behaviour. "How could we have been so dumb?" they'd say. "It was just because we mean so much to one another that we were so dumb." "And it's much better now, isn't it, because of that?"

"So, so much better."

In two weeks' time, fourteen days.

He had slept badly the night before, but he did not doze off on the long drive to Deraa. His nerves were racing still. To left and right of him stretched the flat boulder strewn plain, with the thin yellow mist of chaff hanging over the villages. Was it really only forty-eight hours since he had driven here with Johnson?

In his room at Deraa was a low pile of letters. He turned them over. One from his father, the others looked impersonal. They could wait till later. He went over to the depot. The flow of wheat was being steadily maintained. He watched the weighing of it. He scooped up as much as he could hold between his hands; he tossed it over: there seemed very little sand. He stayed for half an hour, checking, testing; then crossed to the desk where payment was being made. The notes were very flimsy. When would the new issue come? What a hilarious predicament. He could recall the exact pitch of voice on which she had pronounced the word. He repeated it to himself, savouring the pain as one does when one presses one's tongue on a sore tooth. Hilarious. One day he would use that word; and she would look up quickly with a start of recognition. Their eyes would meet. She would smile. Then they would laugh together. "Weren't we absurd that day? Wasn't it hilarious?"

There was a bar in the Mess. But he kept a bottle of whisky in his room. He took his chair out in the garden and poured himself a drink to accompany the reading of his letters. There was a circular from the Athenaeum recounting what had transpired at the Annual General Meeting. The staff was apparently dealing satisfactorily with the difficulties involved by rationing and bombing. The members were thanked for their patience during the exceptional conditions. There was a list of deaths. He knew a bare tenth of them personally. In another ten years, he thought, I shall be finding my friends' names in that list. There was a circular from the London Library, stressing the difficulties under which the staff were working. Mr. Cox was still at his post. At last he came to his father's letter. It had been sent air-mail and had taken four weeks to reach him. It opened with an account of local life in Highgate.

"In some ways, my dear boy, we are hardly aware that there is a war in progress. Bombing has ceased. We sleep well at nights. Rationing is a nuisance and there is a new system of points by which you are allowed a certain measure of choice; but it does not help me very much as the articles I particularly fancy are not available. My only real grievance is the lack of marmalade. I can dispense with eggs, but I do not feel that I have breakfasted unless I have had marmalade. The French prefer jam, so do the Americans. I wonder when our national fondness for marmalade began and why. You probably know. I suggest that you should one day write a history of national characteristics in food-diet. The British habit of being called with a morning cup of tea. When did that start? The East India Company? I don't know. I should like to know."

There was a page of gossip about mutual friends. Then he wrote:

"I paid a visit on Rachel last Sunday. It is very pleasant to have her close at hand. She was very wise to let her house; it was too big for her. Too much housework and she was lonely during the term-time. She is getting a good rent from the Government, though most of it will be consumed, I suppose, by income tax. She will have told you of her flat in Bloomsbury. It is very handy for her work; and I think she is happy at the M. of I. She should be very useful there. I liked the young women with whom she shares the flat. They have friends in for drinks and it all seemed to me cosy and convivial.

"She has, I am sure, told you about all this. And I am sure that she has also told you about her spare work with the Committee of Jewish Relief. But has she told you how very important this work has become to her? She is deeply distressed about the fate of the Jews in Germany and Poland, as we all are, of course. But she is especially distressed because of her Jewish blood. It is something I tend to forget. She never knew her mother. She was brought up in the Christian communion. I have never thought of her as Jewish; and after all we in English do not have a Jewish problem. We think of ourselves as English; which we are. But in fact Rachel is half Jewish and half of her blood relations are Jewish. She cannot help wondering what would have happened to

229

her and them if Hitler had invaded England or if her mother had
married a European. She has also, I fancy, a sense of guilt because
she has not shared the bitter experiences of her race. She feels a
need to make compensation. This is a new side of her that you
would be, I am sure, wise to handle with care. In a sense this
letter is one of warning. Be on your guard when you write to her
not to say anything about Palestine that might offend her. In one
of your letters you referred to the difficulties that the Palestinian
problem was making in your present dealings with the Arab world.
I do not know exactly what you said in your letter; but she was
definitely indignant. 'Doesn't he realise,' she said, 'that the world
has a sacred duty to restore the Jews to their ancestral home?' I
was surprised at her vehemence. So I think, my dear boy, that
you should be on your guard."

Reid frowned as he put down the letter. What had he said
about Palestine? He could not remember. During his few months
in the Middle East he had come to feel, as did most Englishmen
who had lived in the Middle East, that almost every conceivable
mistake had been made at the Peace Conference after the first war.
The Arabs had been deceived, if they had not actually been betrayed. Europe and the U.S.A. had had no more right to create a
Jewish State in the Middle East than in Cornwall, Brittany or
Florida. You had no right to lop off a section of other people's
territory and hand it over to an alien race. Yet at the same time
he was a pragmatist to the extent that he believed that an established fact must be accepted. You could not put back the clock.
All you could do was attempt to lessen the consequences of mistakes. You could not solve your problems; you had to learn to live
with them.

What had he said to upset Rachel? But what he had said
seemed less important than the fact that she had been upset. It
was so unlike her. He had no more than his father thought of her
as being Jewish, but then in England, he, as his father, had classified his compatriots as being English: equal under the Crown.
This was a new slant, a new problem for himself.

He finished his whisky slowly. The sky darkened quickly; the
crested head of the date palm stood in silhouette above the roof,
against orange first, then green, and now a deepening blue. Time
to go into dinner.

The Town Major was leaning against the bar. He raised his arm
in a mock Hitlerian salute. "Heil, Prof. And how was the bright

city? How was Jeanette's, how was the Mimosa? We drank your health last night. Nothing like a professor on the spree. Where did you eat; what did you eat? Was she blonde, a brunette, a red-head? Regale us, let us be seated. Let us eat."

Corned beef had been converted into a cottage pie. There were stewed pears and Bird's custard. There was a sardine on toast. Afterwards tea was served. Throughout the meal the Town Major maintained a flow of heavy-handed badinage. "He won't tell us. Didn't I warn you all last night? Discretion, that's the scholastic line: virtuous as our Holy Father through the week, then when the last desklid drops on Saturday—oh, boy, the purple crescent; come on, Prof, give us the low-down. Cyril's going down next week. Give him the green light. Save him the fate worse than death."

So it ran on, and Reid did his best to reply on a note of appropriate jocularity. A film was being shown that evening in the N.A.A.F.I., but he excused himself. "I'm tired," he said. "I'd only fall asleep."

"I don't suppose you got much sleep last night," said the Town Major. "Come clean, Prof. Why hold out on us?"

In his room awaiting him was the table on which night after night he had poured out on paper the saga of his adoration. As he had driven back that morning he had pictured himself this evening, seated at the table once again, explaining in a contrite mood his ill-humour of the previous evening. A long letter but a light one, not apologetic, not complaining, not self-pitying, lit with raillery; a letter that would woo her back to him. It was barely nine o'clock. He was not sleepy, but now that the time to write had come he was in no mood to write. Better wait until tomorrow. Better wait until his mind was rested. He took his chair on to the pathway, hung the electric bulb over the window so that its light fell upon his book, and turned desultorily the pages of the Oxford Book of English Verse.

He did not write that night, nor the next. "Tomorrow," he would say. But when tomorrow came he would find himself in the same mood of torpor. He was living in a vacuum. He brooded over his father's letter about Rachel. Clearly there was a problem there. But at the moment there was nothing he could do about it. There would be no repatriation from the Middle East until the war was over, and the war had several years yet to run. His English problems had to await his return. So could Diana. So once again day after day, he drove between the depots that lay under his charge, listening to the complaints of villagers weighing the arguments of the Moukhtars, turning the wheat over in his hand, waiting and listening, and delivering himself of fulsome oratorical compliments which the interpreter would clothe in appropriate Oriental symbolism. He would conduct himself as though "time's winged chariots" were reined and bridled, as though Rommel were not beating on the Western Gate, as though autumn would never yield to winter, as though harvests would continue through the October rains; and all day long the sun beat out of a cloudless sky, with the glare of the parched earth dazzling him; and always just before sunset a breeze would blow from the Eastern mountains and the outline of the Eastern hills would merge into a succession of level layers of rich, soft colours, and his palate would savour in advance the sting of the first whisky that awaited him on the paved pathway by the little garden. He was in a vacuum. Let him enjoy it while he could.

Four days before his stay was up, he wrote Diana a brief note.

"You know as well as I do," it ran, "that I'll be coming back on Thursday, but I did want you to be quite sure that I'll be expecting you to dine with me my first evening and get me posted on all the Beiruti gossip. I aim to get in in the afternoon and will be round in the office before six. Let's make it the Lucullus. I need French food—and wine. It will be good to see you. Very good."

He left early in the morning; he did not pause in Damascus; he wanted to make a detour so that he could lunch in Zahlé. He sat in the same restaurant, at the same table, where he had lunched with Farrar and Diana. The restaurant was completely empty. He savoured its coolness, its quiet and its peace, with the rustle of the water cradling his thoughts and the canopy of boughs and leaves dappling the stream's ruffled surface. If Lebanon ever enjoyed a tourist's boom, what a fortune would be made by the restaurants along this bank.

He reached Beirut in mid-afternoon. On its outskirts the smell of stale Arak tickled his nostrils. It was good to be back; and it was good to find his flat looking exactly as he had left it. He had packed away a few personal belongings in a suitcase: a couple of Persian miniatures on ivory; a Damascene dagger; a Turkish prayer rug; a set of liqueur glasses and a decanter. He arranged them on his desk and table and on the mantelpiece. He had bought a bottle of cognac in the N.A.A.F.I. He filled the decanter. It all looked exactly as it had on that last night five weeks ago. He took a long, slow look round him, as he paused in the doorway, before starting out. Soon, very soon, he thought.

It was now mid-summer and Beirut was appreciably hotter than it had been two weeks before. The air had a close, overpowering humidity. The sun was half veiled by the heat. None of the Lebanese were wearing jackets. Most of them had discarded their ties; there was a feeling of languor and exhaustion. The women's hats looked damp, their shirtwaists limp. "I'd been warned about this," he thought. He sauntered slowly along the waterfront. His bush shirt clung against his shoulders. Even so, how good it was to be back here, to be able to accept the present, looking forward confidently into the future; with work that was of interest and value; with the hour to hour routine lit by Diana's presence. Nothing was changed. Everything would be the same.

There was no sentry at the M.B.S.C. main door. That was part of "the purloined letter" system of security. Anyone who wanted could walk in. Suspicion was disarmed. Nor was there any sentry at the office door, on which was affixed a handwritten notice—"I.S.L.O. Walk in." The door was closed. It was very quiet. His heart began to beat faster. It was no good his trying to pretend that he was not excited. The door of Diana's room was open. He looked inside. A female form was silhouetted against the window, facing it. A small and dumpy one. Who on earth was that? He walked on quickly. Farrar's door, too, was open. Farrar was at his desk. He jumped to his feet.

"Welcome back. It's good to see you. I'm getting over-worked. So's everybody else. We've so much work on hand. And the heat. Didn't I warn you? Still, it won't last long. Another month, six weeks."

Reid was not listening. "Who's that girl in Diana's office?"

"Prisilla Marston."

"And who may she be?"

"The new secretary."

"What about Diana?"

"Gone to Cairo."

"What?" He stared, astounded. "When did she go?"

"Last week."

"She never told me."

"She had no time. She left at forty-eight hours' notice."

"Is she all right?"

"Of course she is. Why shouldn't she be?"

"Why did she go?"

"Posted there. You know how it is in our racket. The boys in the small back room have a new idea and we all change seats."

"But why should she go to Cairo?"

"Someone whom she knew in London had been posted there. He asked for her."

"Did she want to go?"

"She didn't have any choice. Cairo has first call on us."

"But all the same. . . ." He was so astonished, so overwhelmed, that he could not realise that it had happened. Beirut and no Diana. He said the first silly thing that came into his head. "I'm going to miss her."

"We're all going to miss her. But Prisilla's very good. As a matter of fact, she's a better typist. Not that Diana wasn't good."

Reid was not listening. Beirut without Diana. "How long will she be gone?"

Farrar shrugged. "Presumably for ever; it's a posting."

Beirut without Diana. He blinked. Mentally he shook himself. "Well, if she's gone, she's gone. That's that. I'd better get those files and read myself back into the picture."

"Let it wait. There isn't all that hurry. You must be tired. Besides, I've got a small party at the flat tonight. The end of term. Aziz is going back to Istanbul. It's to say *au revoir* to him. Annabelle's coming. I was only waiting till you arrived to go. Let's be on our way."

The flat in the Rue Jeanne d'Arc looked just as much the same as his own flat had done. Beirut without Diana. Yet it was the same Beirut. And here was Annabelle with her inevitable brother; and she and Farrar were sparring like lovers in a Congreve comedy, exactly as they had been in December. They had made no progress.

"I am very sorry for Lebanese young men, in one way," he was saying.

"In what way, pray?"

"In the way of love."

"They are not accustomed to complain."

"That is their good manners."

"It is agreeable for young men to have good manners."

"Perhaps they do not know any better."

"Do you think that European young men have greater cause to be contented?"

"They at least have an opportunity of knowing what the young lady whom they intend to marry is really like."

"And do you think, my exacting captain, that that is an advantage? We do not think so here. We consider that the mystery of marriage is one of its greatest charms."

"How can you say that Annabelle?"

"Because that is how we are instructed by our elders. We are introduced to a number of young men, we dance with them, we flirt with them, but we never know what they are like, when they are alone. We wonder, we are curious, inquisitive. We look at those seven, those eight young men. Which shall we choose? Which is the one we really need? Finally we select one. But still we do not know what he is really like. What mystery. What romance. Finally, the great day arrives. The knot is tied. We drive away together. We are alone, to reveal at last our secrets to each other. What mystery, what romance. How can you compare with that your European honeymoon, where the bride and groom can have scarcely a remaining secret for each other: their picnics, their petting parties, their drives in cars. No, I don't envy them."

"But Annabelle, marriage is for life. Do you not run a great risk marrying a stranger?"

"Every man is a stranger until he becomes a husband. You play for safety. We are more romantic. And I suspect that our romantic marriages are more successful than your prudent ones."

Her eyes were sparkling, in her left cheek there was a dimple; and Farrar had an air of gallantry.

"But isn't it tragic," Farrar was continuing, "when you choose unwisely, when the stranger reveals himself to be an ogre?"

"There are remedies."

"Divorce is disagreeable medicine."

"There are medicines besides divorce." There was a look of mischief in her smile.

"If I were a Lebanese young man, and I fell in love with a Lebanese young lady, do you know what I should do?"

"What would you do, Monsieur Nigel?"

"I should wait until she had married, and then I should offer her that medicine."

"How very ungenerous of you, my cautious captain: to wish an unhappy marriage for her. Besides, how unromantic. Surely if you were genuinely attracted to a Lebanese young lady you would want above all things, you would rate it as your highest privilege, to initiate her into the pleasures and mysteries of love, pleasures that I am assured can be considerable. No, no, I am afraid that you confirm my worst suspicions of the English. You belong to a most unromantic race."

"If you would only give me an opportunity of proving that I can be a highly romantic suitor—"

"Ah, there you go again. You are not only an unromantic race; you are an exceedingly immoral one. It is a great pity, I sometimes think, that your father did not settle down after the first war in Lebanon and marry here."

"Or that your mother, during that first war, did not fall in love with an English officer and go back with him to London."

"That might have been a solution, too."

Listening to them, Reid thought, "I was wrong. They are not where they were six months ago. They have advanced a long way along a road." There was a new depth, a new fondness in their badinage. It had been a flirtation then. Now it was a courtship. A kind of courtship that was new to him, but whose attractions he could appreciate. To have to conduct a courtship in public, under the eyes and ears of friends and relatives, required address and wit and fantasy.

He looked round for the guest of honour. Aziz seemed on the immediate surface no different from the young man whom he had met in December on the terrace of the St. Georges. Yet Reid was conscious of a change. He was more self-confident. He was readier to enter a conversation. He did not sit and wait to have questions addressed to him. He asked them himself. Something must have happened while that girl from the Turkish office had been in Beirut. Diana had shrugged when he had asked her. "She said nothing to me. But then she isn't the kind of girl who would."

"And you're not the kind of girl who asks that kind of question."

"Exactly."

"How did they seem when they were together?" he had asked.

"I only saw them together twice. They seemed quite natural."

It might very easily have been a friendship and nothing more. They had seen a lot of one another, but then Eve had a business reason for seeing plenty of him. "I've always found," Diana said, "that when you are sure something is happening, it isn't. And where you are convinced nothing is happening, wedding bells are just about to ring."

For all he knew, nothing at all was afoot between Aziz and Eve. It was every bit as likely that Aziz was involved with a student at the A.U.B.

He went across to him. "I've seen nothing of you for weeks. I've been in Syria on the Wheat Commission."

"So I had been told."

"How did things go this term?"

"Well; quite well, thank you."

"Not having to worry about that exam. must have made a difference."

"It made all the difference."

"You won't have to worry about another one for quite a while."

"Not for a year."

"Does that allow you to mix more in the life of the University?"

"What do you mean by that?"

"If you are not worrying about exams, you have more time to join clubs and groups."

"I'm not interested in clubs and groups. I'm only interested in those who share my tastes."

"And that means music."

"Exactly."

"Haven't you made any special friends?"

"I'm more interested in the music that I hear than in the people with whom I hear it."

Reid laughed. "Haven't you guessed yet what was the point of all these questions?"

"No."

"I was wondering whether you had met the young woman who would have the same effect on you that music does."

"I have met no one in the University who could have that effect."

That wasn't the answer to his question, but Reid did not press the point. Sooner or later he would learn. "How long will you be away?" he asked.

"The new term starts on October the first."

"I'll be in touch with you soon after that."

"I shall be very grateful."

October the first. Two months away. Two months in Beirut without Diana.

237

13

EVE HAD LEARNT through the files that Aziz was coming up to Istanbul as soon as the term ended. Her anxiety had mounted as the last day of term approached. He had promised to come up as soon as his classes ended. But it was easy to make that kind of promise during a long siesta. He might feel very different seven weeks later. It would be stiflingly hot here now in Istanbul. It would be humid in Beirut; but there was the cool of Aley, there were the golden beaches. He might well decide to linger on. The list of passengers on the Taurus was always sent to the office. But it arrived two or three days late, except on occasions of special urgency, and this was not such a case. If Aziz had been a relative, or an English friend, she would not have hesitated to say to Sedgwick, "Could I be told as soon as he arrives?" But she could not display that interest where Aziz was concerned. She had no idea if Sedgwick suspected anything. She did not see how he could, unless Beirut had sent up a report. If Beirut had, it would have been sent up secretly. There were, no doubt, channels that she did not know for such communications. Sedgwick was highly secretive. "At any rate," she consoled herself, "if he does come up and doesn't telephone me I shall know he's here; even if I know it three days late. I shan't be in the dark."

But she need have had no such qualms. On the same day that she had read a list of Taurus passengers that did not include his name, she found a message at the Perapalas. Would she telephone Aziz that afternoon at five?

She telephoned him from the office, on a line that she was confident would not be monitored. She listened, with her eyes closed, to the ringing tone. Fifteen seconds, twenty-five seconds, half a minute. Was he out? But then it came. And the shock along her nerves was so great that she could scarcely speak. "Welcome back," she said. It was like a croak. There was a pause. Then his voice again. "When do we meet?"

"Tonight at nine."

"The same flat."

"Good." And he rang off.

Again she closed her eyes. She was grateful to him for not making conversation.

She returned to the flat to find Kitty standing before her looking-glass, turning first one way then another, patting at her hair, fluffing it, pulling it. "There's no doubt. I'm getting fat. There isn't any doubt about it. I am getting fat."

Eve made no comment. She could not contradict her. There was the evidence of the bathroom scales. But, even so, Kitty was beyond any question a highly appetising object.

"You've nothing to worry over yet," she said.

"Thank you for the 'yet'. The evil day is not far distant. I shall have to diet. How I shall hate it. How I enjoy good food. And tonight at Abdullah's won't do me any good. What are you doing?"

"Writing letters. I'll make myself a sandwich."

"What a hectic life you lead."

Eve had told Kitty that she had acquired a friend in Beirut, but she had supplied no details. She was tempted now to say, "As a matter of fact, I do. My Beirut boy-friend is coming here at nine." Sooner or later she would have to take Kitty into her confidence. But tonight—Suppose he had only come here as Fadhil's representative, to bring her a list of the information that he needed, to arrange a meeting when he could receive her answers. Until she was absolutely certain that Aziz was coming to see *her*, she could not expose herself to Kitty. If she had to be humiliated, let it be in the private hell of her own heart.

I must play it quietly, she thought. Seven weeks is a long time. I must humour him. He will probably be on edge. It is up to me. Everything is up to me. As it always has been. As it always will be. So she argued with herself; rehearsing her part, studying her lines. Thus and thus, it should be, and then. . . .

A bell rang in the hallway. She hurried to the door; she opened it. He stood in shadow; she could not see his features. "Aziz," she started. But that was the last thing that she was to try to say for quite a while. She was in his arms; or at least she was at the mercy of his arms, his hands, his lips, his fingers. She had been half flung, half carried across the room. He had flung off his coat, his jacket. He could not wait. She was on the couch, and he was at his knees beside her. He was ruthless yet he was tender, improvident yet prudent, avid and yet restrained, and suddenly, unbelievably, she was drowned, drenched, in the ecstasy that she had read about;

she was groaning, sobbing, writhing, sighing; and every bone in her body seemed to have been turned to water.

It was the same, but it was completely other.

Rested upon her elbow, she looked down at him, adrowse among the pillows, just as she had in Beirut seven weeks before. "He's mine, altogether mine," she had thought then. She still thought that; but now she thought it in a different way. Before this she had thought of him as someone to be spoiled, to be denied nothing, to be overwhelmed, so that nowhere, never, from any other woman, would he approximate to the raptures that he had reached through her. Now though she still thought of him as "mine," he had become the instrument of her own delight. His body was the violin out of which she struck chord after piercing chord. To him the change in temper may not have been apparent, but to her it was a complete reversal of roles. She was still dominant, still the initiator, the provoker; but whereas before she had schemed how she could create for him the maximum of pleasure, now she devised fantasy after fantasy for her own enjoyment, experimenting to discover what pleased her most, elaborating every ritual of approach. They never talked while they were making love, they never discussed afterwards the details of their love-making. They just made love, following her mood and whim. Did he realise, she wondered, that she no longer had to feign the frenzies that in Beirut had so enchanted him? She even wondered whether those frenzies were as convincing now that they were spontaneous. She had once read that an actress's words rang true no longer when she was expressing an emotion that she was feeling at the actual moment; an actress had to be outside her part. Could that be true in love? She could not think it was.

Back in the office, she would relive the hours that she had spent with Aziz. "He's mine, mine, completely mine." And there in the files was the proof of how much more completely he was hers than ever he suspected, than ever he could suspect. He had brought over from Fadhil a short list of questions, all of them concerned with Turkish exports to and imports from the Axis countries. He appeared to attach considerable importance to these questions. He did not convey in any way the suspicion that the records he received from Fadhil were relatively trivial in terms of the larger rewards that he was receiving from the Germans. He was astute all right.

She reported their meeting to Sedgwick. "How does he seem?" Sedgwick asked. "Is he disturbed about his assignment with the Germans?"

"He does not seem to be."

"I should if I were in his position. Perhaps he doesn't realise what a dangerous game he's playing. When do you see him next?"

"I promised that I would have the answer before he leaves."

"That's early in October."

"The last week in September."

"That gives you plenty of time. And until then. . . ."

He paused: there was a quizzical expression on his face. How much does he guess, she wondered? It was a questioning pause. Better lay her cards upon the table.

"I saw quite a lot of him in Beirut," she said.

"You told me that you had."

"We became quite friends. He has asked me to go to a concert with him. There is no reason why I shouldn't, is there?"

"On the contrary: it would look strange if you didn't go. It's useful to us, too. You may be able to give us some clues as to what's going on. I'm curious to see how he reacts to the treatment he's going to get here from the Germans."

According to Chessman, the Germans were very far from satisfied with the information that Aziz had been supplying. The actual information that he had sent had been of use, but there had been little of it. The German captain was proposing to get tough.

The interview took place during Aziz's third week in Istanbul. Chessman's report on it was added to Aziz's file.

At the start, the German had been cordial and encouraging. "I am very pleased with you," he said. "You have sent up the right kind of information. You have not wasted our time with trivialities. As far as we can check, what you have told us is correct."

"I am glad to hear that."

"But, and there is a but, a large but—you have sent us up very little."

"I have sent up all I had."

"But you should have found more."

"Where should I have found more?"

"In the ordinary course of your social life. You have these friends in the Spears Mission: through them you could meet other members of the Mission. Do you know the Military Ataché?"

"I do not."

"Then you should get to know him."

"We do not move in the same social circles."

"Then introduce yourself into the circles in which he moves."

"That is impossible."

At that point the German began to lose his temper, or to appear to lose his temper. He raised his voice. He shouted and blustered. He stood up. He pounded the table. "Do not use the word impossible to me. This is wartime. I am a captain on the General Staff of the German army. You are a student, a civilian, a boy. I issue orders. I expect them to be carried out. Impossible! Who are you to say impossible to me?"

Aziz remained calm. "I have very little spare time. I have my classes. I have my family. I have my friends. I can only give a limited amount of time to you."

"Then what use do you think you are to us?"

"It was your idea, not mine, that I could be of service to you."

Once again the German lost his temper. "Let me remind you," he thundered, "that you are in a very dangerous position. We hold a document that, if handed over to the Turkish authorities, would send you to prison for the duration of the war. Your education would be stopped: your career would be ruined. When victory finally rewards our arms, you would find yourself without a friend and with no prospects. Your parents would disown you. Impossible! Do not dare to use a word like that to me. You are not in a position to use a word like that. You are in my power."

Aziz did not interrupt. He listened without showing any signs of being cowed by this Niagara of words. When at last the German paused, he said, "Will it do you any good if I am handed over to the authorities? I can do nothing for you in prison. I should have thought that even the meagre information I obtain for you is of more use to you than that."

His quietness left the German without any fuel for his fury. His collar was tight and his neck bulged above it. His eyes glistened. His fists clenched and unclenched. "There is another point, too," Aziz added. "You want me to enlarge my acquaintance. I can only do that by inviting friends to have a meal or drinks with me. I shall need money for that." In the end he secured a monthly allowance of a hundred American dollars to be paid into a numbered account in Switzerland.

"That is a very smooth customer indeed," was Chessman's final verdict.

Eve chuckled as she read the report. It made her feel proud of Aziz. She wondered if he really was in danger. She did not see how he could be. And anyhow, everyone today was in danger in some way or another. The knowledge that he might be in danger pleased her. He was so much hers.

Aziz's time was not completely free. His family made demands on him, and except for her weekly day off duty Eve's mornings and late afternoons had to be spent in her office. But most days they were able to spend an hour or so in a café listening to the music, over a cup of coffee and a plate of sticky cakes, and three or four nights they dined together at Rejans. It would have been pleasanter in the summer heat to have enjoyed the cool of the Bosphorous or the Golden Horn. But neither of them had a car. It was convenient to dine near her flat, and she enjoyed the atmosphere of Rejans—the narrow passage off the Rue de Pera, leading to the short dark stairway. There was nothing romantic about the place. A wide rectangular room with a balcony and no shaded corner, but the menu was in French and the food was French. She loved the fat Russian who played Balalaika music. And the people who went there were sympathic.

One night Aziz nudged her elbow. "Don't look, but over your left shoulder there's a man staring at us."

"Do you know who he is?"

"I've an idea I've seen him, but I can't think where."

Aziz was short-sighted. He wore powerful glasses for reading and found it difficult to recognise across a room anyone whom he did not know well. She let her handkerchief slip on to the floor; she let it stay there for a couple of minutes, then stooped to recover it. As she straightened up she looked across the room. But of course, it was Alexis Belorian.

She caught his eye and waved. "You met him at his cousin Annabelle's and had an argument."

"Why, yes, so I did."

She watched him closely as she spoke. He had probably been speaking the truth when he said that he had not recognised Alexis. But he had not started when she pronounced the name. A very smooth customer indeed. Across the room, Alexis rose from his chair. She half closed her eyes, rehearsing the details of her rôle. She did not know yet whether the Germans in Istanbul had made contact with Alexis, since Alexis had not been instructed to report to the Istanbul office. If he had been contacted by the Germans, he would know that someone in Beirut had reported him, but he would not know who. Aziz, on the other hand, would remember having reported Alexis, but he apparently did not know whether the Germans had acted upon his recommendation. The point had not been raised in the interview with the Germans, according to Chessman's account; and Aziz had not produced his recruitment of Alexis as evidence in his own defence. Everyone was in the dark, to some extent; Aziz most of all. So she reflected quickly as Alexis crossed the room.

He stood looking down, with his mocking, self-confident, appraising look. "I thought it was you. But I couldn't be certain. In this dim room, and almost with your back to me; you do remember who I am, I hope?"

"I remember perfectly. Annabelle Koumayan's cousin. We met there at a cocktail party."

"And you told me that you were stationed in Istanbul and I told you that I was shortly coming here and I made a vow to myself to see you. The first thing I do, I said, will be to ring up that extremely attractive girl who works in the British Council. But, very stupidly, I forgot to make a note of your name. How dumb can one get? When I learnt that I was coming here I rang up Annabelle; she told me that you had left Beirut. She, too, had forgotten your name. She could not remember who had brought you. There was an English officer who she thought might know, but he was in Cairo for the moment. What was I to do? When I arrived here I rang up the British Council. I tried to describe you. No avail. Had you been a redhead or a Swedish blond, identification would no doubt have followed; but your charms, my dear young lady, are elusive. It is even possible that you are not photogenic, though, to those who can appreciate feminine charm, you have the femalest approach to a man's heart. Now let me repair my folly. Let me have, I beseech you, your address and name. Ah, thank you, thank you. Tomorrow, it is deplorable to have to state, I return to Lebanon. But I shall return; assuredly I shall return. My first act will be to telephone you."

He had talked with the confidence of a man who has enjoyed many easy conquests; and there was indeed a masculine magnetism about his self-assurance. She disliked him; she had indeed a definite repugnance for him, but she recognised that he was not negligible. There was a certain relief about a man who knew his own mind, who knew exactly what he wanted and did not depend on a woman to make up his mind for him.

During his rambling speech, he had completely ignored Aziz's presence; now he looked down at him with an air of contemptuous indifference. "It seems to me that I have met you somewhere?"

"We met at your cousin's house."

"Indeed, Annabelle knows so many people. Do you live in Beirut?"

"I am a student at the A.U.B."

"Indeed, indeed. I hope you are taking advantage of its facilities. Yes, I am sure you are. You appear to me the kind of young man who would. Well, I must be on my way. Beirut is a delightful city, but already I am counting the hours to my return here."

Aziz's eyes followed Alexis as he returned to his own table. "I don't like that man," he said.

"I don't think he's very likeable."

"I hope you won't go out with him, when he comes back."

"I don't suppose I shall."

"Suppose, only suppose?"

"I get lonely sometimes. In a foreign country, with no relations. The evenings can be very dreary. It is lonely coming back after a day's work to an empty flat. It can be a relief to go out, even with a man you don't particularly like."

She watched Aziz closely as she spoke. He frowned, and a pleasant glow touched her heart. He's jealous, she thought, that's why he doesn't like Alexis. Alexis is everything he isn't. But she did not linger on the subject. She switched on to a different topic. Jealousy was a dangerous ally. She had done enough. She had planted the seed. Let it grow quietly in the dark. It would not need watering. In its own due time the first green shoots would show.

†

A week later a report came from Beirut. Alexis' mission had been most successful. He had been contacted on the telephone, by a Turk, who spoke excellent English. "You will not know who I am," he said. "But I think we have matters that we can discuss

245

which would prove of interest and profit to us both. Will you meet me tomorrow afternoon in the Café Stanislas? Will you wear a red carnation? I shall be carrying an evening newspaper, and shall be wearing a grey cloth cap and a grey double-breasted coat."

The conversation followed a conventional pattern. "It has been reported here," so Alexis was informed, "that you have spoken in fashionable Beirut circles about the certainty of an Axis victory. You welcomed the prospect of this victory; you felt that a German victory would be of advantage to the Armenians. You dreaded an allied victory in which Turkey participated on the allied side. I do not, as a Turk, share your fear of what Turkey might do if left alone to settle the Armenian problem. I am a young Turk; one of the progressives. I deplore many of the excesses committed in the days of the Ottoman Empire. They will not be repeated by the new reborn Turkey. At the same time I am convinced that a victory for the allies would be disastrous for Turkey. I want to see an Axis victory, and as soon as possible before American intervention can be effective. I am wondering whether you would be prepared to assist the Germans to that victory."

"We have no idea," the report continued, "who the intermediary is. He is not Chessman and Alexis' description of him does not tally with any of the characters in our Rogues' Gallery. But there is no doubt that the German who eventually interviewed Alexis was the same man who interviewed Aziz. The interview followed a different course. This is, of course, only natural; Alexis was there of his own free will, while Aziz had been shanghaied. It was a blackmailing operation. The German was naturally bellicose and authoritative. He could treat Alexis as an associate, as an accomplice.

"The meeting was extremely friendly. The German explained what kind of information he required from Alexis. He asked Alexis a number of questions. He had learnt very little about him from Aziz. It is surprising that the Germans did not ask Aziz for more information about him. They must have had their own reasons for not letting Aziz know that they were proposing to recruit Alexis. We can only suppose that it was a part of their process of intimidation. They wanted to diminish Aziz in his own esteem; also to frighten him by telling him that he had produced no information of any value.

"Alexis' description of himself and of his social milieu impressed the Germans. Here, they thought, was the man who could give them exactly what they wanted. They must have compared him with Aziz, greatly to his favour.

"During the second meeting, they discussed the methods by which he should convey his reports. They are resorting to the device of secret ink, instead of the exchange of newspapers which they were employing in the case of Aziz. That was a clumsy method to which probably they only resorted because Aziz had been led to believe that a letter of his had been intercepted by the postal censorship. There is no such need for caution in Alexis' case. He has been given the number of a P.O. Box (3175), to which he is to write. The Germans are not proposing to write to him at all, unless they have some special reason. They believe that he has been adequately briefed. He has assured them that he will be paying regular visits to Istanbul. This suits our book very well. We shall provide Alexis with some notional characters and we shall maintain a steady flow of the kind of information that we want the Germans to receive. The possibilities of this operation seem to us very great."

Eve chuckled as she filed away the document. In this confused story so many characters were involved; nearly all of them were in the dark to a greater or a lesser degree. She was the only one who was completely in the picture; she alone knew what Aziz was really like.

†

The day of Aziz's return approached.

"I wonder how you are going to feel being on your own again?" said Kitty.

"That's exactly what I'm wondering myself."

"It was one thing to have that succession of empty evenings when you didn't know there was an alternative, or rather when you didn't know what the alternative was. It'll make a difference now."

"That's what I'm afraid of."

"You'd better start going out on dates like I do."

Eve did not answer. She looked thoughtfully at Kitty. She wondered whether Kitty, for all the variety of her experience, knew as much about love and love-making as she did.

"I suppose," she said, "that you find all these men different in some way."

"Of course I do."

"And that's the fun of it, finding in what way they're different?"

"Naturally."

"You look at the man with whom you're on your first date. You say to yourself, 'He looks like a dozen others, but there is something unique about him, something I've found in no one else,' and that's the kick about it, isn't it?"

"Everyone knows that, surely."

"Each man has something new to teach you."

"He's a very peculiar man if he can't. Somehow I don't believe I'd go on a date with that kind of man. Instinct would warn me."

"But don't you think. . . ." Eve paused. She was not exactly sure what she had in mind. She had not formulated to herself in words what she suspected in herself as a conviction. "Don't you think," she said, "that you might be able to find all those differences combined in a single man, if you gave him the chance to show himself?"

"What are you trying to say: 'give him the chance to show himself.' I give him every chance I can. I'm most cooperative."

"Chance was the wrong word: wouldn't it be more exciting to think, when you're with a man on your twenty-seventh date, 'It's going to be different in some way tonight.' Mightn't it be, if you expected it to be?"

Kitty laughed. "I believe you really are in love," she said.

Eve did not answer. Really in love? That was something she did not know. Love! What did it mean; but this she did know, and for very certain: that each date was a fresh date, a landmark, a stage of progress. Why could not one man give you as much as a hundred men? If you were patient, if you waited, if you let the thing go deep. During those two weeks in Beirut she had thought proudly, "No woman will ever be able to give him as much as I have done." Now, with even greater pride, she thought, "No man will ever be able to give me more than he has done, than he is doing."

When the last night came, she thought, "Tonight it will be different. There will be something new." And it was, there was. Often in the days before, she had had the sense of being a horse, ridden by an impatient jockey, goaded towards the winning post. But now suddenly, miraculously, the roles were reversed; he was the charger, she the rider, who was urging him towards the winning post, forcing him, spurring him beyond his strength; faster,

faster; she pressed her knees into his flanks; tighter, tighter. Fantasy lit her frenzy. If only this were a real race she would have a whip, she'd flog him home. "One day I'll buy a whip," she thought. Maybe he'd like it. She could make him like anything she liked. Faster, faster, faster.

Aziz's return to Beirut caused less excitement in the third floor office in the M.E.S.C. building than his last one had. He was not potential, in the way that he had been, in the way that Alexis had become. Reid and Farrar discussed the issue. "His only real use to us now," said Farrar, "is that we learn through him what the Germans want to know."

"That's something, surely?"

"Oh, yes, of course; and we learn how much it's possible for a reasonably bright young man to pick up here in Lebanon, if he keeps his eyes and ears open. But . . . well, it's all secondhand, you know."

"Like Plato's shadows in the cave."

"Probably, Prof., probably, but it's a long time since I was *au fait* with that."

"Whereas Alexis is first-hand. He can send what we want sent up."

"Precisely. We're in control there." He paused. He was sitting on the edge of his desk, swinging his leg. He looked singularly nonchalant, very much the kind of youngish man who would have exasperated one of the older school. "Lounge-lizard. What's he doing here in this playground, fiddling around with papers, when men ten years older than himself are driving tanks in the Western Desert?" But, he had with his elegance and verve very much the air of a crusader, fighting a modern war with modern weapons; there was nothing here of the first war embusqué He looked round the room with its high steel filing cabinets, the repository of the section's work. He wore a pensive, puzzled look; then suddenly his face lit up.

"It's only occurred to me," he said "this very moment. We've reached a watershed; all this time that I've been here—and most of the time that you've been with me—we've been building up a pattern of defence that could switch over to the offensive at any moment. Our traps are baited. We have Alexis trusted by the Germans, ready to tell them anything we want; we've got Aziz less trusted by the Germans, but as far as we are concerned he's a monitored exchange. Then there's Chessman on the Taurus; there are those chaps in Aleppo and Damascus busy spreading rumors in the bazaars. We've got all these vice-consuls and third secretaries in this and the other embassy and legation, wearing uniform, looking like soldiers, but actually assembling information. We have built up an underground; now we've got to find out what we can do with it. We're trained, we're ready, we're on the ball. Where are we to go? You see what I mean, Prof? The water-shed: we've reached it. It's now up to us to find where and how we can attack. Boy, this is where we start."

14

AT FIRST LIGHT on the morning of October 23rd, Montgomery launched his long awaited attack at Alamein. For a week the issue hung in doubt, then the tanks broke through and Rommel's army was in full retreat. "This is not the beginning of the end," announced Winston Churchill, "but it is the end of the begin-ning." In the first week of November a conference of the I.S.L.O. departments was called in Cairo. "You'd better go to that," said Farrar. "You've never been to Cairo."

Reid half closed his eyes. For weeks now he had been wonder-ing how he could wrangle a visit there, and now miraculously the chance had come. "I'd like that very much," he said. Cairo, with Diana a few yards away. Diana in the office where he would be reporting every morning. Diana again, after all these weeks. "When does the conference start?" he asked.

"On Monday week. Why not go down on the Friday train and spend the week-end sight-seeing?"

"That would suit me fine." This time he would not make the mistake of arriving unexpectedly.

"Dear one," he wrote, "I'm so excited. I'm coming to Cairo for that conference. You know what it's all about. I aim to check in at Shepheard's on the Saturday. Which meal will you have with me on the Sunday? Could you leave a message at my hotel?"

He wrote only one other letter, to Gustave. That was at Farrar's suggestion. "I wish that you'd look up that young man who came out with you for the Mission. I forget his name. You called him 'Gustave'. I'm curious about him. I've an idea that we might have a special use for him. Find out all you can."

So he wrote to Gustave, suggesting that they dine together on the Saturday. Gustave could put him wise.

He reached Cairo in the early afternoon. There were two messages waiting for him: one from Gustave, saying he would call for him at eight-fifteen; another from Diana saying that lunch would be fine, that she would call for him at one-fifteen. So that put paid to that. He could siesta and have a bath and enjoy the rare privilege of not having to go into an office at five o'clock.

The light had fadded by the time he came downstairs. The large Oriental lounge, with its cushions, its fountains and its divans, was mainly empty. He walked on the terrace. The evening was warm enough for a man to sit there without an overcoat. He wished that he could have been here before the war, so that he could have compared its present with its past. Was it so different? There were dragomen with smart jackets and tarbooshes; there were shoe-shine boys with their black brass-bound caskets; in the street there were the drivers of taxis and arabanas soliciting custom; there were vendors of postcards, cigarettes and beads; there was a brisk bustle in the streets; but there were not many British officers. Most of them were in their offices. Those who were on leave were resting. It was early yet for them.

He walked into the street, turned right and sauntered towards the gardens. Farrar had given him a map of the city. "Sharia Soliman Pasha," he had been told, "that's what you must make for first." It was crowded now and the shop windows glittered. In Beirut he had often thought, "Who could imagine that there was a war going on five hundred miles away?" Here, it was hard to believe that this affluent international metropolis was the headquarters of an army, engaged in mortal combat. Beirut was a delightful, picturesque Mediterranean township; but Cairo was a city. And once again, looking at the men and women who hurried or loitered past him, many of the women veiled, many of the men in red tarbooshes, many of them wearing the baggy pantaloons that were ready to accommodate the birth of the Messiah, here as in Aleppo and Damascus, he had the feeling of how remote from this people was the war being waged between the Axis and the allies. This was not their war. They had become involved in it, but it was not their war.

He sauntered down Soliman Pasha, till a road, turning to the right, led to the bridge over the Nile. He paused on the bridge looking down on to the brown swirling waters of the river that had coloured so much of his youth's reading: Antony at Actium, the serpent of old Nile, Napoleon at the Pyramids. Had it looked so very different to Cleopatra? Had not the same brown-sailed ships steered down it? The *fellahin* along its banks was growing cotton under the same immemorial tradition. The Pyramids had seen the passage of so many armies.

It was nearly seven before he was back at Shepheard's. The main lounge was more crowded now; the officers on leave had finished their shopping or siesta. He directed himself towards the bar. He would have seventy-five minutes' start of Gustave, but he would make it an early night. He had reached the age when he found it prudent not to drink hard liquor late at night. A voice from the dusk greeted him.

"Hi there, Prof."

It was Johnson. Reid had not seen him since they had driven back together to Damascus. He had heard no news of him, and had assumed that he was still employed with the O.C.P. He was not particularly surprised to find him. There was a disease known to the Middle East as Cairoitis: the periodic and overpowering need to savour the fleshpots of the metropolis. "Have you wangled a conference here too?" he asked.

Johnson laughed wryly. "I wish I had."

Only then did Reid notice that Johnson was wearing three stars instead of a crown upon his shoulder. He waited for an explanation. It came obliquely. "I see that you are in the same spot too," said Johnson.

"What do I take that to mean?"

"That you haven't gone up. Whereas I've gone down, after a whole year in the Middle East. I should think that we're the only two old stagers in the area in that position, Sandhurst, vintage 1916. Something must have gone wrong that year with the harvest."

"What are you doing here?"

"In the pool, waiting for an appointment. Some bloody hopes. If I were in the U.K. I'd be classified as 'temporarily relegated to unemployment.' Not the sack, but the embroidered bag. They can't very well do that here; there's no unemployment to be relegated to. Besides, they don't want the expense of repatriation. So they send me on damned fool courses. Map reading. Sanitation. Aircraft recognition. To hell with it; let's have a drink."

Reid would have preferred to drink alone. It was a pleasure that he could rarely allow himself in the corporate atmosphere of army life. Still, listening to other people's troubles had become his job.

Half an hour later he was feeling that he had never listened to problems for which he could see less of a solution. Many of his pupils had known periods of black despair, and suicide was an occupational hazard of the late teenager. But he had known in their case that there was a sure solution; they had only to be patient; they would get their second wind. They had youth and flexibility and untapped resources. He could encourage them, reassure them in the certainty that there was a cure. It was different in Johnson's case. Johnson was far from being desperate. He was merely moodily discontented. Yet in point of fact he had more need of despair than any of the young students for whom "the pillared firmament seemed rottenness and earth's base built on stubble." There was no future for Johnson, and during the years when he had had youth and energy he had not built up the bastions for his old age.

Johnson had nothing to go back to. "I suppose," he said, "that your University makes up the difference between your salary and your army pay."

"There isn't very much."

"But there is a difference, and if you dropped a pip it wouldn't make any difference to you financially. You started as a Lieutenant, didn't you?"

"Yes."

"So that when you became a captain you weren't really any better off. It simply meant that the University cut your stipend."

"That's so."

"There isn't any real inducement to you to become a major or a colonel. You wouldn't be any better off financially, and rank means nothing to you."

"Why do you say that?"

"Because you're a professor first; there's the handle on your name. The world's lousy with half colonels. You are more important in your own right than you could be in the army. You're in a very fortunate position."

"That's what everyone keeps telling me."

"They're right too, aren't they?"

"We all have our little crosses, even the most seemingly immune of us."

"Even you?"

"Even me."

"I'd like to know what they are. It might give me a fellow feeling. Are you doing anything tonight?"

"I'm dining with our old friend, Gustave. But he isn't due for another half hour yet. We've time for a second drink."

At any rate, he thought, Johnson had the resource of whisky. When a young man sought relief from his troubles in the bottle he drank a great deal too much, he did not know his capacities; the "bender" on which he went had usually disastrous consequences. Johnson knew how to handle his liquor; he could let the smooth distilled produce of malt and barley soothe his troubles and cheat him into a favourable opinion of himself and of his prospects. Johnson's position was not desperate as long as he could afford whisky and provide a reasonable setting for its enjoyment.

"Is Gustave in your racket?" Johnson asked.

Reid nodded.

"How is he doing in it?"

"That's one of the things I'm hoping to find out tonight."

On the surface everything appeared to be going excellently with Gustave. He was wearing a well-cut gabardine uniform; his shoes glistened. He had put on a little weight; it suited him, giving him a sleek, well cared-for look, in tune with his Continental air.

"Where would you like to dine?" Reid asked.

"Not in this caravanserai."

"Where do you suggest?"

"The Turf Club."

"I'm not a member."

"But I am. I'll do the ordering, and you can pay me afterwards. That'll improve my credit there. You'll like it. They've got good wine."

Gustave had been very right. The Turf Club was very much his kind of place. The dining room was dark and panelled. The tables were not close together. It had a thoroughly English air and the wine list included a Krug 1928. There couldn't be much of it left, he thought. Maybe it would be the last bottle of it he ever had.

At the sight of the steaming bucket, Gustave's spirits rose even more. "I'll certainly impress those waiters this time."

It should certainly loosen Gustave's tongue, if it needed loosening. Reid asked him how he liked his work. Did he, at his age, find himself bored by the long hours of office work? Did he wish he had a more active life? Gustave shook his head. "Not here. I might in England, but Cairo is like home; besides, I'm not in the office all the day, not by any means. I have a flat of my own. I'm allowed to wear mufti; the big boys expect me to get around. I'm half Egyptian after all. I know the kinds of joke that an Egyptian will find funny. People are much readier to repeat a rumour if it'll make the hearers laugh. I've got a nose for that."

"I'm told Cairo is very expensive now."

"It's not for me. I know how to do things cheaply; the way you do in London. An American would spend twice as much there as you would. I speak Arabic. That makes a tremendous difference. They feel they can trust me. We laugh at the same things. We're friends. They wouldn't try to pull a fast one on me. Besides, there's the question of girls. I don't have to spend vast sums of money on the women whom half G.H.Q. are chasing. I meet the kinds of girl that the other officers wouldn't meet: you know the kind, shop girls, junior secretaries, the kind that I'd be having affairs with in England. There are a lot of Greeks here. Those girls wouldn't go out with a British officer who only spoke schoolroom French. They wouldn't feel at ease with him. That's what a girl wants: to feel at ease, to be amused, given a good time."

"And you've got yourself that kind of girl?"

"I'll say I have. A Cypriot: half Greek, half Lebanese, lives with her parents, works in a bank; had the dreariest of times till I turned up, never went anywhere, never met anyone."

"How did you meet her?"

"In a cinema; or rather, outside a cinema, waiting for the big picture. We recognised each other right away. It was one of those things. But if I hadn't spoken Arabic it would have been bogged down, never got off the ground."

"And the other officers here, the ones who don't speak Arabic. How do they manage?"

"They don't; or at the best unsatisfactorily. The competition is too great. And there are all those heroes coming in from the desert, with money to burn, vowed on making the most of a ten days' leave. They are entitled to the best and they get the pick.

255

Most of the available English girls are out for marriage. They get their heads turned, too. They were nobodies in England, but here they are the belles of the ball. They've raised their sights. They get my goat."

"But I assume there are affairs going on."

"Of course, there are married men who say they can't get a divorce in wartime; though of course they could. It's their alibi. And there are married women whose husbands are at sea, or prisoners of war or something; then there are others who are out for all the fun they can get until Mr. Right turns up, and of course that kind of thing gets around and my, but aren't they a dish of honey with the bees around it; but the odd thing about it is that with all the world to choose from—I reckon that there's never in any one place been such a congregation of superb specimens of masculinity—in spite of all that they fall, some of them, for the most unlikely males, if male is the right word for them."

"Titania was enamoured of an ass."

"Exactly, and as an example there's that girl in our office."

"Which girl in our office?"

"The one who's just been seconded from Beirut. You must know her."

"Yes, I know her."

"You should see the kind of man she's fallen for."

"What kind of man has she fallen for?"

"A perfect squirt: a Frenchman, a sawn-off job if you ever saw one, and she, as you know, is over six feet high."

"What does this Frenchman do?"

"A vague liaison job, mainly with the French fleet in Alexandria."

"How old is he?"

"Twenty-five, thirty. He's only a lieutenant."

Reid raised his glass to the light. It was darker, deeper in colour than most champagnes. He had drunk it for the first time in the Athenaeum with the Barlow brothers in '38. Alan had said, "This is the only champagne that Tom will admit to being a wine." He held it to his nose, savoured its aroma, lowered it to his lips. It should, at such a moment, have smelt sour, its taste should have been bitter. It didn't, it wasn't; it was the familiar ethereal bubbling nectar. "In two years it'll have passed its prime," he thought. "I may never taste its like again."

"How long has this been going on?" he asked.

"It started within a week of her arrival. The *coup de foudre*. We were all astounded. She's crazy over him."

Reid half closed his eyes. This is the worst moment of my life, he thought.

"A rather similar thing happened in Beirut, with one of the officers in the B.S.M. The girl in question. . . ."

How soon can I call this evening off, he thought.

It was one o'clock before he was back in his hotel; Gustave insisted on showing him the town. "You haven't got to work tomorrow. It's your first night here. A Saturday; and I'm the man to show it you. First we'll go to Bardia's . . . then. . . ."

And when it came, Reid did find the Bardia cabaret entertaining. It was the first time that he had seen Oriental belly dancing. It was, he could appreciate, exceedingly well done. Just as he could see that the small *boîte* where a Russian emigré in a long white smock was strumming a guitar had an authenticity that he had not found in Paris or Beirut. Later, Gustave was for driving out to the Seraglio near Mena House. "Really, Prof, you should see what an Oriental cat house is like."

"I'm sorry. It's too far, and I'm too tired. It's been a long day for me."

"Has it? I suppose it has. And, after all, that kind of thing could not mean anything to you."

"No?"

"You are very lucky in that way."

"I am?"

"You are settled down; children and a wife, established. That side of life has ceased to worry you; yet you are not so old that you can't play golf and cricket."

"Not quite senile yet?"

"Exactly. I've watched you. You really do enjoy yourself at times. Frankly, I envy you."

The next time I have that said to me, thought Reid, I'll scream.

Next morning as he sat on the terrace of the hotel, he thanked heaven that he had had that warning. He was on his guard. She would not know he was. He held a tactical advantage.

The clock moved round. Half past twelve, twenty to one, ten to one. She had a punctual nature. She had not in that connection reacted against her father. It was as likely as not a working day for her. She would come by taxi or in an office car. Not in a ghary. He begun to watch each taxi. Every third one seemed to draw up here. It was, for the most part, officers who got out of them. They came in threes and fours on the way back from their offices; some of them being dropped off at the Continental. A long, low car, chauffeur driven, flying a foreign flag he did not know, drew up. The door opened and a long slim leg slid out. He blinked. Yes, it was she all right.

She stood on the pavement, her back to him, talking inside the car. She remained as the car drew off waving; then she turned. And he was right back, in heart and spirit, to those enchanted Beirut days.

It was cool though the sun was shining. She was wearing a rough off-white woollen coat and skirt; there were large buttons on the jacket and wide bands of a dark blue material stitched across it. It gave her the look of an hussar. And she was wearing a small white hat, side tilted, its narrow blue ribbon adorned with a pheasant's feather. She was half smiling as she walked up the steps with her lips parted; her eyes were clear and wide; there was a glow and gloss about her.

At the sight of him, her half-smile became a real smile. She held out her hand. Because of her height she never kissed friends in public. Her handshake was firm and friendly. There was no doubt that she was glad to see him.

"That was a very smart car," he said.

"The Brazilian Minister's."

"You're moving in high circles."

"Our fathers were good friends. Brazil was an ally in the last war, remember?" She sat beside him on the terrace.

"What'll you have?" he asked.

"A Tom Collins."

"So'll I. That's a new scent you're wearing."

"Do you like it?"

"It's rich and heavy, and it's right for you."

"I got it in the Souks. They're experts at that kind of thing."

"They should be: they've been at it longer. The Arabs discovered distillation."

They sipped through straws at the cool sweet liquid. He watched her over his glass's rim. She had a radiant look. Was that because she was in love? Had she looked like this to strangers after that first trip to Damascus? He had been too much in love to notice.

"How does Cairo compare with Beirut?" he asked.

She shrugged. "There's no comparison. It's a bigger place. It's a centre. It's more important than Washington or London at the moment. It's where things are happening. It's the one place where there is fighting, apart from the Russian front, of course. Everyone has to come here, sooner or later. Beirut was small and provincial. The French wanted to keep it that way. There's a King here and a Court; there are Ambassadors instead of ministers; there's another thing, too: I hadn't realised it when I was actually in Beirut but I feel it now. For we English, Beirut was a sideshow, a backwater. It was French, not English. Cairo is an extension, of the British raj; it's the centre of the British war effort. You keep meeting here people whom you've known all your life; you can talk about your acquaintances and friends. You never could do that in Beirut, could you? We have a personal life outside the office, in a way that we never did in Beirut. One's in touch with the big world here."

He asked her where she would like to lunch.

"Why not here?" she said. "It's really very good. I like all this grandeur, and you don't want a small French restaurant. You have enough of that. You'll hear people say, 'I can't bear hotel food,' but the Ritz is a hotel, after all."

She was curious to hear all the Beirut gossip. "Tell me about Nigel Farrar. Is he ever going to do anything about Annabelle?"

"It's hard to tell. Sometimes I think yes, sometimes I think no. They always flirt when they're together."

"He'll be a fool if he doesn't marry her."

"Lebanon's a long way from England."

"That's not going to matter so much after the war. England's going to be a different place. We may not recognise it."

She was animated, friendly, gay. The talk did not flag for an instant. It was just as it had been in those first days, nearly a year ago. Yet there was a subtle difference. He had been always conscious then of a progression; they were moving towards a point. Each lunch, each dinner, was a stage, a landmark. Each time they had revealed a little more of themselves, or at least she had of herself; and through that revelation they had drawn closer to one another. Later, when the final landmark had been passed, though their meals had started as today's had done with easy animated gossip, there had come a point when suddenly the whole spirit of their meeting underwent a change, when they would cease to be friends and become lovers, even though they did not talk of love. She had a habit, when they were sitting side by side, of lapsing into silence and leaning forward across the table, her elbows on it, her hands closed and her chin rested on them. It was a signal, an invitation. And the tone of his voice would change; he would begin to woo her; with a difference not so much of words as of approach. He might be talking of poetry or of politics, but he would have the feeling that he was swinging incense before a shrine: he would be bathed in the memory of the previous night and the prospect of the enchantment waiting him.

"You are looking wonderful," he said.

"I'm feeling wonderful."

Jealousy stabbed at him. He longed to question her, but knew he mustn't. If she had anything to say, then she would tell him. He tried to put himself in her position. She had come here on her guard. As she drove that morning from her office she must have thought, "This is going to be one of the most awkward two hours of my life. He will imagine that we are going to pick up the threads where we left them. I don't want to hurt him. I shall have to be tactful, diplomatic. What a strain." Well, he could spare her that. And maybe, just for that, she would be grateful to him, until the story closed.

He asked her about the work. Was it more interesting here in a G.H.Q.? She shrugged. "It's a circle with a larger radius, but what's most fascinating for me, anyhow at the moment, is seeing how our Beirut problems appear in the Cairo office. I get all your reports, of course, and I think of you and Nigel drafting them, and then discussing them, and then that staff-sergeant putting it on the machine. It makes me nostalgic. But what's really entertaining is to see how certain things that seemed very important to us in Beirut don't seem so important here, and vice versa."

"Can you give me an example?"

"That Turkish student. You put in so much work on him and they're not very excited over him; whereas they rate that cousin of Annabelle's very highly."

"Can you explain why?"

She hesitated. "It's the new policy. You'll hear all about that tomorrow. Michael Stallard's here."

"Michael Stallard?"

"The controller. Don't you remember? He got you in our show."

"Of course."

Stallard. That lunch at Ajalami's. The prelude to so much. Stallard. An idea came to him suddenly. "Do you remember a Major Johnson?"

"I don't think so. Why?"

"He was one of those Spears Missionaries who were sent out by mistake. He's at a loose end here in Cairo. He was a contemporary of mine at Sandhurst. I was wondering if there was a possible vacancy for him with you. Stallard would be the best man to ask, wouldn't he?"

"I'd say so. He likes you."

They talked easily, cosily; they might have been cousins, enjoying a family gossip. She was completely self-composed, but then she always had been. What was she thinking behind that mask? Was she wondering how she could maintain this calm, uncontroversial level? Like the heroine of a Victorian novel, hoping to avoid a proposal that she had no intention of accepting?

"How long are you staying here?" she asked.

"A week."

"That's fine. Did you hear that there's a cocktail party on Tuesday evening?"

"Yes, I heard."

"Have you seen a programme of the conference?"

"I haven't, no."

"I thought you might not have. I've brought along a copy. Your address is tomorrow afternoon. I fixed that. I thought you'd like to get it over early, so that you could relax and enjoy the rest of it."

"That was very thoughtful of you."

"I'll look forward to hearing what you have to tell us."

"It'll be familiar ground to you."

"Something new must have happened since I left. Besides, I want to hear you lecture. I never have, you know. I've always wanted to."

It was almost the first thing that she had said to him. He recalled the tone of voice in which she had said it, recalled the light in her eyes and the way her lips had parted; recalled it with an overpowering sense of loss. Maybe he would never see that light in her eyes again, never hear that tone in her voice. She looked exactly the same, sitting beside him at a banquette table, her elbows rested on it, a glass of red wine cradled between her hands. But he was seeing only the shell, the surface; the Diana that her

261

relatives knew and her acquaintances. The essential, the inner Diana had disappeared. He had taken the miracle of her for granted. He had not realised that she was the outcome of her mood and now that her mood had changed, she had become no different for him from what she had been all her adult life to a hundred others. Would he ever again see the Diana he had known in those enchanted days?

The meal moved to its close. He glanced at his watch. Twenty to three. Time hadn't dawdled this time as it had at Sa'ad's.

"When's the Brazilian Minister calling for you?" he asked.

"He's not. I'll have to take a taxi."

He was about to offer to drive her back, but checked; he did not want to sit beside her in that enclosed proximity.

"I'll give myself an industrious afternoon, working on that lecture."

"You do that. I don't want to be disappointed and I don't want them to be. I've sung your praises till they're bored with me."

He walked out on to the terrace with her. A small bare-footed boy ran forward. "Taxi! Taxi!" She turned and they faced each other. He held out his hand.

"This has been fun," he said. She did not reply. She looked at him, very directly; almost questioningly, as though she wanted him to say something, something that would make things easier for her. He did not. He felt that by his silence he had gained not only a tactical but a strategic point.

She was sitting in the third row of the conference room. There was an audience of about a hundred. Representatives had come from the various D.S.O. (Defence Security Office) organisations in the Middle East. There were a number of staff officers from G.H.Q. Middle East, also a few from H.Q. eighth army. He was relieved that Diana was sitting close. It meant that he did not need to look at her. He always addressed himself to someone in the back two rows. He knew that if his voice was pitched to the back of the hall he would be audible in the middle rows. If he became conscious of personalities in the front row he might not be heard at the back. And it was his practise while the chairman was introducing him to search the back two rows for a sympathetic face. If Diana had been at the back he could not have helped but be aware of her right through his address. As it was, he would only have to look at her three or four times during the half-hour that had been allotted him.

He rose to his feet with the self-confidence that came from long familiarity with the handling of an audience. He explained how the problems that had faced his organisation in Lebanon and Syria were basically different from those which were presented to the D.S.O.s in Egypt, Cyprus, Palestine and Iraq. He reminded them of the difference between M.I.6 and M.I.5. "M.I.5—and all our organisations are branches of M.I.5—is concerned with defensive security and it operates in those countries which are British colonies or are a part of the British raj. It is counter-espionage, but it works through the local police which it controls or supervises. M.I.6, on the other hand, is counterespionage, working in foreign countries. It cannot work openly with the police. It directs activities into enemy territory. Its representatives run the danger of being arrested as spies.

"This difference between M.I.5 and M.I.6 explains the difference between our work in Lebanon and Syria, and that with which so many of you are concerned. In Palestine, Egypt, Cyprus and Iraq, M.I.5 was already firmly established in 1939. In Syria and the Lebanon it was not, because they were a French mandate. M.I.6 was operating there clandestinely. France was an ally, and a suspicious ally. Fifteen months ago, therefore, when the campaign against the Vichy French was concluded we had no existing network of agents through whom we could conduct our operations. We only had a few, a very few M.I.6 representatives. We had to start from scratch. During the last year we have, therefore, been busy building up that network."

He described the methods of recruitment that they had adopted, and the results that those methods had achieved. "Our work," he concluded, "has been exploratory. We now feel ourselves in a position to take a more active part in the bureau's work. We very much hope that during this conference we shall receive some guidance as to what that part should be. We do feel that ours could be important because of the proximity of Turkey. We and Iraq have a common frontier with Turkey. In the interests of our own security, we have to take cognizance of what the enemy are plotting against us in Turkey. We have to send agents across the frontier. In that respect our work at times overlaps the boundary between M.I.5 and M.I.6. We are hoping to receive guidance on this point."

His talk ended twenty-nine minutes after it had begun. He was accustomed to finishing what he had to say within the time allotted him. He did not have as one of the speakers had that morning, to hurry his last sentences. As he finished he looked down at Diana; she made a sign of silent handclapping. Her smile was warm. Well, anyhow, we're friends, he thought.

Stallard came up to him afterwards. "That was excellent. I knew it would be. But I didn't guess that it would be so good. You're the right man in the right job. I can see that. Wish we'd known about you earlier. By the way, I think it's time you put a crown up. It won't make any difference to you financially. You're already drawing more than a major's pay, but if you don't go up after you've been in a show a year, people may think you're not any good. Security can defeat its own ends in that way. Besides, it's high time Nigel had a crown up and you two must keep level pegging. I'm going to be run off my feet these next three days, but let's have a quiet dinner on Friday, after the last meeting. You can? That's fine. In the meantime, is there anything on your mind?"

Reid thought quickly. He had Johnson very much upon his mind. His first instinct was to leave Johnson till the Friday; but he wanted to enjoy that dinner. He wanted to hear about London and discuss mutual friends. He did not want to have to employ diplomacy. He wanted to let the talk flow spontaneously. Best deal with Johnson now.

"As a matter of fact, there is," he said. "There's a man who came out in the same convoy that I did. A Sandhurst contemporary of mine." He explained the position in which Johnson found himself. Stallard frowned.

"Would he be any good at our kind of work?"

"On the administrative side he would. He knows his way about regulations. He could wangle allowances and cars; that kind of thing."

"I see." He paused, reflecting. "You've nothing for him in Syria?"

"It's a very small organization."

"And here in Cairo they've got more bodies than they can really use. Their establishment needs cutting down. The only opening I can see is in Paiforce—the new Persia and Iraq command. We are extending ourselves there." He explained briefly the situation. "Iraq has been an independent country for ten years, but we had certain treaty rights there: an Air Force station, thirty miles from Baghdad at Habbaniya; we had technical advisors and a military mission. We had an intelligence organisation, an Air Force one, and when the Rashid Ali revolution came along, it was India—the tenth army—that took over. It was all very tentative; we waited to see which way the cat would jump, too many irons in too many fires, but now with Persia under our control, America in the war and a kind of condominium arranged in Tehran with the Russians, Paiforce is going to grow. Yes, I think we could manage with a regular army officer in administration. Johnson, you say. Tell him to ring me any morning between nine and ten. I'll do my best for him, and I look forward to Friday. I won't ask anybody else. At the Mohammet Ali Club, eight-thirty."

Relax and enjoy the peace of it, she had said. He did just that; as far as he could, that was to say. He had made his contribution to the conference; now he could accept "the glow of after-battle wine". Cairo had much to offer: golf at the Gezira Club; Groppi's pastries and iced coffee; martinis at the Turf Club and the knowledge that at any moment he might be running into someone he had known for half a lifetime. There was also the sense of victory in the air. The Eighth Army was sweeping past Benghazi on the way to Tripoli. After three years, first of stalemate and then defeat, the tide had turned; and it was from Cairo that the direction came. Cairo made fun of itself, talked of the "gaberdine swine"; wrote Ballades, "Up the Gehzire, up the Continental"; yet Cairo was the dynamo that drove the war machine. Cairo in the late autumn of 1942 was the most dramatic city in the world. Its atmosphere was contagious, and yet all the time Reid had a sense for himself, of profound unreality. Beirut without Diana. And it was not simply being without Diana during a few weeks. It was Beirut without her permanently, where not only the office, the work in it, the files, but every street and every restaurant in it reminded him of her. He had to reconstruct a life without her, but how could he do that when her ghost was at his side at every crossroads. It was more than he could take. At the moment he was too dazed to know what was happening. He would come out of that daze, but when he did, it must be somewhere that held no memories.

The Friday came and Stallard rose to address the final session.

"In my speech of welcome, I was very brief," he said. "I wanted to hear what you all had to say. I didn't want, at the start, to impose London's point of view on yours. I knew that I had more to learn from you than you could possibly have to learn from me. The man on the spot knows best. I have been very impressed with the appreciations you have each of you made of your particular situations and problems. In particular I was impressed by the distinction that Major Reid drew between his position in Syria and the Lebanon and the position of other branches in Palestine, Cyprus, Egypt. He presented an admirable over-all picture of the security situation here in Middle East. But that does not mean that I have not learnt a great deal from every one of you, and we in London will be enormously helped by the deliberations of this conference. I hope that you will find us in the future, I won't say more sympathetic—we have always been that, I hope—but more intuitive in our approach to and in our assessment of your problems. As I said, I have learnt more from you than you could possibly learn from me. At the same time there is something I can give you, and that is a global picture of this war; or rather I can show you the part that Middle East fills in the global picture of the war. The war is directed from Washington and London. That you must bear in mind. Even though at the moment Middle East is the most active area in the war; it is only a part of the war; it is a preparation for the major campaigns that will be launched later on in Europe. Middle East will then play, I will not say a subsidiary role, but at least an ancilliary role in the main strategy. But for the next six months at least it is the Middle East that will make the headlines, and by next spring the Axis should have been driven out of North Africa. I do not think that there is any doubt they will be. We have, for the first time, an immense superiority in men and in materiel; and the inexhaustible resources of America are now being tapped. Winston has said, 'This is not the beginning of the end; but it is the end of the beginning.' A new war is beginning and in that new war our security forces will have a new role.

"Major Reid said very pertinently that in Syria and Lebanon a network had been finally created, but that he was not yet clear as to the best use to make of it. He presented this fact modestly in support of his contention that the other offices had a long start of him. But all of you are in the same boat really. You have each of you a network and you have to put it to a different use. We are now on the attack. We have ceased to be on the defensive. We are no longer protecting ourselves against attack. We no longer need to consider the danger of being overrun by an invasion. During the last two years we have given a great deal of time to the organisation of a scorched earth policy and the creation of guerrilla bands to harrass back areas and L. of C. There is no longer any need for that. We are no longer trying to discover the enemy's intentions. We are trying to conceal our intentions from him, to mislead him and to misinform him. In one sense our need for internal security is the greater. We must conceal the presence and the movements of troops. Our order of battle is even more important than it was a year ago. We have to be on our guard against sabotage, particularly in Paiforce where we have the oilfields of Kirkuk and the refinery of Abadan. There must be no relaxation in postal censorship. At the same time we must not confine ourselves to the defensive. We must be active. We must not only conceal our intentions from the enemy, we must mislead him as to our intentions. Deception. That is our motto for the immediate future. Get the enemy guessing and keep him guessing. We have the initiative. He must never know where we are going to strike. Will Turkey join us and will we launch an attack through the Balkans? Where shall we open the second front or the third front: in Italy, in Greece, in the south of France? As long as the enemy is uncertain of our plans he will have to disperse his troops. His defences will be thinly held.

"That indeed, gentlemen, is the chief message that I bring to you. Do not relax conventional security, but make deception your middle name."

For several weeks now the roof garden of The Mohammet Ali Club had been closed. The days were warm but it was chilly in the evening. The high ceilinged dining-room was ornate with Edwardian decoration. Only a few high ranking British officers were members; it was patronised by Embassy officials, Egyptian notables, and a sprinkling of French refugees. Apart from the uniforms there was no sign that a war was being fought a few hundred miles away. Stallard studied the menu for several minutes. "You order what you like. I'm looking for what I can't get in England. Anyhow, we'll have champagne; that goes with anything."

"I had a bottle of Krug 1928 at the Turf Club the other night."

"You won't get any here. Too many of the members know what's what."

"Can you get it still in London?"

"If you know your way about. I do."

"How is London now?"

"Dreary; and it's going to get drearier. Nothing's happening; and nothing is likely to happen for a while. They talk about the second front next year. I'm not in the know, but I don't think there's the slightest chance of it till '44. It's very hard to keep up the spirit of the troops under those conditions. And all the time there are more shortages. Things are wearing out. Clothes look shabby. It's getting harder to get anything done. The food is dull, and there's not enough of it. You can only get a meal in a black market restaurant, and only the few can afford that. Liquor's getting scarce. Every restaurant is crowded; the streets are full of foreign troops. Everyone's overworked. They have to wait in queues to get to their offices and get back from their offices. Fire-watching and the Home Guard make for a corporate spirit, that I will concede. Class barriers are going down, the blacksmith and the squire meet on equal terms; but it's all a wearing away of nerves and patience. You're lucky to be out here, in many ways."

"Would you come out here, if you could?"

"I wouldn't, but then I'm lucky. I'm having a very interesting war. I meet more important people than I did in peacetime. I'm in the centre of things."

They continued to talk of England. It was barely fifteen months since he had left, yet to Reid his life there seemed immeasurably remote. He could scarcely believe that the familiar life was going on there much the same.

They talked about personalities. They had not, in fact, a great many acquaintances in common, but they knew about a great number of the same people. He had heard about or met casually a great many of Stallard's friends, and vice versa. It was very true, Reid thought, that England was so small, its social life so interknit that everyone knew or knew about everybody else. He had once pointed out in a lecture that English society often divided itself into the King's set and the Prince of Wales' set; and this cleavage could be observed even in the unaffluent group that was not within range of Court circles; the improvident Bohemian on the one hand and the law-abiding conformist on the other. Two apexes widening to broad bases. In the same way the governing class in London—the word establishment did not then exist—was divided between two types of man: the type that belonged to White's and the type that belonged to the Athenaeum. He and Stallard belonged to different worlds, yet they were members of the same family; in separate pyramids but on the same level; opposite numbers to each other to that extent. It was a relief to meet again someone on that level. He had been able to so seldom since he sailed for the Middle East.

"Oh, I forgot to mention," Stallard said, "that fellow Johnson. I've fixed him up. He should be all right, shouldn't he?"

"I don't see why not. Do you?"

"No," Stallard hesitated. "One can't pick and choose these days. Besides," once again he hesitated, "one should back the kind of person that one knows."

They looked at one another. They said nothing. They could talk in shorthand.

"He's going to Paiforce, is he?"

Stallard nodded. "As far as we're concerned, Paiforce is developing. As you know, Paiforce was formed last summer when the Germans were advancing into Russia and it looked as though they might swing southwards through the Caucasus. There's no danger of that now. They were stopped at Stalingrad, and most of the troops who were rushed to Paiforce have been withdrawn to the Western Desert. There's a new development there: aid to Russia through the Persian Gulf. The Americans are creating P.G.C., Persian Gulf Command, at Khoramshar; we've got our base at the Shatt-al-Arab. The security of those bases is of first importance; and so is the security of Iraq and Persia. We don't want unrest on the L. of C. Oh, yes, Paiforce is going to be exceedingly important for the next two years, at least."

It was the opportunity Reid had been waiting for. "Do you think that there'd be a place for me in our outfit there?"

"For you?"

"For me."

"But I thought you were getting on so well with Nigel."

"I am, but there's a personal equation. I've very strong personal reasons for wanting to put quite a stretch of desert between myself and the Levant."

"I see." Stallard looked at him, ruminatively. "How'd Nigel take this?"

"He'd understand, the way I put it to him."

"In that case. . . ." Stallard hesitated again, his forehead creased. "You're actually the last person that I've thought of moving. You and Nigel were a team. You were the complement of one another. But if you want to move, if you've a personal reason for wanting to move that Nigel would understand, which wouldn't leave him disgruntled . . . and, as a matter of fact, we are increasing our establishment and the chap I was proposing to send as G.2—he's a sound man, of course, but you'd be infinitely better. I was most impressed by your address on Monday. You are in the top grade, after all. But apart from that, he's from Cyprus. He's not in the Arab picture and a lot of the work in Baghdad is along the same lines as your work in Beirut—as regards Turkey certainly. I see it as a triangle: Beirut, Ankara, Baghdad. I'd be delighted to have you there; provided you can make it right with Nigel."

"I'd prefer to tell him myself, if you don't mind."

"Mind? I'd be furious if you didn't. Yes, you can take my word for it, I'm delighted about this. Next year we'll have our conference in Beirut."

†

Reid had talked lightly enough to Stallard of how easily he could explain to Farrar that he needed on personal grounds to transfer to Baghdad. He had visualised himself bringing up the subject at the close of a cordial dinner at the Cercle. But it seemed a rather different matter when he was sitting at the office at nine o'clock on a Monday morning, with Farrar asking him about the conference.

"Now tell me everything," he had said. "Who was there, what did the controller say, what was the Palestine point of view?"

It took Reid half an hour to put Farrar in the general picture. Then Farrar started upon personalities. "Did you see Diana?"

"Yes, I saw her."

"How was she?"

"She was looking radiant."

"And how was Gustave?"

"On the crest of the wave. He's got a Cypriot girlfriend."

"Having a lovely war, in fact."

"Having the war he wanted."

"No qualms about not being in the Western Desert?"

"None that are apparent."

"Precisely as I planned. He'll do anything to preserve that lovely war of his. We've got him where we want him."

"What do you want him for?"

"I don't know yet, but we may find a use for him. And what about old Adams?"

The discussions of personalities took quite a little while. "Well, and I guess that's everything," Farrar said at last. "Unless you've anything on your mind?"

It was the worst possible moment to bring up the question of his transfer, but he could not go back to his own desk and heap of files and begin a morning's work as though he were still a permanent member of the office. He could not wait till lunchtime.

"There is one other thing," he said. "It's rather complicated. It'll take a little time. I don't want to be disturbed when I'm explaining it."

"If we can't have privacy ourselves, what is security about?" He rang the bell under his desk. A corporal answered it. "No telephone calls for the next half-hour and no visitors. Not even the Minister himself. Well, and what is it?"

"It's about Diana."

"Ah . . ."

"Did you . . . I mean . . . about us . . . did you guess anything?"

"I'm not blind, dear boy."

"In that case, you'll understand. The first thing I learnt when I went to Cairo was that she was having a wild affair with a Frenchman."

"And that surprised you?"

"Doesn't it surprise you?"

"Not in the least."

"But . . ." There was nothing he could say.

Farrar was smiling. "Diana's a young person in revolt. She's of her day and hour. And that's a very different day and hour from the ones in which you were a young man. Before World War I there was no general knowledge about contraceptives. A girl couldn't make love with impunity. The consequences could be disastrous. An affair could be a very serious matter for her. But now she has immunity. She can live as freely as a man, if she's so inclined."

"I'm aware of that."

"You may be. But are you aware of the consequent corollaries to this immunity? If you were, I don't think you'd be surprised. We've always been told there was a basic difference between men

271

and women, and of course there is: women bear children and men don't. There is a corollary to that difference, the fear of pregnancy, now that that's been removed there's no reason why a girl shouldn't live as a man does: experiment and have affairs until she meets the man she wants to marry. That's why I wasn't surprised to hear that Diana was having an affair in Cairo."

"But she was having an affair with me."

"While she was here, she was. But she's in Cairo now. An affair isn't like a marriage. It's on a short-time basis; that's the whole point to it. So as I said, I'm not in the least surprised that Diana has a beau in Cairo."

"I was."

"I know you were. So, what . . . ?"

"I suppose I'd taken it too seriously."

"That's the chief snag about affairs. You go into them light-heartedly and one of you takes it more seriously than the other. It really was a shock to you?"

"So great a shock that I don't feel I can work here any longer."

"I see."

They looked at one another. At any rate I've said it now, thought Reid. "It's the being reminded of it all the time," he said. "In the Cercle, at Sa'ad's, at the Lucullus; all the restaurants we've been to; and here in this office, with all the reports she filed and people talking of her. I've got to get over it; push it into the background of my mind. I can't do that here."

"I see that."

"That's why I want to go to Paiforce. I've discussed it with Stallard. There's a vacancy in their establishment."

"You haven't wasted any time."

"There wasn't any time to waste."

"What did Stallard say about it?"

"He didn't want your feelings hurt."

"My feelings aren't hurt easily; and in a case like this . . ." He paused and grinned. "Prof, old boy. I'm going to miss you damnably. I didn't want you in this outfit to begin with. But that was only because I thought we'd have more fun together in that flat with you still in the Mission. And I'm not sure we wouldn't have. But it's worked out thunderingly well, and I shall miss you. But we shan't lose touch with one another in this racket. Let's have dinner tonight, and I'll put it on the house, since I'm now dealing with the G.2 Paiforce."

272

They dined at the Cercle, as they had on that first November evening. "We'd best have something good to drink," said Farrar. "You won't find anything in Baghdad. Their Arak's foul; made out of dates. Beer comes from Turkey and costs the earth. You'll have to rely upon your N.A.A.F.I. ration. Let's make the most of this. The city of the Caliphs isn't what it was."

Farrar was in lively spirits. "I'm depressed as hell about all this," he said. "I'll be waking up in the morning with a bright idea; 'It'll be fun to learn what the old Prof. thinks of that,' and then I'll remember that you aren't here any more, that you're on the banks of the Tigris, plotting heaven knows what mischief. But there's one good thing about all this: it's better to leave a place three months too soon rathar than three days too late. Nothing's worse than spoiling something that was fine by repetition or by hanging on too long. That's what Diana was so afraid of: having it hang on too long."

"What do you mean? Having what hang on too long?"

"You and she. It could have no future. You're not free to marry; even if she had wanted marriage, which she most likely didn't. Can you picture her a Professor's wife? She was crazy about you; from the start; long before you knew about it. She got you into our office. And that trip to Damascus was her idea. But she knew it couldn't last. She was resolved that it should end on a high note, because it had been so glamorous; because it was continuing to be so glamorous. That's why you were sent off to the O.C.P."

"What on earth had she to do with it?"

"Everything. She came to me about it. She was worried. 'This is getting too serious,' she said. 'For whom?' I asked. 'For you or him?' 'For both, but more for him—or rather it's more serious for him, if it gets serious.' She wanted to end it without hurting you. She said she wanted a posting somewhere else. That was easy to to arrange, of course; but she made it more difficult by insisting that it should take place while you were away. There would be too much tension if you were in the office. Besides, she had a sense of dramatic irony. She wanted the last night to be an occasion that she would know was the last night, but you wouldn't. So we concocted that jaunt of yours with the O.C.P. Ingenious of us, wasn't it?"

"It seems inconceivable to me."

"That's because you haven't tumbled yet to all the opportunities this racket offers. Provided you are on the ball when you need to be, you can do anything. On the day after you went she and I dined together. We both got rather high. She was delighted with herself. 'He'll remember this as long as he remembers anything,' she said. 'And so shall I.' "

"I thought that was the way men felt. I didn't know women felt that way."

"Doesn't that bear out what I said? There may not be so much basic difference after all. Anyhow, not where a girl like Diana is concerned. About ten days after you'd left, she came into my office with a large fat letter in her hand. 'Look at the weight of this. Wasn't I right to call down the curtain?' "

"She didn't show you my letter?"

"Of course she didn't. She wanted me to feel the weight of it; to show me how seriously you had begun to take it. She was so pleased with herself. My, but was she furious when you came back unexpectedly for the night. She was almost in tears next day. It spoiled everything; it ruined what she had planned as the perfect curtain. 'I behaved abominably,' she said. 'But I couldn't pretend. I couldn't put on an act.' "

"You don't mean she put on an act that last night before I went to Deraa?"

"Good heavens, no; except in as far as we all put on acts when we flatter ourselves that we are controlling our own destinies; but . . . you see how it was. She had created the ideal memory for you both . . . and then suddenly finding that she had to do a repeat performance. It was beyond her. She felt so guilty the next day. How was she in Cairo, by the way?"

"She was very gracious. She was. . . ." He checked. "I didn't know that you knew Diana as well as that."

Farrar smiled. "Prof," he said, "you're one of the big thinkers of our day, as a historian. What was it they said about Lucullus: *rerum cognoscere causas*, knowing how things come about; but I really am amazed sometimes at your . . . no, that's the wrong word . . . innocence . . . that's not right. There's something about you that makes me feel rather humble. I'll tell you what it is. You're the only person I know in this damned Middle East who hasn't a personal axe to grind."

PART II

The City
of the Caliphs

1

FOUR MONTHS LATER IN BAGHDAD, on a bright March morning, an orderly brought a long envelope to Reid. "The adjutant says this is important, sir."

It was one of Johnson's chores as adjutant to sort out the mail each morning and despatch it to the officers concerned. Reid opened the envelope. It was from the Istanbul office. It was addressed to the bureau's H.Q. in Cairo, with a short distribution list. It was a short letter. That was one of the points on which Sedgwick was insistent. "V.I.P.s are busy men. That's why they are V.I.P.s. If you are going to attract their attention, be brief and to the point." Reid put the file he had been reading back into his intray. "O.K." he told the orderly.

The letter did not fill half a page. "Chessman has informed us that the Germans are about to send a wireless transmitter from Ankara to Baghdad. He does not know to whom it will be delivered. The German plan is this: Chessman will smuggle the wireless set through the Customs. The agent to whom he is to deliver it will join the train at Mosul. He will have a sleeping coach reserved on the train. The coach will have been reserved from the frontier. Shortly before the train reaches Mosul, Chessman will place the set in the coach. Chessman will never see the agent. Chessman presumes that he will be told the number of the reserved compartment in time to warn us. The operation is expected to be staged in a month's time. We await your instructions."

At last, Reid thought. At last. His spirits rose with a heady exultation. He could picture Nigel Farrar striding back and forth up and down his Beirut office. "At last, at last" he would be thinking. And Reid knew exactly how Farrar would see the issue, in terms of the deception campaign on which his heart was set. "Capture the agent; capture the set; force the agent to transmit the messages we want." That indeed was the obvious Beiruti answer. But it was a Baghdadi not a Beiruti problem; and Baghdad was very different from Beirut. That was one of the first things he had learnt in the Middle East.

Two years ago in London reading the accounts of the two campaigns, he had thought of them as being similar, short compact actions against negligible opposition, to remove German influence in the two key cities of the Middle East. They had only lasted a few weeks each. They had seemed side shows to him; minor successes to compensate in part for the grim series of setbacks in Greece, in Crete and in the Western Desert. But as he realized now, they could not have been more different. The action in Syria and the Lebanon had been fought by the British against the Vichy French with a certain measure of assistance from the Free French Forces. It was part of the European War; it did not concern the Syrians and the Lebanese. In Iraq on the other hand, the British had put down an armed revolt by the Iraqis against an Iraqi regime that had been established by the British, was backed by the British and was basically pro-British. The revolt against the Prince Regent had had the backing of a large section of the Iraqi people. Rashid Ali who had instigated it was the elected Prime Minister. The revolt had been encouraged and aided by the Germans. But it had been essentially an Iraqi revolt. And there must be now in Iraq a great many people who regretted the defeat of Rashid Ali. The Syrians and the Lebanese on the other hand had stood outside the battle. They had only been concerned with the extent of the profit they were likely to be able to extract from the eventual victors. There was no fifth column in the Lebanon. There was in Iraq. That was why the arrival of a wireless set in Baghdad was an entirely different project here from what it would have been in Beirut. "I've got to think this out" Reid thought. "I've got to get by myself."

He put the letter in his tunic pocket and stood up. The centre was billeted in a series of old Turkish houses, on the west bank of the Tigris, a mile south of the Maude Bridge which linked the old city with the new residential section. The offices were in a house very similar to that which he had occupied in Deraa; two-storied, with a balcony running round its upper floor, and set round a garden out of which a date-palm grew. The officers at work in their separate rooms looked like monks in cells, and indeed the place had a monastic air. He walked across to the main entrance. "I'll be around out here, if anybody wants me" he told the sentry.

A narrow path ran along the river, immediately before the office, the bank shelved to a sheltered pool that served as a harbour for a small fleet of boats—bellum was the local word—that plied across the river. A boatman hailed him, but he shook his head. The mess and dormitories of the centre were in a large house that in Turkish days had been a Prince's mansion. A low wall ran round its gardens; he sat there, looking northwards to the low skyline of the ancient city.

When he had first arrived, he had thought Baghdad the ugliest and the dirtiest place that he had ever seen. He had come by air from Cairo. Heat and glare had beaten up at him from a mud-caked road down whose centre ran a low hedge of oleanders; their drooping pale-pink blossoms were discoloured under a film of dust. On either side of it were drab one-storied villas. A large ceremonial arch, the entrance to a projected park, stood on the edge of a wilderness of small garden plots and discarded vehicles, symbols of abandoned enterprise. A cluster of dingy cafés were crowded with long-skirted Arabs, their heads wrapped in long black-and-white handkerchiefs. They were seated on rectangular wooden settees, sipping at their coffee while a radio deafeningly blared out either a scream of oratory or one of those cacophonous Oriental dance tunes that always seem about to reach a rhythm but never do. Everything was shabby; there was a complete absence of bright colours; and from the broad and sluggish Tigris had risen a cloying smell of drains. The centre of the city was even more discouraging. Its central thoroughfare, Al Rashid Street, cut by the Germans for military purposes during World War I, through a labyrinth of narrow streets, ran from the north gate to the south; it was lined by a succession of one-roomed, one-windowed, tastelessly decorated shops, that was interrupted every twenty yards or so by a café or hotel, a cinema or an ampler store. The pavements were flanked by pillars, under a roof, which imprisoned the air and rendered it more pungent. The roadway was thronged with all manner of decrepit vehicles. Along the pavement small boys were propelling laden donkeys. Old, bent men shuffled at a kind of trot under the weight of brushwood and incongruous articles of furniture that they carried knotted upon their backs. Arabs in long-skirted robes moved with sedate tread,

279

telling their yellow beads. Westernised government officials in ill-cut European clothes threaded their way gingerly to their offices. Voices were raised. Horns were honking. The thermometer stood, in the shade, at 110 degrees.

Reid had wrinkled his nose. "Well, I have been warned," he thought. He had gone on feeling like that for the first two weeks. But gradually he had come to feel a kinship with this city whose many changes of fortune had in part reflected the changing fortunes of the human race.

Normally, Iraq was a country that you saw in pastel shades, water colours rather than oils, through a fine haze of dust. But today, in the fresh, spring air, the domes and minarets stood out in clear, sharp outline, across the river.

On that first evening in Beirut, Farrar had told him that he had made a practice of sitting in Arab cafés watching the stir of life around him, because it helped him to understand the problems that faced him in his files. He, in his turn now felt that sitting on this low wall, looking northwards at the crowded city, he was more likely to see his problems through Baghdadi eyes than he would back there in his office among his files.

He remembered that first talk of Cartwright: about taking a long view in the Middle East. Iraq had been one of Britain's problems for a quarter of a century and it would continue to be long after the Nazis had been overthrown. Iraq with its oil, Iraq on the road to Suez, the gateway to the East, to India and Malaya, was the fountain of a great deal of Britain's wealth. First things first. Beat Hitler, then decide how to deal with such of the world as had survived him. That would be Farrar's argument, and Reid could recognise its validity. But the winning of the war would serve no purpose unless the world that we were to inhabit afterwards was stable. The prosperity of Iraq would always matter; and if that prosperity was to be protected, it was important to know how great was the opposition to the Hashimite regime.

This wireless set might be the clue to that opposition. They could discover who was the agent who joined the train at Mosul. They could keep track of his correspondence and his friends; they could discover who were the enemies of the regime. Some of these would be enemies because they would prefer to have the Germans win the war; but a large number would be pro-German because they were against the Royal Family. To be able to make these discoveries would surely be of greater value than to operate a wireless on behalf of the "deception" programme.

After all, the difficulties of conducting such an operation were very great. Not only would they have to shanghai that agent and persuade him to transmit the news they wanted, but they would have to conceal from the Germans the fact that he had been shanghaied.

The operation might easily misfire. If the Germans were to discover that we were operating that set, without our realizing that they knew, how desperately we should prejudice our own security. The dangers might be greater than the rewards.

There was, of course, a third alternative: to catch the agent red-handed, to stage a public trial, to have an excuse for strengthening security precautions, to impress on dissidents the power and efficiency of our intelligence machine, to frighten the opposition. Arabs more than most races respected power. And it might well be that the agent under cross-examination would betray his accomplices. He would be cross-examined by men whose fathers had been trained in a Turkish school. The successors of Abdul The Damned's experts had not much to learn from the S.S.

There was, he felt, more to be said for that alternative than the deception campaign that Farrar would be sure to favour, but even so, he preferred his own solution.

The final decision lay with Cairo. Yet it was a Baghdad problem. Baghdad should have the louder say.

On his way back to his office, he put his head round the door of the clerks' office. He looked for the staff-sergeant, saw him by one of the filing cabinets, walked across to him. "I'm opening a new file, Staff. Operation radio. Can you enter it?"

He took the folder back into his office. On his desk were a couple of letters from the U.K. which had arrived while he had been sitting on the wall. The top one was a blue airletter form from Rachel. The other a typewritten envelope that had come by surface mail. They could well wait. He spread out the new folder on his desk. He entered the letter from Istanbul, marked it No. 1. On the cover he inscribed: Operation Radio. Opened March 17, 1943. He passed his hand across it lovingly. Entry No. 1. How many and how varied would be its entries. He envisioned all the letters that would come from all those centres, from Beirut, Jerusalem, Damascus, Cairo; with he himself at the core of the operation.

He could picture Diana in Cairo, eagerly opening one of his reports. "Ah, Baghdad. I wonder what they've got to say." That was an exciting sideline to the issue. He had been brought back into her orbit. During his months here, she had seemed far away. He had had only routine matters to report. He had been grateful, in a way, to this new work that had forced her into the background of his routine. But his heart was beating fast at the knowledge that once again he was in touch with her; that every week, in some way or other, she would be reminded of him. "Now for the boss" he thought.

His Colonel, Mallet, had his office on the first floor. When he wanted one of his officers, he would come out on to the balcony and shout his name, always a Christian name or nickname. He himself was approached through his secretary—an English woman, the wife of one of the Anglo-Iranian executives. Reid handed her the file. "This really is immediate."

The adjutant's office was on the other side of the secretary's. (He had got back his crown.) Reid paused there on his way downstairs. "Thank you, for marking that top urgent."

"Delighted. I'm here to help." Johnson was nowadays in the best of good humour. He had not a great deal of work to do; and the little that he had was within his compass. He had an air of authority; of the man "on top of his job". That's one thing at least that's turned out right, Reid thought.

Back in his office he picked up the two letters that had arrived while he was sitting on the wall. He opened the typewritten one first. It was a circular from M.C.C. about the matches that it was proposed to play at Lord's during the following summer. Cricket. Two years ago when he had been stationed in London he had played a few matches against schools. There was a local side here, The Casuals, run by one of the men in Anglo-Iranian. He supposed he would turn out for it. It was difficult on a cricket ground to realize that there was a war in progress.

He picked up Rachel's letter. He slit the flap. It was a short letter. It did not turn on to the second page. "My dear" he read. "In novels women who write this kind of letter always start off by saying: 'This is the most difficult letter I have ever had to write'. Do they in real life, I wonder? I know that this is the most easy letter I have ever written. It is so straightforward. I have fallen in love. It is the real thing. I have no doubt about that. I want to marry him as soon as possible. There are no complications on his side. He is an American; a Colonel: four or five years younger than myself. He hasn't been married before. He is a lawyer. He belongs, he tells me, to what is called 'seaboard society'. Do you know what that is? I don't know what is the divorce procedure for soldiers serving overseas. But there must be one. I leave all that to you. Good luck. Rachel."

From the balcony above, a firm, masculine voice shouted "Prof." He put the back of his hand against his forehead. "She should have died hereafter." He hurried up the stairs. "Sit down, Prof." the Colonel said. "This is going to take a little time." His Colonel, a regular soldier, in the 60th, was a few years younger than himself. After a decade of regimental soldiering, he had specialised; taking language courses. He had worked in intelligence and liaison: much of his service had been spent in the Middle East. He had never married. Reid had been told that he was homosexual; which was why he had never been given command of his regiment; why he had been always employed on extra-curricular appointments. Reid liked his Colonel well enough; he was a good man to work for, but there was always a slight barrier between them.

"Now tell me how you feel about all this?" Mallet said.

Mallet sat forward in his chair, his elbows rested on the table. He nodded his head from time to time. "Yes, yes" he would interpolate, "yes, yes. I see".

"Don't you consider that it would be dangerous to have an enemy wireless operating here in Baghdad?" he said at length.

"If our defensive security is sound, and we must presume that it is sound, a spy should not be able to find out much. And it would be interesting to learn how much a spy is able to find out."

"You are assuming that we shall be able to discover the wavelength he is using. That's a big assumption. I think you will have to accept that as a risk and explain when you make out your case, why you think that risk worth running."

"You'd like me to argue the case that way, sir."

"Why, yes, Prof, certainly. This is your show."

"But it's you who'll have to sign the letter."

"A C.O.'s always responsible for what his men do, isn't he? Let's run over the thing again and see that we've got all the points."

Reid repeated the main headings of his argument. Sometimes at Winchborough when he had been delivering a familiar lecture, he had had the sense of being outside his role as a professor, following his own thoughts, while the lecture continued like a record he had put on a gramophone. He had that sensation now. His mind was on that airgraph.

"How should I have felt" he asked himself "if this had happened nine months ago, when my love for Diana was at its peak, when I believed she was in love with me? Wouldn't I have welcomed this news as the door to freedom?" He could picture himself telling Diana at a carefully chosen moment, at dinner or at lunch at Sa'ad's; at the high crest of intimacy. "Dear one, I've never talked about my home." "I know, I'm grateful that you never have. I don't want to hear." "But now you've got to. My marriage is over. It was never a happy one, or rather, it was never right. The chief thing was missing. But it's over now. She's asked for a divorce. I can start again. We can start again." He could hear the duologue. How else could he have re-acted? The temptation would have been over-powering. Thank heavens he hadn't had this news nine months ago!

"Yes, that's fine, Prof. I think you've made every point." The Colonel was concluding "and don't try to minimize the risk of having a wireless set transmitting information that we can't control, or may not be able to control. It's the point that some of those security minded boys will jump on. Call it a calculated risk. And let's get this appreciation off as soon as possible. Let's get our punch in first: before young Farrar's plea for his deception programme."

"I'd better mention the two alternatives, hadn't I?"

"Briefly, yes, to show that you're aware of their existence. But concentrate on your solution. Let them argue their case for themselves." He handed the file back to Reid. It was quarter to twelve. The office closed for lunch at one. In seventy-five minutes he should be able to sketch out a rough draft; provided he could concentrate upon it. Could he though?

He stood outside his office watching an Iraqi orderly, trying to fix the heating. It was a curious contrivance, a low brick coffin roofed with tin with a round hole the size of a billiard ball at the top. In front was a narrow aperture the width of a man's hand. Through a narrow tube, oil dripped into the hole. Inside the tin was a bizarre contraption for regulating the flow of oil. On the floor of the coffin a small saucer was set to catch the flow. Once lit the oil was supposed to heat the tin covering the coffin and keep the room reasonably warm.

It rarely did. Either the saucer spluttered like an inferior firework or it emitted a raging furnace that converted the room into an oven. It depended on the wind, the temperature, or the extent to which the pipe and saucer had been cleaned. It was very difficult to adjust the flow of oil. It stopped or poured and when it poured, it would seep through the brickwork and ooze in a thick black stream across the floor. From the balcony offices it would, as often as not, drip into the rooms below.

There was a school of thought that considered that water should be mixed with the oil and in some offices a second petrol tin was arranged through which water dripped simultaneously with the oil into the saucer. The flame under this treatment was often more consistent, but it produced its effect through a series of small explosions that were not only noisily disturbing but emitted a volume of malodorous smoke.

Reid spent quite a little time during the week looking at this contraption. It served as a corrective to his files. It reminded him of how backward a country this was in many ways.

The orderly straightened up. His fingers were covered with grease. He rinsed them at a tap. Then dried them in his hair.

I must get back to my desk, Reid thought. But he knew that he could not concentrate upon his report, as long as that airgraph was unanswered. An idea occurred to him. He went back into his room, picked up the telephone directory, and looked for the number of the Advocate-General's office. He had not a branch telephone in his room. He went into the main office. The telephone was in an annexe where he could not be overheard. He knew one of the A.G.'s captains. "One of my men has a problem," he explained. "His wife is carrying on with a Pole. She wants a divorce. And he's more or less agreed to give her one. He does not have to go back to get it, has he?"

"Good heavens, no; if he had, half the army would be applying for repatriation on compassionate grounds."

"Is it a difficult procedure?"

"Not particularly." He explained what it was.

"Does it take very long?"

"It can do sometimes. Papers get lost. Enemy action. All that kind of thing. It's safer to send everything in duplicate by different mails. One doesn't always know if the papers have arrived. We ask them to acknowledge the receipt by airgraph. But the airgraphs themselves get lost. Sometimes the people forget to send receipts."

"Would you say it would take a year?"

"On the average, yes. It can take longer."

"Thank you very much."

He took an airgraph from his drawer. "Dear Rachel," he wrote, "I have just received your letter. I am writing to Jenks. He will get in touch with you." He paused. Jenks was his lawyer, an old family friend, he was the godfather of their second boy. Jenks could see how the land lay. He would be the go-between. There was no point in his starting with Rachel a long correspondence that might well become acrimonious. Jenks could argue his case better than he himself could. Rachel would listen to him. He concluded the letter briefly. "I send you my love and my best wishes, now and always." And now he thought, the rough draft of that appreciation.

The half of it was finished by one o'clock and he was able to mingle with the straggling group of officers that was on its way to a preprandial session. There were some twenty officers in the centre, half of them R.A.F. in view of the preponderant position occupied by the air force in Iraq. The mess consisted of a series of two-storied balconied houses, each one set about a garden. There was a broad terrace above the river, where the centre dined in summer and met for apéritifs in winter. Through its various links with the Intelligence units of other areas, the Mess was enabled to enjoy a variety of apéritifs denied to other messes. Vodka from Iran, Arak from Syria. The centre had a monastic air, and it is traditional for monks who are denied the pleasure of the bed to enjoy the pleasures of the table. In Iraq there was a complete unavailability of female company. The shuffling, veiled Moslem women were strictly chaperoned by their menfolk. The climate was considered too fierce for A.T.S. units to be stationed there. There were a few female secretaries, the wives of oilmen, for the most part; but the proportion of men to women was a hundred or so to one. Reid, before he left for Paiforce, had been told: "The wise man recognises that as far as he is concerned, that side of life is finished for the duration." "That's all right by me" said Reid. "I'm in the late forties, and I'm married."

He had indeed found the complete sexlessness of Baghdad a relief after the restless atmosphere of Beirut, where women were accessible, but where the ratio was fifteen to one; and nearly every serving soldier was basically dissatisfied because he was within the range of temptations that he could not assuage. Reid was grateful for that atmosphere today. Problems such as his present one had no status here.

That afternoon, just as though it had been any other day, he took a "bellum" across the river for a round of golf on the nine hole course that ran round the Casuals cricket ground; and by his own low standard he played rather well, although all the time he was phrasing and rephrasing the letter that he would write to Jenks.

The office reopened at half-past four; and he set himself to the drafting of his appreciation.

"An F.S.P. corporal," he wrote, "usually travels on the Taurus. Chessman will give him the number of the agent's compartment. It is customary for that corporal to search the kit of any suspected passenger. He will, on this occasion, be on his guard against waking the suspicions of the agent. Another F.S.P. corporal will join the train at Mosul and pay particular attention to any Iraqi who is waiting on the platform. These two N.C.O.'s should between them be able to identify the agent and point him out to a detective who will be waiting for him at Baghdad station. This detective will be chosen by our own city representative; or if it is intended to take the Baghdad police into our confidence, we can borrow one of their detectives. Once we have found who the agent is, we should have no difficulty in spreading our net wide."

He took the draft to the staff sergeant. "If you can get that done for me by ten o'clock to-morrow, I'll be grateful." It was now quarter to six; at half past, the office closed and the clerks went back to their evening meal. But the officers did not dine till half past eight, and most of them stayed on at their desks, tidying up the remains of the day's work. It was, Reid had found, the most productive hour of the day. Then would be the time to write to Jenkins.

"Dear Jenks", he wrote, "Rachel has told me that she is in love with an American, a Colonel and a lawyer in civil life, and wants to marry him. She has asked me to give her a divorce as soon as possible. I have acknowledged her letter, telling her that I am writing to you about it and asking you to get in touch with her. Will you do so, please? Rachel has given me very few details except that he is a few years younger than she and that he is, as we used to say, 'well connected.'

"In my opinion, the idea of a divorce is most unwise. Things

287

are bound to seem different in peacetime, for both of them. Whatever he may think now, he will surely want to get back to America as soon as the war is over; and will he want to shackle himself with the responsibility of another man's children; foreign children: I think we should do nothing. I rang up the advocate-general's office to ask what the procedure was for soldiers serving overseas applying for a divorce. You have probably had cases of this kind already, but in case you haven't, this is the procedure." He repeated what the A.G. had told him. "It is quite a straightforward process, but it can take time. Papers get lost. Enemy action, that kind of thing. He said a year on the average. I suggest that we should be dilatory.

'Thou shalt not kill yet need not strive
Officiously to keep alive.'

Give them time to get over it. He'll probably be posted overseas as soon as the second front is opened. I leave the tactics to you, but that's the strategy I should suggest. I very definitely don't want a divorce myself. And I don't think it would be fair to the children. What a long time I shall have to wait, damn it, before I can get an answer to this letter."

I think that covers everything, he thought, which was precisely what he had thought an hour earlier when he had read over his appreciation before taking it to the staff-sergeant to be typed. He could wish that he felt as certain of the outcome of the letter as he did of the appreciation.

2

HIS APPRECIATION REACHED ISTANBUL six days later. Copies had also been sent to Beirut, Cairo and Jerusalem. Sedgwick rang for Eve. "Operation Radio", he said. "Baghdad's in first again. You might as well take it round to the Embassy and let them have a look at it. Read it yourself first. I'd like to know how you feel."

The document was signed by the Colonel, but Eve knew that it would be the Prof's handiwork. There had been a change in the Baghdad summaries since his posting there. The style was more concise, less colloquial; with a pruning of adjectives and adverbs, coupled occasionally with the use of an unusual word that she had to look up in the dictionary; always to find that it conveyed an exact shade of meaning. There was a change, too, in the summaries that came from Beirut; there was a certain jocularity about them. She wondered if they were Nigel Farrar's work. She did not know, except by name, the man who had taken the Prof's place. She wondered sometimes about the Prof. How was he liking it in Baghdad? And Diana, in Cairo. What was happening to her? She had heard hardly any gossip for a long time from there. She had expected some from Martin Ransom. But he had been transferred to Ankara a few days after his return. He had rung her up to say "Goodbye" but he had clearly been in a great hurry. She had no time to ask whether he had met Jane Lester. She wondered what they had made of one another. There were times when she felt very out of things in this neutral country, surrounded by pro-Axis nationals. She wished she were more in the centre of things; in an area that was at war, and where British troops were stationed. There were times when she wondered whether she hadn't had enough of Turkey. She had been here for three years. That was a long time. Last summer Sedgwick had offered her a transfer. She had refused it then because she was on the brink of her romance with Aziz; that was nine months ago. A good deal could happen in nine months. She was as excited as ever about his visits. He was, too, she fancied. Yet at the same time, in retrospect, now that the first ridges had been scaled, one visit was like another. She was not headed anywhere. Nothing could come of it. He was due up in May and then there was his long vacation in the summer. Perhaps that should be the end. October would be a good month to leave. It was time she got back to England, to her real life. She did not want to become an expatriate. October would be a good time to go.

She re-read the Baghdad appreciation; then put on her hat and coat. It was a bleak, chill, day. She still enjoyed her visits to the Embassy, but they had lost much of their savour. Life generally indeed had lost a good deal of its savour since Martin had left. It was not till he had gone away that she had realised how much had meant to her their infrequent dinners and the chance meetings that they had at cocktail parties and in office corridors. She had always been given a sense of anticipation on starting out for an Embassy occasion by the knowledge that he might be there.

Although it was cold, she did not hurry down the Rue de Pera.

She enjoyed looking at the shabby figures who shuffled or strode past her, with the uneven walk that they had acquired through a lifetime of stumbling over cobblestones. Most of them wore long black overcoats with dilapidated dark hats pulled low over their eyes; their hands were often clasped behind their backs, fingering at their yellow beads. Their faces were stolid and unsmiling. Turks rarely laughed. They despised men who laughed. They thought them frivolous. They set high store by dignity. They must have been very impressive in their imperial days when they had worn tarbooshes, coloured trousers and bright sashes.

She turned right by the flower market, following the dark alley's course past its succession of restaurants and beerhalls to the fish market. She lingered there, then turned into the narrow high arcade, with its little statues set in niches under the roof. She walked slowly down it, looking into the windows; at the pictures, the ornaments, the jewellery that were on offer. In one there was a display of leather necklaces. "You could make a whip out of one of those," she thought. A look of mischief came into her eyes. She hesitated, started to walk on, then stopped. "It might be fun at that. Why not?" She pushed open the door.

She returned to her flat to find a message on her desk. "Please ring Kitty Lang at once." Kitty was in a bubbling mood. "I've been talking to a friend of yours," she said, "a foreign friend. He was most anxious to get in touch with you. He was convinced that you were working with the council. He couldn't be persuaded that you weren't. He was so persistent that the telephone girl put him on to me."

"What's his name?"

"I don't know. He kept on trying to spell it and I couldn't get it. An Armenian name. It started with a P. He met you in Beirut, he said."

"I know. Belorian. Alexis Belorian."

"That would be it. P's sound like B's."

"I hope you didn't give him my address."

"As a matter of fact, I did."

"Oh, why?"

"He sounded fun."

"He did?"

"And really he was so persuasive. I thought he deserved a break."

"I see."

"So I asked him round for a drink this evening."

"In that case you'd better be a chaperone."

"But it's you that he wants to see."

"It may be, but I don't want to be alone with him. He's a champion wolf."

"What's wrong with that?"

"You'll see what's wrong when you see him. What time did you ask him for?"

"Seven thirty."

"Well, mind you are back by eight."

"That dangerous, is he?"

"I suspect he is."

"Oh, very well then, eight."

Eve shrugged. She had known that this was bound to happen some time. She was lucky it had not happened sooner. She took the Belorian file out of the cabinet.

For five months now he had been sending up a steady flow of information through the notional characters that Farrar and the Prof had created for him. The Germans had been satisfied with the information. There had been no need for him to come up to Turkey. But to maintain his persona he had to make an occasional appearance. She was surprised that Beirut had not warned them that he was on his way.

She looked down the passage. The light was green above Sedgwick's door. She tapped on the door. "Come in." He looked up always as though he had all the time in the world to spare. "Ah, back so soon. What did they say about it across the street?"

"Nothing. He read it and handed it back to me."

"No comment?"

"No comment."

"What did you think of it?"

She had expected this question and was ready for it.

"If we have time to spare, if we can afford to take a long view, then Baghdad is right."

"Do you think we can afford to take a long view."

"We're better able to now than we were a year ago."

"That's very true."

He looked at her quizzically. Then smiled. "I don't really know what I should do without you, Eve. You bring everything down to earth."

"Am I to take that as a compliment?"

"In this connection, yes."

His eyes were twinkling. "How's Farrar going to feel?" he asked.

"He isn't going to like it."

"That's what I'd say." Sedgwick paused. "It's curious, isn't it, to think of those two working against each other? They were such a success together, as a team. They complemented one another. Why did they split?"

She did not reply. She had wondered that herself. "There must be some reason we don't know," he said. "There always is. How did Farrar strike you?"

"Someone you had to like."

"And the Prof?"

"Someone you couldn't not respect."

"That's hit it on the head, and the way things are now . . . of course, we don't know how Cairo'll feel: the decision lies in their hands. But I've a suspicion that they'll back the Prof. Is Farrar the man to bear a grudge?"

"Not where the Prof's concerned. Not anywhere, I'd say, as far as that goes."

"Yet he's someone, isn't he, who might if pressed do something flighty, so as to show the rest of us where we all get off, for the hell of it."

"He might, indeed."

"That's what I was thinking." He paused. He looked at her, then smiled. "I really don't know what I'd do without you. I can think aloud to you. Some man's going to know himself to be very lucky someday."

It was her dismissal and she knew it, but she had not finished yet. "Alexis Belorian's in town," she said.

"So I have been informed."

"But his visit isn't on the files."

"There are files within files, you know."

He pointed to a small grey cabinet in the corner. "It holds quite a lot," he said.

She had seen that cabinet every time that she had come into his room, but she had never given it attention. It had never occurred to her that he had files that she had not seen. It sent a little shiver along her nerves. How much did he know that she did not know he knew; how much did he know that she did not know herself? She felt herself on shifting ground; not only she but Aziz.

"Alexis Belorian is coming round to have a drink with me tonight," she said.

"I think you'd be justified in charging that against expenses."

"There's no reason why I shouldn't see him, is there?"

"None at all. It would only make him suspicious if you avoided him. Where did you meet him, by the way?"

"At an afternoon party in Beirut."

"Of course, yes. I remember. He met Aziz that day. And you've not seen him since?"

"Once only, here, for a few minutes."

"You weren't, were you, with Aziz by any chance?"

"As a matter of fact, I was."

"Ah, you were."

"It doesn't matter, does it?"

"Of course not, no. Just something that occurred to me, that's all."

Once again, she had the sense of the ground shifting under her. Yes, she had better get out of here in October.

She had half a bottle of whisky in her flat, but she was not going to waste that on Alexis. Vodka was good enough for him.

"I hope that you are going to like this," she said. "The only thing I can guarantee is that it's not harmful. I made it myself."

"Made it yourself."

"Of course, didn't you know that? We live on the starvation fringe. We do and make do. It isn't difficult. Filtering's the only problem. You put a wad of cotton wool at the bottom of the funnel. Let the Vodka seep through drop by drop and don't use glycerine. It spoils the taste."

"Good. I'll remember that. Not to use glycerine."

There was a twinkle in his eye. He was not unattractive. She could recognise that; he was flamboyant: he almost had elegance: almost but not quite. His clothes did not look quite new. Though his shoes shone, they had the wrinkles of a year's use at least, and though his collar and his cuffs looked as though he had put on a clean shirt that evening, they did not glisten with starch. He was plump, he would probably be fat at forty and obese at fifty, but his weight gave him a look of health and of well being. Most women would consider him attractive; but his assurance irritated her. She was conscious of a definite recoil. He probably was aware of it, which might be the core of her attraction for him. She was a challenge. He wanted to break down that barrier.

"Have you seen anything of that Lebanese friend of yours?" he asked.

"What Lebanese friend?"

"The one I saw you with here."

"Aziz?"

"Yes, that's his name, I think. Does he come up here often?"

"Not very often. He's at the A.U.B."

"That's what I heard. Not very bright, I gather."

"Isn't he? I wouldn't know."

"I thought you saw him quite a lot."

"Only now and then. He cares for music; he likes to play my records. Do you ever see him in Beirut?"

"Never. We move in very different worlds."

"You seemed to be moving in the same world the time I met you."

"At my cousin, Annabelle's? I've never quite understood what he was doing there. Nor had she."

There was the click of a lock outside. Kitty. Thank heaven she had kept her promise. "This'll be my room mate, Kitty Lang. It was she who talked to you on the telephone."

"So that explained it. I was wondering . . ." He did not finish his sentence. He had risen to his feet as the door opened. He checked at the sight of Kitty; he stood, gaping. His eyes wide and his mouth half open. Kitty had checked too, astonished by her effect on him. They stared at one another. Eve looked at him. Then looked at Kitty. "This lets me out," she thought.

He recovered himself quickly, with his charms in full deployment. "Now this is a surprise. And what a delightful one. When I heard your voice, I thought: 'Now that must belong to a very charming person.' Voices can be deceptive. A woman of fifty can have a very lovely voice. Yet somehow I felt it was a young voice that I was hearing. I wanted to find out who you were. I was planning to ask Miss Parish. Of course, voices can be deceptive in another way. A pretty voice doesn't necessarily mean a pretty face. Though if a woman has an attractive voice, she almost certainly has an attractive nature. If she hadn't an attractive nature, it would betray itself in her voice. There'd be a disagreeable under-tone. So I was pretty certain that I should want to meet you; but how could I have guessed that your face would match your voice, that . . . it takes my breath away."

Kitty laughed. "It doesn't seem to have."

Inwardly Eve chuckled. Most certainly this let her out. "And now I see why I thought that Miss Parish worked with the British Council. It was a flat that you two were sharing. I thought it was an office."

"Oh, no," Kitty said. "Eve's one of our hush-hush girls."

"She is?"

"She tells everyone she is in the Foreign Office. A very funny foreign office I should say. I've no idea what she does, or whom she does it with. But she certainly gets a lot of perquisites that we don't get at the Council. That's why I bothered to come back early. I felt sure she'd have brought out her Dimple Haig."

"I'm afraid that Mr. Belorian isn't one of the friends that I can enter on an expense account."

"I on the other hand can put you down," he said. "I have to know about local trade conditions. You can tell me a great deal I didn't know. You already have, about filtering Vodka. I might have guessed about the wad of cotton wool at the bottom of the funnel. But avoiding glycerine, no, that I'd not have thought of. It'll look very well in my report. It'll show them that I'm *au fait* with the local market. I can give us a good dinner on the strength of that. Where shall we go? Abdullah's? That's got the best food. But we might want music. Rejans? Why not. We might like to dance. It's only one man between two ladies, but I assure you that I shall be equal to my responsibilities."

"You needn't worry about me," said Eve. "I couldn't have come out anyhow. But I've an idea that Kitty's free tonight."

The alacrity with which Kitty accepted proved that she would have made herself free if she had not been.

Next morning, Kitty's bedroom door was still ajar. Eve pushed it open. The bed had not been slept in. On her return that evening, she recognised from the lack of bottles in the bathroom that Kitty had returned for a hurried packing. Next morning, she rang up Kitty at her office. "When are you coming up for air?" she asked.

"He's leaving Tuesday morning."

"Then I'll be seeing you that night?"

"And mind there's some whisky in that bottle. I shall need a stiff one."

Kitty invariably returned bright eyed from a romance. On this occasion she was radiant. "I've never seen you look so good," said Eve.

"I've never felt so good."

"I can't wait to hear all about it."

"I can't wait to tell you. Have you got that whisky?"

"I've got Dimple Haig."

"Bless you, that's heaven. My, but he was wonderful."

"He's a quick worker seemingly."

"And I wasn't dilatory. What's the point? Why be coy? They say that a man doesn't respect you if you go to bed on your first date. Why should I want to be respected, anyhow by an Armenian? If it had been an Englishman or an American that I had an idea of marrying, it might have been different: though I guess it wouldn't, me being what I am. Why waste time? Particularly with Alexis."

"Where was he so special?"

"That's what I'm coming to; it was the first time I'd been with . . . well, I suppose you'd call an Armenian an Oriental, wouldn't you?"

"He might not like being called that."

"What does he think he is?"

"A Levantine."

"That's the same thing almost. Let it pass. Anyhow, I'd always heard that Egyptians liked their women plump. You remember those dancers at the Bardia cabaret. Nobody would call me thin. No, don't say that I'm just right. I'm not. I've five pounds too much, at least. Someday I'll have to do something about it. I'm always a little shy about that with a man. I'm afraid that he'll be disappointed in me. I've never told you this before. Somehow I couldn't, then. I'd have been ashamed. One's Achilles' heel you know. And I've developed my own technique, in self defence. I've heard women say that the preliminaries are the best part of all. And I can see that it is so for most women; not for me. I'm always afraid that the man's going to be disappointed. The first time anyhow; so I cut the preliminaries down; no long, garment by garment, tussle: straight to the battle; when it's once begun, and he's having a good time, and I make damn sure he's having one, he won't be noticing whether I'm five pounds overweight; he'll have too much else on his mind; besides, it'll be my face he's looking at; most of the time anyhow, and no one's complained about my face. That's my secret. Get started fast and make it last for ever; that's how I was planning to have it work with him. But was Alexis letting me?"

She was lolled back in the chair, her legs stretched out, her eyes half closed; a dreamy reminiscent expression on her face. She took a long, slow sip at her whisky; she shook herself as though she were coming out of a doze. "That's how I'd meant to play it. Did I get a chance; hell, I didn't. He liked me just the way I was; he couldn't have too much of me. Preliminaries. I thought they'd never finish; the way he gloated over me, over every inch of me. It drove me mad. His hands, did you notice his hands? No, of course, you didn't; they're short, pudgy hands, very soft. You'd think he'd never done a thing with them; those fingers, the way they kneaded me; that's the word, kneaded. He made me feel as though I were Cleopatra, an object of idolatry. You know how it is to have someone crazy about the very thing that you're uncertain of yourself; a society beauty wants to be complimented on her conversation, a blue stocking on her eyes; to have someone crazy about my figure; nobody's been crazy about me for that before. And it wasn't as though he didn't like the rest, my God it wasn't.

"Do you know one thing he said? This really got me. Almost the last thing he said, early this morning. 'I'll be away a month,' he said. 'At least a month. I wish I were a Sultan and could shut you up in a harem in my absence.' 'So that nobody could get at me?' I asked. 'Partly; but more to have you looked after, by a slave; who'd massage you and give you baths; and cover you with scent and keep you out of the sun, and feed you with honey cakes; and you'd get so white and soft and plump.' That sent me. Can you guess how that sent me. 'But darling,' I said, 'I am plump already.' What do you think he said? 'Not really. You could do with five pounds more.' To be asked to put on weight! Do you see that box on the table; Turkish delight. His goodbye gift to me. Just pass it over."

Later, a long while later, Eve brought up another subject. She had been more than a little disconcerted by the remarks he had been making about Aziz. Kitty had come into the room at the very moment when she had been on the brink of learning something.

"What did you talk about?" she asked. "In the intervals. Don't tell me there weren't any intervals."

Kitty laughed. "There weren't so many; after all we had to sleep a little, or at least I had. I had to work next day."

"Did you talk about Beirut at all?"

"A little, why?"

"It's useful for me to get information about other countries, from foreigners. It's useful for my job, I mean."

"I never know what your job is. As a matter of fact that's one of the things in which he was interested."

"One of what things?"

"Oh, you know, things. He wondered what exactly it was that you were doing."

"I hope you didn't tell him."

"How could I? I don't know. Hush-Hush. That's all you tell me. I sometimes think that you defeat your own ends by telling us so little. We tend to blurt the wrong things out. If you'd tell us where to pipe down, we could pipe down. As it is you leave us to our devices. At your own cost, maybe."

"That's very true . . . I guess. . . . Maybe you've something there. What did he say?"

"Nothing that added up to anything. He was inquisitive, that's all. He wondered about Aziz. He wondered how you came to know him. He didn't like Aziz. I gathered that they'd quarrelled at some party."

"That's true. They quarrelled at some party."

"It wasn't anything particular. You asked me; that's why I'm telling you."

"I know. I'm grateful. It's a help. I can't explain. But in my racket, it's like an elaborate chequerboard. Unexpected things fit in. Have you ever done jig-saw puzzles?"

"I never have."

"You've missed a lot. And there's a parallel. You have all these odd bits in front of you. You get the greys together and the blues and greens. The shapes make a pattern. Then suddenly you see the picture. It's not just a group of greens and browns and whites and reds. It's a child with a red skirt, feeding a white rabbit with a lettuce. That's how it is with us. We collect a group of colours. Then suddenly when we expect it least, lo and behold, a picture takes shape under our eyes. I'm very grateful to you, Kitty. You can't guess why and I can't explain it. But it has been helpful to me to learn that Alexis was interested in . . . well that he did happen to be interested, just in that."

Next morning, Eve was summoned to Sedgwick's office. "Here's Beirut's appreciation of the radio issue. Just as we would have expected. A deception offer. Poor Farrar."

"Why poor Farrar?"

"A signal's come in from Cairo approving Baghdad's scheme. As we expected, didn't we? So will you get busy, laying this one on?"

"When's the machine being shipped?"

"That we don't know. Not for three weeks at least. That leaves us all the time we need."

"There isn't much we can do, is there?"

"I wouldn't say there was. It's a Baghdad problem. Only. . . ." He checked. He looked at her quizzically. "If anything blows up in Baghdad, it's going to be awkward for us here."

"I don't get that."

"You don't? If the Germans here were to feel that we had penetrated their organisation, as they would do, if they realised that we had been watching for their men in Mosul, they'd start shifting their defences. We wouldn't know where they'd moved. It's something for us to keep in mind, you know."

"Have you by the way heard anything about Belorian's visit?"

"I'm expecting to hear from Chessman in a day or so."

"Nothing from Beirut yet?"

"No, nothing from Beirut."

Nothing anyhow that had appeared on the main office files; but how could she tell what there might not be in that small corner cabinet. She had felt apprehensive ever since she had learnt of its existence.

Eve would have been more apprehensive still could she have been an invisible witness of the scene that was taking place at that moment in Beirut in the apartment in the old town that the office had taken over for Reid's successor. Belorian had just reached the end of his report on his visit to Istanbul. "That sounds most satisfactory," Farrar was saying. "This is working out better than I had dared to hope. We'll carry on the way we're doing. Is there anything you've on your mind?"

"There is one thing. Do you know anything about a girl called Eve Parish?"

"No, I don't think so. Should I?"

"She was down here last summer."

"A great many people were down here last summer."

"I met her at a party of my cousin, Annabelle. Annabelle did not seem to know much about her. She said she was a friend of yours."

"I wonder how that happened. Tell me more about her. What does she look like, what does she do? What age is she?"

"In the early twenties. Small, darkish, not obviously attractive, but I wouldn't be surprised to learn that someone had gone for her in a big way. I rather thought I'd have a bash myself, but I got side-tracked."

"You mean you met someone better."

"Someone a great deal better."

"Poor, poor Miss Parish; what was it you said she did?"

"That's what I'd like to know. I got the impression when she was down here that she worked for the British Council. I'm sure she told me that she did. But when I rang up the Council in Istanbul, they'd never heard of her. But I was so insistent that they finally put me on to someone whom they thought might know. It turned out to be the girl that Eve shares a flat with. This girl told me that she was employed in something very hush-hush. Now why should she have told me that she worked in the British Council?"

"Perhaps because she didn't want to have you make a pass at her."

"But I hadn't started to make a pass at her."

"My dear Alexis, do you think that you're the kind of man who would ask a girl out to discuss modern painting. Girls know these things."

"Do they? Maybe they do. Anyhow I felt it rather fishy. There's another thing too about her that made me curious. At that party she was with a young Turk who was studying at the A.U.B. I met them together up in Istanbul."

"Ah, wait a moment. I think I know who you mean. Was his name Aziz?"

"That's it."

"Ah, now I've got it. Yes, it all comes back. Aziz was one of the Prof's protégés. He seemed a bit of a misfit, and the Prof was trying to find friends for him. He asked me if I couldn't get him invited to Annabelle's. I remember the girl too now. He asked if he could take her."

"I think there's something on between them."

"It's not impossible."

"No, I don't mean in that way: I wouldn't have thought he was her dish. An insignificant little squirt. She could do better than that with such a lack of females everywhere. No, I meant in terms of our line. I can't see why else she should be bothering to see anything of him."

"You think she's getting information out of him."

"I don't see any other explanation."

"You may be right."

"I half thought of putting the Germans on to him. Then I thought, no, I'd better ask you first."

"Quite right. You might have landed in a hornet's nest. The trouble about this racket is that there are so many different rackets and no one knows who's working for whom. I can give you an example. There was a man down here, a Turk, a survival of the Ottoman Régime, who was sending up messages in secret ink to Turkey. We didn't know if his information was going to the Germans or the Turks. It wasn't very valuable information and if it was going to the Turks themselves, we didn't mind, but if it was going to the Germans, we thought we'd better stop it. So we asked our Turkish friends in Ankara if they knew anything about this chap. They said they'd never heard of him so we arrested him. The very next day we got a frantic message from our Turkish friends saying that the fellow was employed by their naval branch. They only knew about the military agents. Of course it was too late then. I'll make enquiries about this girl and her Turkish boy friend. Are you likely to be seeing more of them?"

"I'm hoping to see a lot more of the girl she shares a flat with."

"Fine, keep us posted. I'm very grateful to you for putting us on to this."

Back in his office, Farrar sent for the Aziz file. There were not very many recent entries on it. Chessman reported that the Germans were far from satisfied with him. He did not seem to be of much use to anyone, and he was costing quite a lot of money. Alexis' casual remark had started him on a new train of thought. It might be that quite a different use might be made of young Master Aziz.

3

JENKINS HAD ASKED RACHEL REID to call on him at half past ten. It was now quarter to eleven, but punctuality was impossible in wartime, at any rate for civilians. Jenkins was in the middle fifties. During the first war he had served in the same regiment as Reid; at that time they had seemed contemporaries. Front line subalterns met on equal terms. But now Jenkins thought of himself as belonging to another generation. He was ten years older, but felt twenty. He was rheumatic. He moved slowly. He had put on weight through eating too much starch. He had had his clothes let out because he had no coupons to buy new ones with, but his cutter had been called up for military service and his replacement had done the job clumsily. He was conscious of looking shabby, he who had prided himself on his neat, military appearance. His chief clerk was in the army. He had to work twice as hard as he had before the war, and taxation had reduced his income by half. Because of his rheumatism, he had not joined the Home Guard, but he was on fire-watching duty two nights a week. One of his sons was in the R.A.F. The other was in the Western Desert. His daughter was a clerk in the Admiralty, stationed in Bath. She came back for a long week end leave once a month and slept the clock round. She never seemed to have time to talk to him. He lived in Pinner; before the war he had enjoyed his daily train journey, with a corner seat in a first class carriage, and the Times Crossword Puzzle to occupy his thirty minutes run. The journey now lasted fifty minutes. He rarely got a corner seat and often failed to get a seat at all and had to stand. He walked to and from the station to save petrol. At home he had no servant living in. A woman from the village came in once a week to scour the living rooms and kitchen. The house was too large and it was impossible to keep more than one room warm. They sat in the library. His wife had become a household drudge. She grumbled about chilblains in the winter. It was her first experience of daily cooking; he presumed that she did the best she could with the scanty material at her disposal; but he never sat down to the table with a sense of anticipation, nor did he rise from it feeling that he had been fed.

Wine had been one of his favourite pre-war hobbies; he had already drunk all the wine he had laid down. His wine merchant sent him a monthly parcel of twelve miscellaneous bottles. He would say, "I think I shall be able to give you a little Burgundy this month . . ." with the word "give" underlined. He had to drink beer every other night, thin weak beer tasting of watered straw. He never felt well. Gastronomically, he had the sensation of being simultaneously stuffed and hungry. His weeks were occupied in a series of minor frustrations. He never seemed to be able to get anything he wanted done, whether it was a boiler to be repaired, a jacket to be let out, a car to be overhauled, a rebate supplied by the Income Tax Authorities.

At his office, he found his temper short. He had little patience with his clients' preposterous demands upon his time and patience: estate duties, death duties, wills, conveyancing, trust funds, mortgages as though any of these things mattered now in wartime. He often found it difficult to keep his temper. And he had to admit that he took a certain satisfaction out of being able to say "No". He was relieved when his clients were unable to do what they wanted. He warned himself that he had to be on guard against this predilection. "You are paid", he would tell himself, "as your father was before you, and your sons will be after you, by men and women who rely on you to smooth out their problems for them. That is your function, your purpose in the world. You depend on the gratitude of your clients." He knew that; yet he could not help chuckling when he unearthed a new regulation that prevented a landlord from evicting a tenant who would not pay his rent. "He's in the same boat too," he'd think, and sitting now waiting for Rachel Reid, he found it impossible to care whether she got her divorce or not. He presumed that she was sleeping with this American. Why couldn't she be content with that? Was that not one of the blessings of wartime conditions that you were spared the hole and corner subterfuges of an intrigue? All those inconvenient trysts that, after the first rush of emotion, made a sensitive person think, "either we've got to call this off or cut and run". In wartime you could have your cake and eat it.

The bell at his side rang. "Mrs. Reid." "Please show her in." He had not seen Rachel since the war began. He was astonished at the change in her. She looked ten years younger. There was a glow about her, a kind of incandescense.

"You're looking wonderful", he said.

"That's how I'm feeling. Love works miracles, I'm told. Everyone's saying that to me. I'm starting to believe it." She sat down and crossed her legs jauntily.

"If I were to tell you how smart you looked, you'd tell me that you'd had that frock of yours six years."

"Not a bad guess. Seven. I was wise to store up well during those safe years. Were you wise too? How's your cellar?"

"Empty. I wasn't wise enough."

"Too bad. When this case is through, I'll give you some of ours; don't they call that a "refresher"? Or is that only where barristers are concerned?"

"Only where barristers are concerned. And you do realize, don't you, that I'm Ned's solicitor, not yours? I can't work for you both. You'll have to get a solicitor of your own."

"I know, I know; when I walk out of that door in half-an-hour's time, I'll walk out of your life for ever." She was bubbling over with high spirits. He had never seen her in a mood like this. She had always been quiet and reserved.

"You've realized, I suppose, all the complications that are involved," he said.

"I hadn't thought there were any. It seems so straightforward. Don't tell me he's going to make difficulties."

"I didn't say he was; but . . . he isn't happy about this, you know."

"I didn't think he would be."

"He doesn't want a divorce; he instructed me to tell you that."

"Naturally, it'll take him a little while to get used to the idea. It must have been a shock. It was quite unexpected. It surprised me as a matter of fact, and I'd had a chance to see it coming. What else did he say in his letter?"

"Not very much."

"He wasn't angry; he wasn't indignant. It must have hurt his vanity."

"Do you think vanity rates very high with Ned?"

"Do I? . . . well, no, you're right, it doesn't. He's got less vanity than any man I know. Perhaps that's his trouble; or rather what makes him difficult for other people. Anyhow that's neither here nor there. Of course, it was a shock; but he'll get used to it."

"He doesn't want to break up his marriage."

"He never set much store by it."

"How can you say that?"

"If he had, he wouldn't have gone off and left us."

"He did not leave you. He was a serving officer. He was posted overseas."

"Oh come now, come now. That's a first war argument. He wasn't in his twenties, he was too old for combat stuff. He need never have gone back into the army. He could have got exemption. They told me that at Winchborough. And even if he joined the army, he could have found a post in England. He'd have been much more use to his country in the Army Education Corps, in his own field."

She talked with an assurance, with an authority that surprised him. Young though she looked, she was talking to him as though he was her junior.

"What about the children?" he asked.

"He can see them whenever he wants. I shan't raise any difficulties."

"Don't you think that children need their own father to look after them?"

"It's better if they have, but that's another thing. He didn't only leave his marriage. He left his children. During the very years when they most needed him. He hadn't got to go. I don't feel that he has any reason to complain."

"Have you told the children?"

"Not yet. There isn't any need to worry them. They've got used to their father being away. For the first two holidays after he went away, they'd say, 'When Daddy's coming back?' They don't any longer. They say, 'When we go back to the farm'. That's what they're dreaming of. They love their home."

"And what about their home?"

"They'll be going back to it. It's my home, remember. I hold the title deeds."

"Won't you be settling in America?"

"We don't know yet. We'll wait and see. Charles has a good many irons in the fire. He's what they call well-heeled. That's another lucky point. There won't be any difficulties over money. Ned won't have to worry about alimony. I really don't see any difficulties. I'm sure Ned won't be tiresome. He's not that kind of person. And I want you to see Charles. I've brought him round. That's why I was late. He's waiting in the office. I wanted you to be able to tell Ned what a fine chap he is; that he won't have to worry about the boys with a wrong kind of step-father. Is there anything more you want to ask me before I bring him in?"

"Just this. It's the chief point Ned made and it's the point that has counted most with me. Why be in all this hurry, in wartime, when everything is so uncertain? Nobody knows how long the war will last. The end of the beginning. That's only as far as we have got. After three and a half years. Nobody knows what kind of a world it'll be when the war is over. Ned is in the Middle East. He won't be repatriated for at least three years. Your American is a soldier. As soon as the Second Front is open, he'll be overseas. He may be overseas a lot. There'll be steady fighting somewhere from now on till the war is over. At this moment you and he are free. You can see as much of each other as you want. No one's interfering. Think of all the people before the war who fell in love outside marriage. Wouldn't they have envied a couple in your position. What do you stand to gain? Nobody considers appearances in wartime. Why be in such a hurry to get married?"

"Because he wants it so." She was smiling and once again he had the feeling that she was giving a lesson in psychology and behaviour to someone who was barely adult; who had to have everything explained to him.

"Why?" he asked. "Is he afraid of losing you?"

She shook her head. "No, it isn't that. It's his conscience. He genuinely thinks all this is wrong, and that it's only justified because it's going to end up in marriage. As he pictures it, we are an engaged couple who can't get married right away and have anticipated the church ceremony. He thinks it all right for fiancés to make love."

"And he thinks it all right to break up a marriage?"

"Divorce doesn't carry any stigma in America. Wives go off to Reno and plead mental cruelty. And no one thinks any the worse of it. But affairs are frowned upon, I gather."

"Not by you though."

She shrugged. "Does it matter how I feel? If he had been a different kind of man, if he'd been a Frenchman or a Pole or even an Englishman, I'd have followed your advice. I'd have lived in the moment and thanked God for it. I'm in love and the whole thing's fine. But he's not that kind of man, he has got this conscience, perhaps it's a national way of seeing things. I'm crazy over him. I'll do anything he wants. I don't want to lose him and I'm afraid that if I hedge, if I make delays, he won't think as well of me. He'll think I'm light. This may seem strange to you, but it's a tremendous thing to him that I should, well, go on week ends with him. I fancy he's not had very much experience. He feels that I wouldn't be going on week ends with him unless I'd been bowled over. I want him to go on thinking of me that way. I find it rather sweet. Look here, you'd better see him, then you'll understand. Can you ring for him?"

He was tall, broad shouldered, trim. He was handsome in a clean, straight-cut way. He had a broad friendly grin, but what struck the lawyer first and most powerfully was his air of healthiness. He was vibrant with vitality. Rachel had risen to her feet as he came in. She moved into the centre of the room. He stood beside her, put his arm around her shoulder and she snuggled against him, looking up at him. They smiled at one another. There might have been no one in the room beside themselves. The whole thing was touchingly spontaneous. Then the American turned to face the lawyer. "I'm lucky. I sure am. And don't I know it," he began. "What have I done to deserve this, I ask myself. You've known Rachel all these years. Maybe you've got used to her. I don't think I ever shall. Every time I see her it's a shock, right along my nerves. We're sitting in a restaurant. I look down at my plate, cut off a piece of meat. Then I look up and there she is across the table; and I'm transfixed, frozen with that piece of meat suspended in mid-air."

"It's true. He really does. And people stare at him. They must think he's mad."

"And so I am. Crazy. That's what being in love is. Being crazy. I'm in the clouds. She is so wonderful. I can't wait to have my mother meet her. I've sent her photo over. But photos aren't the same thing. I'll say they're not. I know, Mr. Jenkins, that you must be a bit suspicious of me. An American taking away one of your girls. But don't think of it that way. No, sir. I'm not taking her away, not unless she wants it that way. We can make our home as easily here as in America. Where she is, my home is. Whatever way she wants it. My firm has a London office; I could transfer to it; nothing simpler. And as for those boys of hers, what fine fellows they are. I think they should finish their education here. The beginning of it anyhow; but they might do worse than go to Harvard later. Two strings to one's bow, you know. But that's a long time off. We've got to get this war won first. I want you to realise, Mr. Jenkins, that I'm going into this campaign with an open mind. What's best for Rachel's best for me. And it's for Rachel herself to decide what's best."

He showed no trace of guilt. He talked as though he were rescuing a damsel in distress, not as though he were breaking up a marriage, as though he were stealing a man's wife. Yet he was a man with a strong conscience. Consciences worked on different wave lengths, Jenks supposed. "You do realise, don't you," he said, "that I'm working on behalf of Major Reid; that Rachel will have to have a lawyer of her own?"

"Of course, of course. It's the same practice on our side; but before we start, I did want you to know what kind of man you're dealing with. I'm going to be the step-father of your godson, after all. I hope when it's all over we shall be meeting often. Very often. And there is one point I did want to raise with you; between ourselves. Rachel honey, I wonder if you could leave us alone for just a little. I won't be five minutes. I promise you." As the door closed behind Rachel, a puzzled frown displaced the broad grin on the American's face. It made him look boyish.

"One thing I'm not quite happy over; the actual procedure in this divorce," he said. "It's different over here from the way it is with us. And frankly Rachel does not see eye to eye with me on this point. I haven't thrashed it out with her. But you as a lawyer will see my point. You know in the States it's very rare for a husband to divorce a wife. It's almost always the other way about."

"It's more usual here."

"Then surely can't we . . . ?"

Jenkins shook his head. "In this case it isn't practicable. The judges are very down on trumped-up cases, in which a husband goes away to Brighton with a prostitute for the week end. They want to be convinced that the husband is serious about another woman. That could not happen in this case."

"Why not?"

"Because there is no woman in Baghdad in whom Major Reid is interested. It would be possible for a British officer serving abroad to fall in love with an A.T.S. girl or a nursing sister or an Egyptian lady or a Lebanese. He might want to marry her and his wife could divorce him on her account, but there are by all accounts very few available females in Baghdad. It would be impossible, under the present conditions, for Rachel's husband to provide evidence that would satisfy a British judge."

"In the United States . . ."

"In your country the laws are very different and much more sensible. Rachel would take a train to Reno and plead mental cruelty, but over here, even if Major Reid were to provide evidence from Baghdad, you and Rachel would have to ask for 'the discretion of the Courts'. You'd have to put your cards upon the table."

Charles shook his head despondently. "I know it's very awkward. My mother isn't going to like this at all. Adultery's not a pretty word."

"Adultery isn't a very pretty thing."

"And it's not a word that I can associate with Rachel and myself. It does not seem to apply. It all seems so different in our case."

"That's how the things we do ourselves usually do appear to us."

"And in Rachel's case one needs to be particularly chivalrous."

"Why in Rachel's case?"

"All those terrible things that have happened to her co-religionists in Germany."

"But . . ." Jenks checked. He was too astonished to complete a comment. He did not know what to say. It was a point that would never have occurred to him. Oddly enough he was rather touched. This American of Rachel's was a damn decent fellow. He tried to be consoling. "I wouldn't worry too much about all that," he said. "When so much else is happening elsewhere, nobody is going to worry about the exact whys and wherefores. People have short memories. In a year's time, you and Rachel will be married and no one will be bothering about how it all came about. Good luck to you."

And now, he thought, that letter to old Ned. Half an hour earlier, waiting at his desk for Rachel, tired, listless, recriminatory, he had felt that he could not care less what happened to any of the three. Everything about it had seemed trivial and pointless; all this fuss about an emotion that subsided as quickly as it sprang into action. In three years time Rachel and her American would be wondering what it had been all about. Then he had seen that look that they exchanged; it had carried him back twenty years. A curtain had been suddenly drawn back, giving him a glimpse of an enchanted countryside from which he had long lived in exile. It might be all over in three years time, but that did not minimize the intensity, the heartbreaking absorption of those first

309

weeks and months. He had been moved; he had felt sorry for them; he wished them well.

"Dear Ned," he wrote, "I have seen Rachel and her American and I have no doubt at all that they are genuinely in love; that they are serious. Rachel looks ten years younger. I would not say that he was more than thirty-five. From one or two things he said I suspect that he has been very much under his mother's influence and that the war has given him his first chance of breaking free. He has probably not had very much experience of women. He is a very decent sort of fellow. He is chivalrous about Rachel. Perhaps Americans are more chivalrous about their women folk than we are. Rachel is touched by his chivalry; it is something new to her. She would have been quite contented to live in the moment; but since he has been so insistent about marriage, she is delighted. Can you blame her?"

He hesitated. He wondered if he should tell Ned about Charles' belief that Rachel was entitled to special treatment because of her Jewish blood. He decided not to. It might make Ned think Charles ridiculous. He did not want him to do that. Charles was not ridiculous. He wondered whether Charles' venerable mother would altogether approve of a half-Jewish daughter-in-law. Possibly Charles' own sense of personal nobility was flattered. Most motives were mixed. He did not want to present Charles in an unfavourable light. There would have to be contact between them eventually through the children.

"You will be wondering, of course, as to what kind of a step-father this man will make," he wrote. "I don't think that you need have any qualms on that account. He is very conscientious, and will make extra efforts on their behalf. He won't try to move them to America unless he is convinced—and of course you will have a say in that—that it is to their advantage. He talked about Harvard when they leave Fernhurst. Two strings to their bow, he said. He is a thoroughly responsible person. His law firm has a branch in England and if it seemed expedient, he could take it over.

"And now you will be asking, 'how do I advise you?' You don't need telling surely that I as a lawyer nearly always disapprove of a divorce. I am dedicated to the protection of property and the safeguarding of the family. Nine times in ten I should say to a man in your situation: 'Let it ride. They will get over it. Let them have their affair.' Nine times in ten a love affair has run its course within eighteen months. Don't they say that a married couple makes love more often during their first year of marriage than in all the rest of their married life? Nine times in ten, I keep saying, nine times in ten, but that's merely to underline why I think this exceptional.

"After all, I've been sitting at this desk in this office for a quarter of a century; and that means that every day for five days a week I have had clients coming into me with their problems; they're usually money problems. I won't say they're squalid problems, but human beings are at their lowest when money is concerned. Money brings out the worst in them. For a quarter of a century I have been consistently in touch with the lowest common denominator in human beings; why shouldn't I be cynical? But now and again, once in many times I meet humans who are living on a higher level. That's what I felt when I saw Rachel and her American today. There was a glow about them. I can't explain it in any other way. There was a glow. You've got to give them what they want. It may work out badly. In five years you may all three of you be saying: 'Why didn't we play it slow? Why were we in such a hurry?' That may well happen. I pray it won't; but even if it were to happen, you'd all of you be better off than you would be if you tried to thwart them. If you did, there would be rancour left that would poison everything, between you all, for ever. And that poison would percolate, would penetrate into your children's lives. They'd sense it; they'd resent it. Shall I tell you what, as a lawyer, I've found to be the greatest mistake that any couple can make: to stay together for the children's sake. The children aren't going to thank them for it. They don't want to have sacrifices made for them. They don't want to carry their parents' responsibilities.

"Ned, I don't know in what temper you'll be reading this. You're away on service, and you may feel that you've been let down behind your back; but don't forget this, will you? Rachel doesn't think you had to go abroad. And is she wrong in thinking that? You left her vulnerable. I am not saying that she has a grievance, now. But she would have a sense of grievance if you were not to fall in with her plans. If you play for time, probably what you expect to happen would happen. He'd be posted overseas; they might be parted for two years; he might be posted straight back to America. They'd barely see each other, if they saw each other at all, and by then you'd be home from the Middle East. By then it would be all too late. And for the rest of her life she would feel cheated. She is in love now; and though you and I both know that that kind of love doesn't last for very long, no one in love is going to believe it doesn't. They say 'this is different; this is the real thing.' Rachel will feel that she's lost the real thing through you. She would always hold it against you. It would poison your whole life together.

"It's a bad business. I'm not pretending that it isn't. It's a question of making the best of a bad job. I know it must be miserable for you, out there, to have the roots of your life suddenly pulled up; to have to think 'What am I going back to?' But nobody knows what's waiting for us when the war is over. We shan't be living on the same salary, in the same houses; any way not on the same terms in the same houses. We'll have to build up a whole new life. It won't be easy. It may not be pleasant. It is possible that it may be easier for you, starting again from scratch. And after all, you will be still a relatively young man in your middle forties. Please, please don't think I'm not sympathetic. I am. But one has got to be practical. I believe that I am giving you sound advice."

He re-read the letter. Would it seem very cold and matter-of-fact to Ned? He tried to picture Ned, far from home, cut off from his friends and family, in his country's service. He checked. That was the way one had talked in the first war. It wasn't true in this. This was total war; total conscription of man power. Everyone was serving his country in one way or another. Ned did not need to be coddled, because he was in khaki.

He lifted himself gingerly out of his chair, straightened himself slowly, with his hands in the middle of his back, remembering a twenty-year-old advertisement for Kruschen salts: "Every picture tells a story." Damn this rheumatism, damn this climate, damn this diet. No wonder he had too much uric acid in his veins. Ned was well fed and in the sun. Ned wasn't plagued with rheumatism.

He walked down the passage to his secretary's room. "Could you type this, please, as a draft, and could you give it precedence?"

His secretary looked up crossly. "That's what you said about that letter to Mr. Crossley."

"I know I did. Now I say give this letter precedence over Mr. Crossley."

"O.K., as long as you hadn't forgotten Mr. Crossley."

"I hadn't forgotten Mr. Crossley."

She was barely civil. Nobody was more than barely civil nowa-

312

days. They lived under too tense pressure. He had not been affable himself. He ought to make allowances for Miss Scudder. She was a dreary, soured little woman who looked after a widowed mother. For her mother's sake she had not undertaken war work. War work might have been the saving of her. It would have taken her out of a groove. She might have been presentable in uniform. She would have met men. She might have been posted where there was a dearth of women. Some sex-starved officer might have fancied her. She had always been a dreary little thing. Ned and he had made an adjective out of her name to describe anything that was colourless and toneless—"a Scudderish day," "a Scudderish suit," "a Scudderish cricket match." The war was her last chance and she had missed it. No doubt she resented having to work in wartime for a drab solicitor on the edge of sixty, typing out title deeds, wearing shabby, thread-bare clothes when her contemporaries in air force blue were carrying "top secret" files to heavily moustached squadron leaders with wings and medals on their chests. Poor, poor Miss Scudder.

He settled himself carefully into his chair. A twinge cut across his back. Why had he bothered to go down the passage? Before the war he would have rung a bell. But now there was a wartime idea of sharing out the work. Why? Did it save any time? Did it improve anybody's temper? His bell rang; a shrill, peevish summons. Surely his bell had been more mellow in '38; or had he welcomed it, then, as the harbinger of variety. "Sir Francis Faversham to see you, sir."

"Right, send him in."

The presence of Sir Francis rarely cheered him. Sir Francis was a baronet with a large estate in Worcestershire which he was selling off piecemeal, field by field, avoiding income tax and slowly disinheriting his son. He was a man of forty who had got himself a staff appointment that entitled him not only to wear red flannel on his tunic but to make frequent trips overseas. He was having a thoroughly good war, and Jenkins found his cheerfulness as exasperating as Miss Scudder's listlessness.

"I suppose you're planning another sale of property," he said.

"In one sense yes, but in another, no. I'm doing a King Lear, or rather thinking of doing a King Lear. I want to make over a certain amount of property to my son. It'll save me income tax; and eventually save him death duties. I'd like you to work out how much I can afford to give him."

"Providing you continue in the way you're doing, cutting into capital every year?"

"Precisely."

"And giving yourself another forty years of life?"

"I don't suppose I shall have such expensive tastes when I get to seventy."

"Don't be so sure of that. Certain tastes can become very expensive in the sixties."

Sir Francis laughed, the full rich laugh of a man who gave full rein to his capacities for self-indulgence. "That's why I'm doing this now," he said. "Most fellows leave it too late. They die within two years and their children have to pay death duties all the same."

"On the other hand, they can be very sure that their children will take good care of them for those statutory five years. They ensure that you survive."

"And that's exactly what I want to avoid; they'd put me on a diet. I'd sooner die."

He stretched out his legs luxuriously. "Just back from ten days in Moscow," he informed Jenkins. They know how to do you well. I bet Stalin does his visitors much better than the Czar did his in the last war. Didn't the Czar prohibit Vodka? No lack of Vodka with Uncle Joe. And their wines aren't bad; from Georgia, very tolerable; table wines of course; to be quaffed rather than sipped, but there's nothing wrong with that, as long as there's enough of them; and there was. We had three full staged banquets. Just let me tell you what we had."

Sir Francis stayed for half an hour. As soon as he had gone, Miss Scudder bustled in with the draft of the letter. She wrinkled her nose distastefully. "That man makes the place stink like a barber's shop," she said.

It was quarter past twelve. His club—the Isthmian—was twenty minutes away. The bell went for lunch at one, and there was an immediate rush upstairs. Late comers tended to find anything palatable was "off". He might as well leave now. It would give him time for a pink gin. The Isthmian was in St. James' Square. It had been bombed in October 1940. One wing was out of action. The front windows were covered over with brown papered cellophane. The library and the coffee room had been filled with dust and rubble; no restoration had been possible. The rooms were very shabby, but they were so dark with the covered windows and the restricted lighting that one scarcely noticed it. Before the war, Jenkins had rarely gone there; he had preferred an oyster shop in Chancery Lane where he was allowed to keep his own store of wine; but he was no longer able to maintain the supply and since the autumn of 1940 he had lunched regularly at his club. It was the one part of the day that he enjoyed. He sat at the long table. He met the same men every day. They were perfectly familiar to him by sight. He knew their habits and their tastes, their particular branch of war work. But he knew very few of them by name. Some of them were, he supposed, men of considerable distinction. But he was not inquisitive. He enjoyed the atmosphere of friendly anonymity.

He ordered a pink gin. The club had an ample store of gin and it had a stock of vintage port, but there was no vermouth so that the only possible cocktails were those made with rum. And Jenkins did not like rum. Whisky was not available till six o'clock. Wine was in short supply. It could be only ordered three days a week; this was not a wine day.

The gong sounded: and everyone gulped down his drink and hurried to the staircase. A long buffet table was set with a succession of hors d'oeuvres dishes. The members helped themselves on plates so small that no one could give himself very much. The display would have looked appetising in a colour photograph; there were sardines, marinated herrings, Russian salad, onions, beans, tomatoes, spaghetti, slices of salami, but there was no variety from one day to the next; nothing seeemd to taste of anything, except the mayonnaise which had a rancid flavour. Jenkins thought of Ned in Baghdad, drinking Vodka in the sunlight; then repairing to a long refectory table that would be set like a banquet in the Old Testament with spiced meats and venison. There would probably be carafes of cool wine. The sweet wine of Shiraz. He carried his plate of hors d'oeuvres to the long table and took an empty seat. He had known for twenty years the man who was sitting on his left. He fancied he had known his name in the days when as a new member he had tried to find out who everybody was, but the name had meant nothing to him and he had long since forgotten it. His fellow member greeted him with a friendly smile. "This is a nice surprise; it's a long time since we sat together." Jenkins wondered if the man knew who he was. He did not suppose he did. He wasn't any one.

At each plate there was a slip of paper on which a member

could write out his order. Jenkins and his fellow member looked over the menu. There was not much choice. A mushroom omelette, it would be made of dehydrated eggs. Jenkins remembered the cook's farm eggs that had come in packets after the last war; they had been infinitely superior. There was cold meat; that would be spam and salami. There were sausages and mashed potatoes; the sausages would be stuffed with sisal. There was a risotto. That would be mainly rice. There was a joint of beef; the beef would be overcooked so that the meat could be sliced thin. There was macaroni au gratin. There were potatoes, cabbage and brussel sprouts. Well enough on paper but it was not surprising that members looked either thin and drawn or pallidly overweight. Nobody looked well. They did not get enough fresh air; they did not get enough daylight in their darkened offices; they did not get enough exercise; they did not get enough wholesome food. They were all over-worked. It was not surprising that they were short tempered sometimes. He chose the cold meat. There was no shortage of Worcester sauce; and he ordered a pint of draught beer. The Isthmian, through a link with the directorate of a brewers' company, still managed to obtain quite reasonable beer.

"What kind of beer are you getting at your local?" his fellow member asked him. "I never risk it. I get bottled beer. How much wine does your man give you every month?"

"A miscellaneous dozen."

"The same with me. But I'm in luck. I've several men. I scattered my credit before the war."

"You are in luck."

They discussed for a few minutes the universal problem of "how they managed." Then they talked of the war. They wondered when the second front would be opened. "Don't you call Italy a second front?" asked Jenkins.

"I don't. Do you?"

"No, I suppose I don't."

"I shan't feel happy until those channel ports are in our hands. They're far too close to us. Have you heard any more about Hitler's secret weapon?"

"I haven't heard anything at all."

"You haven't?"

"How could I in my line of business?"

"No, of course, how could you?"

316

Jenkins wondered whether his fellow member had any idea what his line of business was. He did not see any reason to enlighten him. If he were to, his fellow member might pounce with a "A lawyer; how very interesting; there's a little legal point that has been worrying me," thereby getting free advice. Doctors and lawyers were constantly exposed to that kind of treatment.

"I must say I hear worrying accounts about it," his fellow member was continuing. "I suppose I shouldn't talk about it, but it doesn't matter here, and you're discreet, but the highups are worried. They don't know how long it will be before the new weapon is ready. It can't be long now, they say, and it's going to make that 1940 blitz seem like pantomime."

Jenkins wondered whether this man really had access to secret information. If he had, he shouldn't be so voluble. Everyone claimed to be "in the know". One thing was certain, of that there was no doubt, there were rumours in plenty in circulation about this secret weapon. But then in the first war there had been rumours of Russians with snow on their boots, and in November '40 there had been rumours of the invasion that had been driven off by a flame barrage, on the sea; stories about scorched Germans' bodies being washed up in Normandy. There might be nothing to these rumours; but they made for anxiety all the same. London's morale had been high in 1940. Would it be so high now, after three years of rationing and frustration?

By the time he was back in his office, he had returned to the mood of misanthropical discontent in which he had awaited Rachel. The draft of the letter to Reid lay on his desk. He read it slowly, modified a couple of phrases. He seemed to have touched every aspect. He re-read it, trying to picture its effect on Reid. Would it seem unsympathetic? Would Reid feel that he was being deserted by his friends? If he did feel that, was he justified in feeling that? He had chosen to leave them after all. Rachel had been right there. He had not had to go. He was not in the position of a twenty-two year old subaltern. For the third time he read the letter. It still seemed to him all right.

He walked down the passage and handed the draft of the letter to Miss Scudder. "Do three copies of this on airgraphs. Post them at intervals of ten days." One of them should be certain to get through. He went back to his office. It was chilly, but he did not care to light a fire. Coal was a munition of war. Don't waste it.

He moved his shoulders inside his coat. Three more hours of interviews, of drafting letters, of concentrating upon other people's problems. It was a Scudderish world all right.

4

AS JENKINS SETTLED DOWN in London to his afternoon routine, Reid was waiting on the platform of Mosul station for the arrival of the Taurus. It was six o'clock in Iraq and the train was due. On that train, if the plans held, Chessman would be travelling with the wireless set. Or rather would be travelling without the wireless set which he had deposited in the reserved compartment. The platforms and the waiting rooms were, as always, crowded. To welcome and to see the Taurus off was part of the Moslowi pattern. Very few of the group there would be travelling on the train. It was no use for Reid to scrutinize them, even had he wanted to, which he did not. It was his role to appear unconcerned. There had been no need for him to come down to Mosul. But the temptation to be a part of the operation had been too great. He had made an excuse of a conference with his Mosul representative. And it was high time, at that, that he did see his representative.

From far down the line he heard the long high whistle of the train. Another minute and it would be here. He slung his bedding roll onto his shoulder. He had not reserved a sleeper. He would lie out along the seat of a first class carriage, as he had done twenty years ago on the Riviera Express, booking himself second class but moving into a first class carriage at Dijon for the sake of four clear hours sleep between there and Avignon. In those days of second class European travel, he had always tried to prolong his visit to the dining car where he could sit in luxury, but he was not this evening going to put himself to the expense of a railway dinner. He had brought sandwiches.

A British Major, a G2 in Administration whom Reid knew slightly, came down the platform. "Travelling alone, Prof?"

"Yes."

"Shall we share a carriage then?"

"Of course."

He would have preferred to be alone, but it was not necessary. He did not want to appear standoffish; besides the other, his junior in years, would be more agile and adroit in getting an empty carriage.

The train had a fifteen minute wait in Mosul. It was the third time that Reid had caught this train. There was no difference in this departure from the other two; there were the same mixed group of Arabs and Europeans; the same vendors of brightly coloured soft drinks and cakes and rolls; the same chatter, the same pushing and shoving. He wondered how often he had been on a train in Paris or in England when, for three or four fellow passengers, that trip so ordinary to him had been a high adventure. He might have brushed shoulders with that adventure; he might, as this young staff officer had done, have forced his company upon an acquaintance who had wanted to be alone.

The whistle shrieked and a flag waved. The train drew slowly from the station. Reid sat back in his corner, opened his haversack and took out a book. He did not want to make conversation for very long. He felt restless and on edge and he did not want to appear restless and on edge. He did not want to have this officer saying in his mess to-morrow; "I travelled up from Mosul with the Prof. He was like a cat on hot bricks. I wonder what mischief he was cooking up." At the same time he did not want to appear unsociable. He had a flask of Canadian whisky. He offered it to his companion.

"That's very nice of you, Prof. That's very nice of you indeed. But I don't want to rob you of your ration."

"Don't worry about that. In our racket we have our own sources of supply."

"I bet you do. You don't have a bad time, you cloak and dagger boys. You can go about in mufti, can't you?"

"When we're on duty."

"And that's an elastic term, I'll bet."

"It can be made so."

"I bet you make it so."

"Wouldn't you, if you were in our position?"

"I'll say I would. I often wonder what you cloak and dagger boys really do."

"That's what we ask ourselves sometimes."

The other laughed at that. "I'll say one thing about you chaps.

You've got a sense of humour. You can laugh at yourselves. Well, here's cheers and thank you, Prof."

They gossiped over their drink, indulging in the kinds of gossip that two men share who share nothing beyond the fact that they are stationed together in wartime in a foreign city. By the time their glasses were empty, they had come to feel very much in tune. There was a disparity of fifteen years between them; they had not a mutual friend in England; they had not a common interest. If they were to meet in London after the war, they would have nothing to say to one another beyond "Do you see anything of the old crowd now?" "I wonder what became of Gerald." In five minutes they would have exhausted one another, but here, cut off from their "real lives", they had momentarily and on the surface more in common with one another than they would have had with their oldest friends. That was one of the pleasant things about a war. You were conscious of an instantaneous fellowship with any one of your own race and rank. Reid dropped into a vernacular he would never have used in peacetime. "You'll have the other half," he said.

"If you will."

"I'm certainly going to."

"Well, cheers again then, Prof. Bit of luck my meeting you. You must come round to my mess and have the return match one day."

"I'd love to."

"It isn't as grand a mess as yours. But it's all right. We've got some pretty decent fellows there. I expect you know some of them."

"I expect I do. Who have you?"

But as a matter of fact, he did not know very many. Through the nature of their work, I.S.L.O. officers lived apart from the main traffic of G.H.Q. life. They saw a number of civilians, and of Iraqis. They also had their own representatives in the city who did not wear uniform. But he had met one or two members of the A. mess on the golf course and at the Alwiyah Club. The length of a drink occupied them in personalities. There was still some whisky in his glass, but two highballs were enough for Reid.

"Now for my sandwiches," he said.

"Aren't you going to the diner?"

Reid shook his head. "That's one of the things that I can't charge against the house."

"I'm so tired of eating in a mess that I can use a change."

"I'll see you later then."

Which suited Reid's plans well. His companion would be away at least an hour. And he had warned the F.S. Sergeant that he would not be going to the diner.

The F.S. Sergeant was a brisk, lively Cypriot; dark and neat with a sense of mischief. He had a lengthy name which no one attempted to pronounce. He was known as Frisky, because part of his job on the Taurus consisted in the "frisking" of the passengers. It was held that he particularly enjoyed his work when he had to deal with female passengers. A diplomat's wife had complained of the thoroughness of his attentions. But no one had questioned his efficiency.

Reid was munching his last sandwich when Sergeant Frisky tapped upon the door. "Coast clear?" he asked.

"Coast clear with you."

"All fine and dandy, Sir, everything under control. Can I sit down?"

"Of course, and leave the door open. Keep it aboveboard. He's on the train?"

"Yes, Sir, and have you seen him?"

"No, not yet."

"Are you going to?"

"In a routine way. No search of course. After all, he joined the train at Mosul. There shouldn't be anything suspicious there. It's passengers from across the frontier that we question."

"Has Chessman seen him?"

"To check his ticket, yes."

"What does he report?"

"A man of about forty. An Iraqi. A stranger to him."

"How was he dressed?"

"As a European. The clothes that Iraqis wear; dark, the kind you wouldn't notice."

"Have you got his name?"

"I've got the name he uses."

"I see. Reid paused. "There really isn't any problem, is there?"

"There shouldn't be."

The plan was very simple. Frisky would move into the next coach a minute or two before the train reached Baghdad. He would get out of the train, as it was stopping. He was to stand outside the agent's carriage long enough for the detective who

321

was waiting in the crowd to recognize the carriage. Then he would move quickly away without looking round. The detective in the crowd would follow the agent and see where he lived. The plan was cut and dried. It should work smoothly. "When are you going to see the chap?" Reid asked.

"I thought I'd go right away, before he turns in for the night."

"You might come back and see me when you have."

"Right, Sir, certainly."

"But if I'm not alone, don't come."

"Right, Sir. Right."

Frisky was back within ten minutes. Reid was still alone. "Well?" Reid asked.

"Just as Chessman said, Sir. The kind of guy you wouldn't notice in a crowd."

"Would you recognize him in a line-up?"

"I doubt it."

"Do you think our man at the station will?"

"Well enough to track him to his house, and anyhow that's his job. He knows how to pick out a distinctive trait."

"Fine, thank you, Sergeant; now you can concentrate on the side of your work you really can enjoy."

"Ah, come now, Sir. That isn't fair. How could I have guessed she was a high-up's wife?"

"She didn't look it?"

"I'll say she didn't. And I don't mind betting that she hadn't been it long."

The train was due to reach Baghdad at seven. It was on time, Reid learnt. He had been awake since daybreak. His companion, who had not returned from the dining car until he had himself curled up in his bedding roll, was still asleep. It was a brisk, clear morning and the sun glittered on the golden domes of Kahdimain. The agent's compartment was only two carriages away. From his window he would be able to watch the entire drama. There was no need for him to get on the platform. "The entire drama." But probably it would seem far more dramatic in the report that he would be writing in his cell-like office, than it would here on the platform.

The train's pace diminished. The scattered mudhouses became more frequent; imperceptibly a village became a suburb, which became a town. The carriages were now level with the platform.

The train was scarcely moving. He saw Frisky's door swing open, saw Frisky jump out on to the platform, to stand with his back to the train, his eyes searching the waiting room as though he were expecting to be met. He did not once look behind him. He appeared to have judged exactly how long it would take the agent's coach to reach him. All down the train, doors were flying open. The door behind Frisky remained closed. The platform was beginning to empty before it opened. A man of medium height stepped out. He was wearing a black coat and a Sidara hat. He was carrying a small black suitcase. For a moment he was standing beside Frisky. Then he moved slowly towards the waiting rooms. No one came out to join him. Frisky did not move. He stood as though he were still expecting some one. Then he moved away, at an angle from the man whose name on the pullman porter's list had been entered as Majid Semal. Reid turned to watch Majid walk towards the exit. His walk was leisurely and unconcerned. No one came to welcome him. He was enveloped by the crowd. No one detached himself from the crowd. I was right, thought Reid. Nothing could have been less dramatic.

The office car was waiting for him. In ten minutes, he was at the mess. He had already shaved and he went straight in to breakfast. The Colonel had finished his eggs and was consolidating his powers with toast and marmalade. The Colonel raised his eyebrows interrogatively. Reid nodded. And in return the Colonel gave him a congratulatory nod, then said: " I've a message for you, Prof. Judge Forsyth wants you for golf this afternoon. You can? I thought you could."

Reid was not hungry. He was too excited to be hungry. "No, no eggs," he said. "Some coffee and some toast." Besides, he was anxious to see if there was any mail for him. An answer from Jenks was overdue or at least he felt it was. He had been away two days. He went to his office before unpacking. There was a small pile of letters. Nothing, though, from Jenks. Nothing from Rachel, either. He wondered if she had decided not to write to him, till the case was over. That seemed incredible. There was so much they had to write about; about their boys, about the house, about their joint responsibilities. A marriage, even if it ceased to be a love affair, remained a business partnership. Or did it suddenly cease to be that, when a marriage broke?

There was a letter from his elder son. Had she told the boys, he wondered. And there was a letter from his father. How shaky his handwriting had become. This would be a blow to him. He hoped Rachel had said nothing to his father. Why should she have? Why worry him? It would all come to nothing. Surely it would all come to nothing. He had been so certain of that when he had written to Jenks. But now he was less certain. This silence had lasted for too long.

It was eight o'clock. The clerks were filing into their offices. He put his letters in a drawer. Time for them later on. He crossed to the main filing room. "Anything of importance come?" he asked.

"One thing, yes, Sir, from Beirut."

"Good, I'll take it with me."

He was in a mood for work; for the impersonality of work. He would have to wait at least an hour before any news reached him from the detective. The detective was a member of the Iraqi police. The Centre's and British relations generally with the Iraqi police were excellent. An Englishman, a career policeman called Forester, had been seconded to the C.I.D. division. It was through Forester that the Centre maintained contact with the Police Force. Forester had supplied the detective who had followed the agent from the station. Reid knew that Forester would telephone as soon as he had received the detective's report. There was plenty of time to spare before that happened. He looked at the cover of the file that the staff sergeant had brought him. It was headed: Aziz. It was a little time since he had had news of Aziz. He began to read with a quickened interest. The letter was addressed to the Istanbul office.

"We are puzzled as to what is happening to Aziz. Three weeks running he went to the restaurant, but no one contacted him. He has not been to the restaurant since. We wonder whether the Germans have lost interest in Aziz, or whether they have found another channel of communication. We do not see how they could have done this, but if they have, we do not see how we are going to find out. We have asked Chessman but he has no information. He has simply not been given any newspapers to bring through. We are worried at the possibility that a channel of communication is in existence of which we are unaware. This is a considerable danger to security. We ourselves are in touch with Aziz, both socially and through Fadhil. He listens to Fadhil's records, and occasionally obtains records from Fadhil. But now that correspondence with Aziz's Turkish friend has been discontinued, there is no contact for us with Turkey through Aziz. It is in fact a highly ridiculous situation. Every month or so, we provide Aziz with a series of questions, the answers to which are supplied by the British Council. In return for this, Aziz is supplied with gramophone records.

"Aziz occasionally visits the Centre's flat here in Beirut. We are supposed to be one of his sources of information. At one time, we talked rather openly to see how quick he was at putting two and two together. We do not do that any more. He seems unchanged. If he is at all changed, it is only through his air of being more relaxed. He was ill at ease originally, possibly because we were foreigners; and he had not met many English then. But he certainly does not seem to have anything on his mind. We are in a difficult position because we must not let him suspect that we suspect him.

"We are in fact feeling that this particular operation, which promised so hopefully, has somewhere along the line gone wrong. We are afraid that we have a liability on our hands. We shall be most grateful if you can give us any clue as to what is happening. If you are unable to, and we are left in the dark, we shall, we feel, have to take steps to liquidate this liability."

Reid raised his eyebrows as he read. Everything seemed to be happening at once. Rachel asking for a divorce, the wireless set, and now Aziz in trouble. Over the balcony, the Colonel shouted, "Prof". He picked up the Aziz file and took it with him. "Well, how's our Sherlock Holmes?" the Colonel said.

Reid made his report. The Colonel nodded as he listened. "That sounds all right; provided our friend with his black suitcase hasn't vanished in those back streets."

"We shall know in half-an-hour, Sir."

"Exactly. That's the soldier's point of view. Launch your attack, and wait in your dugout. There's nothing you can do."

Reid handed over the Aziz file. "Have you read this, Sir?"

"Yes."

"What did you make of it?"

"There isn't any need for us to make anything. It's not our pigeon. It's Beirut's and Istanbul's. We are only being kept in the picture."

"I can't help feeling some responsibility. I began this operation."

"I know you did. But that's the Army. With each new job you start afresh. Think how a colonel feels when he's posted to another unit on the eve of an attack he's planned. His men are his men no longer. Their fates are in another's hands. It isn't pretty. But he has to forget that and concentrate on the job in hand."

"What do you think Farrar will do, Sir?"

"What would you do in Farrar's position?"

"Farrar and I are very different people."

"I know you are, that's why I'm asking. What would you do?"

"I suppose I'd cut my losses, call the whole thing off."

"And leave that channel open?"

"No, Sir. I'd take Aziz up to the interrogation centre. Those French boys can be tough. I think that he'd break down."

"That's one way, certainly. I'm not saying that it's not the best, but I fancy that Master Nigel has something more dramatic up his sleeve."

The telephone rang. The Colonel answered it. "Yes, yes, I see. It's for you, Prof." He handed the receiver over. "It's from Forester."

Forester's voice was high and harsh; the voice of a man who smoked too much.

"Reid, is that you? When can you come down here?"

"I can come right away."

"Excellent. I'll be expecting you."

"How did it go?"

"Well; better than well. I'll see you."

An excitement that was new to him shot along Reid's nerves.

"He says it's gone all right, Sir."

"Congratulations. I'll be on tip toes, waiting. Leave me that file though, by the way."

On his way down the balcony, Reid checked. There was something he had forgotten. Johnson's door stood open and he went in. "Can I have twenty dinars, please, on secret funds?"

"Certainly, certainly, all the cash you want." He counted out four notes. Then handed Reid a slip of paper on which was written: Dinars twenty, and the date. Reid signed the receipt. "It's really worth it this time," he told Johnson.

"It's not for me to question you."

Johnson made an entry in his ledger, then lit a match and burnt the slip of paper.

The C.I.D. offices lay in Rashid street on the north of the Maude Bridge. It was two storied, like the majority of Baghdad houses. Reid always enjoyed his visits there. It was a "real" place. He would have found it hard to explain exactly what he meant by the word "real". The Ritz was real, but so was a slovenly tavern on a river, or a congested side street in the slums. Each had grown spontaneously to meet a human need. Each was itself. So many places, like so many people, were not themselves. They were meretricious or contrived or simply down and out, sotted with inertia. The C.I.D. with its rickety balconies and stairways, its crowded hallway, its noise and bustle, its general shabbiness was itself and vibrant.

Forester's office was tucked away upstairs. It would have seemed a comfortably sized office if it had not been filled with books and files and a series of collections of old newspapers. "Always keep a few old newspapers around," Forester would say. "They refresh your memory very usefully; crimes go back a long way. Suppose you're interrogating a man about something that happened in July 1938. It's not a bad idea before you see him to find out what was happening in Baghdad that month. What films were showing. What distinguished visitor was being met by whom, what the gossip was: not important international headline news; little local tit-bits, the kind of things that people remember when they forget when a Prime Minister was murdered. If you bring in a few of those little reminiscences, you'll often disconcert some one you're cross examining. You say: 'July the 20th. I remember that day rather well. They were showing Leslie Howard's "Romeo and Juliet" at the Rashid Cinema.' It startles him. He thinks if you remember that, you can remember anything. He's rattled and he makes a slip. He's so anxious not to give anything away that he tells a lie. Always keep a paper of some kind for every single week."

Forester had been in Baghdad now for a dozen years and each of those years had its separate stack of papers. Forester was himself very small and wizened, only a few inches over five feet tall. The skin of his face was brown and wrinkled like a walnut. He had kept his hair, and his hair had kept its colour. It was impossible to guess his age; he might have been forty; he might have been over sixty. He always wore brown suits. Reid was not sure what a marmoset looked like, but the word marmoset suited him. He often sat in his chair, with one foot curled under him.

He jumped to his feet as Reid came in. His movements were

somehow like an animal's, abrupt yet rhythmic. He clapped his hands. "Good news," he said. "Good news."

"So your man followed him all right?"

"There was no need for him to follow him. He recognized him; had known him all his life. He waved his hand at him. What luck; sometimes one has more luck than one deserves. No need for the least deception. We've got him where we want him."

"Who is he?"

"A schoolmaster."

"Is his name Majid?"

"It is not: Mulla Hassun."

"Where does he teach?"

"In one of the Kuttabs in North Baghdad."

"Is he well off?"

"He's not badly off."

"Would you say he was doing this for money?"

"That's what we are hoping to find out."

"How are you proposing to find out?"

"Through the usual methods."

"The usual methods?"

"Now surely, Major you know what the usual methods are?"

"When I lectured on Shakespearean history, I would say: 'You all know Henry V's reasons for declaring war on France,' but as I couldn't be sure that they all knew them, I proceeded to outline what they were. I could, if I were put to it, write an essay on the usual methods, but I'd probably make a number of inessential points and leave out two or three that really mattered, so that as I have to report back to my Colonel, I would like to be able to tell him exactly what your methods are."

Forester chuckled. "I see. I see. You want me to do your homework for you. Well, it's very simple. We draw a net. We find out all we can about Hassun. My man will be very helpful there."

"By the way, I've brought a present for your man."

Reid handed across an envelope that contained the twenty dinars. "Thank you very much. He'll be most grateful. As I said, my man can tell us a good deal about Mulla Hassun. We can find out who his friends are. We'll find out who the friends of those friends are. We can impose censorship. If there are telephones, we can have them monitored. We will try to build up a picture of Hassun's life. He is not in on this alone. We must find out how he came to contact the Germans. We must find out who is his contact with the Germans. We must find out if they contacted him or if he contacted them. And first of all the question 'Why?'. Is it for money? I suspect it isn't. An Iraqi student in Ankara who gets in money troubles will undertake an espionage commission to get himself out of trouble, and it is not difficult for the Germans to discover which Iraqi students are in trouble. That kind of fellow is obvious and vulnerable. It's different for some one like Mulla Hassun, who's living here in Baghdad, occupying a position of respect. If he were in financial difficulties, he'd have other means of raising funds. A man like that wouldn't start on a campaign like this unless he were anti-British or pro-German or both. And there's this point too, we must remember: the German Consul here before the war, Grobba, was very efficient and very popular. He had a great many friends. He came back here for those few days of the Rashid Ali rebellion. He had a list of his friends and that list is now in the hands of German Intelligence. We don't know who he saw during those few days. He may have seen Hassun. He certainly will have seen friends of Hassun. I think we can assume that Hassun acted out of conviction. There's a great deal that we may discover here."

"It will take us a long time to discover it."

"It will take rather more than a long time."

"This is wartime; ought we to put pressure on? Can we put pressure on?"

Forester shook his head. "Police work is a slow, slow job. You must be beginning to realise that by now. So much of it is office work. It is a question of files, remembering what is in those files, of comparing notes, of suddenly putting two and two together. Being patient oneself and remembering that criminals get impatient too. They show themselves in the open. This present enquiry will involve a lot of work, we shall be watching not only Hassun but Hassun's friends and the friends of Hassun's friends. Ninety-five per cent of that work will be wasted work. We shall be checking on people who are completely innocent. But we have to do it because we have to see Hassun's life in the round. We have to know all about it. So much of a man's life is submerged; his family may not be aware of a most significant section of it; a part of it that appears trivial but isn't. I was once tracking a Londoner whose whole life had appeared above board. He was so busy that I thought I knew how every minute of his time was spent. Then quite by chance I learnt that as a young man he had gone on a cricket tour. He was no particular good at the game. He went as a twelfth man and played occasionally. Thirty years later no one would have associated him with cricket, but the other members used to play in the evening a game of four-handed chess which one of them claimed to have invented. He took a great fancy to it. He went on playing it ever after, with three other men, one night a month. That was the key to a considerable subversive group. We've got to find Hassun's equivalent for four-handed chess. It will take time."

"But you believe it's worth it?"

"It's one of the most worth while things that has come into this office since I've been sitting here."

"You are sure we were wise to let the set stay with the boys; you don't think we should have rounded them up when we had the chance? Caught them redhanded and then grilled them?"

"And let the big fish escape? No, no. We are better as we are. And do you seriously think that these boys can really find out anything the Germans want to know? What access to information have they?"

"That's not an argument I could put up. Think of all the men who are drawing fat salaries organising campaigns against careless talk, pretending that there's a spy behind every table. Nine-tenths of G.H.Q. would be horrified if they learnt what we had done or hadn't done."

"What does your Colonel say?"

"He believes in giving his officers a free hand."

"Then you're all right."

Mallet had told Reid to report on his return. Reid found him alone. "How does the field lie?" Mallet asked. He listened without interrupting, nodding from time to time. "And Forester's satisfied?" he asked at length.

"Thoroughly."

"I hope that we shall be able to persuade the big brass that we are. You know how well it would read in an Intelligence summary in London: 'Our Baghdad section captured an enemy agent with a wireless transmitter in his possession. Under cross examination, the agent betrayed a number of his accomplices and we can claim to have eliminated a very dangerous group of subversive elements.' "

"Isn't there something in Macbeth about 'we have scotched the beast, not killed it'?"

The Colonel laughed. "I'm not saying that you are not right. I'm telling you how it's going to strike the men whose promotions depend on their presenting effective progress reports. By the way, rising out of that, have you begun to prepare your talk for the Controller's Conference in Beirut?"

"I haven't yet, Sir. It's still six weeks off."

"I know it is. But it's going to be a critical conference for this Centre. It needs careful planning. I'd like to have a quiet talk with you. What day have you free next week for dinner?"

"Any day except Tuesday. I'm duty officer on Tuesday."

"Then let's make it Wednesday. Are you a member of the British Club?"

"Yes."

"Then let's go there first for drinks. Shall we leave here at seven?"

The British Club was in a small, one-storey building, east of Rashid street, a short distance from the South Gate. It was run by civilians; it contained a bar, a billiard room, a card room. It served no food. It was exclusively a men's club, though once a month there was a dinner dance. A few senior officers from G.H.Q. were made honorary members. The two main shipping firms had not raised the price of whisky to their private customers and to the clubs. Whisky cost four dinars a bottle in the bazaars, but it was sold to friends at one dinar two-fifty fils. Military members were however, limited to six glasses a week. "How does your whisky ration stand?" Mallet asked.

"I haven't touched it yet."

"Good, then we can each work on our own. Let's see if there's any one in the annexe."

The annexe was a narrow strip of a room off the card room; six feet across with only enough space for a row of six arm chairs down each side. The walls were decorated with small black and white caricatures of members. It was cosy and often when he wanted to be alone, Reid would consume the half of his week's ration here. It was empty this evening.

"My father told me when I was young," Mallet started, "that you should never bring up a serious matter till you had reached the port stage. That may be very sound advice if you've designs on a young woman, or if you are trying to get a client's signature to a dubious contract, but I don't think it's a good idea when two serious citizens have something serious to discuss. Let's get our shop over first, and then relax over a bottle at the Sinbad. I want to tell you why the Beirut conference will be critical and crucial for this Centre. I'm hoping that by the end of it, I shall have arranged for a transfer to M.E.F."

It came as a complete surprise to Reid. Mallet had run the Centre since Military Intelligence had been merged with Air Force Intelligence in Baghdad after the Rashid Ali coup. That was a long time ago. Reid had thought of the Centre as the apple of the Colonel's eye. The Colonel had been awarded the O.B.E. in the New Year's Honours' List. Reid had fancied that he would want to carry on with his job till the war was over. "That's a surprise to me and a shock," he said.

Mallet shrugged. "I've been here two years. I'm possibly getting stale. I hope I'm not. But I may be. That isn't the real point, however, I'm saying this to you in strictest confidence. You are the only person here that I can talk to. We're not quite contemporaries; but we were raised in the same stable and the others weren't—except old Johnson and, well, old Johnson, you know what I mean. My point is this: the Army's my career. I've got to consider my own interests. I'll be retiring after the war. There'll be nothing in the Army for a man of my age who hasn't commanded a battalion in the field. And the higher my rank now, the higher my pension will be; also the better chance of getting a directorate or two in the city. If I can finish up as a Brigadier with the war substantive rank of Lieutenant Colonel, it will be a considerable help to me. That's why I want to go to Cairo. There is no chance of promotion here. There is going to be a downgrading of appointments. I shouldn't be surprised if Paiforce didn't cease to be an independent command, and we came under M.E.F. I've got to be near a lift that's going up. If I play my cards carefully in Beirut, I think I can swing a transfer. But that doesn't mean that I'm leaving you fellows in the lurch. I've built up this Centre and I want to ensure that it will continue to operate in the same spirit and with the same efficiency it has up to now, to the best of my ability. In my opinion, you are the man to run it."

It was an even greater surprise to Reid than the Colonel's announcement of his transfer. "But surely Maurice is senior to me?"

Maurice Spencer, a flying ace from the first war, was a Squadron Leader in charge of the Political Section of the Centre. He had been stationed in Iraq for several years. The Colonel nodded. "On paper, yes, and though seniority does not count for much in a show like ours, and though a Major's the equivalent of a Squadron Leader, it would cause awkwardness if you were put over him. I'm planning to take him to Cairo and put him up a ring. That would suit him all right."

"I get on perfectly well with Maurice. I'd be quite happy working under him."

"I know you are. I know you would. But you are the man to run our show, not he. You can combine the political and the espionage side in a way that Maurice couldn't. He's not up in the espionage side. But you are up on the political side—in fact with your training you're even sounder politically than you are in the cloak and dagger business, which is new to you.

"When I founded this Centre, I saw it as a two-barrelled gun: we were in danger of a German attack through the Caucasus so we had to have a sound counterespionage organisation, but we had also only recently survived a revolution. The country was full of malcontents. If our forces here were to play their proper part in the Middle East theatre, there could not be political disturbance in back areas; so I started the political branch under Maurice. The claims of the two branches might be in conflict with one another and I should be there at the top to adjudicate. That's why I want you to take my place. You are in a position to adjudicate.

"In point of fact, that's what you have done already over this wireless transmitter. There were counterespionage claims and there were internal security claims: you decided that the claims of internal security were the more ponderable. I'm not saying you were right. I'm not saying that you were wrong. You reached a crossroads. You decided on the road that you thought should be taken and you took it. That's all that you can do at a cross-roads. The important thing is that you were qualified to make that decision. You had both groups of facts at your disposal. I don't think that Maurice would have been in a position to do that. He would not have got the cloak and dagger point of view. And I believe that a great many similar crossroads lie ahead of us here in Paiforce. There's no longer any danger in a military sense. German troops aren't going to pour down through the Caucasus. They are being forced back everywhere on to their bases: yet Paiforce is still important. It is the gateway of aid to Russia. There are the oil fields of Kirkuk and the refinery at Abadan. Ours is probably the most important back area in the war. We must see that that area is not disturbed. I'm only repeating to you what you already know. But I'm leading up to the points I want you to consider making in your speech at the Controller's Conference. You are a good speaker; you made an effective speech in Cairo last year. I was delighted when I heard that you were coming to this Centre. You were the very man I wanted. And I want now to be able after this Beirut Conference to convince the Controller that you are the man to run this Centre. I'm thinking both of my own interests and the Centre's. I want the Centre to continue to flourish. It will, I know, under your leadership. And I want to get to Cairo. They won't let me go there unless they are convinced that this Centre is in first class hands. Your speech should clinch the issue."

"What shall I say in this speech?"

"Pretty much what you said to me when you gave your reasons for preferring those agents to keep the set. Explain how the situation is different in Iraq from what it is in the Lebanon. Explain why we want to keep Iraq the way it is; with a Royal Family that owes its presence here to British influence and to men like Nuri who are convinced that Iraq's prosperity depends on a close alliance with Great Britain. But I don't need to dictate your speech to you. You are much better than I am at that kind of thing. If I outline the general strategy, I can leave the tactical side of it to you."

"I see what you mean."

"Fine; and now we've got our shop behind us and can relax. Let's have a fourth whisky. Then we can go over to the Sinbad."

The Sinbad was not fifty yards from the British Club. It was a still, warm night. In a few days now, they would be discarding Battle Dress for bush shirts, and there would be those three or four blessed weeks of early summer, of which he had heard so much, before the heavy July heat had killed off the flies, when the river sank and the peasants came out to plant vegetables on the islands and along the banks. Reid was in an anapaestic mood because both of the whiskies and of the news that he had heard. He was looking forward to his dinner. He scarcely ever dined in an hotel. They were expensive and he dined well enough in his own mess. It was the first time he had been alone with Mallet, except for occasional periods of a few minutes when the mess was empty except for themselves. Was it true what they said about him?

Nigel Farrar had said all those days ago that schoolmasters had a nose for that kind of thing. He was not a schoolmaster, and very certainly he hadn't. It was in fact something he found it difficult to understand. As a schoolboy he had, as practically every English Public School boy did, experienced a romantic attachment for a younger boy. But in the monastic seclusion of a Public School, a younger boy had the look and appeal of something feminine. He was weaker, needed protection; and moving in a different—since junior—world had the appeal of foreignness. Reid recognised too that certain men had the misfortune to have female temperaments and natures encased in a masculine body. Those willowy young men constituted a third sex, but frankly, he could not understand how someone like Mallet, who was strong, virile, active, good looking and to whom one would expect women to be attracted, could have become homosexual. There was nothing dandified or precious about the Colonel. Was it really true? Might it not be that some men were completely sexless, as certain women were? No one would insist that a woman was a Lesbian simply because she did not marry and have children. In the same way that some men and women were tone deaf, had no response to music, lacked indeed a sense that was for the majority of human beings their greatest source of happiness and rapture, might not some others be born without an interest in and aptitude for sex? A man's reputation in the modern world was more easily tarnished than a woman's. Why should they say this about the Colonel, because he had not married, because he had no obvious liaisons, because he had drifted away from regimental duties? He might be absorbed in his mother. There were so many explanations. Anyhow he was on the brink of a good dinner.

It was nearly eleven before they were back in their own quarters. Reid's head was swimming as it had not done for very many years. He was not a man who had "nights out with the boys."

"I'll be going into my office for a moment," he said. "It's been a great, great evening."

If he went straight to bed, the whole world would be swinging round. He sat down at his desk, his elbows rested on it, his eyes closed. A lot had happened since he had last sat here. Could it really be true that he was going to run the Centre? He had never pictured himself with red flannel on his tunic. He wondered if he could get himself photographed in colour. It would be fun to send one to the boys. They would get a kick out of it. And Rachel. He checked. What would this mean to Rachel? Would this mean anything to her now? He lifted his head; opened his eyes. There were a couple of airgraphs in his in-tray. The top one was from Jenkins.

5

EVE TOO HAD BEEN WORRIED by Beirut's report on Aziz. She wondered desperately what was happening to him. She saw no way of finding out. He was still, as far as she knew, due to come up in May. They never corresponded. She felt that his letters would be stiff and awkward. She did not want to have her letters to him subjected to censorship and read by acquaintances all over the Middle East. He had readily accepted her suggestion that they should not write to one another. He too was afraid of censorship, though he did not know that she knew why he had cause to be. It was always difficult for her to have to remember how little he knew about how much she knew about him. It would have been easier to be in complete ignorance. There was a curious double take, in that way, in their relations. Neither could be completely open with the other. Yet he believed that she was being completely open.

She anxiously awaited her office's reply to Beirut's enquiry. It came ten days later. "We have made enquiries through Aunt Mildred about Aziz and the answer is noncommittal. The Germans have found Aziz an unsatisfactory medium. This is not surprising. Aziz is not a trained spy. He has no access to special information. He is quite clever, but he is leading a busy life as a student. He has not much spare time. He devotes most of that spare time to music. If one tries to imagine oneself in his place, one would ask oneself 'How on earth am I going to find out anything that they don't know already?' Last time he was up here they tried to frighten him. See our report X37/1206 of Dec. 12, 1942. But it does not appear to have had very much effect. The reports that Aziz sent up by the agreed channel (X37/1206 of Jan. 13, 1943 and Feb. 17, 1943) can not have been very helpful to the Germans. Our hunch is that the Germans have lost interest in him. This is not surprising in view of the fact that they have in Belorian a much more productive agent with a far higher potential who is covering the same area. They have in Belorian's case, moreover, a simpler means of communication, direct correspondence by mail with secret ink. The method of correspondence with Aziz was elaborate and occupied valuable time. It may be assumed that Germany is feeling a shortage of manpower. Her casualties in Russia have been very great; her forces are spread so wide that in many places they are being spread very thin. Able bodied men are being combed out of Embassies and back areas. Their places are being filled by the elderly, the less active and the less efficient: sometimes their places are left unfilled, with one man doing the work of three. They can not afford to waste their time and energy. It is very probable that the Germans have decided that Aziz is more trouble than he is worth, and called the whole operation off.

"We shall be able to judge this when Aziz pays his next visit here. It is the practise for them to contact him, not for him to contact them. He presumably does not know how he could contact them. When does Aziz come here next?"

Beirut's reply came a week later. "Fadhil reports that Aziz will be visiting Istanbul early in May. We endorse your appreciation of the situation. If the Germans are no longer in touch with Aziz, how will they know when he reaches Istanbul?"

There was no reference to any plans that Beirut itself might have. When she went into Sedgwick, she looked enviously at the small filing cabinet in the corner. If only she knew what it contained. If only she knew by what channel its contents reached this office.

Aziz on that last visit had said "Early in May." But from the last week in April she began to study the list of Taurus express passengers. She wanted to be on her guard for his arrival. She had given him her telephone number that last time. There had seemed no reason not to. Why waste half-a-day? Next time, she thought, she would arrange for him to send her a postcard telling her the day. Then she could have her hair fixed the day before and get her nerves in order. Next time. Would there be a next time?

She had wondered sometimes during his five months absence whether it could ever be so good again. Kitty had quoted to her a poem of Thomas Hardy's: "Lines on a Departure Platform."

> But why, young man, must eternally fly
> A joy you'll repeat if you love her well?

Nought happens twice on this earth. But why?
I cannot tell.

"It's extraordinary. There's no explanation," Kitty had gone on. "You meet some one. It clicks right away. Your eyes meet across a room. You've absolutely no doubt about each other. It's settled before you've said a word. And the whole thing's wonderful; the way you knew it would be. It goes on being wonderful. Then there's a break. You're frightened. Will things be different? But they aren't any different. They're even better. This is against all the rules, you'll say. There's another break. And you aren't frightened at all. This time it's going to be even better. You count the days until he comes back. You don't have dates with anybody else. You are so excited that you lose your appetite. And then there he is—and suddenly the whole thing's dead. There's no explanation."

The third time was the test, so Kitty said. This was the third time.

But there was no need for her to have been alarmed; it was just as it had been, with an added novelty.

He lay on his face across her outstretched arm; his unstifled sobs, his broken sighs were slowly subsiding to a long even breathing. The leather necklace that was slipped round her wrist dangled to the floor. She shook it loose. She passed her hand slowly, over his back, over the curve of his back towards his knees. To-morrow there would be thin, dark weals there. She would count them, gloatingly. There would be more weals there in three weeks time when he went away. He would be shy of sunbathing lest his friends should notice them. She had set her seal on him. That seal would fade, in two, in three weeks time. But the seal that she had set upon his mind, upon his heart would never fade. He would never forget her, never. He was hers; she had made him hers.

"Have you brought a list of enquiries?" she asked him.

"Yes. I've brought a list."

"I'll have your answers ready within a week."

"Mind they're full answers; or I shan't come again."

"It's really only to get those records that you come here, isn't it?"

"What other reason could have I for coming here?"

They laughed together. And she chuckled inwardly, knowing that he too must be chuckling, thinking to himself: "What would she say if she knew about my visits to the Germans; how trivial are those few records in comparison with the funds that are being paid into that Zurich bank." How completely she had him at her mercy.

Summer came early that year to Anatolia; and it was summer things they did during a halcyon three weeks. He borrowed a car and on working day evenings they drove down the Bosphorus and dined at one or other of the fish restaurants on the water's edge; sipped rakki and ate pleasantly slushy dishes, like Imam Baialdi, the Imam faints; or they would take a ferry down the Sea of Marmora past the hospital where Florence Nightingale nursed her Crimean casualties: they would sup in a café of tea and the white pancakes out of which a thick cream oozed. A cool breeze would blow down from the Black Sea; and she would recall Flecker's poetry. "Rose of cities drooping with the heavy summer's burning dew."

They would get back early to the flat so that they could listen to music with the windows open and the curtain drawn and the room filled with moonlight. And though they never planned to make love, half the time it seemed they were making love. And it was as good as it had been before.

Occasionally he would stay the night. She woke earlier than he and she would slide out of bed and stand at the window, watching the sun rise over the low hills beyond the Bosphorus. Around her the houses rose steeply in a half-closed semi-circle. The sun's reflection on the water rippled on their windows. Below her was a small mosque, its garden shaded by a willow. She could see Leander's tower and the minarets of San Sofia. Ferry boats chunked across the channel. "I'm glad it happened here," she thought.

During working hours at her office, she would wonder how he was spending his time with his family. "I'd like to be able to picture you," she said. "Tell me what you do; from the moment you get up, until the moment we meet in the evening." He laughed. "You Europeans always want to be doing something. You can't realize how much time we can manage to spend, gossiping over a cup of tea or coffee."

She persisted in her questioning, but she got no answer. This was no doubt the oriental reserve that she had heard about; the dignity that must not be disturbed. Yet the Prof. had made him talk apparently. How much of the Germans was he seeing? Was he seeing anything of them? To learn that, she would have to wait for Aunt Mildred's report after he had left. It was a curious position: to be as close to him as she was, so utterly abandoned in delight, and yet to have to rely on an impersonal police report for the facts about him.

"Next time before you come up," she said, "I'd like you to send a postcard. You needn't say that you are coming up on a certain day. That might make the censorship suspicious. But bring the date in somehow. Say: 'My mother's birthday is on the 18th of October. We shall drink you health that day.' Will you do that?"

"I'll do that."

"When do you think you will be coming up?"

"September. October."

"Not in August this time?"

"No, not in August." And it was not any good, she knew, asking him for a reason.

"I may not be here then," she said.

"Oh."

"I've been abroad three years. That's about as long as they keep any of us on foreign service."

"I see."

His face expressed no emotion. "His damned oriental impassivity," she thought. "I wonder if he'll care at all if he never sees me again."

She had warned him that they might not meet again, but she made no attempt to beat up the emotion of their final days with a "last time" frenzy. There was no need for that. Their excitement over one another had been so natural, so spontaneous, that she felt it must of necessity go on for ever. Yet at the same time she felt that it would not matter if it stopped. It could not lead anywhere. They had had all they had to give each other. There could never be any mental companionship, apart from their love of music. With him, there could be no mingling, no blending of two natures till they became one person, so that out of their two lives they could make one life. No, it would not really matter if it ended now.

On the morning that he left, it was in a lighthearted mood that she made her report to Sedgwick on his visit. "It was the same as usual. He brought up some questions about Turkish imports and exports. The British Council gave me a few figures. He seemed quite satisfied."

"Good, fine." He looked at her quizzically. "I must say you always look wonderfully refreshed after he has been here."

A week later, she typed out the official report on Aziz's visit.

"Aziz," the report read, "has spent three weeks here. As Beirut has reported (X/21/3471 of May 3, 1943), he brought up with him a list of enquiries about Turkish imports and exports. We provided him with the appropriate answers. Aunt Mildred reports that as far as she knows there was no contact between Aziz and the Germans. In her opinion the Germans have lost interest in Aziz."

Four weeks later Beirut's reply arrived. "Aziz has now been here for two Mondays. On neither of them has he been to Fawsi Café. As you know our agent makes regular trips to Aleppo where he contacts Chessman on the Taurus. He has received no newspapers from Chessman. Chessman can offer no explanation. Chessman's assumption is that the Germans have lost interest in Aziz. We are inclined to find ourselves in agreement with our adversaries. This seems to be an example of one of those occasions when a highly promising project gets bogged down for no obvious reason. One has to accept the fact; and move on to the next assault. We do not consider however that operation Aziz should be written off as an entire loss. It was through Aziz that we managed to enroll Belorian. And in our opinion he is one of the reddest irons in our fire; we are also of the opinion that there is still some use that can be made of Aziz. We will submit our views of this in a later summary."

Eve's eyes widened as she read that final paragraph. She did not know what Beirut had in mind, but she knew Nigel Farrar. He was bright, brisk, ruthless. He did not spare himself; he did not spare others. Aziz was in danger. "I've got to get out of this," she thought.

She was Aziz's link with Istanbul intelligence. If she were not here to give him the answers to those fake enquiries, a whole new routine would have to be set up. It would not be worth Beirut's time. The enrolment of a successor would be too involved and Aziz might not welcome her successor. As long as she was here, Aziz would think it worth his while to come. And as long as he made those trips he was vulnerable. When she had gone back to England, he might not bother to visit his parents, with whom he was in no great sympathy. Beirut was more fun than Istanbul and almost certainly in a little time, probably in a very little time, he would have found a girl friend there. She had lit in him a fire that would not be easily put out. And if Aziz remained in Beirut, Farrar would lose interest in him as quickly as had the Germans here in Istanbul. He was small fry, and there were big fish in the pool.

So that was that, she thought. She looked down the passage and saw the green light shining over Sedgwick's door. She knocked, was answered and went in. "Yes, Eve?"

"You remember, that a year ago you offered me repatriation?"

"I do, indeed. No one could have been happier than I when you declined."

"Thank you, Francis; I was very happy that you should have felt that way about me; but a year's a long time and these last weeks I have been feeling. . . . Well, I don't feel as elastic as I was. I think I ought to have a change of atmosphere."

"We shall miss you, Eve. When do you feel you'd like to go."

"Before the winter starts; it's the winter that gets me down; it comes so quickly after the summer. If we could say mid August. Then I could get used to England and the blackouts before the English winter starts."

"And that will give me time to find a replacement. The middle of August will suit me very well."

"Thank you very much."

That would be several weeks before Aziz planned to come here. And if she were not here, as likely as not he would not come. He would slide unobtrusively out of Beirut's plans as he had out of the Germans' here in Istanbul. She herself would be ready to make a new start in England. She had got over Raymond. She had rid herself of her schoolgirl inhibitions. She was ready for anything that came.

6

THE NAIRN TRANSPORT BUS in which Reid and Mallet crossed the desert reached Damascus shortly before midday. Farrar was there to meet them. He was looking thin and tired; but he was as voluble as ever.

"We've got a small party on to-night," he said. "Nothing elaborate. One or two of old friends, Prof, who'll be pleased to see you."

"Annabelle?"

"Yes, she'll be there."

"Jane Lester?"

"Yes. Have you heard about her?"

"I've heard nothing in my city."

"You read about those prisoners of war who tried to escape and whom the Germans shot. Her husband was one of them."

"How's she taken it?"

"The last way that you'd expect. She's knocked off the boose and started in on everything else that's handy. She's the most dated lady in Lebanon. So if that's what you're out for, Prof, you'd better weigh in quickly."

"Has Diana come?"

"No, she's in Cairo."

That was a relief to Reid. He did not want to see her till his divorce was absolute. If he were to see her now, he would be unable to resist telling her. He did not want to do that yet. Too many men had said to unmarried women: "My divorce will be through in a few weeks; the moment it is, I shall of course be asking you to marry me." He did not know if he would be asking Diana to marry him. He could not know how he would be feeling when he saw her next. He did not know whether he had got over her or not. But either way his divorce would completely alter the setting of their relationship. They had never discussed his marriage, but she had always thought of him as a married man. She had never thought of him as a man who was likely to become unmarried. When they met next, he wanted to be free; free to speak and act as the mood prompted him. He had been afraid that she might be here.

He asked who had come from Cairo. Farrar ran through the names. "Oh, yes, I'll tell you who else is here. Your old chum, Gustave."

"What on earth is he doing here?"

"I wouldn't know. Cairo sent him."

It surprised Reid that Gustave should have been sent. He had not thought of him as moving on that level. He was not a paper man. His value was in his local contacts. He was probably more often in mufti than in uniform. Still he was glad that Gustave would be there. He was fond of him. And Gustave could tell him about Diana.

"What about Aziz? I don't suppose he'll be there."

"No, he won't be there."

343

Aziz was another person about whom he felt curious. He had been worried by that last report about him. Farrar had something up his sleeve; he wondered what it was. But he could not ask him now, when a chauffeur was at the wheel.

"I suppose I shall find Beirut very much the same," he said.

"No. That's just what you won't find. It's become a very different place."

"How so?"

"Because it's become a different war. Beirut's not important any longer; not in the same way, at least, now that the Middle East has been cleared up. The Australian troops have gone. Ninth Army is only a skeleton formation: like your 6th Ind. Div. The few troops that are left are getting restless, particularly the French. They're wondering when the Second Front will open. They want to get back to France. They feel that the British and Americans are delaying the opening of the Second Front for reasons of their own. They suspect that they, the French, are not being given a square deal. There's a different feeling in the air. And it isn't a pleasant one. Nobody trusts anybody else. There's not the same cooperation. The Lebanese are getting fractious too. They think the French are waiting to pull a fast one on them. I'm not sure they're not right. They're making mischief between us and the French. There's not the same sense of urgency that there was. There's no placard: "Think plan and act in terms of March 1944." The war's gone somewhere else. There's a feeling that nothing that's happening here really matters."

There was an irritated impatient tone in Farrar's voice that had not been there before: dissatisfied and querulous. Perhaps it was not surprising. Farrar's contemporaries were in the field; they were fighting in Italy. Many of them had been killed in the North African campaign. Others were waiting for the opening of the Second Front. It had been all very well for Farrar to have referred laughingly to his "lucky war" when so few of his contemporaries were in action. It was different now. He was feeling out of things. Perhaps he had a sense of guilt; was wondering what his English friends would say to him when the war was over. He remembered those first war recruiting posters: "What did you do in the Great War, Daddy?" Farrar was going to need careful handling.

Farrar had said that Beirut was very different; but it looked completely the same as the car drove down from Aley and the red

344

promontory of sand gave the familiar illusion of rising to a peak; there was the same acrid smell of Arak, and the flat in the Rue Jeanne D'arc was heartbreakingly unchanged. It did not seem nearly two years since he had his first drink there on that first evening in Beirut, the day he had met Diana.

The whole setting of the party was familiar. The mixture of officers in uniform, French and British, the great preponderance of males, the half dozen picturesque young women with their black shining hair, worn loose upon their shoulders. Annabelle was as exquisite as ever. He looked for Gustave. In the nine months since they had met, Gustave had put on at least five pounds. But the additional weight suited him; there was no strain on the buttons of his smooth gabardine tunic. Reid moved across to him. "You're looking very well," he said.

"I'm feeling very well."

"I'm delighted to see you, but I'm surprised to find you here."

"Surprised?"

"I wouldn't have thought this conference was quite your line of country."

"It isn't."

"Then why did Cairo send you?"

"As a matter of fact . . ." he paused, he looked round him, saw that no one in uniform was within earshot. "As a matter of fact, the idea of the exercise was that I should meet your Colonel."

"What on earth was the point of that?"

"They've an idea of posting me to your Centre."

"But my dear Gustave . . ." Reid was astounded. He had thought that the whole point of Gustave, as an independent member of the Cairo centre, was his Egyptian background. He would be no use in that way in Iraq. Besides they talked a different Arabic. "Surely you won't like that," he said. "There are no bints for you in Baghdad."

"I can do without them for a little."

"You think so now, but wait till you've been without them for six months, in that heat too. Do you think you'd like the work, at your age? It's a very monastic life."

"It would be nice to put up a crown."

That, even more, astounded Reid. How on earth did Gustave imagine that he was going to get a majority in their Centre. The Establishment only allowed for a Colonel and two Majors, with Johnson because of his seniority being allowed local rank. There was something very curious here. It was something that Farrar had cooked up, he fancied. Farrar had said that he did not know why Cairo had sent Gustave here, but Farrar only told the truth when a lie would not have been easier. "I hope you do come," he said. "We'll do our best to make you welcome."

"Thanks, but it's off the record; don't say a word to your Colonel till mine's broached the business."

"I won't. Have you seen anything of Diana, by the way?"

"I see her every day."

"How is she?"

"Fine."

"And how's her romance going?"

"What romance?"

"The one with the French naval officer."

"Oh, that's all over. He was transferred to Tripoli."

"Who's taken his place?"

"I wouldn't know. But I guess some one has. There's no man shortage in the Middle East." And Diana was not the woman to let herself be neglected.

He moved away from Gustave. Annabelle was beckoning to him. "Ah, but it is good to see you. We have been missing you. How is it in Baghdad? They tell me it is very hot there."

"It is so hot that the flies die off in summer and go under ground."

"How are the damsels of Baghdad?"

"There are no damsels in Baghdad."

"Then why did you go there, my poor friend?"

"I was posted there."

"You should undo that posting and come back here with us and send that wicked captain in your place. It would be very good for him to be for a little while in a place where there were no damsels."

"It would be very bad for my nerves, Annabelle. And besides, I am no longer a captain. I am a major now," said Farrar.

"I know you are, and I am very happy for your sake. I am very proud for you. But major, that has such a dreary sound; so middle-aged and pompous and unsuccessful. It sounds as though you were retired. I shall always think of you as captain. As my gallant wicked captain."

"Suppose I were to become a Colonel?"

"Ah, that is different. Colonel has a dashing sound. It sounds successful; as though you would go higher still. Yes, when you are a colonel, I will call you Colonel."

"You say 'higher still.' Would you like me to be a Brigadier?"

"That would sound even worse. A Brigadier; a postman or a fireman. I would rather that you were a Major than a Brigadier."

"But if I went one higher and became a General."

"Now that is something, a General is a man of high distinction. A young girl could not be blamed for a *faiblesse* for a General."

"Even if he were thirty years older than herself?"

"Even if he were forty years older than herself, which very well he might be."

"So it is really every other rank that you approve."

"Why yes, now that you point it out. Though it had not occurred to me before. Yes, that is how it is, every other rank. Captain, Colonel, General: yes. Subaltern, Major, Brigadier: no."

"General is alas beyond me. But Colonel. If I try very hard I think I could become a Colonel."

"That is a worthy ambition for you, my idle Captain."

"Then I will achieve it, my beautiful Annabelle; and if I do, will you prefer me then to that ridiculous French flying man?"

"But he is not ridiculous. It is you who are being ridiculous to call him so. You are jealous of him because I respect him as an honourable man, which you, my charming and wicked Captain, alas, are not."

"You say I am not honourable; while he is. But is it honourable to court you because you are rich? He wants to marry you, yes; but would he want to marry you if you were poor?"

"My silly Captain; it is you now who are ridiculous. Would he love me if I were poor? Who could love me if I were poor? I would not be myself if I were poor. Would you yourself pay me these flattering, discreditable attentions if my fingers were not manicured?" And she shook her fingers before his eyes. "If my hair did not shine. If the powder did not lie smoothly on my cheeks; if the black pencil did not mark my eyebrows; if garnets did not dangle from my ears; if garnets did not match them round my neck; if the figure that a kind providence has given me were not accentuated and embellished by a master's craftsmanship? And do you not think it is a little unworthy of a man who claims to love a woman not to want to see what he calls her beauty enhanced perpetually? If he cannot himself afford so to enhance it, should he not be grateful to the parent whose money can do this

347

for her. If a man is poor, if he cannot give a wife all that he would wish to give her, is he not wise to seek a bride who is able out of her own resources to adorn herself? Would it not be ignoble in him to seek a wife who would, through marriage to him, become a drudge, a scarecrow? Would that be generous in him? Surely it is more honourable to seek a wife who is able to adorn herself; so that he can offer her not only the honourable estate of marriage, but through her parents the means with which to make it glamorous. Would you not call that honourable, my wilful Captain?"

It was the familiar eighteenth century badinage, but there was an undercurrent of animosity. There was a sharpness, a readiness, a will to wound that had not been there before. Yes, there was a change in Beirut. He had a sudden feeling that Farrar's life here had gone sour on him.

This feeling was stressed during the conference on the following morning. Once again Stallard opened the proceedings. "Many of you will remember last October in Cairo. I told you that I had come out here not to instruct but to be instructed. That I had more to learn from you than you had to learn from me. The only thing I said that I could show you was how your problems fitted into the overall pattern of the war. We in London, and those others of us who are in Washington, have a sense of the global picture which you here in the Middle East cannot expect to have. That does not minimize the importance of your problems. It only places them in a different focus; so that once again I am going to say very little now. I am going to listen to you all in turn and then at the end I will make a final estimate, showing you how I see your problems in terms of the all-in picture. Last October I learnt a lot and I hope that as a result of what I learnt you have found a readier, a more sympathetic response from us in London. I trust that the next year will show results equally beneficial to us all. I am now going to ask you, centre by centre, to give me your appreciation of the particular issues with which you have to deal."

Iraq came third upon the list. Reid's speech followed the line on which he and Mallet had agreed. "Some of you," he said, "may remember a little of what I said in Cairo last October. I was then speaking in terms of Beirut. I explained how different our position was in the Lebanon and Syria from yours in Baghdad, Cyprus, Jerusalem and Cairo. Each of those countries were part of the British *Raj* and in each of them, in consequence, a security organisation had been built up well before the war began. Lebanon and Syria on the other hand had been part of the French *Raj*. We were treated with very great suspicion and as an example I quoted Pierre Benoit's novel "La Chatelaine du Liban." In Syria and Lebanon, we had no organisation before 1941. We had to start from scratch. I had suspected what a difference it was. But I did not then know that I was going to be posted to Baghdad. In Iraq we had a twenty year old organisation."

He explained in detail where the difference lay. In every district there were men whom we could trust. We had also at our disposal compatriots who knew the country, who had worked there in oil, in business, and in banks. We had moreover a government that was cooperative; that relied on us for its maintenance. That government had had and still had its enemies. And the number and strength of those enemies determined the extent of the government's reliance and dependence on us. Those facts, he argued, were decisive in the direction of our centre's work. "We have," he went on, "two jobs of work to do there. We have the immediate and all important job of making our contribution to the war effort, but we have also a long view to take. We have to remember that Iraq is going for many years to play an important part in our policy in the Middle East. Iraq is going to be very vital to our interests, to our whole national economy. We want a strong and independent Iraq, but we want an Iraq whose interests are identified with ours.

"A year ago, we faced the possibility of battle on our frontiers. There is now no such danger. There are very few active troops there. We have a skeleton force. We have only as many troops there as are necessary to maintain order. We are doing police and garrison work. In view of the actual immediate conduct of the war, we have one function only, to provide safe transport for our aid to Russia. That is our function in terms of the all-in strategy of the war. But in terms of postwar conditions, we have a separate and important function, the safeguarding of the prosperity of Iraq. Let us put ourselves in the position of those Germans who are sitting at the Middle East desk. They are wondering what they can do to damage us in Iraq. They can no longer envisage an attack there, but there is an opening for sabotage on our oil installations in Kirkuk, and in Abadan; in regard to sabotage, we have to consider Persia and Iraq as one, as a part of Paiforce. I am surprised that no attempt at sabotage has been made. Perhaps the difficulties are greater than we suppose; they have a great many irons in a great many fires and I think that we, in defensive security, sometimes make the mistake of overestimating the forces that the enemy has at his disposal. We are so busy protecting ourselves that we hamper ourselves. We become immobile. I try to picture myself as a German intelligence officer in Berlin wondering how he can most hinder our war effort and I imagine I would decide that the best way to do it would be by promoting internal dissatisfaction, by causing political unrest. In the north, there are the dissident Kurds; they have a genuine grievance; those grievances could be fostered. There is dissatisfaction in the army. There always has been dissatisfaction in the army. Think of the revolts there were during Iraq's ten years of Independence. There is also a great deal of poverty and privation among the people. There is a great disparity of wealth. There is a suitable breeding ground for Communism. At the moment, we do not feel that any genuine Communism, in the Russian sense, exists. There was no line of direct communication with Russia; as there was and is in Syria, through France. In Damascus, there are genuine Kremlin-trained Communists. It is not long before there will be such Communists in Baghdad. There are Russians in Tehran and on our frontier in Kannaquin. We have to watch this closely. If I were a German intelligence officer, I should concentrate on three points: I should try to make trouble with the Kurds, I should foment disloyalty in the army, I should spread revolutionary propaganda among the proletariat. And in that respect German intelligence is not ill-equipped. As you all well know, there was a very competent and very popular German consul in Iraq during the war, who can give German intelligence a very useful briefing. He knows whom to approach, and how. That is where in my opinion there lies a danger to our security in Iraq. If we have political unrest there, our war effort will be hindered. The smooth flow of 'Aid to Russia' will be impeded.

"This imaginary German intelligence officer in Berlin is concerned only with the immediate effects of his subversive acts. He has no longer a long range interest in Iraq, no equivalent for the Kaiser's dream of a Berlin-Baghdad axis. He does not care what happens there when the war is over. We do, however. We have a very real responsibility towards the future. We want to help our successors. After all, somewhere or other in Baghdad the work of our Centre will continue. When I came here first in the late autumn of 1941, the walls of the Spears Mission were placarded with notices: 'Think, plan and act in terms of March 1942'. I should like to placard the walls of our Baghdad Centre with 'Your work to-day will bear fruit in 1950'."

Nigel Farrar followed Reid. He still looked thin and drawn, but there was vitality, there was animation in his manner. There was no trace of nervousness. He was completely self-assured. "I was not in Cairo for the conference last autumn," he began, "but I read the shorthand transcript of Major Reid's report to you. I was greatly impressed by it. I have been out here three times as long as he has, but I learnt a great deal from it. I was astonished that he should have been able to catch so quickly the essence of our problems; to distinguish between the essential and the inessential. Yes, I was astonished, but then I reminded myself that. . . . ," he paused, he looked towards Reid, "we must remember that our Prof is really a rather remarkable person." A smile lit his face. There was warmth and affection in it. There was warmth and affection in the little ripple of laughter that ran round the audience. He was surprised as well as touched. He had the feeling that they all rather liked him. He had not expected that.

"Remembering what he said at this conference eight months ago, I was very curious to hear what he would have to tell us now about Iraq. I was as confident that he would get inside the problems of that country as he had, in about the same amount of time, got inside ours in Beirut. I was expectant and I was not disappointed. I learnt a great deal from his report. I more than ever realised how different our work here in Beirut is from his in Baghdad and that of you others in Cyprus, Jerusalem and Cairo. The basic difference being this, that you have post-war responsibilities in your Centres. We have none."

He paused. He looked round him. When he went on, his voice had dropped a tone. He spoke more slowly; he spoke more seriously.

"The moment the war is over," he said, "our office will close down. M.I. 5's role will end. M.I. 6 will take over in a restricted way. I cannot foresee how the French are going to handle their problems here, but I am convinced that they will insist on handling them alone. And I regret to say that I do not have the slightest confidence in their administration here.

"I am almost a fanatical Francophil. You remember Josephine Baker's song: 'J'ai deux amours, mon Pays et Paris'? I would not be so provincial; I would go further. I would say: 'J'ai deux amours, mon Pays et la France.' France is the cradle and guardian of our culture. And many experts agree that her record as a colonising power in Algeria, in the Far East, in the West Indies, and more recently in Morocco, is a very fine one. She is trying to work on the Roman Imperial pattern by which colonies become departments of Rome; eighteen hundred years ago a man born in Spain could count himself a Roman, and today a peasant born in Martinique thinks of himself as a Frenchman. Does a Moslem born in the Punjab think of himself as a Briton? That is a significant difference.

"But here in Syria and the Lebanon the situation is different. Syria and the Lebanon were not colonies. The French only had a watching brief. The French had played a very small part in the Liberation of the two countries. They had only a small cultural stake here. The Syrians and Lebanese did not want them. They indeed appealed against their presence here. Most Arabists are agreed that it was a mistake to grant the French that mandate. It was part of a hurried packaged deal at the Peace Conference with Clemenceau and Lloyd George playing power politics with each other.

"From the start it worked out badly. Although Syria and the Lebanon were not French colonies, the French here behaved as though they were. Yet because they were uncertain of their tenure here, they did not behave in keeping with the traditions of their colonial past. They tried to get as much out of the country as they could during the period of their Mandate. We British can honestly say that we sent to the various Ministries in Iraq technical advisors whose job was to make themselves expendable. We did not try to make ourselves indispensable. The French did. They were rapacious and they tried to maintain their position by dividing the various tribal interests, playing off the one against the other. In my opinion the best Frenchman did not come out here. There was no equivalent for Lyautey. The French are paying the price now for the bad faith they showed. Perhaps bad faith are the wrong words to use. A mandate presented a new problem to them. They had not an effective technique for it.

"Perhaps you will say that all this is beside the point. I do not think it is, because it explains why our problem in Beirut is different from those of the rest of yours. We are not concerned with France's position here after the war. We are concerned only with the winning of the war. We do not take a long term view here; as you others can. We want to avoid trouble between the French and the Syrians and the Lebanese because such trouble would hinder the war effort. I have a hunch that very shortly the French are going to do something very silly and chauvinistic here in Lebanon. I am trying hard to find out what it is; and if possible prevent it, but only because the act will be a nuisance in terms of the conduct of the war. It is no concern of mine whether the action that the French may take will ruin their chances of re-establishing their prestige and power after the war.

"There is a difference of approach; and that difference can be best exemplified by the action taken by Baghdad when a wireless transmitter was sent there by the Germans. Baghdad felt that this set would be of great value because through it they could discover what forces were working against the government and for what reasons. It will be a slow operation and its fruits will be appreciated in 1950. Baghdad's decision was supported by Cairo and I do not question the wisdom of that decision. But if a set had been sent to Beirut, there could have only been one reaction: to capture the set, arrest the agents, grill them, find out all we could, keep concealed from the Germans that we owned the set and use it to send to the Germans the kind of information we wanted them to have. We should have taken the short, fast view." He paused. He looked round him. His face wore a belligerent expression. "As I see it," he concluded, "we have only one concern here in Beirut; to concentrate all our forces on the immediate objective of the war. Let the French clear up their own mess afterwards."

His tone had changed during the last few minutes. It had a very odd effect on Reid. When he came to read it in the shorthand transcript, it would seem, he was very sure, entirely unexceptionable. It had been reasoned, judicious; it had been even conciliatory; but to Reid, who knew Farrar so well, that change of voice had indicated a very real change in Farrar. There was an air of antagonism, of defiance, of resentment; the sense of a chip upon his shoulder. Had he fancied it, or was it really there? Later on he would ask Mallet if he had noticed anything.

The meeting adjourned directly after Farrar's speech. Reid went across to him. "Congratulations; that was excellent."

"I'm glad they put me on after you. It made it all the simpler."

"What you said will make my job a good deal easier in many ways."

"I'm glad to hear it."

"I wasn't quite sure if you had got my point about that silly toy."

"I'm not sure that I had either, until I heard your speech."

"We oughtn't to be far apart, you know."

"I'm glad that you feel that."

"Let's make the most of this time anyhow. Let's have a meal together."

"I'd enjoy nothing better."

Before they could fix a date, Stallard had come across to them. "Congratulations to you both. Excellent. Excellent. You should be proud of your pupil, Nigel."

"We should be grateful to Diana, shouldn't we?"

"I'm going to tell her so when I get to Cairo."

"It seems more than two years since we had that lunch at Ajalami's."

"A lot has happened since."

"A lot can happen in two years in wartime. You wait until you see how London's changed." He outlined some of the ways in which it had changed.

Farrar moved away. Their brief conversation, like the last sentences of his report, had left Reid with the uncomfortable suspicion that Farrar had something on his mind, that he was harbouring a grievance. I must have a real talk with him," he thought.

Yet that was the one thing he found it impossible to do. Farrar always had people around with him, or there were people he had to go and meet; on the one occasion when they did find themselves alone, between sessions, on the terrace of St. Georges, Farrar called someone over. It was a person of no consequence. There seemed no need for him to have been summoned over. Reid could not resist the feeling that Farrar was avoiding him.

One morning he rang up the Amin Maruns. Aziz answered the telephone. "I want to see your aunt," he said. "But I also want to see you. Can you give me a time when you'll both be there?" Aziz laughed. "There's not much point in seeing either of us when the other's there. My aunt's always in on Friday afternoon, at tea time. Why don't I see you in that students' café facing the A.U.B.? Any time that suits you suits me."

They fixed a time. He's growing up, Reid thought. Eighteen months ago he would scarcely have made that remark about his aunt and himself. And if he had, he would not have made it with a laugh. He would have been evasive.

Two days later he was to change that estimate. Aziz was not growing up. He had grown up. They met for breakfast at the café On the previous evening he had taken tea with Madame Amin. She was her habitual phlegmatic self. She asked him about certain of her Baghdad relatives. "It is strange to realise," she said, "that when I was a girl, Baghdad was a city in my own country, as Marseilles is for a Parisian. I wonder if they are happier there the way they are."

"You could ask that about any country in the world. Some are better off, and some are worse off. But on the whole there are more people better off than there are people worse off."

"I suppose so. I suppose so."

"Except in the occupied countries at this moment."

"I am seeing Aziz to-morrow," he told her.

"You will find him very changed."

"How shall I find him changed?"

"He knows his own mind now; or at least he pays us the compliment of confiding in us what is on his mind."

"And what is on his mind at the moment?"

"He has decided to take the advice of that nice young friend of yours, Captain Farrar, and go to Alexandria."

"But I thought he was doing very well now at the A.U.B.?"

"He *is* doing well at the A.U.B., but he thinks that he could do better in Alexandria."

"So you've decided to go to Alexandria." That was the first thing Reid said to him next morning.

Aziz smiled. "It seems a better idea now than it did then."

"How so?"

"The world's a different place. Two years ago I thought that the Germans might win the war; now I know that they will lose it. Two years ago I thought that the future for some one like myself lay with a Turkey that was a German ally. The old partnership that the Kaiser had in view. I did not want to go to Egypt, because I should then be in the British *Raj* and I might fare badly when you lost the war, if I was a student in Alexandria, as a British protégé."

"So you thought we were going to lose the war?"

"Didn't you?"

355

"No, never, but there was a time when I thought we might not win it."

"When did you think that you would win it?"

"As soon as America came in."

Reid was following his own thoughts. If Aziz had believed that the Germans were going to win the war, and that his future lay with a Turkey that was allied with Germany, perhaps he had been spying wholeheartedly for the Germans; had been willing and anxious to be of assistance to them. His father had fought with them against the British. His uncle had been killed at the Dardanelles. He might well have been sincere during those months when Rommel was driving on to the Canal. Had that occurred to Nigel? Of course it must have done. Why hadn't it to him?

"Even so," he said, "I should have thought the A.U.B. now that you're settled down there, would be as useful as Alexandria. Isn't it as well to go on with whatever it is one has begun?"

Aziz shook his head. "A Turk would stand more chance in Egypt than in the Lebanon. There's still a great deal of anti-Turkish feeling here. They remember the way the Turks put down revolt. There's the Place des Martyrs to remind them. Egypt has no anti-Turkish feeling."

"You want to make a life outside Turkey then?"

He nodded. "Turkey is too limited, too narrow, too constrained. There is a great deal I love, a great deal I respect, but I have very little in common with my family any longer. Now that I have seen the way people live here, now that I've met Europeans, I couldn't go back to that old life."

He spoke with an assurance that was new. He was a young man now, not a youth; and a rather striking young man at that. He had lost his pimples. His skin was clear. Twenty months was a short time in the life of a mature man, but in adolescence it could be decisive. The change was no less for a man than for a woman. Aziz had found himself. Reid remembered that quotation from the preface to Endymion that Compton Mackenzie had quoted on the title page of Sinister Street. "The mind of a boy is healthy; the mind of a mature man is healthy; but there is a period in between when the spirit is confused, the outlook muddled, the mind in a ferment, the way of life uncertain". Aziz had been in that period when he had met him first. It was a period that was familiar to schoolmasters and tutors. When a young man was in desperate need of guidance, when he pestered his tutor with that need for sympathy; he could be boring, tiresome, exasperating, endearing; and then suddenly he found his feet, and no longer needed guidance. And very often in his freedom he reacted against the mentor who had given him that guidance. It was human to resent the people you had wronged; it was also human to resent the people who had helped you. You wanted to assert your independence. Very often the mentor felt aggrieved. He inveighed against the ingratitude of the young. The wise man shrugged. The young used the elderly as stepping stones. And it was a privilege to be a stepping stone. Aziz had needed him twenty months ago. He did not any longer.

"Have you any definite ideas yet about what you are going to do?" Reid asked.

Again Aziz shook his head. "I shall find out there. That's what a university is for."

"Did you have any difficulty in getting taken on?"

"Captain Farrar fixed that for me, through the British Council."

Had Farrar still any designs on Aziz; he had said in one of his recent summaries that they would have to see if they could not find some new use for him? But he did not imagine he was any longer thinking of Alexandria as a base for that. Aziz had ceased to be the kind of young man who got into debt and trouble in a foreign city.

"You are not thinking of making a career in music."

"Indeed not. Only very exceptional people can make careers out of music. It will be a hobby; a great and close one, nothing else."

Which was the practical point of view. Most young Englishmen with literary inclinations wrote reams of poetry in their teens and pictured themselves as Poet Laureates. Young men thought themselves remarkable during that "period in between," but very soon "the vision faded into the light of common day." In three years time, he and Aziz would not have anything to say to one another. There might even be embarrassment on Aziz' side, because they had once been close.

"Do you remember that prophesy I made?" Reid asked.

At that point, Aziz did momentarily lose his self-assurance. "Yes, I remember very well," he said, and flushed.

"I hope it turned out satisfactorily."

"Very satisfactorily. I thank you."

And that was that, Reid thought. There was nothing more for them to say to one another; now or ever.

During the morning session, Reid sat next to Farrar. During the first break, he said, "I breakfasted with Aziz to-day."

"You did? How was he?"

"Excited about going to Alexandria. Very grateful to you for having fixed it."

Farrar laughed. "It's funny, isn't it, how often something comes to flower and fruit long after it has ceased to serve a purpose. Two years ago, I was very keen to get him to Alexandria. I set the machinery in motion. Now, when I couldn't care less, the wheels have started to revolve."

"That project didn't work out as well as we had hoped."

"That happens sometimes."

"It seemed so promising at the start."

"It seemed very promising."

"In one of your recent summaries, you said that you might be able to find some further use for him."

"I remember saying that." Farrar looked very straight at Reid. There was a challenge in that look. Reid did not accept it.

On the last morning, as before at Cairo, Stallard summed up the work of the conference.

"For me", he said, "it has been an even more stimulating meeting than we had last year. Perhaps because we have got to know each other better; perhaps because the war is going better; perhaps again because we are able to assess the value of the work we have been doing. At any rate, I myself shall return to my austere life rejuvenated. I have learnt a great deal and I hope that I shall be able to convince my untravelled colleagues in the War Office that what I've learnt was worth their learning too." As in the previous October in Cairo, he ran over the points that had been raised by the various Centres. Once again, he paid a particular tribute to Reid's report and this time he threw a special bouquet to Farrar. "I hadn't realized so fully before where and why the problems in Syria and the Lebanon were difficult. Major Reid did stress that point in October, but the points of difference have been accentuated during the last ten months."

He then came to his summing up. "Nothing," he said, "has pleased me more, has encouraged me more than the hopeful, optimistic spirit which I have found among you all. I hope that

358

I shall find you as cheerful a year from now. Because the next year is going to be difficult for you. The war has moved to other frontiers. You are left behind. You were all of you very proud three, two, maybe as little as one year ago when you were posted out here. You were right to feel proud; you had been handpicked. The situation is different now. Establishments are being cut down, and you who are left may be tempted to feel that it is the best who are being taken away. Cut off from your homes, you are inevitably sensitive to the picture that you are going to cut at home. You want to appear as heroes to your families. You did in the past. Will you be able to any longer? The Middle East for two years was the centre of the war. It is not any longer. England is now the centre. You are going to have the feeling that nobody is interested in you any more. You will feel neglected; abandoned. You remember the jokes they used to make about the B.E.F.? Back Every Fortnight. You'll be making the same crack soon about M.E.F. Men England Forgot. I don't think it's going to be an easy time for anyone in this area; but you've got this consolation: it's better for you than the rest because you are doing something active and creative. Intelligence never rests. You will know that what you are doing is important, even if your families in England think you are on a picnic. And don't forget that we in Marylebone have no doubt how valuable your work is. Good luck to you."

There was a lunch after the final session. Farrar sat at the other end of the table from Reid. Afterwards, Farrar came across. "I'm sorry that I shan't be able to come with you to Damascus; I can't spare the time. Everything's been a rush. I've hardly seen you at all, Prof. I'd been so looking forward to it too, but I've been responsible for so much of the organisation of this show. Why don't you come over quietly one time? Surely you could swing it."

"I might take some leave. I'm due for some."

"Yes, you do that. Then we can have some fun." And he was gone. They had not had five minutes alone together during the entire conference.

"How well do you know Farrar?" he asked Mallet that night at dinner.

"Not very, why?"

"I thought he seemed different somehow. Tired and on edge. There was an aggressive tone in that speech of his. He has got a good deal on his mind, I suppose. He's been out here a long time. He's homesick possibly. Perhaps he has a feeling of guilt about being out here, doing staff work at his age. And then he's quarrelling with his girl. She's flirting with some Frenchman. He's a lot to worry him, I know. But there was something strange about him. It sounds a ridiculous thing to say, but I almost had the feeling that he was avoiding me."

"And so he may have been."

"Why on earth should he?"

"Because. . . ." Mallet checked. His smile was quizzical. "It's not too easy to put into words. But your relationship, yours and his, was an unusual one. The disparity of age and of position. It wasn't only that he liked working with you. He was proud of working with you."

"Oh, surely, now. . . ."

"No, no, please hear me out. I'm glad you brought this up. I wanted to have a talk with you about it. It may become important for you in the next few months. Because . . . I haven't had time to tell you yet, but it's going to be all right about your taking over the Centre. I fixed that up with Cairo and with Stallard, and when you are running the Centre, it's going to make a difference to Farrar. It'll be a challenge to him."

"You don't mean he'll be jealous?"

"Not in the obvious way, but indirectly. There'll be a tension. As I see it, Prof. . . . well, you are, you know, an unusual person. You're someone in your own rights. You've been that for fifteen years and you know exactly what you amount to. And because you know that, you don't altogether see the effect you have upon other people who are not in the same position. You are not a vain man, but you're not a modest one. You know how good you are, in your own job in England, so there's no need to assert yourself. You've got yourself sized up, which most men haven't. And because you have, you didn't realise how much you meant to somebody like Farrar, who isn't anyone, as yet; and may never become anyone. He had probably never met anyone like you. He had certainly never met anyone like you on equal terms. That meant a lot to him. I know from the way he talked about you. He had a proprietary way about you that was rather touching. 'I must look after my Professor,' he would say. Always 'my Professor.' He enjoyed being able to explain things to you, and he did, of course, value your opinion very highly. He was very happy working with you. You were a good team. One felt that seeing you together. It was a blow to him when you broke up."

"But that wasn't on his account. There was a very personal reason. . . ."

"I know."

"How could you know?"

"I shouldn't know and the fact that I do know shows me how very upset Nigel was. Your going away put him on the defensive. He had to justify himself; to prove that it wasn't on his account that you transferred."

"But he couldn't have been easier when I first brought the matter up."

"I'm sure he couldn't. But it was when he thought about it afterwards that he began to feel aggrieved. He found that he was lonely; he was resentful because you had made him lonely. And then you went against him over that wireless set. And Cairo took your point of view, not his. Deception is his special project, and you spiked his guns."

"This is all a complete surprise to me."

"I thought it would be. That's why I want to put you on your guard."

"On my guard against what?"

"Against what Master Farrar is cooking up."

"What is he cooking up?"

"I don't know. But I suspect that it will be something very drastic. Did you notice that he was seeing a lot of Sedgwick during the conference?"

"I didn't as a matter of fact."

"Well, Sedgwick is a tough man to deal with; in the way that only a Wykehamist can be. It's funny about Winchester. There are those four schools—Eton, Harrow, Rugby, Winchester—which produce their special types. Men from the other schools—Tonbridge, Uppingham, Marlborough, Sherborne, Shrewsbury—there's nothing distinctive about them. A man might have come from any one of them. But those four are different. Winchester produces the finest civil servants in the world, particularly Treasury officials: accurate, conscientious, infallible, impersonal, almost a machine; as a contrast to that, on the same occasions, when a Wykehamist goes to the dogs, he does it with a thoroughness that leaves an Harrovian at the starting point. And as a corollary of that, when a Wykehamist gets tough, he is completely ruthless because he is convinced that he is in the right. He is impervious to criticism. Who devised body-line bowling? A Wykehamist."

"But I don't see how all this is going to affect me?"

"It's going to affect you because what Sedgwick and Farrar are cooking up is something particularly devilish and in Farrar's case you are the objective."

"I still don't see. . . ."

"You don't. Perhaps you've got too nice a nature. Farrar wants to assert himself, to make a gesture against you, to prove his independence, to say in effect: 'Don't be so high and mighty. Have a look and see what I can do when I put my mind to it.' I prophesy that what he's cooking up will be ingenious, will be legitimate, will definitely help the war effort. But its main propulsion will be to shock you. So be on your guard, Prof. It'll be devilish."

7

"VERY FINE, COLONEL SAHIB, SIR, very fine." With a proud grin, Reid's Indian servant handed him the bush shirt on whose lapels red flannel flashes had been sewn. Reid slipped it on and stood before the mirror. He felt very much as he had as a schoolboy when he had first put on his first eleven blazer. A mixture of pride and shyness. At his preparatory school, it had been the custom to pinch a boy the day he appeared in a new suit, presumably because he looked awkward in it. Would any one want to pinch him when he walked into the mess at lunch? He felt he wanted to give his shirt an airing; to show it off to the world before he showed it to the mess. He ordered a car. "Drive me to the C.I.D." he told the chauffeur.

It was a very hot day. The thermometer stood at 119°. Forester had had a brushwood screen arranged in front of his window; a water tap was allowed to run on it and the drops fell slowly from one twig to another. It was supposed to cool the room. It was Ramadan so the coffee to which every guest was treated had to be proffered in a cardboard box so that the faithful in the passages might not be shocked by the self indulgence of the infidels.

Reid handed Forester a list.

"Do you know any of these boys?" he asked.

It was the latest list of names that had cropped up in the investigations started through the wireless transmitter. About a hundred men were at the moment being subjected to censorship. Forester studied the list. "Him I know, and him, and him, not him, not him. The last two, yes."

"Shall we put them all on censorship?"

Forester pursed his lips, picked up a pencil and scratched out a couple of names. "You need not trouble about those two. We might watch the others for a little."

They had not unearthed yet any subversive activities, but they had found out a number of facts that the persons concerned would have been dismayed to learn were known to the police; one man was evading income tax; another was smuggling carpets from Tehran; there was a flippantly phrased account of how two university students had picked up an air force corporal in a cinema, taken him back to their flat, given him too much whisky and then made use of him.

"It is really very alarming," Reid had said. "Is there one of us who hasn't got something in his life that he does not want to have known by the police? It might easily get found out through the friend of a friend being under suspicion."

"One must choose one's friends with caution."

"If one had to watch not only one's friends but one's friends' friends, one wouldn't have any friends at all."

"Would one be much worse off?"

Which was the kind of remark made without the flicker of a smile that made Reid enjoy his visits to the C.I.D.

"This correspondence has become almost a whole time job for one of my officers," Reid said.

"I'm not surprised."

"I'm wondering how much we are getting out of it."

"We can't tell how much we are getting out of it until we find something definitely subversive. Once we do, a great deal of all this evidence will become of value."

"We can't be sure that we ever shall find anything."

"As you say, we can't be sure."

"And in the meantime that wireless transmitter may be sending messages to Ankara."

"It may."

"And we haven't the machinery to intercept it. The Germans

in Paris have trucks that can detect transmissions. We haven't here."

"What do you suggest?"

"If we arrested Hassun, we'd find out something."

"We'd also lose the chance of finding out a great deal more."

"We'll have to take action some day."

Forester shrugged. "Police work is a very slow affair. It requires a great, great deal of patience."

"You are quite happy to have it go along the way it is?"

"I'm more than happy, I'm delighted."

"O.K. then. If you are satisfied."

But he could understand Farrar's impatience in Beirut. The need to get on with something; to get something done. He watched a drop of water slowly gathering upon a twig. It would take that drop a long time to reach the bottom of the screen. But it would get there in the end. It was three months since he had watched Hassun carry his black suitcase across the platform. And they were no nearer to any action.

In winter, before lunch, the officers of the Centre gathered on the long broad balcony for cocktails in the mild bland sunlight. They relished the sunlight after the five hours that they had spent in their damp chill offices. They were glad to warm their veins with a glass of Vodka or of Arak. They had need too of hot food. After lunch, they would take a bellum across the river; they would play golf, or squash or tennis at the Alwiyah Club. By half past four, they would be back at their desks, in their chill, clammy cells. In summer, it was altogether different. No one wanted hard liquor before food when the thermometer stood on the brink of 120°. Nor did anyone want heavy, greasy food: a salad, a cold soup, something in aspic, fruit and cheese and then a long siesta. It was in the evening, in summer that you sat on the terrace over long cold drinks, while the now sluggish Tigris slithered towards the Shatt-al-Arab; dinner was a parade and lunch was not. And at his first lunch as the new C.O., Reid hurried through his scamped meal exactly as he had done for the last eight months.

It was different in the evening. This was his first appearance before the Centre as their Chief. And he took care to be on the terrace first; to each officer as he arrived, clicking his heels and bowing before he sat down, Reid said, "All drinks are upon me to-night." He no longer felt shy, as he sat in a long high chair with the red flashes on his bush shirt. He had, instead, an exciting, dedicated feeling, that carried him back to his first night at Sandhurst when the Seniors after dinner in their new found privileged positions had stood round the piano, shouting the songs of the hour, "If you were the only girl in the world and I were the only boy" and "Another little drink and another little drink, and another little drink wouldn't do us any harm." He suddenly saw himself on that 1916 August evening, sitting overawed, with the other juniors on the left side of the anteroom, picturing the day three months distant when he would be a senior, bawling round that piano; and at the same time looking ahead to the hour, quarter of a century away, when he would command a regiment, when he would look back to this first night in the anteroom, thinking "it all started here."

Even when he had thought that, he had known at the back of his mind that the army would not be his career; but who could look far ahead in August 1916, when so very few miles away names like Hill 60, Polygon Wood and Beaumont Hamel were cutting their letters into history. But even so, Sandhurst had taught him to see promotion in terms not of privilege but of responsibility. And between this September evening in 1943 and that August night of 1916, the road ran clear and straight. That had led to this. Because he had been there, sitting in that anteroom, as an apprehensive junior, he was now with red flashes, sitting in this long chair, while officer after officer clicked his heels and bowed; and because he had sat then in that anteroom, he was conscious of his duty now.

Because British forces and British interests had been so long established in Iraq, the I.S.L.O. Centre in Baghdad was a great deal larger than the one in Beirut. There were fifteen officers under him and twenty other ranks. It was a large family, and each member of that family regarded him as a kind of parent. His authority over them was unquestioned, yet he was their protection against the higher authorities that stood over him. They would rely on him to fight their battles. He might "stand them on the mat" himself, but he would argue their case for them against Brigadiers and Generals. He remembered in France in the late summer of 1917, with what excited pride and also with an awed sense of service he had seen his platoon for the first time. "These are my men," he had thought.

It was a feeling he had never had as a Professor when he had stood before his classes. Looking over the rows of faces, he had wondered which would be the ones who would detach themselves from the group, who would become distinct and personal, who would make special demands on him. He could give only as much as they could take. The main effort had to come from them. It was a question of individual approaches. There was no joint responsibility on his part. But with a Centre now, as with his platoon then, every single man depended upon him. He would remember this evening as long as he remembered anything, and he was glad that to-night Johnson should be dining in; Johnson who was of his own generation, who alone would be able to guess at how he felt this night. When they moved over to the long refectory table, he made a gesture to Johnson to sit beside him.

Four days later, Johnson came into his office.

"I'm going to ask a favour. Will you have dinner with me, just the two of us, one night next week?"

"That's very nice of you."

"We ought to celebrate your red flannel; and there's another thing. You know, if you live in the same mess as some one, you're seeing them all the time, but yet you are never seeing them at all. Didn't you ever feel that when you were living in your parents' house? You saw more of them when you had a flat of your own, and only went out to see them on occasions. You made an occasion of those occasions. Let's make an occasion of this dinner. Let's have it at the Sinbad."

They met first at the British Club.

"Let's only have a couple of whiskies," Johnson said. "I got some wine at the NAAFI. They're keeping it on ice for us at the Sinbad."

It was a warm still night; a dozen or so tables had been set out on the terrace. There were fires burning down the east bank of the river, where the large flat fish—the musgoof—was being grilled. There was no moon yet; the sky seemed very low and the stars very bright. "Let's make this a good dinner," Johnson said. "If you were in England and you could order anything you like, what would you start off with?"

"As there's not an 'R' in the month, I can't say "oysters," so I'd say caviar."

"I thought you would. And that's exactly what I've got. An F.S. Sergeant brought a jar of it from Tehran."

366

The jar was in the bucket, cooling beside the wine. "It's Palestinian wine," Johnson said. "It's a toss up, isn't it? Or so they tell me. I don't know anything about wine. In fact, I've brought my hip flask. I'll leave you to finish that bottle. I suppose I miss a great deal of pleasure through not appreciating wine. What's the best dinner you've ever had?"

"One of those gaudy nights at Oxford, I suppose."

"Mine wouldn't be anything as grand as that. I believe that I'd plump for a dinner in Belgium somewhere. I've forgotten the name of the place; about fifteen miles back from Ypres; we'd had a week in the Salient; lost half our company. You were in the Salient, weren't you?"

"I was in the attack on Zonnebeke."

"This was a little after that. God, was it raining. God was I glad to get out of that ruddy Salient. We were going back to the Somme to rest. It was our first night out of the line. There was a Canadian captain, halfseas over; he kept on singing the same song. He only knew the refrain:

'Cheerioh, cheeriay,
A rolling stone gathers no moss, so they say.'

He was going up the line next day. He was probably gathering moss himself within a week."

"What did you have for dinner?"

"Heavens, but I've forgotten. Omelette and chicken, I suppose. But I can see it all so clearly; and the rattle of the rain; and bottle after bottle of champagne; and that Canadian with his rolling stone. Say what you like about that war, there were better times to it than there are to this. More variety and the relief of getting out of the line; going to Amiens for the night. There was leave too, every three or four months. God, the excitement of those fortnight leaves; with a swollen bank balance and everyone thinking you a hero. It's altogether different now. You are ordered to the Middle East and it's a five year sentence but you can't give yourself a good-bye party because that would be careless talk. Nothing to look forward to this time."

They relished their caviar. And the muligatawny soup was hot on the palate with an after-sting. "We don't want any more fish, do we, after that caviar? The steaks are good here."

The waiter asked them how they would have their steaks. Four, eight, or twelve annas, for that was the way you ordered your steak at the Sinbad, as raw, medium rare, or well done. "I'm a middle of the road man myself," said Johnson. "Eight annas for me." With the arrival of the steak, Johnson put his flask upon the table.

"You can manage the rest of that bottle yourself, can't you?"

"I'm sure I can; it's very pleasant."

"I'm glad. I thought it was. I wish I liked wine more. I got started on whisky in the East. If you once feel at home with whisky, wine seems tepid."

Johnson had never talked upon his years in India. "Do you look back on that as your best time?" Reid asked.

He shook his head. "There was an unhappy feeling there. We felt that we weren't wanted. There was a lot of pacifism in the air in England. You remember that trouble at Amritsar. We had the suspicion that if there was trouble, and we took a firm line as we should have to do, we wouldn't be backed up at home. It made one resentful against one's own country. That wasn't pleasant for a soldier. Take it by and large, you know, everything has seemed pretty tame after that first war."

"I can't say I've found that."

"Ah, but you are different, Prof. You didn't stay on in the army and besides you've been a success as a civilian. You found your *métier*. But for the rest of us . . . it wasn't so much that we were having a great time in the war. We weren't. But the good times were so super. And it was easy to believe that peace would be a succession of those super times. Without the grim intervals between them. 'Après la guerre'; how we used to talk about it. 'Après la guerre fini; Anglais soldat parti.' And when it came, it amounted to so very little. Though, of course, that wouldn't be true in your case. I suppose you've had a pretty good life really."

"I have had my difficult times."

"Who hasn't? But if you had to live it over again, I guess you would."

"I suppose so, yes."

"I wouldn't; no, I wouldn't. It's been such an anti-climax. If I'd had kids, it might have all been different; it was bad luck I didn't; we both wanted them. But as it's turned out, you can't think how much time I spend brooding over those war years. And there are a lot of others who feel the same. Were you in London for the Silver Jubilee?"

"I was."

"Did it strike you how much it was a recrudescence of a war-time nostalgia? All that milling round the streets, that crowd in front of Buck House, shouting for the King. The King was the symbol of that time, the survival: the singing of the wartime songs: 'Tipperary' and 'Pack up your troubles' and 'Keep the home fires burning.' It was a living again in the first war. The last time of living again in it. Within a year, the King was dead: another year and the Prince of Wales had abdicated and there was a whole new dispensation. The Silver Jubilee was a kind of requiem for the war."

The eight anna steaks were thick and tender; black on the outside, reddish pink in the centre; and the heavy sweetish Palestinian wine had mercifully failed to become sickly after the second glass. Reid let himself relax. He had talked very little. Johnson had said that he wanted to fête the Prof's red flashes, but it was very clear that what he had really wanted was to indulge in last war reminiscences. A host was entitled to set the tone for his own party.

"You weren't ever wounded, were you, Prof?" he asked.

"No, I was taken prisoner, but I wasn't wounded."

"I wasn't wounded either. I was lucky. Did you ever think that you might get killed?"

"Oddly enough I never did. Though the betting, I suppose, was even."

"Nor did I. They used to say that men always had a premonition. They knew if they were for it."

"I'd heard that said too."

"It must have been a curious feeling for those who had that premonition; sitting in the mess the evening before you're going up the line, listening to the talk of what you'd be doing when you came down again, joining in the talk, yet knowing that though some of them might be still here to carry out those plans, you wouldn't. Isn't that what they call dramatic irony?"

"That's what they call dramatic irony."

"I never had that feeling; yet so often I was so very close: a whacking great shell landing in a trench two seconds after I'd got round the traverse. I remember looking once at a trench that had been blown to pieces and saying to myself: 'I wonder how often I shall find myself, twenty years from now, wishing I'd not moved round that traverse.' Did you ever think that, Prof?"

"I always thought: 'I'm bearing a charmed life'."

"Perhaps that's because you had a different kind of premonition. You knew that you were going to make something of your life. You had a premonition of success."

"Success is a big word."

"You can apply it in your case."

Reid did not answer. He remembered what Mallet had said. "You've sized yourself up. You know what you amount to." And he supposed that was true. He had been born with a certain talent: and he believed that he had made the most of it. He had made the mistake neither of minimising nor magnifying its dimensions. He saw himself in focus. He had thought quite a lot afterwards over Mallet's talk. He had been surprised by Mallet's powers of intuition. He had told him things that he had not realised about himself, and about Farrar too. Perhaps that was the feminine streak in Mallet. He had once heard a Don at Oxford arguing that you knew the other sex much better than you knew your own. "Men put on a mask with each other. They are on the defensive; there's rivalry between them; so they don't give themselves away. What man has ever seen another man in tears? Most women have." Perhaps Mallet who had, so everyone said, this strong feminine streak was able to enter a man's mentality in the way that a woman could. He had brooded a long time over Mallet's warning. What devilment were Farrar and Sedgwick cooking up?

"Do you remember that chateau at Potije, on the road from Ypres?" Johnson was continuing. "Well, I was in charge once there, of an ammunition dump. . . ."

So the flood of memories flowed on, as the Tigris below them swirled south to Babylon; the moon would be rising soon, already a grey brown shimmer flickered on the water and Reid in his turn found himself recalled to distant battles. "Where were you in 1918, on March the twenty-first?" he asked.

A sense of euphoria engulfed him. Across the water came the sound of a clear voice singing from an open air cinema. That must be Deanna Durbin in the film that he had planned to see on Saturday. He could almost hear the words. A waning moon three-quarters full was rising above the low skyline of the city. Its reflection flickered on the rippling water, lighting the islands that rose above its surface. From the date groves round the Centre rose a murmuring of voices and the persistent jangled rhythms of oriental

370

music. It was Ramadan, when no one slept. What peace, what utter peace.

"Believe it or not, I was on leave. I'd only had five days of it. Did they recall me in a hurry."

"Then you don't remember how it was around Arras in those days; an unreal sense of peace; mild bland sunlight after morning mists."

How those mists lingered on the 21st, on the day of the great German breakthrough. Anecdote followed anecdote. The bottle emptied in the bucket and theirs was the last table on the terrace.

"We must be going. It's been a great, great evening."

"It's certainly been that for me," said Johnson.

A staff car was waiting for them in Rashid street. The pavements were empty now. Within ten minutes, they were outside the mess. "I think I'll go into my office for a moment," Johnson said.

"Me, I'm for bed," said Reid.

Reid's room was on the first floor, facing East. His bed had been set out on the balcony. The nights were very hot, but round about four in the morning, a cool breeze would rise, and he would pull a sheet over his shoulders. That was one of the best moments of the day, that waking to a sense of a chill.

He was tired, but he was not sleepy yet. He changed into his pyjamas and stood leaning on the balustrade, looking down on the eternal river. It had been a strange, strange evening, evocative of so much that he had half-forgotten. Would he, twenty years from now, on the brink of age, looking back on the second war, hear himself saying: "Everything has been an anti-climax since"? He did not think he would.

Two days earlier he had learnt that the machinery of his divorce suit was revolving smoothly. He could expect his *decree nisi* early in the new year. Because of this divorce he would on the surface be returning to an entirely different life. Yet he would be still a professor of history and philosophy. He was limited by his very assets. He looked ahead five years; the war would be over. He would be fifty; his sons would be at a university. They would have picked up, he and they, the threads that had been dropped during the war. They would probably be as close to him as they would have been if he had shared their teens with them and he would have been spared that saddening period when a father feels his children growing away from him, needing to assert their inde-

371

pendence, a mental equivalent for the weaning of a child. The bond would never have been so close that there would have been the necessity for that wrenching free.

Some psychologists argued that divorce gave children a sense of insecurity. That might happen when a home was suddenly broken up, when the basis of their existence fell apart. But he felt that that was a more valid argument in the United States, a country of overwhelming territorial vastness, whose citizens, whose very way of life was perpetually on the move, and where the young needed to be assured that they had roots. He did not feel that that argument held good in England, with its inherited culture, with its assurance of survival in every church spire, in every village, in the cities through which for nine hundred years no foreign feet had marched. He did not believe his sons would feel they had been cheated. They might even enjoy having a second home. They might call it "rather fun" or whatever the slang phrase of the moment was.

What would that second home be like. Would he be a bachelor. Would he have remarried? Remarried whom? Diana? Why not, after all, why not? She would want to make an end sometime of her present vagabondage, which was well enough in wartime, but would not be in step with a world that was bent not upon destruction but upon reconstruction. Not that Diana wanted to be in step. But she was a part of the spirit of her day; in her revolt against her father, she was in tune with the moment's mood, reacting against complacence. That battle was now fought out. A new battle would be starting; the rebuilding of a broken world. Why should not he and Diana find themselves in step?

From behind him, seemingly from the office wing, came a metallic bark like the sound of a rifle shot. Which probably was what it was. One of the chowkidars trying to scare off an imagined thief. Two weeks ago, the tyres had been stolen off one of the Centre's cars, under the sentries' eyes. The sentries had been told to shoot. He listened, craning his neck. From his balcony he could see the front of the offices. A light went on in one of the top windows. The door of the office opened. A man stood in the doorway. A white man; in a dressing gown. The duty officer. Damn him; he had no right to undress. He had a bed there, surely that should do. He broke into a run. He was making for the mess. There was something up. Reid hurried down to meet him. There was a lamp over the entrance to the mess; it shone down on the duty officer's face so that the cheek bone shadowed it, giving it the look of a distorted mask. "Yes, yes, what is it?"

"It's Major Johnson, sir. He's shot."

"He's wounded?"

"No, sir. Yes, sir. I mean he's dead."

"You're sure?"

"Oh yes, sir, quite. His whole head, sir, blown right off."

"Who by? What by? That damn fool chowkidar?"

"Oh no, sir, by himself; his own revolver. It was in his hand. He was in his office. He's been over there half an hour; in his office, working. Then suddenly the gun went off."

"I see. We'll go across."

Funerals had to be carried out quickly in Baghdad in the summer. Johnson's was fixed for the following afternoon. A perfunctory inquest decided that he had died by his own hand through misadventure. Subsequently there would be a military court of enquiry. Suicide would constitute that the crime of a self-inflicted wound had been committed. An unfavourable decision that would affect the pension to Johnson's widow, and Reid had no doubt that the court would take a lenient view of the situation. So many juries had ruled that a man had had an accident cleaning his gun. There would be only two witnesses, himself and the duty officer. The duty officer would testify that Johnson had come into the office late, had gone to his own room and worked over his files. Johnson had spoken to him on his way to his office and said that he expected to be there for about an hour. It was half-an-hour later that there had been the report of a shot being fired. He would describe the condition in which he had found Johnson. He would add that there were a number of routine files on the desk. Johnson had clearly spent the last half hour of his life working on those files. At any rate until he had begun to clean his revolver. The cleaning materials were on the desk.

Reid in his turn would describe the dinner at the Sinbad. He would say that Johnson was in the best of humours; that they had had two whiskies at the British Club; that Johnson had had two glasses of white wine and then had drunk whisky from his flask. He could not remember how many whiskies Johnson had nor how strong they were. Johnson had a good head for whisky, but he had certainly drunk enough to be a little careless. "I was glad that I had not got to drive a car myself," Reid proposed to say. He would add that he had known Johnson well. They had been contemporaries at Sandhurst, though they had not met there. On their journey out to the Middle East, they had found that the fact of their being contemporaries had constituted a genuine bond between them. He had received a number of confidences from Johnson. He had the highest respect for Johnson as a man and as an officer. He did not believe that Johnson had any personal worries. A year ago, Johnson had been worried by his inability to find a suitable posting in the Middle East. He had been worried by the report that officers over the age of forty-five were to be relegated to unemployment if they were not needed upon any staff. It was at his own suggestion that Johnson had been offered an appointment with the Centre. It was work that he was admirably fitted to undertake. He enjoyed the work. He was popular with the officers and with the other ranks. There was no reason why he should not stay on in the Centre till the end of the war. He could see no reason why Johnson should have wanted to take his life.

Neither he nor the duty officer would be precise about the condition of Johnson's body. The significant question would therefore not be asked. "Why should a man in the process of cleaning a revolver put its muzzle in his mouth?"

The inquest, and the preparation for the funeral—he was to be given full military honours—made the morning a busy one for Reid. It was not till shortly before lunch that he had time to look through his "In" tray. It was only then that he found among his mail an envelope marked "Personal and Private" addressed to him in Johnson's handwriting. The letter was dated "Just back from the Sindbad." It ran: "Prof, old boy. I'm sorry about all this. And I hope it won't be too much of a nuisance and inconvenience. I suppose it will. But I don't see what else there is to do. I'll be very blunt about it and make no excuses. I have been pinching money from the Secret Fund. What I have done is this. When you or one of the other officers asked me for some money for one of your agents, let us say for 20 dinars, I have marked down in the book 30 dinars and kept the balance for myself. As you know, no details were kept of these transactions; receipts are burnt. At the end of the year, the adjutant hands in to the Colonel the grand and final total. It is quite a large sum, as you will have realised by now, because a number of high-up Iraqis are in our pay. Questions are never going to be asked. That is the essence of secret service work, unless the total suddenly ricochets up. I did not see how an increase of three hundred pounds would arouse suspicions. I did not see how I could get found out if I limited my pilfering to three hundred. And I still don't see how I could. But that's what every criminal thinks, isn't it? Anyhow, as long as I was dealing with a stranger like Mallet, I was prepared to run the risk. But it was different with you. You're rather a special person, Prof, you know. Or at least you've been special to me. You were very sympathetic to me when things were going badly. You found this job for me. And I simply couldn't bear being had up on the mat before you on a charge like this. My pride could not have stood it.

"There was another thing too. I realised that, when I saw you sign the taking over paper. You are now responsible for the moneys held by the Centre. If there's a deficiency, you would have to make good. You, not me. And that was something else I couldn't take, running the risk of letting you in for a large sum. And I couldn't continue as your officer, in your mess, with that hanging over my head. It would have poisoned everything. I wouldn't have had one minute's peace of mind. I am sure this is the one way out.

"That's why I'm writing you this letter; as evidence that will let you out if any prying accountant raises difficulties. I don't see how he could, but he might. If he does, you've got the letter. It's up to you to do what you like with it. You might feel that you should hand it over to the G.O.C. straightaway and he might try to sue my estate for my defalcations. I can't say I'd like that to happen; it wouldn't be very pleasant for my wife. But I've no say in the matter, have I? What I'd prefer, and that's why I'm writing this letter after all: is for you to keep it, in your own interests, in case anything blows up. That way you'll know you're safe.

"I'm sorry about all this. It was good of you to come out to-night. It was good to be able to relive those days when I was a different person, and the world was a different place. It's sad that all that should have finished up like this. But I suppose if it hadn't been this way, it would have been another way. I'd got to the end of the road. Good luck."

Reid read the letter slowly. "This is one of the times," he thought, "when one acts on impulse." He took a cigarette lighter from his pocket and switched it on. He led the flame to the paper and watched it run across the sheet, leaving its black, crinkling edge. He dropped the paper on to the tiled floor, let it burn itself out; then crunched his heel on it. "Now for the funeral."

8

THE REPLACEMENT OF JOHNSON as his adjutant presented Reid with an administrative problem. On paper, the Centre was a part of Paiforce and he should have applied to the M.S. branch at G.H.Q. Paiforce for a new adjutant. Yet in reference to its special activities, its orders came from Cairo, which in their turn came from London. If it had been an Intelligence Corps captain who had died, Reid would have assumed that Cairo could either fill the vacancy or would instruct him to find a replacement locally. Usually in a G.H.Q. there were one or two efficient officers who, on personal grounds, were not quite happy where they were and would welcome a transfer. An adjutant, however, was in a different category. He did not need to have had an Intelligence Corps training. Johnson had not had one. And Reid did not see why his successor should. You needed in an adjutant someone with military training, with a sense of discipline, who would inspire his juniors with a sense of awe, and, which was more important, would know his way about regulations, would be familiar with army orders and the technique of claiming appropriate allowances. Reid would have looked consequently for a ranker officer, a man of twenty years' service, who with his knowledge of how to get things done would not only save the Centre a lot of money, but its staff a great deal of time. Reid, therefore, on the evening after the funeral, signalled to Cairo, reporting Johnson's death and suggesting that he should apply to the M.S. Branch in Paiforce for a replacement. To his complete astonishment, however, he received a signal in reply stating that Temporary Captain W/S Lieutenant A. Q. Sargent had been appointed to fill the vacancy created by Major Johnson's death and would assume the acting rank of Major. Captain Sargent, it continued, would be arriving by the Nairn bus on the following Thursday.

Reid stared at the signal. Gustave to fill a post such as this

376

which required long familiarity with military procedure, and training in paper work. It was a job that he would have hesitated to take on himself. He could think of no one less fitted for the post than Gustave. He remembered Gustave telling him in Beirut that he was hoping to be coming to Baghdad soon with a crown upon his shoulder. He had not understood at the time what it was all about. And at that time Cairo had not known that there would be a vacancy for a major on the Baghdad establishment. He could only assume that for some devious reason of its own, Cairo wanted to have Gustave in Baghdad, with the rank of Major. He could not begin to think what it was all about.

He drove down to the Nairn office to welcome Gustave. Gustave was in the highest spirits; he looked well and healthy and his crown glittered on his shoulder. "This is very decent of you, Prof," he started; then he checked. "I suppose I should call you 'Sir' now, shouldn't I?"

"In the office, yes; in the mess, Colonel; and anything you like when we're like this."

"That's a great deal for me to remember, isn't it?" He looked from left to right as they drove through the quiet, humble residential streets; he wrinkled his nose. "This place smells." He noted the shabby pedestrians, the heavily laden mules, the drooping dust-covered oleander bushes. "Scruffy too," he said.

"I warned you, didn't I?"

"You did. I know you did. But anyhow I don't think I'm going to be here very long."

"What makes you think that?"

"Something that Farrar said. I've got a letter from him, which should explain it. Diana Benson asked to be remembered to you; very specially remembered."

They talked about mutual friends. Gustave chattered away briskly. His buoyancy was in marked contrast to that of the majority of men with whom Reid had been dealing during the last few weeks. Everyone looked drained and exhausted by the heat.

The car drew up outside the mess.

"This doesn't look too bad," said Gustave.

"It was a Palace twenty years ago."

Reid showed Gustave which his room was. It faced not upon the river but the date groves. "This isn't too good a room, I'm afraid," Reid said. "There should be a better one vacant soon. But if you aren't going to be here long perhaps it doesn't matter. As soon as you're straightened up, come over to the office. Have you got that letter, by the way?"

The letter was hand written. "Dear Prof, this will be a big surprise to you; perhaps not a very pleasant one, I'm afraid. But don't worry. It isn't for long. I was very sorry to hear of Johnson's accident. Particularly on your account. I know that you were fond of him. But actually it's an ill wind that blows nobody any good, and in a way it's providential. For quite a while we've wanted to have Gustave in Baghdad, and with a major's rank. And we haven't known how to do it. This is a good opportunity.

"I won't give you any details about the project. The less you know the better. By that I mean the less you know the more peace of mind you'll have. It is a very tricky bit of work, but it is a most important one. It's the kind of thing that I've been trying to bring off for the last eighteen months. All this may be a bit of a nuisance for you. I know Gustave isn't the right man for your adjutant, but I don't suppose that he can do much damage in six weeks."

Six weeks. So that was to be all the time it was.

"Farrar's letter didn't tell me very much," he said to Gustave. "Have you any idea yourself why you've been sent here?"

"I gather it's some kind of mission."

"And they think that you'll be more effective in this mission if you can say you've been here a month or so as a major?"

"That's the idea."

"In that case then, they've probably warned you about this. You must be most careful not to suggest in any way that you are not here for keeps. Ask a lot of questions about Baghdad. Act the newcomer trying to find out all he can. Grumble a bit if you like, say 'I don't see how I'm going to stand this for three years.' Complain about the lack of girls. That should be a sound line in your case. Oh, and about that room of yours. That's a good grumbling point. Say what a smell there is from that Arab farmyard underneath your window; have you noticed how they plaster their walls with dung? Like rounds of bread? That's what they use as fuel. Say how it stinks. And I'll do my best to get you a better room. Have you got the idea?"

"O.K. I've got it, Prof. Sorry, I mean Sir."

"Then in that case I'll show you the kind of thing that you'll be doing. It's difficult not having a proper handing over, but I know pretty well what Johnson was about."

Johnson had always seemed to be fully occupied, but now, as he explained what a secretary's duties were, Reid did begin to wonder how Johnson had managed to fill his time. There seemed very little for Gustave to take over. "It doesn't sound a lot," Reid said. "It's the kind of job that you make for yourself. There are day-to-day things that crop up. V.I.P.'s to be met. Cars to be laid on. Railway tickets booked. The phrase 'Generally keep an eye on things' covers quite a lot."

"I guess I'll manage. It looks the kind of job that runs itself."

"Exactly." But to himself he wondered just how much damage could be done within six weeks by a not very competent young man who took his responsibilities so cavalierly. At lunch Reid could not fail to be impressed by the verve with which Gustave was entering into the role of the displaced person.

"When I was honoured with the King's commission," he was saying, "I was informed that I must never in the mess talk shop, discuss religion or mention a woman's name. But to talk about women, that surely is another matter. Surely I am entitled to ask whether there is any truth in the sad rumour current currently in Cairo that there is in Baghdad no channel of communication between the service officer and the local *bint*."

He had, Reid noted, abandoned his P.G. Wodehouse vocabulary for an elaborate phraseology that might have passed for wit fifty years earlier in the days of "the mashers." He had seen examples of it in old numbers of *Punch*; really Gustave was a clown. He could not imagine on what kind of mission he could serve any useful purpose. Yet he was glad to have him here. Once again he was struck by the contrast in terms of health between Gustave and his fellow-officers. They all looked so tired. He so fresh. Probably a Baghdad summer was a greater strain than any of them recognised.

A week later the Beirut summary arrived with an appendix with a very limited distribution list that Reid would not have seen before he was head of the Centre. Since he had taken over from Mallet, he had realised how much material had passed above his head. The Intelligence rule that you were only told as much as you needed to carry out the work immediately to hand, certainly increased the prestige and authority of the senior officer. A major would hesitate to criticise the conclusions reached by the Colonel because those conclusions might be based on information which the major lacked. And after all, the regimental commander did not necessarily know the battle strategy of the G.O.C. The Colonel might be ordered to capture a certain hill. He did not know if that hill was a main objective or a feint to divert the enemy's attention. If the Colonel were told that the attack was merely a feint, he would conduct it half-heartedly, and the attack would defeat its purpose. There was a sound basis for this doctrine. "Theirs not to reason why." Yet at the same time in Intelligence one did sometimes get a baffling sense of working in the dark. This present appendix was a case in point. "We are approaching," it said, "a decisive moment in our deception campaign. We hope to go into action very shortly and to launch the final assault within six weeks. We hope to make use at last of Aziz."

Within six weeks. That was the time that Farrar had set for Gustave's stay with the Centre. It was in terms clearly of that operation that Gustave was required to have spent six weeks in Baghdad with the rank of major before he left upon his mission. And Aziz was a part of this operation too. He remembered what Mallet had said at dinner in Damascus. "Those two are cooking up something devilish, and as far as Farrar is concerned, it's partly directed against you." Reid had a chill sense of evil omen.

On the same morning, the same appendix reached Istanbul. It was one of the documents that Sedgwick kept in his small cabinet in the corner, but on this occasion he handed it to Eve. "Now doesn't this make you jealous? Just when you are going, the drama starts. You'll miss it by ten days."

"Is it going to happen here?"

He nodded.

"But it doesn't say so in the summary."

"I saw quite a little of Master Nigel during that conference in Beirut. We found we had a lot in common. This is a joint operation."

The same sense of evil omen that had chilled Reid now made Eve want to flinch. But she managed to contrive a laugh. "The annoying thing is that I shall never know what this particular piece of mischief is. If I were to see you after the war, you'd plead the Official Secrets Act."

"I might make an exception in your case."

"I'll never forgive you if you don't."

He didn't guess, he can't have guessed, she thought. But I bet he showed me that appendix just to see how I'd take it. He's never shown me one before. She was trembling as she sat before her type-writer. My nerves are going. It's high time I left, she thought. She closed her eyes. In four weeks she would be away; out of it all; starting a new life. Probably not seeing again a single person she had known here. So she argued with herself; but all the time that chill sense of doom oppressed her. What were they planning to do with Aziz? What was there that they could do with him? What had he really done? Yet even as she asked herself those questions, she knew that she knew the answers. There were so many traps that they could lay for him. And he had done a lot—or at least what he had done could be made to look a lot. She knew how ruthless the high-ups in this game were. They forgot that they were dealing with human beings. To them, Aziz was a file; just as to a General at G.H.Q. the Dorset Regiment was not 1,000 men but a flag upon a map. When a spy had ceased to be of use, he might still be made to serve a purpose by handing over his dossier to the enemy; and thereby sending up the stock of a more valuable double agent. That had been often done. They had a lot on Aziz. And it was because of her they had so much. She had baited the trap. It was to see her that he had come up to Istanbul; that he had become involved so deeply. Hadn't she gloried in that involvement? She had seen it as a symbol of her possession of him; she had tied him with one thong after another. It was her fault. It was three parts her fault.

She opened the shorthand notebook in which she had taken down a couple of letters for Sedgwick. She put a sheet of paper inside the machine. But her hands were trembling and her fingers mishit the keys. It was no good. She had to pull herself together. She stared at the keyboard, trying to recover her self-control, try-ing to think herself back into sanity. There's no need to lose your head, she told herself. There's no danger. Aziz is going to Alexan-dria. He'll be out of reach of Farrar and of Sedgwick. He won't be coming back to Istanbul for many months, and by the time he does, the situation will be different. Farrar will have new irons in the fire. He said "Six weeks." Aziz is only a part of his all-in pro-gramme; a cog in it. They can manage without Aziz very well. If Aziz isn't there when they want him, they'll write him off as a bad debt and when the war is over, or long before the war is over for that matter, he will be able to return here and pick up his old life. The ISLO will be inoperative. The Germans will have gone back to what is left of Germany; there'll be no equivalent in Beirut for

Farrar's organization. There'll be something of course in Baghdad. But Baghdad isn't concerned with this operation, as far as I can see. She had got, she decided, to stop Aziz coming through in September. That shouldn't be difficult. She could write him a good-bye letter, telling him that she'd been ordered back to England. She'd meant to do that anyhow. She'd send it a little earlier. That was the only difference. She would send it now.

She pulled out the official letter paper from the typewriter and slipped in an ordinary sheet. "Dear Aziz," she started. "This is a tragic news, but I am having to go back to England right away. . . ."

She made a two-sided message of it. She signed it: "Tenderly, Imshallah E." That's that, she thought. That should have settled it. But two days later, she received a postcard at her flat. It gave the date: August 18. It was the signal they had fixed.

The green light was showing over Sedgwick's door. She knocked, listened for the "come in," and turned the handle. "I hope that you won't think this is a very frivolous request," she said, "but it seems ridiculous that I should be going back to England without having once seen Ankara. I've been through it in a train. But I've never stepped outside the station. If I could spend three days there, Francis, I'd be very grateful."

"That seems a very legitimate request. When would you like to?"

"I'm leaving on August the twenty-eighth. I'd like to have my last week here to say good-bye to everyone. If I could go down on the 16th, perhaps, and get back on the 20th."

"I've no objection. Find out if there's a plane that you can hitch a ride on. We can make it a liaison visit so that you'll have no expenses. And our friends there should be able to put you up. But don't be back later than the 23rd. I'm planning a good-bye party for you."

She then wrote a letter to Martin Ransom.

"It's only five months since you went away, but it's beginning to seem a lot, lot longer. And me, I'm being posted back to England at the end of the month. I would like to see you before I go and in point of fact I'm coming down to Ankara for three days for what is called a liaison visit. Is there any chance of seeing you? I do hope so. As you know we have a branch in Ankara. They're finding a billet for me."

Martin would tell her if there was any justification for her fears. She could trust Martin. She could not have confided in Sedgwick.

There was a service plane with a vacant seat in it, flying down on the 15th. She could arrange her return trip there, they told her. There was always the Taurus, if she couldn't hop a plane. "I'd like to go on the Taurus once," she said to Sedgwick.

There was a car waiting for her at the airport. Secretaries got so bored sitting in their offices that they welcomed any chance to get away from them. A young woman of whom she had heard but whom she had never met had made the trip out. "There's a spare bed in my flat," she said. "You'll be surprised when you see it; or perhaps you won't be surprised. Perhaps it's what you are used to."

"What do you mean?"

"The place is full of roses. You have an attentive beau."

The place was indeed full of roses. A dozen of them, red and yellow; the note accompanying them said, "I'm thrilled at your being here. Tonight I'm, alas, busy; but I'm taking my day off to-morrow. I'll give you a Cook's tour. Will call for you at 10."

It was a clear, bright day; warm with an early chill in the air that warned of the approach of autumn. He was wearing a light fawn coloured suit. She had half forgotten how elegant he was; half-forgotten, too, how welcoming his smile could be; how charming could be that diplomat's capacity to make you feel that nobody existed in the world except yourself. "You've given yourself just the right length of time to see it all," he said. "There isn't much to see. We'll do the old town first. It's very typical."

Typical in that it was built upon a hill; a cluster of narrow streets, with stout stone walls; in which you would notice now and again a piece of stone with a Roman inscription on it, often upside down. A citadel crowned the cluster. From its walls you could see the new town with its long empty streets running into the coun- tryside. "Ankara was very important once," he told her. "On the trade route to the East. Then it became neglected. Ataturk planned it as a city of 150,000. I've an idea he underplanned it."

The rounded hill facing the citadel was covered with wooden huts. "They call them night built shacks," he told her. "If you can get the whole thing run up during the night, and with a roof on top, you can't be turned out by the city surveyor." The houses of the old town were tiled, with balconies. Ankara stone had a touch of rose-madder. It gave a pastel effect to the whole.

"I told you that there wasn't much to see," he said.

"It's a change from Istanbul."

"At least it's that."

They leant against the ramparts looking over the gently undulating landscape. It was very bare. "Isn't it very bleak in winter here?" she asked.

"It's very bleak."

Every one was taken to the dam, he told her. "They finished it just before the war. It provides half the water for the city." Ten miles from the city, it was set out like a park. Pine scented the air. Below the barrage was a charming oblong flower garden. There were restaurants and cafés. They drank a long cool orangeade. "They go in for picnics here. There's a very pleasant place about fifty miles away. We can lunch there. That'll give you time for a siesta. Then we can dine at Karpiç's. Everybody dines at Karpiç's."

It was a pleasant prospect to have a whole day stretching in front of them. Up till now, they had never had more than a single meal together. "I'll wait till this evening," she thought, "before I tell him. After dinner will be the time." It was good not to be in any hurry.

It was a flat, dull road to the picnic spot. "It's no good my telling you where it is," he said. "It's one of those names that no one can remember."

It was a pine covered hill on a long plain. The road swung and climbed. "It's crowded on week ends, but it'll be quite empty now," he said. They did not pass a single car: only a group of peasants collecting pine cones in large sacks. The restaurant was deserted too. There was a series of terraces under the trees, with tables and benches on them. In the kitchen the proprietor showed them what he had to offer, in terms of meat and fish and vegetables. "That and that and that," said Martin, "and Raki and some rosé wine."

The meal was a long time being prepared. They had a white cheese with their Raki.

"How did your trip to Beirut work out?" she asked.

"That seems a long time ago."

"It is, but I haven't seen you since."

"No more you have. I left three days later. I tried to telephone you, but you were out."

"They told me that you called. I was glad you had. Did you see Jane Lester in Beirut?"

"Only for a minute or so, that first time, but I've been there since."

"How was she?"

"You haven't heard about her?"

"I've heard nothing."

He told her what Farrar had told Reid during the drive from Damascus. "She's knocked off drink, and she's as wild as hell."

"So you didn't waste your time."

"I didn't waste my time." He frowned. He hesitated. "It sounds a silly thing to say, or perhaps it sounds a silly thing for me to say, but I was rather shocked."

"It sounds a *strange* thing for you to say."

"Strange, yes, perhaps that's the right word, strange. It's the opposite of what I was supposed—or at least what I thought—I stood for. The whole thing seemed wrong; the whole approach seemed wrong, for a girl like Jane, I mean. It isn't easy to explain. Where love making is concerned, masculine vanity is limitless. Every man wants to be considered a great cavalier, as he wants to be considered a great cricketer or a fine shot. But the angle of vanity alters with each generation. My father told me that in his day every young man wanted to be a great success in the *demi-monde*, but *sans payer*. When I was at Oxford, it was considered *infra dig* to pick up tarts or go to brothels. Even the girls in those London houses used to despise the men who went there regularly; they used to call them 'housemen.' Why go there, one would say, when there are girls of one's own class who are happy to go away for a week end with you if they like you. And that's how I used to feel myself; . . . but this case of Jane. When you see that someone like Jane can end up like that, I feel that the world of Toulouse-Lautrec was a cleaner one, the world where you had professional entertainers in places like the *Chahbanais*; . . . Does this sound very stodgy and Edwardian?"

She shook her head. "I think it sounds rather sweet."

And indeed there was an engaging boyish quality about the puzzled frown that creased his forehead. There was, too, a new expression in his eyes. "You see," he started. . . . But at that moment the food arrived breaking the current of his mood. She suspected that he had been going to say something that he found important, something that needed the right atmosphere for say-

385

ing. Well, and if he had, it did not matter since they had the whole day ahead of them.

"Are you excited about going home?" he asked.

She shrugged. "Yes and no. It can't be very much fun now in England. But I mustn't be away too long. England's where I've got to make my life. I've an idea that the people who are spending their whole war abroad are going to find it difficult to adjust themselves to life in England afterwards."

He laughed. "That's an occupational hazard for men like myself. We're children of no man's land, and we have to be on our guard against putting down too deep roots in the countries to which we are accredited. Otherwise we find ourselves arguing the foreign country's case to England, instead of England's case to foreigners. How long have you been out here now?"

"Three years."

"You came to get over something, didn't you?"

"How did you know that?"

"Intuition, guess work, one or two discreet enquiries."

He had completely recovered his composure. There was the familiar quizzical twinkle in his eye. "If one is interested, one makes enquiries," he said.

She had suspected long ago that he had made enquiries.

She was flattered that he had. Yet at the same time, she was irritated. It was too much a part and parcel of that thought-out way of life that in one way she respected but in another way resented. It was *too* thought out. He would never let himself tumble into anything.

"And now you've got over it," he said.

"Now I've got over it."

"Ready to start a whole new life?"

"Ready to start a whole new life."

"Let's drink to it," he said, and raised his glass. There was warmth in his smile now and her heart warmed to him. He really liked her. He was attractive. And he was sympathetic. She would have liked to have told him about Raymond. Perhaps she would tonight. After she had told him about Aziz, in explanation of what she had to tell him about Aziz. It was a relief that there was to be that dinner later; that this lunch was not the curtain. So often in Istanbul she had had a sense of awkwardness as the meal reached its close, the foreknowledge that there might be a scene, a situation. There could be no scene today. And it was very cosy sitting here under the trees with little coins of sunlight falling through the leaves across the table, eating these pleasant squelchy dishes, the large stuffed green peppers and the fingers of pastry stuffed with cheese, and the cucumbers swimming in sour milk; slaking their thirst with water, sipping the rough red wine, letting the talk drift lazily from one subject to another. She had never felt more at ease with him. "It could so easily have been you instead of Aziz," she thought. "It would have been you if you had not been an Englishman. If you had been an Irishman or an American or a European." She was glad that it had not been him. You could not help being on your guard with a compatriot. You knew too much about each other. You were afraid that he would despise you afterwards; as he was, it seemed, despising Jane. It was better the way it had been. Perhaps they would meet after the war in London.

Karpiç's was at the base of the old town; in the oldest part of the new town. It was run by a White Russian, white bearded, with a high white Russian smock. It was Ankara's international restaurant; British and French, Germans and Italians dined there at adjacent tables, scrupulously avoiding one another. "With any luck, we'll see Van Papen there; he looks very English in his Anderson and Shepherd suits." There was no near-by parking place. There was a partial blackout in Ankara and Ransom took her arm as they walked along the crowded pavement. He held it close; his fingers stroked her wrist.

Karpiç's was large and rectangular like a Baptist chapel.

"It's not unlike Rejans, is it?" Eve remarked.

"They would both look very drab if they were empty. But they never are empty."

The door opened on a din of voices, to which every recognized language made its contribution. There were not very many Turks; those few were most of them in uniform. There were more men than women. A waiter came across at once. "Over here, Mr. Ransom, Sir."

"Over here" was against the wall. "Would you like a whisky?" Martin asked her. "This is one of the few places where you can trust the whisky. Don't let's bother to look at the menu yet. When Karpiç sees one with an attractive female, he usually comes across and says that he has something special." They lingered over their whisky and soda and sure enough, within twenty minutes, Karpiç had come across and bowed. "I think that this is the first time that this charming lady had dined in my humble caravanserai. I think she should be encouraged to come again. I have some excellent pâté-de-foie gras. I know Mr. Ransom that you take a broad, cosmopolitan view of the problems that distract us. The things of the spirit—and are not the pleasures of the table to be numbered among the things of the spirit—Do not they transcend frontiers? I am sure that your delightful guest would not be shocked that channels, legitimate channels of communication, permit me to serve to special guests a pâté that is authentic, that was made in Strasbourg."

He suggested that a chicken à la Kieff should follow it. "And I do consider that those two dishes deserve a European wine. I should not boast to you of my close friendship with certain wine merchants of Moselle, but am I not entitled to, I who was driven from my own country, to reap the benefits of the neutrality which my adopted country has conferred on me?"

"He's a delightful old scoundrel, but he's genuine and it's well to get away for once from 'swooning priests' and 'twisted turbans.'"

Indeed it was very excellent. "And think what I shall be eating three weeks from now," she said. "Spam and dehydrated eggs and macaroni."

"You mustn't forget to tell me how it is." It was at the close of the meal that he said that; just as she was starting to remind herself that it was high time to tell him why she had come to Ankara. She was thinking it, rather ruefully. It would change the atmosphere and it was a very cosy atmosphere. She had not often felt so close to anyone.

"I don't want to lose touch with you," he said. "I've been thinking about you a lot these last few months; and I've been thinking about myself in relation to what you said to me about myself. You gave me a lecture once, do you remember? Jane Lester was a shock to me. That's what started me trying to think things out afresh. You are so different from Jane; yet you were a friend of Jane's. You liked her. And I had a sense of guilt. I had been trying to turn you into the kind of girl who could become like Jane. But you didn't let me and you weren't sanctimonious about not letting me. You simply said quietly 'That is not my game.' And I've kept remembering the things you told me about myself, about the way I had planned out my career. And you were justified, I could agree to that; but not justified all the way: I wanted to justify myself to you. You said that I was wearing blinkers going down a straight broad road: that's true but it isn't wholly true. It wasn't only what you said but what you implied. You implied that I was a calculating careerist; that when the time came, I would make a marriage that would be an assistance to my career. You did imply that, didn't you?"

"I suppose I did."

"And it's true, but only partly true. And even so, it isn't necessarily, at least not all of it, an entry on the debit side. The word 'careerist' has a nasty sound, but a man ought to be ambitious. We don't think much of a man who isn't, do we? The people whom we are respecting the most at this very moment are ambitious: Winston and Monty, for example. That's true now, isn't it?

"And even in terms of marriage, which was your main point really, is it quite so shocking to be prudent? It's considered discreditable nowadays for a man to marry for money. But it used not to be. And don't we often hear of men whose careers have been ruined by an unlucky marriage? Just as we read of men who owe everything to their wives. In certain careers—and mine is one surely, if there ever was one—a wife is all important. She can make or mar. Don't you think that a man like myself, when he came to consider marriage, would be very foolish not to ask himself whether the woman he was going to invite to share his life was someone who would fit into that life, would fill the role that would be expected of a partner in it? Wouldn't he be foolish?"

"He would be very foolish."

"You wouldn't dismiss him surely on that account as a 'calculating careerist.' It doesn't mean that he looks around for the daughter of a millionaire or somebody in Debrett. He is looking for someone who can be a partner, that's the word, a partner."

He paused; his voice had deepened. It had a sincerity that very rarely showed beneath the official flippant manner. And she knew beyond all doubt that within five minutes, if she played her cards correctly, or even if she played no cards at all, if she merely sat and listened, he would have made her a proposal.

It was the last thing that she had expected of him, when she met him first. Yet she could see how it had come about. He had reached the marrying age. He had been away from England for three years, in a world where there was a great insufficiency of women; where there were only two alternatives in terms of dalliance: the mercenary ladies of the bazaars and girls like Jane or

Kitty. And there were not so very many girls like those. Jane was an exception; and when he had met Jane, he was shocked. She was more than he could stomach. She had forced him to take stock of himself. Martin Ransom was in a vulnerable position; a familiar position in English life, to the Empire builders, the guarders of "perilous outland marshes." Had not parents sent their unmarried daughters on winter holidays to Egypt? All those jokes about "the fishing fleet to Malta." It was a story that had been told in fifty novels, and on the whole those marriages had worked out reasonably well.

"Because a marriage is made thoughtfully, it needn't be unromantic," he was saying. He quoted Tennyson: " 'Don't é marry for money, but go where money is.' I don't believe it need be all that thought out. Ambitious men have a sense of self-direction. They make the right choice when they reach a crossroad."

"It needn't be unromantic." She didn't need to tell him how far marriage to him would be for her the complete opposite of unromantic. There had been from the start a mutual attraction. It was only because she had had this thing about him that she had resented his casual courtship. Had she not been thinking only that morning how easily it might have been Martin instead of Aziz? She had had to make an effort not to let herself fall in love with Martin. And the very characteristics that would have made him unsatisfactory as a lover would have made him utterly eligible as a husband. He would concentrate on, he would bank on the success of marriage. He would give himself in marriage, in a way that he could never do in a love affair—a thing done with the left hand; and where he had given himself completely she would be able to give herself completely in return. She knew now enough about herself to appreciate how much she had to give. Marriage between them would start as a real love affair.

She let her thoughts linger on what life would be for her as Martin's wife. He was a man destined for success. He would be an Ambassador within twenty years. She would be Lady Ransom. She would know quite a lot of grandeur. She would meet prominent people upon equal terms. She would be behind the scenes at a number of big events. It would be a life of movement and activity; with the sense that what she was doing, mattered. And Martin's career would not end with his ambassadorship. It would be a step to further careers when he left the foreign service; in business or in politics. He might well finish in the House of Lords.

Wherever she went, she would be able to take pride in herself because of him.

How happy and proud her parents would be. Her children would start life under the most favourable auspices. She allowed herself to relish with an air of mischief the little satisfactions that worldly success would bring her; what a surprise for all those friends and relatives who had patronised her as a "mousy little thing." They would quote to themselves that venerable adage: "Always be polite to girls; you never know whom they may marry." It would be fun to be well off, to be able to do things for one's friends, to send impressive Christmas presents.

It was the fulfilment of her girlhood's day dreams. I must look at it very carefully, very lovingly, she thought. I must recognise what it is I am being offered. I have been dealt the one supreme hand in the pack that can carry every trick. I must look at the cards carefully before I throw back the hand. Because it had to be thrown back. There was no doubt of that. She could not let Aziz be handed over to a fate whose horror even she, who had had glimpses of what could happen in cross-examination, could barely guess at. She could not do that to him. She had to tell Martin the truth. And she also knew beyond all doubt that those words which were now only five minutes away would remain unspoken. He would not want her after that admission. He was not a Victorian to the extent that he would demand that his wife should be a virgin. If she had had an affair with Raymond, he could have shrugged that off. It was before she knew him. But that she should have had an affair with Aziz in Instanbul when he was himself available, that she should have preferred Aziz to him, for that was what it amounted to, Aziz of all people too, who would be in Martin's eyes a "little dago." It was more than any man's vanity could stand, let alone Martin's.

But she had no choice. I'm going to live with this moment all my life, she thought. It's the chance that any girl would give her soul for—the chance of getting it both ways—worldly material success and love as well. I have only to sit here and say "yes." But I have no choice.

"You do see what I mean, don't you?" he was saying. "It isn't a calculated choice; it's a sense of self-direction, the recognition of one's destiny. Is that too big a word? I don't believe it is."

She had to stop him before he went too far. There had to be a break; just as there had been at lunch. Over his shoulder, she caught their waiter's eye. He hurried across. He stood over the table. "And for dessert, Sir? Shall I show you what I have?"

Martin blinked as though he had been shaken from a trance. "Dessert? Oh yes, of course. Wheel round the tray."

It was the break she needed. She helped herself to a honey cake.

"Martin," she said. "There's something that I've got to ask you. One of the chief reasons that I came here was to ask it."

She told him what she had to tell him. He listened, with his full attention, with his official manner, that she had seen often in his office. He might have been wearing a mask. Yet at the same time, he made himself easy to confide in. He was a good and interested listener. It was one of his most marked assets. The men who called on him in his office went away feeling that they had expressed themselves clearly and that they had made a good impression.

It did not take Eve five minutes to tell her story, and she knew that he had grasped its implications.

"I need to know two things," she said. "One, whether Aziz is in any danger; the second is whether there's any real need for him to be in danger. There *is* a war on. If I interfered with the war effort, with an operation that is a legitimate part of the war effort, then I'd be a traitor. But I can't be certain that it is that. There's so much phoney business in our business."

"That's what we feel sometimes in the Chancery."

"Do you know Nigel Farrar?"

"I met him when I was in Beirut."

"And you've read his summaries. You know what I mean when I say that he's always cooking up some ingenious plan. Some of them are so fanciful that I don't feel they're real. He's fooling himself as much as he's fooling the Germans. You remember that case of the wireless set that went to Baghdad?"

"Of course."

"He was very keen on taking over that set and transmitting false information to the Germans. Then the Germans would have discovered that it was we who were doing the transmitting, so we would have had to start transmitting truthful reports that the Germans would disbelieve. Then the Germans would find out that we knew they knew. The whole thing becomes endless. Everyone is in the dark."

"Do you remember that poem, I think it's Coleridge's, about

a man who kisses in a hammock a girl who's pretending to be asleep? 'I thought she thought I thought she slept.' "

They laughed together easily; it was hard to believe that ten minutes earlier they had been on the brink of a decision that would have altered both their lives for ever.

"This is how I see it," she went on. "If whatever is happening to Aziz is part, is an important part, of an important operation, I've no right to interfere, but if it's only the unnecessary dotting of an 'i', something that Farrar has invented for the hell of it, I don't see why Aziz shouldn't be warned, do you?"

"Officially I should say I do. Unofficially I'd say I didn't."

"Do you think you can find out for me?"

"I'll do my best; now let me see." He pondered. "You know the Ankara Palas? Let's meet there. In the main hall, where they serve tea, at four o'clock." He looked at his watch. "It's getting late. You must be getting tired. It's been a long day, and a very happy one."

It had been a long and crowded day, but its passing had been swift. The next day was endless in its passing. Would four o'clock never come? There was nothing to do, and no one to do nothing with. She pottered round the acacia-lined streets. At the end of every one, there seemed to be either a mountain or a minaret. She noted the elaborate brass bound boxes of the shoe polishers, inlaid with porcelain pictures. She wished she could summon up an appetite for the hollow circular pastries that were on sale at half the corners. In two weeks she would be back in austere England, thinking enviously of those appetizing pastries. She drank a great many cups of coffee. At last, at very long last, she was waiting in the Ankara Palas.

She did not expect Martin to be late and he was not late. He arrived at one minute before four. He did not appear to be in a hurry, but she knew that he had only a very few minutes at his disposal. He behaved as though the whole afternoon were his. He asked her what she would like, as leisurely as though she were selecting a five course dinner, but the moment that the cakes arrived, he handed a note over to the waiter, nodding his head in indication that no change was needed. He had now prepared his exit. She noted and admired his technique. He had a long way to go. He would go most of it.

He was very much to the point. "You're absolutely right," he said. "It's the dotting of an 'i', and an inessential 'i'. It was so involved that it might even have defeated its own ends."

"May I ask what the plot was?"

He shrugged. "I found it rather hazy. Farrar wanted to strengthen the status both of the Pullman porter and that Armenian. The Armenian is important. He is the key figure in the next operation; which does seem to me a serious one. I would not have said that this minor operation was of the last importance."

"What was the idea?"

"The Armenian was going to hand your friend over to the Germans, claiming that he was a double agent working for the English too. In support of that, he was going to produce a report that the English had seen before it reached the Germans. That might have improved the Armenian's status on a short-time basis."

"But the Germans would not have got anything out of that; not on Turkish territory, would they?"

"No, but they could have reported your friend to the Turks, on Chessman's testimony."

"What good would it have done the Germans?"

"In actual fact, none at all; they don't know, at least we hope they don't know, that Chessman is a double agent. Actually he is a treble agent. But it suits the German pattern for the moment to strengthen Chessman's position with the Turks. It would have, in their opinion, done Chessman good to hand over your friend as a spy."

"What do you yourself think?"

"I think that the Turks in the Ottoman days had one of the first Intelligence services in the world and that the modern Turks are finding the old machine works very well."

"So that if you were me, you wouldn't think me a traitor to give that warning."

"No, but if you are caught, I shall say I never heard of you."

He rose to his feet. "I have to rush. You must excuse me. There are a great many things on hand. Don't hurry your tea. I have, as the Americans say, taken care of it."

They stood facing one another. In all human probability they would never meet again. Yet they might at this very moment have been happily planning the details of their own joint life: should she arrange to stay on here so that they could marry right away or should she wait in England till he was posted home? Should they announce their engagement now? . . . All the whens and wheres and hows. . . . It could so easily have turned out that way. It seemed a shame. For him as well as her; he might not do as well elsewhere. She could have been so right for him.

The girl who had met her at the airport took her to the station. Eve wished that she had not insisted, but there was no avoiding her. She would have preferred to stand at the near end of the platform and watch the train come in, carriage by carriage. Aziz might be leaning out of the window; he probably would be. Then she would know in what part of the train he was. It was a long train. She might have difficulty finding him.

For her opposite number in Ankara, however, this visit was an occasion; a break in the day's routine. She would want to dawdle in the station restaurant. The station was impressive; with pillars and rounded towers and marble floors; a tribute to the new born Turkey; very unlike the ramshackle jumble of offices and waiting rooms at Istanbul. "We'll get there early," the girl said. "Your carriage is in the front, a third of the way up; we'll leave a porter with your suitcase. Then we'll have a coffee and some cakes."

There was no resisting her. Nor was there any means of getting her out onto the platform to watch the train come in. "We don't want to stand around. Your seat is booked. The train waits ten minutes here. We can wait till the last minute."

That was how she wanted it and that was the way it was. I've got to relax, she thought. I mustn't fuss her. I mustn't fuss myself. I'm so near a breakdown myself that I might have hysterics right here in the restaurant. So she sat with her back to the railway line and ate an extra honey cake and did not turn round as the train slid in, waiting for the other one to say, "All ready now? I think we should be going." At last, she thought. At last.

It had seemed a long train as it stood along the platform. It seemed a much longer train as she fought her way down its crowded length. She remembered the struggle to get to the wagon-restaurant on the trains bound south from Paris. That was nothing compared to this. Turkey might be a neutral, but it seemed as though the whole army had been mobilized to make this journey. The luggage racks were piled with rifles: the corridors were barricaded with packs and suitcases. Voluminously drapped women were nursing babies. She had to fight her way every yard. And each embattled yard reminded her that she would have to fight her way back every inch; and this time to meet the grumbles and complaints of those who had already had to make way once. Doorway after doorway, carriage after carriage: and each time she passed an engaged toilet sign she would wonder if he were behind it. If he were, she thought, he would have come out by the time she made her return trip. No one on a crowded train could stay there indefinitely.

She had started by moving towards the front of the train. It was the shorter trip. She had no idea in what class he would be travelling. It was not one of the things that she had thought to ask him. "Did you have a good trip?" she would say. "Not bad," he would answer, and they would leave it there. He had not much spare money. She did not think he would have taken a sleeper, but he might have gone first class. Door after door. Carriage after carriage. Door after door. At last she reached the luggage van. The front of the train. The final toilet door was locked. She would have to wait to see if he was there. One minute, three minutes, five minutes. How much longer could one stay? She rattled the handle impatiently. Another minute. She banged her fist upon the door. The door opened. A flushed and shamefaced eleven year old boy came out. His forehead was damp. He ought to be ashamed of himself, she thought.

Slowly, she fought her way back down the train. At last she reached her carriage. She looked at her watch. Thirty-seven minutes since she had started out. And it was only a third of the way. Seventy-four minutes to get to the other end and back. Suppose he wasn't on the train at all. And all this were to prove a waste. She need never have told Martin. She need never have lost Martin. But that again was not a factual estimate. She would not have come to Ankara but for Aziz. And if she had not come to Ankara, she would have gone back to England without seeing Martin. By the time they had met again, they both would have gone separate ways. It was only because she had happened to see Martin at that particular moment when he was vulnerable that he had got the idea that he would like to marry her. A week before, no such idea might have been in his mind. It was the sudden sight of her after a six months' break. Everything in life was timing.

Door after door, carriage after carriage. She reached the restaurant car. It was crowded. It was half past eleven. The regular lunch would not be served till noon and the polyglot group of passengers were taking advantage of the empty period to eat the kind of meal they most enjoyed—coffee and tea and honey cakes

396

and pastries. A waiter tried to stop her. There was no seat. She must wait in the queue.

"I'm going through," she said. He remonstrated, but she got her way. She looked to left and right as she elbowed past. He was not there.

Door after door, carriage after carriage.

At last she found him. Very near the end of the train; in a third class carriage, four aside. He jumped to his feet. The delight in his face was touching.

"Eve, you here!"

He was as surprised as he was delighted. He pushed past a couple of bulky peasants and joined her in the corridor. The corridor was filled with packages and suitcases. She looked about her, suddenly aware of a difficulty she had not foreseen. Where were they to talk? There was no room in his compartment; hers was twelve carriages away and they could not talk there. Her fellow passengers as likely as not spoke English. There was the same disadvantage to the dining car. If they could ever get a seat there. How could they talk with another couple, either across the way or at each other's side, a couple who as likely as not spoke English. There was no alternative to the corridor. She beckoned him to the brass bar that ran across the window. There was a narrow gap, and they leant side by side.

"What are you doing on this train?" he asked.

"I came on it to meet you."

"Why on this train? I sent you a card saying when I'd be in Istanbul."

"That's why I'm here."

"But I don't understand. I came up to Istanbul specially to see you. I wanted to say 'au revoir.' I'm going to Alexandria."

"I know you are."

"How do you know I am?"

"The fact that I do know will prove to you that I am not talking out of a cocked hat. You are in serious trouble and I've come to warn you."

"How can I be in trouble?"

"You've been doing some very funny things you know."

"What funny things? That information you gave me about imports and exports? Surely that can't have got me into trouble?"

"Not only that, though the Turks might not have been too

397

happy about that. It's the stuff that you've been doing with the Germans that's done the damage."

"With the Germans?" He stared; his mouth half open. His eyes wore a bemused expression. "What do you know about all that?"

"All that there is to know."

"How could you; it was between me and them."

"That's what you thought. That's what they thought for a time. It was what you were meant to think."

"By whom? Who meant me to think that?"

"The British in Beirut."

"You mean it was a plant?"

"Exactly. The British found out through you what the Germans wanted to know. And they learnt through you how much a man like yourself could learn without special facilities. It was a pretty set-up for a while."

"And who were the British who arranged all this? That Captain Farrar?"

"Yes."

"And his friend, the Prof."

There was a note of almost indignant incredulity in his voice as he said "the Prof." She had a flash of intuition; he had trusted the Prof. He had been fond of the Prof. He had thought of the Prof as a friend. There was a sacred quality about the very real devotion that a young man could feel for an older man whom he looked on as his advisor, his guardian, his tutor. If Aziz were now to feel that the Professor's friendship for him had been a fraud, a trick, his faith in the decency of human personal relations might be ruined. It might poison his entire life. He must be spared that. She shook her head. "No, the Prof knew nothing about all this. It was Farrar's idea completely."

"But they were always about together. How could the Prof not know?"

"Because that's the very way in which the Intelligence services work. You are only told what you need to know. The right hand does not know what the left hand's doing."

"And how do you fit into all of this?"

"In a minor way: as a secretary. I filed the various reports."

"And you knew about this all along?"

"Yes, in a sense, but. . . ."

She paused. She wanted to defend herself. She did not want him to feel she had betrayed him. But she was very tired. There was only so much that she could take: and suddenly in her exhaustion she felt that in the long run it did not matter how he felt about her. To a man, belief in a man's friendship was of more account than in a woman's truthfulness. The whole literary tradition endorsed this double standard. On the one hand, Samson and Pythias, Brutus and Cassius, Jonathan and David; on the other, Delilah, Cressida and Cleopatra. In retrospect, Aziz would recall the happiness that he had had with her. That was enough. She could not argue her case with him. But she had to make some protest.

"There's so much here, Aziz, that I can't explain, on security grounds, and on other ones. I knew what was going on, but I had no part in it; if you can follow me. I didn't instigate anything. You and I weren't a part of Nigel Farrar's scheme; I don't even know if he knew about us. He may have suspected that time I was in Beirut, but it wasn't part of his strategy. It was ourselves— simply ourselves. Please please believe that."

He nodded. They stood, side by side, pressed very close; with all the electricity that there had been, subsided. Children were squalling, parents were shouting. Every other minute, someone or other on the way past, pushed them tight against the windows; and in front of them stretched the bare, bleak Anatolian countryside across which were wailing the first winds of autumn.

"What's the position now?" he said. "You came on this train to warn me. What against? How has the situation changed?"

She told him, as far as she knew herself. The Germans had ceased to trust him; they were planning their revenge. It was essential that he should not come to Istanbul. "Get off the train at the next station. Go back to Ankara. You may have to wait a little there, but it won't matter. Lie low. Have you any money?"

"I've enough money."

"You've probably a return ticket on the Taurus, haven't you?"

"Yes."

"Then use it on the next train south. Once over the frontier you are safe. But don't come back to Turkey, till the war is over, or till the Germans have cleared out. You've nothing to fear. Everything works on a short term basis. You haven't been reported to the Turks, as far as I know. And all that matters is your status with your compatriots. The war can't last long. The Germans are on the run; or are about to be. They could make trouble for you now. In two years it'll be all forgotten. As long as your name isn't on the Turkish records, and I'm pretty certain that it isn't, you're all right. I know about this record business. You're sure you've money?"

He nodded. "Fadhil gave me quite a lot."

"Fadhil?"

"Surely you remember Fadhil; the man I got information from for you."

"Fadhil. Why yes, of course."

"I told him that I was going to Alexandria and so wouldn't be able to help him any more. He seemed rather worried. He said that there were one or two things that he really needed to know. He told me what they were. I didn't see how I could get back, but I wanted to because I wanted to say 'goodbye' to you. I half explained that to him. By 'half' I mean not telling him about you. So this time he offered me some money. As I think you know, until now he's paid me in gramophone records. I didn't need those any more; or not so much since I was going to Alexandria where I could get them. So this time he gave me money."

"I see," she said. So that was how Nigel Farrar had played his hand. But she could not explain that to Aziz now. It was enough that he had the money to get back safely.

"Dearest," she said, "I wish it all hadn't had to finish up this way. But you see, don't you, that I had to warn you."

"I know. I see, but . . . I had been so looking forward to saying 'goodbye' to you."

He pouted; he looked like a small boy on the verge of tears. His boyishness touched her. His concern flattered her. Only an hour ago he had been thinking "In nine hours' time I shall be with her, in her flat, looking out over the Bosphorus." He was a small child in a nursery, robbed of its promised sweetmeat. It pleased her that he should be that. It restored her sense of power. She raised her hand. She laid it against his cheek. "Don't worry, precious. There are better times ahead."

But were there? Not for a long time: till he had become a different person. She had had the flower of his youth. He could not give that again.

"Darling," she said, "I'm desperately tired; all this has been a strain on me. I've a lot on my mind. I didn't tell you, but I am going away too; back to England, the week after next. So this really is good-bye. I'll go back to my compartment right away.

Let's not drag things out. And you will get out at the next station, won't you? Promise?"

"I promise you."

"I'll wave to you from my compartment. Look out for me. I'm at the head of the train. Good luck, my precious. I'll always think of you."

Slowly she fought her way back to her compartment. Door by door. Carriage by carriage. That's that. She had a corner seat. She lolled back, her head against the cushions. Her eyes closed. Drowsiness supervened.

She almost missed him. She would not have woken if the woman opposite had not been getting out and had not knocked against her as she was lifting her suitcase from the rack. The train was already at a standstill. She pushed past the disembarking passengers, found an open window, craned her neck. Yes, there he was. He seemed, standing on the platform, to be only a few yards away. His features were quite distinct. It was incredible that it should have taken her so long to reach his compartment. She waved and he waved back. It was an unimportant little station. Only a dozen or so passengers got off, and as few got on. There was barely a two minute stop. He did not join the passengers hurrying or shuffling to the exit. He looked a very forlorn figure standing on the platform beside his canvas bag. As the train drew out, she lifted her finger tips to her mouth. She wondered how long he would have to wait for a train back. What a drab return for him. His heart had been beating so gaily three hours back. Well, there was Alexandria waiting.

In three weeks, she would be back in London, with winter coming on; the blackout, the restrictions, the queueing up; with everyone looking shabby, everyone short tempered. Trains late and crowded and the houses cold. Another world, another universe. And which would seem unreal, that one or this? She went back to her compartment. She was very tired.

9

REID RECEIVED IN THE FOLLOWING WEEK the news that he had been granted a *decree nisi*. "It went through perfectly smoothly," Jenkins told him, "as, of course, we knew it should. There was no special reason for hastening the decree absolute, so they did not press for it. That means that you will make your application in the spring. The case got no publicity. That is one of the advantages of these small newspapers."

Reid wondered whether Rachel had told the boys. He had not mentioned it in his letters, nor had he mentioned it to his father. He still could not believe that it was really happening. He was so completely cut off here from his former life. He could not believe in its continuity for others. In the winter of 1917, when he was in the trenches, he had read an advertisement of Rolls-Royce cars. "One day," it ran, "the war will end as suddenly as it began. Then you will wonder why you had not placed your order for your new Rolls-Royce months before. Be prepared. Order now." The advertisement had seemed quite unreal. He had known that that was what would happen; that the war would end as suddenly as it had begun. But there in the trenches, it was impossible to believe in anything but the permanence of trench routine, the reliefs, the takings over, the leaves, the casualty lists. In the same way, though he knew that in a few years time he would be once again Professor Reid giving lectures and tutorials and every four years publishing a scholarly tome that would receive considerable attention in the serious papers and sell a few hundred copies; he knew that as Professor Reid he would take up his personal routine. He knew all that, but he could not quite believe it. Was someone on the Winchborough faculty remarking at this moment: "I heard a rumour that the Reids had got divorced; have you heard anything about it?" It all seemed very far away.

On that same day, he received the latest summary from Farrar's office. The appendix with the limited distribution list closed with the paragraph:

"Our attempt to make a final use of Aziz misfired. Something went wrong; we do not know what or why. Aziz has now gone to the University of Alexandria. He will presumably be visiting his aunt in Beirut for holidays, but he may not be returning to Turkey for a long time. As far as our purposes are concerned, we can, therefore, write him off. We had high hopes of this project when it started and the results have been frankly disappointing, but we must not forget that without Aziz we should have found difficult the recruiting of Belorian, and Belorian has been and is being of the greatest use to us. The project in which we had hoped to make a final use of Aziz had as its objective the strengthening of Belorian's position with the enemy. It was not a necessary operation. It was no more than the gilding of a lily. Belorian's stock stands very high. On the other hand, the deception operation to which reference was made in our last summary is progressing satisfactorily. We hope to be able to report on its successful conclusion in our next summary."

And that referred to Gustave, Reid presumed. In a week or so he would be able to apply for another adjutant, which would be a relief. Whenever he went into Gustave, he found him at work upon a cross word puzzle, and Gustave always left the office at the official hour of 6.30. Reid suspected that the office was like a car that is not getting proper maintenance. Sooner or later, there would be a breakdown.

Reid was at work on his own next summary. It was usual for the heads of organizations to leave the writing of summaries to their juniors. But Reid preferred to write personally anything that he was going himself to sign, though he wondered sometimes whether he might not get better results if he handed them over to one of his staff. There was a certain aridity about his reports. Farrar's were much more readable; there was a sense of anticipation, a feeling of suspense, of dramatic action waiting in the wings. His own reports were bulletins of facts. Perhaps that was what was wrong with his published books. They lacked suspense. He read over the opening paragraphs of his current summary. They were set out in tabulated form; the trial of the officers of the Golden Square who had organized the Rashid Ali revolution was proceeding slowly. Censorship had discovered that a former Turkish national resident in Baghdad was sending up messages in secret ink to a friend in Ankara. A check was being placed on all the acquaintances of this former Turkish resident; also on his family. The correspondence would be watched for a little while; if it provided any useful information, it would be allowed to continue. If it did not, the man would be arrested and cross-examined.

Reid paused as he re-read the paragraph. Farrar would have made more of that. Farrar's approach would have been different; he would have whetted the reader's appetite; he would have written in a far earlier summary: "We have become suspicious of a man in his early seventies who had close links with the Ottoman Empire and himself graduated in Constantinople. He is writing long letters every week to a friend in Istanbul. They are very boring letters; they do not contain friendly or family gossip. There is a lot about the weather and there are a number of comments on current international events. It is hard to see why such an old man should be bothering to write such long, impersonal letters, particularly as he never seems to get an answer to them. We are going to submit his next letter to a test with a V.I. lamp." Then ten days later, Farrar would have written: "As we suspected, a V.I. lamp showed that there was writing in secret ink between the lines in the letter sent up to Ankara by our elderly ex-Turkish correspondent. In appendix A we give a translation of the letter in secret ink. We are clearly on the brink of a most significant discovery."

That was how Farrar had dealt with the case of Aziz. He had written: "We are about to make a use at last of Aziz." His readers were therefore impatient for the next summary. He himself, in contrast, would not have referred to Aziz until he had something definite to report; and he had not referred to his ex-Turk until the correspondence had been submitted to treatment under the V.I. lamp. His reports were shorter than Farrar's and more factual; but they were less interesting. He could imagine a general at G.H.Q. saying: "Ah, good, another summary from Beirut. Let's see what's happening there," while a report from Baghdad would be a routine entry on a file. And one of the objects of a summary was to keep G.H.Q. interested in one's work.

He had now to compose a paragraph about the wireless transmitter set. He had planned to send in a NIL report; to say that there had been no developments in this case during the last two weeks. That was the truth. Yet he knew that Farrar would not have been satisfied with such an unvarnished truth. How would Farrar have treated it? Like this, perhaps?

"We are distinctly worried by the lack of development in the wireless transmitter case. We have now seventy-three individuals under observation, but from none of them are we receiving any helpful signs. We are checking on the friends of friends of friends. This is taking up a lot of staff time that could be employed more profitably somewhere else. We have not progressed beyond our first discovery, that Mulla Hassun was in 1938 linked with the Fattuwa, the youth movement that had been started under the influence of the German Consul, Grobba, on the Hitler model. Hassun was associated in this with a fellow schoolmaster and an Army officer. He is still associated with those friends. We are convinced Hassun had accomplices in this operation. And we still

404

consider that these three were the ringleaders. The Fattuwa move-ment had backing from certain politicians, but we have been unable to detect any links between those politicians and our three suspects. Nor have we found any links between the three suspects and any of the extreme left-wing factions in the city. Such links may exist. But our chances of detecting them are slight. We are in fact bogged down. And we feel that the time has almost come when we should take Hassun into custody for cross-examination."

That was the way Farrar would have handled it; and after all why not? The story had been told in less than half a page and it could be read in less than half-a-minute. It was redundant in that it recapitulated information about the Fattuwa movement that had been told in a previous summary. But a busy man could not be expected to remember everything that he had read two months ago. He did not want to check back to previous sum-maries. A recapitulation saved him time. Was it not part of the technique of the detective story to assemble the evidence half way through the book so as to refresh the reader's memory? Per-haps that was what had been wrong about his books. He had not made things easy for the reader; and he had not quickened the reader's appetite by a maintenance of suspense. He might do worse than remember this when he sat down to unravel the intricacies of Philip II's diplomacy towards the Vatican.

Two days later, there arrived on Reid's desk an envelope in which clearly a number of envelopes were concealed. The penul-timate envelope was addressed *Most Secret: Personal*. He opened it. Inside was another envelope addressed to Major Sargent. Reid read the covering letter. It was personal; from Farrar. "Prof, old boy, this is the works. I only wish that you were here with us to pull the lever. Will you hand the enclosed envelope to Gustave? He is to open it in your presence. You are not to read it. It will be much easier if you do not. The less one knows, . . . you know the drill, old boy. When he has read the letter, ask him if he completely understands its implication. He will say 'Yes'; but insist that he re-read it. When he has, ask him if he completely understands it. It is a short letter. It will not be hard for him to memorise it.

"When he assures you that he knows exactly what is in it, instruct him to burn it in your presence. When the paper is burnt, insure that not a cinder of it remains. When you are satisfied, stretch out your hand, say 'Congratulations, Gustave, and good luck.'

"You will then have set on for him immediate transport by the Taurus Express to Ankara. Signal to Ankara and Istanbul the expected time of his arrival. He will be travelling, of course, in mufti. If his clothes do not seem appropriate to a Major on the General Staff, get a suit laid on for him at once. You could buy a length of R.A.F. uniform material and have a 'civvie' suit made out of it almost overnight. Those boys work fast when their palms are greased.

"I do not fancy that this mission will take very long. Within six days, at the most, you should have your adjutant back with you. But it will not be for long. That's not the kind of work that he's best fitted for. As you suggested, two or three months ago, what you want is a regular officer, promoted from the ranks, who knows his way about Army orders and allowances, maintenance of vehicles and all that kind of thing. I don't think Gustave will be away a week; and the sooner you can contrive to send him back to us, the better it will be for all of us. Give Gustave time for the handing over and then switch him over.

"Once again, good luck, old boy. I wish we were working on this game together. It's terrific; the works!"

Reid read the letter over, shrugged, then walked on to the balcony. If this wasn't cloak and dagger stuff, what was?

Gustave's door was open. He tapped on it and went in. He got the impression that Gustave, from the angle at which he was sitting and the way his right knee was pressed against his desk, had been reading a novel inside a drawer which he had closed as his Colonel had come in. Reid smiled. Poor old Gustave; he wasn't made for paper work. Well, he hadn't got much more of it.

Reid held out the envelope. "Your orders at last," he said. "Congratulations."

He watched Gustave read the letter; he watched his expression change as he read the letter. Gustave looked eager, buoyant, excited. Gustave raised his head; he was grinning; with a broad wide grin that showed all his gleaming teeth.

"Have you got it clear?" Reid asked.

"I have."

"Better read it again."

From the speed with which he re-read it, it could not have been very long.

"Are you ready to burn it now?"

"I've a good memory."

"Have you got a match?"

"I've got a lighter. I'll start the conflagration."

As the sheet of paper shrivelled, Reid remembered how so few weeks ago now he had burnt Johnson's letter. If Johnson had not had to write that letter, Gustave would not be in this room now.

"There was a covering letter," Reid explained. He told Gustave what was in it. "Have you got any mufti here?" he said.

"Plenty. I wore it most of the time in Alexandria."

"Then in that case you can make it your job as adjutant to book yourself a ticket to Ankara. It'll be your last job as adjutant."

"I suppose it will be."

"We'll be sorry to lose you here, but I imagine this new kind of work is more in your line than checking up on lodging, fuel and light allowances."

"I'd say it was."

"I hope you are happy about this"; Reid had a sudden qualm of responsibility. "I don't know what this job is," he said, "but it's not an order. You don't have to go unless you want. It's something you volunteer for."

"I had that explained to me in Beirut."

"Then there's nothing for me to do except wish you the best of luck."

There was a train running two days later. On the night before they gave Gustave a goodbye dinner.

"It's not really a goodbye dinner," Reid explained in his good luck speech. "Because we shall be seeing him back here the week after next; but we are seeing the last of him as adjutant. He's leaving on a mission; I don't know what it's all about. I don't want to know what it's about. But knowing our good friend, Gustave, I can assume that it must be devious. If it wasn't devious, why should they have chosen Gustave. I've known him longer than you have. I travelled out in the same ship with him, and I almost saw too much of him. He has few secrets from me. Devious is the adjective for Beirut. And Gustave was the right man for Beirut. I've noticed that the Army makes a practise of posting a temporary officer to the kind of work for which, by taste and training, he is most unfitted, and for which no civilian employer would think of using him. I hope they have found him some really devious work to do in Ankara; but I suspect they haven't. It is something honourable and straightforward; for which they have presumed that with his open, grinning countenance he is temperamentally suited. You and I know how wrong they are. I hope that he will not get into too much mischief. I hope that the damage he does there to the war effort will not be irreparable."

It was a facetious speech. Gustave's reply was even more facetious. He was a little drunk, his face was glistening. Yes, he said, he was going on a mission. He wished that he could take them into his confidence. But under section 5, paragraph 2B of the Army Act he was precluded from such action. He had also testified to having read the Official Secrets Act. They would not therefore expect him to tell them in exact detail what he planned to do; but they knew as well as he did that laws were made to be bent where they could not be broken. And this he could tell them; that he was going on the kind of mission with which they had all been familiar in school days. How often had they not on Sunday evenings subscribed their pennies to missions for the Fiji Islanders? That was the kind of mission on which he was going—to convert the heathen. "You would have expected," he said, "that one of the officers in the Chaplain's department would have been more suitable for such a posting, but the mission on which I am being sent would not, I am afraid, appeal to the Lord Bishop of the Diocese and those ordained ministers who serve under him. It is not my hope to lead our Turkish Brethren into the Arms of Mother Church, but to redeem them in the eyes of Islam; to bring them back to the sacred teachings of Allah's prophet; to cajole them back on to the road from which they strayed during the powerful but mistaken leadership of Mustapha Kemel. It is the belief of our higher command, not only in Cairo but in London and in Washington, that the restoration in Turkey of the true faith would be a secret weapon driven at the heart of the misguided Fuhrer. Why the higher command should believe that, I do not know; they move in a mysterious way their wonders to perform. It is not for us to question what they, in their infinite wisdom, have decided; the wisdom that passeth man's understanding. Ours not to reason why. I go on my sacred and secret mission to lead back our deluded Brethren into the pure ways of that great, that supreme sultan, Abdul the Damned. How I propose to do it, I may not under the Official Secrets Act divulge, but I go with a clear conscience to rescue the Turks from heresy: to restore the harem and the fez."

The speech went very well. Gustave's high spirits were contagious. He was so pleased himself that the others could not help being happy for his sake. "It'll be my turn next," each one of them was thinking. Reid, as he laughed and clapped, wondered what on earth it was that Farrar had found for this engaging clown to do. He remembered Mallet's warning. But there was nothing that he could do about it.

Gustave appeared at breakfast next morning in a light, fawn-coloured Cairene suit. He looked very smart and very Levantine. He did not look like a British officer on leave. Perhaps that was why he was being sent to Ankara. Gustave's head was heavy, but he was still clearly in the highest spirits. He had no qualms about his mission. But Reid could not restrain a feeling of foreboding as he waved him goodbye from his balcony. What on earth could they have found for him to do? He thought of writing a personal note to Farrar, then thought better of it. He sent an official signal: Operation Gustave launched.

There was a tap upon his door. "I think that this will make you smile, Sir." The Captain in charge of censorship handed him a sheet of paper at the foot of which was the imprint of purplish red lipstick. "What on earth is this?" he asked.

"Some *bint* in Cairo."

He stared. The lips had been pressed so firmly on the paper that you could see not only the full shape of the mouth, but the little minute grooves of skin into which the lipstick had not penetrated. She had certainly kissed this paper as though she meant it. He stared. Then started. The handwriting was familiar. The script he had seen scrawled so often on memoranda in that Beirut office; the handwriting that he had so longed to see during his weeks in Deraa and had not seen there. He read the letter.

"My dear, this is in frantic haste. I have been posted back to London. I leave in three days' time, so it's no good your trying to get that leave in Alexandria. I am disappointed. I'll write. Fondly." There was no signature, simply the imprint of her lips.

"Who was this written to?" he asked.

"A captain in the Iraqi army."

"How did his mail come under censorship?"

"Through the wireless set, Sir. He was one of the friends of that captain who was in the Fattuwa."

"Have you got anything on him?"

"I haven't checked, Sir, yet."

"You might then, will you? No, I tell you what. Let me see his file. I shall have to talk to Forester about this. One has to be careful dealing with Iraqi officers." He handed back the letter. The Captain chuckled. "I thought you'd be amused, Sir."

"I am, exceptionally."

"I wonder who she is."

"It looks like an English handwriting."

"Whoever she is, I'd say he was on to a good job."

"I'd say so."

The file on this fortunate campaigner was not a long one. From it Reid learnt that Shawkat al Maslawi had been born in Mosul in January 1915. His father was a rich merchant, with family links in Istanbul and Damascus. His father had made a great deal of money during the famine of 1918. Shawkat had been educated at the Baghdad University and shortly before the war had been granted a cadetship to Sandhurst. He had passed out well and returned to Iraq in 1940 to take up a commission in the Iraqi army. His regiment had been engaged in the Rashid Ali revolt; and he had conducted himself with credit. As a result, he had been sent to Haifa for a short course at the staff college. "That's how he met Diana," Reid thought. He was a very promising young officer. He did not appear to have any political affiliations. He was a keen polo player, which explained his friendship with Captain Jansull. There did not seem to be anything wrong with him. He took the file down to Forester.

"Do you know anything about an Iraqi captain called Shawkat al Maslawi?"

"Everyone in Baghdad knows Shawkat."

"You would not expect him to be a subversive influence?"

"The last person that I should."

"I'm beginning to feel that this censorship game is getting out of hand. It is taking up a great deal of time and we are getting nowhere."

"That is what every policeman feels about his files. He sits and waits and accumulates stray facts, then suddenly he sees it plain. It is as I told you like a jig-saw puzzle."

"That's all very well for a policeman who stays in one spot for several years, whose office continues when he retires, who is leaving a legacy to his successors. Our Centre is a wartime product. It'll fold up when the war ends or else it will be merged with another Centre. I want to leave everything in a tidy state. Besides, there's another thing I don't much like," said Reid, "and that's this building up of files about innocent people. They may fall into the hands of security officers who don't understand why the names were entered in the first place. They'll think that there's something wrong with them; why else should they be on record. Would you like to have your name on one of our registers? I wouldn't."

"A policeman can't let himself be influenced by humanitarian considerations."

"Aren't we fighting this war to save humanity?"

"I can't think why we are fighting it. But I see that you've set your heart on winding up this gang. I'm not going to hinder you. I get bored too, sitting in this office day after day."

Reid was not bored, but he was feeling restless, as Stallard had prophesied he would; if Middle East had become a backwater, how much more so had Paiforce. He had to do something soon to justify his existence here. One of the Colonels in the British military mission to the Iraqi army was a friend of Reid's. He was a polo player. When they next met, Reid brought up the subject of Iraqi officers who played polo. The name of Shawkat soon drifted into the conversation. He appeared to be an excellent player. On the following Sunday Reid went to a race meeting. He did not find it difficult to have Shawkat pointed out to him. Shawkat was slim, graceful, of medium height; he had smooth, catlike movements. Every muscle seemed under control. He was not very dark. He would have been very goodlooking had not his nose been marked by the scar of a Baghdad boil. He had very white and even teeth. He laughed a lot. Reid felt that he would like him.

Reid had read once that there were two entirely different forms of masculine response to the men to whom a woman that you loved or were in love with was attracted. It might be that she would be attracted in him by the same characteristics by which she had been in you, in that case you would feel a kinship with the man. You were the same kind of person. The fact that the same woman had loved you both was a bond between you. On the other hand, she might be attracted to a man who was the very opposite of you; drawn by the very characteristics in him that you lacked and

411

whose deficiency in you had made her seek a change. He had not given her more or better of the things that you had given her; he had given her the things that she had missed in you; things that it was not possible for you to give. That man you would loathe with a hatred that only violence could assuage. He might have felt in that way about the French naval officer—the "sawn-off job." He might have longed for vitriol to throw in that man's face. But Shawkat could have been his friend. It was ridiculous that men like Shawkat should have their names on a police record.

Gustave returned thirteen days after he had left. He was in a quiet mood; he looked less Levantine; it had been grey and cold and wet in Ankara; he had lost some of the becoming tan that he had acquired on the Gezira golf course. He had lost a little weight too. It did not suit him.

"How did it go?" Reid asked.

"Fine, everything went fine."

"A complete success, as far as you know?"

"Have you heard anything to suggest it hadn't?"

The question was put quietly, almost belligerently. As though he had gone suddenly on the defensive.

"We've heard nothing here," said Reid.

"You haven't? No, of course you haven't. It was only Monday."

He said it as though he were talking to himself. As he spoke, he lifted his left hand across his face, covering the left hand side of his mouth. It was a new trick. Reid, looking at him closely, noticed that he had lost two teeth, one in the upper jaw to the left side of his mouth, the other in the lower jaw more to the centre.

"I see you've had dentist trouble," Reid remarked.

Gustave flushed. "I walked into a door in the blackout and knocked out two teeth."

"What a very curious accident."

"What do you mean, curious?"

The belligerent self defensive tone had come back into his voice.

"I should have thought that when you hit that door, the teeth you damaged would be one above the other," Reid explained. He would have also expected there to be signs of a bruising or cutting on the lip. There were not though.

"Damned fool thing that blackout," Gustave grumbled. "Can't

think why they need one. Who do they imagine is going to start bombing them?"

At dinner that night, Gustave ordered wine for the whole mess. He was in the highest spirits; but Reid noticed that he was not sipping at his wine, but drinking it in fast, long gulps. He also kept moving his hand up to his mouth.

"Tell us about the bints in Ankara," the young officer in censorship was asking.

"Now that's a very big question," Gustave answered. "First of all, ye must ken. . . ."

Two weeks later, the Beirut summary concluded with the paragraph: "Our deception operation was carried out with complete success. We feel that it has made a definite contribution to the success of our war effort in this area."

In a further appendix, Reid supposed, there would be a description of the exact nature of that operation. He would give a lot to read it. He was himself at work again on his bi-weekly summary. He wished he himself had something as dramatic to report. Farrar's report did not make him jealous, but it made him restless. He felt the need for action. It was high time he had Hassun under lock and key. He wanted to round off that campaign. He did not want to have to read Shawkat's letters to Diana or hers to him. That afternoon he sent off a signal asking Cairo's permission to start action. The permission came back at once.

10

HASSUN LIVED IN NORTH BAGHDAD, in a detached two-storeyed house. It was built of the traditional mud coloured bricks. It was indistinguishable from its neighbours. Reid and Forester made an afternoon reconnaissance. It would be an easy house to surround. "Not that he'll try to escape," said Forester. "We aren't arresting Public Enemy No. 1. No sawn off shot gun business."

They made their plans for the next day. The school holidays had yet begun. Hassun's last class ended at half-past four. He invariably went straight home. Two policemen would watch the house. As soon as Hassun returned, one of them would ride on his bicycle to the nearest police post where Reid and Forester would be waiting. The police post was only five minutes' drive away. "It'll work out very simply," Forester assured him.

To Forester it was a humdrum operation. He had arrested hundreds of men and women during his long career in the police force. But Reid's heart was pounding as he sat in the small bare room. He was a reader of detective stories. He had read so many accounts of men being arrested. He had wondered how accurately the author had entered into the mind of a criminal. He had never dreamt that one day he would be present at an arrest. He wondered how Hassun would behave. He pictured Hassun at that very moment in terms of his own routine as a teacher. He saw Hassun seated at his desk, speaking from his lecture notes; looking up at the clock, saying: "Two more minutes. We will stop now. To-morrow we will discuss the implications of Louis XIV's decision to secure for his grandson the throne of Spain. There are no more Pyrenees." There would be a scuffle, a shuffle as the students collected their books, and hurried to the door with their chorus of "Good afternoon, Sir."

He saw Hassun tidying up his desk, glancing at his first notes for the next day's lecture, as he had himself so often done. "There are no longer any Pyrenees." When would Hassun deliver that lecture now? Would he ever deliver it?

He savoured the dramatic irony of the situation, pictured Hassun walking to the common room, knotting his scarf round his neck; it was beginning to get cold; pausing to exchange a few words of gossip with a colleague, making a plan perhaps to take a cup of coffee with him on the following morning. That colleague would wait alone in that noisy café. Hassun would collect his bicycle. He had ridden out of that courtyard on it so many hundred times. How often in the next few weeks would he relive in detail that last ride?

The door bell in the police post rang. The policeman on duty answered it. A policeman with a bicycle stood in the doorway. He spoke to Forester. "That's us," said Forester. "We're on our way."

It all went as smoothly as Forester had promised. The door was opened by a nondescript man of middle age and medium height. He was wearing a dark cloth suit in Western style. He had taken off his collar; and the shirt open at the throat gave him an ill-kempt look. Forester spoke to him in Arabic and Hassun led them out of the small hall into the sitting room. A woman and two small children were sitting over a brazier. It was cold and they were wearing coats; the woman pulled her veil up over her nose and mouth. Reid could not follow the conversation. He watched Hassun's expression. It did not change. The children were staring with wide, goggling eyes. Reid looked round him. The walls were decorated with enlarged photographs, presumably of relatives. Carpets were stretched over the chairs and sofa. There were a couple of low tables; on one of them was a brass coffee set; on the other a number of small articles, match boxes, ashtrays, knives in the black and white Asmara silverware, with the traditional designs of date palms and small river boats. There were no books. Hassun addressed some remarks to his wife. Forester turned to Reid. "We are going to search the house. We are looking for the wireless transmitter."

One of the policemen stayed with the wife and children. The other accompanied Reid and Forester. There was an underground room for use in the hot weather. It was furnished with a table and four chairs. There was a litter of children's toys. There was a small kitchen and an eating annexe next to the room into which they had been shown. Nowhere could a transmitter have been concealed. There were only two rooms upstairs, the parents' and the children's bedrooms. They were tidily kept. Reid was surprised at the small number of clothes on hangers. They kept most of their clothes in suitcases. There was a small black suitcase that might have been the one that Chessman had put into Hassun's compartment. Reid called Forester's attention to it. It contained a collection of shirts and underclothes. Forester looked at the inside of the suitcase. Then he emptied the contents on the bed.

"This may prove useful evidence," he said. "We'll take this with us." There was so little to ransack in so small a house that they were quickly satisfied that nothing was concealed.

"En route," said Forester.

There was no click of handcuffs. They drove, the three of them and the two policemen, in the office car. Hassun was handed over to the police and Reid and Forester went upstairs.

"I suppose," said Reid, "that all I didn't understand was the usual rigmarole warning about 'anything you say will be taken down in evidence against you'?"

"Exactly the way it is in Sexton Blake."

"Now what?" asked Reid.

"Let him cool his heels in jail and let him think. In three days' time we'll have a talk with him."

"And continue to leave his friends at liberty?"

"I'd rather wait and see if they react in any way."

Forester gave Reid a careful briefing before the interview.

"We'll conduct this in English. He speaks perfectly good English. And with English he'll feel in a foreign country. That'll intimidate him. Moreover you'll understand what's going on." Forester explained his plan of campaign. "It is my belief that sooner or later he will incriminate himself. I don't know where. I don't know how. It may take place in the first interview. It may take place in the seventeenth. We are in no hurry. I want to move very slowly. I aim to recapitulate step by step the story as we see it. I will go over it with an elaboration that you will find ineffably dull. I want you to sit at my side. I want you to have arranged before you the maximum possible number of various files. The layman is terrified of files. They are, in his eyes, the pathway to the judgment seat. I shall refer to you quite often. I shall rely on you to consult your files with deliberation; then announce your discovery in a firm, clear voice. You can rely on me to conduct proceedings with the appropriate air of assurance. Sooner or later, in my opinion, he will make a slip."

With seven files in front of him and at his side, Reid watched and listened while Forester conducted the examination. Nothing could have been more informal and relaxed. Hassun was invited to sit down. He was offered a cigarette.

"Put yourself at your ease," said Forester, "and I must apologize from the very start for the discomfort to which you have been subjected. In wartime certain of the safeguards of civilised living have to be relegated to abeyance. The law of Habeas Corpus, for example. We have to fight our enemies with the same weapons that they use. You will, as a historian, agree with me that one of the tragedies of international warfare is that we tend to become the very thing we fight. We go to war in defence of Freedom; and we can only defeat the enemies of Freedom by ourselves curtailing our own rights. I know that you understand that; and that you will make allowances for the rough treatment that you have received at our hands. This is wartime after all. And you have unfortunately placed yourself in a rather awkward situation in view

416

of the fact that Iraq has been at war with the Axis powers since January 1943. I will go over the story step by step. Colonel Reid will prompt me if I make a slip. As you see, he has the necessary files at his disposal. I am an old man. I cannot be expected to remember everything. Let us start now at the beginning. In March 1943. Have you got the exact date, Colonel Reid?"

Reid turned the pages of a file slowly, paused, studied a page, then read out: "April 23, 1943."

"Exactly. Thank you, Colonel. On that date, April 23, 1943, we learnt that a wireless transmitter set was being sent from the Germans in Ankara to one of their agents in Baghdad. We did not then know who that agent was. We took steps to discover who that agent was. That agent was to join the Taurus Express at Mosul."

He went over the operation slowly, in minute detail; frequently turning to Reid for corroboration. "Isn't that so, Colonel Reid?" or "Can you verify that date, Colonel Reid?"

He handed Hassun a sheet of paper and a pencil.

"It will be simpler," he explained, "if you do not interrupt until I have finished my deposition. Will you take notes of anything that occurs to you? And then, when I have ended, you can raise those points one by one."

It took him over an hour to reach the train journey from Mosul to Baghdad. "Colonel Reid was on that train. He saw you get off the train. You were carrying a small black suitcase. I suggest to you that the suitcase which we took from your house three days ago is the suitcase you were carrying that day. Colonel Reid tells me that he did not see you carrying that suitcase when you got on to the train at Mosul. Is that true, Colonel Reid?"

"Yes, that is true. I did not see Doctor Hassun carrying that suitcase when he got on to the train at Mosul."

"It is our contention, Doctor Hassun, that you found this black suitcase in your compartment when you boarded the train at Mosul, that it had been placed in your compartment by an agent whom you did not know and whom in fact you have never met. It is our contention that that suitcase contained a wireless transmitter set. We have examined the suitcase carefully and we have satisfied ourselves that it is not a type of suitcase that can be easily obtained here in Baghdad. We have, however, learnt that this type of suitcase is in general supply in Turkey. It is made in Czechoslovakia and Turkey can conduct trade with Czechoslovakia whereas Iraq cannot. We shall later on ask you how you obtained possession of that suitcase if you did not, as we contend that you did, acquire it on the Taurus Express on the night of May the fifteenth 1943. No, please do not interrupt, Doctor Hassun. You will have plenty of time later on to correct me if I am misinformed on any point."

Hassun was shifting uncomfortably. Reid could see that Forester's technique of not allowing him to speak was working on his nerves. He was becoming restive. At the start he had worn an air of indifference. He had made no notes upon the sheet of paper. But in the last half hour he had begun to scribble. He asked for another sheet of paper; mainly so that he should have something to do, Reid felt. He himself was beginning to feel the tension. His chair was not very comfortable; a draught blew under the ill-fitting door. These Arab houses were not adapted to the few cold winter weeks. He was getting very bored. The interview had been going on for two hours. It seemed to be making no progress whatsoever. Reid, who was used to the methods of the lecture room, where he was concerned with the firm making of his points and the retention of his listener's interest, found the performance insupportable. No one had the right to be such a bore. And the most exasperating feature of it all was that he could not permit his own attention to wander. Every few minutes Forester would be turning to him to corroborate some point.

"I think you have, Colonel Reid, the testimony of your field security sergeant who accompanied the prisoner on the train. Will you read it, please?"

Or again: "Now I think, Colonel Reid, that you have there the receipt for the sleeping car in which the prisoner travelled down from Mosul. Can you tell me its number, please?"

And Reid would shuffle through the papers until he found the pertinent document. Minute after minute, quarter after quarter, on and on it went. Reid was beginning to feel hungry. He knew very well that Forester, the policeman, was trying to weigh Hassun down with the weight of evidence, with the appearance of evidence, with this avalanche of papers; on and on it went.

Forester was now explaining the methods of censorship that he had adopted. "We watch every means of communication, air, mail, road, train, telephone. We learn how you spend your days, we learn what your interests, what your hobbies are. We learn who your friends are: and who the friends of your friends are: the ramifications of this experiment are endless. Colonel Reid has one highly efficient, well trained officer who is occupied with nothing else. Colonel Reid, will you show us the files that that officer has assembled?"

Reid lifted up three bulky files.

"Those files," Forester went on, "are filled. They are well filled as you can judge, with specimens of intercepted correspondence. And they contain only that part of the correspondence that seemed significant. They are only part of what we have examined."

On and on it went. They had been here for three hours now. There was a strain upon his bladder, yet he did not dare to disturb the atmosphere. He supposed he could hold on for another hour; but his patience was fretted to the limits of self control. The strain on his nerves was greater than that upon his bladder. On and on it went.

Forester was now retailing the number of suspects he had under observation. "It is over seventy. Colonel Reid can give us the exact number."

"Seventy three."

"Seventy three; that is, you will concede, a substantial number. Each suspect has involved us in a separate investigation. It has taken time. It has taken a great deal of time. That is why you have been allowed to remain at liberty so long. It is nearly six months since you made that trip to Mosul. There was no hurry. We spread our net wide. We are now drawing it in close. We knew which ones to let loose and which to keep. We have narrowed down our suspects from that long list of seventy-three, down to just five names. The five names we really need. It has involved us in many hours of work, but it has been worth it; it has been well worth it. We have got the men we want."

On and on and on. Must he elaborate, must he over-elaborate every point. He would drive a class to sleep in twenty minutes. On and on and on.

"Five names. But they are names that matter. There is yourself first. The ringleader. There is your colleague, Professor Jamal. There is the captain in the Iraqi army, Baroud el Baghdadi. There is your colleague, Shabibi. There is. . . ."

But Forester was never to reach that fourth name. Hassun was on his feet. He had pounded with his fist upon the table. "No, no, no," he shouted. "Not Shabibi, no, not him. Nothing to do with it. No, nothing."

He stood, his breath coming quickly; his hands clenched. At last his reserve had cracked. Forester had made his point.

Silence followed the explosion. A silence that Forester prolonged. "Nothing to do with what?" he asked, very quietly.

"With all of this. The names, the censorship, the wireless set; Shabibi was not in that."

"And the others were? I see."

There was a pause. Then Forester said, again very quietly: "Now please, Doctor Hassun, please sit down. We will accept what you say about your colleague. I had my doubts about him myself, but I let myself be over-ruled by Colonel Reid; the military are so suspicious; but we have made some progress. We have established the fact that the wireless set does or did exist, and that apart from my mistake about Professor Shabibi, our general estimate of the situation is accurate. We shall make swifter progress now. And I think, Professor, that we will ask you to tell us in your own way, quietly, how all of this came to happen. I have been talking too long, too much; I must give you a chance to talk. But first we would like, all of us perhaps, a little interval; and then a cup of coffee. Shall we meet here again in ten minutes' time?

The atmosphere was now completely changed. There was a sense of relaxation; like rival footballers talking it all over after the match. Forester acted like a host: "Now let's start at the very beginning. Tell us how you came to being mixed up in all of this."

It had started, so Hassun told him, before the war; through Grobba. He had been anti-British. The British were arrogant and offensive. They were also, he had believed, decadent. Germany represented the new idea. He had liked Grobba. He had hoped that Germany would win the war. He had hoped that Rashid Ali would set up a new pro-German administration in which Germany instead of Britain would provide technical advisors to the Iraqi ministeries. It was a great disappointment to him when the British won the campaign and restored the Prince Regent. It was during the last hours of the short German occupation of Baghdad that he had been contacted by the Germans.

"Were you contacted by Grobba himself?" Forester enquired.

"No, by a German officer on the General Staff."

"How did he come to hear of you?"

"From an Iraqi student in Ankara. One of my old pupils. Before the campaign, someone in the German Embassy collected a list of

Iraqis who would be sympathetic to the Germans. I was on the list."

"Do you know who else was on that list?"

"No."

"Did you know Grobba personally?"

"I had met him once or twice. I do not think he would have remembered me."

"How did this German contact you?"

"Through a messenger, sent to the college. Everything was in very great confusion. The Germans were going out; the British hadn't arrived. Jewish shops were being burnt. Jews were being killed. Everything had to be done in a hurry."

"What did this German say to you?"

"He explained that this return of the British was only temporary; that Germany was certain to win the war; that this was a local reverse; not to be taken seriously. The Germans would soon return. In the meantime they would want to be able to receive first hand information as to what was happening in Baghdad. They wanted to establish wireless communication with Baghdad. They asked if I would accept a set if they sent one down and operate it on their behalf."

He had explained to the Germans, Hassun said, that he was not a technician, that he would not know how to manipulate the set. "But you surely have a friend who could. You must have some friend in the Iraqi Army who is trained in wireless." In the end they had agreed that he would try to recruit a small group who would assist him. Then as soon as they could manage, the Germans would send down a wireless transmitter by the Taurus Express.

"How were you going to know when the set was ready to be sent down?"

"They would send me a postcard from Turkey saying: 'I hope Aunt Marian is well.'"

"How were they going to know that you had received the postcard?"

"I was to post a card they gave me saying: 'Aunt Marian is well and sends her love.'"

"To whom was the card addressed?"

"I cannot remember. To someone in Ankara. I do not remember the name."

"And what was to happen then?"

"The Germans were to send me another card saying: 'Shall be

thinking of Aunt Marian with birthday love on . . .' and that would be the day on which the train would arrive in Mosul."

"And you would go up to Mosul and join the train there. How would you know the number of your compartment?"

"The signature on the postcard would give me the number of the compartment, with the letters changed into figures."

"I see. That meant that you would have to arrange your own transport to Mosul."

"Yes."

"Did they leave you any money for that?"

"Twenty-five dinars."

"That was a good deal more than your ticket would have cost."

"There would be a number of expenses. It might be very inconvenient for me."

"Was that all the money you received?"

"Yes."

"Agents do not ordinarily work for nothing."

"I did not think of myself as an agent. I wanted the Germans to win the war. I wanted to help them with it."

Was he speaking the truth, Reid wondered. He might be. And he could have expected to be rewarded when the Germans had won the war.

"Did you only have this one interview with the German?" asked Forester.

"Only that one."

"What rather surprises me is that so much could have been arranged within so short a time. Sending down a wireless transmitter is an elaborate operation. Within an hour the whole thing appears to have been set up."

"There was no time for delay. The Germans were leaving that afternoon. The city was in an uproar. You remember the way it was."

"That is exactly what I do not remember. I was confined, a virtual prisoner, with all the other Britons, inside the Embassy."

He chuckled as he said it, and Hassun chuckled too. There was a friendly feeling in the room. It was difficult to believe that that college professor, a man in background and training very similar to himself, was a prisoner, facing a sentence that was death in war time.

"I see," said Forester. "And then what happened next? You saw about the recruiting of your two partners. Did you have any difficulty about that?"

"No, I knew who would be the likeliest of my friends to join with me."

"You had no difficulty in persuading them?"

Hassun shook his head. "They thought it an adventure. We constituted ourselves a club. You know how keen the Arabs are on forming clubs?"

"What did you call your club?"

"The Wireless Club."

"Now that was in May 1941. It was not till March 1943 that you got that postcard. Were you surprised at the long delay?"

"I was at first. Then a good deal began to happen. The war in Russia was lasting longer than we expected, then America came in. We expected to get that card in the summer of 1942, when the Germans were advancing on the Canal. But after Alamein, when the war started to go badly for the Germans, we began to think that the Germans had lost interest in Iraq."

And that was a pretty sound appreciation of the situation, Reid reflected. It had not occurred to Hassun that it was at that point that the Germans had begun to worry about Allied intentions on the Turkish frontier.

"How did you feel when you got this postcard?" Forester was asking.

"I was surprised."

"You must have wondered whether it was worth while answering it."

"We did. We discussed it for a long time."

"You couldn't have still believed that Germany was going to win the war?"

"No, we had ceased to believe that."

"Then why did you answer the card?"

"We thought it would be an adventure." How frivolous can you get, thought Reid. To brand yourself as a spy, to risk your life, to imperil your children's future, simply because you yourself were bored. For that was what it amounted to, that need for an adventure. Did politicians recognise how powerful an influence upon human affairs was exercised by boredom? There was nothing too silly for people to do when they were bored. The Romans were wise with their formula of "bread and games." Keep the proletariat fed and entertained and they would spare the senators.

"So you sent off that postcard," Forester was continuing, "and a little later you got the message telling you on which day you should go to Mosul. We know what happened next. You found that black suitcase in your compartment; you took it with you when you left the train; you caught a taxi and you went straight home with it. Then I suppose the Wireless Club met and you opened the suitcase."

"Yes."

"There was the set inside it and instructions, I suppose?"

"There was a sheet of paper telling us what wave lengths to use and at what time to use it."

"So you started transmitting on that wave length?"

"We tried to, but we couldn't make it work."

"I thought Barroud was an expert?"

"So did we. So did he. It was a great disappointment."

"What did you do then?"

"We dropped the wireless set in the Tigris."

"You did what?"

"What use was it to us. We could not sell it. It was dangerous to keep it. We were certain by then that the Germans could not win the war. What else was there we could do?"

Farrar would chuckle when he read about this, Reid thought. On the surface it proved that if British Intelligence had taken over the set, British experts with those instructions could have contacted the Germans in Ankara. But Farrar would have his laugh all right. "Well, Prof," he would say, "I hope you learnt a lot about the bad boys of Baghdad with your operation censorship. I question if it did much for the war effort."

The interrogation had lasted for five hours. It was now half past two. "I'm afraid you've missed your lunch," said Forester.

"Well, yes, I have."

"Sorry. I forget that people lunch. My wife makes me up a sandwich, that's enough for me. I work Iraqi hours; seven to two o'clock, and then a little longer. Would you like to share my sandwich?"

"I'd like a whisky."

"Sorry, I can't manage that. They're Moslems, you know. They wouldn't like the smell of liquor in an office. It's bad enough smuggling in coffee during Ramadan. Come on, you'd better share my sandwich."

It was a small sandwich, but a good one. "What happens now?" Reid asked.

"What do you think should happen now?"

"Are you going to arrest the other two?"

"We might have them up for questioning. But what have they done to be arrested for? They didn't contact the Germans. They haven't been paid any money by the Germans. At least, we can't prove they have. I suspect that Hassun was given considerably more than twenty-five dinars, and that they got their share. But we have no evidence of that. They didn't go to Mosul to collect the set. We'll have them up and make them talk. But there isn't much that we can do to them."

"What about Hassun himself?"

Forester shrugged. "I'm not sure that he wouldn't be doing more good at liberty, teaching school, than costing the country money in a gaol. It's for the Iraqis to decide. It's their country and he's one of theirs. But they usually take my advice. I'd be for letting him free. He can't do any harm. I'm not one for punishment for its own sake."

"The whole thing's been rather a disappointment, hasn't it?"

Forester shook his head. "From your point of view, perhaps. But not from mine. You fellows think that you have to justify your existence by trapping spies. The more the merrier. But the more thieves and murderers that I plank behind bars, the more dissatisfied I am. I want a nice quiet law-abiding country where a citizen can sleep well o'nights. This whole case has been most reassuring for me. It has set my mind at rest. If that's the best the Germans can do, we don't have to worry."

"But are you sure that that is the best that they could do?"

"I'm inclined to think so. Planting a wireless transmitter in an enemy country is a major operation. Yet look what a casual amateurish job they made of it. They only cooked it up at the last moment. If they had a genuine subversive organization at work here, they wouldn't have needed to attempt anything so improvised. You know yourself how carefully we had worked out a scorched earth policy in case the Germans broke through in '42. We had a whole underground army of saboteurs waiting to make nuisances of themselves. We would have provided the Germans with a constant and very unpleasant headache. When you compose your Intelligence summary, our rounding up of this 'Wireless Club' may look a rather pitiful fiasco, but I, on the other hand, shall be forwarding to my bosses—the Iraqi authorities—a highly enthusiastic report. We have no need to fear any trouble from enemy agents. In this case a nil report is a positive report. So you see, my friend. . . ."

Reid saw his point. He supposed that his disappointment was that of the small boy who had hoped to play Red Indians. The trip to Mosul and the arrest of Hassun had been in so many ways the most dramatic things that had ever happened to him, yet now at the end of it all, they had proved damp squibbs. Though equally if there had been no wireless set and if he had followed Farrar's advice—and very likely Farrar had been right—Farrar himself might not in his irritation, in his need to assert himself, have embarked on the devious project against which Mallet had warned him, that had so nearly involved Aziz, and had involved Gustave—in what precisely had it involved Gustave?—the project that Farrar was now describing as of such high importance, in the deception programme. So much turned on chance. How could a man call himself the master of his fate when that fate is decided by forces over which he has no control, by people whom he has never met, of whose existence he is unaware? Would he himself have decided on the arrest of Hassun if he had not intercepted that letter stamped with lipstick? How astonished Hassun would have been a month ago could he have known that his future, even his life, was dependent on the amatory caprice of an English girl in Cairo.

"There is one thing," he said. "I would like, if you would let me, to have a talk with Hassun alone."

"By all means, my dear fellow, by all means. Where would you like to see him? Here or in your office?"

"In mine."

It would be more casual there; it might be easier to make Hassun talk, surrounded by British men in uniform. Hassun would feel he was in a foreign country; one tended to relax abroad; to be confidential, in a way that one didn't when one was surrounded with familiar objects.

Hassun was brought up in the afternoon. He looked around him with curiosity. He was probably surprised, Reid thought, by the bareness of the room, by its lack of furniture, by its 'in the field' conditions. Reid rose as Hassun came in; he did not want to create the atmosphere of a cross-examination. "I'm afraid that these chairs aren't very comfortable," he said. "Think of us as

Bedouins, always on the move—though I imagine that a Bedouin's tent would be much more comfortable than a G.H.Q. office, with its cushions and its carpets. I've never been in a Bedouin tent. That's one of the worst things about being a soldier, on a campaign; one never sees the real life of the country, only the towns; in the same way that a sailor only sees the coastline and the sea. I'd like to live with the tribes for a little."

"I've never lived with the tribes," said Hassun. "I'm a townsman too."

"I want to go south to Nasseriyah. I think I shall take a leave down there."

They compared notes on the few sections of Iraq that both had seen. It surprised Reid that Hassun should have seen so little of his own country. "But then after all," he said, "in England I haven't been north of the Thames so very often."

He asked Hassun if he had ever been to England, so many Iraqis had. Hassun shook his head. He had gone to the A.U.B. That was as near as he had got to Europe.

"Perhaps if you had come to England, you wouldn't feel so resentful against the English."

Hassun smiled; a rather contemptuous smile. But he made no answer.

"I was surprised that you should have been so anxious for the Germans to win the war. Why should you prefer them to us?"

"They have done us no damage."

"Do you think we have?"

"You made us promises during the first war which you did not keep."

It was the familiar argument that he had heard a dozen times. Reid had no wish to bring up the counter arguments. He wanted to find out what Hassun thought; whether Hassun, who was an educated man, had anything fresh to say.

"We made mistakes," Reid said. "We made bad mistakes, but at that peace conference there were all those politicians who had to satisfy the voters who had put them into power. If they gave way over one point, they felt they had to stand firm on another. And the trouble was that very few of the men at the top knew anything about the Middle East."

"That may be an explanation; it is hardly an excuse."

"At any rate we freed you from the Turks."

427

"Did anyone ask you to free us from the Turks? They were our co-religionists."

"There was a great deal of feeling here against the Turks."

"There was a great deal of feeling throughout the Ottoman Empire against the tyranny and incompetence of the rulers in Constantinople. The Turks themselves were sick of their own rulers. But that doesn't mean that we wanted our affairs to be managed by Europeans. Hussein and Hussein's sons were glad to follow you because they thought that you would make them kings in their own right; they thought that they would be independent sovereigns. That is what you promised them. But you did not keep your promises. You fooled them and we despise them for having let you fool them. We cannot respect their judgment."

This was more the kind of thing that Reid had wanted to hear; or rather it was on an issue of this kind that he wanted to hear Hassun's opinion.

"Is that why you were ready to back Rasbid Ali?" he asked.

"That is one of the reasons. Feisal and his family either did not realize that they had been fooled by you, in which case they were stupid; or admitted the fact that they had been betrayed and accepted their servitude, which was base in them. Feisal in his time and Abdul Illa now in his are lackeys of your economic policies. You in Britain want our oil, you keep your lackeys in power, with your arms and money. That is why we hate Abdul Illa. That is why we hate Nuri Said."

"How do you feel about the young king?"

"He will always be his uncle's puppet. There will be no health in this country as long as it is run by the Hashimites."

"Do many Iraqis share your views?"

"More and more are coming to."

"I can understand your dislike of the English. I do not see why you should prefer the Germans. It was because of the Germans that Turkey was involved in the first war."

"That was not the Germans' fault. The Turkish leaders were incompetent. They followed what they believed to be their own interests; to their own disaster and their own country's."

"Do you think if Germany had won the first war and the Ottoman Empire had survived, you would be better off here in Iraq now?"

"We would not have an alien Jewish state imposed upon the Arab world."

Now, thought Reid, now at last we're reaching something. "You think that the creation of Palestine was a great mistake?" he asked.

"It was more than a mistake. It was a crime. In the Ottoman days less than ten per cent of the population there was Jewish. It was a small minority, and it lived there happily, as the small Jewish minority lived happily here in Baghdad. But when you turn a minority into a majority, when you impose on the Arabs a completely alien race with a different religion, with different standards, with a different way of living, the two cannot live together side by side. Would you like it if the Americans who in this war are saving you from the Germans decided that as part of their recompense, your county of Cornwall should be turned into an independent Jewish state as a step towards the solution of the Jewish Problem?"

Reid did not answer that. There was no answer to it. And anyhow the analogy was false.

"Would you in the last analysis," he asked, "consider that it was Hitler's anti-Semitism that made you want the Germans to win the war?"

Hassun pondered that question. Then he nodded. "Yes, I suppose in the last analysis I should."

"But you can't approve of what he is doing now—with his mass murder in the concentration camps?"

There was a pause: then suddenly there came into Hassun's face an expression that once or twice already he had noticed in Arab eyes and on Arab lips. It was a smile, curiously compounded of humour, innocence and malice: there was something furtive in it and something brazen. "There is an Arab proverb," he said. " 'To kill one's neighbour is a crime, but the destruction of an entire people is a thing to be considered.' "

It was three months later; operation wireless set was about to be wound up. Shabibi and Captain Barroud had been cross-examined. The interrogation had produced very little. Hassun had been released. Reid had decided to devote a special summary to the case. He wanted to keep separate the various issues it had raised; there had been the rival claims of Farrar's deception programme and his own security programme. He set out the claims of each side, dispassionately, as a chairman would. He then set out the concrete results that had been obtained from Cairo's acceptance of his own point of view. He explained why Forester was satisfied with the results of the whole operation. Finally he tabulated Hassun's reasons for having accepted the German proposition. This he regarded as the most important part of the whole summary because it explained why there was so strong a feeling in Iraq against both the British and the Hashimite dynasty which British bayonets had placed and maintained in power. The summary would have a very small distribution list, but it would reach the British Embassy: it would be registered in the Chancery files. It might contain nothing of which the Embassy was not perfectly aware already. But on the other hand, it might coordinate a number of separate, well known facts in a sufficiently challenging form to attract attention. It might be, if the dark days came as he was beginning to fear they might that, someone turning up this report would understand the better how they had come about and so be put on guard against their consequences. His merit as a historian lay, he knew, in his ability to arrange and coordinate stray facts so that the reader could discern a pattern in the succession of seemingly irrelevant events that comprised the sum of day-to-day existence. As he read over the final proof of his report, he felt that here was his main, perhaps his only contribution if not to the war effort, at least to the confusion that would follow afterwards. This was the justification of his three years in the Middle East, and as he put his signature at the foot, he felt that his own work, as a soldier, had really ended here. What followed would be supplementary; he remembered reading an essay by a novelist on the technique of fiction, that had argued that the climax of a novel should come four fifths of the way through its length; with the last fifth constituting a rounding off. This for him was that peak moment. The war in Europe could scarcely last another year; the second front was open and the Germans were in full retreat. The Russians were pouring westward. The Middle East had been a backwater for several months; there would soon be no need for Paiforce to supply aid to Russia. The Centre would concentrate on political security, protecting British economic interests. He would be working at half pressure; twice as hard as he had worked as a staff captain in the Ministry of Mines, but with nothing like the concentrated energy he had expended during his year in Beirut, and his two years here. It should be a rather pleasant time; a time for reflection, for planning out his future. In a year's time he would have to make decisions but there was nothing he could do about that now. His personal life was in as much of a backwater as the Middle East itself. It was agreeable to speculate on the various possibilities that awaited him, with the world lying all before him where to choose? So he brooded, as he sat at his desk, waiting for his report to come back from the typist's room.

Next morning's mail brought him an airgraph from his lawyer, Jenkins.

"You may not have heard, I myself only heard last week, that Rachel's American had been killed in action. I also learnt that he had left a trust fund for her children. I suspect it will be quite a substantial sum; two thirds of his estate; the remainder to be divided between his fraternity in Harvard and something in New York called the Century Association, whatever that may be. Rachel, with her own money and the use of the children's money till they come of age, will be very comfortably off. So no new responsibilities will devolve on you. Rather chivalrous of that American, don't you think? Your decree absolute, by the way, is due next month.

"I suppose that you will be coming home quite soon. You are well out of London at this moment. Every month it becomes a more Scudderish war. These V.1 bombs have ceased to be amusing. Did you ever meet Sir Francis Faversham, an old friend of mine? He was in the Savoy Chapel when it was hit. Oddly enough the last time I saw him was the morning when Rachel's American came round to see me.

"Well, see you soon. Make the most of your flesh pots. There's precious little to eat here and not much to drink. The Athenaeum has taken its champagne off the wine list and is keeping it for the victory dinner to Eisenhower. You may cash in on that. Good luck."

Rather chivalrous of that American. It was more than chivalrous, it was highly sensitive. He was thinking of Rachel imaginatively. If he were killed and she remarried, her husband might have had qualms about enjoying money left to her by a lover, but he would have no qualms about being spared the support of another man's children. Rachel's American must have been a pretty decent fellow. Poor Rachel, he thought, poor, poor Rachel. He had no doubt whatever of what he had to do. He wrote out two cables. One to Jenkins: Cancel application decree absolute. The other to Rachel: Deepest sympathy your grief. I expect to return next summer. Let us start again where we left off in September 1941.

11

"M.E.F. MEN ENGLAND FORGOT." Stallard was to prove a good prophet during the long slow passing autumn of 1944 and the winter of 1945. The war was not ending as suddenly as it had begun. The check at Arnheim was followed by the Battle of the Bulge. In Europe it was a cold bleak winter; the patience of the English had reached breaking point. Another winter of the blackout, of food shortage, of restrictions. They had been so certain it would end that summer. The men in the Middle East, well fed and warm and sex starved, felt the mounting irritation in the airgraphs that now poured through in such a steady flow; no one was bothering about *them*, they thought; they were all restless and discontented, except those who had achieved a kind of bland "sand-happiness." There were quite a few of these in Paiforce. They admitted they were "round the bend." They diagnosed their complaint as "Paiforcitis." While the Americans in the south, working on Aid to Russia, in their own Persian Gulf Command, said that P.G.C. stood for People Going Crazy. Reid knew that his main job now was maintenance of morale among his staff: of keeping spirits high; of convincing his officers and men that their work was of value.

In August, when the strain of the long summer was at its keenest, when autumn was still a long way off and tempers right through the Command were getting frayed, he assembled the entire Centre in the cool of the evening, on the terrace of the mess. "There are meetings like this," he said, "going on all over Paiforce. Your friends will have told you of them. We are all of us getting homesick; we have been here, most of us, a long time. We are asking why we are still kept on here, when the war in the area is over. We are all 'browned off' and commanding officers have been instructed to explain to their units why their presence here continues to be important. You've heard about those meetings; so have I. The men have listened respectfully, as good soldiers should, but they have gone away grumbling: 'That's all bull,' they've said. 'We aren't doing any good here. We're only here because there aren't any spare ships to take us back and everyone's forgotten all about us.' I can understand how they can feel that, in a regiment, let us say, that was withdrawn from the Western Desert two years ago to meet a drive through the Caucasus, and ever since, while their friends have been charging across Africa and then sweeping over Europe, have done nothing but change billets and go on manoeuvres that seem pointless because they aren't in training for a battle. Who can be surprised if they are 'browned off'?

"But we luckily aren't in that position. We are not soldiers in the line; we are chairborne warriors and our work is every bit as important now as it was a year ago. We are still responsible for the security of Iraq. That security is of great importance to Great Britain. The scale of prosperity that we enjoy in Britain is going to depend after the war on the money that is brought to us from abroad. We are a small country that cannot of itself support a high standard of living. That high standard can only be maintained by our investments overseas. We have a very heavy investment in Iraq. That investment is no longer threatened by the Germans, but it is threatened by a number of subversive elements here in the country and on our frontiers. We have to watch those elements and the system of files that we are building up today will be of great value to the guardians of this country's freedom long after you and I have returned to our civilian employments."

He hoped he had made his point. He had anyhow spoken with conviction. He had believed what he had said, and the conviction in one's voice was more important than the arguments one used.

In the New Year, his name appeared in the Honours List with an O.B.E. Once again he assembled the Centre. "This pretty piece of colour on my tunic is due entirely to you," he said. "It is a recognition of the Centre's work. It is given not to me but to the Centre. And I consider it marks an occasion for the Centre to take a holiday. There wil be no work on Wednesday after lunch. The office will be closed except for the duty officer and duty corporal."

As far as he could see, the Centre was working hard and working happily. Himself, he had a good deal of spare time on his hands. He did not make work for himself, the Centre could function smoothly, scarcely noticing his absence. It was a period of tidying up and rounding off. He went over some of the back files, destroying a number of entries that might be misunderstood by or confuse his successors; conjectures that led into blind alleys, "notional characters" that a future staff might endeavour to identify, causing unjust injury to individuals.

433

He did a certain amount of private reading. He found one of his own books in the British Council Library. He read it with detached curiosity. It dealt with Britain's colonial trade during the Commonwealth. It had been highly praised, and it had involved him in a great deal of research; he had spent many hours in the Record Office. He had consulted every available source of information and .it would be, he believed, of value to any serious student of the period. It was a standard authority and it was very dull. Was it necessary, he now asked himself, to concentrate upon a short period, following every side path? Would it not have been more interesting to have worked on a broad canvas with large strokes, taking a philosophical view of history, showing the interdependence of events? A comprehensive account, for instance, of British trade in the eighteenth century showing how the claims of the East India Company dovetailed with and were on occasions in conflict with the demands of the West Indian sugar planters. He wondered whether for that kind of book, for someone like himself, so much preliminary research was needed. Why not write straight ahead out of his memory, out of the reference books that lay immediately to hand, and when he had finished his first draft, check up on doubtful points and fill in gaps? It was a possible solution. He remembered how he had compared Nigel Farrar's summaries with his own. He must get more life into his histories. So he brooded as the German forces broke and the Russians swept into Austria.

He was living in a vacuum. And he found it not unpleasant. He had resumed with Rachel the weekly interchange of letters that had been abandoned after her declaration of independence. They were as they had always been, cordial and affectionate. They dealt, as they had always done, with the varied interests that they shared. Twenty years was a long time. He wondered if he would find her very different. You would expect an experience such as hers to have made her a different person. But would the difference be apparent to him? Would it show upon the surface? Had he himself seemed a different person after that first night in Damascus? He had been a different person. But had it been discernible? Would he seem different now to Rachel? He shrugged. Either way there was nothing to be done about it now. Everything would solve itself in its due season. In the meantime it was pleasant living in a vacuum; with winter passing; with the Tigris in full flood, with the little walled-in gardens bright with flowers, and the radio, morning after morning, reporting fresh victories on every front.

March became April; it could not be very distant now. G.H.Q. in Cairo was drawing up lists as to the speed at which demobilisation would proceed. Officers and men were being registered under different classes in accordance with their age and length of service. Reid, at the age of forty-seven, who had been called up in August 1939, was in class 6. The first five classes were to leave together. Reid therefore was in the second batch. It could not be much longer now. When the day of unconditional surrender arrived, he let the tension slacken. Now he could start planning for himself. He was entitled to pull strings if he had access to them. The first repatriation class had drifted to Alexandria by dilatory and "laid-on" transport. He could do better for himself than that. Why not a few days in Beirut first? He wanted to say goodbye to Farrar. He had not seen him since that acrimonious conference in Beirut. There had not been another congress; which was proof enough of how unimportant Middle East had become; Stallard had not thought himself justified in taking a free holiday in a congenial climate. His life in the Middle East had begun with Farrar. Of all the men that he had met here, Farrar was the one whom he had liked the most. And Farrar was the one with whom he had found himself "at outs." He would be happier if he could wipe that slate clean.

One of the advantages of working in "cloak and dagger" was that no one quite knew under whose ultimate authority one came. One said: "I'm Broadway," or "I'm Baker Street," or "I'm Maida Vale," and the recognized legitimate channels of instruction and promotion would say: "Of course, ah yes."

Reid went to the D.M.I. and said, "I think it would be simpler from the point of view of the drill of the thing if I handed over to Barnet right away, then went back to Beirut on a liaison visit and sent back to Barnet a report on anything I may find out; there are one or two loose threads that I'd like to get tidied up. Then I could go straight on independently to Alexandria and pick my ship up there."

"Fine. Fine. A very good idea."

The D.M.I. could not have cared less. He was concerned both about his own repatriation and how he was so to organize it that his present acting rank of Brigadier become confirmed as a temporary rank, thereby assuring that he acquired the war substantive rank of Lt. Colonel.

"A sound idea, Prof, very sound idea. Good luck to you."

So once again Reid, his head heavy after a goodbye party, on an evening in early June was being carried westwards across the desert at the Government's expense in the comfort of an air-conditioned Nairn Transport bus instead of limping in open vehicles on a scorched five day trek. And once again at Damascus there was Farrar waiting: a much livelier Farrar than the one he had seen twenty months before; there were no longer taut lines about his eyes and mouth; his cheeks had a ruddy glow and gloss that went with the scarlet flashes on his bush shirt. He looked happy, on the crest of the wave.

All the way over the mountains, across the Bekaa Valley, they gossiped about mutual friends. "Annabelle?" Reid asked.

"You'll be seeing her tomorrow. I've a cocktail party."

"Aziz?"

"The one that got away? They tell me he's passing all his exams with flying colours."

"And Gustave, any news of him?"

"I haven't seen him for a while. They've let him put up a star to join his crown, so they must be satisfied with him."

"I've never quite known what he does for us in Cairo."

"I wouldn't be too sure that he knows himself. It's useful to have someone who can wear mufti and look Levantine. In uniform he looks an Englishman, but put him in fawn coloured gabardine and he looks a 'gypo.' Have you ever seen him dressed up to kill?"

"I saw him the day he went to Ankara. How did that work out by the way?"

"Supremely well."

"You wouldn't like to tell me about that, would you?"

"My dear Prof. I'd hate to."

"I shall be in Alexandria for a couple of days before I sail. I'll try to get in touch with him."

"Do that. He's a very fond spot for you."

"Shall I ask him about that mission?"

"I wouldn't if I were you; no, on second thoughts, I wish you would. Then write and tell me what he says. I'd be amused. Did you hear what happened to that man before you? Mallet. . ."

So it ran on as that car swung down out of the hills towards the haze of heat in which the gay, frivolous little city smouldered. At the sight of its towers and minarets, Reid felt a quickening of his nerves. Of all the places he had seen in the last forty months, Beirut lay nearest to his heart.

They arrived shortly after five. "You've got your old room in the flat," said Farrar. "What a pity we had to break up that arrangement. I've got to look in at the office. I'll leave you to your own devices. Let's meet at eight on the St. Georges terrace. Then dine at the Cercle. And we'll put you on the house for the last time, as we did the first. 'With thee begun with thee shall end the day.' I don't expect you've had anything but Palestinian wine to drink for several months. They've still got some champagne at the Cercle."

It was a very good bottle of champagne. He had not tasted anything to touch it since the last conference. "That's what I've missed more than anything," he said. "Good wine. When my house in England was requisitioned, I got the agent who made the inventory to send out my cellar list. I used to read it over when I felt depressed. That's something to look forward to, I'd think. Now I'm wondering how they'll have stood up to it. Burgundies age fast; I've got some '23s and '26s. They should have been drunk five years ago."

"How are you feeling about going back? Excited?"

"Yes, but apprehensive too."

"Well, aren't we all? But for you it's different. You are established, going back to a settled niche, picking up the threads where you dropped them."

Reid smiled. There it went again; the conviction that his case was completely different because he was over forty, established, with a family. In point of fact, was anyone in Middle East returning to a more uncertain future?

"Apprehensive's the right word, Prof. We've all of us been away too long. It's nearly six years in my case. So many changes have taken place in England I feel they'll have been going six years in one direction and I six years in another. That's a twelve year gap. And there's another thing in my case, my age. Nearly all of my contemporaries will have seen fighting service. Do you remember that first talk we had when I said that someone had to pick up the good hand in every deal. I wasn't boasting. I believed that then. Moreover I was doing much more important work out here than they were at home in England, waiting to be called up or learning elementary musketry. Besides I thought there would be real fighting here, and I'd be in it. But there wasn't; not here at least; while as for all those others who were idling around in England in offices and barracks during the phoney war, think of what they've been through since, in the desert, at Anzio, in France, and now there's Japan waiting. While me, in all this time I haven't even heard a bomb fall. One'll feel so out of everything. One'll have lost all contact."

"When are you going back?"

"Now that's the question," he paused. A mischievous look came into his eyes. "I tell you what," he said. "I'd like you to ask me just that question, in just that tone of voice, tomorrow, at the cocktail party, when Annabelle's around: do it dramatically. You know how I mean, in a pause."

"I'll do just that."

"Ah, Prof, you're wonderful. And I'd never thought of it till this very minute. You solve all my troubles." He paused. He grinned. "I shouldn't get worked up like this. It's only because you're here. I can talk to you. You're older and you're wiser and you amount to something; yet in the military machine we're opposite numbers. We are contemporaries; that's rather special. Why should I grumble because I've had the good luck to have an easy war? But damn it, I've worked hard; even if I've had a lot of fun. Why shouldn't one have fun in wartime, providing one's not shirking? And it has been fun, hasn't it? A lot of it?"

Farrar was once again the laughing congenial companion who had welcomed him to Beirut all that while ago. The angry, self defensive aggressive mood of the last conference had vanished. Mallet had probably diagnosed that mood correctly. It was good to have got back to that old comradeship; it was not likely that they would meet again, other than casually. But this evening together set his whole time in the Middle East within a frame.

He looked round the room. It had not changed in the least degree. It did not even look any shabbier. The tables were as crowded with the same mingling of French and British uniforms, with the same sprinkling of female dresses. There were even a couple of nursing sisters with four male escorts at the table where Diana had been sitting. What a lot had started on that evening. But for her he would never have been posted to the Centre.

"What's happening to Diana?" he asked Farrar.

"In London still, as far as I know. Don't you hear from her?"

"She's not the letter writing kind."

"Isn't she? I wouldn't know." He paused. "Have you got over that all right?"

"On the surface."

"Isn't that all one ever can do when a thing goes deep?"

The cocktail party the next afternoon was very much the same in spirit, as the very first ones that he had known there. Annabelle had put on a little weight, but she was radiantly good looking. She was gay and happy. And there was between herself and Nigel Farrar none of the asperity that there had been on that last occasion; they were back to their old easy eighteenth century badinage. When the party quietens down, Reid thought, I'll fulfill my commission.

There were about twenty guests. He felt that he should know some of them; they looked familiar, but in point of fact there was scarcely one that he knew. "I'd expected to see Jane Lester here," he said.

"She's gone back to England," he said. "She needed a change of air. . . ."

"Have you any idea how she's making out?"

"I've no idea. When people leave, they leave. There are no post-mortems."

Reid looked round him; he should not be surprised, he supposed, that the guests at a Centre party should seem familiar, even if they were not. Farrar was drawing on the same material now in 1945 as he had been in 1941. Still there might . . . yes, there at last . . . there was. A large, florid, youthful figure in a pearl grey cotton suit; the brisk, self confident Armenian whom he had interviewed in that discreet apartment with the independent entrance. The world seemed to be treating him all right. He walked across to him. There was no sign of recognition in Belorian's eyes. "Don't you remember me?" he asked.

"I didn't think I was supposed to recognise you."

"I see that Farrar's acquired an apt pupil."

"I do my best."

"I gather that it's been a very good best."

Reid told Belorian that he was going home.

"That's what you all are doing. I'm going to be very lonely. I shouldn't say it, I suppose, but I'm not enthusing about this war ending. I was having fun and being paid very nicely."

"I don't think a man of your capacities will fail to do very nicely in the peace. Beirut is going to boom."

They gossiped for a moment or two. Then he moved away. Nigel and Annabelle were standing side by side. It was time he fulfilled his promise. He moved across to them. "There was one thing you never told me last night," he said. "You've been out here longer than any of us. When are you due for repatriation?"

"That is what we are all asking ourselves," said Annabelle. "And oh, with what concern and trepidation."

Farrar took a long slow breath and drew himself to his full height. "My poor, my most dear Annabelle," he said, "you are now about to be robbed, you are now robbing yourself of the greatest moment in a woman's life."

"And what is that that I am going to lose, my Captain?"

"My Colonel, please."

"Ah, but to me you will always be my Captain, my dissolute and misguided Captain. Tell me what is this greatest moment in a woman's life of which I am forever to be deprived."

"It is the moment, my most sweet Annabelle, when a man who has been long courting her, but in a devious guise, says: 'I have things to say to you that I must say alone. Will you let me take you for a drive?' And it is a warm, bland summer evening such as this; and he will drive her out of town to a high point on the cliffs; and there will be a gentle breeze blowing from the mountains, and the lights of the town will be twinkling along the harbour; he will switch off his engine; he will place his hand over hers. 'My dear one,' he will say, 'for a long time now I have been courting you; and at the start, I cannot deny it, it was a rather casual courtship; I was a foreigner, here for a brief interval. I hoped to decorate that interval with a little dalliance. But you resisted. You had no use for that kind of decoration. I was disappointed, but I persisted. And the weeks went by, and disappointment became despair. And I tried to leave Beirut. I asked for a posting to Alexandria. But it was not granted. My duty kept me here. And then you began to flirt with a scruffy little Frenchman.'"

"He was not scruffy."

"Please do not interrupt. A scruffy little Frenchman whose intentions you said were honourable because he wanted a husband's right to your inheritance."

"That is not at all the way it was."

"That is how this poor Captain thought it was. He was in a prison from which he could not escape. He longed for the war to end. But when it did end, when he realised that he was soon to go back to England, that he would never see you again, it was more than he could face. Where else should he find anyone so beautiful, so adorable, with such eyes, with a voice that takes on so many tones, with so smooth a way of walking, and with such wit? When he realized what he should have to lose, he knew that there was only one thing in the world he wanted: to stay on here for ever as your husband. And his hand would press firmly over yours. There would be a glow in his eyes; and your eyes too would widen and grow tender. You would lean towards him and his arm would go round your shoulders, drawing you close, close, closer to him. And that is the greatest moment in a woman's life, but that is a moment that you can never know because a respectable young lady of the Lebanon does not go out unchaperoned for a drive with a young man."

"And if permission had been given for a young lady of the Lebanon to make such a hazardous excursion, is that what he would have said to her, my persuasive Captain?"

"That is what he would have said to her; but because it is not permissible, he has had to make her this little speech here in a crowded smoke-filled room."

"And is that what you have in fact said to me? That you want to stay on here in Lebanon for ever and be my husband?"

"That is what I have said."

"Ah, but my silly and long-longed for Captain, do you not think that I am much happier to have it said here and before so irreproachable a witness as our dear Professor?"

Her eyes were twinkling but they were very fond. She raised her hand. She rested it on his arm, above his elbow, pressing it. "Ah, but how happy you are going to be in two years' time that all this has happened in my way, not yours."

Reid had a three days' wait in Alexandria, in a transit camp, before he was due to sail. He had sent Gustave a signal from Beirut, and when he reached the depôt, there was a message saying that Colonel Sargent would call for him on the following evening at seven o'clock. It took him a minute to realize who

Colonel Sargent was. With his first war regard for rank, he found it hard to think of Gustave as a Colonel.

Gustave arrived in a staff car, punctually, in full regimentals. "This is on me," he said. "You did me very well at the Turf Club when I needed doing well. Let's call it quits. Home James and don't spare the horses."

Gustave had acquired a new vernacular since Reid had seen him last. It seemed to be a Victorian style of humour, put between inverted commas. Gustave took him to the kind of unostentatious restaurant that a man of the world recognized at a glance to be certainly very expensive and probably very good. The equivalent of the Maison Basque in London in the '20s.

Gustave waved away the table d'hôte menu that he was offered. "No, à la carte," he said. "I know what's good here, Prof. If you will allow me to make suggestions. They don't mind our sharing a single dish between us, so why not divide a *sole lucullus?* What would you like first, a consommé? A fruit cocktail?"

That's how it started. That was how it went on.

"Do you realize, Prof, it's nearly four years since we caught that Leopoldville at Glasgow? I was a Lieutenant and you a Captain. Not done so badly for ourselves since, have we? Level pegging up the ladder. Three rungs apiece. What'll we take with this, a carafe of 'the widow'?"

Gustave had certainly created a persona.

Reid let him talk, then later in the evening started asking questions.

"What are your immediate plans? When are you coming back to England?"

Gustave winked, knowingly. "Not for a long time if I can help it. I've learnt a lot since I've been in this racket. I know my way around, and I haven't wasted my nights as duty officer. I've nosed around the files. I don't only know what is what, but who is who. There'll be a lot of funny business going on out here after the war. And I, with my Alexandrian mother, sit both sides of the fence. Fishing in troubled waters; that's Gustave's line. And the first come are the first served."

Reid relaxed to this expansive entertainment.

Gustave did not seem to have a trouble in the world, but Reid had not forgotten his promise to Farrar.

"I suppose that star is the reward for your mission to Ankara," he said.

"I suppose it is."

"You wouldn't like to tell me about it, would you?" A crafty look came into Gustave's eyes.

"You wouldn't want me to break the official secrets act, now would you?" Reid laughed.

"I don't know why I shouldn't know if Farrar does."

"Can you be sure that Farrar himself knows everything?"

"If he doesn't, who does?"

"Perhaps there's a man in Ankara who knows more than Farrar does. Haven't you yourself told me that the first principle of intelligence work is the telling a man only so much as he needs to know to do the immediate job in hand?"

Gustave's eyes were twinkling. He was in the stronger position. He was enjoying it. Two can play this game, thought Reid. He said,

"You think that Ankara and Cairo know something that Farrar doesn't."

"It might be."

"Farrar is very pleased with the way it all turned out."

"I'm so glad to hear that."

"And Cairo must be as well, otherwise you wouldn't have that star."

"It looks rather like it, doesn't it?"

"Let's hope that Ankara is too."

Gustave's expression changed.

"What do you mean by that?"

"What do I mean by what?"

"Saying that you hoped Ankara was pleased."

"Don't you."

"Of course, naturally, but still. . . ." He checked. There was a belligerent but at the same time a furtive expression on his face, as though he was afraid of something. "Have you heard anything to make you suspect that Ankara's not pleased?"

"How could I have? I don't know what went on."

"I know you don't, but at the same time you might have heard . . . suppose my name had come up in conversation and some one from the Turkish section had . . . well you know how it is. . . . The way a man looks knowingly and shrugs, and says 'oh Gustave.' You remember that old Latin tag 'Even though they are silent, they say enough'."

"Whatever makes you think they have."

"Nothing . . . only it was a funny thing for you to say. 'Let's hope that Ankara is too.' If you had heard anything, I'd be most grateful if you'd tell me."

"I can assure you that I haven't."

"Because if you had." He paused. "It would make a lot of difference if you had."

Gustave checked again. Reid waited, inquisitive, alert. Gustave wanted to ask him something, Gustave wanted to tell him something. Gustave was anxious, apprehensive. "It's coming," Reid thought. "It's coming."

It didn't though. Gustave blinked and shook himself.

"Forget it" he said. "Forget it. All the same it *was* a damned funny thing to say."

Something damned funny must have happened in Ankara, Reid thought.

PART III
The Minaret

1

A MONTH LATER, on a gray dank afternoon, the convoy in which Reid had travelled home, anchored in the bay of Greenock. The process of disembarkment was swift and smooth. A customs officer came on board. "It seems unfair to take money off you chaps after all you've been through," he explained. "But H.M.'s excises feel that every ship that docks has to pay its way. As long as each ship covers our expenses, we don't care. I don't want to look at anything. Just tell me what you've brought and I'll believe you. It's reasonable to assume isn't it, that each of you will have brought back something dutiable?"

Reid had four Persian carpets. He valued them at a pound apiece, and paid a duty of fifteen shillings on them. The officer was quite satisfied. Within seventy minutes, they were all off the ship in a train. Reid bought a copy of *The Star*. It was the first evening paper he had seen for over forty months. He was surprised both at how small it was, and how much news was compressed within its shortened columns. Such concentrated writing must be very difficult, he thought.

Most of the paper was concerned with the Election. Polling day was the week after next. During the last month Paiforce had been placarded with posters exhorting the troops to 'serve like a soldier' and 'vote like a citizen.' He had registered his vote for the conservatives, not out of any particular conviction but because he wanted to see Churchill still in the saddle when the war was finished. *The Star* was politically liberal. The liberal vote had ceased to be important. *The Star's* reporting was detached and neutral. An editorial note reported that the betting was two to one on a conservative majority of fifty seats.

Young women in A.T.S. uniforms came down the platform with

447

cups of steaming tea. Reid had been warned against the flabbiness of wartime beer, but the tea was as good as ever, strong and hot and sweet. The girls also brought paper bags, containing, each one, a cheese sandwich, a hard boiled egg and a bar of chocolate. Cheese and chocolate and eggs were in short supply. A special effort must have been made to provide this 'welcome home.' It was touching, and rather pathetic too, Reid thought.

They were bound for Carlisle, where they would spend the night in barracks. Next day there would be the handing over of equipment, the final filling in of forms. In the late afternoon, they would catch a train for London. Early on the following morning, they would return to civilian life with the bonus of three months leave on fullpay and allowances. Across the carriage, a major in the Greys was saying: "I can't wait to get my hands on a telephone. I've been away five years. To hear my wife's voice again after sixty months."

It was only then that Reid realised that he did not know Rachel's telephone number. She had changed a flat a few weeks ago. It was a furnished flat. He did not know the name of the owner-tenant. He supposed that he could find the number through directory enquiries. But it would take time. Telephone girls were tired and short-tempered. It would be easier to send a telegram. Moreover did he really want their first meeting to be across a wire. It was not going to be an easy meeting. Four years was a long time, and four such years; with a break in them such as they had had.

On what terms would they be meeting now? Would they behave as though there had been no interval; as though that divorce application had not been filed? Would what the law courts described as 'marital relations' be resumed? Did she want them to be, did he want them to be? Would she seem, would she be a different person? Would he seem different to her? After all there had been Diana. In a sense there still was Diana.

The fortnightly letters that he and Rachel had exchanged over the last year had been cordial enough: they had still a great deal in common. Marriage was a partnership, even if love deserted it.

During the long journey across the Mediterranean, round Gibraltar, he had grown increasingly apprehensive. There was nothing he could do. He would have to await the inspiration of the moment. Balzac in his physiology of marriage had devoted an entire section to the single, trenchant statement "Everything depends on the first night." That was, he was very sure, how it was to be, between himself and Rachel. Everything would depend upon the first few hours. And chance would decide upon their course. Yes, he was glad on the whole he did not know her number.

Her flat was in Bloomsbury Square, on the second floor of a converted Georgian house. The final formalities of his discharge had been carried out with such speed that he arrived there shortly after nine o'clock. She opened the door for him. She was wearing a hat, and a dark coat and skirt. "So early. I was just going out," she said. She had an envelope in her hand. "I'd just written you a note to explain that the key's under the door."

The hall was dark and he could not see the expression of her face.

"Where are you going?" he asked.

"To my office, of course. I'm due at half past nine. I'm almost late."

He knew that she worked in Gower Street, in the Ministry of Information. But he had not anticipated that she would be going there on his first day home.

"Is that all your luggage?" she enquired.

He had only a suitcase and a satchel. "My valise is coming independently."

"You look very smart with your red flashes."

"I'll be glad to get into tweeds."

"You won't find them in too good condition. The moths have got at them."

"At all of them?"

"Most of them. I went down to the Farm to collect them. It was quite a shock. They had been in moth balls too."

"That's a good excuse for getting new ones."

"If you've any coupons. How many did they give you by the way?"

"I've no idea. There were so many forms, including a post office savings account book with my gratuity."

"I hope you've got a ration book."

"Yes. I've got that."

"Good, the sooner you get it round to the food office the better. I'll jot the address down for you. Then I must be running. I'm late already."

"When will you be back?"

"Round about half past six."

449

"Why don't we meet in London and have dinner there?"

She shook her head. "Everywhere's so crowded. Everything's so bad. I've managed to scrounge a chicken: and I brought some of the wine from the Farm. We'll fare better here.—Now I must rush. I think you'll find everything. See you to-night."

She waved her hand, the door clicked behind her, and he was standing in the halflit hall, with his suitcase and sachel at his feet. A soldier's homecoming. He thought of the Great Duke of Marlborough returning unexpectedly from his high triumphs in the Low Countries and pleasuring that great lady, his wife, twice, without taking off his boots. He looked about him. It was a flat like two hundred others. He opened a door; the sitting room: a chesterfield and two armchairs ranged before an electric fireplace: over the mantelpiece a Medici reproduction of the Last Supper. A cocktail cabinet with decanters half and quarter filled: the dining room opened off it: a dark chill room, facing north, that probably could be made attractive at night with candlelight and flowers; a large twin bedded room; with photographs on the dressing table: photographs of the boys, and one of him, an enlargement of a snap taken on a cricket tour in 1935. No sign of the American. And no sign, really here, of Rachel; apart from the silver hairbrushes with her initials, a wedding present. A bathroom divided it from a small dressing room with a single bed: he opened the cupboard doors to see how much of his wardrobe had survived: the blue pin stripe double breasted suit, those well worn tweeds, broad black and white checks; but what had happened to the brown check with the red stripe running through it? A casualty maybe. There was the dark charcoal suit that he had worn for college functions, but where was the bottle green suit that it had amused him to flaunt on stodgy tea parties. He appreciated the moths' taste.

He opened the drawers. Cotton shirts were immune to moths' depredations. What a number of evening shirts he had; and ties, he had forgotten that he had so many ties. Socks? The moths would have got at them, no doubt. But he was well off for handkerchiefs. He went into the kitchen. There was a stack of dirty plates. Had Rachel any help? Did she do all the cooking? There was a large refrigerator. It was stacked with partially consumed morsels: lettuce, potato salad, sardines, canned peaches, sausages. There was a closet containing an iron frame for cellarage. It was well stocked. He pulled out a bottle. La Tache 1926. How well

450

he remembered ordering that. Had it retained its quality? Nine-teen years? Perhaps. But the half bottles of Richebourg 1923 would probably have passed.

The clock over the gas range pointed to half past nine. Perhaps his father hadn't left yet for his office. That was a number that he did remember. The welcome at the other end was reassuringly warm. "Noel, my dear boy. I can't believe it. I knew that you were due back soon; but not so soon. It's wonderful, dear boy. It's wonderful."

"What about lunch today?"

"If I were lunching with the P.M. I'd cancel it."

"The—Athenaeum, then, at half past twelve?"

"At half past twelve, yes, but not the Athenaeum. You must lunch with me. At the Isthmian. What day is it? It's Thursday. We're in luck. We can get wine on Thursdays. At half past twelve. And don't be late, dear boy. All the best food gets eaten if one is."

Half past twelve, and it was not yet half past nine. Three hours to put in, and after lunch, presuming it was over by half past two, there would be another four hours before Rachel's return; before his zero hour. For that was how he foresaw the evening: the hour of crisis on which would depend the outcome of the last third of his life. In the meantime there were these chores ahead of him; the registration with the food office, his visit to Olympia to collect the free suit of clothes—the shoes, the shirt, the hat, the raincoat to which every demobilised soldier was en-titled; and then the visit to Anderson and Shepherd, to hand in his clothing coupons, to place his order for two new suits. In the meantime he could get out of khaki, into that dark blue pin stripe suit. He looked at the date inside the pocket. July 8, 1937. How little he had expected then, that he would be wearing it practically brand new in 1945.

He was relieved to find that it still fitted him. He had not put on weight.

It all took longer than he had expected. He had to wait in a queue at the food office and the girl at the desk seemed incredibly slow in filling in his particulars: there was a series of queues too at Olympia. Savile Row would have to wait till after lunch.

He was glad to be lunching at the Isthmian. He had been a con-stant guest there both of his father and of his solicitor. "I can't think why you don't join us," Jenks had said. "You must eat here at least once a month."

Reid had shaken his head. "One should be a member of two clubs and a guest of three. That's the definition of a Londoner."

As he walked into the hall, a man whom he had known for years without having the least idea who he was, hailed him genially. "I haven't seen you around here for a while."

"I've been abroad, in Middle East."

"In oil?"

"No, in the Army."

"Back for good then now, I suppose?"

"It looks like that."

"Then I hope we will be seeing you a lot."

"That's what I'm hoping too."

The man clearly had no idea who he was and imagined that he was a member. What was the point of joining several clubs provided one had friends?

There was no bar in the Isthmian. Preprandial sherries and pink gins were served in the drawing room. His father was sitting with three other men, one of whom was Jenks. Jenks did not get up to welcome him. "Please forgive me, my dear boy, but getting up and sitting down has become an effort. You know us all, I think."

There were no introductions, in self defence Reid presumed. His father would have felt shy of failing to identify old acquaintances. Reid sat next Jenks. They exchanged a conspiratorial glance. "I suppose that I may expect a visit from you soon," the lawyer said.

"Yes, very soon."

Reid wondered whether when the divorce was underway, Jenks had ever mentioned it to his father. He did not suppose he had. Reid did not indeed know whether his father had any idea that there had been a situation. He had never mentioned it. "Now what would you like, dear boy? Not that there's really any choice. It's either pink gin or sherry. I've caught the waiter's eye. I'd recommend the gin. One doesn't expect it to be pleasant, so one's not disappointed. I've taken the precaution by the way of ordering a bottle of claret. We've still got some '29's I'm glad to say." His father was fussing a little, and Reid noticed that his hand shook as he reached forwards for his glass. He gave the impression of trying to steady himself before each movement. He kept his fingers round the glass, before he lifted it. His father after all, was over eighty now, and each of these last years with their strain and their privations must have been the equivalent of two. Yet his voice was as firm as ever. He was holding his own in the general conversation. He seemed to be enjoying life.

Reid's pink gin arrived. He could not remember when he had drunk a pink gin last. It was not very pleasant on the palate; but it was strong. He needed something strong. In five and a half hours' time, he thought. He sipped at his gin slowly. There had been no bar on the ship. For three weeks he had touched no hard liquor. He wanted to keep his reactions fresh.

His father took out his watch. "Five minutes to. I don't want to hurry you dear boy, but if you could empty your glass within three minutes, I should be grateful. A number of members I regret to say stand at the bottom of the stairs, waiting for the gong. Not very dignified. Looks greedy too, not only looks but is. I like to start moving across the room, so that I reach the foot of the stairs, simultaneously with the gong. I'll give the signal."

Reid realised why his father needed the two minutes. His rising from his chair was a laboured process. And now that he stood up, his son could recognise that he had acquired a stoop. His walk had become a shuffle. Yes, he was an old man now.

His syncronisation was astute. Half a dozen members had a short lead of him. And one or two others pushed their way past him on the stairs, but the coffee room was not a tenth part full when he came into it. "We'll sit at the long table, nearer the buttery," he said. A decanter of red wine was set before them. It was the first wine of quality that he had tasted since his trip to Cairo, in the autumn of 1942. The reserves on the Egyptian wagon lit had been long exhausted. "This is a treat Father. I had forgotten how good, good wine could be."

"It almost makes you forget how bad, bad food can be."

"It doesn't seem so bad."

"You're being polite."

"No really, no."

"You wait, till you've had precisely the same food every day for thirty days and none of it with any backbone. It's the monotony that gets you down. That's been the trouble with everything over here. Monotony. Each day exactly like the last. That's where you've been lucky, you've had variety."

Reid smiled. He thought of those long hot July days when the temperature stood steady around 110° with an occasional jump to 120°; and the only respite to the heat was that little breeze that lifted off the Tigris at four each morning, when you woke with a slight shiver and pulled a sheet over your shoulders. "Yes," he said, "I've been very lucky."

Talk was general, lively, animated. They talked of the election; everybody was agreed that the Tories would get in by fifty. They talked about currency restrictions, about blackmarket restaurants, about income tax; they speculated about how long the rationing of petrol and food and clothing would continue. No one talked about the war. The war with Germany was over; their war, that was to say, was over. The war with Japan was another matter. It was scarcely their concern; it did not affect them personally.

Listening to the talk so brisk, so lively Reid had a surprising sense both of its intimacy and provincialism. The men here really liked each other. They were friends in the way that members of a club were not usually. Max Beerbohm in his essay 'A club in ruins' had said, looking at a ruined building, 'it was more than a home; it was a home against many homes; it was a club.' He had himself thought of a club as a refuge: as a harbour; a place where you went when a date had failed you; when you had nowhere else to go. But for these Londoners during the last six years, the Isthmian had been the centre of their private lives. Their families were in the country, or evacuated overseas. They had come here night after night, after their long dreary hours in offices either underground or with windows covered with anti-blast protection, so that all day long they had had to work under electric light. For long periods the blitz had roared about them. They had not thought of themselves as being in danger, but subconsciously they had been aware of danger. At any moment the building might be hit. Had not the Carlton only a few yards away been reduced to rubble? There was no closer bond than that of dangers shared. It was not surprising that they should have come to feel genuine affection for one another.

Yet at the same time their lives during those six years had been intensely narrow. The circle of their interests had been drawn with the shortest radius. They had commuted between their flats, their offices, and their club. In wartime, with the blackout, with the restrictions, any journey involved difficulties that one was loathe to take. Against the background of great events, these clubmen had been chained to the trivial problems of their day to day routines. Everything from the big world came to them at second hand, by hearsay. "Will I ever," Reid wondered, "find myself at one with them again?"

For coffee, his father took him into the billiard room. They sat at the far end of a raised leather covered settee from which, if they wanted, they could watch the play. "Have you seen Rachel at all yet?" his father asked.

"For a couple of minutes. She was going out just as I arrived."

"How did you find her?"

"She seemed all right. But I scarcely saw her; the hall was dark."

"I suppose that she'll soon be giving up her job at the Ministry?"

"I imagine so."

"She's still very concerned with Palestine."

"So I'd inferred. Do you see her often?"

"Not enough. We are both very occupied. No one seems to have any spare time nowadays, yet no one seems to do anything."

There was a pause. There were several questions that Reid would have been glad to ask his father, but he refrained. He did not want to have this first crucial meeting with Rachel affected by preconceived ideas. He wanted to approach her with an open mind.

"I suppose," his father said, "that you'll be going down to Fernhurst to see the boys?"

It had not occurred to Reid. There was so much already on his mind, but perhaps it should have done.

"I'd thought of going down one day next week."

"That is what I expected. I'd rather like to go down with you if you wouldn't mind."

Reid could not have been more surprised, he was glad that the room was dark with the lights concentrated on the green baize cloth, so that his father could not notice his expression. "But that would be wonderful, of course." He hesitated. "Tuesday's a half holiday. Why don't we go on Tuesday."

"That would be fine for me. We'll take the morning train."

Tuesday. That was five days away. By the time he saw the boys, he would know what kind of life he and their mother would be sharing.

By half past five Reid was back in the flat in Bloomsbury. He unpacked the brown cardboard parcel that he had acquired at the demobilisation centre. The sports coat that he had chosen in preference to a suit had looked well enough against a background of new suitings. Its texture seemed tawdry when set beside his Savile Row tweeds, worn though they were. His tailor had told him that it would take at least a year to get his new suits ready, though they had one or two suits that had been ordered before the war by customers who had never turned up to claim them which could be adapted to his measurements within two months. He should think himself lucky that his 1937 suits, moth-scarred though they were, still fitted him.

The bath was heated by a geyser. He was afraid that in war-time London, bath water would be tepid. But to his relief, it ran steaming hot. He had not had a hot bath since he had left the Beirut flat in the Rue Jeanne D'Arc. In Iraq it had always been showers. He stretched and wallowed. He noticed that the bar of soap had a rubber base; to prevent it getting soggy, he presumed. Soap was a munition of war. Don't waste it.

His bath revived him. He took another look at the kitchen cupboard. There was a third of a bottle of gin and three quarters of a bottle of whisky. He would have dearly loved a whisky, but he did not know how close Rachel's quota was. How long did a bottle have to last her. He wondered what kind of a quota he would get from his own wine merchant. He looked again at the stock of bottles in the wine bin. Rachel had said she had a chicken. How long would it take to cook. Should he open a bottle to let it breathe? But how much air did a 1926 La Tache require? Better leave well alone. Better wait till she got back. He was restless, and on edge. If only it were this time to-morrow.

At last he heard her key click in the lock. He hurried into the hall to welcome her. He took her by the wrists. "I never had a chance to look at you this morning." He led her into the sitting room, into the light. "But you look wonderful," he said. "You're radiant. You look six years younger."

He held her away from him for a moment, inspecting her quizzically, smiling, his head first on one side then the other. Then he drew her close, and his arms went round her. It was a cousinly kiss, upon the cheeks, but it was reassuring. Her figure was pliant. It was thirty months since he had held a woman in his arms, and his senses stirred. Was it after all going to be all right? Was a miracle about to happen?

"It's good to be back," he said.

"It's very good to have you back. I'm ravenous, are you?"

"Ready to eat, not ravenous."

"I suppose you hogged it at the Athenaeum?"

"I lunched with my father at the Isthmian."

"Then you did hog it; I know Poppa; or rather swilled it, in these spartan days."

"What are we going to drink by the way with that chicken that you scrounged?"

"Which would you prefer: a Burgundy?"

"I think a Burgundy. How long will it take to get that chicken ready?"

"Not more than three quarters of an hour."

"Then I'll uncork a bottle."

"Wouldn't you like a whisky first?"

"I nearly took one half an hour ago."

"Why didn't you?"

"I didn't know how long that bottle had to last."

She shrugged. "I get one a month. I keep it for occasions."

"That's what I suspected."

"But this is an occasion isn't it?"

They sat together, sipping at the fragrant liquid. She asked him about his lunch. "Poppa's beginning to show his age. How was he?"

"Fine. We're going down to Fernhurst next week, to see the boys."

"Good, they'll love that."

He asked her about the flat. "Don't you have any help?" he asked.

"There's a woman who comes in once a week. That's all I need."

"What about the holidays?"

"We manage. The boys are very good. They cook their own lunches, or go out. I do their dinners."

"And do you do your own dinners when you're by yourself?"

"I'm not very often by myself. I go out most evenings."

He nearly asked with whom, but checked. A whole new life had started for her since she came to London—with her job and her committee work. Personable women never needed to be alone in wartime.

"Shall I find the boys very different?" he asked.

She pouted. "They seem the same to me but then I'm seeing

457

them all the time. They may not to you. Four years is a long time."

They finished their whiskies slowly. "You'd like a second, wouldn't you?" she asked.

He shook his head. "We mustn't make it too much of an occasion. We must leave something there for other ones."

She rose, and he rose too.

"Can I help you?"

It was her turn to shake her head. "Next time; you watch me now. This is your first day home."

He sat on the kitchen table, watching her fiddle round the stove, watching her lay the table. "Do you realise," he said, "that this is the first time we've ever picnicked—in a house of our own, I mean?"

"Wartime has its compensations."

"We missed a lot when we were young. There were always children and servants in the way."

"There'll be children here again in three weeks' time."

The chicken was on the table and the wine was poured. He held his glass to his nose. "I hope it's as good upon the palate." It was. "We're in luck," he said. He lifted his glass to her. "Let's stay in luck," he said.

He asked her about the farm. How soon could they hope to get it back. "I've my hands on the right strings," she told him. He asked her about mutual friends. She shrugged. "I see scarcely any of them. If I were to make a list of the people who in January 1939 I thought of as my best friends, I'd be surprised if I've seen more than three of them in the last twelve months. Everything is so difficult nowadays. It's a major project to get one's hair done or to see a dentist. One does one thing at a time. One sees the people that one works with and that's all there is to it."

I must ask her about her work with Palestine, he thought. But later, when things are cleared away. When we are cosy over coffee and a cognac.

"Jenks was at the Isthmian to-day," he said.

"Was he?"

"I'll be going round to see him one day next week. I suppose that in spite of taxes, because of that legacy to the boys we are rather more comfortably off ourselves."

"We are very much more comfortably off now."

"Till they come of age."

458

"Exactly, till they come of age."

Should he have mentioned that, he wondered. Perhaps he should have waited. Could he have ignored it though, completely? It had to be brought up sometime. "How do the boys feel about it?"

"They haven't grasped it. They take a very temporary point-of-view. They've never worried about money: they never heard money discussed as though it were a problem. They've always assumed there was enough of it."

He asked about the bomb damage in London. "In point of fact did you know a single person who was killed in an air raid."

"No one that I knew well."

"Not nearly as many as were killed in cars or aircraft."

"No, not nearly."

"But a great number of our friends have had their houses smashed."

"A great, great number."

They talked of the houses that had been destroyed. "You've not been round London yet. In every square and street and crescent it's the same. One or two houses gone. They all look like mouths with a couple of front teeth missing."

The level of the wine sank slowly in the bottle. Its warmth spread along his veins. It was good to be home, even in this furnished flat, which did not contain a single personal possession. The mere fact of eating in a private house, with an attractive woman sitting across the table was a relief unbounded, after the succession of meals in messes that had been his background for close upon four years. Most of the occasional dinner parties to which he had been invited had been masculine, or, when there had been a hostess, with a masculine preponderance of six to one. He had not had a single meal alone in feminine company since he had lunched with Diana in Cairo in the late autumn of 1942, nearly three years ago.

Slowly a deep peace of spirit settled on him. He was returning from a long, long exile: an exile that had taught him to appreciate the things that he had taken for granted six years ago. He was returning to the amenities and graciousness of living. He would set the right value on them now. He had learnt his lesson, just as Rachel had. Diana was his equivalent for her American. For both of them without that experience, life would have been incomplete, would have been half lived. Now they could start afresh, on equal terms, ready to attain the happiness, how was it that de Maurier had put it, "that lies so easily within the reach of all of us once we have ceased crying for the stars." It was going to be all right. Of course it was going to be all right.

The meal ended with strawberries, started after the last drop of the Burgundy had been sipped.

"I'm afraid that I can't give you cream," she said, "but I've saved the top of the milk."

"They're the first strawberries I've had since I left the Lebanon. They seem very good to me."

There was really no fruit like English fruit. The climate that made England so difficult gave it in recompense the loveliest gardens in the world and the richest, most subtle fruit.

"Can I help with the washing up?" he asked.

She shook her head. "Mrs. Gaskell comes on Friday. I leave as much as possible for her, but you can help me clear away. Then we can have our coffee at that corner table."

It was a congenial corner table, with two stiff backed but well upholstered chairs set at right angles to one another. You were comfortable, but you were not lolling back; no one could talk effectively when they were lolling back. "I'm afraid this coffee will seem terrible after what you've been used to in the Middle East."

"England was never good at coffee."

But this particular coffee was worse than anything that he remembered. "The brandy's very good," he said. He had very rarely drunk French Brandy since he had left Lebanon. In Baghdad he had been restricted to South African Brandy, which was well enough mixed with ginger ale but was not a liqueur. "It's a relief to drink cognac again," he said. He took a long slow sip and held the time-ripened liquid against his tongue. How good to be able to do that again, instead of having to swallow quickly for the effect.

"Tell me about this Palestine committee of yours," he said.

"That's exactly what I want to talk about. You can be most helpful to us."

"I, helpful? How? In what?"

"In joining our committee, taking the chair at public meetings, helping us draft appeals. You are the very man we need, with your status as a historian and a professor, then your being just back from the Middle East, and as a Colonel too. You'd carry real authority. How long can you wear uniform?"

"For three months."

"And I know you're sick of it, but just for these few occasions, you wouldn't mind. I know it would make all the difference. We must make the most of these three months."

Her eyes were shining; there was a glow in her voice that he had not heard before. He had not believed her capable of so much enthusiasm; she had always been so restrained.

"But what is your committee working for?" he asked.

"The scrapping of that ridiculous white paper; to let as many Central European Jews as are still alive get into Palestine right away."

"Do you think that is fair to the Arabs?"

"What do the Arabs matter. They never made a proper use of Palestine. They neglected Palestine. Think what the Jews have done there within twenty years."

"We have a treaty with the Arabs."

"Treaties are made to be modified, to suit new conditions."

"It's the Arabs' country."

"Only because the Jews were dispossessed. It is their spiritual home: the centre of their faith and culture. For centuries they have carried round with them their sacred Torahs, sounding the Shofars on the Eve of their Holy Days, The Eve of Yom Kippur, on Rosh Hashanah, praying for the day of their return. Surely you must realise. . . ."

He half-closed his eyes. Her arguments were familiar enough to him. There was no answer to them, any more than there was any answer to the arguments that Hassun had flung in his face in his Baghdad office. It was an impossible situation. There was no solution. He had suspected when he left Middle East that he would be involved in this kind of argument; and he had resolved that he would be noncommittal: that he would stand on the touchline as he had during the Spanish Civil War. He would not take sides, since he could not give himself wholeheartedly to either party. He had foreseen such arguments.

He waited until Rachel paused. "It's a very complicated business," he said. "There are arguments on the other side."

"What are the arguments?"

He gave them to her. In the main what he had to say was a paraphrase of Hassun's denunciation. She listened carefully and

461

her eyes were hostile. She did not interrupt. She waited till he had finished. "Is that what you believe yourself?" she asked.

"You didn't ask me what I believed myself. You asked me what were the arguments on the other side."

"And what do you believe yourself?" Her voice was glowering now not glowing.

"I believe," he said, "that from the beginning the whole thing has been a mistake, a misunderstanding and a profound misfortune. The issue of the Middle East was handled after the first war carelessly and stupidly by politicians who were too concerned with their own European interests to understand the Arab problems that were involved in the dissolution of the Ottoman Empire. I think the Arabs can justifiably consider themselves betrayed, not only by the creation of Palestine, but by the dismemberment of the country into British and French spheres of influence. At that time it was no one's intention to create in Palestine an independent Jewish state. The population of Palestine at that time was only nine per cent Jewish. The Balfour Declaration referred to a spiritual home for the Jews, a national home for the Jewish people, was his phrase, not an independent Jewish State. No one could have foreseen then the Hitlerian persecution; it was that persecution that created an argument for a Jewish State."

At that point she interrupted him. "I wouldn't say an argument for; I would say a need for; I would go beyond that, I would say the necessity for."

"I can see that argument."

"Then in that case, why will you not help with my committee. You would carry so much weight. You can explain the historical background. You can tell them of your experiences in the Middle East, of the wonderful work the immigrants have done with their collective farms, how they have irrigated the land, how they made crops grow where they never had before. The Arabs are slovenly and idle, you know that. They rely on Allah to work miracles. You are the very man we need. You could do so much for us."

Her voice had a rich, fierce urgency. He had never believed that she had a gift of oratory. He knew now she had. He would have given anything to have acceded to her plea. But he shook his head.

"For four years I've been living among Arabs. I have liked them personally. I have respected their way of life. I have absorbed their point of view."

"You are pro-Arab, that's to say."

"Not in the terms of a controversy: as an issue in a conflict. But as I said, I have made many good Arab friends. I cannot testify against them, in public. There are certain loyalties."

"Then what are you going to do? Are you going to write a letter to *The Times* endorsing the Arabs' claims, arguing for the white paper, insisting that every frontier should be watched, that these wretched refugees from terror shall be sent back to another terror, perhaps a worse terror, destitute, homeless, starving. Is that what you propose to do?"

"It is not what I propose to do."

"Then what do you propose to do?"

"Nothing."

"Nothing! With all these fine pro-Arab sentiments, this traditional English respect for the Arab gentlemen: nothing, sit there and just do nothing."

Her voice had struck a sneering note. He felt his temper rising, and he knew how easily when one's temper rose, one lost track of one's own identity in an argument. In order to score a point, one brought forward an argument whose validity one only in part accepted. I must keep my head, he thought. I must, I must.

"I do not believe that there is anything a person like myself can do. It is too late."

"What do you think is going to happen then?"

"I am not a prophet, but this I know, a situation has been created that will constitute at any rate during my life a running sore in Anglo-American relations with the Arab world."

"And you propose to sit there on the touchline and watch it happen?"

"What else can I do?"

"What else can you do? How like you. What else can you do? What else can you ever do, but stand aside; the onlooker: the neutral, the impartial chairman, never losing his temper, holding the balance. That's you all through, as a man and a professor. Catherine de Medici: was she an unmixed evil? That was the kind of thesis you would set your students. And the paper that got the highest marks were those that patiently laid out the credit and the debit entries, setting the one against the other, and finally deciding that the world might have been a worse place if she had never lived. That's you. Professor Reid. I know you. After all these years I know you."

She had risen to her feet and her eyes were blazing; her voice low-toned with scorn and anger. As happened so easily in family disputes, a general issue had become a personal one. The smouldering resentments of twenty years had been quickened into flame. He had read once that there was no personal relationship in the world that could not be ruined by three sentences. I've got to stop her, he thought. I've got to stop her. But he could not see how. Not once in all their years together had she lost her temper. Nothing could stop her now. She had to get this off her chest. And nothing could ever be the same again between them.

"That's you, Professor N. E. Reid, always collected, always calm, judicial and impersonal. Never taking sides. Never losing your temper, never embroiled. A half man, that's what you are. Thank God I met one real man before it was too late: a man who knew his mind; who when he saw what he wanted, went for it and got it. I found him; and I lost him: lost him through those foul Nazis, and how did I come to lose him, because of you, because of people like you, Professor N. E. Reid, who didn't stop the Nazis when you had the chance: who stood aside and weighed alternatives. Nonintervention in Spain. Appeasement at Munich and then when you stumble into war, you dismiss the men who'd warned you as premature anti-fascists. God, but you make me sick, you English; your smugness, your complacence. Thank God, I met one real man once, even though I lost him. It makes the world seem less cheap."

She swung round on her heel and the door slammed behind her. Everything depends on the first night. Of one thing Reid was sure. Never again would he and Rachel live together as man and wife.

2

REID MET HIS FATHER on the Tuesday, at the ticket barrier at Waterloo Station. They had agreed to meet half-an-hour before the train was due to leave. It was a long time since Reid's father had been in a train. He had heard many stories of crowded carriages. It was essential that he should find a seat; but luckily there was no particular crush. They had corner seats in a carriage with the corridor to the left, so that they would get an early glimpse of the square golden tower. The train was due at Fernhurst shortly before noon. It was almost to a minute the same train that his father had caught in 1912 when he had come down to see him, half a lifetime ago. Reid was there before his father. With a wistful look he watched him shuffle across from the ticket office to the barrier. He wondered if his father would have the energy to walk from the hotel to the cricket field. Would there be a taxi? He was as touched as he was surprised that his father should have wanted to come down with him. "Isn't it rather strange," he said, "that we should be catching now for the first time together, the train that we've caught so often separately."

"That's exactly why I thought it would be rather pleasant for us to catch it now."

There must be, he supposed, a 'last-time' quality about everything that his father was doing now. He wanted to refresh his memory, to add to his store of memories, so that he should have more to brood over, during those final months when he sat in an armchair before a fire, listening to the radio, struggling with crossword puzzles, reading the poems read in childhood. Perhaps too, he wanted a reassurance of continuity; to be reminded that things which he had known in boyhood still survived, which was something that England alone could offer now. England whose roads for nearly nine hundred years had been untrodden of foreign feet.

The familiar landmarks approached and faded: Westminster and the River, the Tate and Wimbledon; the Woking golf course on the left, where Joyce Wethered's concentration had been so tense that she never heard a train go by as she sank a crucial putt; the tapering tower of Salisbury's cathedral; Templecombe with its blue faced clock, then the low square tower of Fernhurst Abbey. It was a warm and sunny day. The Abbey was a bare quarter of a mile from the station. The school buildings lay behind.

"Do you feel like walking up, or would you rather wait for us in the hotel?"

Classes ended in the summer at half past twelve. The train was a little late.

"I'll wait," his father said. "I'll reserve my strength for afterwards. You hurry on."

Reid stood in the corner of the courts, in the angle of the library and the sixth form class room, looking across the cloisters, to the School House studies; above whose lichened roofs rose the Abbey tower. It was the view of the school buildings on which photographers always concentrated. In terms of a haphazard architectural grouping, it was unique. He had seen nothing lovelier. He thought of all the European soldiers who would return nostalgically to romantic landscapes and find nothing left.

Stillness brooded over the courts. Then the first strokes of the Abbey clock chimed out, and there was a banging of doors, a clatter of feet, a surge of voices with several hundred boys, running if they were fags, sauntering majestically if they were seniors, across the gravel. Just as they had always done. He hurried to the point in front of the abbey which his sons would have to pass on the way to the hotel. He wondered if he would recognise them, in spite of the constant supply of snaps that Rachel had maintained. But they would recognise him, of course. He hadn't changed.

He need not have worried. He recognised them right away; out of a scattered group of seven or eight who came round the wall. James in the blue hat ribbon of the sixth, Mark with the magenta and black house ribbon. There was less than two inches difference in height between them. At the sight of him, they broke into a run. Mark said, "You're not in uniform." He had deliberated on whether he should wear his uniform. They might have liked showing him off with his red tabs; on the other hand it might be better for them to meet him as the civilian that he was going to be for them in future. He laughed. "After wearing khaki for six years you want to see the last of it."

He asked them if there was a cricket match on that afternoon; yes, they told him: against M.C.C. "Will Poppa be able to walk that far?" Mark asked.

They went straight into lunch. Mark did all the talking. He had a piece of gossip about one of the masters who was reputed to be getting black market petrol for his motor bike, and of a rag perpetrated by the lower fourth against an ineffectual temporary master. Mark was bright-eyed and dark, very obviously his mother's son. James was more like himself: with his high forehead and long nose. A modern psychologist might argue that Mark was loquacious because he was ill-at-ease, whereas James' air of reserve concealed a deep conceit: he could not be bothered to exert himself in public. It was the fashion nowadays to assert that everyone was the opposite of what he seemed, that rudeness was a mask for shyness, and cruelty the self protection of a warm hearted nature. He preferred to think that more often than not people were what they seemed, that James was naturally reserved and Mark naturally was effervescent.

During his four years' absence when he wrote letters to his sons, Reid had kept reminding himself that all the time his sons were growing up, that a boy of fourteen was very different from a boy of twelve, and the changes effected by adolescence were profound and unpredictable. He had been on his guard against writing down to them. Yet he did not think he had ever written to them, otherwise than on equal terms.

Sitting now in this familiar room, where he had sat so often with his father, he remembered himself as he had been at fifteen, absorbed in house and school politics, in games and in promotions, in rags and rows; thinking of Latin and Greek, and history as four subjects, as steps to prefectship. He saw himself at seventeen, with the wide fields of literature opening out before him, discovering a new poet every holiday, returning each term to boast of his acquisition, larding his essays with quotations that he hoped the headmaster would not recognise.

He asked James which of the modern poets he read most.

"Eliot, I think and Yeats."

"The later or the earlier Yeats."

"The later one of course."

Reid smiled. There had been no later Yeats when he had been James' age. Yeats had been "Innisfree."

"I remember reading 'Prufock' when it came out first in the Catholic anthology. I was about your age. I thought it silly."

"It doesn't seem silly to me."

"Nor to me now."

The grandfather intervened. "There's a time lag in appreciating poetry. The poet is ahead of his time. I'm not sure that I've caught up with Eliot."

After lunch, they walked down to the cricket field. It was three quarters of a mile away. Mark and his grandfather dropped behind. Reid remembered what Rachel had said about the advantage of two parents going down to see two boys. They talked much more freely when they were not together. Not that Read had anything in particular to say to James. He felt at ease with James, as he assumed his son did with him. He and his own father had never felt the need for what one called 'heart-to-heart' talks. They had talked openly and friendlily and casually: as he hoped he and

James would. There were no immediate problems. James had taken his school certificate the previous summer. He would be sitting for his higher certificate next week. There should be no difficulty about his satisfying the University requirements. New College was waiting for him. He had another two years of school; then he would decide whether to do his military service first or go up to the University. Now that the war was nearly over, the period of military service was likely to be curtailed during the next year, so that it might be an advantage to get his military service finished first. But that was a decision that could wait.

"I suppose you've no idea yet of what you want to do when you come down from Oxford?"

James shook his head. "There's plenty of time to think about that later."

"And do you realise don't you that owing to this legacy, you are in the fortunate position of doing the work you like without having to worry about the immediate returns from it."

"I realise that all right."

He gave his father a quick sideways look as he replied; a smile flickered on his lips; it had a quality of mischief. Reid had an idea that women would find him attractive later on.

They strolled slowly round the field. James pointed out a man in a dark grey flannel suit, bareheaded, wearing a Hawks' tie. "The new chief." The appointment had been made during the war, and Reid had not met him yet. But they had moved within the same scholastic orbit, allowing for the fact that the new chief was a Cambridge man; they were contemporaries. He felt he knew him.

He introduced himself. The new chief was burly, athletic; he looked an administrator rather than a scholar. Yet in fact he had taken a double first and was a fellow of Trinity. He had an open manner. "The war's stopped at the right time for your young man," he said. "He can now take a shortened military service in his stride."

Reid remembered how at James' age he had been desperately anxious that the war should not finish before he got in the trenches. No one felt that way about this total war, when civilians were often in more danger than men in uniform, when the whole resources of the country were mobilised and you were sent where you were needed most, in whatever capacity you would be most useful; when so much of the fighting was remote, in Burma, in

Malaya, in the Western Desert, when the actual casualties were proportionately so many fewer, and there was no longer that hectic atmosphere of soldiers coming home from the trenches for a two weeks' leave.

"Are you out of the army for good now?" the new chief asked him.

"I sincerely hope so."

"It seems an appalling waste your ever having had to go. But I suppose it was a pleasant change."

"I was on the reserve. I was called up. I didn't feel justified in applying for an exemption."

"You had the first war feeling about that. I had it too at the beginning. But then I wasn't on the reserve. If I had wanted to join the army, I'd have been too old. They'd not have wanted me. It's been a different war, and a much more sensibly run war. In the first war no one looked ahead to the time after the war. This time we didn't rob our schools of their best masters. We let our young men finish or at least partially finish their education. We've given them a base they can return to. In some ways of course life has been very different here, because of restrictions, because of the blackout and boys leaving a year earlier, but those are surface differences. In essentials our life and work here have been going on very much the same."

And, yes, Reid thought, that is what has been going on all over this beleaguered island. The pattern of living has been continued and maintained; each group in its separate niche. There lay the island's strength and there too, possibly, the island's limitations. After four years in the Middle East it was going to be difficult for him to find himself at home here for a little.

On the way back from the field, Reid and his father changed companions. Mark talked incessantly. He wanted to know when they would go back to the farm. He was looking forward to going back. His mother had promised him a gun. It would be fun to have a garden. Yet he would miss London, the cinemas and exhibitions and all the people everywhere. He had an engaging zest for life. Reid felt that he would manage to enjoy himself whatever happened. There was no sign of a sense of insecurity because of pulled up roots.

The evening train left Fernhurst shortly before six; the same train by which Reid thirty years before had so often seen off his father; the old man craned his neck to catch a final glimpse of the Abbey tower, golden in the evening light. He was seeing it for the last time and knew he was.

He sat back in his seat and closed his eyes. Within a minute he was asleep, breathing gently, wheezily; the flesh of his cheeks sagged. He looked very old. Would he last out the winter?

A waiter came round, announcing the first call for dinner. Reid booked two places for the second service. But when the waiter came round to announce the second service, the old man shook his head.

"One meal a day's enough for me. You go alone, dear boy."

"I'm better without a second meal. I'll have Rachel make me a sandwich when I get back."

They scarcely talked during the journey. The lights went on in the carriage after Basingstoke. "What a relief not to have the blackout," Reid's father said. "That got one down more than anything. You were lucky to have been spared that."

Reid smiled. Everyone seemed to imagine that he had been on a four years' holiday.

Rachel was in the flat when he got back. No reference had been made to her outburst on his first night home. No reference ever would be made, and Palestine would never be mentioned; but the pattern for their life together had been set.

She smiled brightly as he came in, and lifted her face so that he could kiss her cheek. "Now tell me all about it, right from the very start," she said.

"If you'll make me a sandwich while I wash," he said. "I've had no dinner."

He opened a bottle of beer and they sat together at the congenial corner table. She was bright and animated; an invisible observer would have found it a moving picture of domestic happiness; they talked of the children and of their plans for the next holidays. "By Christmas," she said, "we should be back at the farm."

They had so much to discuss that it was eleven o'clock before his glass was empty. "With my early start this is late for me," she said.

"Why don't I breakfast at the Athenaeum?"

"Why don't you? That might be easier for us. We can read our papers undisturbed."

470

They kissed good-night as cousins; and went to their separate rooms. And this was how it would be for the next thirty years. He shivered: he had got to see Diana.

He had no idea what she was doing now, or what was her address. But in 'Who's Who' next morning, he found her father's address in Kent. Even if the house was let, as he presumed it would be, the letter would be forwarded to her within a week. "I am back in England," he wrote. "I long to exchange gossip. Please ring me here, any morning between nine and ten."

Four mornings later the hall porter called him to the telephone. The deep contralto voice was as rich, as full as ever. "I can't wait to see you," she said. "When can I?"

"Which meal suits you best?"

"Which meal suits *you* best?"

"Have you time to linger over a lunch table?"

"I have."

"Then let's make it lunch."

"How soon?"

"To-morrow?"

"To-morrow's fine by me."

He felt unsteady on his feet as he walked out into the imposing hallway.

He had invited her to a French-Italian restaurant in Leicester Square. He was unfamiliar with London restaurants. He had little need for them, living in the country. But in the year when he had been stationed in London during the blitz, he had gone to this particular restaurant fairly often. He had become friendly with the manager.

He arrived early. He had been instructed in the technique for wartime restaurants. The customer was limited not only as to the amount he ate but as to the price he paid for what he ate. A manager made his profit on his wines. If you allowed him to make a sufficient profit on his wine, he might embellish your menu with special delicacies.

The manager greeted Reid with warmth.

"It is very good to see you back," he said. "I hope that we shall be seeing you very often."

"I hope so too. I have thought about your restaurant very often, and missed it very much. I have had many good things to eat but nothing that was worth while drinking in the Middle East. In Baghdad there was no wine at all. Now today, to make up for that I would like a very special wine. What is the best red wine you have? You have possibly something that is not on your list?"

"Would you prefer a Burgundy or a Bordeaux?"

"My guest is a lady, so as it is lunch perhaps a claret would be better."

"I have a Poyferré '34."

"That used to be very good."

"It still is."

"We'll settle for that, then."

"I'm afraid sir, that it will not be cheap."

"I should not expect it to be. Now what have you on your menu that would go well with it?"

"As a matter of fact, I do, by good fortune have a very tender piece of steak."

"Nothing could be better, and instead of an aperitif, I will have a half bottle of dry white wine."

The half bottle in its steaming bucket had just been set upon the table, when Diana came through the door. It was nearly three years since he had seen her. He had once again the sense of seeing her for the first time, with the instantaneous shock of recognition along every nerve. It was a cool day and she was wearing a coat and skirt, a dark, rich, brownish red, with a couple of white roses on her lapel. "I've chosen a wine that will exactly match that dress," he said.

She had looked immensely tall as she came through the door, but she seemed of medium height once she had sat down. "Now tell me about everything," she said.

He had so much to tell her. There was so much for him to hear. He told her about Farrar first. "After all these years he and Annabelle really are going to get married."

"They are, I so hoped they would. I was afraid they wouldn't. They were so right for one another. But he couldn't see her in an English marriage. And he couldn't see himself transplanted to Beirut. I suppose that it wasn't till the war was over, and he had to face repatriation, that he realised he had more roots in the Lebanon than in London. He was scared of coming back. At least that's how I suppose it was."

"It *is* difficult to feel at home isn't it?"

"I'll say it is."

"Everyone behaves as though one had been away for a long week end. They are not in the least interested about where one's been. They say 'I haven't seen you for a day or two'. I answer, 'I've been four years in the Middle East.' They say, 'Oh, have you' and start telling me how they've managed to find a part-time gardener."

"Exactly."

"Sometimes, sitting by the Tigris, organising all those subversive activities of ours, I'd think of my former colleagues in their lecture rooms and studios, doing exactly the same things they had in 1935. How they would envy me, I thought. How excited they would be to hear about it all, how careful I should have to be to know where to stop, how to respect the Official Secrets Act. I couldn't have been more wrong."

"You certainly could not."

"They aren't in the least interested in what I've been doing."

"They couldn't care less."

He asked her how some of the others who had been repatriated were settled down. "What about Jane Lester?"

"Jane's all right; after those two extremes, first with the bottle then the bed, she's sailing on an even keel."

The white wine had been quickly finished. The claret had been set on its side in an ingenious silver nineteenth century contraption, that by the turning of a screw lowered the neck and raised the punt of the bottle, so that the wine could be poured without disturbing the sediment. Customers, Reid suspected, often ordered a more expensive wine than they had intended, for the privilege of having their bottle cradled in it. It was a status symbol on a table.

Diana held her glass between her hands, warming it, then raised it to her nose, breathing in its perfume. She took a long deliberate sip.

"This is very good," she said.

"I can't believe that it's nearly three years since we drank wine together."

"It wasn't such good wine then."

"It didn't seem to matter, did it?"

It did not seem to matter either, that there had been not only a three year gap, but a break in sympathy. Three years ago in Cairo they had been watchful, on their guard, almost adversaries. They were back now to their old easy intimacy; there might never have been a gap. There might never have been a break. They were at one again. She was unique. There was no one like her.

"Do you remember Eve Parish?" she asked.

"Eve Parish?"

"She was in our branch in Istanbul. She came down to Beirut on leave."

"Of course yes, I remember. Wasn't she mixed up with that Turkish protegé of mine, Aziz?"

"She certainly was."

"Aziz faded out of the picture suddenly. Something funny happened there, I never knew what it was."

Diana laughed. "I can tell you what it was."

She told him. It was strange, he thought, how in that intelligence racket of theirs, you only knew half the story at the actual time; then gradually you began to fit in the pieces of the jigsaw puzzle; months later, possibly, when the whole thing had ceased to matter.

"What's happened to Eve Parish?" he asked.

"She's married. A major in the 60th, a regular."

"A decent fellow?"

"Thoroughly: the kind of man you'd like to have your sister settle for. You know." He knew, exactly. They didn't need to explain themselves to each other, he and she. They could still talk in shorthand. They were as close surely as they had ever been. This was like one of those winter lunches at Sa'ad's when they had risen from the table at three o'clock, with the office not due to open for two hours and without any discussion had taken an arabana back to the old town. They were back at the beginning once again; he felt himself drawn within the mantle of her magic.

"You remember Gustave?" he asked.

"Of course, what of him?"

"He's a half-colonel now."

"He was that before I left."

"I can't think why he was."

"For services rendered, I suppose."

"I saw him in Alexandria as I came through."

"How was he?"

"He rather puzzled me. He was arrogant and self-important yet he was on the defensive."

"I'm not surprised."

She looked at him thoughtfully. "You saw him didn't you when he came back from Ankara?"

"Yes."

"How was he then?"

"In a jumpy state: either talked too much or didn't say a word; ordered wine for the whole table, and gulped it down half a glassful at a time. He'd lost some teeth and was self conscious about that."

"How many teeth?"

"Two."

"That all?"

He looked at her quickly, searchingly. The phrasing of her questions and the tone in her voice had put him on his guard. The antennae of his intuitions quivered. "I've an idea that you know what Gustave's mission was."

"I certainly do. I was very much in on it."

"Can you tell me what it was?"

"There's no reason why I shouldn't. It's all over now. You were in our show. It was only chance that you weren't in on it. Nigel knew that you would object. It isn't a pretty story."

"I'd like to hear it."

"And I'd be glad to get it off my chest. It was part of Nigel's deception campaign. That was the thing he really cared about. He was very upset when you wouldn't take over that wireless set for deceptive messages. I think he cooked up this scheme as a kind of protest: a gesture of defiance, a revenge. He cooked it up during the Beirut congress with our chap in Istanbul, the tall thin blooded one."

"Sedgwick."

"Yes, that's the chap. They were out to convince the Germans that Turkey was coming into the war on our side and that we were going to attack through the Balkans. If the Germans could be made to believe that, they would have to keep a large body of troops on the Turkish frontier; troops that they couldn't afford to spare. Nigel and Sedgwick decided that the best way to do this, was to send up into Turkey a Briton who would be provided with a great deal of false information in which he would himself believe. He would be instructed to contact in Ankara a member of the Bulgarian underground to whom he would hand over this information. The Germans would be tipped off; they would kidnap the Briton; they would torture him and under torture he would give them the information that he had handed over to the Bulgarian."

"What was to happen to the Bulgarian?"

"He was to go back to Bulgaria."

"Did the Germans mind?"

"They didn't mind what the Bulgarians knew as long as they themselves knew what they knew."

"Didn't it confuse the Bulgarian resistance?"

"Not particularly, not for very long; we could let them know before it was too late, that the deal was off, and in the meantime it didn't do any harm to encourage the resistance movement."

"Wasn't it dangerous to give the Germans that chance of penetrating the Bulgarian resistance movement?"

"We didn't expect to make much use of the Bulgarian resistance. Besides we could trust our friends there to take what is called appropriate action."

"And what about the Briton?"

"He'd be let loose as soon as he had spilled the beans. He wouldn't be likely to confess. It was really a very neat scheme."

"Why had he to be sent to Baghdad?"

"Because the attack could be launched more easily through Iraq which is a British sphere of influence than through Syria which is French."

"So that's how Gustave got his half-colonelcy?"

"Exactly."

"But why Gustave?"

"We had to have a very special person. Someone who would never think of himself as a coward; who would be proud of his rank and uniform; a loyal subject of the crown; yet someone who would crack under pressure: someone who had no idea that he would crack: and who would be so ashamed of himself after he had cracked, who would be so horrified by what he had done that the Germans would be convinced that he had spoken the truth; that was an essential part of the whole scheme; that the Briton should be overwhelmed by the enormity of what he had done."

"And Gustave filled the role in your opinion?"

"Perfectly. He's only half British after all; and there's no type more ostentatiously British than the half-Briton. Gustave was a flamboyant personality. He'd always be the first to volunteer for anything yet he's got that alien weakness, that foreign craftiness: of which he is, or at any rate was, unaware. Let's put it this way, if a general had said to you, 'Prof, can you be sure that you wouldn't crack under torture?' you'd have hesitated. You wouldn't have been sure. You wouldn't have volunteered. Though I'm not saying that if by any unpremeditated chance, you had been exposed to torture, you wouldn't have held the fort. But you couldn't be sure. Gustave on the other hand saw himself in the role of the traditional hero, 'the drunken private of the Buffs.' That's why we picked on him."

"And how did you come into this?"

"I was deputed to find his Achilles' Heel."

"And how did you do that?"

"It wasn't difficult. Everyone has some physical attribute on which he sets high value, on which his enjoyment of life depends; a pianist's fingers, an athlete's ankle. Gustave was crazy about women. It was his sport, his hobby, you knew that. In a curious way it was a bond between us. I like men, though I'm not crazy about them, as he is about women; but we have the same kinds of problem, he and I, and the lucky thing is we aren't each other's tea. We don't attract each other in the least, so we can compare notes about our separate campaigns. It's rather comfortable. One needs to have one person in one's life to whom one can say anything and it's pleasanter when that someone is of the other sex. So it was quite easy for me to say to him 'Gustave, you must have asked yourself what it is that women find most attractive in you, what special feature. Several men seem to have fallen for my voice. What is it about you, do you think?' He answered without hesitation. 'My smile; not exactly my smile; but my teeth when I smile. They are so very white and straight. They suggest strength and health' so there we are, I thought."

He stared at her dumbfounded. "How did you tip the Germans off; through that Armenian, Belorian?"

"Yes."

He shook his head. "To think of you, mixed up with a thing like that."

She laughed. "Don't be so shocked. It was all very practical, and in the last analysis, highly economical. Why waste time on toenails."

He winced. It was the ruthless, brutal kind of remark that shocked him yet at the same time attracted him. She hated war so much that she was prepared to relish its loathsomeness, like Bunyan's pilgrim 'Eyes take your fill of the filthy spectacle.' No bannered broidery for her. Yet all the same. . . .

He remembered Gustave as he had been on the convoy, hopeful and high-hearted; he remembered his depression when he learnt that he had come out on a fool's errand, his dread of going to Egypt as a subaltern. Gustave was so mercurial. He had been on the crest of the wave that night at dinner in Cairo at the Turf Club: how proudly he had carried his crown as adjutant in Baghdad: that last dinner and his comic speech. He had not had a care in the world that night. Never again could he be the same lighthearted person. Forever he carried the burden of a disgrace. How astutely Diana had diagnosed his weakness. He remembered how on his return he had kept lifting his hand across his mouth, in self-defence. Once a friend of his, a man vain of his appearance, had on a tour in the South of France got his teeth stained with a cheap local wine. He had kept lifting his hand across his face; just as Gustave had. Every time that he took out his plate, Gustave would be reminded of that dark hour of shame.

With the eyes of vision, Reid pictured the torturers at work. Perhaps there had been no torture: pain was a challenge: pain was a concentration of reflexes. Very likely they had given him injections, so that the gums were numbed. Then they had taken out a tooth. They had shown him his reflection in a mirror. There had been no hurry. They had inserted the needle in the lower jaw. They had waited till the jaw was numb. Then once again he had been shown his reflection in the mirror. Then the dentist had lifted his upper lip on the other side. The sharp prick once again, and then as he had waited, his nerves had broken and for the rest of his life now he would be spiritually maimed.

"It's pretty grim to think of Gustave idling there in Alexandria with this upon his mind," he said.

"It's grim to think of all the relics from the first war who are still alive, their faces shot away, with half their limbs."

"I suppose one couldn't tell him now; now that it's over."

"Tell him what? That he'd been handpicked for cowardice. And remember this: remember two things, first that he doesn't know that anyone knows that he broke down. As far as he's aware British Intelligence is delighted with his work, they made him a half-colonel. He is perhaps terrified that some document may be discovered in German files, referring to what he did. But the betting is a million to one against it. And that fear will grow less every day. There's that and then there's a second point. There was no advance through Turkey, he has no human lives upon his conscience."

"Do you think he'll ever be the same man again?"

"Are any of us, ever about anything, the same man or woman again?"

She leant forward across the table. There were two inches of wine still in her glass. She closed her hands round the glass and lifted it to her lips. It was an act of ritual. She looked at him, steadily. When she spoke her voice had softened and grown deeper. "Do you remember almost the first day in our office, when you brought me round that file about Aziz, when you were so deeply shocked. It's the same thing again, you know; a general mustn't count his casualties before a battle. He must think of the grand strategy, not the individual. That operation of Nigel Farrar's may have immobilised three divisions. How many allied lives do you think that saved? Can you set the chip on Gustave's shoulder against that."

The sentiment of what she said was harsh, but once again there were those viols in her voice. He half closed his eyes. He remembered that day in Beirut so well; and how he had said "Thank God you are in this office to keep me sane," and they had gone out to lunch at Sa'ad's and that lunch had been the beginning of how much.

How close we are, he thought. He looked at her, with a slow fond gaze. Her beauty was in the early summer of its flowering. Never had she been more radiant. He had lost her once, but that had been in wartime, in a period of shifting sands and on foreign soil. Now they were on solid ground, in their own country, in a land that had become foreign to them both. Their compatriots were alien to them and they to them; but they, he and she, were familiar to each other. They had shared so much. They were bound by the fact that they had been involved in, could understand, and could justify in terms of the exigencies of their particular brand of service, an action for which there was no moral justification whatsoever; an action that was despicable and base in terms of the decencies of human conduct. Could they, who had been through things like this together, ever build a life for themselves with anyone who could not share it with them. Surely they belonged to one another.

Swooningly the memory returned of that enchantment in Damascus, of all those winter afternoons, of all those summer nights in Beirut. Through her he had attained to a whole higher range of living. She had been a gateway to unguessed delights, a window opening on the immortal meadows. She had been, she given him so much, yet somehow, miraculously she had needed him. His staidness had been the complement of her flamboyance. They were a pair. His spirits soared.

Rachel on his first night home had dismissed him as a man who had always stood upon the touchline, who never committed himself, who was the eternal chairman. But that was only because he had never seen anything he really wanted, anything he had to have. But now he had. It had needed this episode to shock him, to galvanise him into a realisation of himself.

He knew what he wanted now, he wanted Diana back, wanted her as his own, for always. Rachel did not need him. She would never do more than tolerate him, any more than he would her. Had she not said "This is the easiest letter I have written in my life." He could do as much for the boys, more possibly, outside the range of their home than in it. He could give them a second home. Before the first war, divorce would have been a scandal for a Professor. It wouldn't now. There was no obstacles. The road stretched clear. His heart exulted; slowly he would woo her back: slowly the radius would be shortened, a month, six weeks: it need not be longer. He sighed softly. Had he ever known such peace of mind before?

He sipped the last mouthful in his glass. "We've been talking all this time about our friends," he said. "We haven't said anything about each other."

"I know, and that was what I was waiting for."

"What are your present plans?"

"I fancy they'll surprise you. As a matter of fact we've only missed each other by a month."

"How, where, I don't understand. I thought we'd just found each other."

"Only to lose each other. I'm bound for Baghdad next week."

"For the same firm?"

"Lord, no. I'm going to be married."

"To whom for heaven's sake?"

"This may surprise you. To an Iraqi officer that I met in Cairo."

His fingers tightened within his palms. Steady now, steady. You mustn't let her know you know.

"Would I have come across him?"

"I wouldn't think you would. He avoids court circles. Very much the army man. He's a Captain. He was trained in England. Shawkat al Maslowi."

"Oh but I do know him, or rather know about him. I've seen him at the races. He's a fine fellow. Everybody says so. Oh, but I'm so glad, Diana. So happy, for your sake."

3

AND THAT WAS THE STORY that Reid recalled, seventeen years later, as he boarded the Beirut bound Pan American clipper at Idlewild. As the guest of the Iraqi government he was travelling first class, a thing he had never done before. He settled himself into the big deeply upholstered seat and stretched out his legs towards the footstool. What a difference was made by that extra allowance of eighteen inches. Four seats instead of five across the aircraft. Precisely the same difference as there was between first and second class in an English railway carriage. The moment that the 'fasten your seat belts' sign had been switched off, an air hostess was at his side. What kind of cocktail would he like?

"Could I have a glass of champagne instead?"

"Of course you could, sir."

It was a Krug '53. Rich, and full: chilled but not cold, with a youthful effervescence. He had effected to despise champagne when he was young. It was only good at eleven o'clock with a dry biscuit, after a heavy night. In *boites* where it was *'obligatoire'* he had said, "You can put a bottle in a bucket if you like; but bring me the wine list, it's burgundy I want to drink." But later in middle age he had come to find that champagne did for him something that no other wine could do. One's palate changed. Also one's metabolism. Many of his friends had to limit themselves to Scotch Whisky now. He was glad to have been spared that fate.

The air hostess came round with a tray of canapés, hot and cold. "I mustn't blunt my appetite," he said. He took only one: a cold stuffed egg, sprinkled with caviar. How different this trip was, from the slow eight weeks journey round the cape. The memory of that journey was very actual to him, as he sipped the cool stinging drink, just as the memory of that whole tract of four years was actual to him. He had relived those years often. They had risen

481

like a range of hills, out of the flat, rolling countryside of his calm life as a professor. He had added to his knowledge, his understanding of them, by meetings with this and the other individual, by the reading of this and that report. Gaps had been filled in, light had been thrown on shadowed vistas. He had learnt a great deal during that last lunch with Diana. He had learnt even more from an unexpected meeting only seven months back. A year and a half ago he had been offered and had accepted an exchange appointment at Columbia. One evening his telephone had rung. A foreign voice that had seemed familiar was at the other end. "You'll be surprised to hear from me," it said. "I'm Aziz."

The voice was still familiar, but he would not have recognised Aziz in the street. He had grown slightly bald; he had put on a little weight but not too much. He had acquired self confidence and a presence. He was a handsome man. He had come over to America, directly after the war, to represent his Uncle's interests. He had felt immediately at home there. He had taken out first papers, to begin with as a matter of precaution, so that he would have a responsible status for his work. Then he had fallen in love with an American. He was a citizen now and the father of three children.

"Do you never miss Turkey?" Reid had asked him. He shook his head.

"There are a number of Turks here. There is a large Lebanese colony in Brooklyn. I can find most of the things I liked about the Middle East, and I'm spared everything I didn't like. New York is the place for those who don't feel quite at home in the country of their birth."

They had a long talk about the past. "You were very kind to me," Aziz said. "You gave me encouragement and sympathy. I might not have passed those exams but for you. You gave me faith in myself. No one like you had ever taken an interest in me before. I had to prove myself worthy of it."

He paused. "I had an extraordinary time there; through that friend of yours."

"What friend?"

"Captain Farrar. I don't suppose you knew. I've always wanted to talk to you about it."

Aziz told him his whole story. That was how Reid had learnt of the part Eve had played on the Taurus, going north from Ankara. Piece by piece, the jigsaw had been fitted in. During the next three weeks, imshallah, he would fit in the rest.

The air hostess handed him a large and elaborate menu. The handiwork of Maxim's of Paris. He could have a cream of asparagus soup, or a turtle soup with sherry. He was offered a choice of three entrees: a steak, a lobster newburg, guinea hen with wild rice. That, he supposed, was the American touch; the menu with a choice of entrees; on even so standardised an operation as a transatlantic flight, national characteristics could be observed. There was a salad with foie gras. There was 'les fromages'; a 'bombe surprise', finally fresh fruit. Three wines were offered. The Krug: a Mersault and a Pichon-Longueville '53. "I'll have the turtle soup, and the guinea hen," he said. "And I'll have all the wines, white, red, and then champagne."

It was now half past eight. It would be half past one in London where he was due to land at half past seven, in six hours' time. When he arrived in Beirut at 6 p.m. Beirut time, the morning's work would have barely started in New York. His colleagues would be finishing their first lecture. During that interval while he was being propelled, above the clouds, eastwards in pursuit of light, he would have consumed the sumptuous dinner that was about to be presented to him. There would be a breakfast shortly before reaching London: there would be another breakfast for the benefit of newly joined passengers between London and Frankfort: between Frankfort and Vienna there would be canapés and cocktails. Between Vienna and Istanbul, there would be a lunch as sumptuous as this present dinner. Beirut was little more than an hour from Istanbul. And there at Beirut Nigel Farrar would be waiting to take him to the cocktail party that would precede a dinner; while on this aircraft, bound for Delhi, another banquet would be being served. He was not only flying but living above the weather. He would have felt himself a disembodied spirit were the needs of his body not being attended to so richly.

The air hostess handed him his cup of soup: another filled his glass with the greenish gold of Mersault. In a mood how different from that first time, he would be arriving in Beirut in fifteen hours' time. He saw himself standing in the hall of that mission building, he heard the clatter of Diana's heels upon the stairway, he saw those notices on the walls 'Think, act and plan in terms of March 1942'; he listened to Cartwright's speech of welcome.

He thought over that speech as he relished slowly, course by course, and glass by glass the meal that was to prove as sumptuous on the plate as it had looked on paper. He could recall that speech paragraph by paragraph. And in retrospect he could not see that the subsequent course of events had falsified a single clause of it. The men who had been in authority in the Middle East had had to look twenty years ahead. They had had to see the war not only in terms of their own immediate European interests, but in terms of the Arab world. It had not been the Arabs' war, and the men in authority there had realised that. They had planned in terms of a long time future. And yet how disastrous from the English point of view had been the outcome of it all: not merely in terms of the liquidation of the Empire, but in loss of prestige and face and faith. There had been the quarrels with Nasser; the fiasco of Suez, the futile, humiliating campaign which had engendered in Arab hearts a distrust both of American and British policy that was as acute now as it had ever been. Then finally in Iraq, which had seemed so securely based as a sphere of British interest there had been that grim July night of regicide.

He remembered the last dinner in London of the Anglo-Iraqi association which had been attended by the young King and Prince Abdulilla. There had been a distinguished list of guests at the high table; he remembered the high oratory, particularly by a former head of the British Military Mission in Iraq, who had lost an arm in the first war and fought at the great Feisal's side, a man with a love of poetry who honoured the brotherhood of arms. His voice had glowed, as turning to the young king he had spoken of "how sire, your grandfather and his men swept across the desert to the sea," and he could still see after the dinner Prince Abdulilla, standing by himself against the wall, very slim and elegant, waiting for his friends to present themselves. There had seemed such warmth, such trust then between the countries, such confidence in what lay ahead: yet two years later there had been that grim night of shame, and there had been nothing the British could do but accept the fact. There were times when it seemed that the work over all those years of all those well intentioned men had been the pouring of so much water through a sieve.

So he brooded as the vast silver clipper slid eastwards through the night.

When the top lights in the cabin were switched off, he took a last sip of his cognac and dozed off. The lights were switched on

484

again three hours later. But he woke refreshed. Nor when the hostess offered him a breakfast, did he spurn it. He felt that it was breakfast time in England and that he should be hungry. It was a grey, bleak morning. Early lights were showing in the windows. There was no fog: he could pick up certain landmarks, the spires of Eton chapel, the rounded towers of Windsor, the curving Thames, the green sward of Twickenham. He was absorbed in a strange euphoria. It was strange to be landing like this, in transit in the country of one's birth; to buy a copy of *The Times* and *The Express* and be offered in return for dollar travellers' cheques, cashmere pullovers at a tourist rate. Forty-five minutes pause: then he was off again. Another breakfast was offered him, and he did not reject it. "No omelette, thank you please."

At what was four in the morning for New York, he was being offered in the vast bazaar of Frankfurt, Zeiss Cameras for a negligible cost. Forty-five minutes and again they were in the air, with canapés and cocktails preparing them for Vienna.

For Reid the sense of euphoria persisted. This was a unique experience for him. Everything seemed unreal. Yet he felt himself to be existing on a high metaphysical level of reality. Vienna lay below him, a patchwork effect of forests upon hills, of lakes, and the broad grey Danube. A pause. Then once again aloft, with another vast embellished menu facing him. He thought as the aircraft touched down in Istanbul, "If my grandchildren could see spread out on a table the amount that old Poppa has put away in the last twelve hours, they would be appalled." Yet he felt quite sober: he had no sense of being gorged. The French spas were specialising now in the 'Cure de detente'—how to relax the tycoon within nine days. He wondered whether the same effect could be achieved within three days, by flying a man to Toyko and back, first class. He remembered how Harold Nicolson as a young diplomat had asked Arthur Balfour for five days' leave, to get his nerves unwound. Balfour had said "Nonsense my dear boy. Take a long week end. Lay in a store of very good Burgundy and some detective novels. Read and drink and you will be fine on Monday." In Balfour's day there had been no first class clipper flights. Reid had rarely felt better than he did when the aircraft touched down in Beirut. "God knows how I look," he thought.

But Farrar was apparently unshocked. "God, Prof, but you look wonderful, for a grandfather in his sixties."

Farrar himself was little changed. His hair was slightly grey, he had not put on weight, but his face was lined now and the lines suited him; they gave him dignity. Farrar had been home on leave several times, and Reid had kept in touch with him. But Annabelle had stayed behind. She had no links with England. Reid had not seen her since his last stay here, the day when Farrar had proposed. He was curious to see her. He was anxious to see them together.

They lived in an apartment house, on the sixth floor, looking out over the Plage Saint Simon. They were high enough to be spared the worst of the mid-summer heat, but Reid presumed that they went up to Aley then. Annabelle was the mother of three children. Reid had expected that she would have put on weight. She had: but not too much. She had a rich late summer beauty. A bloom lay on her cheeks.

"We haven't arranged anything for to-night," she said.

"I'm glad you haven't. I've lost touch with the clock. I don't know if it's day or night."

"But you'll wake up promptly at eight to-morrow," Farrar said. "Your nerves will do that for you. I've done this trip often enough to know. And you'll go through to-morrow with a dragging feeling; nothing in particular; you'll think. You've got adjusted. But that's where you fool yourself. You'll go to bed to-morrow, at the usual time, midnight or eleven and you'll wake up to your astonishment at noon. Then you will be adjusted. So we haven't arranged anything for you to-morrow, only for the day after to-morrow."

"And for this evening," Annabelle said, "we'll be quiet and Lebanese."

"Does that mean arak and tabooli?"

"That is precisely what that means."

It was a simple, spacious flat. It could have been made to look like a European flat; but there were carpets and cushions and low stools. It had a Levantine air, and there was an effect of rooms opening out of rooms.

The children were spaced harmoniously in age, with three year intervals: the eldest one was fourteen. They had not had a child right away. They had given each other time to get to know each other. The children were very well behaved. They sat quiet: they did not interrupt. They answered when they were addressed.

"We'll have some Kibbé and some pastries," Farrar said. "Then the children can go to bed and we can talk."

Reid had had a bare four hours' sleep in the last thirty hours and he had consumed an extra major meal, but he did not feel tired and he was able to eat his share not only of the tabooli but of the kibbé. He did not find himself losing grip of the conversation. They talked of mutual friends and after the children had retired, they talked about themselves.

"One thing does surprise me," Reid remarked. "Twenty years ago I would have prophesied that Nigel would have got fat when he settled down."

Farrar laughed. "Perhaps I should have, if I had settled down. But I never have. Annabelle has kept me on tenterhooks all the time. I cannot take her for granted. I can never be certain that she will not turn those great dark eyes onto some young slim Armenian. I am over fifty remember. I can't afford to give away any points."

It was Annabelle's turn to laugh. "That's what I always knew. I knew that my long treasured captain would make an admirable husband."

"What," Reid asked, "is your definition of an admirable husband?"

She shrugged.

"I want him to be romantic, yes. If he is that to start with, then I can keep him that way, I think. And it would follow from that, that he would make love graciously. I would like him to be generous with his money, not a spendthrift but open handed; I would like him to be kind and tender; and good company; some one who liked parties. I would like him to give me my own way, not always though, and only, and now this is most important, in the things that we can share."

"What do you mean by that?"

"A trip to Cairo, that we could take together: a new car that would look elegant at the race course, but not a boat since he does not care for sailing."

"You asked for a lot, Annabelle."

"If you ask for a lot, you get a lot. I knew what I could get and where. Would I not have been foolish to have taken him as a lover when he could be so much more attractive as a husband?"

Her eyes were twinkling: it was the old badinage of the restoration comedies. "You on the other hand, my dear Professor, would have been, I think, more charming as a lover than a husband."

"That's the last thing I ever expected to have said about me."

"I know; because you are staid and sensible; a dignified member of society, who has a regard for his responsibilities, who wouldn't abandon his wife and children; yes, you are all that I know; if a woman were to ask of a husband that he should be first and foremost a good citizen, then you would stand high upon her list. But that is not really what a woman wants: she wants someone who will give himself to her, so that their two lives become one life. Could you ever do that, could you ever be that, my dear Professor? I do not think you could. You have that secret world of your own, with your books and lectures and it is such a private, such a barricaded world. I would like to ask your wife if she agrees with me."

"I've an idea she might."

"I think so too. And if a friend of mine thirty years ago had begun to take you seriously, do you know what I would have said to her?"

"You tell me what you would have said to her."

"I would have given her a warning: I would have said, 'He is an honourable and upright man: he is a man of talent and as his wife, you will enjoy the glory that is reflected from that kind of man. But be on your guard; six months after your honeymoon, you may find that you have done no more than acquire a new piece of furniture for the house.' That is the warning I should have given her, if her hopes were matrimonial, but if her ideas were less conventional, then my advice would have been very different. 'As a lover,' I would say to her, 'I think he would be delightful. He would for a few weeks break out of that prison house of his. He would concentrate on you, with all the emotion that has been bottled up for months. Nothing would exist for him in the whole world but you. You would be engulfed, submerged; you would be his sun, his moon, and all the stars. And that is what a love affair should be.' "

She paused, her eyes were twinkling still with mischief: but there was a reminiscent almost a wistful expression on her face. "Do you know what I thought, my dear Professor, when I saw you first?" She paused. She turned to Farrar. "This is something, my distrustful captain, that I have never told you; now is, I think a good time to tell you when I have a witness for my protection, but this is what I thought. 'I will have a romance with the Professor.' You well remember, my dearly cherished but insidious captain that you had been harrassing me for a long time with very equivocal suggestions. I confronted your blandishments with a rigid Levantine rectitude, but I was not impervious to their effect. I was not as confident as I appeared. I wondered if you were right and I was wrong: no, I do not mean 'wrong' in resisting you: on that point I was convinced. But was I wrong in resisting everybody else. I was not going to be the easy spoil of some casual crusader; but I was a human being; I assured myself that if an appropriate opportunity were to be presented that I could accept with delicacy and discretion, I would accede; and when I met the Professor I thought 'this is it.' He is over forty. He is married. He has a career. He is not the man to throw his top hat over a windmill: he will not involve me in disastrous consequences. He is healthy, he is handsome. His emotional nature has probably been slumbering for ten years. Why should I not benefit from that long somnolence; why should I not release the avalanche of his devotion. That is what I thought my complacent captain. And do you know why I did not?"

"I should be most interested to learn."

"I did not, because I know too well what you Englishmen are like where women are concerned. The friendship between two men is to you something sacred. You would never let a woman interfere with it. It is, I suppose, because of your imperial training. Men in the jungle, men on lonely frontiers, without another white man within a thousand miles. You have to trust each other. I knew what would happen if I let the Professor see that I might not find his approaches unacceptable: he would have turned to you. 'Farrar old boy,' he would have said, and she raised her voice mimicking the English accent, " 'Farrar old boy, that wench Annabelle. Is the coast clear there?' And you, my chivalrous captain would have answered, 'Of course old boy. Good luck to you.' It is one of the traits about you Englishmen that I find both engaging and exasperating; as for that matter I find so much else about you Englishmen engaging and exasperating; and somehow I did not want that to happen. Because I knew if that did happen, I should lose you, my troublesome captain, irretrieveably; and that was more of a risk than I was prepared to run. So you see, my dear Professor, what a narrow escape you had twenty-one years ago."

As Farrar had prophesied, Reid woke up next morning at his usual hour of six o'clock, which for his colleagues at Columbia was ten o'clock on the previous night. It was a clear, cool sunny morning; very like that of the first Sunday he had spent here. "I've taken the day off," Farrar told him. "I'll show you round the sights and we'll lunch at Sa'ad's. That'll make you feel nostalgic."

It was not only Sa'ad's that made him feel nostalgic. So much was the same, and so much was different. The night club quarter was unchanged. So was the Lucullus restaurant, so was the view from the terrace of the St. Georges; and the main shopping street, and the road along the campus; the feel of the town was the same. The new luxury hotels had not altered that. It was only on the edge of the town that the huge development of apartment buildings had made a new city of Beirut. The Bain militaire for instance had been submerged. Its privacy had vanished; and the white and blue lighthouse could only be seen from certain angles.

"Does it seem very different living here?" Reid asked.

Farrar shook his head; "It's what it's been for centuries; elegant, astute, corrupt; but corrupt in a very gracious way."

Their talk switched from one topic to another so quickly that afterwards Reid could not remember where what exactly had been said. It was a continuous conversation with interruptions.

"How does all this seem to you in retrospect?" Farrar asked. "For me who's never left here, it has a steady continuity. My life during the war wasn't so very different from what it had been before and what it has become since. But for you it was such a break in your routine. Does it seem now a kind of, well, I won't say nightmare, but something that happened to someone else?"

"Sometimes it's so much more real than the things that are happening to me now."

Farrar asked him about his sons. They were both doing well enough, he said. One was in Shell; the other was in the wine trade. They were both married. He had five grandchildren.

"I read a book of yours the other day. The one on Charles V. Very interesting."

"Really: you found it interesting?"

"Well, you know what I mean. Not like a novel, of course."

Reid laughed. "I've tried to make them rather more like novels. I learnt a certain amount about that, out here."

He told him what those summaries from Beirut had taught him about the need to maintain suspense. Farrar was delighted. "To think of a Professor of history and philosophy learning how to write from me. I can hardly believe that."

"I can only assure you that my post war books have done much better than my previous ones."

On the terrace of the St. Georges over a glass of arak, they talked about Baghdad. "You were never there were you?" Reid asked Farrar.

Farrar shook his head. "Oddly enough, I never was. By the way you realise don't you, who is our Ambassador there now?"

"Geoffrey Bennett isn't it?"

He had looked it up in Whittaker's in the Century Club library, and checked Bennett's entry in Who's Who. Farrar shook his head. "There was a change two months ago. Our old friend from Istanbul, Martin Ransom, is in the saddle now."

"I never met him."

"You didn't? That surprises me. He was in on one or two of our things."

"I don't need telling that. I'll be interested to meet him."

"There's something by the way I'd like to have you do for me in Baghdad."

This part of their serial conversation was taking place on the terrace of the St. Georges, the one place where during their morning's stroll they were completely out of earshot.

"I'm an oil man nowadays; oil isn't a cover for me any longer," Farrar explained. "Yet at the same time I have on the side, maintained a few contacts from those days. My advice gets asked occasionally and I get asked for help. I've a finger or two in several pies. I'd like you to take a message for me."

"That's what you said to Gustave."

Farrar looked at him, with a start.

"You weren't meant to know about that," he said.

"So I gathered: but I found out. How's Gustave doing, by the way?"

"Not over well."

"What do you mean by not over well?"

"Oh, several things. His wife divorced him. It wasn't a pretty case. Then he was the secretary of a club. There was some confusion about the accounts. Nothing was proved, but he considered it tactful to resign."

"Do you ever see him nowadays?"

"He doesn't want to see people like ourselves any longer."

"How is he off financially?"

"He's all right there, I fancy. His current wife is comfortably heeled."

"How is he in himself? I was rather fond of him you know."

"And so was I in a way. But one can't worry about feelings of

491

that kind when a war's on. He immobilised five German divisions for half a year."

"That's how Diana argued. She put it at three divisions, though."

"Let's put it at four."

"That's not negligible, to set against one mental casualty. Anyhow what's this message you want me to deliver in Baghdad?"

"It concerns Diana. Her husband is one of the few high up Army officers with a clean record. Certain interested persons want him to stay that way, in view of certain events that may take place in the quite near future. At the moment he's in Suleimania campaigning against the Kurds. They want him to be sure to stay there between January and February: to keep out of Baghdad at all costs. They want the message sent to him by word of mouth. Security up there is very strict. You could get the message to him through Diana. Nobody else could."

"Where was he when the king was murdered?"

"In Suleimania; on every count his record's clean. He's a very sound Army officer. He accepts the Army code of loyalty to the authority in power. They want him to stay that way. They may need him one day; politically. Can you get that message to Diana?"

"I can."

They had their talk on the St. Georges terrace, shortly before lunch. They went straight from there to Sa'ad's. It was impossible to sit in Sa'ad's and not talk about Diana.

"I've often thought about you, Prof," said Farrar. "It was such a strange war for you. You finished up a full colonel with red flannel. I know that. But for about four years, you were in khaki, without any kind of status; you weren't aligned with your opposite numbers; or at least those who would have been your opposite numbers in 1938. You were meeting on equal terms captains like myself, twelve years younger than yourself who were nobodies in civil life. Didn't you find it very strange?"

"Not very. I put the clock back twenty years."

"And that made you vulnerable to the kind of experience that wouldn't have happened to you if you had stayed on in England as a Professor. I mean Diana. She must have given you a terrific jolt."

"She did."

"I don't want to pry or anything, but I imagine that you had led a pretty steady sort of life."

"I had."

"And that in spite of all those novels about the twenties. Flaming Youth, and the Bright Young People, for someone like yourself, who was in his early twenties, who hadn't a great deal of money, who was working very hard to make up the time that he had lost during the war, it can't have been all that hectic, surely?"

"It wasn't."

"So that to meet someone like Diana at the age of forty-three, to have her carry such a torch for you . . . I know what it meant, of course, when you asked to be transferred to Baghdad, but now in retrospect, it's twenty years ago. You're in late middle age. How does it seem to you now. Did it make it very hard for you to settle down to—well, I suppose you could call it humdrum life in England. It's something I've often wondered."

"It's something I've often asked myself." Reid paused remembering that lunch in London, when he had been prepared to abandon his home and start on a new life; recalling the long slow years that followed: years professionally of much accomplishment and some achievement, of work that had both absorbed and satisfied him; years that had been in a way impersonal, when he and Rachel had run their family in an harmonious partnership. He had enjoyed the friendship of his sons; he had enjoyed watching them grow up; in particular he had enjoyed their years at Oxford: they had been so obviously getting so much out of it. It had been in the last analysis, an uneventful time, but it had been unharrassed by the strain that had made him in 1939 welcome the return to uniform. He had got on well enough with Rachel, now that there were no intimate relations. He did not think he would ever have reached this calm of spirit if it had not been for Diana. He could answer Farrar reassuringly.

"If you've once known the very best," he said, "you can be content with, well I won't say the second best, because it isn't that at all, it's something that bears no relation to the best. If you've not known the best, you feel that you've been cheated; or you suspect that you've missed it through some deficiency in yourself: or maybe you think that there is no such thing as the best, that people are lying and pretending when they claim that they have known the best; that life in fact is an imposture: when you're in that mood it's difficult to keep a balance, but," he paused, searching for an aphorism that would explain in a phrase how he really felt; searching and half-finding it, "it's not difficult," he said,

493

"to live contentedly, once you've realised that there is such a thing in the world as happiness even though you've missed it and now won't get it. Do you remember that poem of Newbolt's, 'He fell among thieves,' about the man who was going to die at dawn, brooding 'in a dream untroubled of hope.' That's the point, I think." He paused again. He had found the aphorism. "It's easy to be happy when you know that you never will be happy."

4

BAGHDAD WAS HUNG WITH FLAGS and with streamers stretched across the streets. The city was celebrating the five hundredth anniversary of the Philosopher Al Kindi and its own thousandth anniversary. But in far greater part the celebrations were a display of personal glorification for the Dictator Kassim. His photograph was on every hoarding and in every shop. For every tribute to Al Kindi, there were a dozen to the leader of the glorious July revolution.

Reid landed shortly after ten. From the window of the aircraft, it all looked familiar enough; the yellow ochre countryside, *le pays beige*, the twisting river, the date palms, the low houses, the golden domes of Khadimain glistening in the sunlight, but once on the ground, on his way from the airport to his hotel, he looked in vain for certain familiar landmarks. There were the rows of two-storeyed flat-roofed villas, there were the stunted, blossomless, dust-covered oleander bushes, but where were the statues to Feisal and to General Moude? They crossed the river and there to the right was a fine new bridge. But the East Bank of the river had lost its charm. The picturesque old wooden houses, with their balconies and courtyards were desolate and shabby. Many of them had been replaced by concrete barracklike constructions. The low palm dotted skyline with its mosques and minarets had vanished. The air was heavy with dust. He turned to the right and there was Rashid street with its colonades and shabbiness: its shuffling pedestrians, its bicycles and donkeys. His nostrils wrinkled: that old pungent smell.

He had booked a room in the El Katib. He had been advised to stay in the new American style hotel that had been built between the south gate and the Alwiyah Club. But he wanted to evoke memories in a hotel that he had known in wartime. Twenty years ago the El Katib had been the smartest and most expensive; when G.H.Q. had been billetted in hotels, it had been reserved for officers above the rank of major. It was very shabby now, and was mainly patronised by Russian technicians, who had camped there like Bedouins with their wives and children and had no spare funds for the least personal indulgence. They did their own washing in their rooms, and the bar was desolate. But Reid was content enough to be here. This was the Baghdad he knew. In the American style hotel down the river, he would wake in the morning, wondering at first whether he was in Kansas or Detroit.

His room faced on the river. He walked on to the balcony. The west side of the river was little changed, there were the palm trees and the low houses many of them dating back to Turkish times, some of quite recent structure but all of them blended into the pervading atmosphere of watered dust. The river though was different. Long banks ran down to it, on which small boys were feeding sheep and goats: mud islands in the centre were planted with vegetables; the river itself was narrowed so that it had become a stream, meandering through shallows. This was December, surely the river should have risen by now. Then he remembered: there had been a heavy flood six years ago. Another few inches and the city would have been submerged. A barrage had now been erected to the north; the flow of water had been restrained and irrigation projects were under way that might restore the country to the prosperity that it had known in the days of Haroun al Rashid.

"I must get out into the street and see what it all looks like now," he thought.

On his way through the hall, he was stopped by the room clerk. "A telegram for you, Professor Reid."

He had hoped there would be. In Beirut, Farrar had found out Diana's address from the Iraqi consulate. He had invited her by cable to lunch with him at the Alwiyah club on the day before the celebrations opened. He tore open the envelope. He read 'Delighted, love.' Now he could relax.

He spent the rest of the day, making a long, slow, sentimental pilgrimage. It was a bright cool day; an easy day for walking. During the celebrations he would be taken, he knew, on a tour of the latest developments, but he wanted to see what had happened to the places that he remembered. He crossed the river by the new bridge and turned south towards the centre's building. The Prince Regent had acquired the mess and dormitories and planned to make a private palace there. A high tiled wall over which he could not see had been set across the entrance to the garden. No one was about. The office buildings were also empty. He looked through the windows. The rooms were in disrepair. The garden overgrown. The house would be pulled down soon. No one needed this kind of house any longer. They wanted solid blocks of concrete. Air conditioning had effected more changes in the life of Baghdad in a dozen years, than as many centuries of wars had done. He wondered if well off Baghdadis stlil slept on the roof in summer. There might soon be a generation that did not know about that cool breeze that came off the Tigris at four o'clock. Not far from his old centre was Nuri Said's house. That too was abandoned. The walls and window frames were pock-marked with the machine gun bullets that had racked it on that fatal night.

He crossed the river again and walked north from the Alwiyah club. The East bank was cluttered now with cafés and food stalls. There were flags and photographs of Kassim: many of the streamers had been inscribed in English: in an English that was not quite English, such as 'all homage to the creative thought.' He did not see anyone wearing the high split felt hat—the Sidara—that Feisal had introduced. Many of the men were chewing lettuces as they strolled along.

He lunched in a café facing the river by the south gate. He ordered an arak and a plate of messé; The Café was full of men under fifty drinking beer or arak. Baghdad had a beer factory now. Reid ordered a bottle; it was light and good. Most of the men wore dark Western suits. Half of them had no collars; those who wore shirts with collars attached, left the shirts unbuttoned at the neck. They looked very scruffy. The few who were wearing the traditional Arab dress looked infinitely more dignified.

There were large brown buses running now down al Rashid Street. He took one to the old part of the city, surrounding the bazaars. Here the work of demolition was in brisk operation. Whole sections were being torn apart, to be replaced by tall dun coloured barracks. Never had he seen an uglier city. Yet it had a certain poetic quality in the evening, when the fires were lit along the river, and the broad flat fish were grilled on them.

He acquired a card of temporary membership to the Alwiyah Club. He arrived there early. The inside had been done over. He did not think that had he been brought here blindfold, he would have known where he was. There were a couple of waiters though whom he remembered and who remembered him. And the garden was the same, though somehow he had expected the grass to be more green. It was pleasant sitting there in the sun, remembering how it had been on summer evenings when young officers in bush shirts had danced on the small stone circle. He tried to pretend that he was not feeling nervous. He wondered if he would still recognise her.

But there was no need for him to wonder that.

They had their gin and tonics on the lawn.

"I've something to say to you that I don't want overheard," he said.

He told her what he had to tell. She nodded. "Yes, I understand. Thank you very much."

There were only two other couples lunching and one man by himself. The room was bleak. It needed to be crowded to look gay. The menu was like that in an English railway station.

"I always have cold meat and salad here," Diana said, "and don't order wine. The beer's really better."

The whole thing was very far from seeming an occasion. "Do you know that in all my months here, I never had a meal alone in feminine company."

She raised her eyebrows.

"It was a very celibate world for most of us," he said.

"No little shulamite?"

"No little shulamite."

"Poor Noel; poor, poor Noel, I'd have been very surprised then, if I'd been told I'd be lunching with you here in 1962."

"It would have surprised me too. When I was sitting out there, in the garden, I wondered if I should recognise you."

"I don't think that I've altered very much."

"Scarcely at all."

Her hair was grizzled. She was a little thinner: and her mouth was lined, but there was no real change. He had thought that with her height and having had children, she might have become massive in middle age. She had not though.

Their talk moved smoothly. They talked about the celebrations, a little but not much about the changes since the establishment of the new régime. She had to be careful what she said in public.

497

They were both sufficiently familiar with police procedure, to know that their meeting would certainly be reported to police headquarters. One meeting between two compatriots, between two old friends, was to be expected. But a second meeting would have been suspicious. Besides Diana did not live in Baghdad, but on an estate two hours' drive away. Whatever they had to say, had to be said now.

"It seemed strange at first," he said, "your being married to an Iraqi."

"Why strange. Is there anything stranger about an Iraqi than a Frenchman or a Dane?"

"Surely his being a Moslem makes a difference?"

"Not really, nowadays. One thinks of Moslems in terms of the Holy war, and of all those wives. And I suppose if one were married to a very devout Moslem it would make a difference. But then so would it if one were married to a devout Catholic; there's not very much difference between what Shawkat believes and what the average, casual English churchman does. The forms of worship may be different, but not the essence. Do most of us after all, have much more than a rather vague belief in God?"

She paused. She looked at him, questioningly. He did not reply. He did not know the answer to that question. He had often asked himself why he who had such a definite regard for what are called 'the eternal verities,' had never found it possible to embrace whole heartedly any single creed, though he accepted the communion of the Established Church, and did not consider that his taking of the communion was an act of blasphemy.

"As a matter of fact, you see," she was continuing, "Shawkat is far closer to me in terms of upbringing than a Spaniard would be. He'd been to Sandhurst. He'd had the English grooming. He liked and respected the English way of doing things. But he wasn't a part of it. And that's really what I wanted in a husband. Someone who would understand *me*, through having seen and understood and what is more appreciated a way of life against which I was in reaction. You see what I mean."

"I see what you mean."

"A Spanish officer for example, couldn't have been a real husband for me, for he couldn't understand how I had come to be what I was. His attitude would have been 'let's rub it out and start afresh'; but you can't rub out something you were born to. That's what made Nigel Farrar wrong for me."

"Steady now, steady. You are going much too fast. How does Nigel Farrar come into all of this?"

"Because Nigel, like myself, was dyed-in-the-wool English; he was reacting against England, just as I was, but in a different way, for different reasons. And for the very reason that we were so close, we were not quite close enough. We might have become enemies. Thank God, we had the sense not to marry."

"Was there any talk of it?"

"Indeed, there was."

He could not have been more surprised; a flash of intuition made him ask, "Did you have an affair with Nigel Farrar?"

"Of course. Didn't you know?"

"I had no idea."

She laughed. "Oh, my darling Noel, how innocent you were. We must, all of us, have been a fearful shock to you."

Nigel and Diana! That explained a lot. Why had he not suspected? It was as well probably that he hadn't.

He switched the conversation. He asked her about her children. What were her plans for them? Were they to be exposed to European influences? "The A.U.B. should give them a chance of choosing. That's the best I can do for them. But I hope they'll decide to stay here. This country needs the kind of man I hope they'll be."

"What did your father make of it all?"

"Tickled to death. Just what he's hoped for me. I can hear him talking about it, in the Rag. 'That daughter of mine, no use for the kind of man that she met in her mother's house, picked up a blackamoor in Cairo. Still she was true to her training in her way. The man had been to Sandhurst.'"

"Did he ever meet your husband?"

"No, and I so wish he had. They'd have liked each other."

"He's not alive still, is he?"

She shook her head. "But he died only three years ago."

The talk moved easily enough. There were no pauses. Yet Reid had the feeling that they hadn't really a great deal to say to one another. Though she had changed little in appearance he felt that he was sitting beside a stranger. Neither knew anything of what the other had been doing during the last seventeen years. The friends they had had in common had gone out of both their lives. Their interests were different, too. This is the end, he thought; the last pages of the chapter that had begun in Beirut, on that

November afternoon, twenty-one years before. It seemed appropriate that it should end like this, with him lunching with Diana, the bearer of a message on which the fate and future of a régime might depend.

Next day the celebrations started. They were highly tedious. The speeches were much too long. A remarkable array of Mayors had been assembled from places as remote as Rome, Tashkent and Pekin. Each of them spoke at length. The mayor of Moscow considered it a suitable occasion to deliver an attack on the British colonialism to which Baghdad had been subjected. By universal acclaim the laurels, had there been any, would have gone to the mayor of Damascus who spoke as a scholar and a poet. The receptions were even more tedious than the sessions. Kassim always arrived late, and insisted on long conversations with individual delegates. On one occasion it was eleven o'clock before the guests reached the supper room. There was a dearth of alcohol.

For Reid the proceedings were wrapped in an uneasy atmosphere of foreboding. Kassim was invariably escorted by a heavily armed bodyguard and men with tommy guns stood around the lavatories. Reid wondered if the others were conscious of this omen. Would he have been, if Farrar had not entrusted him with a message? The day after the celebrations ended, the British Ambassador gave a dinner party to which Reid was invited. The old residence had been burnt down during the July revolution, and the Ambassador now lived on the west bank. "I am afraid," he said, "that this house will seem a sad declension from the high days that you remember."

Reid was curious to meet Sir Martin. He was even more curious to meet his wife. She was tall and handsome, some ten years younger than her husband. Arriving at the same time as three other guests, he had no opportunity of talking to her before dinner. But seated three places away from her, he had chances of glancing at her during the meal and of overhearing snatches of her talk. She had a slight trans-atlantic accent: he fancied it was Canadian. She talked lightly, almost flippantly. She was smiling half the time. She was dressed simply, but expensively. She wore little jewelry, but that little looked very good. He assumed that she had money of her own. She seemed a good foil for an Ambassador.

On his left was an Iraqi lady, the wife of a government official. She was in her middle forties. She had daughters in their late teens and early twenties. He asked if they were closely chaperoned. She laughed. "They are by their standards, but my mother's shocked out of her wits. She can't think what's happening. She thinks the world's headed for perdition."

"They don't go out with young men alone, do they?"

"No, but they go out in parties of four and six. At parties they sit in couples. They're freer than late Victorian girls were in England. The next generation will be as free as your sisters were."

On his other side was one of the secretaries at the Embassy. "Were you here on that July night?" Reid asked.

"I'll say I was."

"Was it all a great surprise to you?"

"Yes and no. We had warned Nuri that Kassim wasn't to be trusted. But Nuri said that he had had it out with Kassim and that Kassim was his man."

After dinner, the Ambassador beckoned to Reid to sit beside him. "It's strange that we never met during the war," he said. "I knew of course that you were here, and I've read a number of summaries that I presumed were written by you. As a matter of fact only the other day, I was re-reading one of them. I wanted to recreate the past and I thought I could do worse than see what you chaps had been haying then. I found some of them very helpful. Particularly one you wrote about that schoolmaster with the wireless set."

"I remember that one. What happened to that master, by the way?"

"He's doing well enough. He's a headmaster now. You must have had an interesting time out here."

"It was more than interesting; it was exciting."

"And pleasant too, I'd think."

"Yes, in many ways."

"It's more than it is now. One's virtually a prisoner. If you want to go out for a day's shooting, you not only have to get a special permit, but take a policeman with you, in your car."

"It's sad to think of how little's survived out of all the solid work that was done by sincere and really first class men."

The Ambassador shook his head. "One's taking a short view if one thinks that," he said. "Look back fifty years: read an account of how Baghdad was then, as capital of a villayet in the Ottoman Empire. It was wretched and filthy. And so were the Iraqis. Immense progress has been made; that progress couldn't have been made without us. The Iraqis may not seem grateful now. But the people that one helps rarely do show gratitude. In time they may. The Indians are very friendly with us now. This moment is the lowest point of the curve."

He spoke with authority. He had the smooth easy manner of the diplomat, but he could, clearly, be very firm. Reid wondered how much he knew about what was going on beneath the surface here. During the 1930's there had been an idea that official embassies did not know as much as newspaper reporters. But his experience in the Middle East had taught him that Embassies had access to all the information that a journalist could reach and a great deal else besides. In the 1930's had not Sir Horace Rumbold from his Berlin embassy warned the British government of what the Nazis were preparing, as cogently as any journalist had done. Ransom had probably a very shrewd idea of what the next months held.

They talked for a little about their separate experiences during the war, then the Ambassador pushed back his chair. "Time we were going next door," he said. "Oh by the way, there was a young woman in your organisation who was in Istanbul, Eve Parish. Do you know what happened to her?"

"She married a soldier, someone in the 60th."

"And it turned out well?"

"From all accounts, it has."

"I'm glad to hear that: yes, I'm very glad."

Reid's flight for Beirut left at noon. He was to stay a couple of nights with Farrar, then catch his Pan American clipper. He looked forward to the strange euphoria of that westward flight, with meals following one another in an unaccountable succession, breakfast followed by breakfast and lunch by lunch, with a cascade of champagne restoring every wakeful hour. Then he would think things out. He was too tired now.

His suitcase was packed. He walked out on the balcony: in all human probability he was looking down for the last time on the Tigris. In spring the snows would melt and the gates of the barrage would be opened. Once again these low sloping banks would contain a brown fierce swirling torrent. In his mind's eye he could see it.

The telephone bell rang behind him. "My car already?" But it was not his car. It was the rich contralto voice that he had heard for the first time as duty officer in Beirut.

"Noel, is that you: oh, but I'm so glad I got you. I was afraid I wouldn't. This line is terrible. And there was something that I had to say: that I couldn't say across a lunch table. You remember me. I'm most myself when I'm on a telephone. So please let me say this now. Don't interrupt. Let me say what I have to say. Then I'll ring off."

At the Alwiyah club at lunch, seated beside a woman who had changed in seventeen years inside herself, he had felt that he was with a stranger, but now hearing her voice, not seeing her changed features, he was transported to those early days, to Sa'ad's, and the Lucullus and that dark flat below the minaret. Once again the mantle of her magic was about him. The years slipped away. He was a captain in his early forties. His heart was singing as he listened.

"I had to say this to you. I don't want to be misjudged by you. I told you at the start that I was ruthless: but I'm every bit as ruthless with myself. That's what you've got to realise. You mustn't think those months, that all that started in Damascus, was only a casual *passade*. It wasn't. It was the real thing. And it was the first time that I'd known that. That was why I was frightened. I had to get out, fast. There is a point in a love affair, where you can get out. If you once pass that point you're lost. I couldn't afford to let that happen. Because though it was the real thing, I wasn't convinced it was the right thing, for either of us. And if it hadn't been the right thing for us, we'd have ruined one another. I know myself. I can't live with a compromise. If a thing isn't right for me, then it's more than wrong. But I couldn't have told you that. You'd have over persuaded me. And I'd have so wanted you to do just that. I couldn't trust myself. And so I ran. And even now I'm not sure if I was right to run. I'll never know. We might have been wonderful for one another, but if we hadn't, we'd have been disastrous. And it hasn't turned out so badly for us, has it? I had to say this to you. Now you'll understand. You'll think about me in the way I want you to. And now I'm going to ring off. Goodbye, my darling, bless you."

There was the click of the receiver. He walked out on to the balcony; but he could not see the brown sluggish river, the date palms and the dun coloured houses on the bank. There was a mist before his eyes. Through his ears and along every nerve cell the viols in her voice were echoing.

POSTSCRIPT

This novel is a piece of fiction and all the characters and events in it are fictitious. It is, however, based on personal experiences. I am, myself, of the same age as the central character, Professor Reid. In the first war, as he did, I went to Sandhurst and in 1919 transferred to the Regular Army Reserve. In September 1939, I was recalled to my regiment with the rank of Lieutenant. In September 1941, I was posted to the Spears Mission (Syria and the Lebanon) as a liaison officer with the Free French Forces. After nine months in Beirut and Cairo, I was transferred to Baghdad to work in counterespionage.

The general background of those years is, I hope, accurately reported. But there was in Middle East no organisation whose work bore any resemblance to that of the I.S.L.O. described in this story. None of the incidents I have described took place.

On their arrival in Beirut in November 1941, the prospective members of the Spears Mission were received at the legation by the *chargé d'affaires*, my good friend, J. A. de C. Hamilton. His speech of welcome is here, in large part, reproduced. In retrospect it seems to me that I heard in that speech more sound sense than I was to hear in my remaining forty-two months in Middle East. But the Cartwright of this book is scarcely a portrait of Hamilton.

In Baghdad I worked in close cooperation with the British Technical Advisor to the C.I.D. He bore no resemblance to the Forester in this story.

I was in Bagdad in December 1962, during the Al Kindi celebrations, but I did not attend any of the functions. The British delegate was Professor Max Mallowan who very kindly supplied me with some information about them. The British Ambassador at that time was Sir Roger Allen who honoured me with his hospitality. He bears no resemblance to the fictional character who in this book is accredited to the Iraqi government. As far as I know, no message was sent to an officer in the Iraqi army, advising him to avoid Baghdad, during the early weeks of 1963.

I repeat this is a piece of fiction.

During my years in Baghdad, I became a close friend of Majid Khadduri, now a Professor at Johns Hopkins University and the author of a number of important books. His history of Iraq is essential reading for any student of this area. I am most grateful to him for the help that he has given me. I have also been helped by Peggy Mann's book, *Israel*.

The first half of this book was written and the manuscript was finally revised at the MacDowell Colony, Peterboro, New Hampshire. Once again I must express my warmest gratitude to the Directors of the Association. My debt to them is very great. I simply do not know how I should have managed without the colony during the last fifteen years.